THE SUNSHINE CHRONICLES : FORBIDDEN FUSION

KELSEY LEIGN

Book Cover by Kelsey Leign

Illustrations by Kelsey Leign

Edited by Alexis Augustine

First edition 2025

ISBN: 979-8-89778-699-2

For my Lollipop Gals — Erin, Jenna, Kaley, and Lauren
Thank you for the love, the hype, and the honesty.
This one's for you.

Chapter Playlist

Pull the Plug - Noël Tsoukalas
You Don't Know - Katelyn Tarver
Burning Down - Alex Warren ft. Joe Jonas
Unsteady - X-Ambassadors
Royal We - Janani K. Jha
OK Not To Be OK - Marshmello ft Demi Lovato
Conspiracy - Paramore
I Don't Know What Else You Want From Me - Willyecho
Run Through Walls - The Script
Optimist - Crash Adams
Off the Edge - VOILÀ ft LUNA AURA
Run With Me - Watt White ft Loch
Smoke & Trouble - Society of Villains ft Sam Tinnesz
Legends Are Made - Sam Tinnesz
Another Place - Bastille ft Alessia Cara
All of Your Lies - Morgan Clae
repercussions - Bea Miller
Hands to Myself - Selena Gomez
Steal the Show - Lauv
can you hear me? - Munn
Senses - MICO
Who's Afraid of Little Old Me? - Taylor Swift
Phoenix - League of Legends ft Cailin Russo and Chrissy Constanza
I Am Not Okay - Jelly Roll

Truth Comes Out - Willyecho

Even If It Hurts - Sam Tinnesz

Your Touch - Foreign Air

Nevermind - Ben Barnes

One Day - Tate McRae

Burn It All Down - League of Legends ft PVRIS

Don't Say I Didn't Warn You - VOILÀ ft Craig Owens

Nothing Is As It Seems - Hidden Citizens ft Ruelle

Everything or Nothing - Willyecho

All My Friends - Dermott Kennedy

Anxiety - Letdown

A Little Bit Bad - Kevin McAllister ft Willyecho

that way - Tate McRae

Feel the Light - Jennifer Lopez

Empty - Letdown

Lose Control - Teddy Swims

Evil Is My Middle Name - Society of Villains ft. Sam Tinnesz

My Heart's Grave - Faouzia

Unstoppable - The Score

Friends - Emmit Fenn

Sweeter Than Revenge - Society of Villains ft. Sam Tinnesz

The Rumble - Morgan Clae

Gitapodi
Diplopela
Welcome to
Nicc
Delgia
Nykeraki

Pipistrella
adra
Eliorra
Krevastisto
Zotypas
Entrance to
the Kyllindro

Prologue

The second time death came for me, it wasn't physical, but emotional—mental. Something I never knew existed.

My body felt shattered sitting on the floor of a cold dungeon before a man who shouldn't be alive, yet was still whole. I'd stabbed him. *Through the heart.*

Hadn't I?

It only took three words from him, and my whole world collapsed, along with my knowledge of what I thought love was.

The words clanged through my head.

Guess again, girlie.

Girlie.

The boy I'd grown up with—the one I fell for unknowingly, who said he loved me—he *couldn't* be the one now crouching before me, admitting he betrayed me after all these years.

Then again, maybe he was never the boy he claimed to be. Maybe he was always on the side of treachery and I just was his assignment. Get close to me. Make me love him. Get me to trust him. Then rip it all away at the most opportune moment.

"You seem genuinely surprised to see me." The familiar cadence of Kaleb's voice had changed drastically. It wasn't the voice of the boy I knew. The warm tone, smooth like honey, right with joy—that was gone. This was the gravelly whisper of someone who'd used my innocence to control me. To manipulate me. To get me here—wherever here was. "Tell me, did you ever suspect me? Or did my father train me well?"

I wanted to spit in his face. Slap him. Scream. Do *something*.

But all I did was stare, unwilling to believe it was him. His features were different from the last time I'd seen him. A deathly pale face, one eye swollen, with muscles slack. The face of a boy I loved moments after stabbing him through the chest.

How was he alive? Who was this person in front of me? Was it the boy I loved? Was anything I felt for him real, or was it all fake? What kind of monster could do that?

My breathing became shallow, my body numb. I couldn't form words to say any of what was running through my mind. Black clouded my vision. Oxygen evaded me. Panic consumed me.

He used to be the one to help me through these attacks. Now, he was causing it.

My fingers found the hem of my shirt, running along the rough seam of the strange material I'd been changed into. It was ragged, cool, and slightly damp from being in the dungeon. The cold rock wall against my back was relentless, but I pressed into it harder, if only to clear my head and steady myself.

Thoughts of who taught me *those* coping methods ran through my mind. Had Kyler been on my side the whole time? Had I wrongfully blamed him for this betrayal? Where was he now?

I stared at Kaleb, still crouched before me, and mustered all the strength I could. "How long?" I knew my voice wasn't hoarse from non-use. It was from screaming as the man before me was stabbed by my own hand.

His eyebrows shot up at my words. Whether it was because I spoke or because of what I'd asked, I wasn't sure. The surprise on his face melted into a devious smile. "From the day we met."

The blood drained from my face, but my body grew hot. It was all a lie. Everything. We'd known each other since kindergarten. We were *children*. He'd befriended me only to grow up and betray me. How could a *child* be so manipulative? And what about Arabella? Had he befriended us both only to try and coax us into loving him?

"My father made sure I knew of my assignment from the beginning," he continued, studying me as I processed our fake-to-him friendship. "Trained me daily on how to gather intel and report on my findings. Put me through rigorous exercises. Made sure I wouldn't break if I were ever tortured for information. About you. About me." He reached for my hand, but I yanked it away. A vicious smile spread across his face as he snatched it up anyway, fingering the bracelet still wrapped around my wrist. "He provided the stones for this." I gasped, realizing I hadn't considered the bracelet since I'd put it on. "The stones suppress your powers, but if I made it too obvious, your Omada would notice. So I disguised them as something I knew you'd never want to take off."

I tore my hand free of his grasp again and tried to unclasp it, to free it from my wrist. But the damn thing wouldn't budge. I was frantic, and Kaleb—he was laughing.

"You won't be able to get it off. Not here. Only someone with magic can take it off you now."

I clenched my teeth and gripped the bracelet tightly. "You're a monster."

"Oh, I know. It's what I was trained to be." A small gasp beside me reminded me Kendall was still here, silently observing. Kaleb ignored her. "Father put me through his sessions every time he came to visit. Telling me I had to endure the pain, just in case. It made me who I am."

The mark on his back… His father *had* hurt him, but not in the way he had made it seem. The little boy I grew up with had to endure that, and I knew nothing about it. It disgusted me to realize that, even if I had known, it had all been a ploy to get to me. The thought of someone doing that to their own son—twisting him into a monster in the process —was abhorrent.

"Being chained in that cave had to look legitimate, too. The torture. The pain. That was real. When you found me, I had to look every bit the part. Of course, Koladon had no idea I was his inside source. He thought I was just some human boy you loved and could use against you." He was the one providing them information? The whole time? The store. The courtyard. And they never knew… But why would he keep his identity secret if they were after the same thing? "But my father's voice echoed in my head, reminding me with every slice of the blade and every burn of the brand that it was all to get you back here. You would be my prize in the end. I would claim you as mine and be able to wield your power however I wanted."

I curled my lip in disgust, but an inner battle was raging within me. I had once relished being wrapped in his arms and yearning to be his. Now, I never wanted to feel his arms around me again. How had I so easily flipped from being the person who rushed in to save him from danger to the one who said what I did next? "I will *never* be yours," I rasped.

He chuckled darkly, the sound chilling. "Not like that, girlie." I recoiled at the nickname I had grown fond of. "We are forbidden from intermixing. A curse is placed on anyone who mates with different species." A sly grin made me wonder what that even meant. "No. I will *claim* you."

My heart plummeted. "No," I whispered, remembering Kyler explaining the difference between claiming and choosing—a slave. I'd be *his* slave.

"Yes," he bragged. "Your powers will be mine to control, and there's nothing you can do about it."

"No…" I repeated.

But Kaleb stood, grabbing my chin roughly to make me look up at him. "You will be the most feared Fae in all the realms, making me the most powerful being among all species." I tried to pull my chin from his hand, but he gripped it harder, leaning close enough to feel his breath on my lips. "But first, I have to break that bond my brother has with you."

ONE
Pull the Plug

Brother.

He was his *brother?*

Weeks—or months—had passed since Kaleb dropped that bomb. It was hard to tell with the dungeon being pitch black, not even a flicker of light or window with the sun seeping in from outside. We only knew time had passed based on the ever-changing guards.

Brother.

That word echoed every day since he left—in my mind, in my dreams. Sometimes, it felt as if the dungeon itself softly repeated the word over and over.

He was his brother?

Kaleb hadn't shown up since that night he'd left me dumbstruck on the floor of that damned cell. He slammed the barred door shut, cackling, but not before I vomited all over his boots and myself. He'd rambled something about a welcome-home party, but nothing he said registered as he locked my cell. My mind had shut down, and my body followed suit.

I hadn't left the dungeon, either. Guards brought me filthy water and stale bread at random times, never speaking to or even acknowledging me, no matter how loudly I yelled or screamed at them. They seldom glanced my way, and they never unlocked my cell.

But the others… The only time I could see anything was when they came to retrieve them. By the light of the guards' torches, I was forced to watch as, one by one, the girls were taken away, always in the same order. They returned each time with new bruises or fresh blood staining their clothes. The first few times the guards came, the girls fought back fiercely because they had no idea what was going on. Afterward, they realized that resisting only made their torture sessions worse. They'd beat them until they could no longer move but were still conscious enough to speak. Now they went willingly, fully aware they'd be bruised either way, but less was better.

Ken and Leigh were both sleeping off their latest torment sessions, having come back with broken noses. Again. They always insisted it looked worse than it was, but I never believed their lies. They could barely move when they returned, tossed into their cells like ragdolls, sometimes conscious, other times not.

Ma had it the hardest. Her body wasn't built to survive in this realm. We all got sick when we first arrived, given the change in atmosphere. But while the twins and I adjusted, Ma couldn't stop coughing. She was gone the longest and always returned unconscious when they threw her back into her cell. I tried to ask her what they wanted from her, but she could never remember. It broke something deep within me the first time she was brought back and every time after. I screamed the loudest at the guards for her.

Whenever she was awake, I gave her whatever water I could spare and portions of my bread when I felt I didn't need it as much as she did.

But her body was shutting down.

With the torture and lack of nutrients, whatever sickness she had was progressing much faster than it would have if she had been adequately cared for. I tried to think about why we were all in the dungeon and why, after all this time, I was the only one who hadn't been taken.

There was still no sign of Mitch, but I kept noticing a longer gap between the twins when all the girls were in the dungeon with me. After figuring out the routine, it became clear that Mitch's sessions happened during that time, wherever he was.

The worst part about all of this was that I couldn't do anything to stop it.

I felt powerless. Trapped. I screamed obscenities at the guards as they came to drag my friends from their cells, but it was futile. They still brought them to whatever chamber they used for their sick torture, but I never heard their screams.

The guards learned the hard way to keep their distance from my cell door. I became weary of watching them drag my family away, so one day, I used the floor to sharpen my nails as much as I could. After weeks without any means to care for myself, they had grown long and jagged. One guard made the unfortunate mistake of stepping too close to my barred door, and I lashed out, digging my fingers into his face, clawing at his eyes and ripping away the flesh before another guard pulled him away. Blood spilled from his wounds, and his screams reverberated through the tunnels as they led him away

I saved Ma from her session that day.

As I picked dried blood from my nails later, the girls told me he'd lost one of his eyes before the healers could reach him. I could only grin, laughing maniacally. I couldn't help it. After being locked in a dungeon with no light, food, or clean water, I was spiraling out of control. All I could think about was getting out and saving Ma, my best option being to attack someone who had the power to open my cage.

That guard never returned to the dungeon.

The only time they unlocked my cell was a few hours later when three guards came down, entering my cell one at a time to beat me into oblivion. They weren't allowed to break my limbs, but that didn't stop them from cracking a few ribs or shattering my cheekbone with their feet. I took every hit with just a grunt, absorbing the pain as punishment —not for taking that guard's eye, but for everything I let Kaleb do to get under my skin. For each blow the girls received that I didn't. For bringing any of them into this mess.

The girls screamed as I was ruthlessly abused, helpless on the other side of the bars. I don't recall losing consciousness, but when I woke up, the wounds were mostly healed, leaving only dried blood behind. Shackles had been placed on my wrists and ankles, securing me to the back wall with enough slack that I couldn't get within three feet of my door. I could only move far enough to reach the food tray they slid in. From that day on, I had to sleep curled up with my back against the wall.

The twins begged me not to attempt anything like that again, but I wasn't going to sit idly by while they were tortured endlessly. I had to do everything I could to keep them from coming back with more scars. Even if the chains restricted me, I wouldn't stop trying to protect them.

Today was still uncertain. If they were sticking to their pattern,

Kendall would be called next. However, it felt like more time had passed since the guards dropped Mari in her cell. She returned with a bloodied lip, a cut on her temple, and a black eye. After finishing cleaning her face with her cup of dirty water, I offered her some of mine to drink since hers was gone. She gratefully took a few sips, ensuring to leave me some so I didn't pass out from dehydration—again. The water made us sick, but it was better than nothing. I wouldn't be surprised if they deliberately contaminated the water to keep us weak.

"What did they ask you today?" I whispered through the bars, taking the cup back from her.

She shook her head. "Nothing new. The same questions. How are you what you are? What did I do to help you? Any weaknesses you have that I knew about?" She grinned at the last one, the motion causing pain to flash in her eyes. "I told them you have no weaknesses. They didn't believe me. Gave me this." She pointed to the cut on her temple, which she said almost made her pass out.

I grinned half-heartedly back at her, pulling my knees to my chest and resting my chin on them. "The only weakness I have is falling for a monster." He said everything I needed to hear, doing whatever it took to make me fall in love with him. Every move he made was calculated. The flirting. The touches. The conversations. Perhaps revealing his scar to me, showing he was helpless and wounded—human—was what he thought would really seal the deal. He was right. Even though he never told me what happened, his vulnerability in those moments drew me in even more.

I fell right into his perfectly laid trap. Of course, it never crossed my mind that the kid I'd known since kindergarten could betray me in such a terrible way. Never once had I suspected him of feeding the enemy information about me. But as I mulled over our entire friendship while trapped in this dungeon, it all made perfect sense. He knew everything about me—my weaknesses, my strengths. He knew where to strike to make the most impact. Kaleb knew all there was to know, and he'd ultimately used it all against me.

The first few days, my body ran dry, crying over someone who betrayed me. It was how I dehydrated myself the first time. Every thought of the love I'd felt for him invaded my mind for days, reminding me how much I craved him and needed his touch—his comfort. The way his brown eyes shone and his tender smile made me want to give him everything—to make him my everything.

Fortunately, I hadn't seen his face since that day because I still wasn't sure I could look at him without wondering whether he was the boy I'd known my whole life or the monster who betrayed me. Was any of it real? I didn't know what kind of powers Kaleb possessed, but I wouldn't be surprised if one of them was the ability to manipulate my mind.

Mari reached through the bars and took my hand. "He tricked us all, Rayleigh." She couldn't read minds, even outside the magic-blocking cells we were in, but she had once told me I wore my emotions on my face. "I never suspected him. He hid his true identity from all of us. Even Kyler." The name made my body tense, and Mari noticed. She tightened her grip on my hand. "You still don't trust him." It wasn't a question.

I shook my head. "How can I?" I whispered, pulling my hand from hers. "He's Kaleb's brother. How could he not be in on all of this?"

Mari sighed, pulling her hand back into her cell. "They may be brothers, but I honestly don't think Kyler knows." Her voice was contemplative, no doubt thinking back to the time she'd spent with him over the years. "Even if I hadn't known him for as long as I did and only saw what happened in the meadow… I still wouldn't believe he knew." Her voice had softened. She'd been slowly sharing with me what happened in the meadow while I was running my own rescue mission to the cave. There was only so much I could take, so I usually stopped her mid-story to process everything. It was already hard enough to deal with everything concerning Kaleb.

But she was only awake for short periods, her sessions leaving her exhausted or unconscious. For some reason, we seemed to have a bit of extra time now. I took a deep breath, planning to ask for the whole story, but I stopped myself. Would knowing what happened that night make any of this better? Or would I end up regretting ever going into that cave to save Kaleb? Even if I had suspected him, the fact that Koladon had Ma and Mitch would have led me to that meadow.

I watched Mari closely. Even if she told me what happened, would I believe her? I didn't have to because in my mind, she wasn't blameless yet. But she was sitting in a cell just like mine. There had to be a reason she came back as beaten up as the twins and Ma. She had been locked up and tortured, too.

I took a deep breath, letting it out slowly while watching her face in the dim light of the nearby torch. One of the guards left it behind in the bracket on my cell door—a mistake they'd never made before, but I wasn't about to remind them to take it. It was the only light source we'd seen since being here.

"Tell me what happened," I said carefully. "From the beginning."

Mari's eyes shone with tears. There was no mistaking the caution in her voice when she spoke. "We knew the meadow was a trap but thought we could handle it. We weren't expecting so many others to show up." She sighed heavily before continuing. "With Bastiel and Stefano not coming, that left three of us against nine others that Koladon had summoned from Niccodra. He wasn't stupid. He prepared well for a battle against three of the strongest warriors in the Kidemos."

She was referring to Theo, Kyler, and herself with those words. I remembered this part of the story. I knew they were strong from my time with them, but I wasn't aware they were *all* top warriors. And they were all assigned to me…. That explained why Aaidan was so curious about my powers.

"We landed in the meadow among those dragons and their Doulos." The word sent a chill down my spine, knowing that was what Kaleb intended for me. "Aaidan gave us a chance to surrender, offering safe passage back to Niccodra instead of fighting. Kyler's dragon shot a blue fireball at his head in response." That alone should have erased any doubt lingering in me, but was it different because his dragon was in control? "None of us were going to walk away from that fight. We knew that. But Aaidan didn't know you weren't on that field with us. He even mocked Kyler's illusion of you from the ground in his human form. We used it to our advantage. Kyler and Theo both took on four of the ten Kidemos, leaving two for me to fight. Ken and Leigh used their vantage point to help us against attacks we couldn't see coming from the Fae warriors."

"I saw you fall from the sky," I interrupted her. "Leigh wasn't with you."

"That must have been when Aaidan slammed into me and knocked her off my back." I gasped, glancing at Leigh's sleeping form two cells down. This was a part of the story she hadn't shared with me yet.

"Thankfully, Theo caught her and placed her out of harm's way until I could get back to her." Mari's voice had softened. I turned back to see her watching Leigh, too. "I can't imagine ever letting anything happen to her."

I gave her a weak smile, hearing the truth in her voice. At that point, I wondered how much time Mari and Leigh actually got to spend together. I never really got the chance to ask. "What happened when you returned to the fight?"

She took a shuddering breath. "Koladon showed up. We knew immediately you were free to make your move. But when Kyler tried to confirm with you, he realized something was very wrong. He felt your bond go silent, and something in him snapped, forgetting to maintain the ruse that you weren't there. As soon as your mirage disappeared, so did Koladon. Kyler went feral, tearing into Aaidan's wings to prevent him from flying after him. He found an opening and tried to take off, but the other dragons caught him before he could escape. Kyler unleashed blue fire, but they still managed to drag him back to the forest floor. The only reason he lost was because they managed to get a gonos on him, which forced him to shift back to his human form. Even then, he fought with all his might to escape." Her eyes found me through the bars. "To get to you."

I wanted to believe those words, I really did…

"He tried yelling your name to warn you, but with all the noise from the fight, it was impossible for his voice to reach you." If we'd had our connection—if the bond hadn't gone silent—would it have made a difference? Would we have escaped? "Unfortunately, one of the other dragons had powers like mine and flooded his body with every emotion possible, overloading his senses. He collapsed to the ground, writhing in pain until he passed out. Theo and I tried to keep fighting, but without Kyler, we had already lost."

Mari pulled her knees to her chest and wrapped her arms around them. "The rest of what happened was a blur. They somehow got the gonos on both Theo and I, flooding our bodies with emotion and knocking us out, too. I woke up when someone tossed me into this cell. I knew nothing about Kaleb or what happened to you until you were dropped in the cell next to mine. When your Ma was thrown in next, I realized that something went wrong long before Kyler lost contact with you." Her eyes shone as the firelight flickered in them. "I wouldn't be surprised if Theo and Kyler are in cells like these with Mitch somewhere, but I have no idea where we are. I never knew there were dungeons in Niccodra. Not like these, anyway." She held up the shackles that suppressed her magic. We found that out the very first night when she tried to heal my injuries, but she couldn't. Her magic wasn't there.

I let Mari's story sink in, reflecting on everything she said about Kyler. About all he'd done for me. To me. With me. Kaleb's confession of betrayal made it harder to find Kyler at fault, but my anxiety stemmed from the fact that they were brothers. There was no way Kyler didn't know Kaleb was his brother. Unless…

"Do you know anything about Kyler's parents?" I asked Mari.

She furrowed her brow, silent for a moment before finally answering, "No." She tilted her head. "Come to think of it, we never discussed his family. He was my Lochi and—"

"What's that?" I asked, remembering Aaidan refer to Koladon as one, too.

"It's like a general among warriors." Kyler was a *general?* "Anyway, he never mentioned his family, and I never thought to ask. Family matters were private during training. But even after all these years…" She trailed off, appearing to ponder that topic.

My shoulders slumped forward as I hugged my knees closer. "I never got to ask him where he's from or about his family, either. I don't even know his last name." My eyes found hers. "Or yours, for that matter. Do Drakalasson have last names?"

Mari chuckled half-heartedly. "You were too focused on discovering who you were to ask about us. We didn't really have much time together, if you think about it." Her eyes sparkled with the little humor she could muster through the pain. "My full name is Amarietta Manteio. I come from a long line of pure-blooded healers on my mother's side. My father was also a healer but hailed from a mixed line. His other family lines never developed in him, allowing him to focus on healing alongside my mother. He became part of the royal council, using his ability to sense and manipulate emotions during trials because he excelled at remaining neutral." Mari rested her head back against the bars and sighed. "Mother warned him against it, saying he would be corrupted if he spent too long in their company. But he said he would be the one manipulating emotions, not the other way around. If anything, he claimed he would corrupt the council with his way of thinking. My mother laughed, yet he never once swayed to the wrong side in that council chamber. He was honest and truthful in every trial and made sure that those witnessing or testifying were too."

Goosebumps rose on my arms at the thought of what might happen next—why I was being held in this cell. "Will I be put on trial?" I whispered.

Mari snapped her head to me. "Why would you be put on trial?"

"Why am I in a dungeon? Why are we here? Why do all of this?" I gestured to the entire structure around us.

She gazed at me with her mouth slightly agape, unable to find the answers to my questions.

"The only reason I can think of is the last thing Kaleb said." When he claimed Kyler was his brother, he said he wanted to sever the bond between us. The thought sent a chill down my spine as I whispered to Mari, "Is there a way to break a bond like the one Kyler and I have?"

Mari stared at me for what felt like an eternity before whispering, "I don't know. I've never seen a rider bond, much less seen one removed." The sigh that followed made me furrow my brow.

"What aren't you telling me?" I pressed my forehead against the bars between us, striving to meet her eyes as she turned away from my gaze. "Mari, please," I urged. "I can handle it."

"That's the thing… I don't think you can." Mari's voice was barely a whisper. She'd seen how my anxiety had worsened since we arrived. She watched the panic attacks through the bars as I calmed myself down, pressing my hands so hard into the rock that the cuts on my palms were almost always bleeding. It kept me grounded, though. She told me I needed to move around so my muscles wouldn't atrophy, but I could barely stand, much less lift my legs for exercises. I'd picked my nails to the point of bleeding. My hair was patchy in places where I'd pulled it while screaming during my attacks.

When Mari's eyes finally met mine, I whispered, "Please." She knew something about bonds being destroyed, even if it wasn't a rider bond. I needed to know.

She sighed heavily, ready to answer.

But then the dungeon door down the hall creaked open, and her head whipped in the direction of the sound. Footsteps echoed off the walls —more than one set. Kendall stirred awake, knowing it was her turn. I reached for her hand through the bars as she opened her blackened, swollen eyes to meet mine. She offered me a weak smile and gently squeezed my hand before releasing it and using both hands to push herself up, gritting her teeth and hissing in pain.

Tears welled in my eyes as I watched her stand with a strength I'd always known she possessed but had never wanted to see her use. She took two steps, standing just inside her door, and waited.

The guards came into view, and Ken tensed where she stood. There were four guards, all dressed in the same type of hooded jacket Kaleb wore that first day. I recognized most of them by their physical build. Usually, there were three: two to hold the girls and one to unlock and relock the cell doors.

With a fourth one appearing, my heart quickened. This wasn't a typical session.

Something else was going on.

They passed Leighton's door.

Kendall's.

They stopped outside mine. My blood ran cold.

That wasn't right. I was *never* let out. For anything. I had a chamber pot in the back corner of my cell, which the others didn't have. They never gave me a place to clean myself. I was filthy, weak, tired, and hungry. It didn't matter. I never left. What made today different?

One of the guards lifted the torch from the bracket and used it to help the other find the key he needed.

When my door swung open, I summoned the little strength I had to push myself to my feet, using the bars when my legs couldn't hold me properly. I learned from watching my friends being dragged away that fighting accomplished nothing. Gritting my teeth, I glared at the guards as two of them entered my cell, each grabbing an elbow roughly so that the third could unlock the shackles chaining me to the wall. They then led me toward the door, carrying most of my weight as I struggled to walk.

Mari and Ken whispered words of disbelief as I walked out the cell door with what little strength I had and faced the final guard.

The shadows concealed the face of the fourth, shorter guard from a distance, but when I halted right before them, I could see long, curly blonde hair peeking out from beneath the hood.

A shuffling sounded, and then Leighton's raspy voice echoed, "Ray? What's going on?"

Ignoring Leighton, their head tilted back to reveal a beautiful female underneath. Her pale skin was dotted with freckles, and her brown eyes glimmered with hatred. She was smaller than me but looked like she could knock me out with a single hit, especially given my current state. She grinned wickedly as she spat, "His Majesty requests your presence."

TWO
You Don't Know

"His Majesty?" I sputtered, my voice hoarse. "As in the King?" But she didn't respond. Instead, she turned and led us down the hall, away from my friends and Ma. I glanced over my shoulder to see Leigh, Ken, and Mari standing at the doors to their cells, peering out with anxious expressions. I tried not to dwell on what awaited me and refocused on what my feet were supposed to be doing.

Why would the King want to see me? I'm Fae, not a Drakalasson. What could he possibly want from me? And what did Kaleb have to do with it?

My already weak body trembled, partly from fear, but I was certain it was also because I hadn't used my legs in weeks. Standing in that cell, as Mari had instructed, could only do so much for my muscles. I had never thought of myself as frail or skinny before, but with only bread and dirty water to fill my stomach, that's what I'd become. I had never felt weaker. Even after my accident, lying in a hospital bed for days, I felt stronger than I did walking away from my cell. Nothing in my body seemed to function properly, and who knew if I'd ever return to my normal self?

After several turns through the dark dungeon halls, we finally came to a staircase carved into the rock. I stopped voluntarily moving my feet and groaned. It was one thing to walk on a flat surface in my weakened state and another to climb stone stairs. The guards, however, didn't stop; their constant movement meant I would be going up, even if they had to drag me. My legs wouldn't lift for the first step, and I whimpered as my knees slammed against the sharp corner. I struggled to get my feet under me, but the guards were already two stairs ahead. I cried out in pain as my shins and knees slammed into stone as they ascended. After several stairs and bruises, one of the guards stopped, forcing the other to halt as well. Tears were forming in my eyes from the agony, but I gritted my teeth, determined not to let them fall. I could feel the blood trickling down my shins as I tried to adjust my feet beneath me again.

Nothing was worse than what my friends experienced. I could manage this pain.

The guard who stopped first waved for the other to let go of my arm. It hit the stone step with a smack before I could stop it. Then I was lifted off the ground and cradled in the guard's arms. I would have been embarrassed if I hadn't already been grateful that I didn't have to walk anymore. Although, if they wanted to keep me weak, dragging me up the stairs would have made more sense. Still, I wasn't about to give them any tips.

My mind drifted back to why I was being hauled up the stairs. Were we in the King's dungeon? Did he know Kaleb, Aaidan, and the Kool-Aid Man? Had he been the one who ordered my capture? Was the King the elusive Gustav? What did they want with me?

I wish I had my notebook… Not that I'd be able to write anything in that darkness.

The female in front pushed open a heavy door, and light flooded the stairway, causing me to close my eyes instantly. The sound of rushing water filled my ears. I tried to squint to see what lay beyond the door but could only make out a wall of white. My eyes burned as they tried to adjust to anything other than darkness. The guard set me on my feet, while the other resumed his position at my elbow. As I became more accustomed to the light, I realized that the white wall was not a wall at all but the source of the loud noise: a waterfall. We emerged from the stairwell into a cave-like space, far enough away not to get drenched, yet close enough that I couldn't see around it as the guards led me along.

Our walk along the sliff was silent. The mist skittered along my skin and the thought of washing away the dirt and grime had me wishing to get closer to the falls. Before I had the chance, I was ushered through another door behind the female. She walked as if on a runway—chin held high, each step exuding confidence. With her fitted jacket, black leggings, and high boots concealing weapons, she resembled an assassin. Around her waist, she wore a belt adorned with several small daggers and a long sword at her hip. Why would Drakalassons need someone dressed like that, armed with so many weapons, to escort me? I couldn't even access my magic. I didn't want to ask, fearing she might press one of those many weapons to my throat for speaking to her.

The stone door scraped against the ground, closing with a thud and leaving us in near total darkness, the only light emanating from the torch carried by the guard behind me. Our shadows danced on the walls as we navigated the endless corridor. My legs felt ready to give out, but the guards kept me moving forward, their grip on my arms tightening with each lagging step. A sliver of light up ahead told me we were close to the end.

The assassin pushed open a door several feet ahead, allowing a softer light to illuminate the corridor. As I stepped through the doorway, my jaw dropped when I saw the beautiful hallway before me. The ceiling was high and covered in stained glass windows, which made the white walls and flooring take on multi-colored patterns. The walls bore paintings of various sizes depicting beautifully crafted dragons and portraits of what seemed to be their human forms side-by-side.

We walked silently down the hall, the only sounds being our footsteps and the occasional dragging noise of my foot as it failed to lift off the floor before moving forward.

The female guard stopped several feet ahead at an open archway, turning to face me with a sneer. "His Majesty wants you presentable." Her gaze traveled the length of me, her disgust deepening. "Not sure a bath will do much, kató." She spat the last word like a curse, so I didn't need to know what it meant to respond.

Without flinching, I said, "If you're going to insult me, do it in words I'll understand, bitch." Thankfully, my voice didn't betray my false confidence. The hiss and snarl she returned indicated she wasn't accustomed to being spoken to that way, but as she raised her hand to retaliate, someone caught her wrist from the archway.

"Enough, Naila." A tall, gorgeous female towered over Naila, her brown hair framing her round face and stopping just above her shoulders. She had a solid build and her curves spoke of a love for good food and big hugs, but the authority in her voice told me there was much more to her than that.

Naila snarled as she tore her hand from the female's grip. "She's all yours." With one last sarcastic smile, she sashayed away, the other guards following in her wake.

With the guards' support gone, I placed a hand on the wall beside the door and turned to find the other female staring at me with a soft smile. "I'm Libella." The name sounded familiar, but I couldn't quite grasp it amidst the chaos in my mind. I wanted to thank her for stopping Naila, but I had no idea why I was brought to her. Libella turned and extended her arm to guide me into the room from which she had emerged. When my legs nearly gave out on the first step, I reached for the door frame again. She extended her hand to stop me and asked, "Do you need assistance?"

Puzzled, I stared at her for a moment because the answer seemed obvious. Yet, she hadn't touched me at all, not even when I almost fell. She was essentially giving me the opportunity to ask for help, so I nodded slowly.

"May I?" she asked, her arm reaching for my waist. Again, I nodded, surprised by the sudden opportunity to consent to help—or was it consent to touch?

Her arm wrapped around my waist, and I positioned my arm to encircle hers since her shoulders were level with my head. I leaned into her embrace as she bore almost all my weight to assist me across the room. She reminded me of an Amazon goddess, tall and fierce, appearing youthful—just a few years older than me—but her eyes reflected the wisdom of many more years than that.

"Who are you?" I asked softly.

She didn't look at me as she replied, "I am Libella, handmaiden to the Queen."

Queen? My heart raced. If she was close to the Queen, maybe she could answer some of my questions. I swallowed hard. "Why am I here?"

"His Majesty has requested your presence," she stated plainly.

I rolled my eyes internally, her short and quick answers reminding me of someone else I once asked that question. "Yes, but why?"

"Because he believes you to be one of the most powerful Fae in all the realms." Libella's words echoed so closely to Theo's that I stopped breathing. My body froze. The room spun. The edges of my vision blurred.

I sank my toes into the plush carpet, feeling the soft fibers caress my bare feet. Mustering my strength, I turned in Libella's grasp. "What did you just say?"

Her eyes sparkled with a knowing look as she repeated the words verbatim.

She knew. She *knew* I had heard those words before, almost exactly, from someone I still didn't believe I could trust. Yet it gave me hope that maybe I could. That they were still on my side. Or at least he was. I studied her face for a moment longer and decided to ask my first question again. "Who are you?"

A small smile played on her lips. "I told you. I am Libella, handmaiden to the Queen." I heard what she was saying, but her eyes conveyed a different message. Something like, *Yes, I know you've heard those words before. How would* I *know that?*

But she didn't say anything more. Perhaps there was a reason… fear of being overheard? Or of revealing herself? Was this some kind of trick? I narrowed my eyes, but she continued to smile as she watched me. I chose my words carefully. "Can I trust you?"

Libella looked as if I'd just told her something amusing while raising a brow. "Yes."

My eyes narrowed even more as I asked again, "Can I trust *you?*" I hoped she would understand the implication of my repeated question—who I might be referring to instead.

She tilted her head slightly, a sparkle of mischief in her eyes. "Absolutely, dearie."

The nickname did it. Even though I had no idea how she knew him, I knew Theo orchestrated this moment. After weeks in the dungeon, not knowing what was happening or what to believe, I decided Theo had never betrayed me. I was still uncertain about Kyler, but Theo was here. He was safe, and he was trying to reach me. "Thank you, Libella," I whispered as a considerable weight lifted off my chest.

Her smile widened as she nodded. "Call me Bell."

That struck another chord I didn't want to address, and I winced.

"No. Libella is good."

She frowned slightly but nodded, offering me her hand again. I accepted the help, and she led me to the bathroom. A tub filled with steaming water was set into a beautiful tile floor. Sunlight poured into the room through a stunning crystal window in the ceiling. The way the light refracted off the crystal created spots of rainbow colors around the space. The walls were made of a material I'd never seen before, resembling swirls of black within shiny white stone. The sink was set into a marble vanity, with oils and soaps lining the edge, along with crystals similar to those Theo had shown me weeks ago.

As I sniffed the air, expecting to catch the scent of the bath oils, I detected food instead. Real food. I followed my nose and found a tray next to the bath filled with meat, vegetables, and some fruit. I turned to Libella, my mouth watering as I asked, "Is that for me?"

She nodded. "But eat it slowly; it might upset your stomach after only having water and bread for the last few weeks."

The smell of spices I didn't recognize filled my nostrils as she guided me to the water's edge. The food didn't look like anything I'd eaten before, but my nose was never wrong about food. Libella helped me ease down to sit at the edge. Her last words echoed in my mind as I speared what appeared to be a potato with my fork. "How long have I been here?"

"Four weeks." She walked to the faucet, turned on the hot water, and poured more oils into the mix.

I brought the potato to my nose and inhaled its aroma, wondering if asking her anything was worth it. She might not be able to respond for whatever reason. I took a small bite. It tasted sweeter than I was used to, but its spiced, buttery flavor made me want to shove the whole thing into my mouth. I forced myself to nibble, even though my stomach begged for more. "Where did they take my brother?" I asked between bites.

Libella was retrieving small soap bottles from the intricately patterned cupboard attached to the vanity. "A separate wing. Closer to His Majesty."

Goosebumps crept over my skin. "Why closer to him?" I asked, finishing my potato.

She pulled a towel from the closet. Its door was made of dark wood with carvings traveling down its surface, as if to tell a story. If I ever came back to this room, I'd have to remember to study it closer.

Libella took a deep breath, returned to the tub, and turned off the water. After setting the soap bottles and towel on a small table by the stairs, she faced me. "His Majesty doesn't believe your brother is fully human."

I nearly choked on my potato. "What!?" I sputtered between coughs. "He's human! My parents are human. How could Mitch *not* be?"

"There is speculation that the man you claim is your father may not be human. They suspect he was part of the Omada that accompanied your mother to Earth."

"Excuse me?" I couldn't believe it. But Libella said it as if she'd done so countless times, as if it were normal for me to discover yet another truth I'd known my whole life was a lie. "My dad was human. He never showed signs of—" I was about to say magic, but the more I thought about it…

"Nothing is for certain yet. But that is why your mother has been…" She trailed off, looking at me with pleading eyes.

"Tortured the worst?" I finished for her.

Libella nodded. "She insisted he's from Earth and that he's human, but there's no way to prove it since he's dead."

The harsh words rang through my head as the other ones Libella said clanged around them. My dad could have been Fae. Or was he Drakalasson? Both were part of my Omada, but would my birth mother have had the same protection? "Why does it matter to the King if he's half-human?"

But as soon as I asked the question, I knew the answer before it came from Libella's mouth. "Because there's a law against intermixing with humans."

Okay…maybe I didn't know. "I thought it was a curse."

"Between Drakalasson and Fae, it's a curse." Libella extended her hand to help me up. "Between humans and the races of Niccodra, there's a law against procreating with humans. It's said that the offspring become the monsters of this world when their magic begins to develop. Not being able to use their magic properly…it takes control of their body and makes them forget who they are." She sighed, a sense of calm about her, but I was trembling at her words. "It might as well be a curse."

If Mitch wasn't fully human and turned into a monster because of it —no. He was human. My dad, Greg, was *human*. There was no way he could keep that from us if it were true. Even if his job was super secretive and we knew nothing about it, that didn't mean he was from a different realm… right? As I prepared to ask my next question, I fought the urge to scream that it was all nonsense. "What will they do to Mitch if he isn't fully human?"

"I don't know," Libella said softly. "But if the King has taken a special interest in him, I can only assume one of two things: he'll keep him close, or he'll send him away." I had a feeling the latter didn't mean a trip back to Earth, and the unease I felt led me to my next question.

"Why does the King want to see *me?*" He had to know by now that I wasn't part human, so why was he interested?

"He only asked me to prepare you. I know nothing else." She helped me remove the clothes I'd worn for the last four weeks. When I'd flown into battle with Kyler, I wore the leathers he had given me. But sometime between the cave and the dungeon, someone had changed me into linen clothes that were now filthy and clung to my body in places where I'd been injured. As she peeled the clothes from my skin, I realized I wasn't wearing anything underneath. My cheeks burned as I tried to cover myself with my hands. Libella didn't seem to notice, though, tossing my dirty clothes into a bin near the door and returning to guide me into the large pool of now milky water. I was left wearing only the bracelet of betrayal. Libella eyed the bracelet and sighed. She must have known what it was.

I hissed at the first step into the bath. The steaming water scorched my skin, but I reveled in the pain because it was vastly different from sitting on the cold dungeon floor. Taking another step down, another hiss escaped my lips as the water climbed higher on my legs. Libella assisted me down each step, walking into the water with me up to her knees before helping me lower to sit on a ledge in the tub. The water felt silky and smoother than the water back home, but maybe that was due to the oils she added. My skin prickled under the water, and my body relaxed into the feel of the slick water around me. It felt like magic.

"Keep taking small bites," Libella said, sliding the food tray closer.

"And drink some of this." She placed a glass and pitcher next to the tray. "I'll be right back." With that, she left the room, closing the door behind her.

The water felt incredible, but I knew I wouldn't be able to relax until I knew what was happening. I turned to the tray behind me, sliced off a piece of meat, and brought it to my nose to smell before putting it in my mouth. I chewed slowly at first, even though my stomach growled at the taste of the protein. The taste was unique, but it was delicious all the same. I cut off another piece, eating slowly as I digested the new foods and Libella's words.

She knew Theo. Well enough to know exactly what to say for me to figure that out. She didn't hesitate when I asked if I could trust either of them. My mind wandered back to everything Theo had said and done for me since I met him. When he talked about the fastest he'd ever won a match, he mentioned a partner, but had he said their name? If he did, I couldn't remember. Libella… it sounded so familiar.

And what she said about Mitch…could it be true? Could he be half-human? I mean, I wasn't even human, and signs of me not being human didn't start until I was his age. But nothing about him made me question

—

His accident. He should have died. Could his genetics be related to his survival?

The door creaked open, and Libella stepped in once more. "You didn't drink any water," she remarked, shutting the door behind her.

I sighed, shaking the thoughts from my mind, and reached for the glass she'd poured to take a sip. The sweet water was familiar, and I immediately felt its effect throughout my body. It was the same water Mari had given me after Aaidan kidnapped me. My weakness and hunger vanished the moment a full gulp hit my stomach. "What is this?" I asked, downing the rest of it and refilling my cup.

"It's called glykos. A sweet water from the crystal caves. It has magical properties." Well, that explains it. She handed me a washcloth and soap. "Use this to scrub your body." I placed the empty cup beside the food and took the items from her. "Do you want me to help with your hair?"

"Um…" I hadn't been able to see myself in the mirror, but I could only imagine how I looked after weeks of accumulating dirt, grime, and probably blood. The thought of someone else touching my dirty, tangled hair… on the other hand, it might be nice to have someone else deal with the tangles while I tried to relax. "Yes, please," I said meekly.

She smiled, grabbing a small pitcher and brush before sitting on the edge behind me. "Tilt your head back for me." She dipped the pitcher into the water as I did, then poured it over my head, careful to avoid my eyes. As the warm water cascaded down, the same tingling sensation followed in its wake just like when I stepped into it.

"Does the bath water have magical properties too?" Libella hummed in affirmation. It was strange that they wanted to heal me before sending me to see the King. "Why go through all this healing when I'll just be put back in the dungeon?"

She was silent as she poured another pitcher of water over my head, running her fingers through the knots in my hair while doing so. Maybe she hadn't heard the question. I almost repeated it when she softly said, "We don't think you'll return to the dungeon."

Despite the warm water, my body became rigid and cold. "What do you mean?" I asked breathlessly.

Again, Libella remained silent as another pitcher of water flowed down my head. She poured soap onto my scalp and gently massaged it in. It felt miraculous, but I didn't want to be lulled into a state of relaxation any longer. I needed answers. I stiffened, turning where I sat to meet Libella's gaze. Finally, she sighed. "There's a rumor that the King has plans for you. They are just rumors," she said firmly as I gasped in horror, "but most things spoken in this palace turn out to be true." She gently turned me back around and continued with my hair. I was shaking under the water. Kaleb had mentioned something about claiming me, but he needed to remove the bond between Kyler and me before he could do it. Had he figured out a way? Is that why I was being brought to the King? But why would he be involved in this? Unless…

"Does the King want to claim me?" My voice was barely above a whisper, echoing Libella's.

She finished scrubbing my head and rinsed it with more water as she said, "I don't think so, dear." Then, she poured the contents of another bottle onto my head and rubbed it into my scalp again. I had to fight the urge to relax in the water. It was only natural to assume the worst if she didn't know what the King wanted with me. Kaleb could be working with him.

"Do you know Kaleb?" I asked softly. Libella nodded. "Does he work for the King?"

Her fingers froze, tangled in my hair, and met my gaze. She shook her head, but her eyes seemed to be trying to convey something different. They were wide, shining with something I couldn't decipher as she locked her stare with mine.

"Then why did Kaleb visit me in the King's dungeon as if he had put me there?" I wondered aloud, searching Libella's eyes for an answer.

She must have realized I wouldn't be able to figure it out because she leaned down next to my ear, her breath warm against my cheek as she whispered, "Kaleb is said to be the King and Queen's lost son."

THREE
Burning Down

My brain turned to mush, clouding my mind from everything happening around me. I didn't remember the rest of the bath. Libella must have coaxed me into using the soap and washcloth because I was clean when the tub started draining. So many questions raced through my mind as I waited for Libella to help me.

If Kaleb was the King's lost son, and Kyler was his brother, that meant Kyler was *also* the King's son. That whole not asking about his family thing was really backfiring. But the King's son? That made him a *prince*. Why was he part of my Omada? Was he in line for the throne? Did he have any other siblings? Was being part of the Kidemos part of his princely duties? Did the King and Queen send him to "protect" me? How were Aaidan and the Kool-Aid Man involved in all of this?

The questions were endless. I was about to ask Libella for a notebook, but she was holding a towel for me outside the tub. I took a deep breath, my mind still reeling, and slowly stood up. I barely noticed how easy it was to walk out of the water. My body felt like it had a few weeks ago: full, strong, and eager to move. I turned my head to look at Libella. "What's in that water?"

She gave me a knowing look, extending the towel further. The mysteries of this place were only increasing. Would I have time to sit and learn everything like I had at the Dengalow? Probably not, but I was starting to miss Theo's quirky lessons. Libella wrapped the towel around me and guided me into the main room. I hadn't noticed much about it when I first arrived, but it was enormous—a room fit for the guests of a

King and Queen.

But I am no guest, I reminded myself. *I'm a prisoner.*

The foyer featured an armchair and a long couch positioned against a floor-to-ceiling window. The curtains were drawn, yet streamed through the sheer fabric. Similar to the bathroom, a window adorned the ceiling, casting fragments of rainbows around the room. Several paintings hung on the walls, portraying the Drakalasson in both forms—which I realized were now royal, complete with crowns and elegant attire. Aside from the bathroom door, there were two other doors off the foyer. One stood open, revealing a bedroom where I spotted a standard bed and a large cushioned bed like Kyler's back at the Dengalow. I wondered if it was scattered with crystals as his was…

The other door was closed. It resembled the closet door in the bathroom. Even if I couldn't interpret the story, I wanted to examine the carvings and uncover their meaning.

Libella handed me undergarments, and I skillfully held the towel in place with one hand while putting them on. Even though she had already seen me naked, it was still a bit embarrassing. It was a miracle I could do any of it by myself. I wasn't sure if I had the bath to thank or if it was the delicious food and the glykos. Maybe it was a combination of all three.

I exchanged the towel for a dress made of sage green linen. The bodice was fitted, featuring an asymmetrical layered skirt. Nothing fancy, but also not something I thought a slave would wear. In fact, it resembled what Libella wore. As a handmaiden to the Queen, I wondered what that could signify.

"Put it on and sit here so I can braid your hair back." She motioned to the chair in front of a vanity just outside the bathroom.

The dress fit like a glove, reminding me of Mari's special skills. She always had the perfect size for me. Of course, that was all before we ended up here in a dungeon. "What will happen to my friends?" I asked as I sat down. They probably thought I was being tortured like they had been. I hated that I would have to tell them I was given a bath and food and treated with kindness after what they'd been through.

She brushed my hair and began the braid before answering. "They are to be brought before the King for questioning."

"For what?" I balked, knowing they'd done nothing wrong. Ma was close to dying.

"If Kaleb is the King's son, he will likely want to inquire about his kidnapping and torture."

"My friends didn't do that!" I nearly pulled away from Libella's skilled hands, but she placed a hand on my shoulder to stop me. "That was—all of that was fake! Koladon and Aaidan did that. None of my friends even knew Kaleb was from here."

"I know," she sighed as she continued my braid. "But the King doesn't know that. He only believes what he's told. And Kaleb is a very skilled liar."

Don't I know it... I looked at her in the mirror. She seemed to be on my side, but there was still no way to tell. "No one will go against him?" Blaming my friends for his kidnapping... He probably orchestrated that to pull my friends away from me. To keep his story consistent and prevent other versions from circulating. The King had to know that my friends hadn't done anything. But the only person I could think of who the King might believe... I didn't want to ask because I never wanted to say his name again, but I said, "What about Kyler?"

Libella's fingers paused in my hair for a moment before resuming slowly, yet she remained silent. It made my skin crawl, as if there was something I didn't know about him. Then she whispered, "We have company on the way." She completed the braid and turned me to face her. "Hold out your wrist," she commanded softly. Furrowing my brow, I complied. She swatted my hand away. I barely had time to gawk at her before she pointed to my other wrist.

The one with the bracelet.

I extended my trembling hand, and she quickly unfastened the clasp. The bracelet slipped from my wrist, and I stared at her in shock as she produced an exact replica to replace it. The original vanished into a pocket on her dress just as the sound of boots echoed in the hallway.

Before I could say thank you, she put her finger to her lips and shook her head. The door creaked open behind me, and my mind was racing. How did Libella know about the bracelet? Did the new one have magical restrictions, too? Would she be punished if they discovered what she did? I barely knew the female before me, but something about her entire presence made me want to trust her completely.

But being betrayed by one of the people I trusted most made me hesitant to trust anyone new. I hated it.

Removing the bracelet was one thing; she'd need to do much more to prove I could trust her. As soon as the gonos was gone, though, it felt like a huge weight had been lifted. I knew my powers weren't blocked anymore, but I still couldn't feel them; they seemed to be sleeping.

Before I could take any more time to process, Libella spun me around to face the door. Naila leaned against the doorframe, a sneer already plastered on her face. "She's ready," Libella said before Naila could speak.

"Good. I was going to take her even if she wasn't." Naila's sassy tone made it clear this was the last place she wanted to be. Her eyes locked onto mine, filled with hatred, though I had no idea why she felt such strong animosity toward me. It seemed like whatever it was, she took it as a personal insult that I even existed. "Well?" she demanded. "*Move.*"

Slightly taken aback, I stared at her, but a hand on my back nudged me forward. I gritted my teeth, holding back a retort, and crossed the room as Naila spun on her heel, flipping her hair over her shoulder in the same motion. The same guards from earlier were waiting outside the door. They took their positions beside and behind me, and I followed the sway of Naila's hips through the twists and turns of the palace.

Hoping to find my way back to Libella later, I tried to keep track of the path we were on, but it felt like I was being led in circles. Instead, I observed the paintings, committing them to memory and hoping I'd actually remember them. None of them were the same, which meant we weren't actually going in circles. That's when I noticed the path slanted slightly upward.

We were climbing higher in the castle.

But that didn't make sense. The windows on the ceiling reflected light onto the walls. That was sunlight shining through the glass. I was sure of it.

My mind was playing tricks on me.

"Stop trying to memorize the way," Naila said knowingly over her shoulder, a lazy smirk on her face. "It won't matter."

What did that even mean? Did the hallways *change?* No magic that I knew could do such a thing. Then again, I didn't even know magic existed until a month ago. It was a strange feeling, knowing there was magic now but having no idea what the possibilities were. Sure, Theo gave thorough presentations on the Fae and Drakalasson's magic, but he never mentioned there was other magic! Maybe he never actually intended for me to end up in Niccodra. Maybe he only showed me the magic he thought I would encounter back in Wisteria Falls.

Who knew what other kinds of magic I would encounter here?

Naila suddenly turned off the hallway and into a doorway I swear wasn't there a moment ago. I shook my head, as my mind was *clearly* playing tricks on me. Doors didn't just appear…

I had halted at the sight of the magical doorway when one of the guards roughly grabbed my elbow and gave me a not-so-gentle shove through the door. I shot him a nasty look over my shoulder and shrugged off his hand as I followed Naila into the room beyond.

A massive dining hall spread out before me. The long, white marble table in the center had twelve chairs surrounding it. The vaulted ceilings were adorned with colorful crystals that reflected the light, but a barrier prevented the colors from staining the room. The black and white marble swirled along the walls and floors, but one wall was solid glass from floor to ceiling, offering an incredible view. From where I stood, all I could see was a vibrant sky with a setting sun. No land in sight, but the clouds were stunning.

Someone cleared their throat, bringing my attention back to the table where several people now sat—or had they been there the whole time? Naila had casually thrown herself into a chair, her leg draped over the side as she examined her nails. Clearly, she was comfortable in the presence of—

I realized I had no idea who was sitting there. From their attire alone, I could only assume I was standing before the royalty who requested my presence: the King and Queen, and several others.

Only one of them was familiar to me, and I quickly turned away. My heart hammered in my chest as I stood there, waiting for something to happen or for someone to speak. But they were all staring at me—as if in a trance. I felt the gaze of the one I recognized burning a hole in my head as he watched me, but I couldn't bring myself to look at him. I wouldn't.

Naila broke the silence. "Can we stop staring at the least interesting person in the room and get on with this?" she sneered. Her words shattered the gazes of many, but the one I assumed was the King—the gaudy crown gave it away—stood and moved around the table. He didn't take his eyes off me as he closed the distance between us.

I hadn't moved from right inside the door, but he stopped several feet away. He opened his mouth, closed it, and then tried again. "Welcome back to Niccodra, Rayliana."

"My name is Rayleigh," I said before I could stop myself. It was one thing to believe Koladon had gotten my name wrong; it was another to think he was using a name given to me by someone I never knew existed. My tone was somewhat harsh for addressing royalty, but he wasn't my king or leader, so why should I address him as such? Then again, I had been in his dungeon. He had Mitch and my other friends too, so I added, "Your Majesty."

His eyes sparkled at my near defiance, but he offered a curt nod and a small smile. "Rayleigh. Welcome. Please," he stepped aside and gestured to an empty chair beside him at the table, "have a seat."

I stood there, staring for a moment. Why on earth did these people bring me here? Could I even use that expression anymore? My day just kept getting weirder. But I made my way to the chair and sat cautiously on the edge, still avoiding the gaze of the one person I never wanted to see again.

The Queen also couldn't take her eyes off me, yet she seemed to observe me in a way that made me feel slightly uncomfortable.

"I apologize for the poor greeting into our realm, Raylia—ehm. Rayleigh," the King said, drawing my attention away from his queen. "There were measures we had to take to ensure you were who you claimed to be."

"Why would I lie about something I just found out myself?" I asked, trying to hold back the sass I wanted to add to that question.

"One can never be too cautious." He shot me a knowing look. A sinking feeling in my chest made it hard to keep my eyes off the one person in this room who had lied to me about who they were.

Before I could process his words, the doors behind me burst open. "Sorry I'm late, Majesty," a familiar voice called out. "I had trouble tracking him down." Out of the corner of my eye, I glimpsed long blonde hair and quickly squeezed my eyes shut. I wasn't sure I could bear to see Koladon's face after everything. I wondered where Aaidan was—he wasn't among the people at the table. The Kool-Aid Man spoke to the King in a relatively friendly manner. "Next time, send someone else to fetch him. I'm tired of scouring the endless rows of the library to find him."

The King sighed amusedly. "Thank you, brother."

Wait. He was related to all of them, too? What kind of family history had I been pulled into? If what Kaleb said was true, how could Kyler not have been part of this all along? He *had* to know…

Koladon's presence had my body trembling with anger. I sat on my hands, trying to process everything that was happening while avoiding the sight of the two males who had upended my entire life.

A hand on my shoulder startled me. I opened my eyes wide and turned my head to find Koladon's wicked grin just inches from my face. He whispered, "I wouldn't get too comfortable. You'll be back in the dungeons soon enough." The promise of those words rang through me. He released my shoulder and took a seat across the table from me. My eyes followed him against my will, a nasty snarl crossing my face.

Unfortunately, he sat down right next to the person I had been avoiding all this time. As soon as my eyes landed on Kaleb's face, I couldn't look away.

He now sat between Koladon and the Queen. Everything about him reminded me of the boy I fell in love with. The softness in his gaze was one I remembered all too well. His honey-brown eyes sparkled, a cautious smile on his lips and a subtle glow to his face. A different image of his face flashed in my mind—pale, clammy skin, a swollen eye, and a bloody cheek. As his sweet, clean, smiling face reappeared, warmth rushed to my cheeks as everything he'd done flooded back. How easily I fell for that false tenderness. Or had it been real?

Kaleb held my gaze. Was that hope in his eyes? He leaned forward to say something, but I averted my eyes before he got the chance. The King had taken his seat at the head of the table, chatting idly with Koladon as if he weren't quite ready to begin whatever meeting this was. If Kaleb was the King's son, it meant he was the one trained to manipulate me into falling for him. He was beaten and "trained" to endure torture. Yet, by appearance alone, he didn't seem to fit the role: jolly, boisterous, and rotund—the King appeared to enjoy laughing more than torturing people. Then again, so did Kaleb.

Against my better judgment, my eyes found him again. He watched me with those beautiful brown eyes, still hopeful yet cautious. Why was he acting as if nothing had happened between us? He gazed at me as though I had just confessed my love for him, not as if he had just faked his death at my hands. Not as if he had betrayed my entire family and brought them to a world where they were never meant to survive. Did he really think we could just go back to the love story he'd masterminded me into?

As thoughts of our relationship flooded my mind, my vision blurred. The boy who comforted me through the deaths of the family he probably helped kill stood up abruptly. My breath caught in my throat. The boy I fell for, who gradually tricked me into believing he was worthy of the love I could give, slowly rounded the table, a worried expression on his face. I couldn't take a full breath to clear my head. The boy who called me "girlie" and made me feel alive, yet somehow orchestrated the kidnapping of my entire family from the world I knew, spoke my name with such kindness as he hurried toward me. Blackness replaced my blurred vision, and I felt myself swaying from the lack of oxygen in my brain. Someone repeated my name, but I couldn't tell where the voice came from or who said it.

The world tilted beneath me.

I was going to pass out.

What do you feel?

The words were barely a whisper in my mind. Nothing more than a caress of a thought.

The question echoed in my mind as the swaying slowed. I wiggled my fingers beneath my legs, feeling the soft, padded chair I was sitting on. The cold, smooth floor pressed against my bare feet as they rested on the marble tiles. Hands were resting on my knees, their warmth seeping through the soft fabric of my linen dress.

My vision cleared. The scene at the table came back into focus just as I sucked in a huge gasp of air. The Queen stood, leaning across the table with a wary expression. The King and Koladon remained seated in their chairs, the former displaying a cautious look, the latter sporting a wicked grin. And directly in front of me, with his hands on my knees—

I stood up abruptly, knocking my chair backward and scrambling far from the honey-colored eyes of betrayal. He had the nerve to look shocked as I put space between us, but he still asked, "Rayleigh, are you with me?" That sweet, gentle boy I knew remained kneeling on the ground.

With each retreating step, I reminded myself that he wasn't the innocent person he pretended to be. He was a monster, and the people around the table *had* to know that.

I looked from him to each person around the table, knowing that one of them must have whispered those words to me. The ones that so quickly brought me back from my panic attacks. But none of them seemed to know what was happening except for Kaleb. He couldn't have been the one to say that, though. He didn't realize I'd discovered a new way to calm myself. So, who whispered it?

Unless…

Unless it wasn't a whisper at all.

As I retreated further from Kaleb, I glanced at the bracelet on my wrist—the one he had given me. Only… Libella had removed the real one. Which meant my magic wasn't blocked anymore. That meant—

I hit a wall behind me. The familiar scent of strawberries and smoke filled my nose. I turned slowly toward the source and saw a wicked smile on that familiar, handsome face.

He pulled a lollipop from his mouth and said, "Hey, Sunshine."

FOUR
Unsteady

I took a stumbling step back from Kyler's tall frame. He smirked, then looked past me to the King. "Finally decided to let her out of the dungeon to play?"

So he *was* in on it…

I was still trying to find my feet and where to go as Kyler loomed over me, and Kaleb stood behind me within arm's reach. I felt trapped.

The King sighed, "You seemed to have missed the memo of why we're here, Niko."

Kyler simply chuckled. "Oh, no, I'm fully aware."

My brain started churning over what this could be about. Why did they drag me up from the dungeons, bathe and feed me, then bring me to a meeting full of mostly people I didn't know?

"Then please, sit," the King said. "All of you." He gestured for Kaleb to return to his seat next to the Queen, but his eyes were on Kyler, glowering.

Kyler raised an eyebrow at him. "What's wrong, bro? Not feeling mouthy today?"

Instead of answering him, Kaleb turned sharply to the King. "Can Rayleigh be moved to the seat next to mine?"

A sharp laugh echoed in the room, and it took me a second to realize it came from me.

"Not a chance, kid," Kyler said. Not sure if I should be grateful or not, I narrowed my eyes. What the hell was going on? Kyler referring to Kaleb as "bro" may have confirmed many things for me, including knowing Kaleb was his brother. Had they been in on it together the whole time? There were too many possibilities to consider, and I couldn't handle any more surprises.

"She will remain next to me, son." I whipped my head back to the King. There's another theory confirmed…I think. "Now, both of you sit so our guest feels more comfortable."

Guest? He couldn't be referring to me, right?

"She won't be comfortable either way," Naila chimed in from where she sat, still examining her nails. "She's like a wingless dragon in the sky." Well, she wasn't wrong, even if I had never heard the metaphor before.

Kaleb lingered for a moment longer, eyes darting from Kyler to me and back, before finally returning to his spot between the Queen and Koladon. The latter had been watching with rapt attention the entire time, and I wondered if everything he did was under the orders of the King he sat next to.

Kyler moved to take the empty seat that was unfortunately next to mine, but as soon as he sat down, Naila shot up out of her seat and into his lap. She wrapped her arms around his neck and kissed him full on the mouth.

My jaw dropped.

He didn't pull away, but when she did, she gave him an evil grin. "She's perfect." He grinned back but didn't say a word, only lifting her from his lap and pushing her toward her chair again. She gave him a pouty lip, but he waved her off. She sat heavily and turned her greedy gaze to me.

Okay, *what the hell?* Who was this chick? Why was she kissing Kyler? And why did she act like I was a prize for *her?*

The King cleared his throat. "Rayleigh, if you will." He pointed again to my chair, and I realized I was the only one still standing. Too many things just happened. How was I supposed to accept all of them for what they were?

Knowing I wouldn't get any answers even if I did ask, I closed my eyes, took a deep breath, and slowly sat on the edge of the chair again.

"Fantastic. Now," the King said, turning to Kyler, "You said you were fully aware of the premise of this meeting."

Kyler gave an exaggerated nod.

"I'm not," I chimed in, fully aware that I was not privy to such information but not caring. "I was in the dungeon an hour ago, and now I'm sitting at a table full of people I don't know as if I'm an esteemed guest, with no idea why I'm here." I caught the eyes of those I thought I knew and saw a pair of brown eyes shining with sorrow and blue eyes shining with—

Blue eyes. I blinked.

They were green. I narrowed my eyes at him, but the King answered my non-question as if it were obvious. "You are here because of your bond to Niko."

Of course. The bond. The one Kaleb had taunted me about in the dungeon weeks ago. That conversation came rushing back to me, and a sickening feeling settled in my stomach. That Kaleb—the one from the dungeon—was different from the one sitting before me now. From the one I knew on earth. The question was, which one was the *real* Kaleb?

"Yes, but you said we were here to break that." Kaleb had leaned forward with a face of steel to catch the King's attention.

"I said we would *discuss* such things. But there is protocol to follow."

"I'm sorry," I interrupted, pinching the bridge of my nose. "Can you stop acting as if I'm impertinent to the matter?"

"You aren't," the King replied. "In fact, you are *very* pertinent to this decision." He gave me such a sincere look that I thought perhaps he meant it. That everything he'd said about me tonight was true. I was a guest in his castle and daresay more than a prisoner. "To claim a Fae, there is a small ritual. The same goes for undoing the bond. Both the Drakalasson and the Fae have to relinquish their connection."

Silence filled the dining hall, allowing me to process what he said. If I wanted to break the bond with Kyler, all I had to do was say it? That seemed odd since the connection we'd made during our flight felt so... final. Strong. Unyielding. Like nothing could ever break it. If all it took to rid myself of him were some words, wouldn't that be too easy?

"Rayleigh," Kaleb whispered from across the table. I met his eyes. They shone with innocence and love for a person I no longer knew— one who had stabbed him in the chest. My heart started beating wildly. "All you have to do is say you don't want it." I took a deep breath, taking in the words as I stared into his deceiving gaze. The boy I'd fallen in love with was a two-faced liar. He manipulated me into loving him to get me here. To this point. Where he could break the bond between Kyler and me. To claim me for himself—

Wait a second. Did the King think Kyler *claimed* me? As in Doulos? I glanced at Kyler, who seemed indifferent to the conversation, distracted by Naila's hands running through his hair. *Gross.* I returned to my thoughts. Does the verbal decline of a bond work for Kavaltis as it does for Doulos? When I could read nothing in Kyler's expression, I faced the King. "What will relinquishing my bond to him mean for me?"

He raised a brow in shock. "It will free you, of course. Leaving you free to bond with whomever you choose." I mimicked his raised brow, looking to where he now gestured, and he continued, "Kaleb here seems to think you two had a special connection, and you may want to bond with him instead."

I narrowed my eyes at the boy who claimed such nonsense. He gave me his most innocent expression, and I would have believed he was the same person. I would have—if it weren't for the slight twitch of his eye. The left one. The one that always gave away when he was acting. It was something I noticed when he would make a joke but try to be serious about it. His left eyebrow would move ever-so-slightly and usually cause me to burst out laughing. But this time…

My gaze fell on Kyler again, whose lap was now occupied by Naila's feet. His eyes had a steely look to them as they locked on mine. He smirked, and something about that smirk told me it wouldn't matter what I chose. Because he still had to release me.

There didn't seem to be a way out of this situation. Either way, I wouldn't be my own person; I would belong to one of them. Kyler made the Kavaltis sound much more pleasant than the Doulos, having described the latter as a glorified slave. I didn't even want to think about what these creatures would force me to do if I were under their control, especially as I turned back to Kaleb and noticed a tiny glint of something terrible beneath his well-played-out façade.

"Well?" The King broke the silence. "What is it going to be, Rayleigh?"

I made one last sweep of the room, seeing the hunger in Naila's eyes as well, and turned back to the King with my chin lifted. "I do not wish to break the bond."

"What?" Kaleb shot out of his seat, thrusting his arm at me but addressing the King, "She doesn't know what she's saying!" He shifted his arm to Kyler. "He's probably controlling her!"

The outburst had made the Queen jump in her seat, and she reached for Kaleb's arm, trying to make him sit back down. She'd been sitting quietly, watching the whole scene play out like a tennis match. But she never made to say anything nor act like she was a part of it. She tugged on Kaleb's arm again, but he pulled it from her grasp and waited for the King to answer.

When I turned to him, there was a curiosity in his eyes as he took me in. He glanced at Kyler and said, "*Are* you controlling her?"

Kyler's grin was that of someone who'd won. He was watching me with a sparkle in his eye that I'd seen before, but I had no idea what it meant at that moment. "No."

Naila scoffed and pulled her feet from his lap. "But Niko, you said—"

"Enough," the King cut her off. I whipped my head to him, and a small smile spread across his face. "Rayleigh seems to have made her choice. The bond will stay." Kaleb and Naila tried to interrupt again, but he held up a hand to silence them. "The matter is not up for discussion. If she changes her mind, she will inform me. For now," he gestured to Kyler, "she is yours."

Kaleb sat heavily in his chair, glaring at Kyler, while Naila sat back in her own, arms crossed, and stuck her lip out again. Kyler dipped his chin, acknowledging what his father said, but his eyes were still locked on mine. He tilted his head, and a devilish grin slowly appeared as he took me in with a hunger in his eyes I'd never seen before. Maybe I'd made the wrong choice...

"Now, for the next matter of this meeting." The King snapped his fingers, and the doors flew open.

My hands flew to my mouth as I gasped. Several guards hauled Kendall, Leighton, Mari, and Ma into the room. Their bruises and cuts looked much worse in this light. Some even looked fresh. Ma was still unconscious and being dragged through the room between her two guards. Mari and the twins mustered whatever strength they had left, walking with a rigid posture as they were led to a spot near the King where everyone could see them.

Mitch still wasn't there.

I pressed my fingernails into my palms to keep the panic at bay and myself present. What were they doing here? The King stood and walked over to Ma. I clenched my teeth as he bent before her and lifted her chin. If he hurt her or said one thing against her, I would—

"What happened to her? Why is she unconscious?" he demanded, looking between the two guards holding her up. My jaw slackened at his tone. It almost sounded like he cared. The guards exchanged a quick glance but said nothing. The King stood and waved his hand, causing a small couch to drag itself from the wall to directly behind Ma. Gosh, I'd forgotten all about magic, but seeing him do it with a literal wave of his hand was insane. "Lay her there and go fetch her some glykos."

The guards gave him a questioning look, which seemed to be their mistake. One minute, they were eyeing the King as if he'd told them to swallow a horse. The next, their heads twisted, and the crack of their necks echoed through the hall. They fell to the ground in a heap, and my jaw dropped. Someone gasped, but I couldn't comprehend who. *Did he just kill them?* Their bodies didn't move from their crumpled position, but I stared for a moment longer just to be sure.

Oh my God. He did! He hadn't moved a muscle.

I pulled my eyes from the dead guards. Ma hovered where they had been holding her up. The King lifted his hands, and she floated toward the couch behind her. He laid her gently on the cushions until it looked like she could have been asleep.

The King dropped his hands and turned to one of the guards holding Ken, whose face mirrored my shock. "Go fetch the enhanced glykos." The King's tone differed this time, almost amused. That guard seemed more intelligent than the others because he gave a short nod, released Ken's arm, and disappeared out the doors a moment later.

The King turned to Kyler, who had barely moved since sitting down, and said, "Niko, if you will." He gestured to the unmoving bodies, and in an instant, they were gone. My mind was going a million miles a minute.

I took a deep, shuddering breath and held it.

One.

What just happened? The King obviously knew we were in the dungeons, but he acted as if he wasn't aware of how we were treated. Like he didn't think we were beaten, starved, and dehydrated.

Two.

He just *killed* those guards, and for what? Because they didn't listen to him? Or was there some other reason he just casually snapped their necks? Had I missed something?

Three.

Was he genuinely upset that Ma was unconscious? Or was he expecting me to think he was actually a good guy here by trying to avenge the way my mother was treated?

Four.

Whatever the reason, I knew I never wanted to get on the King's bad side. Not if he did that with barely a thought.

I released my breath as quietly as possible, turning to the girls and seeing Mari watch me intensely. I furrowed my brow, but her head moved slightly back and forth. I don't know what it meant, but I cautiously turned back to the male who was now rubbing his hands together as if wiping them clean of the deaths he just caused.

He caught my eye and dipped his head slightly. "I apologize you had to witness that." My god, he sounded sincere. "Regardless of what you must think of me, you and yours were not to be harmed while you were in the dungeons."

My eyebrows shot up so high. "Just starved and dehydrated then?"

He furrowed his brow, looking at the rest of the guards. "Were they not given the food and water I sent for?"

"You mean the moldy bread and the water that tasted like piss?" I scrunched my eyebrows. "No offense, Majesty. I didn't expect a five-course meal in your dungeons, but I could hardly call what you sent us 'food and water.'"

"I see." The King had not taken his eyes off the lineup of guards. Some of them had the sense to be nervous, shifting their stances and avoiding eye contact. The guard that had gone to retrieve the glykos returned and walked straight up to Ma. "Stop," the King demanded. The guard froze just before the couch Ma lay on. The King turned to me. "Please. Come care for your mother."

Eyeing him warily, I slowly pushed myself up and stepped toward Ma. The guard held out the glykos, which had a straw that I gripped between my fingers before kneeling in front of the couch. Her ragged breathing reached my ears, and my eyes burned as I lifted the straw to her lips. Realizing she might not be able to drink through it, I plugged the top hole and pulled it from the glass, lifting the bottom to her mouth. Once it was inside, I unplugged the top hole. At first, nothing happened. "Come on, Ma. Drink it," I pleaded.

Suddenly, her body convulsed in a coughing spat, the liquid sputtering out of her mouth as she nearly fell off the couch. I put an arm on her shoulder to keep her in place. She coughed several more times before finally taking a deep breath and sinking into the couch again. I watched, waiting. Nothing happened. I took another strawful and dropped the liquid in her mouth as tears burned my eyes. "Ma, please."

The liquid disappeared, and her throat worked to swallow it. A breath of relief washed through me as I prepared another sip for her, putting it in her mouth. After a few more, her eyes fluttered open, and they wandered around the room, finally settling on my face, where tears streamed down my cheeks. "Ray?" Her voice was raspy and broken, but a happy sob burst out of me.

"It's me, Ma. I'm here." I brushed her matted and dirty hair from her face, then lifted the cup and placed the straw in her mouth. "Drink this. It'll help." I smiled through my tears.

"Where are we?" She tried to look around, but I covered most of her field of vision, making her focus on drinking the glykos. As the water took effect, color returned to her face along with some of the strength I knew she had lost. She was still frail, but she was no longer on the brink of death. When she finished the glass, I helped her to sit up against the arm of the couch. When she could take in the rest of the room, her face went slack, and she repeated her question.

"Niccodra," I answered, having come to that conclusion myself.

"You're safe here." The King's voice broke me from my concentration on Ma. His claim had yet to be seen, as she was just beaten so many times under what I thought was his orders. I was questioning that now, though. "You may sit there with her, Rayleigh. I can conduct this meeting regardless of where you are."

The way he spoke seemed as though I was co-leading the meeting. I sat gingerly next to Ma and wrapped my arms around her elbow. After not being able to comfort her for the last few weeks, the need to do as much as I could overwhelmed me.

The King turned to the rest of the table, his eyes landing on Kaleb. "You claimed to have been kidnapped and tortured by some of the people in this room," he stated, the words so formal that I wasn't sure if the King viewed him as a son or not.

Kaleb's face turned red. "I only recall being tortured, not by whom." His eyes flickered away from the man he claimed was his father. "My vision was mostly obscured due to my injuries." Something seemed off. The way the King was questioning him and acting toward me made me think he knew something else. But wasn't he also the one who trained Kaleb to endure torture? Didn't Kaleb tell me his father prepared him for moments like that because he knew they would come to pass? My questions were spiraling out of control with how much information was being dumped on me.

The King nodded, turning to Kyler. "You claim you were attacked in your attempt to get Raylian—ehm, Rayleigh back safely?"

I sat up quickly at the question to see his response. His eyes met mine. "Yes." So he *was* trying to get me back to Niccodra!

His Majesty finally turned to me. "And what were you doing in the cave where Kaleb was being held captive?"

My eyes widened. I remembered Libella saying something about Kaleb spinning lies about my friends. What had he said about me? My gaze found his where he seemed to be sitting on the edge of his seat. He nodded as if permitting me to tell the truth. "I went there to save him," I said, knowing the whole thing had been a charade. But if he spun some tale about him being the King's son and that's why he was captured, I wasn't sure what else I could say. If I tried to tell the King that Kaleb came to visit me in the dungeons to torment me and tell me I'd fallen for his trap, then where would that leave me? My friends were still in danger. Ma. Mitch. If I said anything against Kaleb right now and the King honestly thought he was his son, he might give up all pretenses and think I was trying to sabotage his reunion with him.

So I kept my mouth shut.

The King seemed to contemplate what we said, looking between all of us. Then his gaze fell to his brother. "And you?"

Koladon lifted his chin, a grin playing at his mouth. "I was following orders, as I said earlier. You wanted answers and Rayliana. I got them the best way I knew how." What he didn't say was apparent enough to me:

the King didn't know that Koladon was the one who did the torturing. He obviously didn't realize Kaleb's part in it, either. The silence between them stretched before the King once again took in each of us.

Finally, he turned to me. "May I have your permission to view your memories, Rayleigh?"

Cold water trickled down my back. View my memories? Could they do that? I should have seen that coming. At least he was asking for permission...But if he saw what happened in that cave, he'd see me stab Kaleb through the heart—or who I thought was Kaleb. But then, where would that lead us? Because, obviously, Kaleb is alive and well, sitting right across the room from me. How would he play that off?

On the other hand, maybe it would expose him for tricking me into thinking I'd killed him...

I found the King's gaze again and nodded slowly.

He dipped his chin and reached his hand out. I lifted a shaking hand toward him, but he hesitated when he saw me trembling. His face spoke volumes. Something in his eyes told me he understood something I hadn't meant to communicate, and he stepped back. "Perhaps you will feel more comfortable if Niko did this part." He didn't give me a chance to respond as he motioned for Kyler to join us.

My heart jolted as I turned to find him standing from his relaxed position at the table and strolling over to where I sat next to Ma, a smug grin on his face. Ma gently squeezed my arm as she lifted it from where it wrapped around hers. I could sense her strength returning from the way she nudged me to stand.

The King had stepped back to his chair but didn't sit down. Kendall, Leighton, and Mari silently watched from where they stood next to me. I wished I could reach out and hug all of them. Tell them how happy I was that they were alive. But I couldn't do that. Not yet.

Kyler stopped several feet away from me, taking me in from head to toe, and then chuckled before extending his hand out to me. Not having the energy to care why he laughed, I sneered at him, wondering if choosing the King might have been more comfortable after all. When Kyler gave me a knowing smirk, I finally slapped my hand into his as if giving him a stupid high five. His thumb held my fingers in place as he leaned in slightly, saying, "This might be a little invasive."

But I barely registered what he said. Because the minute my hand touched his, my body exploded with a euphoric feeling I'd only felt once before. Every nerve came alive, and the world around me disappeared.

I knew what this was. I *knew* what was happening.

And it was difficult to hide what I felt rushing through my body.

My powers.

FIVE
Royal We

My grip on Kyler's hand tightened as the feeling intensified. It was *not* this extreme when my powers appeared that night before our flight. Something about this felt like *more*. Like my powers on earth were muted, and this was the true strength of what I could do. The trembling started at my legs and moved up my body until I felt I would collapse.

A strong hand grasped my elbow, keeping me upright, and the world around me came back into focus. Kyler was standing before me, still holding my fingers but also holding me steady at my elbow. His face still had a stupid smirk on it, but something in his eyes—

I blinked, and it was gone.

"Didn't know I made you so weak in the knees, Sunshine." I wanted to wipe the smug look from his face with a solid fist, but I knew it was a bad idea. My powers settled into every part of my body, his grip never wavering.

It didn't stop me from sneering at him. "Yeah, that's not attraction—that's fear." The shaking slowed as my body absorbed the power thrumming through me. It was a new feeling, but it also felt so *right*. Like everything had just fallen into place.

Kyler chuckled, "I'm not so sure that's fear causing your body to tremble at my touch."

I was fully present now, and heat rose up my neck from the anger now surging through me. I forgot how much I hated his insinuations. Instead of falling for his bait, I bit out, "Can we please just get this over with?"

His eyebrow twitched, and he released my elbow, sensing that I was steadier on my feet. As soon as he let go, my powers fell quiet again—not sleeping, but…hiding. Kyler reached his free hand toward the King, who waited patiently behind him.

Someone in the room let out a tiny gasp, and the silence that followed was overwhelming as the King placed his hand in Kyler's. Kyler turned to me. "I'm going to pull the memories from your mind, transferring them to my father." There was that confirmation I was looking for earlier, but I didn't have time to process that right now.

A gentle caress down my temple made me close my eyes. I remembered the last time I felt that touch on my mind and how different everything had been. I also remembered what that caress meant and went searching for the detailed oak door, finding it almost immediately. But I hesitated a moment before opening the door to the eyes I knew were waiting on the other side. I had no idea what would happen or what the King was about to see. All I knew was I did nothing against him or the two-faced liar who claimed to be his son. And he would soon see that.

I took a shuddering breath and opened the door to my mind.

Those stark blue eyes bore into me, taking me back to that moment in the school courtyard—when Kyler needed into my mind so he could save me from Aaidan. Was all of that really an act? Or was that who Kyler really was?

Instead of an invasion, like the one I felt that day, there was a slight tug on a place in my mind where I assumed the memories were kept. It was gentle and seemed more like a stream of consciousness floating through the door to that corner where I'd hidden away the memories of that night in the cave.

Afraid I'd have to relive those memories, I tried to retract from that small presence in my head. But Kyler held fast, still gently pulling those moments in the cavern from their hiding place. The conversations from the cave filtered through my mind as they were dragged from my memory, but the words disappeared when they passed over the threshold of the oak door.

As if the memories had been taken from my mind completely.

I jerked my eyes open as Kyler dropped my hand. His face was inches from mine, but I couldn't read the expression on his face before he turned and retreated to his spot at the table.

I sank back down next to Ma and took several deep breaths, trying not to think about what was about to happen.

The King seemed to be in some sort of trance. His eyes darted back and forth, as if the memory was playing like a movie in his mind. I tried to recall what he could be seeing but came up blank. He blinked, took a deep breath and opened his eyes to focus on the guards holding the girls. "Release them," he said.

We let out a collective sigh of relief, and I tried to hold back a happy sob as I sat up to look at them. The guards holding them didn't dare make the same mistake as the ones who disobeyed the King earlier and let them go. The twins reached for each other, trying to keep the other from collapsing.

But the King wasn't done. He lifted a finger, pointing at the table. And with a voice full of disdain, he said, "Seize him."

I snapped my head in the direction he pointed and couldn't believe my eyes.

Koladon shot out of his seat, but the guards were already there, grabbing each of his arms. "What is the meaning of this? What did he show you?" he yelled, trying to break free from their grasp. "I did what you asked!"

"You tortured my son," the King seethed. "And three innocents. I will not stand for it."

"I didn't know he was your son!" Koladon screamed as the guards started dragging him toward the doors. Trying to face him again, he screamed over his shoulder, "She stabbed him!"

"Do you think me stupid, brother? You were clearly controlling her. She wouldn't have done that on her own because she loves him."

My jaw hit the floor. What *did* the King see? If he saw me stab Kaleb, how did that explain him sitting at the table in perfect health? What was I missing here? Something had been twisted in the story. Not only that, but the King just claimed that I loved Kaleb, which meant he had no idea about his betrayal and how I felt now. Was it possible to tell him without being sent back to the dungeons?

Something inside me told me to keep quiet. He would get what was coming to him.

For now, I'd have to play along. As if what I did in that cave were still the only truth.

Koladon screamed several obscenities, mostly aimed at me, but his last words before the doors closed behind him were snarled at Kyler, "You'll regret this."

"Doubtful," Kyler mumbled, a lazy grin on his face.

Kaleb, who had been on the edge of his seat the entire time, stood as Koladon finally disappeared from the room. "I'm sorry, father. I truly had no idea."

Damn, he's really laying it on thick.

The King held up a hand. "It's alright, son." He released a long breath and then turned to me. "I knew my brother was capable of such things, but I never thought he would do something like this. You have my sincerest apologies for everything that happened in that cave."

I honestly had no idea what to say, but the words that fell out my mouth were, "I thought I'd killed Kaleb."

"You nearly did," he said as if expecting me to say that. "His wounds were nearly fatal, but he got to a healer in time."

I coughed, trying to cover the shocked noise that escaped me. "How did he get here?" My curiosity was getting the best of me. I needed to know what went down after I was brought here weeks ago.

"My healers returned with him a few days ago. They didn't want to risk traveling with his injuries."

A few *days?* Kaleb visited me the night I arrived in Niccodra. How did he trick the King into thinking he was on earth this whole time? How deep did this plan of his go? Was there any way to expose his true nature to the King without him misinterpreting my intentions?

For a King, he sure did seem pretty thick.

He straightened, took a deep breath, and turned to the twins as they stood huddled a little closer. "Please accept my apology for the torment you've endured these last few weeks. If you'll accept, I would like to offer you a place to get cleaned up and properly recover." They gave him a questioning look but nodded slowly. His eyes fell on Mari. "Your mother pleaded your innocence, and now that I have seen that truth firsthand, I ask for your forgiveness," he paused, closing his eyes to take a deep breath, then opened them to find her watching him closely. "I am giving my son first choice, but you may claim the other as my apology."

I furrowed my brow, having no idea what he meant. But Mari straightened to her full height, clenched her jaw, and nodded.

Kaleb eyed the exchange and mirrored my confused look, aiming it at the King. "First choice in what?"

"I know it is not what you hoped for," he sighed, "but since Rayleigh has already been claimed, you may choose one of these two." He gestured toward the twins. "Both are strong warriors, from what I can tell."

Hold on… What was he talking about?

Kaleb looked to the twins and Mari, who was trying not to meet his gaze and instead found Leighton's. An emotion passed over her face, disappearing quickly when she looked away. But that expression was one I knew all too well.

And apparently, so did Kaleb. "I choose Leighton," he said.

Leigh knew of his betrayal. Even though she wasn't conscious when he came to my cell door, she knew. So when he said her name, her body collapsed in fear. Ken grabbed her from behind, shaking from the same fear.

The King nodded. "As you wish." He motioned to Mari. "Please, show Kaleb how it's done."

Mari swallowed thickly and gave the King a look of defiance, but her words sent a chill down my spine. "I wish to claim Kendall."

The blood drained from my face. I surely hadn't heard her correctly. 'Claim' was the wrong term. She meant to say she *chose* Kendall, right?

Mari pursed her lips, her eyes finding mine. A sense of dread filled my body as her determined gaze turned from me to Kendall. When Ken saw the look in her eyes, she shrank away from Mari, pulling Leigh with her.

No. This can't be happening.

Kendall backed further away, but her retreat made no difference. Mari was quick. One second, she was several feet from them; the next, she wrapped her hand around Ken's forearm.

A scream ripped from her throat.

"No!" I cried, tears welling in my eyes as Mari caught Kendall with her free arm before her body gave in to the pain. After several seconds of the blood-curdling scream, Mari finally released her grip. As she lifted her hand away, it revealed a burn mark in the exact shape of her handprint. She shook her hand, wiping it on her leg, and made to pull Kendall closer to her.

Leighton had regained her strength the minute her twin screamed and whipped around in her arms to hold her up. When she tried to stop Mari from pulling Ken away, the look she received made her freeze.

Purple eyes blazed where Mari's blue-green eyes used to shine. *Oh my God.*

Shock washed over me, and tears spilled down my cheeks.

Mari's dragon had just claimed my best friend.

Wherever I thought this day would go, this was not on my list of possibilities.

Leighton released Kendall with a look of betrayal, tears building in her eyes as she watched Mari pull Ken to her side. Mari's eyes faded from purple fire to the blue-green I knew, but she could no longer look at Leighton. She turned her gaze to the far wall, keeping her arm around Kendall and her chin up.

"It's okay, Rayleigh," the King said, breaking the silence, and my head whipped toward him. He held up his hands as if to show me he meant no harm. "She's safe now—protected." I glared at him. Safe? She was nothing more than a slave to Mari now. How could she do this to us? I had just started trusting her again, and the moment we escaped the dungeon, she did *this?* The King held my gaze. "And you're safe with Niko."

He really did think the bond between Kyler and me was the same as what Mari had just done. Why hadn't Kyler told him? Or perhaps our bond was what he claimed. The burn seemed the same. I had no idea if Kyler verbally claimed me before he caught me. The difference between the bonds was murky, and Kyler never explained it thoroughly. The way the King described it made it seem like being a Doulos was a privileged position. What if the lies truly ran that deep? What if Kyler's dragon *did* claim me, and it was all part of the manipulation?

As I recalled those moments outside the Dengalow when I first met his dragon, I remembered he told me how to reach him—how to call him without Kyler's interference. Perhaps he could tell me the difference.

But that would have to wait because the King was now motioning

Kaleb toward Leighton.

"Stop!" Several heads whipped in the direction of my outburst, but I was standing now. Whatever trance I had been in when Kendall was claimed seemed to have broken. "Please—"

"Rayleigh," the King interrupted me, giving me a stern look. "This is the highest form of protection and privilege I can give them in this castle." He seemed to think that was enough explanation and turned his attention back to Kaleb, gesturing toward Leighton again. Her eyes darted around the room, looking for a way out of the shitty situation we'd been dropped into.

"How does it work?" Kaleb asked with a tone of innocence that turned my vision red.

The King stepped up beside him to walk him through the process. "First, you must declare your intent as Amarietta did."

Kaleb swallowed thickly. "I—I wish to claim Leighton."

Leigh started backing away from the traitor. He stalked toward her but went slowly as if trying not to scare her. My feet wouldn't move. I felt frozen in place, and some part of me whispered that was highly probable. There was nothing I could do. I couldn't even voice my objections, the words getting caught in my throat. Silent tears tracked down my face as Kaleb followed Leighton like a cat tracking a mouse.

"When you touch her, you'll be able to feel her powers," the King informed him. "Reach for that spark within her and use your powers to pull it to you. The magic will do the rest."

Leigh's foot caught on the step behind her, and she fell, trying to scramble away as Kaleb grabbed for her arm. When she snatched it out of reach, his hand wrapped around her exposed calf instead. Her scream erupted in the dining hall, sending chills down my back.

Kaleb's scream echoed hers, and my jaw fell open in shock. "Why does it burn?" he yelled, trying to release his grip on her but unable to pull it free from the pain.

"It's how the connection is made," the King yelled over the screams. "Your xousía is being branded onto her, marking her as yours."

Finally, Leighton stopped screaming as Kaleb ripped his hand from her leg. "I'm sorry, Leigh. I didn't know that was going to happen." He stepped toward her cautiously, but she sat up slowly and looked at him with a drastically different expression than the one she had moments ago. Her face was relaxed, her head seemingly floating above her body.

As if she were in a trance.

I found Kendall leaning into Mari for support, and her face was the same. *This cannot be good.*

"What did you do to them?" I whispered, glancing between the twins, trying to find some semblance of sanity within their gazes. But when Leigh took Kaleb's outstretched hand and let him pull her up, I stopped searching.

Because there wasn't any sanity left in them. They *belonged* to the dragons who claimed them.

Bile rose in my throat as Leigh leaned into Kaleb's strong embrace. I remembered what those hugs felt like. I used to think his arms were where I felt the most safe. But as Kaleb wrapped his arms around her, I saw the possessiveness in that hold and knew—I never wanted to feel his arms around me again.

His face betrayed nothing. But his eyes? Those told me everything I needed to know as he met my gaze.

Everything was going according to plan. His plan.

I opened my mouth to say something to the King, but again, the words escaped me. I decided to try a different topic. "What will happen to my ma?" I whispered, watching the twins unwillingly accept their fate of being bound to dragons.

The King glanced at Ma, still leaning weakly against the arm of the sofa. "She can be sent back to her home. But her memory will be wiped."

I jolted. "Wait. What?"

He sighed as he stepped up to me, his hands clasped behind his back. "She cannot go back to Earth remembering anything about Niccodra." His eyes met mine, and a glimpse of sadness flashed. "Nor can she remember anything about you."

"*What?*" I repeated, swinging back to Ma, whose body revealed her weakness. The glykos helped, but only so much. She wouldn't be able to survive here much longer. But that didn't mean I wanted her to leave here and forget all about me. Her eyes found mine, and she gave me a weak smile. "She won't remember anything?" Tears burned my eyes, but

I choked them back. Ma's eyes spoke volumes as they bore into mine: she knew it would come to this.

"It's too big of a risk. She will be taken back after we determine what to do with your brother."

My head whipped around to face him, and I felt jerked around by all these revelations. "My brother? Where is he? What did you do to him?"

The King held up a hand to stop me. "Your brother is in my wing of the castle under close watch. I have done him no harm. I swear it. But, we have reason to believe he is not fully human." His eyes turned to Ma. "You were interviewed by ou—"

"*Interviewed?*" I seethed, all thoughts of Mitch vanished as memories of Ma's bloodied body being thrown into her cell replayed in my mind. "She was *tortured!* Every day! For the last four weeks!"

The King furrowed his brow as he met my fiery gaze. "My investigation squad only met with her twice."

"Well, your investigation squad lied to you. She was dragged away far more than that. All my friends were. I had to watch them get taken away and come back with new injuries *every single day*. For *weeks!*"

He closed his eyes, scrunching his forehead at the words. As if he had no idea.

"Koladon set the guards on them," a small voice said from the table.

I turned toward the noise. It didn't seem as if anyone said anything, but both Naila and Kyler were looking at the Queen. She was staring at a spot on the table, her eyes pinpointed there.

The King straightened. "You witnessed this?"

She shook her head, her eyes finally lifting from the table to find the King's. "He told me, but I couldn't say anything because he—" she cleared her throat, "—he was controlling me."

Rage seemed to fill the room as the King took a slow, deep breath. His whole demeanor changed, reminding me of when Kyler threatened Aaidan in the courtyard. This version was someone I never wanted to mess with.

The Queen lifted a hand. "But when the gonos were placed on him, it freed me. I can tell you—"

"Not now," the King snapped, making the Queen recoil. His tone softened at her reaction, but only just. "We will talk about this later." His body shook as he tried to calm himself, rage still clear in his eyes as he turned back to me. "The things done to your mother and friends were not ordered by me. I hope you believe that." His voice turned more business-like, "We asked your mother about her husband, and she claims to have no idea about him being from Niccodra. However, there are signs from Mitchell that tell us otherwise. If they are confirmed, we must proceed with our protocol."

"Which is what?" I asked.

"We will cross that bridge if it comes," he replied, his tone ending the conversation. Before I could beg him to tell me more, he clapped his hands. "You are all dismissed to your chambers. Mari, please take the rooms adjoined with your mothers. She has set everything up for you there. Bring Kendall with you. Food and attire will be brought to you both."

Mari nodded, mustering her strength to haul Kendall's arm around her shoulders and gripping her around the waist. They were both weak, but Ken still stared off into the distance, her eyes unfocused. She seemed unaware of her surroundings, but when Mari started walking, Ken followed suit.

As they made their way to the doors, the King addressed Kaleb. "Show Leighton to your chambers. Food and attire will be brought for her as well." Kaleb nodded and held Leighton upright as she, too, had unfocused eyes. I watched my friends go with their dragons in a daze, wondering if there was anything I could do to help them. Would I even be able to see them? Talk to them? What was going to hap—

Wait… If they were bringing them to their chambers, that meant—

My gaze shot to Kyler, watching me with an evil grin plastered on his unfortunately beautiful face. *No.*

The King waggled a finger between Kyler and Naila, now standing near the table. "If you two would like to continue sharing a bed, we can move you to a chamber with an extra one. But it would take a few weeks to prepare." *No, no, no…. This was not happening.* "Or perhaps you can use Naila's chambers for such… activities." He cleared his throat, which made Nalia and Kyler smirk. "I will have a separate room set up for Rayleigh's mother." *Please don't say it. Please don't say it.* He met Kyler's gaze. "But for now, please escort her and Rayleigh to your chambers."

Shit.

SIX
OK Not to be OK

The King didn't give me time to protest. He offered his arm to his queen and left the dining hall without turning back. I was left standing there, staring at Kyler, who was fiddling with the empty lollipop stick in his mouth.

I took a moment to collect myself, closed my eyes, and took a deep breath. This was bad. Everything that just happened was *bad*. But I *still* didn't have it the worst. Kendall had to stay with Mari after learning she was never really on our side. And Leighton… I know why Kaleb chose her. He saw the same look in Mari's eyes that I'd seen. She cares for Leighton. And apparently, Kaleb is a master at stabbing people in the back. Not that him taking Ken would have been any less awful, but I know he did it to separate Mari and Leigh—

"Stop wasting time, Sunshine."

Just block him out. He was trying to rile me up again. Like he used to. I wasn't about to let him do that. Not after what just happened. Not in front of Ma. Not in her fragile state. I needed to care for her and figure out what to do about the twins. *How am I going to do any of this?* Ma needed to get back home. Ken and Leigh needed to be released from their captors. And Mitch—

"You have five seconds to start moving," Kyler growled, "before I drag you both down to my chambers. I have things to do."

I squeezed my eyes tighter, gritted my teeth, and swallowed the words I wanted to yell at him. He could wait a few more seconds. I just needed one more—

"Five. Four—"

My eyes snapped open, shooting daggers at him where he leaned against the archway. "Are you seriously *counting*?"

His green eyes narrowed, barely containing the fire in them. "Three. Two—"

"I'm not a child!" I stomped my foot.

He raised a brow as he looked at my feet, then back up at me. "Then stop acting like one."

"Oh, screw you, jackass!" I turned to reach for Ma, who still looked unstable. She probably couldn't even walk on her own. Nevertheless, she pushed herself to her feet, and I moved quickly to wrap my arm around her waist and hers around my shoulders. I pulled most of her weight onto me and headed toward the door where Kyler was waiting.

"Sweetheart," Ma whispered, her voice strained. "You can't let him get to you." She coughed. The energy to talk as we walked across the dining hall depleted her strength. "You're giving him power over you by reacting."

"I know," I sighed. "I just can't stand to be around him."

"Well, it doesn't look like you'll have a choice." She coughed again.

I groaned at the truth in that statement. My sleeping arrangements wouldn't be like they were at the Dengalow. I wouldn't have my own room, no balcony or private bathroom. No privacy—

Ma stumbled, and I stopped to readjust, helping her lean most of her weight on me. She could barely grip my hand. Her body was shaking as she tried to use muscles she hadn't in weeks. She'd been through so much, and there I was, worrying about sleeping arrangements.

I huffed loudly as we approached Kyler, who turned swiftly into the hallway before we even reached him.

Of course, he wasn't going to help. What did I expect? That didn't mean I couldn't be mad about it. Once Ma was comfortable and taken care of, I was going to let him have it. No holding back. It didn't matter that he was back to being an asshole again. He could have at least taken some of her weight off me.

Naila was standing outside the doors, apparently waiting for him. She immediately grabbed his arm and draped it around her shoulders, wrapping hers around his hips as they started down the hall. "Care to explain?" she said, glaring up at him.

"I don't need to explain anything to you."

Ma and I exchanged a glance. Whatever their relationship was, it was weird. But for some reason, that made me more intrigued. I hated that I wanted to know more. Especially because I already knew they *slept* together. *Ew.* But the way they treated each other didn't seem like they really enjoyed each other's company. It was more like he tolerated her, and she was obsessed with getting what she wanted, which seemed to be him. And me.

I struggled with Ma's weight behind them as we trudged down the magical, everchanging hallway. And I listened.

"But you said you would bring her back for me," Naila said.

"I said no such thing, babe." *Babe?* I hated pet names. Hearing him call her that was almost worse than when Aaidan called me love. Kyler wasn't even looking at Naila, though. His arm was still draped across her shoulders, but he stared straight ahead. She, however, watched his face carefully as he said, "I was told to retrieve her. Her power was my reward."

Oh my God.

"Yes, but you could have released her for me," she practically whined.

He shrugged. "You heard her. She didn't want to break the bond."

Her voice raised slightly, but it was enough to tell me she was done begging. "You have *mind control.* Make her choose differently."

Kyler dropped his arm from her shoulders. "It doesn't work that way, babe. You should know that."

His arm falling away from her was the final straw. She gritted her teeth and said, "You don't even need her power! You're strong enough without her." Naila whipped around to me, stepping right into my personal space. I stumbled backward at her sudden closeness. "Let me have a taste," she whispered, her voice hungry. I tried catching myself to back away, but between Ma's weight and Naila's closeness, I couldn't move in the right direction to get away. Naila reached for my bare arm, but Kyler snatched her hand from the air and pulled her away so fast she slammed into the wall.

Kyler's shoulders rose and fell with deep breaths as he growled, "You will not attempt to claim her again. Do you understand?"

Naila was not going down that easily. She leaned forward, stopping inches from his face. "You can't be there to stop me every time," she said. "I have direct access to your chambers, remember?" She was daring enough to tiptoe her fingers up his chest. "She'll be all alone in there." Her voice had gone soft, but her eyes found me as she said, "Vulnerable."

The word made me shiver, wondering what she had planned if she ever did get her hands on me. My power.

"If you touch her," Kyler's voice was low, almost seductive, when he said, "I'll have no choice but to cut these off." He gently grabbed the hand on his chest and traced her palm with his fingertips. My jaw dropped at his casual threat of *cutting off her hands*. She gasped, but not out of horror. Kyler leaned in and whispered, "Be a shame to lose such *lovely* hands."

Naila's eyes were back on Kyler's, and she grinned. "I love it when you talk dirty to me."

"Oh my God," I sputtered. "Can you please stop whatever the hell this is and get me back to your chambers?" I'd seen enough of that to last me a lifetime. I don't know what took me so long to say something, but I wish I could scrub those memories from my mind.

Kyler chuckled and straightened, catching Naila's chin. "Go back to your chambers, babe. I'll meet you there later." For a second, I thought he would kiss her, but thankfully, he dropped her chin. She collected herself, slipping on the face of the assassin I met earlier. With a wild grin, she flipped her hair over her shoulder and turned back the way we came, disappearing down the hall.

I rolled my eyes. She was definitely going to be a problem.

Realizing just how heavy Ma had become on my shoulder, I looked over to find her eyes closed and her head lolled to the side. "Ma?" My voice cracked. Her eyelids fluttered but didn't open. "Ma, please," I whispered, lifting her head with my semi-free hand. "We have to get back to the room. I can't carry you—"

Suddenly, her weight was gone, and I was tipping forward at the difference in gravity. I caught myself in time to find Kyler throwing Ma over his shoulder and continuing down the hall. She groaned at the movement but still seemed unconscious.

"Hey!" I shouted, catching up to him and yanking on his arm. "Put her down!"

He didn't stop. "She's unconscious."

"Thanks for stating the obvious, jackass. But you're hurting her!"

"I'm *carrying* her, Sunshine. Not torturing her."

"Yes, but—"

"She's fine. Stop arguing."

"She's not *fine!*" I yelled. "She's clearly sick. Or dying. Or both!"

Kyler didn't respond. He just kept walking.

"She can't stay here," I went on. "You have to take her back! She needs to leave. *Now.*"

Silence. Was he really that heartless? Would he really let her die? I thought about what Mari said in the dungeon and wondered if it was even true. Did Kyler really fight for me in that meadow, or did she make it up to get me to trust her? I was starting to feel like nothing they ever told me was the truth.

But what if it was true? What if Kyler did care about me?

I let out a long breath. I didn't want to resort to begging, but Ma didn't belong here. She had to go back. "Kyler, please—"

"Don't call me that," he snapped, not turning to me.

I jolted at his tone. "By your name?"

"My name is Nikylo."

I raised my eyebrows at his back as he picked up his pace and put several feet between us. "*You* told me your name was Kyler."

He turned sharply into a doorway that had appeared, and my thoughts of his name were gone. I was never going to get used to that. Used to magic.

I went to follow Kyler through the door, but something made me stop.

The archway. The paintings surrounding it.

I'd been here before.

I stood there frozen, taking in the familiar space even though I'd only been here once.

It was the room I met Libella in.

Voices came from within the room and practically tripped over the entrance when one of them was hers.

"Libella!"

She smiled from the bathroom doorway. "Hello again, dear."

The fact that she was still here brought a smile to my face. Maybe she'd answer more of my questions.

Then I remembered why I was brought here—whose chambers I was in. I looked around the room and found him depositing Ma on the sofa near the window. As soon as he released her, the room constricted. There was a rush of air. A moment of darkness. Just like that, Kyler was gone.

I stood rooted to the spot. I'd forgotten he could just do that. Teleport—or whatever he called it.

"Rayleigh, is everything okay?" Libella's voice broke me from my stupor.

I shook my head to clear it, finding her earnest gaze across the room. "Honestly?" My shoulders sagged as everything sunk in. I looked at Ma, unconscious once again, and went to kneel beside her, taking her hand in mine. Tears stung my eyes as the events of the dining hall replayed in my head. Ken and Leigh were under the control of two dragons, neither of which I could trust. Kyler was being an ass again—or maybe he never stopped being one. Kaleb was acting like nothing happened. Ma couldn't even sit on her own. And Mari... "No," I finally said. "Nothing is okay."

Even if I couldn't trust Libella, what was the harm in being honest? I'd been holding on to too many emotions over the last few weeks, trying to put on a brave face so the girls wouldn't see how much their pain was torturing me. No matter what I was going through, they always had it worse.

Watching them come back to their cells with new scars and bruises was a different kind of torture, though. One that never pierced the flesh, but it pierced the mind and soul. I wished I could have taken their place. But every time I tried to offer myself, I was ignored or told to shut up. Nothing I did could save them. I was powerless. Weak. Trapped.

I still was.

Libella was kneeling next to me on the ground. Her closeness surprised me, but I didn't jump away. "How can I help?"

Her kind words did nothing to stop the tears from falling. I choked on a sob. "I don't know." There was nothing I could think of aside from a hug, but I didn't know if that was weird to ask. So, I focused on Ma.

"Will a bath help my mom like it did me?"

"Oh, I think so," her cheery tone made me turn to her, tears still lining my eyes. "It might not do as much, but it will certainly heal her injuries and help her to feel more relaxed."

"Okay." I gave her a weak smile and turned back to Ma. "Is there anything I can do to help?"

Libella placed a gentle hand on my shoulder. "I'll take care of her. You need to rest." That tone, that sweetness in her voice, felt familiar. As her words sank in, a yawn forced its way out, and she helped me stand. "Come. Lie down while I look after your mother. I'll bring her to rest beside you when I'm done."

I nodded, another yawn taking over. "Okay. Just for a little while."

Libella led me to the enormous bed and pulled back the covers. "I'll be here when you wake up."

A thought from our conversation earlier made me ask, "Aren't you supposed to be the Queen's handmaiden?" I crawled into the bed and sank into its fluffy mattress, pulling the pillow comfortably under my head.

"She has other handmaidens. I was instructed to be here. With you." She pulled the blankets up to my shoulders and laid a hand there. "Sleep, Rayleigh."

The bed shifted.

I dragged my eyes open to see Libella lying a freshly cleaned, wound-free Ma next to me. Whatever soap she'd used smelled wonderful—something floral and sweet, like what I'd used earlier. Libella gently moved Ma's hair away from her face and tucked her in. The actions were so tender and nurturing, like Libella was tucking in her own daughter—though she looked to be about the same age as Ma.

My body felt like it was weighed down by a million bricks, but I forced myself to shimmy closer to Ma and draped an arm across her waist. She was still out cold, but her body was warm.

I gave Libella a weak smile from where my head was still stuck on the pillow. She returned it, then walked out of sight, and the room grew darker. The sun must have been going down.

I pulled myself closer to Ma, listening to her steady breathing.

She was okay.

For now.

१ में २ र

Kendall and Leighton were screaming. Their tortured cries filled my ears. I tried to block them out, but it was no use. I couldn't move. I tried to stand, to go to them, but I was chained to the wall, helpless.

Ma's fragile bones smacked on the cement. *Crack* — on the cell bars. *Crack* — against the rock wall. Koladon tossed her around—his powers throwing her this way and that.

Mitch was bleeding out, lying in a puddle of his own blood. A gurgling sound escaped his mouth as he choked on his cry for help.

The dagger in my hand was flying toward Kaleb's chest. His wide honey-brown eyes shone bright. He was begging me to kill him.

I screamed, needing to wake up from the nightmare.

None of it was real. I knew that.

But I was paralyzed.

I couldn't move.

My body started shaking.

Violently.

No wait. That wasn't me.

Someone else was shaking me.

I shot up in bed, my eyes flying open. The hands on my shoulders fell away.

The room was still dark. My eyes were trying to adjust.

A small light flickered on the table next to me. I turned toward it and found someone sitting beside me on the bed.

I jumped back a little, careful not to scream. I tried to focus on whoever it was with what little light I had, and a sob escaped me. "Kendall?" She couldn't be here. There was no way. I was still dreaming.

This was a trick my mind was playing on me. A hope that could never come true. I reached out to touch her. Slowly. My hand met her warm cheek, and her hand covered mine. I met her sad, wide eyes. "Oh my God, you're here!" I scrambled to pull her closer and wrap my arms around her tighter than I'd ever held her. Tears streamed down my face as I sobbed into her shoulder. Her body shook against mine as she returned the embrace. Hot tears soaked my shirt, but I didn't dare let go. If I let go, she could disappear. "How are you here?" I asked into her hair.

She sniffled but made no move to release me. "I don't know. I woke up to you screaming. I don't even remember falling asleep."

Mari. She could make people sleep. I'd seen it. Felt it. Did she knock Ken out and leave her alone in her chambers? But then, how did Ken get here? Even if she were conscious, she wouldn't have known where to go in this castle. Did Mari know she was here? Did someone bring her here? What was going on?

As much as I wanted to know, I also just wanted to cling to her and not think about anything that happened before falling asleep. She was here. She was safe. She was ok—

I pulled away to look at her. Grabbed her face with both hands, turning it this way and that, finding no black eye, no scratches or scars. She seemed perfectly healthy. "Did you take a bath?" She eyed me warily but nodded. "Who helped you?"

"I don't know her name. She didn't say much, and I couldn't really speak." She grabbed my hands from her face and brought them down between us. "But she said she was there to care for me and that the bath would help."

"What did she look like?"

Ken shrugged. "Tall. Strong. A goddess." She cracked a grin, "A thick, curvy goddess."

"Libella," I whispered.

"What?"

"Her name is Libella," I said a little louder, wondering how she helped Ma *and* Ken. Is that who brought Ken here? If she was with Ken, who was here with me? Or did she feel like she could leave me here alone?

"It was really strange," Ken said, returning my attention to her. "I barely remember what happened after Mari touched me. One second, I was backing away from her as she grabbed my arm. The next, I was being led to the bath by Libella."

Fire lit my veins as the events of the dining hall replayed in my mind. Ken's scream echoed in my head. "She claimed you," I bit out.

"She what?" Ken's face went slack. That's when I realized that she had *no* idea what that meant. Theo never told us about the bonds in the sessions we had. I hadn't known to ask about them.

I took a deep breath. "Back on Earth, Kyler told me about this thing called a Doulos bond. It's something a Drakalasson can do to Fae." I thought about what the King said to Kaleb. It was easy enough to put things together. "They claim them and their powers as their own. To control them. 'A glorified slave' is how Kyler described what they were." I realized that was where my knowledge of the Doulos ended, but then I remembered what Mari had done. I reached for Ken's arm and turned it over several times. Running my fingers along her smooth, healed skin. Searching. *It has to be here.* But Ken's skin looked normal. There was no red mark, no lingering outline of a hand. Nothing.

"You won't find anything."

I whipped my head in the direction of the new voice. It came from a dark corner of the room where I could barely make out a shadow sitting in a chair. It didn't move, but I knew someone was there. And if that voice told me anything—

"What do you mean?" I whispered to the shadow, squinting to see if I could make out the person sitting there. "Why not?"

The shadow moved, causing the light to reveal familiar features. When the light hit the blue-green of her eyes, I sucked in a breath. "Because I didn't claim her."

SEVEN
Conspiracy

My jaw dropped. Mari watched me carefully from across the room. She seemed regretful and full of sorrow, but her look was determined.

"You *didn't* claim her?" Mari shook her head. I sighed, "Then what the hell happened in the dining hall?"

Mari touched her fingers to her lips. "We can't speak freely here. No one can." She looked to the doorway and seemed to make a decision before looking back at us. "But we may have a few minutes if we speak quietly." She stood and crossed the room. I pulled Ken closer to me, and Mari froze midstep, her blue-green eyes lined with silver. "I would never hurt Kendall."

I eyed her, unsure of anything anymore. My voice was barely a whisper when I asked, "Why did she scream like that?" The memory of the noise that had erupted out of her echoed in my head, and I tried to shake it away.

"I had to make it believable," she whispered. Swallowing thickly, she went on, "The King would have killed all of us if I didn't do it." My hand covered my mouth. The King was becoming more and more terrifying with each moment I spent here. "So I flooded her mind with pain, but I didn't actually hurt her. I think she passed out." She looked to Kendall, whose eyes were wide with terror. "I'm so sorry you had to endure that. This was never supposed to happen." She looked defeated and dropped down to the ground cross-legged in front of us.

"What do you mean?" I asked, knowing there was no way they could have all worked this out—not with the way the King reacted to everything. "What about the red mark I saw in the hall?"

"My dragon provided the heat to make it look like a burn mark. Just enough to turn it red."

I shook my head. I always seemed to be questioning Mari's loyalty, but she kept coming back. Every time something would happen to make me suspect her, she would say something to prove her innocence. And she never expected me to believe her. She was never surprised when I was suspicious. I wondered what that said about me. About her. Yet here she was, making me question her again. "How do I know you're not lying?"

She shrugged, but it was Kendall's quiet voice that answered. "I don't think she's lying, Ray." I turned to face her and saw the genuine look on her face. "Right before she grabbed me, she whispered something… that she was sorry, I think." She looked to Mari for confirmation.

Mari smiled slightly. "If I could have given you more warning, I would have. But I was alone in there." She closed her eyes and dropped her voice even more. "My mother told me this would be difficult."

I scrunched my eyebrows. "Your mother?"

Mari nodded, saying nothing, but her eyes communicated so much. They seemed to tell me I had all the information I was seeking. She watched me, waiting to see if I could piece it together. I narrowed my eyes, thinking of how I could possibly know who her mother was. But as I thought about who Mari was and how she acted, the answer dawned on me. I said, a bit disbelieving, "Libella."

Mari nodded again.

"But then how could you not kno—" I started, my voice slightly raised.

But Mari shushed me almost immediately. "I told you, we have to talk quietly," she whispered, then pointed to the open door where the distant sound of footsteps rang.

I pursed my lips, nodding. I was about to ask how the hell she didn't know Kyler was the King's son. Especially if her mother was the Queen's handmaiden. But then, if someone were listening, why did she tell us she didn't claim Kendall? I eyed her suspiciously and whispered, "What can you tell us?"

She closed her eyes, taking a deep breath before opening them again. "That you're safe," she said as if it were the only truth she'd ever told me. "My mother is Kyler's attendant. She's the Queen's handmaiden, yes. But when Kyler is around, she is assigned to him."

I clenched my teeth and thought about the moments in the hall. About the way Kyler acted. The voice that whispered in my head. I found Mari's eyes and searched them for a moment before asking, "Can I trust Kyler?"

Mari held my gaze for a moment but then dropped it. "I don't know."

I let my head fall back. That wasn't the answer I was hoping for. After all, I was now stuck living in his chambers for the foreseeable future. If I couldn't trust him, I would adapt. I wanted to know what the hell was going on and why he was acting like a jackass, but there was no way to find out. I would have to move on with the only certainty being that Mari was on our side… or so she said.

My mind wandered back to Libella and I thought about how she got me to trust her. The words she used.

I found Mari watching me intently. "How does Libella know Theo?"

Mari's eyebrows shot up before she pursed her lips, suppressing a smile. "She's his mate," she whispered.

I squinted at her. "Mate? What does that mean?"

She gave me a small smile, speaking fondly, saying, "It's complicated. But basically, their souls were made for each other."

"So he's your dad?" I asked, scrunching my brows together. Mari's complexion didn't match the mix between Libella and Theo. Not only that, our conversation about her dad earlier didn't match what Theo was capable of.

"No, no. My father…" she trailed off, her smile fading. "My mother found Theo after her…relationship with my father. He's no longer in my life." She took a breath, shaking her head from whatever thoughts came up, and said, "Theo has taken me in as his daughter since they mated, though."

I let her words sink in, memories of their interactions flooding my mind. It made sense now why I always thought Theo was silently reprimanding Mari and the sweetness I'd seen between them at the Dengalow. It reminded me of me and my dad.

A pang of sadness pinched my heart. I missed him. I looked over at Ma, still silently sleeping beside me. Her breathing was steady and she looked to be okay right now, but I knew it wouldn't last much longer. I reached to brush her hair from her face. Did she know something about Dad that she was protecting? Was he from this realm, *my* realm? Was Mitch going to be okay? If he wasn't fully human, he might survive here longer than Ma, but if they were wrong… if he was just human…

"Rayleigh," Kendall's voice broke the silence as she touched my arm. "She's going to be okay. She's going home, remember?"

The tears I'd been trying to hold back were suddenly streaming down my face as I choked out, "But she won't remember me. Or Mitch, if he stays here. And if he goes too, neither of them will remember me." I swallowed my panic, trying not to let my emotions overwhelm me. Ken took that as a sign to pull me into a hug, and I felt the bed shift slightly as Mari sat beside her.

"The memory modification will only make her forget her time here. It won't wipe you from her memory, Rayleigh."

"But the King said—"

Mari held up her hand. "I know what he said. But he never plays with memories himself. The person who does will make her temporarily forget you so the King sees fit, but she will remember you." I eyed her suspiciously. There was something else she wasn't saying. I could tell by the way she watched me. Like she was waiting for me to connect the dots again. But then her head whipped to the door. "Someone's coming." She stood from the bed and reached out to Kendall. "Time to go."

Ken still had her arms wrapped around me, and she squeezed me one more time. "I'll visit when I can."

I looked at her sad eyes and realized we hadn't discussed the biggest issue of all. "What about Leighton?" I asked Mari in a whisper, whose face dropped immediately, along with her eyes to the floor, but she didn't answer me. "Mari." She didn't look up, but her shoulders moved in a deep breath. "You can't just leave her with that—that *monster*." My voice raised slightly, causing her head to snap up, and she jammed a finger to her lips. I dropped my voice again, "Please tell me there's something you can do."

A single tear fell from her eye. "Right now, there's nothing I can do. It would seem too suspicious." She took in a shaky breath. "There is one possibility. But we will have to talk about it later." I opened my mouth to ask when, but she hurried on before I could protest, "In a safer place. My mother is in the process of setting up a space for us. For now, Kendall and I must go."

I stood as Ken did and made to follow them to the door, but Mari held her hand up. I swallowed thickly and asked, "When will I see you again?"

"I don't know," she said, sighing. "But I'm sure it won't be long. Doulos are meant to follow their bonded ones throughout the castle." She saw my body slump and stepped toward me, her arms extended but stopped a few inches from me. I looked up at her face, so open and vulnerable, and decided that a hug couldn't hurt. I stepped into her embrace and it felt like being wrapped in a warm blanket. "You'll see us again soon. And I'm sure we'll see Leigh, too. Whatever Kaleb is up to, he still seems to think he will get away with it."

My mouth was pressed into her shoulder, but I mumbled into it anyway, "I think I'd like to try stabbing him again."

Mari's answering chuckle was unexpected but light. "I think we all would. But that's not a great idea right now."

"We'll take turns," I said, pulling out of her arms and wrapping my own around me. Mari had a brilliant smile on her face, and so did Ken.

"We'll make him pay for what he did to you," Ken nodded. "To all of us. Together."

The footsteps in the hall clicked closer and I suddenly didn't want them to be anywhere near me. "Get out of here. Quick!" I shooed them toward the archway, but Mari headed toward the bathroom instead. I hurried after her and whisper-shouted, "Where are you going?"

Mari didn't answer me. She headed to the door with the intricate patterns, stopping in front of it. She reached out and quickly touched three symbols, causing iridescent light to flash through the cracks. When Mari opened the door, another bathroom appeared on the other side. Once she pushed Kendall through, she stepped in and turned to shut it. I watched, slack-jawed, as she grinned at me and closed the door behind her. The click of the door caused another flash of iridescent light, and they were gone. I walked over to the door and turned the handle, swinging it open. It was a typical bathroom closet with soaps, towels, and extra bed linens.

How in the world did it just change from a bathroom to a linen closet? As I shut the door, I almost opened it again to double-check, but someone cleared their throat behind me.

I whipped around to find Kyler leaning on the doorframe of the bathroom entrance. How long had he been standing there? Did he see Mari and Ken escape? What did he—

"What're you doing?" The accusation in his tone told me he knew exactly what the door did. But he had to know I didn't have the slightest idea how to use it, right? I had to come up with something quick because the longer he looked at me, the more irritated he seemed.

I crossed my arms and scowled at him. "I was looking for a towel."

He raised a brow, then smirked. "No, you weren't." My face dropped, and I suddenly remembered that he could read minds. *Shit.* How was I supposed to keep secret meetings with Kendall and Mari from him if he could find the information whenever he wanted? "You were snooping," Kyler said, pushing off the door frame and walking toward the closet the girls had disappeared into. Toward me.

My body instinctively wanted to shrink away from him, but I hated that. My brain said I should be scared of him, but my inner pride whispered, *Screw that.* I took a deep breath and stood my ground, keeping my arms crossed and tilting my head. "Can you blame me? You left me alone in a place I've never been."

He stopped inches from me, narrowing his eyes. "I see you've got your sass back. Good." He reached behind me and pulled open the closet door. I had been standing against it, so the sudden movement pushed me right into him.

I threw my hands up to stop myself before my face hit his chest and shoved as hard as I could. He didn't move a muscle and I was now trapped between him and the door. "Ugh! And you're still an *asshole!* Move!" I tried shoving him again to no avail.

He chuckled darkly, reached into the closet, and pulled out a towel. I hadn't realized I had put my weight against the door until he released the handle, and I stumbled backward as it slammed shut. As I found my footing, he placed his arm above me on the door and leaned down to whisper, "Best go back to bed, Sunshine. We've got a big day tomorrow."

My face heated as I felt his breath on my face, but I couldn't move, and it didn't seem like he was about to move either. I decided to push his limits and stood up straight with my hands on my hips. This alone caused our faces to almost touch, and a look of surprise crossed his face as he drew his head back an inch or two. I raised an eyebrow, "What do you mean, big day?" Instead of sounding sassy like I'd intended, it came out genuinely curious, and I mentally rolled my eyes.

His eyes traveled down my body as I waited for his answer, and I realized I was wearing one of those silk nightgowns again. I didn't remember changing into one, but Libella must have changed me while I slept. I moved my arms to hug my waist, and as my hand touched my ribcage, a warmth radiated through it. Kyler's eyes found mine, and a flash of blue made my eyes widen. *His dragon.* The blue was gone in an instant, but as his breath hit my face again, the faint smell of smoke filled my nostrils. *Shit, what was his dragon's name? Mushudo? Massmido?* Kyler must have realized my thoughts because he pushed off the wall and walked toward the vanity. I needed to remember that name.

He didn't say anything; he just laid the towel on the counter near the sink and turned on the faucets for the tub. When the water was running, he started removing the belt around his waist, littered with several weapons I hadn't realized he had on him. He set it on the counter near the towel. I hadn't taken the time earlier to look at the intricate and regal outfit he wore. The dark green material ran down his back, almost like a cloak, fastening tightly around his body with several buttons in the front that he was slowly undoing. His tan pants fit him snugly and were tucked into his knee-high brown boots. He slid off his jacket, dropping it to the floor and revealing a loose white shirt tucked into his pants. As he untucked it, and a small glimpse of his abdomen peeked through.

"Are you going to stand there and watch me undress?" Kyler's voice was rough and cocky. I ripped my eyes from the spot where his muscled torso had been exposed to find a smug look on his face.

"I—no, you just—I was—" I pointed to the door, but my feet wouldn't move.

His raised brow and smirk told me one thing: he was loving this. Before I could say anything, he pulled his shirt over his head in one swift movement, and it took everything in me not to take in what that single move exposed. I lifted my chin and stared at the ceiling, trying to find the will to move my feet. "You looked away at the best part, Sunshine."

The soft pop of buttons filled the space, and I realized he wasn't going to stop just because I was standing there. It was like he didn't care that he was stripping down naked in front of me. I still couldn't move my feet, so I just kept my eyes on the ceiling as I listened to his pants hit the ground and his footsteps move toward the running bath. Ripples in the water broke the silence, and I cleared my throat. "Will you please let me go now?"

His answering chuckle was enough to let me know I was right. "You wanted to know what was happening tomorrow, so I thought I'd tell you before you go to sleep."

"While you're naked in a bathtub?"

"What can I say? I like it when you get nervous around me."

"You're delusional."

"Am I? Your cheeks are still red."

"That has nothing to do with nerves!"

Kyler mused and was quiet for a moment. Then he let out a hefty sigh. "You can look now."

"I'm not interested in looking."

"Are you sure about that?" His sure tone made me clench my teeth to keep from swearing at him. He sighed, "You won't see anything. I'm fully immersed."

The idea of talking to him while he bathed was still ridiculous, but I knew he wouldn't let me go until I heard him out. He was holding me there on purpose and for a reason I had yet to learn. Slowly, I lowered my chin, eyeing his form, where he relaxed in the huge floor tub. His arms were resting on the edge, making his shoulders peek out above the water and part of his muscular chest, but he watched me as I made sure the rest of him was concealed beneath the milky water. My eyes met his.

"Well?" I asked, wanting to get to the bottom of this as soon as possible.

Kyler raised a brow at me before he leaned his head back, closing his eyes. "The start of Kaleb's welcome home celebration." My eyebrows shot up, and I stumbled forward a step. Kyler's eyes popped open, finding mine immediately. "How did you do that?"

"Do what?" I asked, still in shock from his previous statement.

"Break my hold."

"I fell forward in shock!" I retorted, but I wasn't letting him off the hook. "A celebration? For that manipulating liar?"

Kyler narrowed his eyes at me, but after a moment, he shook it off. "My brother is not a manipulating liar," he stated as if I were crazy. "He has been lost for years and has finally come home." I could've been mistaken, but it sounded like there was a slight sarcasm in his voice. He laid his head back again. "The celebration will consist of many things but mainly a dinner, a ceremony to meet his dragon, and then a ball, all over the course of the next three days."

My eyes bugged out of their head. "Meet his dragon?" Remembering how Kyler's dragon had acted and what he said, that sounded like something I didn't want to be a part of.

"Yes." Kyler's eyes found mine again. "Don't worry, though. You'll be safe." He winked at me. I rolled my eyes. As much as I knew that was true, I didn't want it to be because of him. Libella and Mari would keep me safe, I couldn't care less what Kyler did.

Something occurred to me then. "Wait, if he hasn't met his dragon yet, how did he claim Leighton?"

Kyler didn't answer. Instead, he lifted his arms and head from the side of the tub and slid off the seat and under the water. He didn't emerge right away, but the last thing I was going to do was panic. I would not worry about him or his safety anymore. He clearly didn't need my help here. I wouldn't be saving his life in this realm—or any realm, for that matter—not after what he did.

When he finally resurfaced, he stood up in the middle of the tub. The water cascaded down his body as he slicked back his hair, squeezing the water out. I mentally scolded myself for watching it trail all the way down his torso until it disappeared into the water just below the dimples on his back. *Look away, Rayleigh,* I seethed at myself and finally tore my eyes away from his bare muscled back and found him reaching for soap on the countertop that was just out of reach.

"Should have grabbed it before you got in, dumbass," I said, hugging my arms tighter around my body.

He slowly turned to face me, a smirk gracing his unfortunately handsome face. "You could get it for me, Sunshine." He gestured to himself in the water. "Or else you'll see everything you missed earlier while staring at the ceiling."

I gave him a mocking smile and said sweetly, "If I could move on my own, I would." I blinked rapidly to complete the act. "Or you could use that thing called magic to get it."

With his torso fully exposed and his smile turning a bit more wicked, he leaned back on his elbows. I swore violently as my feet moved involuntarily across the room. "Thing is, I have more than one type of magic. And I'd rather you get it for me."

"Jackass," I mumbled as I fought my body's movements toward the sink. "I said I would do it and you still feel the need to control me."

"It's more fun this way," he mocked. As I reached the soap, I turned to chuck it at him before he could sense what I was doing. It flew straight for his face, but he caught it inches before it hit its mark. Instead of growling like I expected, he lowered the bottle to reveal a full smile, and his stupid dimples appeared. "Fiesty tonight, aren't you?"

I let out a noise of frustration. "Can I go to bed now?"

He raised a brow, ignoring me for a moment and putting the soap to use. I looked away, taking advantage of his loose control to lean against the sink. "Not yet. I haven't told you your responsibilities for tomorrow."

"Responsibilities?" Then I remembered: I was his Doulos. I had to do whatever he said. I closed my eyes and sighed. "Let me guess, I have to be at your beck and call?"

He was scrubbing his head with soap when he gave a small laugh and set the soap down, dunking himself underwater again. I shook my head. This had to be the most annoying conversation I'd ever had with him. Was this what it would all come down to? Him being the asshole I met in school, controlling me because it was easy, and me doing anything he said, whether I wanted to or not? At least now, my body wouldn't be betraying me. It seemed just as repulsed by his betrayal as I was. Even though Kaleb was the real traitor, Kyler wasn't far behind with his actions. And here I thought we'd become friends.

Kyler's head popped out of the water, and instead of being entranced by the water again, I kept my eyes on his face, waiting for the answer to my question. Instead, he turned to walk out of the tub, and I grabbed the closest thing to cover my view of his naked body as he emerged. "You couldn't have waited until I left to get out?" I basically shouted.

His answering chuckle came from close by, and I wanted to slap the smirk I knew was on his face. He tugged on whatever I was holding to hide from him, and I screamed, not letting go. "Let go of my towel, Sunshine. Unless you *want* me to walk around naked."

I immediately released what I now registered was the towel he'd set by the sink and covered my eyes with my hands instead. "You're despicable," I spat.

His voice came from directly in front of me. "Watching you get flustered has been my favorite thing since that first day in chemistry class," he taunted.

I huffed, "Are you covered now?"

"Do you want me to be?"

"*Yes!*"

"Then yes."

I uncovered my eyes slowly to find him several inches from me with the douchiest smile, the towel secured low on his hips, and droplets of water still covering his chest. That's all I let myself take in before looking back at his face. "Responsibilities?" I said through my teeth, trying not to register the way his hair dripped water or how his face was literal perfection as the water gleamed on it.

His grin slowly faded as he dipped his chin, his voice dropping so low that it made my chest vibrate. "You are to do everything I ask, never leave my side, and let no one else touch you." He stepped closer, although I wasn't sure there was any more space for him to do so. "And don't do anything stupid," he growled.

The command rippled through me, and I suppressed the shudder I felt making its way to the surface. Those were his last words to me before I was captured. I wondered if he remembered that. The way his eyes bore into me made me think he did, but he was still pretending to be my friend then. So why use the exact phrase? Was it because my reckless behavior made him lose control of his "prized possession," as his dragon called—

His dragon! Dammit, what was his name! Massimo? Mossduo? Knowing I wouldn't remember tonight, I focused on Kyler's instructions. "Wouldn't dream of it."

His eyes flashed with recognition of my last words to him, but he went on in that deep voice. "If somehow you end up *not* by my side and someone *does* touch you, you are to inform me. Immediately."

"Like you care," I sneered.

"Oh, but I do care, Sunshine." He leaned in, and I couldn't back away. He was holding me in place. His whisper tickled my ear as he growled, "No one touches what is mine."

The scent of smoke reached my nose as Kyler shoulder-checked me on his way out of the bathroom. As he walked into the main bedroom, I suddenly thought that both Ma and I would have to share a bed with him. But he passed the bed and went straight to the room with the giant cushion, slamming the door behind him. I felt his control over me disappear, and I released the breath I'd been holding since he'd leaned in. I put my hands on my cheeks, feeling the heat that had filled them in his presence. Perhaps my body *was* going to betray me again, but this time, I couldn't let it win.

EIGHT
I Don't Know What Else You Want From Me

"Good morning, dear."

Light filled the room, and I opened my eyes to find Libella pulling back the curtains. I gave her a small smile as I stretched, wanting more than anything to learn more about her and Mari, and ask about Theo — where was he? Was he okay? But before I could even greet her back, she was by the bed and pulling the blankets off. "You've got a big day ahead of you. Nikylo requests that you be presentable. He has provided your attire for this evening's dinner as well as your daily duties."

"Daily duties?" As the cold air hit my skin, I sat up to wrap my arms around my legs. "He didn't say anything about daily duties," I said plainly. Ma stirred in the bed next to me at the loss of the warm covers and I reached out a comforting hand as her eyes fluttered open weakly. I reached over and grabbed her hand, squeezing tightly. Tears lined my eyes as I thought about what was to come. "What about Ma?"

Libella rounded the bed and helped Ma sit as I released her hand. "She will be left in good hands. We have been provided some necessities from her world to help with her health." *Her* world. Not my world. Not our world. *Hers.* Libella talked so much like Theo that it was almost scary. Always direct and to the point, even if it seemed harsh. "I will set her up in her new room with that and breakfast while you take care of your morning needs. Your breakfast is on its way up."

"Her new room?" I stared at Libella. Her instructions were clear, but sleepiness still fogged my brain, making her words feel as if I'd been hit by a truck. That meant I would be left alone with Kyler. I should have known that was coming. Refocusing on Ma, I asked, "Where are you taking her? What things did you get for her? How will it help her—"

"Rayleigh," she held up her hand to stop me. "Your mother is in good hands. I promise. Please do as I ask." Her gentle reprimand made me shrink into myself. She wasn't mean, per se, but it seemed like a different Libella than the one I met yesterday. Her gaze softened when she took me in, and her eyes flicked to something behind me. I slowly turned to find the door to Kyler's chambers still closed.

Oh. I nodded dramatically as I glanced back at Libella, who returned my gaze with a small smile. I swung my feet to the floor and headed to the bathroom.

The empty tub made me roll my eyes as I tried to burn the image of Kyler sitting in it from my brain. He had some nerve, exposing himself to me like that. I shivered as my bare feet touched the tiled floor—or maybe it was the memory of him being a cocky jackass. Ugh, I had a feeling it would come back to haunt me.

There was a mirror behind the sink I hadn't noticed before, and it showed me someone I didn't recognize. My cheeks were sunken, my eyes were hollow, and my body still showed signs of having eaten very little over the past several weeks. The healing waters could only do so much, it seemed. I leaned in, noticing new scars from the single beating I'd received in the dungeons. I pushed back from the sink, thinking of how awful the twins came back every time they were taken away. *None* of my scars compared to what they had gone through in a single session, let alone four weeks' worth. Our quick healing hadn't prevented the jagged cuts from turning into nasty scars or the shattered bones from healing crooked.

There were times I wondered why the twins didn't end up in the hospital as much as I did growing up. After all, if being clumsy was a trait of a young fae, why were they different? And how did they end up on Earth? They only had one elemental power, which meant they weren't being hunted for their powers… so why were they there?

That would be a question I'd have to ask Theo—if I ever saw him again. Maybe if I asked, Libella would let me see him… I didn't want to get my hopes up, though, so I added the questions to my never-ending list instead.

Taking a deep breath, I splashed some cold water on my face and took care of my needs before returning to the bedroom. Libella was sitting alone at a table that hadn't been there before. I sighed. Trusting Libella was difficult enough, but trusting her with Ma? She hadn't said anything this morning, but she was weak. I hoped that whatever was brought from Earth would help her regain some sense of self because it was hard to find the Ma I knew in there. Who knew how much longer she'd be here? It could be hours, it could be weeks. I only hoped they would let me see her again before she left.

I took in the table filled with various foods. They looked familiar from a distance, but as I followed Libella's beckoning to the table, I didn't recognize any of them. What looked like an extra thick slice of bread was a piece of toast filled with colorful fruits. The thick pancakes were filled with a pink cream that melted in my mouth. There were slices of meat I wouldn't have touched because of the blue tint, but Libella told me I needed the protein and promised it wasn't poisonous. After eyeing her suspiciously, I placed a small bite in my mouth and discovered it tasted like a mix of beef and chicken.

A door opened behind me as I finished my plate full of food. I didn't have to turn around to know exactly who it was. His presence filled the room with tension. I kept my eyes on my plate as his footsteps slapped on the floor behind me. Too late, I realized the only open chair was beside me. I made to get up, seeing as I was done eating, but a hand landed on my shoulder.

"Don't stand on my account, Sunshine." Kyler had a gravelly morning voice, and I curled away from his touch, making him chuckle before he sat casually next to me. So casually, he hung one leg over the arm of the chair and draped his arm over the back. "What did Chef make for us today, Libella?" he asked, popping a pink berry in his mouth.

I glanced up at Libella, who only raised an eyebrow at Kyler before stating, "Exactly what you asked for, Nikylo. With the addition of some milot because—"

"Thank you, Bell," Kyler said, cutting her off with a raised hand and then waving it in the air. His plate floated around the table, food jumping off its place on the table to fill it. My jaw fell slightly open as I watched the ease with which he used his magic. I wondered if I would ever learn how to use *my* magic. "You are to report to Libella today," he said, stabbing a piece of blue meat from his plate that just landed before him. "Wear the attire provided, listen to her, and talk to no one else. Understood?"

I blinked at him slowly, raising my eyebrows. "Aye, aye, Captain Asshole." I gave him a one-fingered salute using my middle finger.

He gave me a dark smile, leaning toward me. "Careful. It sounds like you're warming up to me again."

"You wish."

"It would make things so much easier."

"Well, I'm not one to make things easy."

"I would hope not." His eyes traveled down my body slowly, making my skin prickle. "I love the hunt."

"Eh-em." I jumped at Libella's clear interruption, finding her scolding Kyler with her eyes as he slowly turned to face her. I shook my head free of the trance I'd been in. "If you're done eating, Rayleigh," she said, turning to me, "we best get on with your day." I gritted my teeth and stood from the table as Libella did. "Your clothes are there." She gestured to the bed, where the dark blue material was folded neatly.

I picked up the top piece and found it had a soft linen texture. As it unfolded, the intricate details within the fabric looked oddly familiar. When I turned it around, that side had different symbols. "What do these mean?" I asked, not bothering to turn around for the answer. I traced the first symbol, full of lines intercrossing with no visible pattern.

Kyler's whispered explanation made me turn sharply to find him watching my every move with a smirk. "I'm supposed to walk around the castle wearing this?"

"Yep." He popped the end of the word and gave me a wild grin, taking a bite of the stuffed toast.

"This is degrading. I'm not wearing this. I'm not your property." I crumpled up the shirt and chucked it at him, but he caught it, holding it up to see the symbols of his powers stitched into the fabric on the back. Then, he flipped it around for me to see the front, where the other two symbols he translated for me were displayed for all to see: "Nikylo's Property."

"Actually, you are." He stood, covering the distance between us. "In this castle, you are *mine*. And when you're not by my side, everyone needs to know. So, while you go about your daily duties, you will wear this shirt. When you walk this castle without me, you will wear this shirt. If you do *anything* without me, you will wear this shirt." He was so close that his eyes shifted focus between mine, his breath hot on my face. "If I hear that you took this off or covered it, there will be consequences. And you won't like them." He stepped closer, bringing his mouth to my ear. "Is that clear, Sunshine?"

The whisper tickled its way through my ear, but I refused to shudder the feeling away and stepped as far from him as I could, saying through my teeth, "Clear, Asshole." I ripped the shirt from his hands, grabbed the pants off the bed, and shoulder-checked him on my way to the bathroom.

Degrading wasn't a strong enough word for what the outfit made me feel anymore. Even if he hadn't claimed me as his Doulos, he was treating me like one now. I felt like a bug he was slowly squashing under his foot. The Kyler I thought I knew didn't exist anymore. The friendship we developed back on Earth was gone. He would have never talked to me like that. And if he was going to make my life miserable… well, two could play that game.

There was a moment when I thought about calling his dragon, but with Libella present, I didn't think it was a good idea. Who knew what the dragon might do to someone else? I didn't want to risk her life. She seemed like the one person I could trust right now, outside of Mari, even though they were both under the impression that Kyler still cared about me. I hoped I wasn't wrong about either of them.

When I emerged from the bathroom, Kyler was gone, but Libella waited patiently by the door. "Your shoes are here." She pointed to a spot near the archway, where a pair of shoes that matched my outfit sat. They were flexible, light, easy to slip on, and more comfortable than I imagined.

Glancing down at my now complete wardrobe, I eyed Libella through my brows. "Why am I wearing this?"

"You have duties to attend to. This outfit is practical for those."

"And what are these duties?" I asked a bit sarcastically.

She smiled. "Follow me." And without giving me time to protest, she led the way out of the room and into the never-ending hallway.

I had no idea what Kyler had lined up for me to do, but I was mostly glad I didn't have to be with him all day. Mari said we were supposed to be with our bonded ones throughout the castle, so why was I going with Libella? What was she going to have me do? Was there something I missed from Kyler's instructions? He only told me the duties during the ceremonial events. Whatever I was about to do, he gave no actual instructions or clues except that I had to make sure no one else touched me. I did not believe for one second that his biggest concern was my safety, but the fact that Libella didn't counter Kyler's instructions told me it was probably for the best.

Libella and I walked in silence for a while before I decided to ask some questions. Her hands were clasped in front of her, resting on the top of her skirt as she followed the curve of the hallways. Half a step behind her, messing with the hem of my shirt nervously, I asked, "Libella, can I ask you some questions?"

Her head turned slightly to acknowledge she had heard me, and she nodded. "I'll do my best to answer."

Even though she didn't outright say it, I knew she meant she would answer what she *could*. I nodded and took a deep breath. I didn't think she'd be able to answer my questions about Kyler and whether or not I could trust him. So, I went down to the next topic on my list of things I needed to know. "Where did you send my mom?"

"She is down the hall with one of the other handmaidens."

"What did they bring from home for her?"

She eyed me sideways but answered, "They brought an oxygen mask and some other essential vitamins not provided by the atmosphere here." When my only response was scrunching my eyebrows together, she went on. "Her lack of nutrients for four weeks drained her body's immune system, so even if she gets back to Earth soon, she would be very sick. She needs to build it back up."

I nodded, knowing that was the best thing for her. "So she'll be better before she goes back?"

"She will be in a better condition, but the environment here will prevent her from getting stronger physically. The vitamins will only prevent her from getting worse."

"When will she be sent back?"

"After your brother's trial."

"And when is that?"

She hesitated a moment before lifting her chin and saying, "Tomorrow. After the ceremony."

My blood ran cold. I only had one more day with Ma. And I hadn't even seen Mitch since we were brought here. "Will I be able to see him before his trial?" I asked, wondering what state he would be in, what kind of torture he'd been through over the last month.

Libella sighed, turning to face me. Her eyes were big and round, a warm chocolate brown. They spoke volumes above what her words conveyed. "He's in the King's wing of the castle. You are not allowed access, I'm afraid." But what I saw in her eyes said, *There may be a way.*

I played along with her outspoken words, sagging my shoulders and dropping my chin. "Okay." Thinking I could hit two birds with one stone, I asked, "Would it be possible to get a notebook or something? To write him a letter?"

Libella took me in for a moment and gave a single nod. "I will see what I can do." She turned and continued up the hallway, and I fell into step behind her again.

Thinking I'd be brave, I watched her face as I asked, "How did you meet Theo?"

Her cheeks flushed slightly, and she pursed her lips to keep the smile there from forming completely. It tugged at my heart to see her reaction, even so many years after they'd been together. Was it always like that when someone fell in love? Or was it just a "mates" thing? Thinking about love made my thoughts fall back to Kaleb. No matter how much I hated him for his betrayal. There was still a lot of hurt, too. My love for him had been real, and seeing him try to replicate the gentle Kaleb I knew made my heart hurt, remembering how he used to calm me and hold me. I shook the thought away and focused instead on Libella, who was still trying to keep herself from smiling. Maybe I could have what she had one day instead of the regret I felt for loving someone who just stabbed me in the back.

Libella still hadn't said anything, collecting herself and perhaps some thoughts. "We met at Mari's dragon ceremony two centuries ago."

My head snapped to her, my eyes wide. I had forgotten about those moments with Mari in the room full of paintings. She told me the painting of Niccodra was from over a century ago and that she *remembered* when it looked like that. My next question came out in a whisper. "How old is Mari?"

Libella looked over her shoulder at me with an eyebrow raised and a slight smile. "You never asked her." It wasn't a question, but I still shook my head. "Mari is two hundred and eighteen years old this year."

I blinked so slowly that I thought my eyes wouldn't reopen from the shock. "There's no way," I whispered. "She doesn't look a day over seventeen."

Libella laughed through her nose. "We age much differently here than what you're used to."

"Yeah, no kidding," I scoffed. "How long can your kind live?"

She weighed her head back and forth, "It depends, but most of us can live to be over a millennia."

My jaw dropped. Living to that age was unheard of. To think that someone could have been alive for that long was insane. What did they do with their lives? It seemed like so much time to fill with the same old things in life. On Earth, you had milestones every ten years or so. Was there something similar here? Did they go to school? College? What kind of jobs did they have? Was retirement a thing? How did this world work with all the years people lived? Did they have children like we did on Earth? If so, how many of them inhabited this realm? The notebook couldn't come fast enough. I already knew some of these questions wouldn't make it to the list because too many filled my head.

As I slowly shook my head, I thought back to her answer to my initial question. "What can I expect of the dragon ceremony?"

Libella looked down at her feet and took a deep breath. "You won't experience much of anything unless Nikylo lets you see."

An archway appeared on the left side of the hallway, and we turned into it, following a narrower corridor with windows on both sides. The sky displayed beautiful shades of purple and pink, making me wonder just how early we were up for the daily tasks. My sense of time had disappeared since being released from the dungeons.

From the castle's location, which seemed to sit atop a high mountain in the center of the island, I could see a great distance in either direction. The floating island was bigger than I had imagined, having only seen the painting of Niccodra back at the Dengalow. I couldn't see any of the others, but from this vantage point, I could make out the edges of this one.

"But if he does permit you to see," Libella continued, drawing my attention back to her, "it will be through his Lunnoxia powers."

"His what?" The word sounded familiar, but it seemed like ages ago I learned all the dragon's powers. I couldn't remember which line had which powers.

"His Lunnoxia powers. The ability to influence your mind."

Right. The one that allowed him to read my mind, plant images and thoughts, and control what I saw—

Wait a second. Is *that* what happened the night I stabbed Kaleb? Did someone make me see myself stabbing him? Was it Kyler? Or did one of the other dragons have that power? Koladon didn't even know about Kaleb. Did that mean someone else was involved? It was too dangerous to ask Libella now, as we were still traveling through the castle. I made a mental note to remind myself of the questions I needed to ask and returned to the reason his powers came up in the first place.

"So if Kyler allows—"

"Nikylo, dear," Libella interrupted. "I know he asked you to stop calling him by his false name."

I raised my eyebrows at her, slightly taken aback by her brash tone. Out of respect for her, I decided to listen. But *Kyler* would not hear the end of this. "So if *Nikylo* allows me to see this ceremony, what will I experience?" I glanced out the window, trying to keep myself from glowering at Libella. It wasn't her fault Kyler was such an ass, but him telling her to make sure I don't call him Kyler made me want to punch him. Maybe I'd try later.

Libella took a deep breath as we exited the narrow, windowed hallway into another one similar to the first, but this time, we descended. "Our dragons have been with us since birth, but during the ceremony, there is a ritual that brings whatever Drakalasson is in attendance to the dimensional plane where the shifters are linked. Those transported watch as the dragon reveals themselves to their shifted form. Kaleb will be positioned on the ceremonial dais where his dragon will come forth to make the final connection."

I thought there was already a lot going on with different realms…now there were other dimensions? What was the difference between realms and dimensions? Another question to add to the list… "The sooner I can get that notebook, the better," I mumbled, hoping Libella would take the hint. "What do you mean by final connection?"

"After it is made, they share one mind. While the dragon has been linked to them since birth, the ceremonial connection bonds their minds. Before that point, communication, if any, is limited."

Limited? What did that mean? Libella was answering questions that I didn't think Kyler would, so I decided to ask her the one he didn't answer. "How could Kaleb claim Leighton if he wasn't fully connected with his dragon?"

"It is a necessary step for shifters to take before their final connection. It is what brings the dragon forth in preparation for the ceremony. That is why Kaleb's ceremony is happening so closely after he claimed Leighton: his dragon is now primed for it."

This was a lot to remember when I couldn't take notes. "I know you said communication is limited, but can dragons…appear before that?" I asked, knowing Kyler's dragon pushed through to see me whenever he could. I wanted to know if Kaleb's dragon ever came through, and I just wasn't paying enough attention.

"It is rare since the final connection gives them the shared mind and ability to shift. But it is possible, under the right circumstances." Libella stopped in front of a doorway. "This is where you will spend most of your days in the castle," she said, gesturing to the closed door. "At least until Nikylo says otherwise."

I raised my brows in question, waiting for her to go on, but she didn't. "What's in that room?"

"It's not a room," she said with a smile.

The door swung open to reveal a prairie of grass and trees, flowers, and a small lake, colors so bright that even in the early morning hours, it was vibrant. The scene seemed oddly familiar, though I couldn't quite place why, other than it reminded me slightly of my meadow. Libella held the door and ushered me through it, revealing the mountains on either side of the grassy plain, the castle towering above and behind me. It was beautiful.

The momentary distraction of my awe didn't prepare me for the scream to my left, right before being tackled to the ground.

/ NINE
Run Through Walls

Someone wrapped their arms tightly around me, but not in an "I'm fighting you" way. It was more like they were happy to see me. As soon as I turned in their embrace and figured out who it was, I returned their embrace, and a happy sob escaped me.

"Oh my god, you're here!" I screamed, pulling Leigh close and feeling her hair to make sure she was real. I pulled her away from my shoulder to see her face. Her blue eyes shone with tears, but the bags under them made them duller than usual. "You're here!" I repeated, wiping the tears from her face, moving my hands to her shoulders, then grabbing her hands to put them to my face. "I'm here too!" I assured her, her face scrunching up in confusion. "I didn't think I'd see you again," I whispered the truth I hadn't wanted to accept, knowing it was more than possible that Kaleb could have kept her from me.

"Me neither, Ray." She pulled me into another hug as her sobs of joy continued. She jerked back, and her face suddenly went slack, terrified. "Is Kendall okay? I had no idea Mari was going to do that," she paused, clenching her jaw before continuing. "How could she betray us? I thought she was our friend. I thought she—" Her voice caught in her throat as her eyes filled with tears again.

I cupped her face and gave her a bright smile, even though tears had filled my eyes, too. "Mari had to do that, or else we could have been killed." Leigh's eyes widened. "She put on a show, Leigh. Kendall is fine. Mari didn't claim her."

"Then what happened in the dining hall?" she whispered. A haunted look filled her eyes as they grew unfocused. "Why did Ken scream like that?"

"I asked her the same thing. But she promised it was all a show, and nothing really happened to Ken."

The words must have struck a chord because she suddenly sank into my arms again, hot tears hitting my shirt. "But it really happened to me," she whispered against my shoulder. My heart sank to my stomach. She was right. It happened to her, and there was nothing we could do to help her—at least not at this moment.

I wrapped my arms around Leigh as her body trembled and laid my head on top of hers. I knew what this betrayal felt like, how it felt to be stabbed in the back by someone you trusted—someone you thought was your friend. Nothing prepared us for that and it seemed there was nothing we could do, either. But Mari had given me a sliver of hope, and that's what I needed to give Leigh. "Mari said there might be a way to help you," I said into her hair, running my fingers through the strands to calm her more. "She didn't give me specifics, but there might be a way, okay?" Leigh didn't sit up but kept her head against me as she nodded. "Just hang in there, Leigh. We'll figure it out." She nodded again, and as we sat there, something occurred to me. "What does it…feel like? To be bonded to him?"

She took a shuddering breath. "I don't think it feels much different," she said. "The mark on my leg is still tender. It feels like a bad sunburn." She lifted her loose pants that were similar to mine to show me the mark on her leg. It looked just like mine did the day after Kyler caught me. "Other than that, I don't feel any different." She sat up and looked at me through her bleary eyes. "To be honest, I don't think Kaleb knows what he's doing."

To that, I rolled my eyes. "Yes, he does. He knows exactly what he's doing. It might be new territory enacting it, but he definitely knows what he's doing."

"He seemed pretty lost when we returned to his chambers yesterday." Her voice was timid.

"Yes, but Leigh, you heard what he said—" I paused, catching myself… because she *hadn't* heard what he had said in the dungeons. "He admitted to betraying me—that he was behind it all along. He's been against us from the start. Leigh," I paused, swallowing the lump in my throat, "he's the reason Arabella is dead. That my dad is dead. Your parents!"

Leighton looked me squarely in the face and shook her head. "Maybe he was tricked? Or manipulated?"

"Leigh! Are you serious right now? You were just upset that he had claimed you, and now you're defending him? He was—" That's when it hit me—when the sincerity in her eyes didn't waver. "Oh my God…" I whispered, closing my eyes and letting the tears pool behind my eyelids as I dropped my head back. I took a slow, deep breath and brought my chin back down, grabbing her hands in mine. "We are going to get you out of this. I promise." Because those weren't Leigh's words coming through. That was the bond. The one that tied her to Kaleb, made her defend him and take his side, believing everything he said, no matter what he'd done. It had to be. She knew what happened in that dungeon, how he'd confessed to everything—practically bragged about it. Ken and I told her. She *knew.* There was no way she would defend him after that. Maybe that was another reason he chose Leighton because she hadn't been conscious when he was there. Even though we told her, she still only knew the Kaleb that the bad guys captured, the silly, goofy, warm-hearted Kaleb that we all loved. I let the tears fall on her head as she sniffled again. I could only hope we would figure it out sooner rather than later.

"Who let the crying fest start without me?" I whipped my head toward Kendall, standing with her hands on her hips by the castle door, a shaky smile on her face and tears pooling in her eyes. When I turned back to get Leigh's reaction, she was already on her feet and running to her sister, who was lucky enough to have braced herself for the impact, catching her around the waist.

I let them have their moment and stood to brush myself off. When I looked up, Libella's quiet stare caught my eye, and she gave me the slightest nod. I tilted my head at her, my eyes flicking to Leigh and back, only to receive the same slight nod. I pursed my lips and dipped my head, knowing exactly what she meant. Leigh couldn't help but be on Kaleb's side with the Doulos bond in place.

After a few moments of catching up with Ken and Leigh, I gave Ken our signal of needing to talk privately and she nodded. Then Libella stepped forward and motioned for us to follow her. I let the girls go first, arm in arm, taking in their outfits from behind. They were similar to mine, the only difference being the colors. Ken's was a silvery white, the symbols on her back in lavender. Leigh's was a coppery orange color, with her symbols in a slightly darker shade of brown. I squinted my eyes at them. Did the colors represent their dragons? Did that mean Kaleb's dragon was orange? When they turned around to sit where Libella indicated, I looked for the symbols on the front, but they weren't there. No fancy symbols to indicate who specifically claimed them. Clenching my teeth, I opened that little door I'd made inside my mind and screamed down the hatch. No words, just a blood-curdling scream. I slammed that internal door shut, but not before laughter rang through. I stomped the remaining length of the field, throwing myself onto the ground next to Ken and crossing my arms tightly around myself.

"This is where we will do your lessons," Libella said, and my head snapped to attention, finding a huge smile on her face.

That was the moment the puzzle pieces started falling into place. *Libella. Ma* told me about her. She'd *met* her before. Libella was the one who came to Earth to help my birth mother learn to wield her powers. No wonder I recognized her name. Libella seemed so familiar with Ma when caring for her, and it's because she'd known her for years. Any lingering doubt in trusting Libella vanished at that very moment. Not only did she know Ma, but she trained my birth mother, and now she was going to train me, too. A rush of excitement went through me as I smiled at Libella. She returned it, knowing I'd finally pieced it together.

"I have invited some of the other residents of the castle to demonstrate their powers for you," Libella stated. "One of them is an Omonian, who will demonstrate for the twins. The other two are Annysian and Udarian, for Rayleigh."

I shifted my gaze from her to the girls quickly, wondering if she knew I also could wield fire or if that had been kept from her. Or perhaps there weren't any more Ignalians around because I was truly one of the last ones…

"If you have any questions, they will be happy to answer, but they will not stick around for your training exercises. They will only demonstrate for you, as they have their duties in the castle. Understand?"

We all nodded, and Libella beckoned to someone behind us. I looked over my shoulder to see three Fae walking into view, and Kendall and

Leighton gasped. The portraits we saw at the Dengalow didn't do them justice. They were stunning, each with unique features, but the pointed ears peeking through their hair categorized them all as Fae. Their eyes each held a vibrant color; even the brown eyes of the darker-skinned male were a copper shade. Each one was immaculately groomed, and their outfits were nothing like ours. They each wore something different, likely signaling who they were in the castle. They crossed the field and turned to face us, and I snapped my mouth shut quickly, pursing my lips.

The first Fae stepped away from the others. She wore a blue outfit that resembled the workout gear I would wear to the gym. The blue top rimmed with gold hugged her neck, exposing her shoulders, and cropped just below her ribs. The matching leggings fit her perfectly. Her bright blue eyes found Leigh and Ken. "I will be demonstrating water wielding for you." The twins nodded, and the petite female faced the small lake full of water.

My jaw dropped in silent awe as water lifted from the lake at the motions of her arms and made its way to her. The water pooled itself into a ball in front of her, and she moved her hands in intricate patterns, her legs doing what seemed to be some heavy lifting. Considering the weight of a gallon of water, it didn't surprise me that it took strength to lift what looked like at least five gallons high above her head. She kept her gaze on the ball of water, bringing one hand down with a good portion of the water while keeping the other above her head, holding up the big ball. She made a pinching motion and swiped across her body slowly. The smaller ball transformed, stretching out and becoming more translucent. As it took on a different shape, it floated toward Leigh, who stood in awe at the fully formed sword as it stopped in front of her. She looked from the sword to the Omonian, who smiled and nodded in encouragement, already pulling another portion of the water down to shape into something else.

Leigh reached forward and wrapped her hand around the hilt of the water sword. Her hand didn't go through the water as I thought it might, but wrapped around the solid hilt. The weight shifted, pulling the tip to the ground as if it were real steel. After her initial shock, Leigh used both hands to lift the sword again and swipe it through the air a few times. Ken had a bow floating in front of her, and she reached to grab it, along with the quiver full of arrows that the Omonian had sent over.

"Will these actually do any damage?" Leigh asked, feeling the blade of the water sword for its sharpness and answered her question when the blade produced blood on her finger. She inhaled sharply at the pain and immediately put her finger in her mouth to ease the pain. "Well, that answers that," she whispered as both Libella and the female giggled.

Ken had pulled an arrow from the quiver, rolling it between her fingers before testing it out on the bow. She hadn't ever taken an archery lesson, but she seemed about ready to ask for one. "This is incredible."

The Omonian dipped her head.

"What's your name?" I asked, and she whipped her shocked face to me. If I were staying in the castle, I wanted to know the people here, which meant knowing their names instead of referring to them by their Fae lines.

"My name?" she whispered as if she had never been asked, but I nodded and stood to walk toward her. Her hands shook as I approached, and I stopped a few feet from her with my hand extended.

Her hands dropped to her side, and the ball of water above her collapsed, drenching her and me both as I was close enough to feel its splash. The twins laughed, and I couldn't help but join them as I noticed their weapons had returned to liquid, too. The sweet Omonian looked embarrassed, but I kept my hand extended anyway. She only stared at it before looking at Libella. I followed her gaze and saw Libella demonstrate shaking my hand. I turned back to find the Omonian slowly bowing her head to me and taking my hand as if she'd never shaken someone's before.

"My name is Cleo." Her meek voice made my smile widen.

"It's very nice to meet you, Cleo." She pulled her hand from mine and backed away, bowing her head several times as if apologizing.

I let her, turning to the other Fae, who both were shifting on their feet as they watched me approach them. "And what are your names?" I reached my hand out to them as well, waiting for their hesitancy with a smile.

They glanced at each other, then back to me again. The darker-skinned young male stepped forward first, hands clasped behind his back and bent at the waist. He wore linens similar to ours, but his were a dark green. No symbols adorned his shirt, though. "It is not customary for us to greet one another in such ways, miss." His black hair was in twisted braids, and brushed his shoulders as he bowed, then straightened.

I tilted my head, retracting my hand. "How is it you greet one another?" It hadn't occurred to me that their customs might have differed, but that didn't mean I couldn't learn. After all, I was one of them. I should learn their ways, especially if I was forced to stay there.

Surprisingly, the young male grinned and approached me, exposing both palms. "Take my hands," he instructed, and I should have noted his devious smile or the sparkle of mischief in his eyes.

But I did as he said, and the moment my hands were in his, he spun me around and dropped me so suddenly that I thought I was falling. But he had caught me in a dip, pulled me up slightly, and then his lips were on mine. Before I could protest, I was spun again to face him with my hands still in his, as if we hadn't moved at all. I stood there, frozen in place, staring blankly at the young male who now wore a triumphant grin. *Did he seriously just kiss me?* My ribcage heated a bit, but I ignored it, gazing at the male who still held my hands.

Laughter broke out behind me, and I turned to see Libella holding her stomach as she tried to control herself. The twins' shocked faces took her laughter as a cue to join in, and I pulled my hands from the young man's to cross them over my stomach as I tilted my head at him, trying to mask the red I knew was patching my face.

"*That's* a customary greeting?" I accused, knowing full well that that couldn't be true.

He chuckled, mimicking my crossed arms. "It's a cultural greeting, yes. We faeries are affectionate beings." He winked.

I couldn't help but roll my eyes as I bit back a smile, thinking that was a crazy way to greet someone. "Why didn't you greet the twins that way then?"

"They weren't eager to greet me." He turned to the girls, hands outstretched, but they stayed where they were, hands up in an "I'm good" gesture. Romeo let his hands fall to his side, shrugging. "I suppose mine is a bit more dramatic than some, with the dip and whatnot."

"Well, he has used the dip and kiss on a few unsuspecting in the castle!" Libella said through her lingering laughter. I was glad to know I shouldn't expect to be spun, dipped, and kissed by every Fae I introduced myself to, but it did make me more wary of introducing myself to others of my kind. "I shouldn't have doubted his courage when it came to you, though. Even with that outfit on. I have to say I enjoyed watching your reaction." She laughed again, more of a high-pitched giggle this time that was becoming more contagious by the second. I couldn't help but join in.

Raising my brow at the young male, I said, "If you don't give me your name, I'm just going to call you Romeo."

He clasped his hands behind his back and mocked another bow, smiling. "I've been told by many that I live up to the name my parents gave me."

My jaw dropped. "Wait, your name is *actually* Romeo?" He winked and I just shook my head, smiling to myself. "Well, don't try living up to the name too much. Sacrificing yourself for love isn't all it's cracked up to be." My smile faded as the truth of that statement sank in. Isn't that exactly what I'd done? Sacrificed my freedom for the love I had for Kaleb? I had gone into that cave knowing that I likely wouldn't come out, whether I died or got captured. I had sacrificed myself for him because I didn't want to lose him. Even though it wasn't how I expected, I still lost him, and in the end, my sacrifice was for nothing.

"Don't worry—I don't plan to," Romeo said, returning my thoughts to the present. He pulled a hand from behind his back, his fingers pinched together as if he were holding something. There wasn't anything there, but he extended it to me anyway. Before I could question his gesture, a rose bloomed from his fingertips, and I was only slightly taken aback by the magic as I plucked the flower from his hand.

"You know," I mused, plucking a petal from the red rose and watching it drop to the ground, "I actually think roses are overrated. Perhaps you have something a bit more unique here in Niccodra?"

Romeo's face lit up, and he pulled his other hand from behind his back. The flower that bloomed in his cupped hand was magnificent. It had reds, oranges, and yellows, all shimmering in the light of dawn. The petals extended down over his hand like water as he presented it gently in his palm; the green leaves that draped over the edges of his hand seemed steadier than the petals but just as elegant. He extended the flower toward me, and I cupped my hands to receive it. He laid it in my palms and quickly retracted his hand, staring at the flower, but after a second, his shoulders dropped in disappointment.

I squinted at him, "What's wrong?" The flower looked completely fine as I brought it closer to my face to examine the intricate details of the petals. The red petals were the outermost layer, and some of the veins that ran through it were orange, yellow, and white. The orange ones had yellow and white veins in the second layer. The layer closest to the middle was yellow with white veins, and the very center held three small petals, all white. The petals were softer than satin and draped over my fingers like the fabric. No flower I knew had any similar properties. It was unique, just like I asked.

"Nothing," Romeo finally said, pursing his lips but glancing at Libella again. When I looked at her, her head snapped to attention, but she seemed to have been shaking her head. I squinted at her, but Romeo spoke again, "Keep the flower though. It's yours." It might have just been my imagination, but he genuinely seemed disappointed.

Libella walked up next to me with a small pot, and I gave her an incredulous look while laying the flower in it.

"Later," she answered my silent question. "Write it in your notebook." And with a wink, she turned back to where she had been standing before, the pot and flower vanishing instantly. I hoped it was sent to Kyler's chambers, though I didn't think Libella had that kind of power...

"Now that we've introduced ourselves—" Romeo started, but I held up my hand to stop him, giving him a look while pointing to the only Fae who hadn't introduced herself. She dipped her head slightly and gave me a grimace of a smile.

"It's okay. I promise I won't bite," I said, smiling.

The girl just scrunched her eyebrows at me, then turned to Romeo and quickly made a few small gestures with her unusually tiny hands.

Romeo rolled his head. "Ugh, fine. This is Tietra. She can't speak." He held up a finger before I could say anything and went on, "But don't let that fool you! She knows every little thing that goes on in that castle." He shot her a look, daring her to contradict him, but she just gave him a smug smile.

Ken stepped forward and signed something to Tietra. I had forgotten she knew sign language, but she had taught me some things so we could communicate in class without getting caught. That's where our secret hand signal came from for when we needed to talk privately. Tietra watched Ken's hands carefully but ended up just shaking her head. Ken switched to letters of the alphabet, which had Tietra's face lighting up. She signed back several letters, too fast for me to keep up, but Ken smiled and nodded, signing something else quickly before turning to me. "I told her I'm a listener too and asked if she'd teach me her language. She agreed, asking if you and Leigh wanted to learn, too."

Leigh and I both nodded quickly, knowing signing could be helpful in the future. I used the sign I knew for thank you, to which she bowed her head slightly, and then I turned back to Romeo. "*Now* that everyone has been introduced," I gave him a sassy smile, "Please, continue the lesson."

"I already showed you how to wield earthly magic." He crossed his arms, but it was Libella who cleared her throat.

"Romeo, I can always find someone else in that castle who will provide more help than you've been." She gave him a knowing look and I knew she'd won when he scoffed.

"Fine. I'll demonstrate *a little* more." He scrunched his whole face in a sarcastic smile and backed up a little. I did the same.

He slipped off his shoes and dug his toes into the soft grass, closed his eyes and—

"Why did you take your shoes off?" Leigh interrupted.

Romeo's eyes snapped to Leigh, blinking a few times. "To be grounded, of course."

"Well, why can't you do that with your shoes on?"

"Because. They interrupt the connection." His tone was dripping with sass as he took a step toward her. "Any other silly questions, *ritsi?*"

"What did you just call her?" Ken snapped, stepping between Leigh and Romeo. No one messed with Leigh in front of Ken. I'd seen what happened to those who did and was glad I would never be on the receiving end of her wrath.

But Romeo smirked, looking Ken up and down. "*Ritsi.* It's an endearing term. But you?" His eyes took a slower rove over Ken this time, and she seemed a bit taken aback by his brashness. "I'm going to call you *fimora.*"

"Ew. No thanks." She stepped back and pulled Leigh with her, but

Romeo just smiled through pursed lips.

I sighed loudly, pulling Romeo's attention from Ken, and said, "Can you please just show me how you wield?"

"With pleasure."

With his feet once again planted in the grass, he clapped his hands in front of him, causing the ground to jolt and me to lose my balance. I caught myself and widened my stance, watching as he threw his arms back over his head, pulling a solid post of dirt from the ground. He made the same motion again, another pole popping out of the ground about six feet from the other. With a matching set of steady-looking poles, he reached his hands out to either side of him toward the lines of trees there. A steady flow of large leaves flew from the trees and neatly arranged themselves together. Although I couldn't really tell how they connected until they were directly in front of me. Vines were pulled up from the ground and weaved up and down through the leaves, sewing them together. The blanket of leaves sinched together at the ends and connected to vines that had braided themselves into a thick rope. At the end of the rope was a loop, which made its way around the tops of the poles of dirt. Once it settled in place, Romeo dropped his hands and hopped up into his contraption, clasping his hands behind his head.

"A hammock? Really?" I sighed, "How is that going to be useful in fights?"

"Who said I had to show you how to fight? I was told to show you how to wield." He closed his eyes, "Besides. Udarians don't really go to war with their skills. We mostly just like to build things."

A breeze blew past me and flipped Romeo's hammock so fast that he didn't even see it coming. But he righted himself quickly and whipped his head to Tietra, who gave him a close-lipped smile. *I like her,* I smiled to myself.

"It seems Tietra would like a turn now." Romeo practically spat her name, returning her mocking smile, then positioned himself in the grass, crossing his arms as he waited for her demonstration.

I smiled at Tietra and gestured for her to proceed. She nodded, lifting her arms in a wide arch above her head. When her palms met, she brought them in front of her face as her eyes locked on me. She twisted her hands and then separated one away, twirling it as if to tell me to turn around. But she wasn't gesturing to me; she was commanding the air that wound its way around me, starting at my feet and working up to my hair. The braid Libella had put in it the night before came undone as the air ripped away the ribbon and twirled my hair above my head. I giggled as the air traveled up my face and hair, the feeling slightly tickling me as it caressed my skin. The breeze disappeared as quickly as it came, and Tietra gave me a huge smile, seeing I was impressed by her show.

"These are incredible powers," Libella started. "And while what we did today was more playful, it is important to know that you shouldn't be playing around when you aren't fully aware of how they work. We will start small with things like these three just taught you, but know that there will be more power in your reserve when practicing and not overdo it. Thankfully, none of you can wield fire," she seemed to purposely avoid my gaze as my eyes widened, "so we don't have to worry about anything getting too out of hand. Do you have any questions for our demonstrators before they are dismissed back to their duties?"

"What does it feel like?" Ken asked abruptly.

"What does what feel like, *fimora?*" Romeo smirked, taking her in once more.

She only squinted at him before saying, "Using your powers, *coqueto.*"

Romeo's face dropped, taking her in. "You can't insult me with words I don't know."

"Then don't call me things I don't want to be called." Ken crossed her arms, and I couldn't help but gawk at my friend's boldness before laughter bubbled up.

"It's, um—" Every head turned to Cleo, whose face turned red, but she continued, "it's kind of like... like feeling your own heartbeat, but everywhere. Like your blood rushing through you, only... stronger." She paused, seemingly searching for the right words, then her face brightened. "And—and you can push that feeling outward! Like reaching with something that isn't quite your hands." Her eyes darted to Libella, who offered her an encouraging nod. "It gets stronger when you're near water," she added, her voice gaining confidence. "You'll feel it pulling at you—calling you, almost. Like it's a part of you, and you're a part of it."

Ken smiled at Cleo's nervousness and nodded slowly, as if what she said made sense. "How do you... extend it?"

"That is something I will walk you through in our lessons," Libella answered, making Cleo shrink back into herself. "If there are no more questions regarding the demonstration, I must send our friends away."

Of all the questions I had, none of them pertained to the demonstration, so I just kept them to myself. Leigh and Ken didn't seem to have any more either, so Libella dismissed Cleo, Romeo, and Tietra. The latter smiled as Ken signed goodbye. Romeo blew Ken a kiss, then Leigh, then me. Cleo walked straight up to me and grabbed my hand again. She didn't shake it, though. She just squeezed and gave me a warm smile before following the other two back into the castle.

Once the door closed, we all turned back to Libella. "We will start one at a time to make sure you get the feel of it before I let you practice on your own." Thankfully, she wasn't letting us go about it alone because my last failed attempt at air-wielding almost knocked me off the back of a dragon mid-flight. "Which of you is brave enough to try first?"

Nervous to go first based on Libella's statement of fire wielders, I hesitated a moment before raising my hand. But Leigh beat me to it. "Can I go first?"

"Absolutely, dear." She opened her arm to gesture toward the small lake. "Come join me at the lake."

TEN
Optimist

Leigh confidently followed Libella to the lake. A glance at Ken told me she wanted to follow, but I grabbed her wrist. I pulled her close enough that we could see what was happening but far away enough that Leigh couldn't hear our whispers.

"I think the Doulos bond does more than just make us slaves," I whispered, watching as Libella crouched to run her fingers through the water and encouraged Leigh to do the same.

"What do you mean?" Ken asked, her voice laced with worry.

"When I tried to tell her we'd get her away from Kaleb, she started defending him—saying he didn't know what he was doing. That he was manipulated or something."

Ken didn't say anything for a while, entranced by Leigh's movements in the lake. She was cupping the water in her hands and letting it slip through her fingers, listening to Libella explain what she was searching for within herself. I cleared my throat, and Ken shook herself from the trance. "Maybe he was manipulated," she shrugged. My mouth dropped open, but she put a hand up before I could protest. "That doesn't mean what he did didn't hurt you or that who we saw in that dungeon wasn't the true Kaleb. But we know he wasn't doing this on his own. And Koladon didn't know Kaleb was the King's son, so we don't know who he's working with."

I bit my tongue, wanting to scream that he definitely could have been working alone, but she was right. Even if he wasn't being manipulated into it, he had to have a connection with someone to get me back here.

Because if Koladon didn't know that Kaleb was feeding him information, then Kaleb had to have another informant—or at least someone he was communicating with. That only raised my suspicions about everyone who was part of my Omada again. But even if Kaleb wasn't doing all this on his own, he had to have something to gain from it… but what?

Ken noticed my internal debate and wrapped an arm around my shoulder, pulling me close. "You have every right to hate him and be suspicious of the bond messing with Leigh. And who knows? Maybe the Doulos bond does make us defend our…" she trailed off, searching for the right word, "bonded. But until we know for sure, we will just have to remind Leigh who he is every chance we get."

I wasn't sure "bonded" was the right word choice, but I nodded. "I just hope it doesn't get stronger and she stops listening to us."

"Well, if Kaleb really doesn't know what he's doing, maybe he won't try to use that against her," Ken suggested.

But I gave her a look. "I have no doubt that Kaleb knows what he's doing. Not after what he said to me. Not after he faked his death by my hand." The image of my dagger going through his heart flashed in my mind, sending a shiver through me. "Nothing he ever says will make me think otherwise." Ken nodded slowly, and my shoulders sank as I pleaded, "Please don't tell me you agree with Leigh."

Ken's eyebrows shot up. "Of course I don't, Ray." She grabbed my shoulders, turning me to face her. "Whether or not he's working alone, I don't believe for one second that he is being forced to do this against his will." Her eyes got a faraway look to them. "The Kaleb we knew… he's gone. He would have never talked to you like he did in that dungeon." She focused back on my face. "They say eyes are a window to the soul, and his were dark and empty that night. There's no way—"

"What are you two whispering about over there?" Leigh shouted. We both whipped our heads toward her to see her beaming as a single droplet hovered above her hand. The minute she saw our solemn faces, though, the droplet and her face both fell. "What is it?"

But Ken and I stared at where the water had just been floating. "You wielded?" Ken marveled, walking toward her.

"Yeah…" Leigh trailed off, eyes still darting between Ken and me, but I just gave her a big smile, hoping she would let it go. "You missed it?"

Ken reached her hands out to her sister's, studying them before looking at her face. "We looked away at the wrong time, Leigh. That's all." Leigh finally found Ken's eyes and gave a weak smile, so Ken opened Leigh's palms toward the sky and said, "Show me again."

Libella gave me a look past the twins but said to Leigh, "Remember what you're searching for?"

She nodded and lifted her hand, palm up between her and Ken. At first, it didn't seem like anything was happening, but then there was a slight movement in her palm. Moisture was collecting in the center, and Leigh turned all her focus on it. The tiny puddle that formed lifted off her hand and became a single drop of water. Leigh locked her gaze on the floating bead, shifting her eyes slightly to the left and back. The water followed. Ken's face lit up, likely mirroring my own, as we watched in awe.

"This is incredible," Ken muttered, reaching her hand toward the droplet. As soon as it touched the tip of her finger, it slid over the top and trailed its way up her arm. She giggled as she looked at the culprit and found Leigh beaming again. "You're using *magic!*" Ken squealed. All thoughts of the water subsided, and she threw her arms around Leigh, a mix of laughter and tears coming from them.

I watched as they celebrated Leigh's victory and, for a brief moment, wished Arabella could have been there with us. Would she have had multiple powers like me? Or would she have wielded less? Would they be the same? I let the questions pass through, realizing that no one would know the answers, and they wouldn't matter in the end anyway. But that wasn't even the point. She wasn't here to celebrate these big or small victories with me. She wouldn't ever know what it was like to wield magic or even know magic was *real.* I had no doubt she would have loved it, though.

But Kendall and Leighton had each other—in this moment, anyway. Come to think of it, why had Kaleb even let Leighton come to these lessons? Why let her learn her magic if she could use it against him? I thought about asking Libella, but she probably wouldn't know the answer either. So I kept it to myself and watched as the twins whispered in hushed excitement to each other.

Leigh lifted her head from Ken's shoulder to find me smiling softly and reached out to me. I hadn't noticed the tears that had formed in my eyes until they fell at her offer. I put my hand in hers, and she promptly pulled me into their embrace. Leigh whispered, "We're all here for each other. And blood-related or not, you're our sister, too."

"Yeah," Ken whispered. "We're in this together. You're stuck with us."

How they knew where my thoughts had led, I had no idea, but I laughed halfheartedly through tears and ducked my head into the hug. "I know. I just wish Bell could have been here to experience all this."

"We do, too, Ray," they both chimed in.

"She would have been so proud of you—for how far you've come, everything you've gone through, and how much stronger you are because of it," Ken added.

"You haven't even seen me wield yet," I stated plainly.

"We don't have to," Leigh muttered. "We know you'll be better than both of us," she lowered her voice even more, "especially with three elements."

My head snapped up at the reminder, and I pulled away from the girls to find Libella standing several paces away, watching us. She had to know I could wield fire, and I needed to confirm that — but without directly asking. Keeping my voice as low as possible, I asked, "You know I am Evanian." She nodded, holding my gaze. I narrowed my eyes. "So you *know* what I wield."

Again, she nodded, smirking, then said, "You were shown what you will be learning today." Her emphasis on "today" made me cock my head slightly. "Nikylo specified that he wanted you to be shown both today but that you only focus on learning *one* each training session." She kept her gaze locked on mine.

Then it dawned on me: Koladon must have told the King that I only have two elements. When he asked me in the cave what I could wield, he hadn't questioned it when I said I could only wield air and earth. He merely acted as if he knew I had more than one element, which meant he knew I was Evanian, but not one capable of wielding three elements. With the Lunnoxia powers that some had, I thought they would have known that already, perhaps even extracting the information from my mind somehow. But maybe they didn't even think to look. Maybe they just believed me. Maybe...

But Kyler knew I had three elements. If he knew, everyone else had to know…right?

From the way Libella was looking at me, though, I knew they didn't. But *why?* Why hadn't Kyler told them? Knowing I wouldn't get an answer even if I asked, I nodded. There would be no fire-wielding lessons. At least, not today.

I turned back to the girls. "Ken, do you want to go—" I stopped short. Ken was grinning at me, a droplet of water hovering above her palm. My jaw dropped. "How the hell?"

Ken raised her other hand and positioned it behind the floating water bead. "Tom taught us a lot about ourselves without exposing that we could wield. So when he finally told us what we were, he said everything he taught us was a part of Fae training." She shrugged as if wielding magic wasn't the coolest thing. She moved the droplet back and forth between her hands like a tennis ball. "I guess you could say I've been studying. Cleo's confirmation of how it felt was the final piece of the puzzle. And Leigh told me what Libella told her."

I marveled at my friend, knowing she was incredibly talented, but this was different. She basically taught herself how to use magic. "You're incredible, you know that?"

Ken winked. "I know." Then she flicked her fingers, and the water droplet flew toward me, smacking me straight in the forehead. My jaw dropped as both she and Leigh burst into laughter. Even Libella started giggling. I bit my bottom lip in an effort to hide my smile, but I failed miserably. I decided to show them exactly what I knew how to do.

The girls screeched as they lost their balance against the wind I swept at their legs. They were so close together that they knocked into each other and fell to the ground in a fit of giggles.

"Hey!" Leigh shouted through her laughter, pushing herself up. "When did you learn to wield?"

"Tom taught me too, remember?" I teased. "And Kyler and I went—"

"Eh ehm!" Libella interrupted, suddenly very serious. I turned to look at her and saw the caution in her eyes.

I had forgotten where we were. Forgotten the situation we were in. I had almost revealed that I used my powers the night Kyler and I went flying. Was that even real? It seemed like a fever dream, riding on the back of a dragon, filled with euphoria and power and… something else. It was hard to believe that the Kyler from that flight and the asshole in the castle were the same person.

I couldn't question that right now, nor could I reveal it. Even with no one around, it seemed there were eyes and ears everywhere. Could we even trust the Fae that just demonstrated for us?

"Shall we continue our lesson?" Libella asked, the warning in her voice evident.

We all nodded. Libella led the girls back to the water, and I sat in the grass as instructed. Tom had only taught me how to control air with his lessons, not anything to do with earth. Romeo didn't help at all either, as he only strived for attention. Libella told me to connect with the grass, whatever that meant. So, I sat there, feeling the blades run through my fingers as the girls did the same with the water in their hands. Libella said that even though they could control a droplet, that was nothing compared to what they should be able to do if they truly connected with their powers.

The grass tickled my fingers and the palms of my hands. Even though I thought Romeo put on quite a show, he was right about being able to feel the ground with no interruptions. The little I could feel with my hands was going a long way, so I slid off my shoes and dug my toes into the ground. I instantly felt *more*, like the vibrations of the Earth were speaking to me, waiting for my silent command. But I had no idea how to control it or what part of myself I could use to make it do my bidding.

I spoke to it with my mind. *Move.*

Nothing happened.

I lifted my hands and pulled the ground with me. Nothing.

I thought back to what Romeo had done, conjuring a flower in his hands. How had he done that? It seemed to sprout from his fingertips and that was before he took his shoes off. As soon as his toes hit the dirt, a hammock popped up. Maybe it was a type of energy that passed through him… Or perhaps I just needed to wait for Libella to tell me exactly what to do. Deciding that was best, I laid back in the grass, closing my eyes and taking in the scent of the field, feeling the power it held.

The grass didn't smell like the meadow back home. It was somehow earthier and sweeter. I dug my toes and fingers deeper into the soil, which shifted around me, soft and pliable. The moisture made it stick to my fingers, and the vibrations changed as my hand closed around a clump of dirt. I kept my other hand open in the soil. The dirt grew hot in my hands as the vibrations intensified, almost as if it were angry. I loosened my grip on the dirt, letting it fall back into place. I swear I *felt* it sigh in relief. Apparently, the earth didn't like to be forced to do something.

I used my other senses to better connect with the earth, listening to how the grass swished against itself, licking my lips to taste the air now filled with the sweet, earthy taste of freshly dug-up dirt. I waited to feel the sun on my face, the day's heat starting to increase, but then a shadow passed over me and stayed there. I opened my eyes, expecting clouds in the sky, but found someone standing over me instead.

Sighing dramatically, I closed my eyes again. "You're blocking my sun rays."

"Get up," Kyler seethed.

"No. I'm connecting with the earth."

The heat I'd felt moments ago was suddenly overpowering. "I said, get. *Up.*" His demanding voice was deeper—and closer. So close I could smell the smoke on his breath.

I peeled my eyes open to find him crouched over me, eyes a blazing green as he stared me down. Oh, he was *pissed.* I rolled my eyes and pushed myself to a sitting position, turning around to face him on the ground. "What?"

He took a crouched step forward. "I thought I was clear about your responsibilities today," he growled.

I opened my arms in a gesture to the field around me. "Yeah. That's why I'm out here *connecting with the earth.* I'm doing what Libella told me to."

"Those aren't the responsibilities I'm talking about." His whispered words sounded more threatening than his normal voice.

That didn't stop me from crossing my arms over my chest and pulling the sass card. "Well, then, I have no idea what you're talking about."

"Bullshit, Sunshine." His glare told me he wouldn't tell me.

In my head, I ran through what I remembered of my responsibilities. Don't leave Kyler's side, do as Libella says, don't talk to anyone, don't take off the ugly outfit, don't have any fun, don't do anything stupid, don't let anyone touch me—

I clicked my tongue. "You're upset that I *shook someone's hand?*"

"That's not all you did, is it?" he grinned, the look terrifying.

How could he *possibly* know what happened in the field? He wasn't even there. "Why does it matter?" My voice was louder than intended, and I didn't necessarily want the twins to hear me, but I couldn't help it. "You can't be bothered to be nice to me, but the minute someone else is friendly with me, you're suddenly upset about it?"

"Oh, they weren't just being friendly, Sunshine."

"How would you even *know?* You weren't out here!" I pushed myself to my feet, and he followed suit. I forgot how much he towered over me, but that didn't stop me from walking right up to him and jabbing my finger into his chest. "You can't pretend to care about me like you did at the Dengalow. It's not going to work. You got me to trust you, to be friends with you, and then you went and stabbed me in the back!" I blinked back the tears that threatened to fall as something unreadable flashed in Kyler's eyes. I pushed on. "In no world will I ever fall for that façade again. So, yes. I shook some people's hands, and Romeo caught me off guard with his *cultural* greeting. But you're right, I didn't stop him. Because *I don't care.*"

Kyler hadn't backed down or moved in the slightest, but he leaned into my finger and bent down to say, "Newsflash, Sunshine: We were never friends." I don't know why my heart sank at those words, but it did. "And you shouldn't trust me. But if you ever want to see your brother or mother again, you'll do as I say." The last command rumbled in my chest as I looked up at him through my eyebrows, hating that he was using my family against me. "Understood?"

I clenched my teeth. There was only one more day until my brother's trial, and by the end, I would never see him or Ma again, regardless of the outcome. Arguing now wouldn't do me any good, and I couldn't bring myself to answer Kyler, so I just glared at him.

But that wasn't good enough for him. He stepped closer, his mouth next to my ear, as he bit out every word he said. "Is that understood, Sunshine?"

"Yes," I said through my teeth, taking a huge step back from his overwhelming heat. "Can I get back to my lessons?" My tone was dripping with a sweetness I knew he'd hate.

He gave me a wild grin. "Absolutely." He gestured with his arm toward Libella and the twins, who I'd forgotten were even there. But they hadn't even seemed to notice Kyler and me arguing.

They were waist-deep in the lake, soaked to the bone and laughing. Had they not heard any of what just happened? Libella wasn't even looking our way. She seemed to be smiling at whatever progress the girls made, unaware of Kyler even being present. I turned back to Kyler to accuse him of whatever he might have done, but he was gone.

"Ugh." I turned back to watch as the twins took each other's hands, and the water around them rippled away. Libella was standing close enough to them that the water rippled around her, too. Her mouth was moving, likely guiding them with her words, but I couldn't hear her from where I was.

I stepped toward the lake and heard her reassuring, instructive voice, "You'll start to feel the power running through you faster now, like the blood in your veins."

Both the girls nodded as they smiled at each other, and the water spun around them like a whirlpool. "How do we make the water go higher?" Leighton asked, her voice shaking with excitement—or was it fear?

"If you feel like it will listen, just tell it what you want it to do." Libella watched as the girls nodded at each other and closed their eyes. I waited to see if the water would move, hoping it wasn't just me who couldn't make anything significant happen. But as the water rose around them, my shoulders dropped. "That's it, ladies! You're getting the hang of it!"

My jaw dropped as the water climbed up over their heads. There was no reason for me to be upset. They were using *magic*. After a few seconds, the water separated, revealing the twins and Libella in the middle. The water moved behind them in a big wave, and the girls turned to smile at me. It took me two seconds to realize what they were planning, and I whipped around to sprint in the other direction but ran into someone immediately. She grinned, grabbed my shoulders, and whipped me back around to face the wave coming our way.

"Mari!" I laughed, struggling against her hold, my ribcage suddenly heating up at her touch. I ignored it and shouted through a smile, "Don't do this to me!" She laughed in my ear as Ken and Leigh threw their arms downward, and the water came crashing down on Mari and me.

The twin's laughter rang out as we shook off the excess water drenching us. I couldn't hold back the happiness I felt for them, being able to control water like that. "Not cool!" I shouted as I sputtered water. "But also, *incredible!*" I ran up to where they were stepping out of the lake and threw my arms around them. "How does it feel to wield water like that?" I stepped back as the heat flared again on my side. I was going to kill Kyler for this new development.

They were both out of breath as they smiled. "Surreal," Kendall said while Leighton said, "Like I can do anything."

Her eyes weren't on me, though. They were focused on the only person I knew was behind me. I stepped out of her way, and she didn't hesitate. She walked straight to Mari, who didn't dare move. She just stood there with her hands clasped in front of her as Leigh approached, a wary look on her face. "Hi," Mari whispered, giving Leigh a shy smile.

I could no longer see Leigh's face but heard her say, "Thank you. For saving my sister."

Silver lined Mari's eyes as she nodded. "I wish I could have done the same for you."

"You did what you could," Leigh said, her voice soft. Her gaze dropped to her leg, where Kaleb's handprint was still visible. "I'm not sure there's a way to save me now."

Mari stepped forward and lifted Leigh's chin with a single finger. Her eyes locked on Leigh's. "I will find a way." Her voice broke, like something got caught in her throat. "I promise." Leigh nodded, and Mari lifted her hand to swipe her thumb across Leigh's cheek. "Don't cry, *meli.*" Leigh leaned into her hand, and Mari used that to pull her into a loving embrace. Leigh's arms wound around Mari's waist, and she buried her head in the crook of her neck.

Not wanting to invade their privacy any more than I already had, I turned to Kendall. Tears welled in her eyes, too. "She truly cares about her, doesn't she?" Ken whispered. All I could do was nod as tears tracked down my face. I missed so much of their relationship because I was blind to it back home. There had to be more to their story that I didn't know, and I hoped that one day, Leigh and I would get time to talk about it. But first, we had to save her from—

"What are you doing?" A sharp male voice echoed across the field. I whipped around to find Kaleb charging across the lawn to where Leigh and Mari had just broken apart. His eyes were raging. "Step away from my Doulos, Amarietta."

"That's it," I muttered, stepping toward Kaleb, but someone caught my wrist. I turned to see a strong warning in Libella's eyes. Something in her gaze made me stop. What would happen if Kaleb got too close? I'd risk not seeing Mitch and Ma again if he touched me… But something else in her eyes told me there was more danger than that. I clenched my jaw, and took a deep breath. Leigh was strong. She could get through this. She knew what she was doing…right?

"It's okay, *meli.*" The sound of Leigh's voice made me turn back to them. Mari stood protectively between Leighton and Kaleb, but Leigh had her hand on Mari's shoulder, gently pulling her back. "I know my place." Reluctantly, Mari let Leigh move her.

As soon as she was out of the way, Kaleb lunged forward and snatched Leigh's wrist, pulling her to him.

"Hey!" I shouted, unable to contain myself. "Don't you *dare* touch her like that!" Knowing I couldn't go near him, I stood my ground and lifted my hands, ready to strike with my power. Kaleb didn't have to know I'd learned hardly anything yet.

Kaleb spun around, and his eyes widened, his pupils shrinking to reveal that deceitful honey-brown color. When he saw me there, poised for action, he immediately dropped her wrist and held his hands up in surrender. "Sorry, I—"

"I don't care what you are." I decided to use his game against his actions. "She is your *friend*, remember?" When his face dropped, I asked Leigh, "Are you okay?" She nodded slowly, likely under some spell of his and thinking he did nothing wrong. But we couldn't have that. I turned back to Kaleb. "If you *ever* touch her like that again, I will never speak to you." I knew Leigh could take care of herself, but that didn't mean I couldn't defend her in my own way.

Kaleb took a tentative step toward me, an apology written all over his face, but I raised my hands higher. "Don't," I warned.

He froze, pursing his lips. "I didn't want Amarietta to try anything rash before the ceremony."

"What could she possibly do?" I asked, curiosity getting the best of me.

Kaleb dropped his shoulders, eyes shifting as he said, "I don't know. I just…" he trailed off. "I was told not to let anyone touch her until after the ceremony."

"*Liar.*" The word didn't come from me but from Kendall. I turned to find her failing to fight back angry tears, and her body shook as she took a few brave steps forward. "I've known you for over ten years, which means I know when you're lying." Her arms were raised now, too, but her movements actually did something with the water behind her. "Tell us what you know, Kaleb."

He stumbled back, watching the wall of water climb high above Kendall as he murmured, "You learned how to control your powers." It wasn't a question.

"Do you want to find out how much I've learned?" Ken's voice rumbled and even I got the chills.

"Don't, Ken," Leigh whispered. "It's not worth it." She motioned for Ken to put her hands down. Kendall looked at her twin, who gave her a slight nod of reassurance and then lowered her hands, causing the water to drop unceremoniously behind her. Leigh gave her a small smile. "I'll go with him. I promise I'll be okay."

Ken bit her bottom lip, trying to hold back the tears already spilling down her cheeks, but she nodded. I reached out to Ken and pulled her into a side hug. Kaleb's awed expression slowly faded as he turned to Leighton and motioned her toward the castle. It didn't go unnoticed that he didn't attempt to touch her. Good. Leigh gave us one more look, then turned to Mari and gave her a tearful nod before turning to the castle and disappearing through the door with Kaleb.

"Mari, dear. You and Kendall must go too," Libella instructed, her motherly tone similar to Ma's. "You're needed to help with preparations for the ceremony."

"I know," Mari breathed. She lifted both hands to her face and wiped it clear of any remnants of tears. She took a deep breath and let it out slowly before turning to Kendall. "Come on, Ken. Let's go."

I gave Ken one more reassuring squeeze. "She'll be okay," I whispered.

"You don't know that."

I dropped my arm from her shoulder and faced her. "No, but I have to believe she will be. Because if we lose hope, then so will she." Ken was still staring at the door Leigh disappeared through, so I grabbed her shoulders and turned her toward me. "Kaleb may have just given us information without meaning to. There's reason to believe we can do something, right?" Ken gave me a slight nod. "So keep your head up. We will figure this out." I smiled, deciding to use her usual word on her. "Together." She gave me a teary-eyed smile as I pulled her into another quick hug, ignoring the pain in my side, and then gave her a little nudge toward Mari. I met Mari's gaze as Kendall walked over to her. I could tell she wasn't convinced either, but gave her an encouraging nod before they both turned toward the castle.

If I had to figure it out on my own, I would. The notebook I was promised might help me get the answers I needed if I asked the right questions. And if they were answered.

"Come on, Rayleigh." Libella wasn't ushering me toward the castle where the others disappeared, though. She had turned and motioned toward the forest. "It's time to begin your training."

I took a deep breath, releasing all the emotions that had just built up. Stepping toward the forest, I promised myself to do everything I could to learn my powers, just like Ma had made me promise her. I straightened my back and made a more confident stride toward the forest, but then the image shifted, causing me to pause. A shimmering line appeared, and then it opened into a black hole where Libella was ushering me. I groaned loudly as Kyler stepped out of the portal he had created, a shit-eating grin on his face.

ELEVEN
Off the Edge

"No," I said simply, crossing my arms over my chest and glaring at Kyler.

"Rayleigh, you cannot practice here," Libella sighed. "This is the only way."

I eyed Kyler, grimacing. "And why does he have to come?"

"Because you can't seem to follow simple instructions," Kyler snapped.

"They're *dumb* instructions."

"Enough," Libella ordered, holding her hand up to Kyler. He worked his jaw, glaring at me instead. She turned to me with a stern look on her face. "Rayleigh, your power is stronger than the twins." My jaw dropped. I knew it was possible, but hearing Libella confirm it had me swaying where I stood. "You cannot practice near the castle, especially with your earth magic. It could disrupt the foundation if we aren't careful."

Well, when she said it like that... that still didn't answer my question of why Kyler had to join us. "Fine, but Kyler can't come anywhere near me."

Libella pursed her lips, glancing at Kyler, who met her with a tight-lipped grin. She closed her eyes and turned to me. "I'm afraid that's impossible, as we need to fly to our location."

The blood drained from my face. "What?" The thought of flying again gave me mixed emotions—remembering how it felt but also who it was with. "Can't we just, like, portal there or something?"

"No, dear," Libella said. "You've never been conscious during a—"

she stopped herself, latching onto my word, "—portal transfer, and we don't know how it will affect you."

That sounded scary enough that I didn't press the issue, so I took a different route, asking Libella, "Can't I just fly with you?"

A low growl rumbled from Kyler's direction. When I turned to sneer at him for being so possessive, blue eyes stared back at me, burning like a fire and I swallowed my insult.

"That is not an option," Libella stated, again pulling my attention to her. Her face had turned ashen at my request. "You must fly with Nikylo."

I crossed my arms but couldn't find it in me to be annoyed. I hadn't seen his dragon break through like that in a while, so maybe he *did* choose me, and the Doulos bond was a ploy…

But that didn't stop me from wondering why I couldn't ride with Libella. Was there some unspoken rule about flying with a dragon you weren't bound to?

"I suggest you put these on." Kyler snapped his fingers, and a pile of clothes fell next to me. I gave him a wary look, noticing that his eyes were back to their piercing green. I was slightly disappointed but shook it off and picked up the clothes, similar to the riding leathers he'd provided for the first flight—the color of his dragon's scales.

As much as I hated being close to Kyler again, I knew being with his dragon might be the perfect scenario. I wouldn't have to summon him to ask what the hell was going on with Kyler or why he was back to being an asshole. I could just do so during our flight to…wherever we were going. "Okay," I said, softer than I intended, remembering the last time I'd seen his dragon was our parting near the meadow. I wondered what he would have to say about me not following his last instructions.

"You can change over there." Libella pointed to a small wooden shack near the castle doors.

I nodded and turned on my heel, avoiding Kyler's gaze, even though I could feel it burning a hole into my skull. I didn't want him to know I planned on talking to his dragon, but I also didn't know what I would say when I finally got the chance. How does one apologize to a dragon for thinking they were the bad guy?

The shack contained various weapons, and again, made me wonder why Drakalasson needed weapons of any sort when they had their powers and shifting abilities. Ignoring the question, I stepped inside and shut the door behind me.

Pulling off the linen clothes, I slipped on the riding leathers, which fit like a glove around every curve. The bottoms stretched enough to pull up into place and were strangely breathable. The top was sleeveless and zipped up in the front, a bit snug, but I knew it would fit comfortably once I got it on properly.

I was struggling with the zipper over my chest when the door creaked open. "Hey!" I shouted, assuming it was Kyler coming to tell me to hurry up, and scrambled to finish zipping. "I'm almost done, jackass!"

"Almost done with what, princess?" The familiar male voice made my blood run cold as the door clicked shut behind him. But it wasn't Kyler's voice.

I whipped around to see the familiar blonde hair and stark blue eyes of my beautiful torturer, Aaidan. "What do you want?" I snapped, wondering how he got into the shack without Libella or Kyler noticing. Then I remembered he had shielding. He could make himself invisible.

Aaidan stepped closer, a grin gracing his face. "We never got to finish our conversation."

"What conversation? All you like to do is monologue."

He scoffed, "So you've said. I guess that means it's your turn to talk."

If Kyler and Libella didn't know he was in there with me, I had to let them know somehow. I crossed my arms over my chest. "What could I possibly tell you?" The last time Aaidan shielded me, Kyler reached out to me through our mind link. But that hadn't worked since before the meadow... Was that a fluke, or did Kyler block it off permanently—

"No use trying to reach out to your dragon." He took another step closer and pointed at my bracelet. I tried to hide the fact that the bracelet wasn't what he thought it was, but when my face didn't reflect the fear he was expecting, he squinted at me. "You already knew that, though, didn't you?" When I didn't answer him, he went on, to no one's surprise. "Does that mean you know your powers aren't working and that you can do nothing to defend yourself?" He grinned as he took another step toward me. "Or did someone switch it out for you?" I felt the color leave my face as Aaidan took his final step into my space and stopped mere inches from me. How did he always know things that happened behind closed doors?

"I'm training today," I said boldly. "If this stops my powers, why—"

"Oh, it doesn't just stop your powers, princess. It prevents you from accessing any magic and, in turn, stops any magic from reaching you." He looked down at the bracelet again, studying it. "But if it were switched out and you *can* use your magic," his eyes lifted back to mine and I gasped as a burning red color had replaced the icy blue, "that means you can be affected by magic. But there's only one way to find out." I tried to take a stumbling step back but only backed into weapons, knocking them from their places on the wall. "This might be a little unpleasant," Aaidan's voice had dropped to something much more sinister.

Kyler! I screamed down the bond. I hadn't used the bond to talk to him since before coming here, and I wasn't sure if he could hear, so out loud, I also screamed, *"Nooo!"* It was preemptive of whatever Aaidan was going to do, and I didn't know if he would let me scream or if Libella would even be able to hear me through his shields, but it didn't hurt to try. Aaidan reached for me just as my ribcage heated, and before he could grab hold of me, some sort of light shot out of me and threw him backward. I took the opportunity of him being thrown back into the wall to run out of the shack and onto the field where Kyler was rushing toward me, Libella hot on his heels.

"What happened?" Kyler asked, a hint of worry in his voice but eyes focused.

Breathless, I said, "Aaidan. In there." There wasn't much of a fight between us, but the slight panic he caused left me trying to catch my breath.

Kyler flew past me while Libella stopped beside me, gripping my elbow for support. Once I was steady, she quickly released me. "Are you okay?" she asked, looking me over for any injuries.

"I'm fine." Those words were more surprising to me than Libella, who nodded and then looked to where Kyler was emerging from the shack empty-handed.

"What did Aaidan want?" Kyler demanded, also giving me a once-over.

"I don't know. He said something about my bracelet blocking magic from touching me and from me using it." Kyler and Libella exchanged a glance, but I had already known this information thanks to Kaleb. "He suspects it's been switched out and tried to prove it by grabbing me."

"What happened when he tried?" Kyler said, still in that demanding tone.

I ignored how it irked me and said, "Some sort of…light came out of me? Almost like a shield."

Kyler loosed a breath and nodded. "Good."

I balked at him. "What do you mean 'good'?"

"It seems the means I've taken to ensure you're not touched are working. Even though you haven't followed the clear instructions I gave you not to let *anyone* touch you, someone you don't want touching you, cannot, thanks to my precautions."

"What *precautions?*" I snapped, forgetting that I should probably be thankful for his insane possessive qualities, if only for them saving me from Aaidan.

He stepped closer, his smoky scent washing over me as he said, "Everything you wear has my xousía woven into its threads." At my furrowed brow, he clarified, "Magic, Sunshine."

"Why not just call in magic then?"

"Because it's not *just magic—*"

"*Enough,*" Libella cut in again, taking the both of us by surprise and letting out a hefty sigh before mumbling to herself, "Now I know what Theo meant about you two." Before I could ask what that meant, she asked Kyler, "Where is Aaidan?"

He crossed his arms, shrugging. "Who knows? But he wasn't there. The only sign of him was the knocked-over weapons throughout the shack." He turned to me. "You sure he didn't touch you at all?"

"No," I said. "The magic knocked him backward before he could."

"Good."

I glared at him, trying to remember that he had probably just saved me, but also not wanting to thank him for being insane.

"Let's get out of here before someone else sees her and tries to do the same," Libella instructed.

Apparently, we were just going to accept that Aaidan had disappeared and not ask questions about where he went…

Libella turned to the open field and took a few steps before her body shifted into its dragon form. A beautiful jade dragon landed in the clearing where she had been, and I stared in awe at her majestic beauty. But before I could admire it too much, I was knocked backward hard enough that I fell on my ass. I looked up to find Kyler had shifted right next to me, not bothering to step away for more space.

"Screw you too, jackass!" I said more to myself, hoping his dragon didn't think I insulted him for Kyler's poor judgment. I helped myself up and dusted off my hands right before a tail snaked around my waist. I gritted my teeth, knowing it was Kyler's control issue because it wasn't the blue eyes I'd been hoping for, watching my progression to his back. The thought of him not letting his dragon have control didn't even cross my mind. *Guess I won't be able to talk to his dragon after all.*

As he set me down in my spot between his shoulder blades, I felt a strange tingling along my body where it met his smooth, warm scales. I shivered to rid myself of it and settled in. I didn't want to think about what that meant, even though it felt warm and comforting.

Kyler spread his wings and launched us into the air. I wasn't prepared for him to take off so suddenly, so I found myself scrambling to find my grip on his spine as he climbed higher into the sky. I knew he couldn't hear me, but that didn't stop me from slewing a string of curse words his way or from adding it to the list of reasons why I wanted to punch him.

Once he leveled out in the sky, I took a moment to look around. My jaw dropped in awe, all anger leaving my body.

The castle sat atop the hill we circled, and I recognized the crystal palace from my dream back at the Dengalow. The dream version looked exactly like the one before me, and it didn't take me long to realize why. Kyler was able to give it so much detail because he lived in it.

Trying to ignore that fact, I turned my attention to admire the rest of the world around me—*my* world.

The castle sat atop a mountain situated in the middle of the island. More hills and valleys spread out around the base of the mountain, and the trees were thick down the slope, but when they thinned out, I could see several lakes spread out toward the edges of the island. Before I could wonder where the water came from, we rounded to the front of the castle, and a beautiful waterfall came into view, cascading down into a dark hole in the ground. But from where we soared above, I could see that the waterfall fell straight through the ground and into a mighty river that split into several smaller rivers spreading around the island. We were so high up that I could almost see the entirety of the island, including where the rivers branching off from the lakes fell off to the planet below. It was stunning, especially as the sunrise shone on the water.

The sun hadn't moved from its half-risen state, which made me think maybe the days were different here. Half the sky was still dark, while the other half was filled with clouds of pink and blue, resembling cotton candy floating in the sky. As much as I wanted to know how this world worked, I wasn't about to ask Kyler through the bond. Even if it was accessible, his behavior lately made me think he wouldn't answer me anyway.

We continued circling the island, and I reveled in the feeling of gliding through the air and how it made me so incredibly happy. Regardless of who I was flying with, it gave me a feeling I never knew I needed — It felt like *home.*

The air flowed through my unbound hair, and I closed my eyes to breathe it in. A spark came to life inside me, and I reached for it, knowing exactly what that feeling was. Without opening my eyes, I followed the path of the spark through my body and into the beast's scales beneath me, finding my way to where I wanted to go. I found myself feeling the wind along the wings of the dragon as they moved. The way it flowed around them. His dragon might have been right under his skin, but I was pretty sure he and I were on the same page— and he'd find it funny, too. With a smirk to myself and a tightened grip, I called the wind to do my bidding.

A surprised roar sounded as we jerked to the side midair. I opened my eyes as a slight laugh escaped through my nose. My tight grip kept me on as we leveled back out, and the dragon's head whipped around, his bright green eyes tearing into mine. *I suggest you don't do that again,* his voice rumbled down the bond.

My heart dropped and chills ran down my spine at the feeling of hearing him in my head again. But I just smirked at him, knowing that being a menace to a creature that could light me on fire at any minute was walking a thin line and not caring. Mostly because I knew his dragon would never let him torch me, but also because I knew Kyler likely wouldn't have the guts to try. I may be a pain in the ass, but for whatever reason, he wanted to keep me around. That gave me all the confidence I needed to annoy him. That and his dragon also seemed to find it hilarious as a rumble of what seemed like laughter resounded in my head.

He faced forward again and dived almost vertically. Thankfully, I was still braced from my jest, so I only had to hug my legs tighter to keep myself from lifting off his back. We hurtled toward the ground at a speed we'd never reached before, and as the ground got closer, my heart fluttered. We weren't slowing down. I internally screamed, not wanting to give Kyler the satisfaction of my fear because I knew it was payback.

A clearing came into view near the island's edge, and the trees surrounding it became more detailed as we zoomed toward them. He spread his wings at the last possible second and landed hard on the ground, shaking it beneath us. Libella came in for a landing next to him, barely making an impact.

My legs were shaking from the adrenaline, so I didn't immediately swing them off him to slide down but carefully unwrapped my arms from his spine. He didn't even let me catch my breath before he wrapped his tail around me and yanked me off his back. He didn't bother setting me down gently either, causing me to stumble over my feet and land on my ass, *again*.

I was so preoccupied with my stumble that I didn't even notice Kyler had shifted until he was stalking toward me. "Do you have *any* idea what you've just done?" he yelled.

I pushed myself up, trying to ignore my shaking legs. "What I've just done?" I balked, making myself meet him in the middle so I could shove my finger into his chest. "You basically crash-landed us and almost lost yourself a rider!"

"Are you insane?" He swatted my finger from his chest and got in my face. "*You* tried to knock me out of the sky!"

"Well, if you weren't being such an ass, I wouldn't have done it!" I screamed.

"Stop blaming me for *your* stupid decisions!"

I recoiled. "Excuse me?"

"You heard me," he snarled. "Every time you make a stupid decision, and I call you on it, you blame me. But *you* made the choice. Not me." When I didn't respond, he went on. "Anyone in that castle could have sensed your magic."

Shocked by the subject change, I yelled, "Why does it matter if they can? Obviously, I have magic. Aaidan is probably already telling them the bracelet is a fake because *magic* threw him away from me! Did you even think about that?"

"My xousía is *nothing* like your magic," he bit out. "So he'll think the bracelet was real, and that's what threw him back. Not your powers."

Oh. "Well, no one could have known I was the reason you were blown off course," I sneered, trying to recover from the slight embarrassment. "You could be a lousy flier."

"Me? A lousy flier?" he laughed heartily. I raised my eyebrows as if to suggest it were plausible. He stepped closer and whispered, "I'm about as lousy at flying as you are at jiu-jitsu, and everyone in this realm knows it."

My jaw dropped. "Did you just say I was good at jiu-jitsu?" I didn't try to hide the smirk on my face.

He furrowed his brow but recovered quickly. "Don't let it go to your head. You're in my realm now."

My brows lifted higher, "What's that supposed to mean?"

"My powers on Earth were weakened. Here? There's no way you can beat me."

"You forget. This is *my* realm, too," I taunted. "I'm sure that means my powers are also stronger here than on Earth."

It was his turn to smirk. "If you don't start obeying simple orders, you won't get to test that theory."

I squinted at him. What was the point of all this? Why was he acting like the Kyler I knew back at the Dengalow? As if everything in the castle hadn't happened? It was almost as if…

No. There was no way. He would never have treated me the way he had. There was no excuse for that, not if he genuinely wanted to be my friend.

But the sparkle in his eye was so similar to the Kyler I had grown fond of…

That spark disappeared with a blink, and his energy changed from teasing to hostile again. How could he switch from one to the other so

—

"Are you two done with your lover's spat?" Libella asked from right next to me. I jumped away from her, my cheeks heating at her insinuation, but Kyler gave her a look that made her mischievous one disappear.

"Not lovers, Libella," Kyler said, straightening and clasping his hands behind himself. "Now that we're far enough from the castle," Kyler addressed me, "you can start training with your earth-wielding."

I crossed my arms. "It wouldn't work back at the castle. What makes you think it'll work here?"

"Because I'm not suppressing it anymore."

I balked at him. "Why were you suppressing it?"

"Can't have you destroying anything." He gave me a sarcastic smile and turned on his heel to walk away. "Besides, you're mostly blocking yourself."

"What does that even mean?" I yelled, stalking after him. Libella caught my elbow and turned me to face her.

"Libella," Kyler warned.

She let go of me immediately, hands up as if in surrender. "My apologies, Nikylo. You know I would never—"

"Yes, but if I let you, others will think it's okay, including her."

"Yes, sir." Libella turned back to me, and I eyed both her and Kyler. She ignored my unspoken question, "Something within you is blocking your magic—suppressing it—that you must face and let go of."

That sounded like something Tom told me, and it made sense, given my circumstances. With my family's lives at stake and my friends under the influence of monsters, there was a lot of stress and anxiety in my life. The stress from the past month alone could have been what was blocking me from using my abilities.

I nodded at Libella but said, "Why did my air magic work then?"

"You have already worked past the anxieties blocking your air magic back at the Dengalow." It didn't pass me by that Libella knew far more than she should for not being at the Dengalow. "Earth and fire magic have their own temperaments, especially fire, which can be tricky to navigate and overwhelming if you aren't careful." She eyed me cautiously, but it disappeared as she went on, "Earth magic is a bit easier to handle and will come to you better if you're grounded, as Romeo said. So start with your shoes off and sit on the grass with as much of the ground touching your bare skin as possible."

"That won't be much with this outfit on," I mumbled as I slipped out of my shoes.

"Actually, those leathers are meant to be like a second skin and absorb the same as your own skin would."

I furrowed my brow. No wonder being on the dragon's back felt so intimate. It was basically skin-to-skin contact. I shook the thought away, not wanting Kyler to pick up on the thoughts. I dropped to the ground rather heavily, still shaking from the rough landing, and sprawled out like a starfish.

Libella crouched next to me. "Feel for that spark of magic that comes alive at the feel of the earth. Once you find it, follow it back to see what's blocking it and try to push past it." She stood again and stepped back. "Once you think you've got it, try moving and shaping the dirt around you. The magic will show you how."

I nodded and tuned in to what my body was feeling. The grass tickled me everywhere it touched, confirming Libella's statement about the leathers, but once I settled in, it felt more like a comfortable bed of grass. It was strange to be fully clothed and suddenly feel like I was wearing nothing. My face flushed at the idea, and I found myself wishing for the linens instead. While those literally named me Kyler's property, these leathers made me *feel* like his.

I ignored the thoughts crowding my mind and tried to rid myself of the idea of him, focusing on the ground beneath me instead. I closed my eyes and let myself sink into it.

At first, I felt nothing but the cool and soft grass beneath me. I moved my fingers through the blades, hoping that would help me feel something more. A spark reached out to me from deep within, and I knew I wouldn't have felt it if I hadn't been paying attention. I found the path from which it pulsed and followed it back within myself to where it was settled in a dark corner. I extended a mental hand, but something prevented me from getting to it.

That's when I realized a dark cloud was hovering between my stream of consciousness and the deep green orb glowing just out of grasp. I tried everything I could to reach around the darkness to free the magic, but it felt like hitting a wall. After several more attempts, I gave up and faced the black void before me. From the energy of the void, I could tell whatever I was about to experience wouldn't be easy.

I wiggled my fingers, digging myself deeper into the ground before reaching out in my mind toward the darkness.

It didn't take long for it to consume me.

TWELVE
Run With Me

The truck's headlights were visible right past my sister's head. I honked the horn as it barreled toward us, ensuring the driver saw us. But he didn't stop. Instead, he flashed the lights, which reflected off the rain, blinding me completely.

What was this?

I screamed as the truck struck us with full force, yet I felt no pain as I was jerked around the car, soaring through the air. My seatbelt did an incredible job of keeping me secure as the car flipped.

No... *No.* Not my sister's death. My eyes stung with tears as the memory I had suppressed for so long continued playing in my head.

I gripped the steering wheel tighter, flexing every part of my body before the top of the car slammed into the ground. The roof caved in near my head, and I glanced at Arabella, who had been on the side of the car where the truck hit. She was being tossed around too, but she was dead on impact—

Her eyes found mine.

No, that wasn't right. Arabella died the minute the truck hit us. People confirmed that. Theo confirmed it—he'd found us. Arabella was *dead* when he arrived. Wasn't she?

Arabella didn't break eye contact, even as her head whipped this way and that, until the car finally landed on its roof again and skidded to a halt. She immediately reached for her seatbelt and fell against the roof as it clicked open. It was as if the accident hadn't even fazed her. Her head snapped toward me, and she said—

The sound of my name from a voice I hadn't heard in almost two years echoed in my mind.

"Rayleigh."

Tears pooled in my eyes at the sight of my sister before me, unharmed after an accident I thought had taken her life. They streamed endlessly down my cheeks and into my hair and ears as I lay on the ground, mentally absorbing her presence, watching her mouth move but unable to believe it.

"Rayleigh, focus!" Arabella grabbed my shoulders, shaking them. I looked her dead in the eye as her panicked expression became more intense. "You have to run," she insisted. Run? Run where? From whom? We had just been hit by a truck and should have been seriously injured, yet she was acting completely fine. I felt completely fine. No pain, no injuries, nothing.

Arabella reached up and found my seatbelt. "Put your hands on the roof," she instructed. I blinked rapidly, still unable to grasp whatever was happening. How were we alive? "Ray!" she yelled, pulling my attention back to her memorable face. The scar just above her left eyebrow—I'd given that to her in a wooden sword fight just two weeks ago. The person in front of me was definitely her, even if my mind kept insisting she should be dead.

I followed her instructions, pressing my hands against the roof and pushing myself up just before she unlatched my seatbelt. I crumpled to the car's ceiling, bracing myself as best as I could before pulling my legs beneath me to kneel. Something crunched under my knee, and I lifted it to discover glass all over the ground. I brushed at my knee to clear away any sharp fragments, but none pierced my skin. Strange. I glanced at Arabella, who was gripping my shoulders once more.

"Listen to me. You can't let them catch you," she said. What was she talking about? Who was trying to catch me? "Ray, no matter what they say, you can't go with them. They'll use you—"

Arabella screamed as she was yanked backward through the shattered window behind her. She let out another blood-curdling scream as her body stiffened and then started writhing as if she were in pain. The glass showed no signs of blood, so that couldn't have been the cause of her screams. When she cleared the window, the scene behind her came into view, and I gasped as another pair of legs appeared on the wet pavement. Her scream echoed louder as thunder rumbled in the distance. I could hear the cadence of the other person's voice, but between the rain and Arabella's scream, their words were drowned out

I tried to crawl out after her, but my body wouldn't move. It was stuck in the 'freeze' part of fight, flight, or freeze. Her rigid body seized against the mysterious person's grip on her ankle, her scream still echoing but getting lost in the sounds of the storm. I couldn't tell what the stranger was doing to her. Maybe they were twisting her ankle or something—but that wouldn't cause her to scream like that, would it?

Thunder rumbled in the sky again, and Arabella finally stopped struggling, her scream fading and her body going limp in his grip, but she was still breathing. I could see her chest rising and falling quickly, breathless. The other person's feet turned toward the lightning crashing to the ground, as if they were searching for something. I tried to shift again in the car to get a better view of my twin's attacker, but I couldn't move an inch. Something felt wrong with me. Maybe I had been injured. Paralyzed, even. But no, I'd moved earlier, so why couldn't I move now?

The stranger's voice echoed in the rain, a curse so colorful I thought it might be a prayer. They released Arabella's leg and stepped back toward the car—toward me.

Arabella screamed once more as her body rose off the ground on its own, and a sickening crunch resounded in my ears. Her scream abruptly stopped, her body fell limp, and she collapsed to the ground, not moving.

"NOOO!!" I screamed, pushing through the fear and lunging for the open window. "Bella!" She didn't move, not even to take a breath. "Bell!!" I sobbed, army-crawling toward the shattered window. I knew it was futile, but I had to reach her. She couldn't die alone on that pavement! My forearms crunched against the glass and debris in the car, feeling no pain; I blamed it on the adrenaline.

The stranger's head popped into my line of sight, their face obscured by shadows, but I could hear the smile in their voice as they said, "Hello, Rayliana. It's so nice to finally meet you." Their hand shot toward me, and I flew back against the opposite side of the car, my hip catching on the steering wheel with a crack. "I hope you don't take this personally," they said. I tried to scream, but a weight like a cinderblock landed on my chest, pushing me down into the roof of the car. I reached to remove the weight from my chest so I could get a breath, but found nothing physical there. What was happening? My hip throbbed in pain as the invisible weight continued to crush my ribs, cracking a few in the process and pulling a scream from my lips with my only breath. The stranger's voice sounded strained as they said, "For what it's worth, you would have—"

A roar echoed in the sky outside, similar to the thunder I'd heard, but it sounded closer…angrier this time. And nothing like thunder.

The weight lifted from my chest, and I scrambled to push myself up. But the instant I put pressure on my arm, it was knocked from beneath me with another crack. I moaned as the pain from my broken arm shot through me, but I still tried to focus on what was happening outside. A maniacal laugh filled the air right before my head was slammed against the car window, and everything went black.

I withdrew from the darkness. That couldn't possibly be true. Arabella died in the crash, not because some psycho killed her with magic. I would have remembered that. I would have recalled the sound of her body breaking, the sound of my own bones snapping. I was unconscious the moment the car was hit… wasn't I?

The scene replayed in my mind, and I realized it wasn't just a vision—it was a memory. One I'd suppressed all this time because no one wanted to relive the memory of their loved ones dying. No one wanted to remember watching their twin die. Or any loved one, especially so brutally. Reliving Dad's death was bad enough. It might have been what unlocked my air magic, I suppose, but I hadn't forgotten any of those details. I'd just shoved them into the chasm I'd created.

The memory I just witnessed was something I didn't even recognize. Bella was *alive* after we'd been hit. And she was trying to warn me about someone. But who was she talking about? How did she know? We weren't told anything about our magic or where we came from… or was she? She never told me…why? Why wouldn't she have told me we were from another realm? The way she warned me made me think she knew everything—that we were being hunted, that we were powerful, and that they were trying to use our powers. If she knew all those things about our true identity, someone must have told her.

But who?

The answer was right in front of me. It had to be. We knew all the same people. She had hardly left my side when she was alive. We were attached at the hip. So who could have told her—

It hit me. *Hard.* The pieces falling into place. There was no denying it now.

I took a deep breath, accepting the truth, and watched as the black void before me slowly disintegrated. The green orb behind it floated freely from the pocket of my mind where it had taken up residence and moved toward me. The energy from it was warm and comforting as it glided my way. I reached out a hand to grasp it—

A wave surged through me, filling me with a buzz of built-up energy that I needed to release. I focused on the power coursing through me as I returned to consciousness. I was still lying in the grass, eyes closed, fingers dug into the dirt—which was filling me with *more* power. Grounding myself had completely connected me to the forces I had been blocking, and once they were free, the magic flowed through me effortlessly, allowing me to feel the movement of the island beneath me.

The magic led me, my fingers digging further into the ground, and I felt it respond instantly. The ground trembled as my powers sang, moving the earth as the energy flowing out of me intensified.

Someone shouted my name, but I couldn't tell who it was, as the roaring in my ears drowned out all senses except power. More. I needed more. It surged through my veins, demanding to be released. Something inside me warned that if I didn't release it now, it could become more dangerous later. I pulled and pushed the ground with my mind, with my magic, shaping it as best as I could, hoping it was responding to my commands because I couldn't bring myself to open my eyes.

Suddenly, strong arms lifted me off the ground and drew me into his chest. The severed connection to the earth caused my powers to subside but not disappear, and the ground stopped shaking as a breeze whipped across my face.

"Rayleigh! Open your eyes!" Kyler's voice echoed above me. I should have known he'd break the connection to my powers. I struggled to focus on him, fighting against the force keeping my eyes shut. When they finally cracked open, the world around me was no longer the clearing we had reached, but a vibrant, multi-colored sky surrounding Kyler's face as he looked down at me. "You have to stop!" he shouted, as the breeze swirled around us.

I looked at my glowing hands, gripping fistfuls of grass and dirt—

Glowing hands? Again?!

When I opened my fists, dirt and grass flew away in the wind, making me realize he hadn't merely picked me up. A wing flapped in and out of my view—a jade wing.

Wait. We were *flying?* But Kyler wasn't in his dragon form. He was cradling me in his lap on the back of—

"*Libella?* You said I couldn't fly with her!" I shouted.

"Focus, Sunshine," Kyler's instructive voice brought me back to him. If I wasn't mistaken, he seemed a bit ashen. "Whatever you're doing with your powers, you need to stop."

"I'm not doing anything!" I shouted over the wind, convinced I wasn't directing the magic anymore.

"That can't be true! Look at the damage you've already caused!" he shouted, gesturing toward the ground.

I peeked over Libella's wing and sucked in a breath. The clearing we had been in just moments ago had a crack running through the middle, and pieces were tumbling off the edge of the island. I didn't think we'd been that close to the edge, but trees were crashing into the water below, and the ground crumbled away with them. Half of the clearing was already gone, and the edge inched farther inland as we circled above it.

My eyes shot to Kyler's, and I whispered, "I can't stop it." Tears brimmed in my eyes as he held my gaze. "I don't know how to control it." A single tear rolled down my cheek. "Please... Help me," I pleaded.

He dipped his chin, resting his forehead against mine. "It's like your panic attacks. But you have to let go of the power." His whispered words brushed my lips. *Take a deep breath.* His voice in my head surprised me, especially with how calm it was, but I followed his suggestion. *Good, hold it for four seconds, and when you release it, try to let go of your hold on the magic.*

But what if I lose the connection to my earth magic?

Letting go of it now won't break the connection again. It will just stop whatever you're doing in this moment.

I closed my eyes, nodded, and followed his breathing pattern. It was different from my panic attacks, where I could learn to manage it on my own. This was something I had never encountered before, and having someone guide me through it, even if it was Kyler, was more than I could have ever hoped for.

Another one, he instructed. *This time, open your hands to let it go.*

I hadn't realized I was clenching my fists again. After taking a second breath, I felt the magic settle within me. When I opened my eyes to inspect my hands, they weren't glowing anymore. The power had been released. I still felt it inside me, but it was calm and resting.

The full circumstances of the situation hit me. I had just destroyed part of the island instead of creating something from it. My body slumped in defeat. Maybe I wasn't ready for such power. There was too much to learn with so little time. I took a shaky breath and found Kyler staring at me. *Thank you.* Even in my head, the words sounded unsteady. Tears spilled down my face as I thought about what I could have done, how much more damage I could have caused if he hadn't been there. Trying to make it a little lighthearted, I said, *Libella was right to bring me there. The castle would be in pieces.*

That was my idea. When I looked surprised, he raised an eyebrow at me. *I felt your power that night before our flight. If you're not the most powerful fae, I wouldn't want to meet the one who is.*

Was that another compliment?

He scoffed, *More of a warning.*

Oh. I sighed internally. Meeting someone who could do more damage than that? And I'd done that accidentally... *I don't want to meet them either,* I agreed. Only then did I realize Kyler was still cradling me against his chest. And I could feel every part of our bodies touching. My skin grew hot, and I could tell he noticed because he smirked. *Can I sit normally?* I only asked before squirming for two reasons: because his dragon basically yelled at me, and because we were mid-air. Knowing myself, I'd fall right out of the sky if I tried to readjust on my own.

I could have sworn he chuckled before letting my legs dangle over his and sliding his hand up to my waist, never breaking contact. I suppressed every instinct to shiver at his touch, especially since the leather made me feel everything. He lifted me effortlessly from my crossed position to sit in front of him, as if I were riding a horse... and I suddenly realized that it was much worse. There wasn't much room between the spines; in fact, there was barely enough space for the two of us, so every part of my backside pressed against him.

Better? He asked, a smile in his tone.

No.

Liar.

I swallowed every retort on the tip of my tongue and reminded myself he was not my friend. Unless he had some sort of split personality... I couldn't let him get under my skin. I would only get hurt in the end, and I wasn't about to put myself through that again. I found my grip on the spine in front of me, but his hands didn't leave my waist. *Can you let go of me?*

You can't expect me not to hold on, he said smugly.

You were perfectly fine without holding on when you were, I swallowed, not really wanting to say what I did next, *holding me.*

Alright, fine. He released my waist, but then his body leaned even closer to me, and his hand gripped the spot below my hands along the spine in front of me. *Happy?*

I rolled my eyes. Obviously, he wanted to provoke me. So I just huffed and kept my response to myself. I didn't understand why I allowed him to affect me like that. He severed my connection to my powers because it was spiraling out of control, but he didn't do it for my benefit. He did it to prevent me from destroying the island—for his own sake, not mine.

When we get back to the castle, Kyler interrupted my thoughts, *don't say anything about your mishap in the glen.*

Why? That was such a strange request. I was ready to be reprimanded and locked away for destroying a part of the island.

Don't worry about why, he practically snapped. *Just let me handle it. If anyone asks you about it, refer them to me.*

Why wouldn't he let me take the blame for that? It made me nervous. *Would it be worse if they knew I caused it or if they found out about my magic?*

Both. He was silent for a moment before explaining. *There has only been speculation about your powers and their strength. No one has seen them except me, and now Libella. Without confirmation, most won't attempt to attack you like Aaidan did earlier.*

But if they know I'm training—

No one outside of who was in the meadow knows you're training. Kaleb doesn't even know.

I gulped. *How can he not know? I was in the clearing with Ken and Leigh.*

He only knows you were there to learn, not to practice wielding.

Oh. Something else hit me then. *What about Aaidan?*

He doesn't know anything. It seems like he was just testing a theory.

But in the shack… I pursed my lips.

What? Kyler didn't sound worried but annoyed. When I didn't respond, he said, *Spit it out, Sunshine.*

I bit my lip. *I may have accidentally said something.*

What did you say? he snapped.

I didn't think it was important since your xousia knocked him back!

What, he bit out, *did you say?*

I sighed to myself. *I said I was training today.*

Shit. He was silent for a moment, making me wonder what he was thinking—or saying to Libella—as we took a sharp turn off course, and

Kyler tightened his grip around me. The gesture made me glance over my shoulder, but I quickly faced forward again when I realized how close that put my face to his.

Something caught my eye just under Libella's wing. A glimmer off the water below? No, there it was again. Movement. *My heart skipped a beat. Kyler. I think someone is following us.*

A low growl rumbled against my back where it pressed into his chest. *Where?*

The fact that he didn't doubt me made me question him, but I pointed. *Below us, about halfway to the ground. There was a strange movement in the air.*

Kyler leaned over to follow my pointing finger and emitted another growl. *Dammit,* he growled. *Okay, here's what's going to happen.* He let out a hefty breath on the back of my neck before saying, *I'm going to shift, and you're going to transfer to my back—*

"*What?!*" I shrieked aloud, forgetting where we were.

Shh! He'll hear you!

Who? I yelled back. *Who's following us?*

What do you mean, who? It's Aaidan!

Well, I guess that explains his disappearance. He wanted to follow us, so he probably made himself invisible. But how did Kyler not notice? *Why do I have to transfer to your back? Why can't I stay with Libella?*

Because you can't talk to her, and I'm going to need her.

Need her for what?

Would you stop asking so many questions! he demanded. *We don't have time!* He shifted his hands to cup my hips on either side, the sensation feeling very intimate since the leather didn't offer much of a barrier. *I'm going to jump and shift, settling right below Libella, and you can do one of two things.* This already sounded like I'd go splat on the ground if I made one wrong move. *The first option is that you jump, and I'll catch you.*

Jump?! Are you crazy? I was back to shrieking again, but this time I made sure to keep it in my head.

You will have to trust me. Those words brought back the moment in the courtyard when I let him into my head, which, in this case, seemed like we were trying to make the same kind of connection. *As my rider, this is what we were meant to do.*

I took a deep breath, recalling him sharing all this information, but never imagining I'd actually have to do it. *What's the second option?*

He sighed, *I'll teleport you to my back.*

Nope! I blurted. Libella said she didn't know how I would manage portaling, and I took that to mean teleporting as well. But that meant I had to jump. And jumping from the back of one dragon to another just didn't seem like something I could do. Yet, it felt like I didn't have a choice. Alright. *What do I—*

Just follow my lead, Kyler said quickly, and his hands slipped away from my hips, taking his entire presence with them. I didn't realize how cold it was at this height without his warmth. For some reason, Libella's dragon form wasn't nearly as warm as Kyler's.

Where did you go?

Are you ready? Wait, had he already shifted? I peered over the side of Libella's flank and saw Kyler leveling off below us. The air beneath him still pulsed with the rhythm of Aaidan's invisible wings.

Won't Aaidan suspect we know he's there? I asked, stalling for the time I needed to hype myself up for the insane jump I was about to make.

No, Drakalasson don't usually ride each other. I snickered a little, my nerves getting the best of me. *Really?* I know he was deadpanning, but I swear I heard a smile in there, too. *We don't have time for you to stall any longer. When I count to three, all you have to do is slide off Libella's back. I'll catch you.*

Oh my gosh, this is crazy! I did not wake up this morning thinking I'd be riding a dragon, let alone jumping off one. *Don't you need to be, like, in my mind or something so you can see where I'm falling?*

Don't worry. I'll catch you. He no longer sounded irritated or angry at my questions. He just sounded—*I promise.*

For whatever reason, I completely believed him. Even though he hadn't been the Kyler I thought I knew these past few days, a glimmer of him appeared earlier today, and it was showing again now. That protective side, not the possessive side. The side of him that he claimed was his dragon, though he hadn't let his dragon come through to talk to me… I took a deep breath and let it out slowly. *Okay. I'm ready.*

When I count to three, Libella will tilt, and you just let yourself fall, okay?

Well, at least that meant I didn't have to jump myself. But it sounded like Libella wouldn't give me a choice. I wasn't sure which was worse, so

I decided that the less time I spent thinking about it, the better. *Okay.*

One, he didn't count quickly, but I wish he had. *Two.* I took a deep breath and closed my eyes, but I immediately opened them again. I couldn't do this without looking. I'd need to hold on once I landed. *Three.*

All the breath left my body as I felt Libella tilt, my body with her. It took everything in me not to grab hold of her spine and keep myself on her back. I felt her cool body slip away from mine, and I was free-falling.

The air whipped around my face, but I summoned my powers from within to shield my eyes from the wind so I could concentrate on Kyler, whose dragon form was drawing closer by the second.

Spread your arms and legs wide like a starfish. I followed the instruction, wondering how that would help me land on his back. But I realized a moment too late that he wasn't planning on me landing on him. His body flipped over so he was flying upside down, and his forelegs reached out for me.

A huge gust of hot wind knocked me off course, and I screamed, closing my eyes as I flailed in a different direction. A roar sounded behind me just before claws wrapped around my torso, nicking my skin and holding me tightly in their grasp. I let out a sigh of relief and opened my eyes.

But my relief was short-lived when I noticed the color of the claws around me. They weren't the midnight blue I had expected, but a fiery red. And the leathers I had been wearing had vanished.

THIRTEEN
Smoke & Trouble

Kyler! I screamed, struggling against Aaidan's tight grip. *Kyler! Where are you?!* The cold air bit into my bare skin as we soared higher.

Rayleigh! he shouted back, not bothering to conceal the panic and anger threading through his voice. *He's shielding you. You need to let me in!*

As he spoke those words, I felt that familiar and comforting caress in my mind, and I didn't hesitate. I found the door and let the blue eyes in, feeling him invade my mind. *Can you see me?*

No, but I know how to find you. His voice sounded strained in my mind. *I can feel you, but you have to get out of his grip.*

I'm—trying! I grunted, my bare skin scraping against the claws around me, leaving burning cuts wherever they caught me. The dragon's claws wouldn't budge. *His grip is too tight.*

Try using your magic, he said, as if the answer was obvious. Reaching for my air magic— *Wait! Not yet. Build it up and wait for my signal!*

I did as he said, building my energy by coaxing the white thread of power to my fingertips. As we ascended, breathing became more difficult, but I sensed the power growing within me as I waited for the signal. I could still feel Kyler's presence in my mind, but the longer Aaidan flew without Kyler giving the signal, the more anxious I became. *Kyler?*

I'm right behind you, but he's trying to jump with you. I'm currently preventing that. The thought of teleporting sent chills down my spine. I absolutely didn't want to vanish anywhere with Aaidan. Who knows what kind of torment he'd put me through if he got me alone again? I was already bleeding from where his talons snatched me out of the air. I couldn't feel the pain due to the adrenaline, but I knew I'd feel it all later. *Okay, on the count of three—*

The last time we waited until three, we got interrupted! Just say go! I yelled, not caring about his reaction.

Fine! Go!

His presence left my mind, and I did my best to channel the built-up energy blast toward the talons. I knew it had worked when the dragon roared and his grip loosened. However, his claws didn't fully open, forcing me to wiggle my way out as quickly as I could. Once I was free from his grasp, I found myself free-falling once again.

Brace yourself! Kyler yelled in my mind. I had no idea what I was bracing myself for, but when Kyler's tail reached for me, I raised my arms and braced for the impact.

Instead, I felt the air around me constrict, and then there was nothing for about half a second before I sensed his tail wrap around me. I relaxed, recognizing the familiar warmth of his dragon's scales. I felt faint and had to fight the wave of nausea threatening to take over. That must be what teleporting does to those who aren't used to it.

Blinking rapidly and taking deep breaths, I finally managed to open my eyes and take in my surroundings. The world had changed. The sun shone brightly behind me, and the air felt hot and dry. The island we were approaching didn't resemble the one I had just partially destroyed. It appeared barren and desert-like, lacking any live vegetation. All the visible tree trunks and bushes were bare, and the ground was pale brown dirt with cracks running through it. There was no sign of water anywhere on the island.

Where are we? I asked, genuine curiosity shaping my tone.

But no response came. I looked up at the dragon holding me, and my entire body felt as though it had been plunged into ice-cold water. Because it wasn't Kyler's tail that had wrapped around my bare body—it was Aaidan's.

Kyler! I shouted into the void of the bond, not knowing how far I'd just been taken away from him. Silence echoed back. *Kyler!!* He said he could reach me from miles away, so why wasn't he responding?

Rayleigh? A faint response came, and I exhaled. *Are you okay?*

No. Where are you? Where am I?

I don't know, Kyler's faint voice replied. *Aaidan somehow blocked me out. Before I could grab you, he teleported you both. I'm trying to track you, but tracking teleportations is almost impossible.* His voice was so faint that I wondered how far we'd traveled. *What do you see?* he asked.

I described the island and its stark qualities. *It appears deserted,* I added. *And it's much smaller than the one we were on.*

Are there any mountains or lakes?

No. I searched the small island for landmarks and spotted a small dome that resembled a cave. *There's one small cave in the center, but the island looks like it's mostly dried up with no water in sight.*

Shit. The soft voice answered, pausing for a moment while I surveyed the rest of the small island. Aaidan circled the center of the island where the cave loomed, and I shook my head. What was it with caves and me being captured? *I can't teleport directly to that island. I have to fly in. It could take almost an hour.*

What?! I screeched, dreading every second I would have to spend with Aaidan. Admittedly, I would prefer to endure that torturous time with Kyler, but I wasn't about to tell him that. *Why could Aaidan teleport here if you can't?*

He didn't.

Clearly, he did. We are flying above it now!

No. You've been gone for hours. My stomach plummeted. Hours? Only seconds had passed. How did hours feel like seconds? Unless *that's* what teleporting did to me. *I'm as close as I can get without teleporting in.* His voice in my head seemed louder. *I fly faster than Aaidan, but not that fast.*

My heart pounded in my chest. *What should I do?*

Do what you do best, he said simply. *Keep him talking. Distract him. But try to keep your temper in check.*

I don't have a temper!

Sure you don't, Sunshine.

I mentally flipped him off, wondering if he would even notice, but his faint, dark chuckle confirmed it. Aaidan descended toward the sand, his tail still tightly wrapped around my bare body. I wondered if he would be kind enough to provide me with clothes, but I kept my hopes low. Just before his clawed feet touched the sand, he spread his wings to glide just above the ground. His tail loosened as he flew over a small hole I hadn't noticed, unceremoniously dropping me in.

A scream barely escaped my lips before the hole in the sand enveloped me. I didn't fall very far before landing with a big splash in a pool of water. I hadn't expected it, so I didn't have time to close my mouth before plunging into the unusually warm water. As soon as my feet felt the rocky ground beneath me, I pushed myself up and shot through the surface, sputtering out the water I'd swallowed. Wiping my eyes and coughing up the remaining water, I tried to take in the cave. *He dropped me in an underground pool,* I told Kyler.

Figures. His voice was slightly louder than last time, yet still barely above a whisper.

What do you mean? I shot back. *What's so special about this place?*

Long story. Is he down there with you?

No. I looked around to see if there was another entrance besides the hole directly above my head. There was light coming from one end of the pool, but it wasn't directly in the sun. There must have been a tunnel from the cave entrance leading down. *At least, not yet.* I stayed where I had been dropped into the pool, treading water, not wanting to get out for two reasons. First, I was still naked. Second, it would bring me closer to Aaidan.

Try not to provoke him. He's more powerful there than anywhere.

How is that possible? I practically yelled. But my answer came as soon as my eyes adjusted to the darkness of the cave. It wasn't a rocky floor I had pushed off of to reach the surface. Lining the pool above and below the water were the colorful crystals I recognized as those the dragons used to recharge their powers. *What are these crystals called again?*

Xouta. The ones that are a blend of blue and red enhance his shield, which I'm sure he'll have up. The ones that resemble fire boost his Parevim powers.

I scoffed. *And how am I supposed to know which powers those are?*

Physical manipulation, Sunshine. I swear I could hear him roll his eyes.

How can you expect me to remember all that? Everything I had learned practically melted from my brain as soon as I went into survival mode in the dungeon. I couldn't recall much about my own powers, let alone the dragons. Looking around the cave, I noticed that most of the crystals were the colors he mentioned. Great. *So how are you going to get in here if his shields are up?*

You need to distract him enough to lower his shield.

And how do I do that?

I'm sure you'll think of something.

An idea flashed in my mind, and Kyler swore colorfully. *What?* I asked, feigning innocence. *It would work.*

Well. You're not wrong. Aaidan is a simple male.

And you're not? I chided.

It would take more than that to distract me, Sunshine.

It was my turn to smirk. *I seriously doubt that. Especially if it were Naila.*

He scoffed, the sound off-hand, but I knew I was right. *That—*

He's coming, I interrupted as the entrance to the cave darkened. The shadows on the wall danced as Aaidan walked in, rounding the corner to stand on the shore of the pool where I was still treading water.

He grinned at me. "Nice of you to drop by, Princess." He crouched at the edge of the water and dipped his fingers in, dragging them across the surface to make ripples. "Do you like my hideaway?"

I considered making a snarky remark but thought better of it and chose a completely different approach. "I would have preferred an invitation rather than being dropped in, but it's nice, I suppose." I gave him a smirk.

"Better than that tiny cave back home," he taunted, ignoring the bait I'd offered him.

I chose to change the subject instead of gracing him with a response. "Why did you bring me here, pretty boy?"

"Pretty boy?" He raised an eyebrow on that flawlessly angled face, his blue eyes standing out. "Since when do I have a nickname?"

Yeah, since when does he have a nickname? Kyler butted in.

"Since I just gave you one." My smile dripped with false sweetness, knowing Kyler heard my response too. *Jealous, much?* I tossed at him. "Besides, you've already got one for me."

"Huh." He squinted at me. "No sassy remarks or clever comebacks today?"

"I'm just waiting for you to begin your monologue."

He chuckled briefly and grinned, "I'd rather listen to you stumble over your words again."

I narrowed my eyes at him, then remembered I was supposed to distract him. Keep him occupied. So, I swam a little closer and found my footing on the Xouta, creating a floor beneath me. I got close enough to shore that I could stop treading water, but not shallow enough that anything below my shoulders was above water. Teasing my bare shoulders above the surface seemed to grab his attention; I just hoped the dark water concealed what I wasn't ready to reveal yet. "Thing is, I'm not as nervous around pretty boys anymore. I seem to have gained some confidence in that area."

"Have you now?" He tucked one leg under himself, sitting on it, and propped his arm on the knee still raised in front of him, his eyes roaming over my bare shoulders.

"Why did you bring me here?" I repeated, my voice light, curious.

His bright blue eyes found mine and twitched slightly before he tilted his head and said, "Because you're the most powerful fae, and I intend to take advantage of that."

I tried not to gulp as I swallowed my retort. Instead, I dragged my fingers across the surface of the water and watched their progress to keep my eyes away from his. "And what do you *intend* to do?"

He didn't even take a moment to consider his response. "Claim you."

I met his gaze, trying not to let mine betray me as I suppressed the fear evoked by those words. "Why does everyone want to claim me? Why doesn't anyone just ask if I want to join them?" Thankfully, the words slipped out casually, just as I had intended. But internally, I was trembling.

Aaidan raised an eyebrow. "*Do* you want to join me?"

"Depends." A low growl echoed in my head, but I brushed it aside. He was the one who told me to distract him, after all. "What can you give me that Kyler can't?"

Nothing, the voice in my head rumbled.

"Power," Aaidan shrugged.

It was my turn to raise an eyebrow. "Kyler is a prince. As far as I'm concerned, the only one with more power than him is the King."

I'm flattered, Sunshine, really, Kyler mocked.

Aaidan smirked and stood, shoving his hands into his pockets. "Their power comes from politics." He walked along the shore, kicking a crystal as he went. "The power I'm after will not limit your strengths." He turned to face me again. "You destroying part of the island today was just the tip of the iceberg. Your power runs much deeper than that."

I wasn't sure where this was headed, but he finally seemed to be starting his monologue, so I gave him more to talk about. "And how would you know how much power I have?"

"Oh, there are rumors about you all over this realm. 'The young Fae girls, hidden away from our world.' We hadn't seen the likes of you two for many centuries." I furrowed my eyebrows. He was part of the team sent to kill my sister and me, wasn't he? So why was he acting like that wasn't the plan at all? "Now, when I was assigned to your case, I was only given the basics. My superiors said it was a top-secret mission, and that was all I needed. But now that I've met you—now that I know what you're capable of?" He flashed me an evil smirk. "There is so much more to you than I was told."

He didn't seem likely to elaborate, so I asked, "What *were* you told?"

"That you were protected by the highest in the Kidemos because you were Ignalian." He halted abruptly and turned to me sharply. "But you aren't Ignalian, are you?" He barely paused for breath, let alone enough time for me to respond. "You are clearly Udarian based on what I saw, and Koladon mentioned you were Annysian as well. But nothing more?"

I lifted my shoulders above the water, catching his glance again. "I only know about the two," I said, recalling what I had told Koladon.

He squinted. "Then why would they put you under the guise of an Ignalian?" he mused to himself, holding up a finger. "You see, I've asked myself that question a lot over the past few weeks. And while I was healing," a low chuckle reverberated in my head. *It's a wonder he can still fly.* Kyler's mocking tone hinted that he wasn't sorry for what his dragon did. Or maybe he was in control at that time... "I decided to do some research. Thankfully, your book-hoarding dragon left a wide selection of study material in your realm."

Wait, is he talking about the books at the Dengalow? I asked Kyler, knowing that my notebook, where I had made extensive notes about my lineage, was there too. The only response was a low growl, which meant I must have been right. I tried to mask my emotions with a smile, but I was almost certain it couldn't hide the blood draining from my face. I lowered my voice and adjusted my shoulders again, "And what did you find out about me?"

His eyes didn't drop to my shoulders again but maintained their hold on my gaze. "It wasn't so much about your power as it was about your little *bond.*"

Shit, Kyler's voice echoed in my head at the same time my breathing shallowed. Kyler's outburst confirmed my questions: It wasn't a Doulos bond between us, but a rider bond—a Kavaltis. I wasn't sure what that meant for me and him, but it felt like something Aaidan shouldn't know at all. *He can't leave that cave alive.*

You can't be serious!

If he lives, you will be in more danger than you are now.

You almost sound like you care. I mumbled, knowing that wasn't the case at all. His dragon? Maybe. But Kyler made it clear I was his property, not someone he cared about.

We don't have time for this. You need to get his shield down and be ready. Five minutes out.

You said it would take an hour!

Yeah, well. I lied. How he shortened the time from an hour to less than twenty minutes blew my mind, but—

"I assume you're talking to him right now, huh?" Aaidan interrupted, continuing his pacing along the shore. "Is that why you haven't responded to my discovery?"

"No," I lied, trying to think of something quickly. "I'm just trying to remember what kind of bond Kyler and I share. Could you remind me again?" I fluttered my eyelashes but was almost certain my tactics weren't working.

"Liar," he sneered, baring his teeth and confirming my theory. "Why don't you come out here so I can see your fancy Kavaltis bond?"

"No thanks. I like the water."

"Oh, it wasn't a request, Princess," he grinned. Then, my body was no longer mine to control; my legs moved of their own accord—or rather, Aaidan's accord. I tried to resist but remembered he was most powerful within the confines of his little cave. The walls glowed as the fiery crystal's energy intertwined with Aaidan's powers. The red and blue crystals also glimmered faintly, indicating that his shield was still active. As my body rose above the surface, I tried to cover myself, but even my arms wouldn't respond to my commands.

"What is it with men and their need to control women?" I said, still trying to break free from his grip.

What is he doing? Kyler's voice was much closer than it had been before.

He's using his powers to make me get out of the water.

Kyler's voice dropped, *Fight it. With everything you have, fight it.*

I'm trying! I didn't mention that I wasn't really fond of Aaidan seeing me naked, seeing as I had suggested it in the first place.

Whatever you do, don't let him touch you.

Stop being so possessive! My chest was now exposed above the water, and I tried again to drop below the surface or raise my arms to cover myself, but it was no use. The only things I could control were my mouth and my eyes. "Can I at least get some clothes, pretty boy?"

Aaidan grinned as he watched me make my way out of the water. "Nah, you're more vulnerable this way. You're less likely to try something if you're not wearing anything."

"You're the one controlling me! I can't even cover myself with my arms, much less attempt anything!" Suddenly, my arms were free to move, and I quickly crossed them over my chest while continuing to wade out of the water.

"Happy?"

"No, I'm still naked and being put in an uncomfortable position!"

"Good. At least if I release you, your hands will already be busy." He winked. I wanted to slap the wicked grin off his face—badly. That would distract him, perhaps enough to get the shield down. But more likely, it would anger him, which Kyler had suggested avoiding.

Recalling what Kaleb had said in the dungeons, I asked, "How can you claim me if I'm already bonded to Kyler?"

His wicked grin widened. "Someone's been running their mouth, haven't they?" Aaidan tilted his head. "How *was* your visit with your old friend?"

My jaw dropped, and my eyes grew wide. "How did you—"

"You didn't think I found those books on my own, did you?" At my silence, he chuckled. "As much as I hate to admit it, I was left to die on that battlefield. Shredded wings, bleeding out. If Kaleb hadn't found me,

I'd be dead. Or at least, I wouldn't be able to fly."

My mind was racing. So neither Aaidan nor Koladon knew it was Kaleb who had been secretly informing them of my whereabouts. But he revealed himself to Aaidan afterward. Why? Why would he expose himself to Aaidan and help heal him? And how?

"Wondering how an undeveloped Drakalasson healed me?"

"Get out of my head," I snapped, locking eyes with his bright blue ones.

"I don't possess Lunnoxia powers, Princess. You simply struggle to conceal your thoughts from your expression." If I had a dollar for every time I heard that... "His partner came to retrieve him, given that we were both too injured to travel."

So I really stabbed Kaleb... but how did he survive? Especially when the dagger I used was supposed to be fatal to Drakalasson. Then again, maybe his undeveloped powers were still strong enough to deceive me. Or maybe... I glanced at Aaidan. "Who is his partner?"

"No idea. Never showed their face. Wore a hoodie that obscured their features." Goosebumps prickled my skin, reminding me that I was now completely out of the water, stepping onto the shore just a few paces away from him. I kept one arm covering my chest and let the other drop to hide what little I could of the rest of me. The hooded figure was Kaleb's partner? That explained a lot, but it still left me wondering who the hooded figure really was. "But they brought us both back to that house you were staying in, healed Kaleb quickly, and then they disappeared for a while, leaving me in my dragon form to recover. They returned days later in high spirits, the proper Xouta in hand and a plan. You were in high demand back here in Niccodra." He raised a hand to drag a knuckle down my face, but I jerked back, causing him to lift his eyebrows before he dropped his hand. "The King tried to squash the rumors about you and your twin early on, but it seems Kaleb and his partner knew about you long before any of us."

Is his shield down yet? I had forgotten Kyler was still in my mind.

I stole a glance at the crystals, still seeing the red and blue ones glowing. *No.*

What are you doing to distract him?

Making him monologue.

He can still talk while shielding. You need to try something different. That image flashed in my mind again. *Shit, Sunshine.* He sounded tense. *Seriously?*

I'm telling you, it would work.

You can't think of anything else?

Not unless I want to try to take him down. I pursed my lips at my own suggestion, realizing I didn't even want to touch him, much less get him in a headlock.

"So Kaleb isn't the King's lost son?" I asked, trying to seem like I wasn't engaged in a full conversation with someone else in the silence.

"Oh no, he definitely is. When I told Kaleb about my discovery of your bond, he said he wanted proof before he would believe it. Said that if it were Kavaltis, we would need to find a way to break it so he could claim you during his ceremony." He scanned my bare body. "Now, where is it?"

I tried not to cringe at how callously he examined me. Kaleb had really been acting his ass off in that dining hall. He had a plan all along to involve me— "Hang on. What do you mean, during his ceremony? He claimed Leighton in the dining hall."

"It all happened sooner than planned, so he had to improvise. With you refusing to give up your bond with Kyler, he could do nothing. His father forced that moment upon him. Knowing his ceremony was approaching, claiming a Fae within the timeframe was crucial, and he couldn't simply allow Kendall and Leighton to remain unbound in the castle."

"Why not?" I interjected, genuinely curious. Aaidan was always so good at answering questions that he probably shouldn't.

He raised an eyebrow. "Unbound Fae have free will. Can't have that in the castle."

"What do you mean? Does Leighton have to do everything Kaleb asks? And Kendall with Mari?" I added the last part hastily, remembering the roles we all had to play.

"They don't just have to; they'll *want* to."

I held back the gasp that wanted to escape. That was why Leighton acted the way she did in the field earlier—why she defended Kaleb and wanted me to believe he was still in there. It was because she had no choice, no free will. She couldn't think for herself. Her Doulos bond made her believe those things. The bond was forcing her loyalty to him.

Distract him, Sunshine! Now!

I tried not to huff at Kyler's command. "So," I lowered my voice and gradually pulled my hand away from where it had covered my chest, running a finger down Aaidan's chest that was mere inches in front of me. "If I were to join you," I said, looking up through my eyelashes at him. "I would want to do everything you asked?" I hated making myself more vulnerable, using my body as a distraction. It felt disgusting, especially with him. But I had no choice. I was without clothes, without help, and my powers were nothing compared to his—not here. The best distraction was using what I had, and that was all I had. Literally. I would deal with my humiliation later. For now, I just had to get out of that cave.

His blue eyes burned as they traveled down my bare body, just as I expected. It almost made me feel empowered, if I weren't so disgusted by it. These creatures were accustomed to nakedness, and I knew I'd have to get used to it someday, especially since I was likely going to be living there. I tried not to hide my chest again, and instead laid my hand flat on his, taking a deep, shaky breath. I hoped he perceived my nervousness as a reaction to being close to him and not for what it truly was—the lies.

"Yes," Aaidan breathed. "If the bond between you and Kyler is broken, you're free to choose me." He reached up and wrapped his hand around mine.

"But wouldn't Kaleb be upset if I chose you?" I pouted, uncertain why he was falling for this. Maybe Kyler was right, and Aaidan was just a simple male.

His hand wrapped around mine possessively, lifting it from his chest and bringing it between us. "He doesn't have to know," he whispered, taking me in once more. His eyes found the slightly discolored skin on my torso where I knew the bond mark lay. He traced a finger across my ribcage, but the goosebumps that followed were nothing compared to when Kyler did it. I forced myself not to pull away from his touch. "Besides," Aaidan's eyes found mine again as he dropped his hand from the hidden madí. "It won't work if I can't break the bond."

"Break the bond?" My eyebrows knitted together, nearly betraying me. "I thought it had to be given up mutually?"

"That's how you release the bond. To break it," Aaidan grinned, his fiery blue eyes finding mine before shifting to a burning red. "A stronger dragon must claim you."

A scream erupted out of me.

Pain. That was all I knew.

As my vision turned black, I screamed, the pain radiating from where Aaidan grasped my hand and coursing through my whole body. He was yelling, too. Although, he seemed to enjoy the pain he felt, laughing through the screams as his grip tightened on my hand. There was a fire consuming my hand, crawling up my arm. No—worse than a fire. It was internal. Like lava invading my veins. My screams echoed through the cave just as Aaidan's did, alongside his sinister laughter.

My body seized in his grip, and I crumpled to the ground, causing his hand to release mine. The burning sensation and my screams lingered, though. His laughter faded away, and I wondered how long the flames beneath my skin would last. The overwhelming heat seemed to take over my bloodstream and had just reached my shoulder when it finally slowed. The pain subsided, my senses returned, and I realized his control over me was gone. I scrambled back from the monster before me.

Aaidan's body tensed; his power coursed through him, yet he remained still. The energy seemed to hold him in place while his body absorbed it, flowing through his veins. I could *see* it. It was like his veins radiated a lavender glow as it traveled up his arm.

The pain in my arm made me look down to see the damage he had done. Streaks of red traveled up my arm, resembling the burning I had felt. But as I stared at them, they began to retreat from my shoulder, back toward where he had held my hand, trying to claim me.

"No!" he roared, and my gaze snapped to him, watching as the faint glow beneath his skin faded. "No!" He shouted again, looking at me as if I were the reason it hadn't worked. Which I very well could have been. He stalked toward me as I crab-crawled away, hitting the wall of Xouta hard. The cave glowed brighter as he closed in on me, making me wonder what he would do when he caught me. And even more, why he wasn't using his powers to bring me to him.

A shadow passed over the hole above the pool and suddenly crashed to the ground between Aaidan and me.

No. Shadows didn't growl like that. Or have shiny scales running along them.

The figure rose to its full height, facing me and swinging its powerful head closer to mine. A sob of relief escaped me as I looked into those fierce eyes.

"Theo."

FOURTEEN
Legends Are Made

Before I could celebrate his arrival, he whipped around to where I had last seen Aaidan.

"How dare you take what belongs to me!" Aaidan's voice was deep, and his eyes glowed red.

A roar escaped Theo as he lashed his tail into Aaidan's stomach, the spines that usually lay flat shooting straight out to become a deadly weapon. Aaidan's roar of pain made me cringe as he collapsed to the ground, blood gushing from his new wound. His head shot up to Theo, red eyes glowing as his expression shifted. I scrambled to my feet, desperate to stay away from Aaidan's dragon. Pressing against the wall, Theo charged at the half-shifted dragon with his s-curved horns. He aimed directly for the exposed underbelly of the dragon, striking his target before the full transformation could even take effect.

The injured dragon's roar shook the walls, causing several crystals to splash into the water, with one or two striking my head before I could protect it.

Aaidan's tail wrapped around Theo's smaller figure and flung him into the pool, drenching me where I stood on the shore. I tried to sneak toward the cave entrance, but the red dragon slammed his tail into me, sending me back into the cave. A scream erupted from me as I soared through the air and landed hard on the rocky shore of the pool. I rolled several times, and when I finally stopped, I pushed myself into a sitting position and cradled my arm. I wasn't sure if it was the impact of the tail that shattered it or when I hit the ground, but my adrenaline was too high for me to feel the pain.

When I looked up at the thunderous footfalls, Aaidan's dragon was stalking toward me, a possessive fire in his gaze. The brief distraction cost Aaidan, as Theo had regained his footing and slammed into him again, horns first. He struck almost the exact same spot, causing the already bleeding wound to open further.

The red dragon slammed into the ground at Theo's impact and attempted to roll with him in its grasp. However, Theo leaped off quickly, jumping in front of me. The dragon's head whipped around swiftly, and if I hadn't been paying attention, I would have missed the object flying out of its mouth. It struck Aaidan's neck just as he managed to right himself on all fours. The collision sent the dragon back, and as it fell, time seemed to slow. His body shifted back into human form just before hitting the wall and crumpling to the ground. The wound in his stomach wasn't as fatal as I had expected, but it was still oozing blood as he lay still.

I shouldn't have cared, but I breathed a breath of relief when his chest rose and fell in rhythm. I didn't want my friends to become killers, even though Aaidan was on my list of people I thought deserved it, alongside Koladon and another person I couldn't name. My eyes drifted to his neck, where a metal band was now wrapped around it, resembling a collar of black metal.

Theo turned to face me again, and I swallowed my emotions as I held back the urge to throw my arms around the dragon's neck, aware that his dragon might not care for me as much as Theo did. His eyes locked onto mine, then moved over my body, taking in all the scrapes and cuts I'd acquired since the fiasco in the sky. Tears filled my eyes, knowing this was the second time he'd saved my life from that monster, and in a cave, no less. Yet, this time, I was happier to see him than I'd ever imagined. His gaze landed on the arm Aaidan had seized to claim me, and he took his time examining it, undoubtedly noting every detail and mark there. Then it shifted to the arm I still cradled, and a long sigh escaped him, smoke wafting through his nose.

When his eyes found mine again, his body shifted, and the familiar man in the tan beanie, a white tunic, and flowing brown pants stood before me, a slight crinkle in his eyes as he smiled. "Hello, dearie," he said, his arms slightly open in greeting as he let out an exhausted breath, likely from the fight he just had.

I laughed through the tears streaming down my face and stepped hesitantly into his arms, sobbing onto his shoulder as he gently wrapped his arms around me. He patted my back, speaking in his sing-song voice, "There, there. No need to cry. I've got you."

"How?" My voice was muffled against his shoulder, but I didn't want to pull away. I hadn't realized just how much I'd missed him over the past few weeks. I hugged him tighter as I asked, "How did you find me?"

Theo's chuckle shook us both. "I'm not ranked among the highest in the Kidemos for nothing, dearie." He placed his hands on my shoulders and gave me a slight push back so he could see my face. "I've been nearby since they let you out of those dungeons. As part of your Omada, I'm *always* close by."

"How did you get here before Kyler, though? He said he was five minutes away—"

Theo raised a hand. "I was five minutes away. He's still making his way here."

"But how?"

He sighed, "My ranking comes from my tracking abilities, in addition to my speed."

I nodded as if I understood, but I recalled his presentation at the Dengalow. "But you only mentioned having one power."

"No. I just didn't disclose that I had multiple."

My jaw dropped. Of course, he didn't have to share his entire lineage, but I would be lying if I said I wasn't a bit hurt that he didn't confide in me.

He reached for my hand while I continued to process and asked, "May I?"

I raised the injured arm with the one that had felt like it was on fire moments ago, placing it in Theo's outstretched hand. Then I looked at the man still lying behind Theo. "Is he dead?"

Theo took my hand and lifted it higher to inspect my shattered arm more closely. "You already know the answer is no. But he shouldn't be waking up anytime soon. Aside from his injuries, that collar drains his powers, and I'm pretty certain I threw him hard enough against the wall that he will only wake when Niko gets ahold of him."

My eyes snapped back to Theo. "What do you mean?"

Theo's eyes met mine again, but the sparkle was gone. "Aaidan won't live another free day in his life. Niko will question him—" I knew that was not all Kyler would do, "—but he will never know freedom again."

You're going to kill him, aren't you? My soft tone gave away my concern.

Unless you'd like to do the honors.

A shiver ran through me. *Is it necessary?*

Yes. The finality in his tone resonated like an echo in my soul.

Theo gently lowered my arm back to my side. "Would you like to wait for Niko or come with me and—" He stopped abruptly, pursing his lips and nodding at my widened eyes. "Never mind. I will prepare Adarachi for transport."

Theo didn't respond that way because of my expression…

Possessive asshole, I muttered. *What did you say to him?*

That you would be riding with no one but me ever again.

Theo wandered over to where Aaidan lay. *You know Theo is harmless.*

No. I don't.

So, why did you let him save me if you didn't trust him?

I never said I didn't trust him. I just said he wasn't harmless.

Are you serious? Theo has been watching over me my entire life—

And yet you have been captured, tortured, and nearly killed multiple times.

You're one to talk! I shouted. *How many times was I captured while you were there?*

I followed Theo's orders in the other realm. The only time I didn't was when I listened to you. And look where that got you.

Careful. You're starting to sound like you care again.

A frustrated sigh traveled down the bond. *You're riding with me—Dragon's orders.*

I wasn't sure why that felt like a punch to the gut, but it did. I shook off the thought and made my way over to where Theo was working on tying up Aaidan, stanching his wounds in the process. "Where did you get the rope?"

Theo sighed, "Seems you're not the only one he's brought back here as a prisoner. There was some stashed in a makeshift hole over there." He gestured to a dark spot on the wall.

I walked over to the hole, peering in to see if anything else was there. The longer I stared into the darkness, the more I could see of the empty hole. There was a smoothness to it that seemed strange, especially if Aaidan had dug it out, but maybe he just used his powers. I glanced around the rest of the cave, noticing that the crystals no longer glowed but sparkled along the wall. It wasn't a huge cave, nor was it something I had seen before, but it did look oddly familiar. "What is this place?" I asked, still admiring the structure of the underground cave.

"This is one of those caves I told you about." At my lack of recognition, he said, "It's a Xoutallos harvesting cave."

"I thought those were at the center of each island?"

Theo's raised brows told me he was surprised I remembered that, but not about the caves. I shrugged, knowing sometimes it just took a piece of a conversation to remember everything that was said. "It is in the center of an island."

"I don't remember any of the islands being desert-like…" The painting Mari showed me flashed in my mind, where all the islands were lush with green vegetation. But when Mari tried to say something… "You stopped Mari from telling me what happened to Niccodra, didn't you?" Theo dropped his gaze to the cave floor. "Does what she was going to say have to do with why this island is covered in bare trees and dry, cracked earth?"

"Yes," Theo admitted. "There's a right time for this discussion, but now is not it."

"But—"

"Rayleigh, you have no idea what this realm has endured, and I'm not about to enlighten you on its tragedies when you're set to return to the castle within the next few hours." He took a deep breath and stepped toward me, pressing his palms together in front of his chest. "Sorry for my outburst." I chuckled a bit at what he called an outburst. "There will be time to learn, but, again, now is not it. I'll bring a notebook so you can jot down those pesky questions." He winked, and I could only smile. "For now, let's get you back to the castle in one piece."

"Can you at least answer one question?" I pleaded.

He looked at me cautiously. "One question for you means twenty follow-up questions."

I cracked a smile, knowing he was right. "Just one. I promise." At his nod, I took a deep breath. "Why can't anyone teleport to this island?" The question had been bothering me since Kyler mentioned it. It didn't seem like their teleportation powers had limitations on locations, but this island didn't seem like one that needed guarding. There was no one here. The castle was on the larger island, and the only thing of significance seemed to be the crystal cave—one that Aaidan appeared to claim for himself.

Theo took a deep breath, taking in the cave around us before his gaze landed on mine. "This island was where the core of the planet's magic is housed."

My eyebrows furrowed. "This tiny, deserted island is where the magic comes from?" Theo raised his eyebrows. "But how is that possible? There's no life here! It's dry and hot, and this planet consists of floating islands above water. How can the magic be here?" Theo's expression didn't change, and I understood why. "I'm sorry! But you can't expect such a small answer to satisfy the big question I asked!" When there was still no change in his expression, I replayed his answer in my mind. One word stood out: was. "Oh." I pressed my lips together against the many other questions that surfaced. *I really need that notebook.*

No. Kyler butted into my thoughts again.

Stay out of my head.

Unfortunately, that's impossible.

I mentally rolled my eyes, then had a brilliant idea. *If you don't give me another notebook, I'll be forced to ask you all the questions.*

Mitera save me, he mumbled. *Fine. Another notebook it is.* I celebrated my small victory with a clenched fist at my side. *I saw that.*

Saw what?

"That." Kyler's physical voice was jarring compared to our internal monologue, even in that single word. I spun on the balls of my feet to face him. When his eyes met mine, they didn't linger long before traveling down the length of me, examining the cuts and bruises along my bare—

It took everything in me not to hastily hide from his gaze or the way he prowled toward me from across the cave. I had forgotten my clothes were missing until I felt his eyes examining every part of me. The adrenaline from the fight must have wiped that thought from my mind. Kyler's gaze felt different from how Aaidan's eyes wandered, making me feel even more vulnerable. As his eyes trailed back up my body, I could see the fire in them before they even returned to my face. Seeing as his eyes hadn't left me since I turned around, I tilted my head and lowered my voice, "I thought you couldn't be so easily distracted."

His eyes instantly locked onto mine, still ablaze with intensity in that green hue. He stood right in front of me now, his eyes smirking even though his mouth wasn't. "Don't flatter yourself, Sunshine," he whispered, his breath warm against my face. "I'm just making sure what's mine is in one piece." He reached a hand behind me, and something warm and soft brushed against my shoulders. He pulled it around me and secured it under my chin.

I broke our gaze to look down at my newest wardrobe. It was a robe, similar to the one I remembered seeing Theo in after he'd shifted, but this one was midnight blue with silver threading for the details. A realization dawned on me. "Is this yours?"

He didn't respond, but he reached to tie the belt around my waist. It was only then that I realized just how close we were. His fingers lingered on the tie as I stood frozen, forcing myself to appear confident instead of shying away. Kyler met my gaze again, his jaw clenching a few times before he opened his mouth. "I thought I told you not to let him touch you." His words were low enough that I don't think even Theo could have heard them ten feet away.

I gritted my teeth. "I did what you asked. Distracted him." When he raised an eyebrow and just stared at me, I cursed under my breath. "But now I can see that's probably exactly what he wanted me to do." Here, I thought I was doing a good job distracting him, but he was the one who played me. By getting me to touch him, he was able to easily try his hand at claiming me without me putting up a fight.

"Next time, listen to me."

"You didn't give me any better ideas!" I shouted, shoving him with my good hand.

But he caught my wrist, pulling me right back to where I was. "I didn't say, don't touch *him*." My eyes widened at his tone. "I said, 'Don't let him touch *you*.' See the difference?"

I bit my tongue but then thought better of it. "Yes, dumbass. Now let me go." I tried to pull my wrist out of his grip, but he tightened it.

"Do you, though?" he snapped, yanking me back into him, leaving no space between us. I could only see his face. "Do you see why I said not to let him touch you?"

"Yes!" I shouted, still trying to break free from his grip. "But you could have told me what would happen if he did!"

"Would it have made a difference?" Before I could give my obvious answer, he cut in again. "I'm trying to *protect you*. If you would just listen —"

"Stop trying to protect me and just tell me what's going on!" I stopped struggling in his grip and looked at him earnestly. "Please," my voice barely rose above a whisper. "You know what happens when you don't just *tell me* what's happening."

He glanced over my shoulder.

"Don't look at me, Niko. She's right," Theo said, and I couldn't imagine loving him more.

"Kyler, please," I didn't like begging, but I just needed to *know*.

His bright green eyes bore into mine, and an emotion filled them that I'd never seen before. He blinked, and then it was gone. "We have to go."

I dropped my shoulders in defeat, my arm falling beside me as Kyler released it. I sighed heavily and returned to cradling my arm. The urge to escape the cave was pressing, but I wanted an answer, so I stood my ground. "I'm not going with you unless you tell me what happened." I crossed my arms over my chest carefully.

He tilted his head at me, fighting an inner battle as he held my gaze. He knew I wasn't joking, and I knew he could move me even if I didn't go willingly. This was more of a battle of wills, deciding whether or not he wanted to fight me all the way back to the castle.

Theo's voice shattered the tense silence. "A Drakalasson can override the bond between a Fae and another Drakalasson if they are the more powerful of the two."

Our heads turned towards him as he stood near the tunnel that led out of the cave. I tilted my head and asked, "But does that include the Kavaltis? Or just the Doulos?"

Theo glanced at Kyler, who was glaring at him but likely communicating something telepathically. When Kyler's gaze met mine, he clenched his teeth before responding. "A Doulos bond cannot override a Kavaltis, but the opposite is true. However, that does not mean it won't inflict pain on the one they are attempting to claim." His eyes drifted to my arm, where I had noticed the red streaks earlier.

I would have let the subject drop if his eye hadn't twitched. "You're not telling me something."

His eyes met mine again, and it felt as if he were reading my soul. I stifled the shudder that coursed through me. "I've only read a little about Kavaltis bonds, but from what I understand, they used to be combined with a Doulos bond." He took a deep breath, and his eyes momentarily shifted focus between mine before locking in again. "It is *possible* to be both under different Drakalasson."

My eyes widened, and my breath caught before I could take a full one. "Are you telling me," I swallowed the lump in my throat that threatened to prevent me from speaking, "that even though your dragon chose me, someone else can still claim me?"

His simple nod sent chills down my spine. The same emotion from earlier flickered in his eyes, and I realized then what it was: *fear*. He was afraid of... what? Someone else controlling me?

I clenched my teeth, running my tongue over the front of them before spitting out, "Why don't you just claim me if you're so afraid of someone else doing it?"

His gaze shifted so quickly from that fear to something else that I couldn't catch it before the fire returned to his eyes. "If you don't start listening, maybe I will."

"My *friends* can't claim me. I won't stop them from *hugging* me just because you'll throw a temper tantrum."

"Well, then, I guess you don't want to see your mother or brother again."

My jaw dropped. "You wouldn't keep me from them," I whispered, anger radiating through me.

"I can, and I will." With that, he pivoted on his heel and made his way to the exit.

"Screw you, jackass!" I shouted after him, hot on his heels.

Theo had thrown Aaidan over his shoulder and followed both of us out of the cave. Kyler stalked up the tunnel, the muscles in his back tensing and flexing with every movement, and flipped him off. I hated that I had to ride back to the castle with him. A pain in my ass was an understatement. I'd have to bite my tongue the entire ride home, not wanting to insult him in case—

A slow smirk spread across my face. Oh, I was going to be in big trouble later, but I didn't care. At least I wouldn't have to endure Kyler.

I made sure he was outside the tunnel and looked ready to shift before calling his name. He turned to face me, a clear scowl on his face. "What?"

I smirked, already a few feet away from him. As soon as his eyes met mine, his face dropped, knowing precisely what was happening. Before he could take a breath to stop me, I lifted my chin and said, "Mosmudo."

His green eyes held a fierce fury for a split second before shifting to a burning blue. I grinned as his human form morphed into his dragon right before me.

I had remembered the dragon's name just before drifting off to sleep last night, my eyes shooting open as the memory of him making me repeat the name replayed in my mind. There hadn't been anywhere to write it down, so I repeated it to myself as I fell asleep, and thankfully, that worked.

The dragon's front feet landed on the dried-up earth, stirring up loose dirt as he regained his footing, breathing smoke from his nostrils and lowering his head to meet my gaze.

You possess quite a fire within you, Little Ember. His deep blue eyes sparkled with a wink. A nickname from his dragon? I couldn't decide if it was better or worse than Sunshine… *Brave of you to risk angering him at a time like this.*

"Well, he made me angry." I shrugged, crossing my arms. I knew it sounded a bit petty, but the whole back and forth of 'Is he or isn't he my friend?' was driving me nuts. "I didn't want to spend an entire flight back without a decent conversation." I paused for a moment, then added, "Plus, I kind of missed you."

I have missed you, too, Little Ember. I am glad to hear you enjoyed our last conversation. Smoke filtered through his nostrils, and a deep rumbling reached my ears. *He is not happy with you, that is for certain. But I am grateful you finally remembered how to call me.*

"Your name isn't easy to remember."

Mosmudo is not my name.

I scrunched my eyebrows, replaying the conversation he and I had back outside the Dengalow. "But you said to say that to call you forward."

I told you to call to me, and nothing could prevent me from coming to you.

I squinted my eyes. "Does that mean you…have a different name?"

The dragon mirrored my gaze, his bright blue eyes narrowing. *I do, but only Nikylo or other dragons can call me by that name.*

"Why?"

We can continue this conversation on the journey back to the castle, but we are running out of time. His tail curled forward, poised to lift me to his back. *May I?*

I nodded, lifting my wounded arm away from my body to avoid getting caught. The adrenaline was finally fading, and the pain was beginning to settle in. His tail coiled around my abdomen, and the familiar heat of his scales seeped through the robe Kyler had given me. "What are we late for?" I asked as he lifted me off the ground and onto his back.

The dinner to celebrate the return of the one you call Kaleb.

"Oh yeah…" That was the last place I wanted to be, but it seemed like I had no choice in the matter. I would be attending whether I wanted to or not. "What can I expect at the dinner?" I asked, unsure of what else to discuss for the hours we had left on this trip.

That is not the information you wish to ask about, is it? The dragon spoke with an air of omniscience. I suppose he could read my mind. As he unfurled his wings and took off, I noticed that Theo had shifted and was carrying an unconscious Aaidan in his claws.

Why does Aaidan have to die? I asked, knowing that switching to our mind link was more effective for traveling. As we ascended from the tiny cave entrance, I took one last look at the deserted island. How could such a small island be so guarded by magic yet serve as the home base for Aaidan and whoever else was on his team? Wouldn't it be easy for anyone to come in and take control?

Adarachi has witnessed your power and is now aware of our Kavaltis bond. His knowledge of both makes him a formidable enemy for you and Nikylo.

Why, though? They already knew I was powerful. Why does his knowledge of the Kavaltis bond also mean he needs to die?

Careful, Little Ember. You are beginning to sound as if you care for Adarachi.

Ew, no. I just... The words got stuck as I tried to express them. Because while I didn't care for Aaidan, I didn't want Kyler to become a murderer. Then again, maybe Aaidan wouldn't be the first person he's killed. From the guy I met back on Earth and everything I'd seen him do, he was certainly capable of it. But if Aaidan had to die just for my safety, it didn't seem worth it.

It is not just for your safety. The dragon interrupted my thoughts, forcing me to focus on him once more. *Even if Nikylo were not in danger, I am certain Adarachi's life would still be at risk.*

What do you mean?

After everything that tavi has done to you... I am surprised Nikylo has allowed him to live this long.

Please don't try to convince me that Kyler actually cares. I rolled my eyes, watching the water flow beneath us as we flew. *There is already so much evidence against that.*

As you wish. The dragon fell silent, leaving me to consider a new topic for discussion.

Why can only other dragons call you by your name? I asked, returning to our conversation before he interrupted me.

It is out of respect that no one but our kind calls us by our names.

What an interesting concept. *So, I can't even know your name? What if I came up with a nickname for you?*

A nickname? The question sounded as if he had never heard that term before.

Yeah, like a shortened version of your name or a term of endearment. I shrugged, suddenly wondering if calling a dragon by a nickname was insulting. If it were, I'd probably have been barbequed by now. *You have one for me, so it's only fair, right?*

A deep chuckle rumbled through the dragon's body. *Fair point, Little Ember.* He enunciated my new title with smoke trailing from his nostrils. *However, you must promise never to call me by my full name.*

I promise. A nickname will be more fun anyway. I winked, and that chuckle vibrated through him once more.

My name is Valisdrako.

I repeated the name to myself several times, thinking of the different, easy names to pull from it. Val felt too feminine, so I chose the other obvious choice. *I shall call you Drako.*

Drako hummed beneath me, and I took that as his approval of the nickname. *No one has ever given me a nickname before.*

Well, now they have. I smiled and looked around at the world we still flew over. If the trip was supposed to last hours, I'd need to think of a lot to say to keep the conversation going. The first questions that came to mind were about him. *Why does Mosmudo bring you to the forefront?*

The word coming from you is a summoning to me. If another rider bonded with a dragon, they could use it to summon their dragon as well.

So, even if I say Drako, you can't break through Kyler's control?

A scoff reverberated in my mind. *Nikylo has been particularly stubborn lately. He does not want me to reveal his secrets.*

What secrets? I asked a bit too quickly to seem nonchalant. *I mean… what could he possibly be keeping from me?*

I am no gossiper, Little Ember. The dragon seemed to scold me with those words. *Nikylo's secrets are his to share. In time, I am certain you will learn what you must.*

I doubt it. I mumbled. I should have known better than to ask. While I am Drako's favorite, Kyler and he are of one mind, which meant the secrets would remain so until Kyler chose to reveal them.

The silence stretched as I looked below us at the world of water. The deserted island had vanished behind us, and in the far distance, I could see another island—the one we were on earlier. The only reason I recognized it was that the crystal palace atop the hill reflected the sunlight vividly. I scanned the sky for the ball of light and found it nearly setting again. I hadn't been gone that long, had I? Kyler had said I had been gone for hours, but the dinner was still planned for that night. We were running late, yet I could have sworn the sun was rising while I was learning and practicing my magic.

Does time work differently here? It was the only thing that made sense, and I hoped Drako would answer at least a few of my pesky questions, as Theo called them.

Our sun no longer measures our days, if that is what you are asking.

What do you mean, 'no longer'?

Niccodra is in a state called Palikleido. Great. Another big word to remember. *The time it takes our planet to rotate is the same time it takes to orbit our sun, Andromeda.*

The concept seemed familiar, but I couldn't quite place it. *What does that mean, exactly?*

He seemed to take a deep breath. *It means that only one region of our planet can see Andromeda fully in the sky.* That didn't sound good for the planet's health. *There are three regions: Imera, which is in constant daylight; Nychta, which is in darkness; and in between the two is the region called Lykos, which is in constant twilight.* This was starting to sound increasingly familiar. *Lykos contains the mainland and one other island, while the remaining six are divided between Nychta and Imera.*

I thought back to when Mari showed me what Niccodra used to look like. Under the sunshine and lush vegetation, all the islands looked green. It made me wonder... *How did Niccodra end up like this? Is there nothing that can be done to fix it?*

No one knows what caused the slowing of Niccodra's rotation, nor if it can be restored to its original state. I gazed at the water far below us, wondering if the planet's core was impacted by the atmospheric changes. *Nikylo kept a journal of the events as part of his princely duties. Perhaps you could ask—*

Drako went silent, and I turned my head to look at him, but nothing seemed off. *Drako? Did something happen?* I scanned our surroundings for any sign of danger but saw nothing except the water beneath us, Theo behind us with Aaidan still in his clutches, and the islands far off in either direction. *Drako?* The worry in my voice was clear, but—

I must go, Little Ember, Drako's voice was shallow and small, nothing at all like the deep, rich voice I knew. *Ask the journ—*

A low rumble coursed through the dragon beneath me, and his head snapped back to face me. Green eyes drilled into mine, igniting my soul. But I didn't cower, refusing to reveal the slightest bit of fear Kyler had instilled in me. I sucked on a tooth and smacked my lips before saying, "Welcome back, Asshole."

FIFTEEN
Another Place

Silence stretched for the rest of the journey, but that didn't mean nothing happened. The rage radiating off Kyler was palpable. His reaction was a bit over the top, in my opinion, but he didn't seem to think so. I didn't attempt to talk to him, but the amount of disgruntled noises I didn't hear but felt from him were insane. I bit my tongue, fearing he might make me swim part of the way back. I wouldn't have put it past him, considering that any time I let go to rearrange my hair or adjust the robe around me, he would jerk one way or the other, forcing me to scramble as I tried to find my grip again. Words weren't exchanged, but clear disgust and annoyance definitely were.

When we landed back at the castle, it was in the same field where Ken, Leigh, and I had been earlier with Libella. He didn't give me time to swing my leg over before lifting me from his back. Secretly, I was thankful because the robe would have slid up on my way down, but he didn't set me down gently either. That caused me to stumble, and when I turned around to flip him off, he had already shifted into his human form and was storming toward the castle without a single glance back at me.

"Hey, Asshole!" I yelled, but he didn't stop. "Where am I supposed to go?" He clearly wasn't going to wait for me, and Theo had vanished as soon as we neared the island. I figured he was taking Aaidan to wherever Kyler would "question" him.

Kyler reached the castle door and wrenched it open, revealing a slightly panicked Libella. He murmured something under his breath as she passed by him, and she nodded, heading straight for me. "Oh, dear. I'm so sorry about earlier. I should have—"

I raised my hand. "Please, don't apologize. You did nothing wrong."

She stopped short, tilting her head at me, then shook the look of confusion from her face. "Okay, dear." She extended her hand toward my injured arm. "May I see your arm?" I placed it in her hand, and she called over her shoulder, "Do you want to help?"

Little did she know, Kyler had already vanished into the castle. "He wouldn't even if he were still there," I said confidently, not holding back my hostility toward him. However, considering how adamant he had been about people not touching me, you'd think he would have stayed. Maybe the secret to making him forget about it was to anger him enough that he wouldn't bother paying attention.

"Well," Libella sighed, placing both hands under my arm as if holding a platter. Her eyes met mine, "A warning for you then: this will not be pleasant."

I nodded and clenched my jaw as her gaze shifted to the bruise forming on my arm. A warming sensation spread through my arm from where Libella's hands rested, drawing my attention to her actions. It flowed to the area where I knew the break was, gently probing each part as if her magic were searching for the precise location of the break. Thinking it would help, I concentrated on the spot that had snapped and sensed her magic immediately latch onto that area. Libella peered at me through her lashes, a slight crease forming on her brow, but then the most excruciating pain kicked in, and I bit my tongue to stifle a scream.

Through gritted teeth, I asked, "Why does Kyler's help make such a difference in the pain?"

Libella's eyes met mine, shifting focus between them for a moment before she said, "Each bond between fae and dragons has its perks, just as it has its downfalls." She looked back down at my arm but continued, "The Kavaltis bond is unique. Your magic chose his, and his chose yours. The power within the connection helps you heal faster and alleviates the pain associated with the injury."

The pain radiated up to my shoulder, and it took everything in me not to jerk my arm away. It felt like sticking your tongue to a battery, but ten times worse. "How?" I managed to ask.

Libella didn't look up this time. "The one situated between the

Dynkoi and the injured bears the pain themselves."

My jaw dropped. There was no way… My thoughts returned to that day in the Jeep — when Mari used me to heal Kyler. I had been so worried about him that I hadn't thought to pay attention to how it actually worked. And when Kyler healed me, I didn't get to see it, nor did I feel any pain… But that was a different time, when I believed he might have actually cared for me. Clearly, that had been a misunderstanding on my part.

I felt that power surging through me to heal him, but I didn't recall any pain… "I helped heal Kyler," I said, forcing myself to ignore the pain in my arm. "Why don't I remember feeling any of his pain?"

She glanced at me briefly before turning her attention back to my healing arm. "You were probably too focused on the fact that he was dying," she whispered. She wasn't wrong. His pulse had been weak, and the cut was deep. Realizing he was dying had sent me into a frantic state. Mari had warned me it could be painful, but all I'd felt was the energy pulsing through me. I remembered yelling, but was that from the pain or the force of energy coming out of me?

The last time *I* was healed like this, I was unconscious. Now I understood why. Mari healed many of my injuries that day, and I knew that had I been awake, I probably would have fainted from the pain. Adding magic into the mix would have made me think I was dead or dreaming. The pain didn't come solely from the healing; instead, it felt like a pressure on the already painful wound, pulling it back into place. I could feel the magic knitting the bones together. It felt completely different than when Kyler healed me. When my back was sliced open, I only felt an indescribable bliss throughout my body after that warming sensation.

"What does the healing feel like to you?" I asked, trying to turn my attention from the pain.

Libella kept her eyes fixed on my arm, watching as the glow from her hands pulsed. "It begins with a warmth pooling in my core and flowing into my hands, gentle yet steady. Sometimes, there's a faint hum, a tingling in my fingers, as if the magic is searching for the pieces it needs to mend." The pressure on the wound eased along with the pain as Libella traced her fingers along the length of my arm. "But when it's a clean break or a messy injury, it almost feels as if the wound resists. I have to push through, like trudging through mud—thick, slow, and stubborn until it finally gives way."

The warming sensation in my arm vanished as Libella let go. The sharp pain from the break was gone, but a dull ache still radiated down to my hand. "Is it fully healed?" I asked, glancing back up to find Libella studying me.

"The break is mended, but the bone is probably still tender. Nothing a bath and a glass of glykos won't fix." She offered me a tight smile and turned toward the castle. "Come, we must get you ready for tonight."

Right. The dinner. The absolute last place I wanted to be, especially if I had to stick next to Kyler all night. As I trailed Libella to the castle door, I realized I had no idea what the night would bring. "What should I expect at the dinner tonight?" I had already asked Drako, but something else had taken priority.

"Did Nikylo not inform you?" Libella asked, though somewhat sternly.

"He just told me I had to stay with him and do whatever he says," I said, not hiding my annoyance. His possessiveness was starting to feel repetitive.

"The dinner is to celebrate Kaleb's return."

When Libella didn't expand on that, I sighed. "Okay, Kyler mentioned that mu—"

Libella turned on her heel to face me. "Rayleigh, you must not call him by that name."

I stopped just before I ran into her and studied her. The strictness in her voice almost hid the emotion I could see in her eyes. Almost. I narrowed my own. "Why?"

She straightened, locking eyes with me. "That is not his name. You must call him Nikylo."

There was something she wasn't telling me. What was it with people and not telling me things? Why was she getting so upset over his *name?* He had also snapped at me for calling him Kyler… "Okay. Fine. *Nikylo* told me what the dinner was for, but not what I could expect."

Satisfied with my correction, Libella continued down the hallway. "The King and Queen will address their court and the Fae Councilors, followed by a celebratory dinner—"

"The Fae Councilors?" I gasped, trying not to trip over my feet. That meant everyone I had learned about who held power in leadership would be at this dinner. "Why are they coming?"

"Because the King and Queen are respected by their fellow leaders, the Councilors attend all events involving the royal family." Libella turned onto the bridge connecting the hallways. "The royals will also attend events hosted by the Fae for their leadership."

Tucking away that nugget of information, I asked, "So the dinner is just that? A dinner? And some sort of speech?"

"Yes, there will be some mingling afterward, but you don't need to worry too much. These dinners are common, and you might find yourself attending another one while you're here."

My eyebrows drew together. "What will that one be for?"

"We will cross that bridge when it comes," Libella said, her tone final, indicating she wouldn't elaborate further.

As we exited the bridge and entered the familiar hallway, I kept my eyes on the walls, aware that there were doors yet seeing none as we walked past the portraits. "How do the doors to different rooms appear along this hallway?"

Libella glanced back at me with a hint of a smile. "Ah, the castle has finally piqued your curiosity enough to ask?" Her smile broadened slightly before she turned back to face forward. "The door will only appear when someone with permission to enter is nearby."

"Permission from who?" I asked, aware that not everyone held the authority to grant such permissions.

"Whichever royal deems it necessary." The hallway felt more familiar, suggesting we were likely close to Kyler's room. "Any royal can grant permission to any room, to whomever they choose."

I narrowed my eyes at her, recalling the secret door Mari and Kendall used last night. "Is there a way to bypass the permissions?"

Libella stopped walking, causing me to bump into her. I stumbled back when she turned to face me sharply. "No. If you are not allowed in a room, you will find no other way in. If you are in a room and suddenly denied access, you will find yourself outside of that room, likely not unharmed." She eyed me with suspicion. "Don't attempt to enter rooms for which you lack permission. Do you understand?"

The blunt reprimand caught me off guard, but I nodded. I had only wanted to ask about the secret magical doors. As her expression softened, I realized it might not have been a reprimand so much as a warning. The castle seemed to hold more magic within its walls than I had given it credit for. If it could remove me from any room on its own, then I definitely needed to be careful going forward. Still, I didn't expect to be granted access to many rooms, given my status in this place.

"Good." Libella pivoted on the ball of her foot and continued the rest of the way in silence. We hadn't been very far from Kyler's rooms, as I had suspected, and she entered the archway moments later. "The bath is ready for you. I will prepare your outfit for this evening."

I blinked. "What kind of outfit am I supposed to wear tonight?" Knowing Kyler, he probably picked out something else ridiculous that marked me as his property.

"Go bathe, and I will show you when you're done." With that, she vanished through the door with the big cushion.

Instead of satisfying my curiosity, I entered the bathroom and loosened the robe that was still wrapped around me. I hated that he had given me his own robe but understood that it was likely infused with his magic, or whatever he called to it. Xousía?

I stepped into the steaming bath, and every injury I had sustained that afternoon suddenly came to life. My adrenaline and distractions faded away, and the throbbing and stinging kicked in. I hissed at the heat as it crawled up my legs and onto my torso. I sank beneath the water and allowed it to heal the scratches and bruises across my body before coming up for air. I felt the magic now, having experienced what it did without the distraction of Kyler touching me or him dying. The warming sensation was the most prominent, acting like a quick-acting salve. The pain vanished almost instantly as I positioned myself at the edge of the tub to grab soap for my hair. It smelled oddly like the one I used back home. Dismissing the question that arose, I lathered my hair with it and ducked under the water, taking my time to rinse it out.

When I emerged, there were feet right outside the tub. Thankfully, I hadn't stood to my full height, but my eyes traveled up to find Kyler standing there with his arms crossed over his bare chest. Did he not know what a shirt was?

"What do you want, *Nikylo?*" I sneered, knowing that his presence at this exact moment was no accident.

His eyes flashed at my use of his proper name. I figured that if I was going to get scolded for calling him Kyler, I might as well start using his proper name in every circumstance. He held my gaze briefly before asking, "Do you remember your responsibilities for this evening?"

"Yes."

"Good." He walked to the sink, grabbed a bottle of something, and shook some onto his hands before applying it to his wet, curly locks, as if he had just finished his own bath. "In addition to the duties you're already aware of, I will introduce you to the Councilors. None know for sure about your powers, but they will sense it. You must not confirm your Ignalian lineage." His eyes met mine in the mirror. "Understood?"

Great. The demanding asshole was back. But what would be so bad about confirming my Ignalian lineage? And why were we suddenly able to talk about it so openly? I hadn't even been able to mention it to anyone, let alone him. But I wasn't going to question him on that or stop the conversation. "Yes, but if they can sense it, how will me not saying anything make a difference?"

He picked up another product from the sink and applied it to his neck and chest. The sweet, smoky scent drifted across the room, and I resisted the urge to take a deep breath. The smell was so familiar and comforting. I hated it. "Fortunately, that power is still suppressed and not as noticeable. However, the Ignalian Fae Councilor may still sense it. She hasn't encountered another one in a long time, but that doesn't mean she won't recognize it right away." He turned and leaned against the sink, crossing his arms again. "I will also work on concealing it. My recent research indicates that it's possible for me to hide an element, but I have no experience in doing so. It will be something I learn as we go."

I studied him from my position crouched beneath the water, remembering that my nakedness held no significance for him, yet I still felt the need to hide. He seemed to be in a strange mood, open to conversation. Not an asshole, but not the friend I once knew either. Some weird in-between. I could work with that. "What about my Udarian and Annysian lines?"

"There are already rumors circulating about those, but it's just speculation. Most people won't believe it until they see it. But the Councilors? They'll know. Especially Marta and Oliver." When I gave him a questioning look, he clarified, "Udarian and Annysian Councilors, respectively."

"Oh." A thought struck me, and I selected my next words carefully, unsure if he would respond. "The Omonian Councilor..." I trailed off, but Nikylo understood where my thoughts had wandered.

"Yes, Tom will be there."

A mix of relief and sadness washed over me. "Do the girls know?"

"No. He probably won't be pleased to discover that they have been claimed. This may create tension at the gathering."

I chewed on the inside of my cheek, then looked back up at Nikylo. "Why so forthcoming with all this information?"

"You need to be ready for tonight."

"Five minutes ago, you threw me from your back."

He slightly tilted his chin down, the corner of his mouth lifting. "That's a bit dramatic, isn't it?"

"It absolutely is not dramatic. My arm was broken, and you just threw me on the ground, fully aware that I was injured and weak."

He raised an eyebrow at my tone but nodded slightly. "I apologize for throwing you from my back—"

"Twice." His eyebrows shot up at my interruption. "You threw me off twice today."

His smirk grew. "I apologize for throwing you from my back *twice*. My temper tends to flare up when Valisdrako is involved."

I raised my brows at the casual use of his dragon's full name. When I considered calling him out for it, I remembered he was allowed to use his dragon's name, according to Drako. "That's a shitty excuse for your behavior." I crossed my arms over my chest, realizing that the bruise on the mended one was completely healed with no lingering pain. This bathwater really was magical.

"No excuse, Sunshine. Honest truth. He dislikes when I interrupt him or keep him from you, and you already know that his temper tantrums require something I can't access here." I held back a chuckle that bubbled inside me. Were the lollipops the only way to tame his dragon? "You might want to remember that. He's not impossible to control, but it's definitely harder when you're around."

I smirked, knowing that Nikylo hated not having that control. Sure, his power was stronger here on Niccodra, but that meant Drako was also more powerful. I decided right then to use my power to summon him only when absolutely necessary. "Got it. Anything else?"

"Just remember everything I've told you, and you may find a visit to my father's wing of the castle in the near future." The sparkle in his eye made me question why he was acting so—

I gasped. "Mitch?"

He pushed off the sink and stalked toward the door. "Behave tonight, Sunshine." It wasn't confirmation, but I knew that's what he meant. My heart was racing wildly in my chest. I wasn't sure what had gotten into him to make him have a normal conversation, even if I was in the tub and vulnerable. Perhaps that's why he approached me then, because he knew I wouldn't do anything rash.

But none of that really mattered. *I was going to see Mitch.*

As soon as the door clicked shut behind him, I hurried out of the tub and grabbed the towel from the sink, wrapping it around myself before entering the bedroom. Libella waited patiently by the vanity, which had replaced the table from this morning. I paused when I saw what hung from the wall. "I'm supposed to wear *that?*"

Libella motioned to the chair in front of the vanity, inviting me to sit. "Yes. Special request from the Royals."

My jaw dropped as I sank heavily into the chair, staring at the crimson dress hanging on the wall. It was like nothing I'd ever worn before. The material shimmered in the light and featured a slit up one side of the skirt, but not high enough to reveal anything. I wondered what the purpose of wearing that dress was and why the Royals had a say in it. Wasn't Nikylo the one in charge of my outfits?

When I voiced my question, Libella sighed, a sound unlike any I'd heard from her before. "The King and Queen gave me the orders. I simply follow them." I almost interrupted, but she continued. "My guess is they are showcasing you as their prize. They won."

I shifted my gaze from the dress to her reflection in the mirror while she ran a comb through my hair. "What do you mean?"

"The rumors that have been circulating around the castle have reached the ears of the Fae, somehow." A glance in the mirror told me she might know how they found out. "Ever since it became known that Fae children were hidden in your realm, they have been trying to reach you. To find you before we did." She used 'we' in a way that suggested she didn't include herself.

"But why would they want to find us if we were purposely hidden away?"

"The Fae are protective of their kin. Their familial nature is affectionate and protective, and knowing you were alone in another realm triggered their instinct to bring you back home safely."

"But we weren't alone. Our…well, my Omada was there to protect me. Tom was there with the twin—" My eyes widened at a sudden thought. "Wait, were the twin's parents part of my Omada?"

She looked at me in the mirror with approval as she began a braid on one side of my head. "Yes. Originally, you had Taj and Lysan alongside Theo, Stefano, Bastiel, and a few others. But due to your lineage, the mission was top secret and couldn't be discussed by anyone who knew. It was a binding magical contract, that is until you turned sixteen."

"What happened when I turned sixteen?"

Libella pinned the braid halfway back on my head and began working on the other side. "That's when your Omada members were supposed to inform you about your lineage."

I thought back to the days around my sixteenth birthday. No one ever tried to sit me down and talk to me about anything. I hadn't even met any of my Omada properly at that time, let alone known anything about them. I was pretty sure Arabella would have told me if she had known

—

The memory of the car accident replayed in my mind, the one I had apparently suppressed. Arabella was urging me to run, to not let them catch me. She knew. For how long, I wasn't sure, but she knew we were Fae. That people were hunting us. Had she found out on our birthday? Why hadn't I been told? Why hadn't she told me? Had she already met Theo? No, that was impossible. She wouldn't keep someone like him a secret from me. In my mind, only one other person made sense. It was the same conclusion I'd reached when the memory first resurfaced. I found Libella's eyes in the mirror again. "Who told my sister?"

Her eyes softened, filled with sadness as she whispered, "I think you already know, dear."

I shook my head slowly, "No… no, because that means… that means…" I searched her eyes for some sign of confirmation, but Libella turned her gaze to my head instead. "Why?" My voice cracked as I raised it. Libella still wouldn't look up, focused on pinning my hair. I spun around to face her, her hands freezing in midair as my hair slipped through her fingers. "Why didn't you tell me?"

When she met my gaze, her hands dropped to rest on her stomach. "I can't."

Tears welled in my eyes. "You said you didn't know if he was Fae."

She shook her head. "I said there is speculation he might not be human."

"But that means…" I trailed off. My dad had been part of my Omada all along. His secret job was to protect Arabella and me. All the signs pointed directly to it. How had I not realized? Would it have even mattered if I did? I couldn't save Mitch. Not on my own. But who could I even talk to about this? Who would be able to rescue him from whatever fate awaited? "What was my father?" I asked, looking up to find Libella studying me.

"I can't say," she replied plainly.

"Can't or won't?"

"I *can't.*"

I squinted at her. "Something is preventing you from saying?" I guessed, based on what she had said earlier about the binding magical contract. She just held my gaze. "Magic of some sort?" No confirmation or denial. But I figured she could deny it if I were wrong. Sighing in frustration, I turned around in my chair, studying my hands in my lap. "What will happen to Mitch?"

Libella's hands hesitantly returned to my hair, wrapping a strand around her finger. "I don't know. That will be decided at the trial." She let go of the strand, and it sprang back into a perfect curl.

I blinked dramatically. "How did you do that?"

She chuckled softly at my reaction. "My dragon provides warmth to my finger for this," she explained as she wrapped another piece.

My jaw dropped. It seemed silly for a dragon to lend its heat for curling hair, but a smile formed on my face. "Interesting." I focused back on our conversation. "Will I be able to attend Mitch's trial?"

"I'm sure they'll want to ask you some questions, so yes."

I chewed on my cheek while she finished curling my hair and pinning it in place on my head. There wasn't much else to say, and I knew she wouldn't answer all the questions I wanted to ask. I was starting to forget some of the questions I needed to write down by this point. *I need that damn notebook*, I thought to myself.

A small *thunk* pulled me from my thoughts, and I glanced at the vanity to find the pot with the flower Romeo gave me. But that wasn't the source of the noise. Right next to it was a notebook. I attempted to suppress a smile but failed miserably. *You just couldn't stay out of my head, could you?*

I told you, Nikylo's voice echoed down the bond. *It's impossible.*

Why are you being so cordial? I asked, not bothering to beat around the bush.

Because it's just us.

That didn't stop you from being an ass earlier.

Do you prefer when I'm an ass? I could hear the smirk in his voice.

Ignoring his question, I picked up the notebook and asked another. *Are you actually going to answer my questions?*

If I can.

I clenched my teeth. Something felt off. He was being too open. It reminded me of the friend I thought I'd made back at the Dengalow. But I'd promised myself I wouldn't fall for that. He couldn't be trusted. Not if he knew Kaleb was his brother. Not with the way he'd been treating me. *Thank you,* I said curtly. *And to answer your question, yes.*

He didn't respond, so I opened the notebook and wrote down what I could remember while Libella finished styling my hair. She then worked on my face, using their version of cosmetics, which mostly consisted of lining my eyes and adding a bit of color to my lips and cheeks. When she stepped back, I glanced at my half-finished look in the mirror. Libella truly worked her magic, and as soon as I had the dress on, I knew it would tie everything together. I gave her a small smile, set the notebook on the vanity, and stood so she could help me with the dress.

A knock sounded at the door just as Libella finished lacing up the back. "One moment, please," Libella called out, loud enough for whoever was waiting to hear her. She tied off the laces and turned me toward the mirror so I could see myself. The surprise on my face spoke volumes. I looked absolutely stunning. The dress was low-cut but not too revealing, and it flared slightly at my waist. I ran my hands along my stomach, feeling how the fabric hugged my skin. It was soft as velvet but not nearly as thick. It felt similar to the material my riding leathers were made of. I could feel every touch as if the dress weren't even there.

I was so busy admiring myself in the mirror that I didn't remember someone had knocked on the door until Libella called my name. "Someone is here to see you."

A butterfly fluttered from my stomach to my heart. I turned and walked toward the door, and that butterfly disappeared as I took in my visitor.

"Libella, please wait outside," Kaleb said with a warm smile on his face.

SIXTEEN
All of Your Lies

"What are you doing here?" I asked, crossing my arms tightly around my body, mostly to showcase my anger toward him but also to hide the way my hands were shaking. I no longer knew what this person in front of me was capable of, and that terrified me.

"I needed to see you," his gentle voice reached my ears. Unfortunately, Libella could do nothing against Kaleb's request, so she stepped outside, where Leighton waited, her eyes cast to the floor. Every part of me wanted to scream at Kaleb as soon as the door clicked shut, but with Leigh in his possession… There was no telling what he might do.

I raised an eyebrow at his words, not believing their gentleness for a second, and repeated my question.

"I needed to see you, to see if you were okay," he said. When I didn't respond, he tried again. "I haven't been able to talk to you, and after what happened to you in the dungeons—"

"You mean what happened to the twins, Mari, and my mom," I interrupted. "Because all I did was sit and watch as they were dragged away."

"Still," he reached out to comfort me, but I couldn't help flinching. He froze, his eyes filling with hurt, then dropped his hand back to his side. "I can't imagine how hard that was for you."

"Nothing that happened to me down there can compare to what they went through," I argued.

He held my gaze and took a deep breath. "I'm still sorry you had to go through that."

Did he forget that he came to visit me in that very dungeon the night we were thrown in? I almost called him out on it but decided I wanted to see how long he would drag this out. As he held my gaze, my skin crawled and my anger simmered just below the surface.

When he realized I wasn't going to say anything more, he sighed and looked down at the floor. "I know you don't believe me—"

"So stop pretending!" I shouted, unable to hold it back any longer, and his head snapped up at my tone. "Stop pretending like you didn't betray me! Like you didn't betray your friends of over ten years! We were locked in a dungeon for a month. *Tortured* for a month!" Even meeting his gaze was difficult because the honey brown used to soothe my soul in so many ways. Now, I couldn't trust the person they belonged to—the person I once trusted the most. "You broke everything between us," I choked out. "Everything. I don't even know who to trust anymore. I have to question that *because of you.*"

He stepped toward me, but I stepped back in response. "Please, just let me explain."

"I already know enough," I countered.

He clenched his jaw, his eyes drifting around the room before settling on me once more. "What did he tell you?"

"Nikylo? Nothing. No one has said a word to me," I replied. "Except Aaidan."

A fire flashed in Kaleb's eyes. Through clenched teeth, he said, "And?"

"Your lies won't work with me. He told me enough to understand that the person I knew, the one I loved—my best friend—is gone."

A light faded from his eyes, and his shoulders slumped. He took another step toward me, reaching out once more, but I stepped out of reach. "Rayleigh, please. Just…" He kept his hand extended as if I would finally come around and lowered his chin to meet my gaze. "Just let me explain."

"There's nothing you can say that will make up for what you did!" I seethed, swatting his hand away. "You lied to me. You told me you loved me." The emotion choked my throat, causing the words to come out as a whisper. "How could you do something like that? How could you be my best friend for years, only to betray me to these *monsters?*"

He shook his head. "It's not that simple, Ray."

"No, you don't get to call me that," I snapped. "You're not my friend. That name is reserved for those closest to me."

He closed his eyes and pursed his lips before saying, "There is so much you don't know."

"Again. Nothing you say will change my mind."

"Will you at least listen?" he pleaded, his honey-brown eyes fixed on mine with a sincerity I recognized. "He won't—" he paused, clearing his throat. "I can't tell you everything, but will you *please* just listen?"

I didn't speak for a long moment. My curiosity urged me to hear him out, to understand his reasoning for everything he did. However, I also knew it was nearly time for the dinner celebrating his return. *Nikylo?* I whispered down the bond, reinforcing my walls against Kaleb. As much as I wanted to believe his words wouldn't change anything, the person in front of me was someone I had been close to for years. I'd trusted him with everything. He had seen me at my lowest because I had allowed it. He brought me through some of the hardest times in my life without asking for anything in return. He never opened up to me like I did with him, even though I thought he had. So much of his life remained a mystery to me, but now he wanted to share it? After claiming our entire relationship—our whole friendship—was a lie?

Yes, Sunshine? Nikylo's smooth voice brought me back from my thoughts.

I hesitated to tell him what was happening only because if I did, I knew he would show up. That would cause Kaleb to shut down and not say anything. I wanted to know why he betrayed me, but I wouldn't find out if Nikylo interrupted. *How much time do I have before dinner?* I knew I might regret the choice to keep him from knowing Kaleb was here, but I needed to know.

Someone will be retrieving you in ten minutes, he said. *Why?*

I was on the verge of telling him the truth, but I also knew that if anything happened, he would be there in a heartbeat. *I just wanted to know how long I had to write my questions.* Before he could respond or try to figure out what was really going on, I did my best to block my thoughts from reaching him and turned back to Kaleb. "You have five minutes."

He sighed with relief and gestured toward the chairs in the room, but I shook my head. "You can say what you need to right here."

Pursing his lips, he nodded curtly and began his tale. "I was brought to Earth at the same time as you. Some say I was sent away. Others say I was stolen. I'm not sure which is true, as I was so young." When I merely stared at him, he continued. "When I was old enough, I was told the reason I was brought there: I had to become friends with you and Arabella and learn everything I could about you."

"I already know this," I started.

"But what you don't realize is that I actually grew to care about both of you," he interrupted.

"*Bullshit.*" Though his words seemed sincere, all I could think about was how he spoke to me in that dungeon. The look in his eyes when he bragged about tricking me my whole life.

He worked his jaw but pressed on. "I made friends in a world where I felt alone. I got to experience a childhood I never could have because of you two and the twins." At the mention of the others he betrayed, I felt a surge of anger but kept silent. "You brought me in, and I set my mission aside. I was just a kid! I wanted friends." He sighed, realizing his words weren't having the impact he hoped for. "Our backyard battles and adventures were things I knew we would have done here, but only because that's what I was told. It would have been different, with magic and other elements in this world, but I knew I had that to look forward to for whenever we all returned to Niccodra together."

"So you've been here before?" I pressed, not allowing him to believe it would have been the same if we were all here instead of on Earth.

"Yes," he confirmed. "The family vacations I took were to bring me back here."

The way he said it suggested that the trips were anything but vacations. "And who is your family?"

His eyebrows pulled together as he studied me. "The King and Queen. And Nikylo."

I raised an eyebrow, still questioning how the King I met in the dining hall could be the same one that Kaleb claimed put him through rigorous training. The King did kill two guards without moving a muscle, though. I chose to focus on the other part of his 'family.' "Then why didn't

Nikylo recognize you on Earth?"

"Because he never knew me," he said simply. "I was just an infant when I arrived on Earth. He was one of many who believed I had been lost."

My eyes narrowed. "You weren't lost, though, were you?"

He locked eyes with me but didn't respond to my question. "The people who took care of me on Earth weren't the King and Queen, but they were familiar with them—close to them."

"So you were kidnapped?" He still didn't answer me. "If you really want me to believe you, your best chance is to answer my questions. Avoiding them just makes me think that everything you're saying is a lie."

"I can't say what happened. I was too young," he countered, his voice rising. "What I told you about my training is true. I was tortured to endure the pain. I played the role of my father's spy because I had no choice. If I didn't make my reports, I would be beaten into oblivion."

"Your father, the King?" I finally asked, seeking clarification about the man who trained and tortured Kaleb, turning him into this… monster.

"He never told me he was king." He cast his eyes down to the floor. "But his lessons were brutal. Some of the 'family vacations' were just me recovering." When he met my gaze again, tears lined his eyes, and I almost felt sorry for him. Almost. His voice dropped to a whisper, "I didn't think any of what I reported would actually make a difference." He took a hesitant step forward as he noticed my expression shift to realization. Surprisingly, I didn't step back but stood my ground.

"And the day Arabella died?" I wasn't certain he was involved, but when he stumbled back a step, it gave me all the confirmation I needed.

He looked at me as if I'd hit him. "You can't seriously believe I did that," he said, his voice barely audible.

"What about my father?" I continued, stepping closer to him, forcing him to back away as he shook his head. "Mitch? Ma? Ken and Leigh? Their parents? What about them, huh? Because I'm pretty sure that the day you came down to that dungeon and told me it was all a lie from the beginning, you sealed your own fate." My voice rose as I backed him against the wall. While the terror on his face grew with each accusation, his eyes betrayed him. The tears were gone, and there was nothing there. A darkness stared back. "The look on your face tells me everything I need to know. Whether what you're saying is true or not, you still played a part in telling them what they needed to know about my family to get them killed or captured. So, no, Kaleb. I won't listen to what you have to say anymore. Stop trying to convince me you're a good guy in a bad situation. Stop trying to convince me it wasn't all an act. Because I know you. I know your tells. I know when you're lying. You may have helped me through things in my life that I could have never done on my own, but you no longer have the privilege of being that close to me. So I suggest you stop acting like a lovesick puppy because I won't fall for it again."

I tried to catch my breath, controlling the anger that had spiraled into backing him against the wall. His face dropped, then his chin, and he finally closed his eyes. We stood there for a moment—him backed against the wall, me standing my ground before him, trying to compose myself and waiting for him to concede.

He took a deep breath, and when he met my eyes again, he did so through his eyebrows. A window to his soul opened… and that darkness flowed out as a slow grin spread across his face.

My breath caught in my throat as I stepped back, a chill racing up my spine. His face morphed from the gentle, kind, and loving friend I knew into the monster that had used me my entire life. Kaleb was gone. I had already mourned him once. I wasn't about to do it again. "Leave," I demanded, thrusting my arm toward the door.

The smirk remained on his face as he pushed off the wall, towering over me while I tried not to back down. His head tilted slightly as he assessed the fear I was sure was evident on my face. "Like I said, there's so much you don't know, girlie," he said, his voice a haunting version of the one I once loved so much. I shivered at the nickname, contemplating how I'd grown so comfortable with it. "As long as I have one of you, I have all of you." He reached to touch my face, but I slapped it away. Before I realized it, he had caught my wrist with one hand and my waist with the other, twisting us around and throwing me backward. I let out a cry of pain as my head slammed into the wall, making me see stars. He was there immediately, pinning my arm above my head while his other forearm pressed against my collarbone, keeping me in place. "There is no stopping this, Rayleigh," he whispered in my ear. How did he pin me so easily? I tried to knee him in the groin, but he shifted his hips to block me and chuckled. "I will get what is owed to me in the end. And if I don't, at least I have leverage." He unfurled the fist at my shoulder, revealing his palm and the madí that appeared there.

I sucked in a breath, swinging my eyes back to his. "You wouldn't." But I knew he would. The day he claimed Leighton, he acted like he had no idea what he was doing. He played his family like a violin. He knew exactly what he was doing when he chose Leighton over Kendall and how that would affect not only me but also the twins and Mari.

"Until you release yourself from that bond with my brother, you will keep your distance from Leighton. You will not speak to her, you will not train with her, and you will not be allowed near her unless I am present." He stepped back just enough to meet my gaze. "You will watch me break her in ways you never thought possible."

"No…" I pleaded, searching his eyes for any trace of the boy I once knew. But there was none.

"You *will* break that bond with my brother and choose to be *mine*. Because, in case you forgot, I know you, too, girlie. You won't sacrifice your friend's safety for your own." He released my hand above my head and ran his finger down my face. I tried to jerk away, but there was nowhere for me to go. "It's only a matter of time." His finger left a hot trail down my cheek. He gave me another wicked grin, pushed off of me, and straightened the copper tunic he was wearing, pulling his cuffs down to his wrists as he walked back to the door. "See you at dinner," he smirked, opening the door to reveal Libella and Leigh waiting patiently outside.

I caught Leigh's gaze, and tears filled my own eyes. Her face showed no emotion until she offered me a warm smile. A normal one. One that told me she had no idea what was about to happen to her. I couldn't do anything to warn her, and there was nothing I could do to help. Even if I tried to free myself from the bond Nikylo and I shared, he would never let me go. He'd made that clear enough with every rule he imposed on me.

Leigh gave me a small wave before stepping in line behind Kaleb. I waved back, even as tears streamed down my face, watching my friend follow the person who had promised to hurt her. I knew in my heart that it was all part of his plan, his twisted way of tormenting me in the process—I understood there was nothing I could do, but I couldn't just stand by without her knowing I was here for her. I had to try.

"Leigh!" I shouted as I rushed into the hall to stop her. Both she and Kaleb turned around at my call. I ignored him and focused on Leigh's bright blue eyes. "I love you." With those three words, I tried to convey everything else I wanted to say: *Don't trust Kaleb. Nothing he says is true, and he only wants to hurt you. I promise I'll get you out of there. Just hold on a little longer. And remember, you're not alone. You're never alone.* I knew it wouldn't change anything—that she would probably still get hurt and might not be the same when I finally got her back. But I *would* get her back. I wouldn't leave her with that monster. There had to be a way to rescue her, and I would find it. I had to.

"I love you too, Ray," she smiled, then turned at the sound of Kaleb beckoning her to follow.

A hand settled on my shoulder, and I turned to see Libella watching me intently. "What did he say to you, Rayleigh?"

I turned to watch my friend and my enemy disappear down the winding hallway and sniffled. "Nothing I didn't already know."

SEVENTEEN
repercussions

The only reason I didn't curl up into a ball was because of the hard work Libella had put into my look for the evening. When my escort knocked on the door, Libella found me studying my thumbs after sinking to the floor when Kaleb left. "It's time to go, dear," she said quietly, having said nothing since we watched them walk down the hall. There was no telling what was going on in her mind. For all I knew, she had informed Nikylo about Kaleb's visit. I did not look forward to his reaction to me not telling him.

But I had to set all that aside and focus on more important matters— like the fact that if things didn't go well tonight at the dinner, I wouldn't be able to see Mitch before his trial tomorrow. I folded and unfolded the short note I had written to him. It wasn't much, but it was enough to warn him of what was to come and to tell him how much I loved him. I refused to say goodbye because there was still no telling what the King would do. I just hoped tonight wouldn't be the last time I saw him.

I took a steadying breath and stood, following Libella to the door. I groaned at the sight of Naila waiting for me on the other side.

She waggled her fingers at me, a big grin on her face. "Hello, Kató."

I plastered a smile on my own face. "Hello, Bitch."

She blinked, seemingly unfazed, and scanned my outfit slowly from head to toe. "Nice dress." The insincere compliment made me roll my eyes.

I took in her dark blue dress, which left little to the imagination as it hugged every curve and featured slits on both sides that went uncomfortably high. The neckline plunged almost to her navel, and it had no sleeves. I met her eyes again. "Wish I could say the same," I shrugged, pushing past her into the hall.

The disgruntled noise she made had me giggling to myself. This girl wanted to mess with me today? Oh, she had no idea what she was in for. I didn't wait for her to catch up; I just kept walking until she finally stepped in front of me, shoulder-checking me as she passed. Deep down, I hoped that I could spar with her one day. I wanted to show her exactly who she was messing with and the mistakes she was making in doing so.

When the archway to the dining hall appeared, she vanished inside without waiting to see if I would follow. My nerves had intensified the closer we got, fully aware of who would be present. Not only Kaleb with Leigh, but the entire royal family, their court, and the Fae Councilors. I didn't know if anything specific rested on my shoulders during the dinner, except that I had to keep my Ignalian lineage a secret and stay with Nikylo so I could see Mitch. I focused on making those my only goals and trying not to give Kaleb the satisfaction of knowing that everything he said earlier weighed heavily on my heart.

Taking a deep breath, I stepped toward the idle chatter emanating from the hall.

I wasn't prepared for the transformation the entire room had undergone, nor for the number of people within.

Every decoration and piece of furniture was different, and even the flooring had been altered. There were a mix of colors, with the most prominent being copper—such a strange color for royal dining. Swirls of ivory, turquoise, and midnight blue flowed throughout, and the main table was made of a marble-like material, combining all four colors. I had never seen anything like it.

The crowd fell into a hushed silence, and I realized it was because everyone was looking at me. I glanced around the room and then down at myself, sighing. The red dress was certainly intended to make me stand out since everyone else wore colors that matched the room. Swallowing hard, I tried to calm my nerves as I lifted my head and walked alone into the room toward the second-to-last person I wanted to spend the evening with.

He stood near the dais where a smaller table was set up, his back turned to me as he remained engaged in conversation. He must not have realized everyone else in the room had stopped talking. Even the person he was speaking with wasn't paying attention to him. When he finally seemed aware of this, he slowly turned to see what everyone else was looking at.

My breath caught as he met my gaze. Why did he still have that effect on me? My heart raced wildly as one corner of his mouth tilted higher and higher. If he wasn't careful, that dimple would pop out, and I'd be toast. I forced myself to look away from him and dragged my eyes down to take in his detailed midnight blue tunic. It fit snugly against his torso and flared at his hips, accentuating his fit figure. The front extended down to the top of his thighs, while the back split in the middle and reached the back of his thighs. The pants matched the top, and his dark boots reached his knees. An interesting wardrobe compared to what I grew up with, but it seemed to be the normal choice in this realm, as most of the men in the room wore something similar.

Nikylo met me halfway, his eyes slowly trailing from my face to my toes and back. When his gaze found mine again, there was something there I'd only seen a handful of times. Something I could never quite place. "You certainly know how to make an entrance."

"All I did was walk into the room, just like I'm sure everyone else did," I whispered back.

"Yes, but not everyone can silence a crowd like this." He casually waved toward the room around us.

"Didn't seem to stop you from talking."

"That's because my back was turned."

"So if you'd seen me walk in, you would've been speechless?" I raised my brow. "That'd be a first."

He scoffed, "Guess we'll never know."

"I guess we won't." My nerves had gotten the best of me, and I realized how easily we had slipped back into our old ways. I cleared my throat and lifted my chin. "My responsibilities?"

He lowered his chin, his green eyes darkening slightly as he offered his elbow to me. "You're not as snarky as usual," he whispered.

I gently grasped his elbow. "It's the nerves."

"That hasn't stopped you before," he glanced at me sideways, guiding me deeper into the room.

"I've never felt this nervous around you," I retorted, locking eyes with him.

A smirk played on his lips as he guided us to the table. "Oh, I'm certain you've been this nervous around me before." He winked, and I could only roll my eyes.

"Don't flatter yourself," I attempted to tease, but it fell flat. I realized he was trying to distract me from the crowd around us, but it didn't seem to help as much as he'd hoped. My heart was still in my throat at the thought of meeting every leader in this realm.

"I'll gladly show you the memory," he chided, not pausing for any of the people who appeared to be waiting to speak with him. When I glanced at him sideways, he grinned, and a vivid image flashed in my mind.

We were in his bedroom at the Dengalow, and he was kneeling in front of me.

I pressed my lips together, shaking the image from my mind. "That was a different time."

"Was it?" he asked, attempting to catch my eye again.

"Yes." I had intended to say it confidently, but it didn't come out that way at all. In fact, I seemed to be questioning it myself as he pulled a chair out at the head table for me.

Stop being nice, I scolded down the bond.

Surprise flashed across his face. *Don't get used to it.* His eyes gazed out at the crowd, still watching us. *Tonight is about Kaleb, but Father never wants to upset the Councilors, for fear they might start something.*

What does that have to do with you being nice to me?

If they notice you're unhappy or being treated poorly, things could go south quickly. He guided me to the chair he had pulled out, and I took a seat as he pushed it in behind me.

So, his actions were all about formalities. Good to know. I glanced out at the crowd, which had begun to whisper among themselves, still stealing glances at me. Libella hadn't lied about the rumors; these people already knew who I was and had been eagerly awaiting my arrival. I tried to spot familiar faces in the crowd, but most were new. From what I knew of the people in this realm, I could see Fae mixed in with the

Drakalasson. There was something about their physiques that made it easier to distinguish between them. The Fae were lithe yet toned, with sharper features and pointed ears, while the Drakalasson were broader, their rugged features giving them a rougher appearance. Both were beautiful in their own ways, but I could definitely see the differences watching them mingle together.

A head with black braids came into view, and I recognized Romeo as he navigated through the dining hall with a tray of food resting on his shoulder. He paused to offer his food to several people as he walked by. I turned to see Nikylo sitting next to me. "Romeo works in the kitchens?"

Nikylo worked his jaw, focusing on the dark-skinned male as he approached us with the tray. "Yes. It's one of his many duties in the castle."

"What else does he do?" I wondered aloud, but he was now climbing the stairs to our table. Instead of waiting for Nikylo's answer, I offered Romeo a warm smile. "Hi, Romeo."

His eyes shifted to Nikylo, who merely stared at him before turning to me and giving a brief nod. "Good evening, Rayleigh. I hope you're enjoying being back in Niccoddra."

A small laugh escaped me. Such a tame greeting compared to his last one. If only he knew what I'd been through since being brought back. But I nodded, saying, "It's different from anything I could have imagined." Which wasn't a lie, because I don't think I could have envisioned being in this realm, let alone the events that had occurred to me since arriving.

His smile widened as he lowered the tray for me to see. "Would you like a zymi?"

"A what?"

"They are similar to your pastries from the other realm," Nikylo's low voice rumbled. I shot him a dramatic side eye, aware that he was still glaring at Romeo.

Shaking my head at his obvious dislike for the young Fae, I grabbed a couple of pastries from Romeo's tray and thanked him before he vanished into the crowd again. I placed one of the zymis in front of Nikylo and said, "Eat. It might help with the frown lines on your face."

Nikylo instantly relaxed his face, making me suppress a giggle.

I took a bite of my pastry and sighed as the flavors danced on my tongue. I hadn't tasted anything this delicious since arriving in Niccodra. Nikylo's comparison to pastries wasn't far off, but they were much less dry; they practically melted in my mouth. The fruity center reminded me of raspberries with a hint of dark chocolate. I devoured the rest of it in one bite, licking my fingers clean.

A chuckle next to me made me whip my head to Nikylo. He wore a smirk and had clearly been watching me enjoy my treat.

"What?" I snapped, my cheeks already burning.

The smirk deepened as he leaned closer and whispered, "I wasn't aware you were capable of such cute and innocent noises."

The heat from my cheeks spread to my whole face. "I don't make cute and innocent noises!" I whispered angrily, making sure no one else was close enough to hear. When I looked back at Nikylo, his expression was nothing short of mischievous.

"Oh, I'm sure you don't." My jaw dropped as he chuckled darkly, hooking his finger under my chin to close my mouth. "Best keep that conversation for when it's just the two of us, Sunshine." He grabbed a glass that had appeared in front of him at some point and downed the contents in one gulp.

"What is that?" I asked, doing my best to push away the thoughts that flooded my mind from his comments. Why did he always have to fluster me so much?

"Libations. And no, you can't have any," he said before I could even ask, because damn—I desperately needed something to help me forget.

"Why not?" I wasn't certain whether alcohol laws were the same in Niccodra as in my hometown, but it didn't seem like it as I looked out at the crowd and saw a young girl down one—

"Kendall!" I made to stand, but a hand landed on my arm. I glared at Nikylo as he pushed me back to my seat.

"You stay here. She can come to you."

"Why can't I go down there?"

He raised an eyebrow. "You said you remembered your responsibilities."

"I do," I snapped, pulling my arm free. "If I have to be next to you all night, then *you* can follow *me*." I pushed myself up again before he could stop me and hurried down the stairs, hearing a grumble of protests behind me as his chair scraped against the floor, presumably following me.

Weaving through the crowd, I tried to focus on where I had seen Kendall. The number of people hadn't seemed so large when I entered earlier or while I was sitting on the dais just now. But as I found myself in the middle of it, I felt overwhelmed by the sheer number of bodies surrounding me. They were all quite a bit taller than I am, not to mention larger. Who knew dragon shifters had such imposing statures?

I stood on my tiptoes, trying and failing to see above or between their bodies to where I had seen my friend just moments ago. I thought I was headed in the right direction, but with my senses overwhelmed, I started second-guessing myself. Were there really that many people in this room? How had I lost track of her? I spun in a circle, thinking I'd missed her by accident, but found the people around me closing in. They weren't looming over me or even looking at me, but every way I turned, I bumped into someone.

My breathing quickened as I struggled to push my way out, but I couldn't even see where the crowd ended. There were too many of them. My vision faded from the outside in—

A hand closed around my wrist, making me scream before arms wrapped tightly around me, pushing my face into their chest so I couldn't see anything around me. "Shh… you're okay." The familiar voice helped me relax in their arms, and I let out a choked sob into their shoulder. "Where were you heading?"

"Kendall. I thought I saw Kendall," I whispered, pulling back to find blue-green eyes locked onto mine. "Did you bring her with you?"

Mari smiled, "Yes. She's right over there." She pointed over my shoulder, and I turned to see my friend shoving a zymi into her mouth just like I had. A laugh escaped from me as I made my way through the clear path to Kendall. When our eyes met, she quickly put down everything in her hands and ran to wrap her arms around me. A low growl rumbled in my head, and I mentally flipped off Nikylo.

"Ray, I'm so glad to see you!" she said, her voice muffled against my hair. "I heard what happened, but I wasn't allowed to visit you." She pulled back, gripping my shoulders to look me over from head to toe.

"Are you okay?"

"I'm fine. Lucky to be here, I guess, but fine." I gave her a weak smile. Tears brimmed my eyes as my thoughts drifted from what had happened with Aaidan to my conversation with Kaleb. I turned to Mari, who was just a few steps behind me, her eyes scanning the room until she noticed me looking at her. "Can you two come to Nikylo's chambers tonight? Like you did last night?" Mari sighed, starting to shake her head. "Please. It's important."

She studied me for a moment, then whispered, "I'll see what I can do."

"Ah, Mari," Nikylo's voice called from behind me. "Fancy meeting you here."

Mari straightened and moved quickly to Kendall's side. "Niko," she said, nodding in my direction. "You should keep her away from the crowds. Her anxiety is still just below the surface."

My eyebrows knitted together at Mari's observation, but Nikylo didn't miss a beat. "She was fine. I was steps behind her. Besides," he took a sip of his new drink, the glass already half empty. "She won't need me if she's got you controlling those emotions."

Mari's face turned pale as she met my gaze. "Ray, I would never..." She looked back at Nikylo. "Why would you say that?" He didn't respond but took another drink while holding her gaze. "What's gotten into you?"

Nikylo raised his brows, surprised by the change in Mari's tone—or perhaps it was the way she spoke to him.

I raised my hand to stop him from answering and Mari from continuing. "It's fine, Mari. I know you wouldn't do that. Nikylo is just... well, Nikylo." I stepped closer to the girls and whispered, "I'll see you tonight." I met Ken's gaze; she must have seen the emotions in mine because the light in her eyes dimmed. I reached out to touch her cheek, but Nikylo cleared his throat behind me. I clenched my teeth, dropped my arm, and huffed loud enough for him to hear. When I opened my eyes, I put as much as I could into my eyes. "I love you. I promise I'll fill you in later." Ken nodded, and I turned back to Nikylo. "Stop being rude, or I'll take your *libations* for myself." I stormed past him, but he grabbed my elbow.

"You will do best to remember what's at stake, Sunshine." His eyes pierced into mine. The green shimmered in a way I hadn't noticed before, and I understood it was likely due to the liberties he was taking with his drinks.

I yanked my arm from his grasp and got in his face. "I remember just fine, *asshole*. Do me a favor and keep your hands to yourself. Your drunkenness is not an excuse to put your hands on me." I didn't give him time to reply as I spun on my heel and headed back to our table.

Thankfully, the crowd seemed to be dispersing to their seats as well, creating a clear path to the dais. I perched precariously on the edge of my seat, watching Nikylo trudge up the stairs after me. He practically dropped into the seat beside me, casually draping a leg over the arm and looking nothing like a member of the Royal family. I wondered if the drinks he'd had should have waited until the food was served. He downed his drink, slammed the empty glass down, and called over one of the Fae carrying a drink tray. He grabbed two more glasses before shooing them away, lifting one to his lips and placing the other in front of him.

I reached across him, saying, "I think you've had enough," and grabbed the one in his hand along with the one from the table as he observed my careful movements. I was setting both down on my other side when I felt one of them vanish from my grasp. Initially, I thought it had slipped, but when I didn't hear it crash onto the table, I glanced back at Nikylo. He was swirling the liquid in the glass with a smug grin on his face.

"Cheers, Sunshine." He raised the cup to me and then to his lips. Fine, if he wanted to be drunk off his ass, who was I to stop him? I set the full glass down in front of me and leaned back in my chair with a huff.

An eerie voice echoed through the room, "Announcing His Majesty, King Gustav, and Her Majesty, Queen Kahlea." *Gustav?* As in the one Kool-Aid Man and Aaidan were working for? Now I really had questions… The sound of chairs scraping had me leaping to my feet as I turned my head toward the entrance. He wore an ivory outfit, similar to Nikylo's, but he also had a golden crown on his head, the tines resembling swords as they jutted off his head.

The Queen wore an elegant turquoise off-the-shoulder gown. The train was a lighter shade of turquoise, sheer yet breathtaking. The threading along her neckline was ivory, complementing the King's attire, along with the stitching on the sash across her waist and the intricate design down the overlapping slit of her skirt. My jaw dropped at the sight of her. She was a beauty like I'd never seen before, and I wondered how I hadn't noticed her the other day.

She and the King approached the dais and sat in the chairs on Nikylo's other side. His mother cast him an apprehensive look, which made him adjust himself in his seat to look more proper.

Then, the same eerie voice echoed, "Announcing His Royal Highness, Prince Talekor.

EIGHTEEN
Hands to Myself

The moment the doors opened, my heart sank to my stomach. Kaleb—or should I say Talekor—strolled in with a confidence I had never seen from him. The copper tunic and matching pants highlighted the honey-brown color of his eyes. It featured the same intricate detailing as Nikylo's, though slightly different. I couldn't pinpoint why at this distance, but when I lowered my gaze to examine the midnight blue tunic—

"There he is!" A loud, slow clap echoed through the quiet dining hall as all the faces turned to Nikylo, who was now standing next to me. *He* was the one clapping, staring at Kal—Talekor as he entered the room. "So nice of you to finally make your appearance, brother."

My eyes widened at Nikylo's obvious drunkenness. I reached to pull him down into his seat, but he shook me off. I grabbed the water that had been placed in front of me, instead, needing something to stifle the laughter. I had never seen him that... well, drunk. He raised his glass toward his brother, who had slowed his entrance due to Nikylo's outburst.

"To your safe return! Oh, and if you ever get lost again," Nikylo made a grand hand gesture, and a thick, folded piece of paper appeared in his hand. "Here's a map to help you find your way back."

"Nikylo!" the Queen scolded, her dark green eyes swirling.

"What?" Nikylo drawled, flinging the map across the table as Talekor pulled out his chair to sit. "Thought he might need it anyway since he's never been here before." He shrugged, dropping back into his seat and finishing off his third drink.

That was an odd statement, especially since he had told me less than an hour ago that his family vacations were to Niccodra. Did Nikylo really not know he was alive? What would Talekor have done during his time in Niccodra if he hadn't spent it with his family?

"Mind your tongue, Niko," the Queen's whispered reprimand pulled me back. "Or I will make sure you are the one assigned to his tour of Niccodra."

Nikylo all but rolled his eyes as the other glass I'd taken appeared in his hand. His mother gave him a look but didn't attempt to snatch it from him. She must have known he would have taken it back just the same. I sighed loudly. If there was one thing I didn't want, it was to deal with a drunk, possessive asshole while meeting new people later. Before the cup reached his lips, I snatched it from his hand, holding it just out of his reach as he tried to grab it back. He raised an eyebrow at me, and I knew a second before it happened that he would just use his powers. I felt it slip from my fingers just as it reappeared in his hand. When he lifted the cup to his mouth again, eyes on me the entire time, I made a bold decision and snatched it again, this time downing the slightly purple liquid myself before slamming the cup on the table.

His reaction time was slow, so by the time he realized I had a different plan and reached to snatch the cup back from me, it was already gone. I flashed him a wild grin as I swallowed the last of the sweet, fiery liquid. "If I can't cut you off, I'll just steal your drinks for myself. You're not the only one who can be a pain in the ass."

His glossy eyes locked onto mine, more focused than any other drunk might have been. A smile danced on his lips. "Good luck keeping up, Sunshine," he whispered. "You'll be throwing up all night if you try to keep pace with me."

He was probably right since the only time I'd ever drank was a sip of beer at my parents' house. It was disgusting. Whatever I just downed… it already felt different in my body. I wasn't sure what kind of drinks they served here, but I was beginning to understand why Nikylo had told me I couldn't have any. I shook my head and regretted it immediately. It felt like it was floating and heavy at the same time. How could one drink be this effective so quickly?

The sound of clinking glass caught my attention, and I turned my head slowly to find the source. The King stood three chairs down, holding his glass and a small knife. Although he had stopped tapping the glass, the clinking noise echoed in my mind like a melody. I looked at the crowd, which had started murmuring among themselves at Talekor's entrance, and they quieted, turning to face the dais where we all sat.

Almost everyone had a floating cloud of color around them… Had they always had that? I turned slowly to Nikylo, whose cloud color matched his tunic in dark midnight blue. "Why do you have a cloud of color above your head?" I whispered—or at least I thought I did. Many heads near the dais turned hesitantly toward me, including the Queen's. She did not look pleased. I pursed my lips as my eyes met Nikylo's, noticing a stupid grin on his face.

Best to keep our conversation private. You're yelling.

I wasn't yelling! I shouted down the bond.

Your face is yelling.

I dropped my expression into a neutral one. *Why do you have a colorful cloud above your head?* I repeated, now unable to focus on anything else. It wasn't moving, per se, but the cloud also wasn't completely still.

His eyes sparkled as a smirk lingered on his lips. *It's our dragon aura.*

Your what?

Dragon aura.

I squinted at him, then at the crowd, where I noticed all the different colors: deep purple, pink, black, and even silver. It was almost like a rainbow made of tiny storm clouds. *Do they only appear when you're all in the same room?*

He let out a light chuckle. *No. You can see them because you stole my spondí,* he gestured towards the cup in front of me. What a strange name for a drink.

That drink makes me see dragon auras?

Yes. Well, he paused, scrunching one side of his face. *Technically, it awakens your sixth sense.*

Sixth sense? I scoffed, leaning forward to see the bright auras floating above the other royals. The queen's aura matched her dress, the king's matched his tunic, and the prince… *Why doesn't Kaleb—er… Talekor have one?*

Because he hasn't solidified the bond with his dragon yet.

Talekor must have sensed my gaze because his eyes suddenly locked onto mine, revealing a wicked gleam despite the seemingly genuine smile on his face. I quickly shut my eyes and leaned back in my seat, letting my head fall against the chair while I took a deep breath. Nikylo clearly hadn't heard about Talekor's earlier visit; otherwise, he would have mentioned it by now. I wasn't planning to bring it up, but if he found out from someone else that Talekor had slammed me against the wall and touched me... I dreaded to think of what he might do. I decided it would be best to tell him after dinner, as his intoxication made him act irrationally.

I tried to shift my thoughts to something else when the King's voice reached my ears. "...and luckily for us, we also found Rayliana." My head shot up as I looked at the King, who had extended his hand toward me. Did he just say he found me? I scoffed. That wouldn't be the word I would have used. More like kidnapped. "We weren't sure who she was right away," the King continued, a warm smile on his face. But something about the way those words seemed to squeeze out of his throat made me narrow my eyes. "But after some thorough investigation, we confirmed her to be one of the children lost during the spectacle sixteen years ago."

As my eyes slowly drifted to Nikylo, filled with a question, I noticed him pursing his lips. I suppose I'd be adding that to my list of questions later... I squeezed my eyes shut against the dizziness from all the quick movements. I turned back to the King, whose gaze remained on me before shifting to the crowd once more.

"A few other Fae children were found hidden away as well." The King nodded to someone in the crowd, and I turned to see Mari standing, with Kendall following suit. At the same time, the doors to the dining hall opened, and Leigh walked in. Tears welled up in my eyes as the twins saw each other and... nothing. They did nothing. Because they couldn't. Leighton's gaze shifted away from Kendall far too quickly, finding Talekor instead, and she made her way to the open chair next to him. I ground my teeth. "These two are the daughters of the late Fae Councilor, Lystian, and his wife, Tynoja." I scrunched up my face at the unusual names. Nikylo, Talekor, and now Lystian and Tynoja? No, they were still Taj and Lysan in my mind. Would I *ever* know all there is to know about the people I thought I knew?

Careful, Nikylo's voice made me turn to him. *Your face might get stuck like that.* I stuck my tongue out at him. A low chuckle reached my ears as he watched my tongue disappear back into my mouth. Before my cheeks could heat at his gaze, I turned back to the King, trying to concentrate on his words. His mouth moved, but all I heard was, *Best keep that distraction away.*

There went my chance to hide the heat in my cheeks, which now spread down my neck. Gah, that drink was making me really hot. I avoided whipping my head to Nikylo and did my best to focus on the speech again.

"That said, please," the King remarked, clapping his hands. "Enjoy."

The tables in the dining hall suddenly filled with a variety of foods, and ours was filled with smaller platters of the same. Some looked similar to what Libella brought me during my first bath, others similar to foods back home, but some were odd colors and shapes. They didn't necessarily look edible, but everything smelled delicious. I reached to put some food on my plate, only to be slapped on the hand.

I bit my tongue to avoid shouting obscenities at him and reached for the serving spoon again. I was ready for him the second time, my other hand gripping his wrist before he could hit me again. Out of the corner of my eye, I noticed his jaw slacken as I spooned what appeared to be potatoes onto my plate. He was so clearly inebriated that he didn't remember we didn't like each other. This guy, the one teasing and bullying me? That was Kyler. The other asshole? That was Nikylo. His expression shifted back to a sly grin, and my gaze shifted above his head to the floating, midnight blue cloud. "I wish you were here instead."

Laughter, loud and long, rang out in the dining hall, and it took me a moment to realize it was Nikylo. I'd never heard him laugh so freely. His face was glowing with joy I had only remembered seeing once. Yet, I still didn't know if it was real—if Kyler was real. The one who walked toward me on the lawn of the Dengalow after our first flight, wearing a grin that could melt all worries away. It had felt real. Everything about that night had felt real.

But then again, so had everything with Kaleb. All the comfort, fun and the love I felt for him. That was why his betrayal hurt so much, because for me? It had all been real.

I sighed. I wasn't drunk enough for this. Fortunately, a Fae carrying drinks walked by just as Nikylo was using both hands to grab food. I wasn't sure if he would, but I didn't want to risk him intercepting my need for another. I reached for the purple drink—What did he call it? Spondí?—downing the whole thing in one gulp. A loud sigh had the hairs on my neck standing on edge.

"Really? The first one wasn't enough?" Nikylo sighed, placing the food on his plate and reaching for a slice of what looked like bread with a pink tint to it. His eyes hadn't left mine, and wow, were they a gorgeous green. The edges were so dark they resembled pine needles, almost blue in hue, and as the color flowed toward the center, it lightened to resemble the clearest waters of a turquoise sea in the moonlight. One eye had a faint speck of amber. Had that always been there? I'd gazed into his eyes enough times; I should know—

"I'm going to add this to the list of things we should do when it's just the two of us, Sunshine." Nikylo's voice was rough, and my full attention returned to him, still holding my gaze. And as we stared at each other, I realized… he wasn't going to look away. I had to do it.

Okay, on the count of three, I told myself. *One.* I blinked. Those green eyes were shining bright, with a hint of amusement. *Two.* I blinked again, slower this time, noticing the corners of his eyes crinkling slightly. I took a deep breath. *Three.* I closed my eyes and turned my head slowly, unable to move anything quickly as everything felt glued to its current position. Once I was sure my head was turned fully away from Nikylo, I opened my eyes… only to find I was still facing him, and his eyes were dancing with amusement.

I pursed my lips. "I can't look away," I admitted.

One corner of his mouth lifted too far, and that damn dimple appeared. "Clearly." I was going to melt from embarrassment.

I tried not to smile, but something was bubbling inside me that I couldn't suppress. His eyes remained locked on mine, so I closed my eyes again, battling the laughter. I grabbed my chin and forced my head to turn, peeking with one eye to make sure I was looking at the crowd and not Nikylo. I sighed in relief and opened both eyes. I needed to eat something before things got even more out of hand.

We ate in silence, but I couldn't shake the feeling of Nikylo's gaze on me every once in a while. Thankfully, I kept my head forward, concentrating on my food because there was no way I would be able to regain my focus if I so much as glanced at him. The food was delicious. I should have focused more on what I was eating and the flavors that danced on my tongue, but my thoughts kept drifting back to Nikylo. Again.

What was wrong with me? He was a possessive asshole who'd already proven he wasn't messing around. His being inebriated shouldn't have changed that. The clothes he made me wear, the fact that he claimed me as his property, not allowing me to hug my friends, wearing clothes that fit him too well, keeping me from Mitch and Ma, having such perfectly toned muscles under that tunic, preventing me from having any fun, smiling with those stupid dimples, the other dimples I'd caught a glimpse of on his back—

Nikylo cleared his throat.

I stood up abruptly, which was a mistake because I wobbled in place. Thankfully, I caught myself on the edge of the table. The Queen glanced at me along with both of her sons, but I ignored the boys and gave her a small smile before stepping out from behind the table. "Excuse me. I need to use the restroom."

The heat on my face made it clear that my embarrassment was visible for everyone to see. As I stepped down the stairs, I realized I had no idea where the bathroom was. Clenching my teeth, I turned back to Nikylo. He wore a smug grin, and his cheeks were flushed pink. Obviously, the drinks were getting to him, too.

Go. I'll guide you. Nikylo's eyes pointed to the far end of the dining hall. I squinted at him, uncertain if I could trust him, but I turned to head that way anyway. Some people looked up as I walked past, and whispers followed me. It was a bit unsettling, knowing they were talking about me but not knowing what they were saying. *They are whispering about your lineage,* Nikylo informed me.

Stop that! I huffed, hurrying faster to the back of the dining hall. *How can you possibly know what everyone is whispering about? Are you in everyone's head?*

I can be. He went quiet, leaving me to listen to the whispers again. *When you pass between those pillars, turn left.* I spotted the pillars and nodded, the spondí still making me regret moving my head in any direction.

Why can't you stay out of my head? I asked, annoyed that I could hardly think about anything without him knowing what it was.

It keeps me entertained.

My thoughts are not meant for your entertainment.

I disagree. I find it very entertaining that you think about my back dimples.

I rolled my eyes, flipping him off over my shoulder as I walked through the pillars and turned left. The pillars lined the back of the hall until they met the windowed wall, where the sky beyond was full of clouds—not the pretty cotton candy clouds that I had seen earlier in the day, but a storm brewing in the distance. I smiled softly at the thought of rain. How it would cascade down my skin, just like the water had down his—

A dark laugh interrupted my thoughts.

I stopped in my tracks. *I don't think about your back dimples,* I blurted, stomping my foot in frustration. I really needed to find a way to block Nikylo out.

I could hear the grin on his face as he hummed and said, *There will be a doorway along the wall right before the windows.*

I blame the drinks for those thoughts, I said, continuing along the wall.

Ah, see, I would be inclined to believe you, but you had that memory readily available. Which means you stored that image—

Stop! I yelped, not wanting him to finish that thought. His chuckle echoed down the bond. *You're an ass,* I said, turning into the doorway. I tried to block out every thought I had of him, to prevent him from seeing any of it. He hadn't responded, so I assumed it worked. There was only one other door in this hallway, but it was closed. I reached for the handle, but it disappeared before I could grasp it. "Huh?" I pulled my hand back. The handle reappeared. Was the spondí playing tricks on me? Slowly, I inched my hand towards the handle again. "What the—?" The handle was there. I *saw* it. But the moment my hand got close, it vanished. No handle, just smooth wood. "This is ridiculous," I muttered, setting my jaw as I reached out one last time. Maybe if I went fast enough...

Just as my fingers were about to grasp the handle, the door swung open and a familiar female jumped back in surprise. "Oh! Um—sorry!"

I stumbled back, glaring between Cleo and the perfectly ordinary handle that had magically reappeared. "You were in there?"

Cleo nodded, her cheeks flushing. "Um... yes?"

"How did you get in when the handle keeps *disappearing?*" I marveled, suddenly needing to know her secret.

"Oh!" Her face brightened, something shifting within her as she realized I was just confused. "Um, so—so the castle kind of... helps with privacy?" She twisted her hands, smiling softly. "When someone's inside, the door handle just—poof!—disappears when someone tries to open it. It, um... it won't let you grab it until whoever's inside is finished." She glanced at the door I was staring at and then back to me. "I—I guess no one told you that?"

I crossed my arms. "No, I just thought the door had a personal problem with me or something."

Cleo giggled, covering her mouth. "Oh! N-no, no, it's not you!" She shifted on her feet, still smiling. "It does that to everyone. But, um... the castle values privacy."

"Huh." That was all I managed to say. The same was definitely not true for Nikylo's bathing chamber. An awkward silence lingered for a moment before I said, "Well... I'm going to use the bathroom now."

"Oh, gosh. Yes, yes, of course. I'm so sorry!" Cleo ducked her head and hurried down the hall without looking back. I smiled. She might be a little odd, but I was beginning to like her.

I stepped into the bathroom, closed the door behind me, leaned against it, and breathed hard as I felt for my head to see if it was still attached. It seemed like it was floating away, and I needed to catch it, but all I felt was the intricate braid that Libella had styled along my scalp.

I dropped my hands, refocusing on not allowing any of my thoughts to slip down the bond following my encounter with Cleo, and turned to see my face in the mirror above the sink. I braced myself against the counter and leaned in closer to examine the effects of the drinks reflecting back at me: glossy eyes and bright red cheeks. I blinked hard, trying to concentrate on my reflection, but the room spun slightly. I turned on the cold water, splashing it on my face while carefully avoiding the little makeup Libella had applied. When I caught my reflection again, I realized the cold water made absolutely no difference except slightly cooling my cheeks. Great. I was clearly more drunk than I thought. I scolded myself for thinking I could have a single drink without consequences, let alone two. I was glad, though, that the disappearing door handle wasn't just a result of drunken foolishness.

After taking care of my needs, I washed my hands and splashed my face again trying to cool down. I took a deep breath and stepped out of the bathroom. I let out a tiny scream as someone shoved me against the wall, bracing their hand above my head. I placed my hand on his chest and pushed, only to find the midnight blue tunic beneath my fingers. My eyes shot up to Nikylo's, noticing the same glossiness I'd seen in my own.

"What are you doing?" I asked, breathless from the panic that had surged upon being ambushed.

"You blocked me out," he whispered.

If I wasn't mistaken… "You're hurt by that?" I asked incredulously.

He squinted at me, his eyes shifting focus between mine. "How?"

"I don't know," I shrugged, my voice more confident than I expected. "I just didn't want you to hear my thoughts anymore."

"Did someone teach you?"

"No, K—Nikylo. I just wanted you out of my head."

His eyes narrowed, and I suddenly realized just how close we were. His warm breath brushed against my face, unsteady and erratic. My gaze dropped to where my hand rested on his chest. A few buttons had come undone, allowing my fingers to graze his bare skin. I'm not sure what compelled me or why I thought it was a good idea, but I lightly glided my fingers along the seam of his tunic up to his collarbone. He took a shuddering breath, or perhaps that was me. His skin felt warm and soft, something I hadn't anticipated from such a toned body. A familiar scent enveloped my senses, intoxicating me. The strawberry note was more muted compared to what I was used to, but the smoky, sweet scent of meadows and books was strong. I traced my finger back down his chest to where it first landed, pressing my palm flat against where his heart beat beneath. The rhythm I felt was much faster than I expected—

"Your drunkenness is not an excuse to put your hands on me." His voice was deep and husky as he echoed my words back to me. My eyes slowly tracked back up to his. Words and breath abandoned me when I met his gaze. It had darkened under my touch. I ran my fingers along his bare skin again, uncertain whether I was still intoxicated from the spondí or if it was him I was drunk on. It had to be the spondí. His face was mere inches from mine, and I couldn't muster the strength to push him away or remove my hand from him. He tilted his chin down, bringing himself so close that his breath skated across my lips. "Those people may have been whispering about your lineage," he leaned even closer, bringing his mouth next to my ear, "but all I could think about was this dress you're wearing."

A shiver raced down my spine at his confession. What was happening? Why was I allowing him to keep me here? He pulled back slightly, only to rake his eyes down my body, and all I could do was swallow hard. He hadn't touched me at all, even while crowding me against the wall. He merely walked toward me and placed his hand above me, his closeness making me retreat. In fact, the only contact was my hand, which remained on his chest, despite his entire body being just inches away from me at every possible angle. He lifted a hand as if he were going to change that, but he halted, hovering right above my hip.

"Oh!—Oh, gosh."

I jumped at the noise but was pressed against the wall and couldn't move away from Nikylo. He didn't even seem surprised by the interruption. He grinned at me, then slowly shifted his gaze from mine to see Cleo standing at the end of the hallway with her hands covering her eyes. "Yes?" he said smoothly, taking in the embarrassed Fae at the end of the hall without shifting from where we were. Although she was embarrassed, she didn't seem particularly surprised to find us in this position, but I certainly didn't want to stay like this. I tried to squirm my way out, but the hand he had been hovering above my hip now rested on it, holding me in place. The warmth of his hand seeped into my bones, and I suppressed a shudder.

Her face was bright red as she awkwardly shifted on her feet, staring at the ceiling, the floor—anywhere but at us. She cleared her throat, her voice small yet high-pitched with flustered energy. "Um—s-so, the Fae Councilors, uh—they're expecting you," she said, wringing her hands together and sneaking a quick glance before immediately looking away again. "L-like… right now."

He gave a brief nod and a lopsided smile to Cleo. "We'll be there in a moment."

She didn't wait for any further details, hurrying back the way she came.

My gaze shot back to Nikylo's. "The Fae Councilors? Oh my god… I *drank* before meeting them. *You* drank before introducing me to them!

How are you going to hide my lineage from the Ignalian Councilor, Kyler?" The name slipped out, but I didn't have time to think about it. "I am not prepared to meet the leaders of the Fae like this." My hands flew to my face, feeling the heat in my cheeks. I had no idea what the Councilors expected of me, but I knew that being intoxicated was probably not on their list. Especially Tom. He would be so disappointed in me.

A heavy sigh brushed the top of my head, and his hand slipped from my hip. "Here, take this," Nikylo said, pulling my hand from my face and pressing something into it. I opened my eyes to see a small vial of golden liquid resting there.

"What's this?" I asked, shaking it in his face. "How is another drink supposed to help me?"

"It's not a *drink*," he snapped, working his jaw. "It will sober you up."

"What?" The tone of genuine surprise escaped.

"Just… drink it. Please," Nikylo said, finally pushing off the wall to step back. He closed his eyes, stretching his neck to both sides as he shook out his arms, seemingly attempting to shake the drinks out of himself.

"Where is yours?" I asked, still gripping the vial tightly.

"In your hand."

My jaw dropped, but I quickly composed myself. "You had more to drink than I did. You should take it." I shoved the vial back toward him, but he stopped me, wrapping my fingers around it instead.

"No. Just drink it. I'll be fine." He flashed me a wicked grin. "It'll be more fun this way."

"You're supposed to help hide my—"

"I know what I'm supposed to do!" he snapped, pressing me against the wall again. It didn't scare me, but I noticed a flicker of fear in his eyes again. His voice turned into a whisper as he continued, "You need to be sober for this. I do not." He lowered his gaze. "This," he said, reaching for my dress again but stopping just a hair's breadth away. "This is intertwined with my xousía, and the fire will appear as my own." I could still feel the heat of his hand through my dress, even though he wasn't touching me. "If even a small amount of fire magic comes off you, my xousía should conceal it. My soberness won't matter."

"Then why did you have this?" My voice came out softer than I meant. "There's no way you could have known I would drink tonight."

When his eyes met mine again, I knew I was right. It was written all over his face. He hadn't anticipated my drinking tonight, which meant the vial had been for him because he knew he would need it. But why had he anticipated drinking so much? Who prepares themselves to get drunk? "Trust me. Please." His voice was low as he reached up to tuck a stray piece of hair behind my ear. I opened my mouth to reply, but he cut me off. "I know I've given you no reason to, but I need you to. Just for this."

It could have been the drinks, his scent, or maybe even his words—heck, it was probably all of them—but I nodded, realizing that I likely would have done anything he asked in that moment. The pleading in his voice, his closeness, and my fuzzy brain—they all contributed. I pulled the small cork from the vial and tipped the concoction back. Nikylo watched as I swallowed the contents, sighed, and took a measured step back.

My body reacted immediately when the liquid hit my stomach. It felt like coming down from an adrenaline high. My body felt heavy, and I tensed up, knowing that I didn't want to appear depressed going into this meeting either. The effects of the spondí slowly faded away, and the midnight blue cloud above Nikylo's head vanished. Heat flooded my cheeks for an entirely different reason as I realized exactly what I'd done while inebriated. I dropped my chin, avoiding eye contact with the male before me. What had I done? Was I really that weak to give in to my thoughts and feelings so easily? It was embarrassing—

A finger hooked under my chin, lifting my gaze back to his. "Spondí gives you the freedom to do the things you may not have the courage to do without it. It's not embarrassing to feel what you feel. Inconvenient? Sure," he shrugged, a smile tugging at his lips. I attempted to drop my gaze again, but he tilted my chin higher to keep my eyes on him. "You are not weak, Sunshine. And you can't let these Councilors think that either."

I swallowed the lump in my throat and grabbed his wrist to pull his hand away. "Stop being nice," I whispered. "It's not helping."

He nodded and stepped back. My grip on his wrist lingered until he was too far for me to hold on. "Shall we, then?" he asked, straightening his jacket.

I almost nodded but then wondered out loud, "Why is it so important for me to make a good impression on the Councilors?"

"Because," he said, his hand guiding me down the hallway, hovering over my lower back. The sensation it caused made me want to lean away from him. "You will likely be joining them on the council in the future."

NINETEEN
Steal the Show

"What?" I exclaimed, the breath in my lungs suddenly gone. "You can't be serious." At eighteen, I was in no position to lead anything, especially in a world I had only just discovered existed. The only reason I could think of for being in power was that I was the most powerful Fae. And that didn't make sense. My nerves got the best of me as I said, "I—I thought the Fae chose their leaders based on—on leadership qualities, not—not the strength of their power."

"That's true," Nikylo said calmly, guiding me along the pillars back to the dining hall.

When he didn't continue, I halted in my tracks, my voice trembling, "I'm not going out there until you explain what the hell you meant by that."

My stopping caused the hand hovering over my lower back to make contact, but it didn't linger; instead, he clasped both hands behind him as he faced me. "There she is." His sarcasm made me roll my eyes, but I crossed my arms, waiting for his answer. He sighed, "Being Evanian makes you a different kind of Fae than they have a leader for. You are the only Evanian right now, so you're already speaking for your kind." The muscles in my face went slack at his words, and I opened my mouth to say something, but he raised a finger. "I realize you're not ready to lead. They also know this. But your existence raises the question of whether *other* Evanians exist."

I blinked at him. That hadn't even crossed my mind. If Arabella were still here, I wouldn't be the only one in existence. In fact, there were more before me… My eyes met Nikylo's. "What about my mother?"

Nikylo dipped his chin, appearing impressed by my question. He lowered his voice, saying, "As far as we know, she is no longer in Niccodra. We do not know her whereabouts; therefore, we cannot assume she's alive." My heart skipped a beat, and something deep within me nearly flickered out. I hadn't realized I'd been holding out hope that she was alive somewhere, that perhaps I'd get to meet her. "That leaves you as the one to speak for your Fae line."

"Ugh… I didn't ask for this!" Panic laced my voice. "Can't I just fall under the Annysians or Udarians?" *Or Ignalians?* I thought to myself, not wanting anyone nearby to hear.

He shoved his hands into his pockets and shrugged. "As far as I'm concerned, the choice should be yours." My eyebrows shot up. "But be ready to make a choice there, too."

"A choice between what?"

"I'm sure any of them would make their offers convincing to have you on their side."

"I don't want to be on anyone's side! I just want to live a life where I can learn about my powers and the history of my people!" I surprised myself with those words. I hadn't admitted that I wanted to learn about their history or really having anything to do with them. I'd been so focused on what was happening with me—with Nikylo and Talekor, Ken and Leigh. But being here? Seeing the world I belonged to? It made me yearn to know it all. To visit the places where Fae lived. To see the places I should have grown up. But perhaps all of that came at a cost… I turned my attention back to Nikylo, who was still patiently waiting for me to process everything. "I don't want to lead," I whispered.

He nodded, a level of understanding in his still slightly glossy eyes. "Feel free to tell them that. The Fae are all about expressing yourself, after all." The tightness in his voice puzzled me until I noticed a head peek around the pillar a short distance away.

Romeo gazed directly at me, motioning me to come closer while flashing a wide smirk at Nikylo. "You shouldn't keep them waiting," he whispered.

Nikylo gestured with his hand to continue down the hall, although his movements were a bit stiffer. Maybe he needed another drink. I took a deep breath, held it for four seconds, and then let it out. It was just an introduction, nothing more. They simply wanted to meet me because I'm Evanian and one of the most powerful—

The *most powerful,* Nikylo corrected.

I shot him a glare. *Don't make me shut you out again.*

I think that was just a fluke, he smirked. *You won't be able to do it again.*

I raised an eyebrow at him. *Wanna bet?*

He mirrored my expression. *Sure, why not make things interesting?* He smirked, looking ahead as if he weren't talking to me at all. *If I win, I get to train you tomorrow.* I scrunched my face. That seemed like a strange thing to win in a bet. Why would he want to? A wicked grin appeared on his face, and I knew that meant he had something up his sleeve. All I knew was that I didn't want to be on the receiving end of whatever that might be.

I tapped my finger on my chin, considering what I would actually want to win. *Okay,* I finally said, *if I win, you have to take me to the library.* His shock mirrored my own. *It beats me having to ask you everything.* I shrugged as we passed between the pillars and into the dining hall, now full of people again.

Deal, he said, his voice smug. I glanced at him as he guided us back toward the front of the dining hall.

How will I know if it worked?

He looked up as if pondering it and then said, *If I can recall a specific moment or thought while you were trying to block—*

Successfully blocking you out, I countered.

He simply smirked. *If I can recall a specific moment or thought, you lose.*

Deal.

We stopped at a table where several Fae stood by their chairs. I recognized them as Fae due to their pointed ears and sharp features. However, the most astonishing aspect of their appearance was just how magnificent their beauty was. The paintings I had seen were gorgeous but didn't capture their essence, nor did seeing them from across the room. My gaze was fixed on the female in the center. Her curly ginger hair framed her face and fell to her shoulders. She had light, bright blue eyes that sparkled against her freckled skin. A subtle smile played on her lips as someone behind her whispered something into her pointed ear. She nodded and then turned to step toward me.

"Hello, Rayleigh," she said, extending her hands. "My name is Kaledra, but you may call me Kaley." I placed my hands in hers and leaned forward as she kissed both my cheeks, mimicking her movements. When she stepped back and let go of my hands, she said, "I represent the Ignalian line."

My breath caught, but I forced myself to breathe normally as I wrung my hands in front of me. Naturally, I was introduced to the person I was supposed to keep my lineage from first. Hopefully, whatever Nikylo had done with his xousía and the dress worked because I had no clue how to hide it myself. That reminded me... I shot a sideways glance at Nikylo before turning my attention back to Kaley.

She slightly bowed her head from where she stood, and I almost told her not to bow, but then she said, "Prince Nikylo."

"Councilor Kaley." He bowed in response. I supposed it made sense that they were on good terms with each other. Running an entire realm required cooperation among different leaders. Kaley's eyes darted back and forth between Nikylo and me enough times to make me want to squirm, but I recalled him mentioning that they wanted to ensure I was treated fairly. So, I smiled and waited for her to speak again.

Her sky-blue eyes met mine. "I hear your journey back to Niccodra wasn't easy." It wasn't a question, but it made me curious about what she'd heard regarding my "journey" and whether any of it was true. I really had nothing to say, so I just held her gaze. "How has training with your powers been?" Her eyes subtly shifted to Nikylo mid-question, but she was still looking at me for the answer.

"I've only just begun, " I said, not knowing what she was aware of. "Unfortunately, my powers were suppressed for quite some time. Between that and only discovering I had powers a little over a month ago, I haven't been able to practice much."

Kaley nodded, as if my words confirmed something for her. She turned to Nikylo. "And you're giving her enough time to train?" she practically snapped.

"Now, now, Kaley," the woman beside her said, placing a hand on her arm. After being distracted by Kaley's beauty and the fact that she was Ignalian, I had forgotten to take in the rest of the Fae at the table. The one who interrupted had dark skin and hair as black as night. She had braids like Romeo's, but hers almost reached her navel and had pieces of something orange woven into them. Her features suggested she was likely in her mid-thirties, but I knew that probably wasn't the case, especially when her deep brown eyes held so much wisdom. I knew the Fae could live quite long lives, but I wasn't about to ask how old she was. "You know Romeo, Cleo, and Tietra were sent to the training grounds this morning," she said. "They are the best teachers they have here at the castle." Best in the castle? They seemed so young... The female turned to me, and a bright smile lit up her face. "Hello, child. I'm Marta, the Udarian Councilor." She greeted me in the same way Kaley had, her hands and cheeks warm against my own.

I smiled at her, grateful for her stepping in when she did. Ignalians were powerful, and I didn't want to know what happened when one lost their temper. "It's nice to meet you," I said, then added quickly, "Both of you."

A tap on my shoulder had me turning to find yet another Fae with hands outstretched. This one was male, with white-blond hair and a lighter complexion. I placed my hands in the handsome young male's, worrying for a moment that a repeat of Romeo was about to unfold, but when he leaned in, it was a gentle cheek-to-cheek greeting. A slight burning sensation manifested on my ribcage, and I mentally scowled as the male spoke. "I am Oliver, Annysian Councilor. I look forward to hearing more of your story." Oliver gave me a charming smile, and that alone indicated he was probably one of the younger Councilors. His gray eyes sparkled in the light as he held my gaze. "Your eyes are like the oceans below, a blue not often found among our kind."

My brow furrowed. "Blue eyes seem pretty common here," I said, glancing at Kaley's again.

"Blue, yes. But your shade of blue?" His eyes darted between mine again. "I've never seen the likes."

"She takes after her mother with those eyes," said a voice I recognized.

I turned around to see Tom walking up behind me. He had a huge smile on his face and his arms open, waiting for a hug that I launched myself into. He held me tightly, so much like my dad's hugs that I had to hold back tears as I clung to him. I had almost forgotten what it felt like to be embraced by a fatherly figure. Sure, Theo was there, but I had known Tom longer. Even though he was my coach, he stepped in during the months after my dad passed to help me navigate my emotions in the best way he knew—through training. I hadn't realized how much he meant to me until this very moment.

I pulled away as the burning on my torso intensified, but I didn't let go of Tom's shoulders. "I've missed you," I said, tears welling in my eyes as I took him in and was physically taken aback by his appearance. Because while he looked the same… "Since when do you have pointed ears?"

Tom chuckled, grabbing my wrists and pulling my hands off his shoulders. "I've always had them, but back on Earth, I kept them hidden." He let my arms drop to my sides.

"How?" I asked, knowing that was outside the realm of Fae powers.

He smirked. "A potion, if you will, with… special ingredients. It suppresses my Fae features until the reversal potion is taken."

"Huh." I stared at him a bit longer, my eyes adjusting not only to his pointed ears but also to how his beauty had become magnified. If I thought he looked like a board shorts model before… "Will my ears look like that someday?" I meant to sound excited, but I ended up sounding slightly disgusted as I reached up to feel my still-rounded ears.

There was another chuckle, but this time, it came from the table where Marta was now sitting. "Yes, child, your ears and features will change slightly when all your powers have properly settled in." A knowing look crossed her face, and my eyes widened slightly, but she just winked. Her eyes focused on something behind me. "Does Rayleigh have her own quarters?"

"No," Nikylo said. "She stays in my wing but has her own bed." I recoiled at the statement, glancing over my shoulder at him with confusion. *Later*, he said down the bond. Marta's question had seemed innocent enough, but Nikylo's response didn't quite add up. I mean, I had a bed, but I was pretty sure it belonged to him unless he was recharging in his dragon form. But why did he feel the need to specify that I had my *own* bed?

When I turned back to Marta, she was nodding. "And what about the other two Fae that were brought back?"

"Ah, yes, my girls," Tom said as he looked around the room. "Where are they? I only just arrived a few moments ago, so I haven't had a chance to look for them."

My heart dropped into my stomach, and my eyes began to burn. He didn't know… He didn't know Leigh was bound to Talekor. When the joy in his eyes sparkled, the hope of seeing the twins again, I realized I couldn't let someone else break the news to him. It wouldn't go well. It had to be me. I turned to face him completely. "Tom," I whispered, drawing his attention away from his search. "I have to tell you something." My voice cracked, instantly making me fight back tears. This wasn't going to be easy.

He lowered his chin, watching me cautiously. "Rayleigh? What's the matter?"

I bit my bottom lip and released a breath. "It's Leighton." Tom just stared at me, a question in his eyes. "She…" I sniffled, trying to figure out how to word what I needed to say next. I took a deep breath and reached out to place a hand on his elbow. "Talekor claimed her as his Doulos," I whispered.

A dark expression settled on his face. I had never seen Tom upset, much less angry. His nostrils flared, his jaw tense. His voice had fallen from its usual cheerful tone to match the darkness in his eyes. "Where is she?"

"Tom, there's nothing you can do," Nikylo said next to us, his tone firm. It wasn't a friend talking to a friend or even peer to peer, but a Prince to a Councilor. A warning, by the sound of it.

He turned sharply to Nikylo. "Where is she?" he reiterated, his tone just as firm. "I have a right to see my daughter."

"Daughter?" I stuttered. "But you never—" I stopped abruptly when he turned back to me. The look in his eyes had softened, and that was silver lining them. "When?" I asked softly.

"The night before…" He trailed off, glancing around the dining hall, clearly unsure if he could trust anyone present. But I understood what he meant without needing him to finish his sentence. The night before we all vanished. He hadn't seen the twins since adopting them. The expression on my face must have shattered his resolve because his voice was faint when he said, "Please. I just want to see her."

I chewed on my cheek, nodding. "She's probably near the dais with Prince Talekor."

Tom immediately stepped in that direction, but someone caught his elbow. We both turned to find Nikylo staring at him. "For the sake of your entire family—" the insinuation in his tone sent chills down my spine, "—don't do anything you might regret."

Tom met his gaze and gave a curt nod. Nikylo released him and reached for a glass on a passing tray, knocking it back quickly. "Shall we return to idle party chit-chat?" he exclaimed, his voice completely shifting from the dire subject. After placing the empty glass back on the tray, he grabbed another one and turned to face the other Councilors.

Tom vanished into the crowd as Nikylo picked up the conversation where we had left off. I knew Tom couldn't do anything to help Leigh, but I hoped seeing him would be beneficial somehow, even if it was just mentally.

"…destruction on the western border. Any idea what happened?" The words snapped me back to the conversation. Because, if I wasn't mistaken, they were asking about the damage *I* had caused.

I glanced at Nikylo and noticed a look of cool indifference on his face. He didn't meet my gaze but replied with a shrug, "I believe someone decided to use the space for a new community or market. That requires some demolition, doesn't it?" He was speaking to Kaley and Marta, the latter sporting a knowing smile on her face.

"I suppose it does. Did your father approve of the glen being used?" Marta challenged, raising her eyebrows.

Nikylo flashed her a sly grin. "I suppose if he hadn't, there would be consequences for whoever destroyed it without permission, no?"

I turned away from their conversation, not wanting to give myself away—even though I was pretty sure Marta already knew. I found Oliver standing nearby, leaning against the table. I stepped up next to him, leaning beside him and surveying the room as he did. After a moment, I asked, "What are you looking for?" His eyes scanned the room as mine would if I were in a crowded space with few people to talk to. People-watching was a pastime I enjoyed, and it seemed to be something Oliver enjoyed, too.

He smiled without glancing at me. "A reason to leave this table and roam wherever the winds may carry me."

I smiled at his aloof answer. "And where do you think the winds would take you?" I asked, still watching the crowd around us.

"Away from the noise, from the politics," I turned to see his thoughtful gaze still scanning the crowd. He was young, so perhaps being a leader wasn't what he had wanted, just like me. Maybe he was someone I could talk to if they ever brought up my taking on that responsibility. He smiled and said, "Perhaps to find the ocean breeze so I may once again marvel at the color your eyes behold."

My cheeks flushed as he met my gaze. Were all the Fae so flirtatious? I pursed my lips, my eyes briefly dropping before I locked onto his gray ones again. "I'm sure you've seen others with eyes just as pretty."

"I do not believe I have. I would have remembered." He didn't break my gaze, his eyes still flicking between mine. A breeze caressed my face, moving several loose strands away from my eyes. My jaw dropped as Oliver whispered, "There. Now there is no obstruction to my view."

His boldness made me break eye contact and giggle. Then I realized he had just used his magic so effortlessly and didn't lift a finger. When I met his gaze again, I was biting my lip. "How… Can you teach me how to do that?"

The soft smile on his face told me he was still captivated by my eyes, but he extended his hand to me, nodding. "The wind is especially easy to control, but I will allow my magic to show yours how it is done."

Without hesitation, I placed my hand in his and immediately felt his winds caressing my skin once more. It reached out to connect with my magic, and I sensed mine react as it surfaced towards where his rested on my arm. My magic greeted his by wrapping around it in what I could only describe as a hug. "How is it doing that?" I asked, knowing I hadn't done a single thing to control it.

"Magic responds to that which resembles itself. My call for your winds granted them their own control, as you see." His winds lifted from my arm, and my magic followed, traveling from my arm to my face, where, once again, the stray hairs were brushed from my eyes. I sensed my magic acknowledge it, and then the presence of Oliver's magic receded from mine, leaving it suspended between us. I couldn't see it, but I could feel it. It was waiting for instructions on what to do next. I smiled, directing the breeze toward the one hair out of place on Oliver's head.

"Uhp, uhp," he raised his hand. "Gentle control. Do not push the winds. Guide them."

I nodded, loosening my mental grip on my powers. I let out a gentle breath, and the breeze flowed exactly where I'd aimed, flipping the piece of hair back into place. "Oh my God," I laughed in awe. "I did it!" Oliver wore a smile that made his eyes crinkle. "Thank you!" I jumped to hug him impulsively, but he didn't hesitate to return the embrace.

"I am delighted to see you have had some proper training; otherwise, that would have never worked," he said as he pulled away.

I took a careful step back when he shared a glance with someone behind me. I followed his gaze to find Nikylo, Marta, and Kaley all observing what had just occurred. My excitement faded as I turned back to Oliver. "This was a test?"

"A friendly conversation that happened to provide an opportunity to see if you have proper control over your powers," he said, his gaze still locked on mine. "Most Fae your age have learned how to control their powers their entire lives. Schooling their breath work and their self-control long before their powers even start to emerge. You did not have such training." His gaze shifted to Nikylo behind me. "Your words hold true, Niko, at least for her Annysian line." Oliver lowered his chin, and at that moment, I understood exactly why he was a Councilor to the Fae. "Be sure the same applies to her other training."

Nikylo smirked, "Don't worry, Ollie. Her instructors are some of the best."

Oliver rolled his eyes before finding mine again. "I did not mean to deceive you, Rayleigh." He extended his hands. I glanced at them briefly before hesitantly placing mine in his, my eyes lifting to his once more. "If you would like to visit that ocean breeze with me sometime, just ask Nikylo to send for me. Teaching you how to hone your powers would bring me great joy. Though I am certain that Tietra will do a marvelous job on her own if you prefer to learn from her instead."

I smiled weakly, "Okay." Even though his test caught me off guard, I knew it was partially his responsibility to ensure I was getting proper training. Between that and Marta asking about my housing, I knew they were just gathering the information they needed to ensure I was being treated fairly. "Promise not to trick me again?"

He brought my hands to his mouth and kissed both. "I promise," he said with a genuine smile. "However, if I am correctly sensing the depth of your power, you will easily surpass my abilities. I may need to deceive you to ensure you do not overpower me." His eyes sparkled with mischief, while mine widened. "Not to worry, though. Our magic has already been acquainted and will likely work well together." He winked as I bit back another smile.

"Okay," I said softly, ignoring the grumble in my mind. The thought of learning to harness one of my abilities from a leader of my people was becoming more enticing. Clearly, Nikylo didn't seem to be on board, likely because Oliver was kind and welcoming—the complete opposite of him. And probably because he kept touching me. "I'm sure Nikylo would be happy to have you teach me." I glanced over my shoulder with a sweet smile, finding blazing green eyes on me. "Right?"

With a forced smile, he said, "We'll have to find a time to make it work."

"Splendid," Oliver said. "I will—"

A loud crash echoed across the dining hall, followed by several screams. My head snapped toward the noise, but I couldn't see anything over the crowd. Someone was shouting, but I couldn't make out the words amid the chaos of everyone rushing toward the scene and whispering about what was happening.

"Shit," Nikylo muttered just before I felt the space behind me constrict. I knew that if I looked over my shoulder, he wouldn't be there anymore. The yelling grew louder as another voice joined in, and I knew it was him. I pushed through the crowd, making my way toward the sound of the initial crash, and people easily moved aside for me. As soon as I squeezed past the last of the crowd, my hand flew to my mouth at the sight before me.

Leighton stood behind Talekor, her hands covering her mouth as she trembled. She watched Tom push himself up from the wreckage of the table he had been lying on. It looked as though he had been thrown violently into it, shattering the table and causing all the plates and food to fall on top of him.

Nikylo held Talekor back, saying, "I think he got the point, brother. Let it go." His voice wasn't soft, but rather a projected demand to direct his attention away from Tom.

"He tried to take her away from me!" Talekor shouted, his face beet red and his eyes dark and stormy, fixed on Tom. I had never seen him like this before. In fact, I don't think I had ever seen him angry at all. The Kaleb I knew never exploded like that. This was…something else.

"It was too loud to talk to her in here," Tom replied, his tone firm but not raised. "I was just taking her to the hallway, where it's quieter." He must have a good grip on his anger because I wouldn't be that composed if I'd been thrown into a table hard enough to break it. Not in the slightest. "She has a soft voice, and she's clearly terrified—"

"Do not speak for my bonded!" Talekor shouted, trying to shove past Nikylo again, but he held firm.

Then the Queen was there, taking Talekor's other hand. "Come, sweetheart," she whispered, casting a wary glance at the watching crowd. "Let's take this somewhere else." She gently tugged on his arm, and he turned to face her.

The moment his eyes met hers, they softened. Then his face filled with shock as he realized the scene he had caused. His mouth opened and closed like a fish before finally saying softly, "I'm sorry, Mother. I… I don't know what came over me."

She pulled him into a hug, patting his hair. "It's all right, son. We can talk about it somewhere else. Come on." She released him but held onto his hand, leading him to the door and signaling over her shoulder for Leighton to follow. She did so without a word but glanced back at Tom. She mouthed the words, "I'm sorry," before turning to follow the Queen and her son out the door.

Tom's shoulders slumped in defeat, but before I could get to him, someone else raced up the stairs toward him.

"Dad!" Kendall exclaimed as she slammed into Tom, nearly knocking him over. As soon as he recognized her, he scrambled to wrap her in his arms. A choked sob escape from both of them. I hadn't realized how much he cared for the twins, having assumed he was only there to look after them after their parents passed away. But hearing that the adoption had been finalized before we left and seeing his reaction when he discovered Leigh had been claimed…

I sniffed back tears, wrapping my arms around my stomach as I walked over to Tom and Kendall. I hadn't wanted to interrupt their moment, but Tom must have heard me approaching because his eyes met mine. There were unspoken words between us because he was one of the few people who understood who Kaleb had been to me. Seeing a perfect replica of him that didn't act anything like him was jarring. The look on Tom's face said it all. He reached out an arm to me, and I let him pull me into their hug.

I knew Tom's intentions with Leigh weren't to cause any trouble, but if Talekor was anywhere near as protective of Leigh as Nikylo was with me, there was no chance anyone could get close to her. I had already seen it once in the courtyard with Mari and Talekor, but the possessiveness was nothing compared to the words he said to me before dinner. They echoed in my mind: *You will watch me break her in ways that you never thought possible.* There was no telling how far he would go, but it only solidified the fact that we needed to find a way to get her back—and fast.

TWENTY
can you hear me?

"Remember the rules?"

"Yes," I said, practically bouncing on my toes.

"Ten minutes."

"I know," I replied, hating that my time was limited but grateful for it regardless.

Nikylo touched three symbols on the door, causing each to light up before a light flashed in the cracks and a soft click echoed.

After the fiasco at the dinner, most of the celebration dissipated. With the celebrated Prince having to leave, many saw no point in staying. I was told the Fae Councilors were staying in the castle for the celebration, so they were all escorted to the guest wing with their families and attendants. Niala must have slipped away at some point during dinner, because Nikylo personally escorted me back to his room, although it felt more like I was escorting him given how drunk he was. He couldn't even walk straight, let alone lead me anywhere. Fortunately, I knew that if I just kept walking down the hall, his door would eventually appear for us. As soon as we got back, he ordered me to change out of the "distracting dress," to which I rolled my eyes but complied, finding a nightgown waiting for me on the vanity chair. I grabbed it and went to change in the bathroom.

When I emerged, he was leaning against the wall near the door with the fancy symbols on it—the one I hadn't had time to explore yet. His hair was tousled from the number of times he had run his fingers through it, his shoes had been shucked off and thrown across the room, and his tunic was completely unbuttoned, leaving his bare chest on display. I quickly averted my gaze to his face, which was pointed at the ceiling as he was clearly fighting off his drunkenness.

"Can't you just take that sober potion you gave me?" I asked, heading for the bed and intending to pass out.

"It's not a potion," he slurred. "It's chrygós. And no," he said, pushing off the wall to take a wobbly step toward me as I pulled back the covers. "I can't take it because *you* took it."

"You gave it to me," I corrected. "Then you continued to have four more drinks, knowing you didn't have it," I murmured, moving to climb into the bed. "Don't you have more stashed away somewhere?"

"No. I can only make one at a—" he interrupted himself. "What are you doing?"

I glanced back to see him watching me from where he swayed near the door. "Going to bed... as should you."

He blinked. "So you don't want to see Mitch?"

I shot out of the bed so fast. "Mitch?"

And that's how I found myself standing before the door marked with symbols in his room, reaching for the handle to pull it open. The only rules he gave me were that his shackles had to remain on, I couldn't give him anything to help him escape, and I had only ten minutes.

Nikylo was once again leaning against the wall by the door, clearly using all his energy and focus to keep himself upright. "Ten minutes," he said again, sounding more like a slur.

I nodded and then entered the dark room on the other side.

The room was spacious, though not nearly as large as Nikylo's. A single candle flickered on the wall, illuminating a small dresser, a bed, and a chair by the tiny window. The window barely let in any light, which explained the burning candle. As I took in the room, I held my breath searching for my brother's familiar face, curly hair, and lanky frame, but there was no one there. I almost turned back to ask Nikylo, but then a soft creak echoed from across the space, and I turned to see another door opening.

A happy sob escaped me as I bounded across the room to where Mitch was emerging from what appeared to be a bathroom. He looked up just as I was about to wrap my arms around him—

And his fist slammed into my chest. I went flying backward, landing hard on my ass, and rolling roughly across the floor. The breath was knocked from my lungs at the impact, and I coughed when I finally came to a stop. I tried to push myself up from the floor, but a foot landed on my back, forcing me back down with a low growl that made my bones tremble.

"Mitch, please!" I cried, struggling to push back against his strength, which was greater than I expected. When did he get so strong? "It's me," I pleaded, wondering if he couldn't see me in the dark. "It's Rayleigh!" I tried to tap into my magic, knowing it could easily help in this situation, but I couldn't find it.

His foot left my back, but then his knee pressed between mine, and his arm wrapped around my neck, pulling me closer as he knelt behind me. Instinctively, I raised my hands to block him from choking me and moved to break his hold. But what the hell was happening? Why was he attacking me like he didn't know—

I stopped struggling. Stopped breathing. My heart plummeted. Blackness closed in on my vision. *No…* Libella warned me about this. She told me this would happen. I didn't want to believe her. I didn't want to see him become—

No. I wouldn't accept this. Not like this. Not if it was the last time I was going to see him.

"Mitch," I whispered, keeping my hands in place so he couldn't cut off my air supply, but I stopped fighting to get free. I let him pull me closer, making it harder to breathe as his arm tightened around my ribcage. "Mitch," I forced out. "It's me. It's Rayleigh. Your sister." I could only get a few words past my lips at a time. I thought reminding him of things from his past might help him remember who I was—who he was, since he had clearly forgotten. I started listing things as they came to mind. "We had—a sister. Arabella. Mom and Dad—used to call you—Little Monster." The mention of the nickname our parents gave him made my vision blur with tears. They didn't know how ironic that name was… I swallowed the emotions building up and tried another approach. "We played games. In the backyard. At the meadow. We played—hide and seek." He kept squeezing, his grip causing my vision to fade and something to pop along my ribs. I ignored the pain, knowing it wouldn't matter if I couldn't get through to him. The arm around my neck tightened. I could only keep him from choking me for so long. "Your favorite—was the Nerf wars—in the backyard," I said, tears streaming down my face. "I got you—a Nerf gun—for your birthday. Remember?" The silence that followed was only broken by the sounds of me struggling to breathe and his strained breathing as he used all his strength to squeeze the life out of me.

Nikylo burst into the room, but I shouted down the bond, *No! Let me do this.*

He only paused to look me in the eyes and say, *He's trying to kill you!* His voice reflected the panic in his eyes as he hurried towards Mitch, who just pulled me back farther, growling at Nikylo.

Don't! I screamed. He paused again, glancing between me and Mitch. I could tell it took everything in him not to take Mitch down, but I pleaded, *Please. Let me try.* Because I knew if Nikylo got involved in this, Mitch would likely end up unconscious, and I wouldn't be able to talk to him at all. Nikylo huffed but clenched his jaw and nodded.

Knowing it might be the last thing I said, I used the only ace up my sleeve. "I love you, Mitch," I rasped. "More—than—the—" He squeezed tighter, and as my vision faded to black, I used the last of my breath to say, "Sun."

His grip vanished, and I felt him scramble away from me as I collapsed to the ground. My vision slowly returned while I gulped down precious air, coughing as I inhaled too much too quickly. When I could finally focus on something other than my breathing, I turned around to find Mitch sitting against the wall, his knees drawn to his chest, watching me intently.

I held back a sob as I took him in. His normally tan skin was pale, and he had dark circles under his eyes. There were shackles on his wrists, not connected, but I recognized them from the cave where I had gone to rescue him. Had those been on the entire time? He looked like he hadn't eaten well in the month since I last saw him, but it was hard to tell because he was curled up, his chin resting on his knees. His hair was wiry and unkempt, and when I met his gaze…

"Mitch," I whispered, moving slowly as I inched toward him on the ground. When the candlelight illuminated his face, I noticed a haunted look there. "Do you know who I am?"

It was nearly imperceptible, but he shook his head.

I closed my eyes and took a deep breath, stifling a cough before meeting his gaze again. "I'm Rayleigh, your sister."

He squinted at me, his eyes wary. "Rayleigh…" he whispered as if it were the first time he had ever said the name. His voice sounded different, raspier than usual. He tilted his head like a predator, and I held my breath, afraid he was going to attack again. But his brow furrowed, and his pupils shrank. Recognition filled his eyes, followed by tears. "Rayleigh?" he whispered again, but this time, my name was punctuated by a sob. When I nodded, mirroring his sob, he threw himself at me.

I caught him, pulling him close in the embrace I had anticipated when I first saw him. Out of the corner of my eye, I noticed Nikylo blending into the background as he witnessed the proper reunion. *Thank you,* I whispered down the bond. He simply nodded back. He likely wouldn't allow us to be alone after that, but it didn't really matter. I only had a few minutes left anyway.

Mitch finally regained enough composure to pull away but continued to gaze at the ground. He sniffled and whispered, "I don't know what's happening to me."

But I did. "I know, Mitch." I brushed the straggly curls away from his face and held his cheeks in my hands. "I'm sorry it took me so long to come see you. A lot has happened since that night at the hospital." That much was clear, but given how little time I had with him… "There isn't enough time for me to tell you everything. But I needed to see you… I came to see you before…" I didn't know how to finish that sentence.

"Before they kill me?" he asked.

"What?" I shot back, my eyes snapping to where he watched me carefully. "No! They… they're not going to kill you, Mitch." I brushed away a stray tear on his cheek, trying to comfort him.

"They should," he said, lowering his head again.

"Hey," I scooted closer, my hands lifting his chin so his gaze met mine as I wiped more tears from his face. "You don't get to decide that. *They* don't get to decide that."

"Why am I here? Why did they lock me in this room?" His voice cracked, and that sound alone nearly broke me. "I don't want to live like this… I don't want to hurt the people I love, forgetting who they are— who *I* am." His tears flowed down his face faster than I could catch them.

I swallowed the lump in my throat as my heart broke for him. He had been locked up here for over a month without any knowledge of why, and his mind was playing tricks on him the whole time. There was no one to answer his questions, no one to talk to… I would have gone crazy, too… There were so many reasons he was locked up, and he had the right to know all of it. "You're here because…" I trailed off, chewing on my cheek, trying to find the right way—

"Just say it, Ray."

I glanced up to find him staring at me, waiting for a response he knew would change everything. I sighed, "Dad wasn't human, Mitch." I expected shock from him but was met only with a nod—like he had already known that or figured it out himself. "And apparently, when someone is born half Niccodran, the magic doesn't develop properly, and they—" I choked back tears, not wanting him to think I was scared of him or that I pitied him. "They become monsters, forgetting who they are." The last words were whispered, but Mitch closed his eyes, and he nodded, somehow accepting his fate. He was already experiencing it, after all. "Mitch," I whispered, trying to get him to look at me again. When he didn't, I said, "I'm going to figure this out. There has to be a way for you to stay…you."

"If there were, don't you think they would have found it by now?" he asked, and I knew there was some truth to that.

"Maybe the right people haven't been looking," I offered. "Maybe they aren't looking because they don't *need* an—"

"It's time, Sunshine." His voice was quiet but urgent.

Dammit. I pulled Mitch into a hug and whispered urgently, "There's a trial for you tomorrow, but I'm going to figure this out." I recalled my bet with Nikylo earlier. "There's a library here somewhere that Nikylo is going to take me to. I'm going to do everything I can to keep you here." Whether that meant in the castle or alive, I wasn't sure. Libella didn't specify the purpose of the trial, other than to determine if he was fully human or not. Since I already knew the answer, and they likely did too, the trial could evolve into something entirely different. "Just keep fighting." I kissed the top of his head, then pulled back, finding his hand and slipping a folded piece of paper into it. "Read this whenever you start to lose yourself." He took it, staring at it for a moment before wrapping his fist around it and meeting my gaze. "I have to go," I said reluctantly, standing from our spot on the floor to help him up. When he rose to his full height, he was suddenly towering over me. Had he gotten taller?

He embraced me one last time and whispered in my hair, "I love you, Ray. More than the sun."

Tears streamed down my cheeks. "I love you too, Mitch. More than the sun."

Voices from another room had my head snapping to a door I hadn't noticed before.

"We need to leave. Now," Nikylo said from right beside me, grabbing my elbow and pulling me toward the door we came through. I met Mitch's gaze as I was dragged away, tears still streaming down my face, but he nodded, his jaw clenched, seemingly assuring me that he could do this. He was strong, and he would get through it.

But would he really?

Nikylo pulled me around the corner and through the doorway, leaving Mitch alone in his concealed room. As soon as I stepped through, Nikylo gently shut the door, ensuring that even the sound of the latch was silent, as if he didn't want to be heard. A light flashed behind the door, signaling that access to Mitch's room was now blocked off.

Nikylo's shoulders dropped in…relief? Had he brought me there without anyone knowing? Was I not supposed to see Mitch? What if the note I'd given him was found? Would I get in trouble? Would Mitch?

The sadness of leaving Mitch behind was soon replaced by anxiety as my heart raced, and I raked my fingers through my hair. "What would have happened if I had been caught in there with Mitch?"

Nikylo didn't respond right away, heading to his room—the one with the cushion I hadn't allowed myself to approach. But I followed him. When he noticed I was right behind him, he sighed and turned to face me just inside the door. "I don't know, probably nothing good."

I squinted at the back of his head as he walked into the room and crossed over to what appeared to be a closet. "Then why did you let me see him?"

"Because that was the deal we made." He vanished into the closet, but not before taking off his tunic completely and exposing his muscular back to me.

Wiping that image from my mind, I stayed in the doorway, hesitant to step further into his room. I crossed my arms and leaned against the frame, waiting. He had promised that I could see Mitch if I "behaved," so I figured it made sense. But if he didn't want me seen with Mitch, why did he even make that deal? That thought led me to the other deal we made, and I asked, "When are you taking me to the library?"

There was a thunk, followed by some colorful swearing before a few more thuds echoed. He stepped into view, hovering in the doorframe and mirrored my lean. He was dressed in loose linen pants... and nothing else. "I think you meant to ask when we're training tomorrow."

I ground my teeth, keeping my eyes above his tattooed shoulders. "Since when do you have so many tattoos?" I blurted, unable to ignore the ink that now adorned most of his torso and arms.

He raised an eyebrow, keeping his gaze fixed on me. "Why? Do you prefer your men tattooed?"

"What? No," I lied, still trying to keep my gaze above his shoulders. The intricate designs remained in my line of sight, and I tried not to commit his bare tattooed chest to memory. I wasn't about to let him think he could distract me so easily. "When are you taking me to the library?" I asked again.

He tilted his head, and his eyes, no longer glossy, locked onto mine. "You didn't win that bet, Sunshine."

"Yes, I did! I blocked you out the entire time we spoke to the Councilors!"

He squinted, a faint smirk tugging at his lips. "Did you?"

"Yes!" I shouted, wanting to stomp my foot for emphasis but holding back the urge.

He pushed off the doorframe and started toward me. "So you didn't think Councilor Kaley was bowing to you?" he asked, taking another step in my direction, and a sinking feeling hit my stomach. "And you weren't so distracted by her that you didn't notice the other Councilors? You weren't afraid Oliver would kiss you like Romeo had?" Another step, closing the distance. "Tom's hugs don't feel similar—"

"Stop," I whispered, choking on the emotions that had built up as he spoke. I wouldn't be able to do any research for Mitch. I wouldn't be able to find out what happens to hybrid children when their powers manifest or what kind of "monsters" they turn into. It meant that the last promise I made to Mitch would be a lie. I wouldn't be able to help him. But I couldn't let that be how things ended between us. I couldn't just sit by and do nothing. And I wasn't about to let Nikylo stand in my way. Slowly, I met his gaze. "Take me to the library."

"No."

I had been expecting that answer, so I said, "It's not a request, Asshole." I stepped toward him, forcing him back. "I need to save my brother, and if you're not going to help me, I'll find someone who will." I held his gaze, knowing exactly what he was about to say.

He leaned down, his mouth just beside my ear. "Good luck," he whispered, causing me to suppress the shiver it triggered. Then he pivoted on his heel and walked toward the giant cushion in his room.

I waited, letting the anger seep off of me, hurt lingering from him telling me no. I forced myself to curse him in my head, which wasn't too far-fetched, considering he had reverted to his asshole ways. He had witnessed Mitch nearly kill me because he was losing himself to the monster trying to break free. How could he not want to help? How could he deny me the chance to help my brother? The answer seemed simple enough: he didn't care. About him. About me.

He was crawling into the cushion of the bed as I spewed some nonsense about him not being who I thought he was—because he had proven to me repeatedly that he wasn't the Kyler I had considered my friend. Of course, all of this was a distraction because just as he was about to settle into sleep, I let myself smile and said, "Mosmudo."

Ah, Little Ember, Drako mused as he appeared before me, his blue eyes taking me in from head to toe. *Taking advantage of our friend's inebriated state, are we?*

"He wasn't drunk anymore," I stated, crossing my arms. "And he's not my friend."

Because he won't take you to the library? As I understand it, a bet was made, and you lost. I rolled my eyes. Of course, Drako would know that.

"Yes, but after what just happened with Mitch, I thought maybe he'd show some compassion," I seethed, aware he could probably hear me. "Mitch is the only reason I want to go anymore anyway."

Smoke filtered from Drako's nose as he settled into bed. He truly took up the entire cushion. *Did it occur to you that he may have already helped?*

I squinted at him, thinking about how Nikylo could have helped since I'd seen Mitch. "Has he helped?" I tried not to snap at Drako, considering he was the only one who treated me the same way he did on Earth. Well, him and Theo. Where was Theo, anyway?

I cannot say, Drako stated, furthering my frustrations with the dragon. *I will say that he will not allow you to do this to him again. He will have learned his lesson this time and prevent you from calling to me again. Especially since you have been using me as a weapon against him.*

"I'm not using you as a weapon!" I started, but then I realized that was exactly what I was doing. "Fine," I conceded. "But I only do it because he's been acting like an asshole. One minute he's flirting with me, telling me how attractive I look in a dress; the next, he's saying he won't help me try to save my brother." I scoffed at the stark contrast in his behavior today. It didn't matter what happened in that hallway outside the bathroom. If he only acted that way when he was drunk, there was no reason for me to believe he actually cared for me. Even if I felt every look like a caress and every touch ignited a fire inside me… When I shook the thought from my mind and met Drako's eyes, there was a sadness there. The energy in the room shifted. "What is it?"

He seemed to sigh as he held my gaze. *I am not certain there will be a way to save Mitchell, Little Ember.*

"No…" The word barely escaped my lips as I crumpled to the ground. My body had given out after such a grueling day of training and capture… the dinner. And now, learning that Mitch was transforming into a monster with no way to stop it. "I can't do this, Drako," I whispered, pulling my knees to my chest, indifferent to the nightgown riding up my legs. "If Mitch… if he doesn't make it, I don't think I will either." Tears streamed down my face as I thought of all I'd lost. "He and Ma are all I have left. I can't lose anyone else in my family. Not like this." I squeezed my eyes shut and imagined a world where none of this had happened. Where Mitch and I were waging a Nerf war in my bedroom on a regular Monday morning, and he hadn't been struck by a car that night. One where Ma made another lousy breakfast, but there was no broken family because Dad never died in a freak accident, and Arabella never got hit by a—

My head shot up, my tears instantly ceasing. "What really happened to Arabella?"

Drako's blue eyes fixed on mine. *What makes you think I know the answer to that?*

"Do you?" I countered.

He didn't say anything for a moment but then dropped his gaze and said, *She was killed by someone in this world who craves power.* The low growl in his voice revealed enough of what he thought about this person. *Not only collecting power, but also killing those who might challenge him. He is the one who has led the hunt for you since he learned of your existence.*

"Who is he?" I asked, fury replacing my sense of loss. Not only had he killed Arabella, but he had tried to kill me, too.

No one knows who he is, but we have concluded that he could be linked to the reason Niccodra is stuck in Palekleido. Drako adjusted himself on the cushion so he could maneuver his tail in my direction. *May I?* he asked, hovering his tail near where I sat on the floor.

I sat up straighter, preparing for him to wrap his tail around me, but asked, "Why?"

One of the perks of the Kavaltis bond is that while I recharge my powers from these crystals, you can recharge yours through physical contact with me, he explained, his tail still hovering over me. *It will also help with the anxiety you are feeling.* He gave me a knowing look. *And you need to get some proper sleep. You have another big day tomorrow, along with some research to do.*

"Research?" I didn't question the recharging part, since my powers actually awakened when I first touched Drako. And every time I'd touched him since then, my powers flared. But sleeping next to a dragon? The idea wouldn't seem so bad if Nikylo wasn't connected to him. Still, I lifted my arms, allowing him to wrap his tail around me, which he did. Maybe sleeping next to him would keep the monsters in my nightmares at bay.

For your brother and the other questions you asked me this afternoon. Have you found the journals yet? Drako asked, lifting me easily and bringing me to the cushion. He set me down between his front and back legs, his tail following the curve of the cushion. The warmth of his scales immediately settled into me, and my body instantly relaxed against his.

"Journals? What journals?"

Nikylo's journals, of course. I told you to ask them for the information you seek.

"No, you didn't. I would have remembered—" But the last time he

and I spoke, he was trying to tell me something. To 'ask the journ—.'
"Wait, what do you mean, 'ask them for information?' How would I even do that?"

Drako gave me a look that I could only imagine as an eyebrow raised. *Magic, Little Ember,* he said, smoke filtering through his nostrils again. *Did you find them?*

I thought the answer was obvious, but I answered anyway. "No, I wouldn't have any idea where to look." Nor would I have had the time or thought to do that since that afternoon.

Look in his closet behind the box on the floor. There should be a compartment in the wall that will open at your touch.

I blinked. That was such a specific place for them to be. How would I have even known to look there? "Why would it open at my touch?" I asked, then added, "And why are you telling me this?"

Because of our bond. I assumed that was the answer to the first question. *You carry Nikylo's magical essence within you, just as he does with yours. Anything he seals with his magical imprint can be opened by you.* His eyes shifted for a moment but then returned to mine when he said, *And just because he has been acting like an ass doesn't mean I have to.*

A giggle escaped me. Hearing Drako call Nikylo an ass had to be the funniest thing I had ever heard him say. I tucked away the tidbits of information he shared with me, leaning more into the warmth of his scales. "How do the journals work? Do I just ask it a question, and it will… answer?"

Speak the questions or write them. Be specific, though, not unlike the questions you were asking me about Niccodra. Perhaps the journals will reveal more than just how Niccodra ended up stuck in Palekleido.

A heaviness settled over me, and I realized my body had relaxed so much against the dragon that I was now nestled against him as his wing came down to block the twilight still slipping in through the windows. Once it was completely dark, my eyes drifted closed while I fought the drowsiness overcoming me. "But what about Mitch?" I murmured the question, unable to forget about him turning into a monster, even as sleep tried to drag me under.

All your questions will be answered tomorrow. Drako's deep voice rumbled against my back where our bodies met. I stopped resisting the exhaustion and let his words gently coax me to sleep. My mind must have been playing tricks on me, though, because surely he hadn't said, *You are strong enough to get through this, Little Ember. I know you are, and so does Nikylo. It is why we chose you.*

TWENTY-ONE
Senses

Nikylo

A body was pressed against mine—something I hadn't awakened to in a long time. Who had I brought to bed in my drunken state? I didn't think I had that much to drink… Naila wouldn't have been sleeping this peacefully; she would have been snoring and kicking me away by five feet. In fact, she should have been off doing her duties overnight and returning for a report this morning, so it definitely wasn't her. But then, who had I allowed into my bed?

Whoever it was moved slightly, and I cracked my eyes open. Long, luscious hair brushed my face, a mix of blonde and brown, smelling of citrus, jasmine, and the sweet grass of the meadow… My eyes shot wide open, the events of the previous night flooding my mind. Rayleigh was sound asleep, curled comfortably against me—and completely unaware that I'd shifted back into my human form. *Shit.*

I admit, being the one she seeks out when she requires friendship is quite fun, Niko, Drako's voice echoed in my head. Rayleigh's nickname for him stuck the minute she said it, making me wonder why I'd gone decades calling him by his full name. He went on, *But I think it is time you come clean with your theatrics.*

You know I can't, I seethed, trying not to move too much and wake her. *There's too much happening outside of what she thinks of me. Why did you shift before she woke?* Because while I controlled the human form—for the most part—he controlled the shifting into and out of the dragon form...for the most part.

She deserves to know everything, Niko.

Obviously, she deserves to know! I shouted, trying to think of how I could escape this situation without her waking up. *But her knowing things in this castle is dangerous, especially since she doesn't have a strong grasp on blocking people out.*

Then teach her to do so, he said plainly.

Rayleigh readjusted again, and man, if that didn't make me want to pull her closer... *Couldn't you have at least woken me up before shifting?* She stopped moving, and a sigh escaped her lips—the sweetest sound. I would have to add it to my list of sweet, innocent noises she makes, right along with that giggle from her conversation with Drako last night. Wait, why do I remember that but not the rest of their conversation?

No, I could feel him smirking. *I was curious to see what you would instinctively do while asleep beside her.* He was taunting me. He'd been doing that ever since we met this magnificent creature who had more surprises up her sleeve than I did—and I had plenty. Drako had never been so communicative with me. Events over the years changed that slightly, but it wasn't until Rayleigh showed up that he pushed to the forefront of my mind and had something to say almost all the time. Of course, the pull toward her was stronger than it had been toward anyone else, including Meg. I shook the thought of her from my mind, instead focusing on what Drako probably predicted.

My legs were tangled with Rayleigh's, and my arm lay protectively around her. It wasn't as if I'd planned it, but damn, I'd be lying if I said it wasn't the best feeling to wake up with her wrapped in my arms like this. Yet she had no idea, and I had no way of shifting out of this position without waking her—unless I used my powers. But I had promised myself never to use them without her knowing. Her thoughts were always intertwined with mine—the one downside of the Kavaltis bond—so that didn't count as using my powers. Fortunately, I knew how to keep her out of my head, or I wouldn't have been able to pull any of this shit off.

She might think I'm the ass, but that comes from you, I shot at Drako.

He chuckled darkly. *She wouldn't be as intrigued by you if I hadn't added that to your personality. You were disgustingly charming before I came along.*

I don't think that part of me disappeared simply because of you. I clenched my jaw. *My father played a big role in that.*

Ah, you mean when he had your brother killed? Drako's voice lost its teasing tone, becoming serious at his chosen topic. *You have to stop blaming yourself for something that happened over a century ago.*

I ignored him and went back to figuring out how to untangle myself from Rayleigh. How had we ended up this close without either of us realizing it anyway?

A door in the other room creaked open, and a soft call of my name made me curse under my breath.

She will surely be unhappy if she finds you in this predicament. He had known she would be coming back all along and probably had planned it for that reason alone.

Again. You're the ass. I quickly disentangled myself from Rayleigh, and thankfully, it didn't wake her. I hadn't realized she was such a heavy sleeper. After rolling away from her and off the bed, she curled up tighter. Before the absence of my warmth woke her, I grabbed a blanket and infused it with my heat signature, laying it on top of her before heading out to the foyer.

With a wave of my hand, I sent a request to the kitchen for breakfast to be sent up. I hadn't expected Rayleigh to summon Drako again last night, nor did I understand his motives for how I woke up this morning, so I didn't have time to warn Naila. She had almost reached my door when I stepped out, and we stopped in front of each other. With her hands clenched at her sides and a scowl on her face, I could tell she had pieced it together and knew where Rayleigh was right now.

"You told me—" she began through gritted teeth.

"Stop," I commanded, raising my hand to silence her. "I know what I told you. It still holds true. This is Valisdrako's doing."

She popped her hip, crossing her arms. "You really expect me to believe that your *dragon* made you sleep next to her?"

"Yes." I grabbed her elbow and spun her around, leading her across the common space toward the table. "Her anxiety was high last night, and he insisted on helping her with that." I lied, waving my hand to light the torches around the room and illuminate the main area of my chambers. The other bed still had the covers pulled back from Rayleigh's attempt to go to sleep before seeing Mitch last night.

That encounter had not gone as I had anticipated. I attempted to check on him over the past few weeks, monitoring his progress in adapting to the changes in his body now that the magic was awakening. During the times I could see him, he appeared to be his usual self, with no indication that the power within him was affecting his mind. However, I understood that being in Niccodra drastically influenced demifae children, so it was only a matter of time before things changed. If he hadn't been brought here, his magic would have remained dormant, manifesting into extraordinary abilities back on Gaia, such as being a super genius or an incredibly talented musician or athlete. There weren't many in their realm, but a few curious Fae ventured to Gaia and mingled with humans long enough to fall in love. Most understood the risks of bringing their demifae back, but some had no choice. It rarely ended well for them…

"Why are you protecting her?" Naila prodded, trying to pull her elbow from my grip. I knew if I hadn't stopped her before she reached the room, she would have woken Rayleigh, and things would have escalated significantly. Not a great way to start a day that was already going to be terrible.

Instead, I took a different approach with Naila and gave her a dark chuckle, "Trust me. I'm protecting you." As suspected, Naila was offended by the words and turned her rage toward me, yanking her arm out of my grasp and getting in my face.

"You think that *kató* is better than me?" she sneered. "She can't even keep her thoughts to herself."

"I never claimed she was better than you," I scoffed, sinking into a chair at the table where the food had just appeared. "But she doesn't take well to people she perceives as bullies."

Naila raised an eyebrow. "She's just jealous of my silver tongue." She snatched a piece of stuffed toast from the table before throwing herself into the chair across from me.

"Trust me, it's not that." The number of times Rayleigh's silver tongue got her into trouble… "But I need you to poke…whatever that thing is in her today, so you're helping out at training."

"But Niko!" she practically whined. "I've been up all night with that rat!" She slumped into the chair, throwing a tantrum, and I smirked. "Can't someone else stoke the fire?"

I raised an eyebrow at the irony in that statement but didn't comment. Stabbing a piece of milot, I returned my face to its neutral expression. "Report?"

With a heavy groan, she sat up and faced me squarely. "Adarachi insists that he only acted on his superiors' orders. He claims there is no reason to imprison him for hunting down the individual he was recruited to track."

"But she's here now, in the castle, where Father requested she be. That doesn't excuse his kidnapping her from me when I already had her in my possession." A shiver tried to creep through me, but I suppressed it.

Naila shrugged, slumping in her chair again. This room was one of the few where she felt comfortable enough to relax. I wasn't sure what that said about the rest of the castle or about me, but her deep breath caused her to sink further into the chair. "I dunno, babe. He's got a pretty compelling case. I don't think a trial for him will go the way you want it to."

More like the way we *want it to.* Drako's voice echoed in my mind.

You don't get to be a part of this conversation, I said before blocking the communication line between us. I could only maintain that for so long, but it was necessary whenever I was near Rayleigh. Otherwise, his commentary would cause me to rethink my choices. "He has to answer for everything he's done to her," I told Naila.

"And you don't think tearing his wings apart was sufficient punishment?" she chided.

I gave her a wicked smirk. "That wasn't necessary, but delightful all the same." I had to adjust the story a bit about how we brought Rayleigh back, telling everyone that Aaidan was trying to stop us from taking her, so we had to remove him from the equation. Fortunately, they didn't question it, especially since he didn't return to Niccodra with us because his injuries were too severe. But now that he was back and I could potentially put him on trial, there was no telling what he might say during it. "I may just have to take care of him myself," I muttered, not really intending for her to hear, but I knew she did.

Naila was silent for a moment, prompting me to look up and meet her gaze. She was studying me. "He did mention one other thing."

I rolled my eyes to mask how my blood ran cold at her statement. It wasn't just the words but the way she said them. "What nonsense did he feed you?"

"He said that if you're going to kill him," I released the breath I had been holding as casually as possible, "he has one request."

I furrowed my brow. "What could he possibly think he would get out of me?"

"He wants to talk to Rayleigh."

"No. Not happening."

"He said it's important."

"I don't care. It's not happening." I stood up abruptly from the table, having eaten my fill, and waved the food away, knowing they would send more for Rayleigh and Bella.

"Hey!" Naila shouted. "I wasn't finished eating!" She jumped up to follow me to the bathing chamber. When it became clear I didn't care about her hunger, she said softly, "Niko, he might have some information for her."

"Naila. Drop it." At the sink, I took the morning tonic and swished it around in my mouth, inadvertently giving Naila a chance to fill the silence.

"What if he has information on Talekor? I feel like that's the only thing he could possibly have. He spent how many weeks getting to know him back on Gaia?" Naila leaned against the counter as I spat the tonic into the sink.

Unfortunately, I believed she had a point. He likely had some information, either about my brother or my uncle. Both were crucial to know, considering one was becoming a prince, and the other was set to be tried for torturing said prince. "I'll go see him alone."

She groaned, "When will you even have time? Your princely duties require you to be everywhere else. You can't just make time to talk to him…" But she trailed off as I gave her a smirk. "No, Niko," she whispered. "You can't do that. It's illegal."

"That didn't stop us last time." When she stared at me in disbelief, I grinned and turned to the mirror. I ran my fingers through my hair, inspecting my reflection for anything that might need attention. When I didn't find anything, I made my way to the foyer, planning to grab clothes from my closet, but halted just short of my door when I remembered who was still asleep in my private chambers. With a heavy sigh, I opened a portal pocket beside me and stepped into my closet, leaving the portal open for light since I hadn't turned on any of the sconces in my room.

Naila was just on the other side, finally able to speak. "Niko, the chances of getting caught this time are higher than usual."

"Adarachi is located in a completely different area of this island. I haven't visited there, nor do I intend to in the future, so there's no chance I'll get caught."

She crossed her arms. "I'm not covering for you."

"That's okay. Theo will."

"*What?*" she nearly shouted, throwing her hands up in exasperation. "How can you trust him not to turn you in?"

"I don't. But if I tell him Aaidan wants to talk to Rayleigh and this is the only other option, he'll cooperate." I shrugged on my dark linen shirt, aware I would need it for training later, and grabbed the matching loose pants.

Naila remained quiet longer than usual before asking, "Why has he taken this assignment so seriously?" Genuine curiosity colored her tone.

This is where I had to withhold information, as the whole truth was far too much. "He believes she is still unsafe in this world." After putting on my shoes, I stepped out of the closet through the pocket I left open, allowing it to close behind me. "The only time he finds rest is when Libella is nearby—or myself. Because, for some reason, he trusts me, even though the opposite is not entirely true."

"Don't you think it's a bit strange that he believes she isn't safe here?" she replied, adjusting my shirt to rest properly on my shoulder. The comfort between us had become somewhat normal over the past several months. Before I left for Gaia, she seemed genuinely worried about me. Ever since the betrothal was announced, she has been more attentive and caring. I would have remained single if Father hadn't forced me into this "for the sake of the Kingdom's future," and Naila, as the daughter of the Dikitís, was a prime candidate. It didn't help that her father believed she needed to be more controlled.

"Not after what Aaidan pulled yesterday." I turned toward the door, realizing I was already late. "You will escort Rayleigh to training this morning. I will meet you there, along with Amarietta and her bond."

"Where are you going?" she asked as she met me at the door to open it.

"I have a meeting with Ollie."

"You look mighty comfortable, Niko," Ollie greeted me when I shifted. He was perched on the edge of the island's cliff, overlooking the sea far below. He was the only other person who had access to this place. This sacred spot was one I hadn't dared to share, as it was the one place where I felt I didn't have to put on a show. Oliver had been the only one I'd ever felt completely at ease with. "No regal ensemble for today's festivities?"

I scoffed, stepping up next to him. "I'm training Rayleigh today, so comfort won this morning. But don't worry, the fancy attire will come later. I know how much you love me in a detailed tunic." I winked.

"I compliment you one time…" he trailed off, shaking his head. Yet, I could see his suppressed smile as he looked back toward the open air before us.

The edge of this island was always so peaceful. No one built homes this close to the coast, and no markets or towns dared to challenge the island's strength. Rayleigh had destroyed that glen so easily that I no longer questioned why people considered the edges of the islands so unstable. A part of me yearned for a place that offered this view year-round, though. The castle was nice if you enjoyed living under my father's thumb and the constant surveillance of his every spy. Even with Naila as my own spy, I still longed for a place with open air just to breathe.

"So…" Oliver said.

I raised my brow at him, curious about how he would begin this awkward conversation. I gave him an easy in. "She's here."

"We got her back," he agreed. "But not without consequences." He glanced down at my hand, knowing my madí lay hidden there. "Your bonding with her was unexpected."

"Unexpected, but not unhelpful," I countered, tensing at where I knew this conversation was headed. *This is not the time to start being possessive,* I scolded Drako. The possessiveness didn't just come from him, but he was a big part of why her madí burned when others touched her for too long.

Our bond supersedes his claim on her, Drako's growl reverberated through my bones.

I don't think that's true, but I also don't believe he'll keep us from her, I said before turning my attention back to Ollie. "When she was captured or held hostage, the Kavaltis proved more advantageous than my powers alone."

"I do not disagree that it was helpful at the time, but our agreement was that you would bring her back unharmed and unclaimed. The other Councilors and I enlisted your help because her original Omada members were being picked off too easily." Ollie was showing his more political side for this conversation, so I did my best not to let my emotions take control. "I understand that your role as a double agent was a risk, and I do not want you to think I am questioning your morality, but our fear of her powers being claimed by a Drakalasson was not, and still is not, unwarranted. Your bond is proof."

"The bond was not something I could have prevented, even if I had seen it coming," I replied.

No, it certainly was not, Drako seethed. *And it is not your decision to make to release her, either.*

I know, I growled back. *Stay out of this.* I took a measured breath, but Ollie cut me off.

"I understand this situation is somewhat different. The Kavaltis is not about claiming but about choosing, for both parties, even if she was unaware that the choice was being made." Ollie clasped his hands behind his back and faced me. "However, she cannot remain at the castle, Niko. She should accompany us to her home, where her parents intended to raise her and where her powers will manifest properly."

"Her powers are manifesting just fine here," I said through clenched teeth, trying to keep my growing temper in check. "You said so yourself."

Ollie dipped his head. "While her powers have revealed themselves, they are far from her full potential. At her age, her voice alone should possess great strength. She ought to be capable of forging weapons using her fire abilities and toppling mountains with just a thought. For obvious reasons, her training has been lacking, but she cannot receive the proper guidance from those who choose to suppress her powers within that castle."

I dropped my head back, having heard this multiple times already. But I knew she wasn't ready for that. She wasn't ready to hold that much power. It's not that she couldn't handle it or that she couldn't do it because I knew she could. But mentally, she was still trying to accept that she was the most powerful Fae in all the realms. I lowered my chin and met his gray eyes. "She's not ready, Ollie."

"You are not allowing her the opportunity to prove that by keeping her in that castle." His tone was close enough to a reprimand.

"I'm not—" I took another deep breath. Keeping the truth from Marta was difficult enough. She always knew how to read me. Keeping the truth from Ollie was impossible. He knew everything about me. We'd been raised together. When his mother stepped down to pursue other interests, he took over her position as Councilor. But before that, we were the rowdy younglings causing trouble around the castle. I'd take him flying, and he would show off his ability to stay airborne using only his air-wielding. We talked about everything because we understood each other. For obvious reasons, I could tell when he was lying, but that also meant I was honest enough with him that he could tell when I was lying—or withholding information. No one was around, but I still lowered my voice when I said, "Ollie, she had the chance to reconnect with her Udara powers and nearly destroyed an entire glen."

"That was *her*?" His jaw dropped, his eyes flicking this way and that, trying to comprehend.

"She needs to accept her powers before thinking about letting them manifest properly." I placed a hand on Ollie's shoulder, bringing his focus back to me. "She's been grieving the loss of loved ones for nearly two years straight. She's on the verge of losing the rest of her family, too. Her anxiety at this point is only managed because she is in close proximity to me."

You? Drako's laughter rang through my mind. You *are the cause of most of her stress.*

I chose to ignore him because a response would have gotten us nowhere. "If you take her away from me, everything could go downhill, causing her to lose complete control."

"You are controlling her anxiety?" Ollie looked genuinely concerned. "She should be learning to control that on her own, no?"

"She *can* control it herself," I began but sighed heavily before continuing. "I'm not controlling anything, but the bond helps keep her grounded, and my *distracting* her keeps her focus off her anxieties."

His eyes darkened. "Distracting her? How?"

I clapped him on the shoulder. "It's harmless, Ollie. But she's easily flustered, in case you didn't notice that when you were flirting with her last night." I smirked, trying to hide the scowl Drako was trying to make happen. It wasn't hard to make Oliver's pale complexion turn a shade of pink, but I'd never seen it turn that hue. Acting as if I had no real thoughts on the matter was tough, especially considering where she and I stood now. On Gaia, she was so open with me, and, damn it, if I didn't think we were friends before we got back to Niccodra. Now? I didn't see any hope of reviving what we had.

"There was no need to call me out so callously, Niko," Ollie mumbled, preoccupying himself by adjusting the cuffs of his shirt and shrugging off my hand in the process. "You cannot blame me for such actions, anyway."

"Yes, yes, I know." I waved him off and then tried to ease back into the reason we had come so far from prying eyes and ears. "Rayleigh will be allowed to choose where she wants to go once everything concerning Talekor is settled. I won't force her to stay here, but keep in mind that her friends are also here. One will have the same choice as Rayleigh, as Amarietta won't stop her from leaving the castle. In fact, she may even join you," I confessed, aware of where Mari stood on the matter. "But Talekor's Doulos won't be so fortunate. Unless someone can break that bond, she will have to remain at the castle, and that alone may be enough to keep both Rayleigh and Kendall there.

Oliver nodded, flexing his hands as he prepared to fly back to the castle. After a moment of silence, he met my gaze with familiar sincerity. "Thank you for bringing her back safely. When her mother returned to inform me of Arabella's tragic death, I worried it was only a matter of time before I lost her."

I tried to avoid clenching my teeth when I asked my next question.

"Will *you* give her a choice in the end?"

Ollie met my gaze, his gray eyes resembling a stormy sky, but I knew his words were sincere. "She will always have a choice, Niko. I will never take that away from her."

I gave a curt nod, not wanting to reveal too much, but I feared I had already given him everything he needed to know. Trying to hide my emotions, I said, "Alright then. I'd better head back to the castle grounds for training, and you should get to the Councilors meeting at breakfast. We can reconvene again tomorrow. Same time and place?"

He nodded and extended his hand to me. "I'm sure we'll both have more to share tomorrow."

I gripped his hand to pull him into an embrace. "Keep your ears open around the castle. Never know what you might learn."

"You do the same, but you know…" he pulled back and wiggled all ten fingers at me, "with your magical powers." He winked, and I laughed at what I used to call my xousía, giving him a shove.

He always teased me when we were younger simply because I couldn't remember the correct names for things, but I could read more books in a week than he had touched during his entire training. Of course, he changed that as we got older, joining me in the library at the castle and accompanying me on trips to the Kyllindro—which I needed to make time for soon. There were things that the castle's library didn't hold, but the Kyllindro was sure to have them in its inventory.

I turned to the clearing behind me to shift, but Oliver called my name before I could. When I glanced back over my shoulder, he lifted his chin and said, "Don't go too hard on my betrothed."

TWENTY-TWO
Who's Afraid of Little Old Me?

Rayleigh

"Sorry we didn't stop by last night," Ken said, releasing me from her embrace. "Mari said the room wasn't letting us in?"

I shrugged, having forgotten about asking them to come by. Although it seemed strange that they couldn't get in, I assumed Nikylo had discovered they had snuck in the night before and revoked their permission to his rooms. I would have to decide if that fight was worth it. Between Leigh and Mitch, I didn't know how to manage my anxiety. Lying against Drako last night had mostly taken away those thoughts, but as the day wore on, they surfaced again. "It's okay. I just wanted you to come because I needed to talk to you about Kaleb—or Talekor. Whatever his name is." Taking a deep breath, I shared everything that happened with him and why Leigh wouldn't be training with us anymore.

I woke up to an empty bed but felt more rested than I had in a long time—going back to even before Arabella died. Nikylo was nowhere to be found, but breakfast had been brought to the room again. I ate silently with Libella while my head filled with the events from the day before. I didn't want to tell her that I'd fallen asleep under Drako's wing, but I was curious how he had gotten out of that bed without waking me.

Naila had reluctantly picked me up after breakfast and taken me to the training yard. I expected her to leave, but she stayed with me as I greeted

Kendall and Mari, who had already arrived. Libella had stayed back, telling me that her duties had changed and she wouldn't be training me anymore. I felt a slight pang in my chest but knew she probably had no control over the situation. I had changed into the stupid linens, hating how comfortable they were, and we waited for whoever was going to train us.

Ken sighed heavily when I finished my tale. "Who is this—this evil person? That's not the Kaleb we knew... How did we go all those years without seeing this part of him?" she asked. All I could do was shrug, wishing I had an answer for her. "He really said he was going to use Leigh as leverage?"

"That's the one thing he said that I'm certain is true," I said reluctantly, reaching for her hands. "She's strong, Ken. We both know that. And we will find a way to get her out. We just need to be more careful now."

"Is that even possible? We can't even get close to her." Tears lined Kendall's eyes, and I pulled her into another hug.

"There has to be something we can do," I whispered, running through possibilities in my mind. I pulled away from Ken and turned to Mari, who stood nearby, watching the castle door. I knew she was waiting for Leigh, but I also knew she had heard Ken and me talking. The pain I felt for her surged through me. There had to be a way to fix this, right? A thought struck me. "When Aaidan captured me yesterday... he tried to claim me," I said thoughtfully, trying to recall what else had been said during that conversation. "Nikylo said if a stronger dragon were to attempt claiming a Fae who is already claimed, it would break the bond and forge a new one between them." An idea formed in my mind, and I knew she was the only person I trusted to try it. There wasn't anyone else I felt comfortable asking, but I trusted Mari and her feelings for Leighton. "What if *you* tried to claim Leighton?" I whispered, not wanting Naila to overhear us. "You have to be more powerful than Kaleb, right?"

Mari met my gaze cautiously. "Don't think that hasn't crossed my mind, Rayleigh. It's the only way outside of him letting her go." Her eyes shone with silver. "But I don't want to take that choice away from her," she whispered. "She's already had too many of her choices taken from her. I want her to choose me, and I her."

The words brought tears to my eyes. "I know, Mari." I took her hands in mine. "But don't you think she'd prefer you to make that decision instead of staying with Kaleb?" When she shook her head, I tightened my grip on her hands as another thought occurred to me. "Then, when she's free of him, you can let her go and allow her to make her own choice!"

Mari stopped shaking her head as the idea settled in. Her jaw dropped slightly as she held my gaze, considering it carefully. I could see the hope swelling in her eyes. "I suppose that sounds better than her being stuck with him…" she conceded, but she immediately closed up again. "But with no way to get close to her… It feels impossible."

Ken stepped up next to me. "There has to be a way, Mari," she said, placing her hands on top of ours. "He can't always be right next to her, right?"

"Yeah," I added, thinking of when I'd seen her away from Talekor. The realization that the only time had been yesterday during training made my shoulders slump in defeat. But then… "What about the ball?" My voice grew more excited as I noticed Mari's eyes widen. "He can't plan to be next to her the whole time. People will be surrounding him, asking him to dance, right?"

"Maybe?" I could sense she was holding back. I knew what it was like to get too hopeful about something, only to have it all ripped away, so I understood her hesitation.

Before I could offer to distract Talekor, someone cleared their throat behind me. I turned around to find Nikylo in his own set of linen clothes. I tried to hide the disgust on my face at the matching outfits we now wore. Looking at the other two shifters, I noticed Naila was wearing similar linens, while Mari was still in a dress like Libella's.

"Today, we are training you in the complexities of what you referred to as jiu-jitsu back on Earth. Here, it's known as Kontas Nami." Shit. I'd forgotten that he was training me today. I didn't think our bet included Kendall, but it made sense since we trained together. He addressed Ken as he added, "Being in Niccodra will have awakened your powers. I'm sure you felt that?" When Ken nodded, he continued, "The movements you were taught were the basic moves you'd need to get started. The complications arise from calling on the element you hone to the movement."

"Why are you training us?" Ken asked abruptly.

He tilted his head at her and gave her a mocking grin. "Because someone lost a bet." His eyes darted to me.

"What bet did you lose?" Ken continued to direct her question at Nikylo. All I could do was purse my lips and avoid her gaze. I hadn't shared anything with her about what happened in the hallway with him. There was no privacy here, and I wasn't sure if I even wanted to share that encounter. It felt too… surreal. I'd tell her eventually… if we were granted any privacy.

"Oh, *I* didn't lose," Nikylo grinned. Ken apparently had nothing to say as her eyes fell on me, so he returned to training. "Libella taught you how to summon the element to your fingertips, right?" Ken simply nodded. "The key is always having it ready during a fight so you can release it with every movement."

"Don't I have to be near water, though?" she asked.

"Not necessarily. That just makes it easier."

That hadn't even crossed my mind. But then, when Romeo demonstrated for us, he only took his shoes off during the second demonstration, when he used more of his power. I almost asked how that worked with the other elements, but since I didn't know what Naila knew of my powers, I instead asked, "How does jiu-jitsu, or whatever you call it, connect with our powers?"

"Kontas Nami focuses the energy into your movements," he explained, surprising me with his teaching tone rather than his snarky one. "If your power is right there, it's easy to utilize. You don't need to put someone in a chokehold to take them down or defeat them because the movements will release the power without even touching them."

"So it's like The Karate Kid?" Kendall asked. When Nikylo gave her a questioning look, she sighed. "I'm not even going to try and elaborate," she mumbled. "But that's what it sounds like."

She wasn't wrong—only, it was slightly different. Learning to spar was just about mastering the movements, much like sparring with the staff. Incorporating elemental powers into the movements makes it effective from a distance, so they can't touch you.

"Shall we get started then?" he asked before turning to Mari. "We'll only take a couple of hours." Mari nodded and headed inside silently. I wondered what she would do during our training. "Kendall, you'll be working with me," he said, and I clenched my teeth as he addressed me. "You'll be sparring with Naila today."

"Great." I should have seen that coming. I didn't know why she hated me so much or what I did to deserve this, but when I turned, I found her watching me with a wild grin. "Are we sparring, or am I actually supposed to learn something?"

The question was directed at Naila, but Nikylo responded. "Both. Start with sparring; she'll add instructive techniques, and you'll go again."

I plastered a smile on my face as I stepped toward Naila. While I wasn't particularly eager about sparring with her, the thought of sparring again thrilled me. It had been a while, and I knew my body wasn't in the right shape for it, but I could still recall all the movements. It was like riding a bike.

We faced off, and she asked, "Which element will you focus on today, kató?"

Great. She hadn't said a single word to me all morning, and this was how she wanted to start? I needed to figure out what that word meant… "Air," I replied through clenched teeth. It was the only one I felt comfortable enough using after yesterday's catastrophe.

She tilted her head, tracking her prey. "Is it at your fingertips?"

"Yes," I said, sensing the energy just beneath my skin, similar to how it felt when Oliver was showing me. I wondered if, or when, Nikylo would allow me to train with him because I would much rather do that than let Naila train me. It was already shaping up to be a terrible idea, but I felt like I could beat her.

"Good," she said just before she struck. She was quick, but I managed to evade her grasp. When I dove for her legs, she jumped over me, turning in the air to land on my back. What kind of move was that? Her legs wrapped around me while her arms reached for a hold. I blocked it, but she still had me in a position where I had to pause and think for a moment. She took the opportunity to whisper in my ear, "You didn't even try to use your power."

Dammit. This wasn't going to be as easy as I thought. I had been so focused on grappling when she dove at me that I lost sight of why we were even training. This wasn't anything like trying to create a shield while flying with Drako—or was it Nikylo? This was to test my powers and see their strength. I immediately tried to maneuver out of her hold, feeding some power into my hands as I attempted to release myself.

It was too much. We both flew from where I had directed the burst of air and landed several feet away, sprawled on our backs. The impact made me cough several times as I got back to my feet.

Naila, however, jumped to hers and brushed off her linens. The motion made me pause. Why was Nikylo allowing her to spar with me in the first place if he didn't want anyone touching me? Especially since she tried to claim me in the hallway two days ago… It didn't add up. I almost glanced at Nikylo but thought better of taking my eyes off Naila. I wouldn't put it past her to surprise-attack me if I looked away for even a split second.

Naila sneered, "Too much power."

"No shit," I scoffed, gearing up to go again. "Got any *good* advice?"

She raised an eyebrow. "Focus on releasing it before I get to you," she chided, then immediately moved again to attack.

Time appeared to slow as I concentrated on my energy, watching Naila's fluid movements toward her destination. I didn't want to use too much power, so I released just a touch as I maneuvered out of reach, moving my arms to focus the energy. While it worked, the energy I released barely moved her hair. I groaned as I turned to face her again, wanting to complain about the sensitivity of my power, but she was already charging at me again.

At this rate, I wasn't even going to catch my breath between strikes. She swept her feet to knock me down while I concentrated on stopping her. As I aimed for her first leg, I wasn't prepared for the second one as she swung it around. "Don't be single-minded," she taunted as I lost my balance and landed flat on my back again. Her teaching method was terrible and was honestly starting to piss me off. What had Nikylo called it? Instructive technique? Well, hers sucked.

I pushed myself to my feet again, crouching low so she couldn't use that move again. "If you would actually *teach* me something, I might catch on."

"You wouldn't catch on even if it were all laid out nicely in front of you," she dove again, but I was ready this time.

I dodged her, moving with the flow and unleashing my power in one of my favorite moves. She shrieked as she was flung across the grounds, landing in a roll and somehow getting back on her feet to crouch with one hand supporting her. "Good," she said, flashing a wicked smile. "Again."

We went through several more rounds of back and forth before Nikylo called for a switch. I was already breathless from fighting Naila, who somehow managed to get me on my back more times than I'd like to admit. Splitting my focus between my powers, my movements, and her attacks took a toll on me. It didn't tire me out, though... No. Because every time I was bested, my anger surged anew. I got back up, fuming and ready to go again, only to be beaten. Again. I was supposed to be good at this! I supposedly had more power than any other Fae, yet I couldn't even use it properly. It was beyond frustrating, and now having to switch to Nikylo throwing attacks at me... This wouldn't end well.

I walked toward him across the grounds, but he raised a hand. "Not switch partners. Switch elements."

My jaw dropped. He couldn't be asking me to use a power I'd nearly destroyed the island with. "You can't be serious," I protested. When his only response was a smirk and a raised brow, I groaned and turned back to Naila. I wasn't ready for that, not after what had happened yesterday. He had to have known that. But there was nothing else he could have meant because my Ignala powers hadn't even surfaced yet.

My hands shook as I approached Naila again, accompanied by shallow breaths and tunnel vision. It had been a couple of days since I'd been on the brink of a panic attack. But I forced myself to breathe and kicked off my shoes to feel the grass between my toes. The cool blades tingled as I reached deep within myself for that green orb, releasing the white one I'd favored ever since realizing my powers. The Udara powers floated easily into my grasp, reaching for the blades of grass that caressed my feet. The earth beneath me sang with each step I took. The power was ready, but my hands were still trembling.

Focus on what you feel, I reminded myself. *What do you hear?* I mentally went through the list, answering my own questions, and finally took a deep breath before focusing on Naila.

She looked ready to strike. "Give me your best shot, kató."

"Bring it on." I squared up and watched as she prepared to move, the world slowing down once more while I concentrated on directing the

Udara magic from my fingers to my target. I was terrified I would cause too much damage if I lost my focus, so when she approached me, a giant wall of dirt shot up from the ground to block her. I hadn't intended for it to be that massive, but it did the job. I concentrated on not using too much power, aware that I had plenty, and instead focused entirely on stopping her rather than attacking. A block is a block, after all.

"We're sparring, not pulling punches," she snarled as the dirt settled between us. "Fight, or I'll make this more difficult."

"More difficult? Does that mean you're pulling your punches?" I teased, placing a hand on my chest. "What's the matter? You afraid of little ol' me?"

There was no warning as she dove across the space between us, as I had suspected. I threw my arms up, summoning the ground that awaited my command. It collided with her leg on one side and her shoulder on the other, flipping her midair. I hadn't expected it to work so easily. Where yesterday I felt these powers overwhelm me, today I felt at one with them. It made me wonder if it was possible to connect more deeply with one element than another. There was probably no way to know since I was the last known Evanian...

Somehow, Naila landed on her feet—again—offering me a wild grin. This one was more of an approving, wicked smirk. "Impressive." She stalked toward me slowly, then suddenly vanished. "Now try when you can't see me," her phantom voice echoed.

"What?" I spun around, looking for where she might have gone, but she shoved me from behind, her arm wrapping around my neck. Instinctively, I grabbed her arm, but when I looked down, there was nothing there. I was holding onto her *invisible arm*. I screeched as I threw all my power into *getting her the hell off*. I sensed my power extending from distant places and felt her invisible weight being lifted off me as I continued screaming.

There's no way to explain why having something invisible latch onto me was so terrifying. It was almost like finding a spider crawling on you, but it vanished the moment you noticed it, making you swat at yourself, hoping to squash it. The panic that set in had me screaming, "Get it off! Get it *off! Get it off!*" as I swung this way and that to try and get her loose.

Finally, her weight completely lifted off my back, and she screeched, "Let me go!"

I couldn't muster the courage to look at her, knowing I wouldn't see anything. It was terrifying, though I couldn't explain why. I crouched down on the ground, trying to catch my breath, but the rage from her relentless attacks still simmered just beneath the surface. I leaned into it, forcing myself to breathe through the heat building up inside me.

"Release me!" Naila screeched, her rage palpable in the air. Or was it mine? "*Now*, kató."

Huh? I wasn't holding onto her anymore since her arm was no longer wrapped around my neck. Slowly, I turned to find her visible body suspended in the air by branches and vines. They were tightly wrapped around her torso and limbs, with one around her neck that was slowly tightening. I stared at her, then traced the paths of the branches and vines to the nearby tree line and bushes near the castle. Had I done that? There really was no other explanation, was there?

I met her gaze once more. It swirled with the rage that filled the air around me. Perhaps it was our anger mingling together as my vision turned red. A slow, wicked grin crept across my face. "Did you still want me to pull my punches?"

"You can't beat me, *kató*," she said, her voice slightly strained from the vine still snaking around her neck.

"It looks like I can, *bitch*." Just for fun, I slowly released every vine and branch, sending them back to their places. All except the one around her neck. She was suspended in the air, gripping the vine that tried to strangle her, as I stalked toward her. "I didn't even *try* to do this." I gestured toward the vines now snaking their way back to their homes. "Imagine what would happen if I actually had full control."

"Enough," Nikylo's voice boomed across the grounds.

But I ignored him and stepped up to where Naila was struggling to breathe. "You tried to claim me once, but let me make this very clear." I was now inches from her face. "I have some control over my powers now, and I will not hesitate to defend myself—"

The vines around her throat turned to ash, and she dropped to the ground, gasping for air. Before I could scream obscenities, a hand grabbed my elbow. "That's enough," Nikylo growled. Then, the air constricted around us, and I lost my balance as my weight vanished, nausea rising in my stomach immediately. For a split second, I thought I was being kidnapped again, but my bare feet landed in the sand, and I fell to my knees and wretched. "Get up." The gentle teaching methods were clearly gone.

I wiped my mouth with my arm and glared at him from under my eyebrows. "No."

"It's not a request, Sunshine." He gestured, pulling me to my feet against my will. He released me unceremoniously and took a step closer. "If you want to fight dirty, fight *me*. I put you in this mess. I'm the reason you're here. Take it out on *me*."

I screamed and charged at him, but he vanished just before I could wrap my arms around him. "Coward!" I screeched, spinning around to find him five feet behind me. With a thought, I made the sand beneath him open up to swallow him whole, but he hovered over the spot with ease. "Stop cheating!" I yelled, charging at him again.

He easily evaded me without his power, shoving me between the shoulder blades as I passed, and I landed face-first in the sand. "You're not even trying to use your powers with your movements cohesively." His tone was *bored*.

I rolled over in the sand, looking up at him, and all I saw was red. I shot up from the sand, concentrating my powers on the ground behind him as I swiped at his feet. He dodged both my feet and the pillar of sand I had sent at his back, making me yell, "Stay out of my head!"

Time and again, he dodged my attacks, each one causing my frustration to swell. When I finally ceased my attempts, I shot him a furious glare across the four feet that separated us as he casually brushed sand off his shoulders.

"You're going to have to hone that rage, Sunshine," he said calmly, clasping his hands behind his back.

"Take me back to the mat, and I'll show you rage," I hissed.

He *chuckled*. "Isn't it obvious? You can't beat me here." He gestured to the world around us. "You may have been trained well on the mat, but that means nothing compared to our power off the mat." He circled me, and if that didn't make me want to strangle him, his next words certainly did. "Your inability to focus makes you lash out. Your uncontrolled emotions make you *weak*. And," he leaned in to whisper, "you're the reason everyone you love is dead."

The rage peaked as sorrow intertwined with it, and the red became tangible as I extended my arms, and fire erupted from within me.

TWENTY-THREE
Phoenix

Heat flowed from my veins, swirling around me in tight coils, transforming the fire into a blazing inferno as it climbed toward the sky. Someone was yelling, but I couldn't concentrate on anything except the power that was escaping from whatever part of me I'd shoved it into. The flames were uncontrollable. I should have known that the moment they erupted from me. Theo had said fire was the most difficult element to control, making it the most dangerous.

The flames blazed hotter, and sweat trickled down my temple. My rage was barely under control. He did this to me. He made me lose myself and unleash the most deadly and powerful magic within me without any knowledge of how to control it. What the hell was he thinking? I could have burned the castle to the ground! He likely got himself hurt, unprepared for the explosion that had erupted. How did he expect me to know how to rein it in? I hadn't had any lessons, or books, nothing to help me understand how to control the fire.

The yelling grew louder, and only then did I realize the sound was coming from me, so I clamped my mouth shut. The inferno's roar didn't help, but I strained to hear any signs of life around me—any sign that I hadn't killed the people I was training with. If I had… No, I would have known if I had hurt them. But I couldn't hear anything or see past the red in my vision, though I wasn't entirely sure if that was due to the fire or my rage.

Before I could decide, a sharp burn prickled across my skin. I glanced down at my arms, where flames were pouring out. They were beginning to blister and redden. I needed to put the fire out—*now*. Ignalians were meant to be unaffected by the heat of the flames, so why was it affecting me like it would any other person? Unless, of course, that's what happened when my powers got out of control. My yelling started anew, but this time, it was out of pain, and the flames flared higher.

"Now!" someone shouted from afar. That meant I hadn't killed everyone with my firestorm! But the voice was lost amid the raging fire surrounding me.

Nothing changed at the command except the height of my pain. It felt as if my flesh were starting to melt. But then something filtered through the cracks of the inferno, sliding across my skin: a cold breeze accompanied by water. It had to be other Fae coming to put out the fire before it reached the castle. So much for hiding my Ignala powers… How did they manage to get through the flames, though? I hadn't even been able to see through it. The cold breeze glided across my skin, soothing the burns that had formed. The water ran down my spine, cooling my nerves from their central point. The red in my vision faded, and the flames stopped at the height of a full-grown oak tree.

The breeze soothing my burns brushed against my face and caressed my cheek before fading from my skin. When the flames weakened, I knew why. I tried to stay upright but collapsed onto the ground as my fire slowly extinguished. My heart raced faster than I'd ever experienced, and my skin remained hot to the touch even though the burns had been soothed. I attempted to regulate my breathing, but hysteria took control. Even though it felt like I was crying, no tears actually fell. The fire had dried up my tear ducts.

I don't know how long the fire raged or how long it took to suffocate the flames, but the minute it was gone, several voices swore violently. I was curled in the sand—wait. Sand? Weren't we on the training grounds? I tried to push myself up to take in my surroundings, but I had no strength left. I could barely see anything, but there were what looked like the feet of three Fae and those of a midnight-blue dragon. When I crumpled to the ground, I hadn't done so gracefully. I landed face-first, possibly explaining why I couldn't breathe properly. I mustered all the energy I had left to shift my head, so I wasn't breathing in the sand, even though I hadn't noticed that through the exhaustion.

"Rayleigh," a gentle voice called. "Can you stand, love?" A breeze swept the grains from my face, and a sizzling sound reached my ears as steam wafted around me.

My tongue was stuck to the roof of my mouth as I tried to open it. The amount of sand I had inhaled didn't make it any better.

When it was clear that I couldn't speak, much less move, the soft voice spoke again. "Just hold on, love. I'm coming to you."

"Oliver, I wouldn't do that if I were you," another voice said, this one sounding more familiar.

"She needs help, Thomas. I am not going to leave her lying there without it." The air around me turned freezing cold, and there were several sharp cracks before one of the pairs of feet landed in front of me. He knelt beside me and gently scooped me into his arms. I whimpered with the movements, pain radiating through my body, but he didn't try to move me any farther. "Shh…I've got you."

I shivered in his arms from the sudden change in temperature. My body was still warm, but whatever he used to reach me made his hands cold. I didn't need to say anything before a blanket enveloped us both. The sizzling around me continued, and I realized water was being fed into the ground where my inferno had burned. There appeared to be something like a moat around me where the sand had been. When my gaze returned to Oliver's, filled with questions, he answered without hesitation.

"Your fire burned incredibly hot, causing the vitrification of the sand surrounding you," he explained gently, brushing the hair clinging to my face with his fingers. I had heard that word before but couldn't exactly grasp what it meant at that moment. "We were prepared for fire, but not at the levels in which you unleashed it." Was there a tone of pride in his voice?

The sizzling around us quieted, and someone handed Oliver a glass bottle. "Have her drink this. Slowly," the voice of the phantom hand said.

Oliver nodded and propped the bottle against my lips. "Open," he instructed. I followed his instructions as he tipped the bottle up, allowing a trickle to flow into my mouth. He then pulled the bottle back and said, "Use that to get the sand out of your mouth."

How did he know about that? I did what he said, swirling it around before he helped me lean over far enough to let it spill out of my mouth. When he pulled me back against him and brought the bottle to my lips again, I eagerly swallowed the small sips he allowed. I recognized it as glykos the moment it hit my tongue and felt grateful for the quick healing it provided, but the liquid hardly quenched my thirst.

He pulled the bottle away again and set it down to help me to my feet, the blanket disappearing as we stood. My joints were stiff, and my skin was hot, but most of the pain from the fire was muted. I glanced around, realizing we weren't near the training grounds but on a flat expanse of sand as far as I could see. Dunes not far in the distance blocked my view of anything surrounding them. That's when I remembered: just before I'd started fighting Nikylo, I had felt the familiar sensation of portaling. I searched outside the circle I'd put myself in, knowing I'd seen Drako's feet moments after the inferno disappeared. I spotted him watching me from a distance, his arms crossed. There was a look on his face that I couldn't interpret from where I stood.

Another voice cleared their throat. I turned to find Tom standing within my circle, but it wasn't him who had made the noise; it was Theo, standing outside the circle across from Nikylo, watching me with his arms crossed. I looked around at the four powerful males surrounding me and dropped my head, sighing. I certainly wouldn't hear the end of—

"Now that her powers are fully awakened, her training should be conducted as far from the castle as possible." My head snapped up at Theo's proclamation.

"*What?*" I looked at each male, waiting for one of them to counteract what he said, but both Tom and Oliver nodded in agreement. When I met Nikylo's eyes, he clenched his jaw, holding my gaze. The look said enough. I stepped toward him, but Oliver caught me from behind. That didn't stop me from snarling across the line in the sand. "You provoked me to use my Ignalian power." It wasn't a question, but I wanted an answer.

"You needed to release it," he said, emphasizing each word.

"And the best way to achieve that was by telling me I'm the reason my family is dead?" I snapped, finding a strength I didn't know I still had. "By saying I'm weak just because I have so many emotions?" Oliver was holding me back now, his arms wrapped tightly around my torso. I twisted this way and that, then shouted, "Let me go, Oliver!"

"I do not think—"

"Let her go, Ollie," Nikylo demanded, his gaze still locked on mine. "She can't hurt me." It seemed there was more to that sentence, but he didn't finish it. I was about to prove him wrong, though.

After a moment's hesitation, I felt Oliver release me, and I closed the distance between Nikylo and me in two seconds. My fist collided with his face, and his head whipped to the side with a wicked crack. He adjusted his jaw and slowly turned back to me, the spot where my fist had hit already turning red. I was either pumped with adrenaline, or my hand was numb because I didn't feel a thing.

"Feel better?" he asked through gritted teeth.

In truth, I didn't. "People could have *died* because of what you did. Do you understand that? You *know* I have no control over my powers, let alone the one I hadn't even tapped into yet." My breathing was ragged, my energy finally wearing thin, but I pressed on. "You could have at least warned me about what you were planning today instead of leaving me in the dark *once again*." I took several breaths, realizing I didn't want to be part of his agenda anymore. Not if he wasn't going to tell me what was happening. "I don't care if you're a possessive asshole. You can't make me do shit anymore." He only held my gaze, his face showing no reaction; it made me want to punch him again. I clenched my fists at my side, choosing words instead. "I am *done*," I spat. The glykos must have replenished my tear ducts because hot tears streamed down my face. "I don't want to see you. I don't want to be near you. I don't want to speak to you *ever* again. If you have something to tell me, send someone else. But I am *done* letting you treat me like a pawn in your plan." I took three measured steps back. "Do I make myself clear?"

Amid all my shouting, he stood there and took it. Never looked away, Never stepped back. Never attempted to stop me. He was biting his tongue. All he gave me was a one-word reply: "Crystal."

Without waiting for more, I turned my back on him and faced the other three men, spotting Oliver first. "How do you know about my fire powers?" Nikylo had instructed me to keep them hidden from the Councilors, except for Tom, who already knew, so why was Oliver different from the others?

Oliver met my gaze steadily. "I know your parents. I am the reason you were so well protected all these years while they have been evading the hunter on their trail." His straightforward answer surprised me, but he continued, "Whether you like it or not, I will continue to provide such protection here in Niccodra. I cannot break the promise I made to them, and neither can your Omada." He nodded toward the three other men, indicating how valid his words were.

My parents. He knew them. And he spoke as if he believed they were still alive. I chose to hold my tongue at that revelation and turned to Tom and Theo instead. "Were you two in on him provoking my powers today?"

They both nodded, but it was Tom who spoke first. "You should know by now that bottling up your powers doesn't bode well for when they're finally released." He had to be referring to my near destruction of the island. "When we saw the havoc you caused just by unlocking your Udara powers, we knew it would be even worse if we waited much longer to unleash your Ignala powers."

"We did not, however," Theo interrupted, stepping closer to me and shooting a glare at Nikylo behind me, "know just how he was going to provoke your powers. You see, Nikylo has this knack for getting under people's skin if you know what I mean."

I did, but that didn't make it any better. I bit the inside of my cheek. "I don't care. He could have told me. I would have cooperated just fine."

"Bullshit, Sunshine," Nikylo shouted at last. I turned to see him advancing on me from where I'd left him. Apparently, I hadn't made it clear enough that I didn't want to talk, but he cut me off before I could remind him. "You haven't even accepted how powerful you are, let alone the power you fear the most." Of course, he knew I feared fire the most... "You are *the most powerful fae*. Do you understand that? Do you understand what it means to hold that title? It took four of us—*four*— each with different powers to fight your fire." He stopped so close that his eyes had to shift focus between mine. "Yes, your fire is dangerous and terrifying, but you cannot let it control you. The moment you give it control is the moment you stop fighting. And the moment you stop fighting is when all of this," he gestured to everyone around us, "was for nothing." He was still only inches from my face, but I couldn't bring myself to speak or step back. "You have to learn to control it because the minute anyone outside this circle discovers that you can't, they will take advantage of that. Of *you*." I tried to drop my gaze from his, fearing he might be right, but he gently cupped my face on either side, lifting my eyes back to his. I stopped breathing, for his gaze was no longer the harsh one. His eyes had softened in a way I'd seen only once before. "Don't let those who would take advantage of you see your weakness. Even if you don't feel strong, like you can't fight anymore, you cannot let them see that." He lowered his voice so only I could hear, his eyes full of emotions I didn't want to process as he said, "You are one of the strongest people I know, Rayleigh. I chose you long before I knew anything about you, and I would choose you again today without hesitation."

My brain must have short-circuited. There's no way he just said any of that, right? Not this person who treated me like I was his to control. But as I stared into his green eyes, mere inches from mine, I couldn't deny he was the one standing in front of me, letting those words fall from his mouth.

What did he mean, *he* chose me? That was Drako… wasn't it? The conversation from the night before came to mind. The one where Drako said, "*It is why we chose you.*" Not I. *We.*

Before I could find the words to ask what he meant, Oliver said, "As sentimental as this is, we need to get her back to the castle."

His voice pulled me from a stupor I hadn't known I was in, reminding me that three other people were here to witness that intimate moment. Nikylo lowered his hands from my face and stepped back, his eyes locking with Oliver's as the hardness there returned.

"With Tom and me both gone, things will start to seem suspicious if Rayleigh is not found on the castle grounds," Oliver clarified.

I hadn't been able to focus on anything since Nikylo released me. It felt like I was staring into nothingness. The thoughts in my head were a chaotic mess, and I wondered whether we had actually had that conversation or if I was delirious from exerting so much power.

"He's right, Niko," Theo said. Somewhere along the line, he had stepped up next to me, making me jump with his sudden closeness. "Her training cannot be near the castle anymore, but she cannot be gone for hours at a time either, especially over the next two days. Yesterday was hard enough to find an excuse for her absence."

"What happened yesterday?" Tom asked from behind Theo, concern evident in his voice.

"I'll update you once we return Rayleigh to the castle," Theo said, turning to Oliver. "Could you please stay here with her momentarily while we do some damage control at the castle? We shouldn't be gone too long."

Oliver nodded and caught my gaze with a slight smile. I attempted to smile back, but my energy and emotions were completely spent. Theo, Tom, and Nikylo huddled together, facing us. Oliver raised a hand, saying, "Before you go, could you please fetch us another bottle of glykos?" With a swift glance at me, he added, "Perhaps two."

"Damn. I must look like shit, huh?" I aimed for sarcasm, but it fell flat.

Oliver chuckled as Nikylo tossed him two bottles he had snatched through a small portal. "I'm going to take her to the Verdanvale," he said. "We'll meet you there."

Nikylo stiffened but nodded, vanishing with Theo and Tom right before my eyes.

TWENTY-FOUR
I Am Not Okay

After the others disappeared, Oliver gave me a bottle of glykos, and I consumed half of it before trying to speak again. "Where are you taking me? And why?"

"The Verdanvale. A small home built into the cliffs," he said as if I should know. "To show you that ocean breeze I mentioned." His tone was laced with a gentle tease, but he continued, "It will be less of a distance for Nikylo to travel back to us. He has used much of his energy this morning already." I almost felt guilty, but then remembered he did that to himself. "Shall we?" With a smile, Oliver offered me his elbow, and I simply stared at it.

Time seemed to slow. The gesture and the kindness that came with it were too familiar. I tracked my eyes slowly back up to his, unable to move from the panic that suddenly hit me.

He tilted his head and dropped his elbow. "Is everything all right?"

I knew this person in front of me wasn't Kaleb, but after the ordeal I just went through with Nikylo and all the emotions from the last few days… A sob escaped my lips as I struggled to prevent myself from collapsing again. He'd only offered me his elbow, and now I was hyperventilating on the brink of a panic attack. Oliver had no idea what was happening. I didn't know what to say, but I knew I needed to say something. Trying to control my sobs, I cried, "N-nothing makes s-sense anymore. Nothing f-feels right." The words were broken, but I didn't let myself stop. "I don't feel like I can trust anyone, not even those closest to me. Not after what Kaleb did. He lied to me for years, being the one I turned to for everything. He was always there when I was at my worst, my most vulnerable, when I lost my sister and my dad. When I almost lost Mitch." I choked back another sob, knowing that was a problem I still had to face. "I thought… I thought I loved him, but now I'm not so sure I even know what love is."

Something soft brushed against my hand, and I gratefully accepted the handkerchief that Oliver offered me.

After wiping my eyes and nose, I went on, waving the handkerchief for emphasis. "Now I can't even decide if someone is genuinely being nice or just trying to get close to me to hurt me. I feel like the only exceptions are Libella, Mari, and Theo. But then again, Nikylo doesn't even trust Theo! And he's been part of my Omada longer than Nikylo has." The constant back and forth about how Nikylo treated me resurfaced. I knew I was rambling at this point, but I didn't care. It felt good to express my thoughts to someone completely unbiased. "And I can't even figure him out! He's incredibly vicious and mean most of the time, but when it's just the two of us…" The moments in the bathroom, the hallway, and even just now in front of everyone ran through my mind. "I don't know! He acts completely different, and I can't decide which of his personalities is the real one!" I was screaming through tears streaming down my face. As I wiped them away, I added, "How do I know who to trust anymore? How do I know what to believe? Anyone here could have the power to manipulate me in ways I can't comprehend, and I can't even keep *him* out of my head. How the hell am I supposed to keep everyone else out?"

Through my blurred vision, I could see Oliver had knelt before me, listening intently and seemingly content to let me keep venting. I let out a shuddering breath, unsure of what else to say. He seized that moment to speak. "All of that happened because I offered you my elbow?" He gave me a gentle smile as a short laugh escaped me. He sat fully in the sand, crossed his legs, and reached both hands out to me. I hesitated, unsure of his intentions, but after a moment, I sniffled and placed my hands in his, still clutching the handkerchief in one. He helped me sit properly in front of him after I had collapsed on myself. "I cannot speak for anyone else, and I know you have no reason to trust me, but the least I can do is try to ease your mind about me."

"How?" I asked, trying to sniffle away the tears.

"By making an *órkomatos*."

"A what?" I replied flatly, uninterested in trying to remember unfamiliar words.

He suppressed a smile. "It is an oath of sorts—one that prohibits me from lying to you, or you to me, without the other being aware of the lie."

I scrunched my eyebrows together. "That sounds…" To be honest, I had no idea what it sounded like, but only one word came to mind: "Dangerous."

"What sounds dangerous about it, love?" he asked sincerely.

I shook my head, searching for the words. "I don't know. Not being able to lie to someone…"

"I did not say you could not lie. I just said I would know if you did."

I squinted at him, sniffling back the last few tears. I knew I wouldn't be able to lie to him, but he also couldn't deceive me without my knowing. It might be beneficial to have one more person I could trust without questioning all his motives. But I barely knew him… "What does it involve?"

He took a deep breath. "A minuscule cut in the palms of your hand and mine, connecting the wounds and uttering a few ornate words."

"You want me to make a *blood oath?*" I tried to pull my hands away from Oliver's, but he held them firm.

"Before you make any assumptions, love," he said calmly, as if he had anticipated my reaction, "let me assure you this is not similar to what you might think a blood oath is. This one can be undone just as easily as it is done. If, for example, you decide that you no longer need or want to keep it in place, there is a ritual to nullify the bond." His explanation seemed simple enough, but how could I know— "Of course, you cannot know if I am telling you the truth about that without the órkomatos in place, can you?" He flashed me a knowing smile. "I will repeat what I just told you after the oath is made if it would make you feel more comfortable."

I chewed on the inside of my cheek. This seemed like a big deal, and he wasn't downplaying it, but he was strangely calm about it—as if he had been in this situation before. But who was I to deny someone who was willingly offering to be unable to deceive me? I took a deep breath.

"On two conditions." Oliver nodded. "I want you to repeat what you said *after* you've told me an obvious truth and a blatant lie."

"Calibrating the oath is essential, but I agree. Next?"

I swallowed thickly. "You have to tell me something no one else knows about you. A secret."

He looked at me with caution. "And what might that have to do with our oath?"

"It gives me leverage over you if I'm ever feeling spicy enough to expose you."

His eyebrows shot up, but a sly smirk quickly replaced his look of surprise. "Clever girl," he praised. He glanced down at our hands and then back up at me with an eyebrow raised. "Do I get the same privilege of knowing something about you that no one else knows?"

"I suppose that sounds fair." I shifted a bit in the sand, uncertain about what I could tell him. "How do we…?"

"Ah, yes." Oliver released one of my hands to retrieve something from the band of his pants. I hadn't noticed that he wore linens similar to mine until that moment. The fabric was a pale blue, with white lettering. I wondered if they signified his power or if he was bound to a dragon as well. He revealed the dagger he had drawn from a hidden sheath. "I will make a small knick in my own hand, and you may do the same for yourself, or, if you would rather I do it—"

"I'll do it," I blurted. I couldn't imagine sitting still while someone else cut into my hand.

He nodded, making a small incision in his palm before handing me the dagger. "You must be quick, as we will both heal rather quickly."

I nodded, making a similar cut and wincing at the slight pain. When the blood flowed from the wound, I extended my bleeding hand to him. He grasped it firmly and said, "Repeat after me. Dhenpsy volégo," he began, and I did my best to repeat it exactly, the language sounding unfamiliar to any I had heard before. He seemed satisfied and continued, "eánto prásko." He paused again, waiting for me to repeat. "Psychosou gnorísi." When I finished the last word, I felt something pass between us. I gasped as it rushed through me and settled right above my heart.

When I found Oliver's eyes, they were already on me. "What do those words mean? And what language is that?" I gently pulled my hand away from his. He seemed a bit hesitant to let me go, but he did.

"The language is ancient, derived from some of the old texts in our Kyllindro. The oath essentially states—"

"Wait!" I said, eager to determine what was true and what was false coming out of his mouth. "Calibrate the oath. One truth. One lie."

"My eyes are gray. Your eyes are red." Nothing happened with his first sentence, but when he said the word "red," a small spot on my chest just above my heart burned slightly.

After a sharp inhale, I reached down to my collar, pulling it back to reveal a small mark above my heart. The tattoo was no bigger than my thumbnail and resembled the top of a scythe hooking around a dash. The mark burned for just a second before the pain faded away. "So it'll burn like that whenever you lie?" It wasn't an intense burn, and I wondered if I would feel it every time or if it might start to feel like mild heartburn.

"Yes, always the same, no matter the lie," Oliver replied kindly. I looked back up to find him watching me with a gentleness I hadn't experienced from anyone in a long time. "The phrase, roughly translated, means 'A lie I will not tell, for if I do, you shall feel it in your soul.'"

I stared at him, unsure of how to respond. In my soul? I was pretty sure that the small spot above my heart wasn't my soul, but who was I to correct an ancient translation of a spell?

"As I promised before the oath," he began, then recounted what he had told me about the oath. The mark remained silent on my chest as he reminded me I could get rid of it if I wanted to. I wasn't sure how long I would keep it, but it occurred to me that I might want to trust him enough one day to free myself from the oath. "And what was the last bit I promised you?" He tapped his chin playfully, smirking.

I smiled back, albeit a bit shy. "A secret," I whispered.

He held my gaze for a moment before hopping up to help me stand. "I shall tell you on our way to the Verdanvale." When he offered me his arm this time, I accepted it. It seemed like such a small thing to feel so strongly about, but walking with Oliver on the sand was comforting. Not in the same way as walking around the courtyard had been with Kaleb, which felt more intimate. He didn't make a big deal out of it; instead, he patted my hand and whispered, "Progress is progress."

A weight lifted from my chest at his words, and I allowed myself to feel proud of the small steps I had taken with him.

"A secret is your price," he hummed to himself. "And no one else can know?"

"Nope." I smiled broader than I had in weeks. Having someone to be playful with again was lovely. Everything had felt so heavy lately, but Oliver seemed to lift my spirits from the depths they had been buried in.

"Alright," he sighed. "I am betrothed to someone I do not yet know."

I balked at him. "How can that be a secret? The people who made the arrangements must know—"

"That was not the full extent of it, love." He glanced at me sideways, his eyes brimming with emotions I couldn't decipher. I pressed my lips together and nodded for him to continue. He lifted his chin and faced forward again as we walked. "I grew up with parents who were madly in love with each other, and even though they had their disagreements, their love always prevailed." A pang of sadness hit me, knowing my parents had the same bond before Dad died. "As I grew older, I knew I wanted to find a love like theirs—strong and unbreakable, where we knew each other intimately and embraced every part of each other. But when I learned of my betrothal, all hopes of finding a love like my parents' were cast aside. I realized that even though my betrothal surprised everyone, it was something that might help unite us all. So, I put aside my hopes of finding someone whose soul matched mine and accepted the betrothal to someone I did not know as my future." He took a deep breath before continuing. "It was not until quite recently that I realized they could be one and the same."

"So you still don't know who she is?" I asked, curious how this remained a secret to everyone else. Didn't he have any friends to share this with? Or did boys just not discuss these kinds of things with their friends?

"Not to the extent most know their betrothed. But I have an inkling that I may have the opportunity to know her soon." He lowered his chin, giving me a playful look. "It is your turn now, love. A secret of your choosing."

I wasn't quite sure I was ready to move on from his. I had so many questions, including why a betrothal was necessary among the Fae. They all seemed to get along just fine. But I wanted to respect the fact that he shared that secret with me at all. "Okay," I started. "My secret." I took a deep breath. "Well…" The truth was, I hadn't really thought about the secret I was going to tell Oliver. His was so deep and profound that I didn't think anything I shared with him would measure up to what he told me. But then I thought of something and whispered, "There is a part of me, deep, deep down, that still cares about Kaleb… even though he betrayed me." My eyes burned, but I blinked back the tears. "I don't know, maybe that just shows how deep his manipulation went, but…" I sniffled, wiping away the stray tears with the handkerchief I still held. "He was my best friend. I don't know how to let go of the person I was so close to so easily."

Silence hung between us as we walked through the sand, but I could tell Oliver was giving me time to process what I had just said aloud. I hadn't fully processed my emotions regarding Kaleb after his betrayal. I went from being his friend to loving him as something more, then losing him. Even before the betrayal, I'd thought I lost him. I believed I had killed him—stabbed him through the heart. The grief that washed over me when that dagger pierced his chest was as horrifying as the other two deaths I experienced in my life. Then—the shock my body felt when he showed up in that dungeon was…all-consuming. Since then, I had only been able to focus on every bad thing he's done since I found out. None of it was about processing his hold on me as someone I loved so deeply.

"A betrayal as intimate as that would indeed make for a difficult recovery," Oliver finally said. "Have you given yourself time to grieve your friendship with him?" After a moment's thought, I nodded, realizing that the time I spent in that dungeon was spent mourning the loss of my friend. "Do not hesitate to take more time if you need it. Grieving looks different for everyone." He gave me a knowing look, as if he understood that I might need more time than I allowed myself. I should have realized Oliver was wise, but I hadn't expected him to be so familiar with grief. "As painful as betrayal is, it can lead to growth, wisdom, and profound maturity. One day, your pain will fade, your heart will heal, and you will see how strong you are because of it." We paused our walk, and he turned to face me. "Kaleb hurt you in unspeakable ways, and as devastating as that may be, forgiveness can only come from those who truly understand what love means." He offered me a small smile. "And that includes you."

He had circled back to my confession. I shook my head slowly, holding his gaze. "I don't know if I'm ready to forgive him," I whispered.

"I know. But one day, you might be. The secret lies in continuing to show kindness to yourself." When I furrowed my brow, he clarified, "Being kind to yourself means extending that same kindness to the person who betrayed you." I tried to interrupt him, but he pressed on. "It may seem impossible when your pain is so raw, but true self-kindness occurs when you extend compassion and understanding to more than just yourself. Otherwise, you are only pretending to be kind."

I blinked at him, absorbing his ability to speak so eloquently while still being completely understandable. I turned away from him, unable to form a response, and noticed where we had stopped. Welcoming the distraction, I took in our surroundings.

A beautiful, cozy home was settled against a cliff at the edge of the island. The view from where we stood was truly breathtaking, and the breeze carried the scent of saltwater and summer days. The waters far below were a deep blue, and I pursed my lips as I remembered Oliver telling me my eyes were the same color. If I wasn't already warm from my fire fiasco, I was sure I would have been blushing.

When I focused on what I assumed was the Verdanvale, I noticed three levels, each with a porch featuring a different seating style. The bottom level had two chairs positioned next to what appeared to be a fire pit. The second level had a hammock, similar to the one I'd seen Romeo build yesterday. And the top level was less a seat than a bed without a roof, ensuring the stars were visible at night—

Hold on. It was broad daylight where we stood. There was no way we could be on the same island as the one with the castle. "Where are we?"

I noticed Oliver had settled into one of the chairs by the firepit, observing me as I took everything in. "This is a home away from home, on the edge of Fotypas Island." It had been a minute since I'd learned about the islands of Niccodra, but I recognized the name as one of them. "This one is mostly abandoned except for the coastlines due to the extreme heat, but I have found it is nothing a little magic cannot fix." He smiled as my hair whipped this way and that in the winds he conjured.

I shook my head, trying to suppress a smile, but he wasn't wrong. The heat felt more manageable with his cool breeze licking away the sweat from my body. I spread my arms and let his power cool me off, taking in the view once more. "It really is beautiful," I said, spinning to take it all in.

"Beautiful indeed," he said softly, his eyes fixed on me. "Nikylo should be back shortly. Would you like a tour of the Verdanvale?" he asked, standing to lead me inside.

"Actually," I said, surprising myself. "I have a few questions." His earlier mention of my parents made me curious about how much he knew about them.

He chuckled. "I am certain you have more than just a few, no?"

I squinted at him, biting back a smile. "For now, I only have a *few*."

His eyes sparkled. "I will happily answer them as we tour through the house?"

Walking and talking didn't seem like such a bad idea. "Sure." I met him on the steps leading into the Bungalow, and we crossed the threshold. The interior was more exquisite than the exterior. I wasn't sure how they constructed things without the same materials we had back on Earth, but this place showcased it beautifully. It was evident that trees were specifically shaped for this home, as they followed the curve of the rocky wall along the back and grew closely together to form the remaining walls. They made excellent use of the cliff it rested against, using it to stabilize the ceiling and carve stairs out of the rock to access the upper levels. It wasn't a large space, just big enough for a few to enjoy, but it felt more like an escape. It made me wonder what the main island looked like for the Fae.

"The first floor features a combined kitchen and living area, as you can see," Oliver started, gesturing toward the counters and seating in the space. Twin blue couches faced each other on a rug, and two matching chairs mirrored them, forming a semi-circle around a coffee table. A shelf along the wall held books, but they looked nothing like those I had seen on Arabella's shelves. Hers were colorful and had beautiful covers. These appeared older and significantly less vibrant. The space didn't offer much more than that, but the details clearly indicated that someone with Udara powers had helped him create this place. "I love to cook," he continued, "so I wanted to have a space where I could do that on my own." He bit his cheek, then admitted, "Sometimes it just tastes better when—"

"You make it yourself," I finished, then pursed my lips when he smiled.

"Baking or cooking?" he teased.

"Cooking is my specialty, but baking is my…" I paused, swallowing hard as I realized I hadn't picked up a spatula in over a month. "Was my passion."

He gestured toward the kitchen. "Well, if you can persuade Niko to bring you here, my kitchen is your kitchen, anytime you would like. It will always be stocked with whatever you need."

"He'll never let me come here," I murmured, opening the cabinets one by one to discover that it was, indeed, fully stocked. However, some of the ingredients appeared different from what I'm used to.

"I think we both know that is not true, Rayleigh." Oliver stood in the center of the room with his hands clasped behind his back. When I met his gaze, I could have sworn there was something there—something he wasn't saying, but I shook my head.

"How would you know what he would or wouldn't allow me to do?" I asked, crossing the room to the bookshelves to see what adventures he liked to go on.

Oliver let out a long breath as he walked with me to the shelves. "I have known him a bit longer than you have, love."

I shot him a sideways glance. "How long are we talking?" I picked up the first book and quickly realized that it was written in a language I couldn't read. I flipped through it anyway.

"Centuries."

The book slipped from my hands. Did he just say centuries? The grin on his face confirmed his comment when I turned to him. I knew Mari was over two centuries old, so I wasn't sure why it surprised me that Nikylo was, too. Perhaps it was because he still acted immature sometimes. Looking at Oliver, I realized that it also applied to him. "How old are you?"

"Three hundred and twelve this year." His eyes sparkled, knowing the number shocked me. He bent down to pick up the book I'd dropped and put it back on the shelf. "Niko is four years my senior." I stared at him in disbelief. Two three-hundred-year-old males had been flirting with me. I wasn't sure how I felt about that. "Shall we?"

He gestured toward the stone steps that led to the next level. I nodded, allowing that information to sink in. After a moment, I brushed aside the thought of their age and remembered my questions for Oliver: "How do you know my parents?"

He didn't respond right away, completing his walk up the stairs and moving to the center of the landing before facing me. He stood in the middle of the sleeping area, and although I wasn't sure why, I suddenly felt the urge to be anywhere else. He spoke as I tried to suppress a blush creeping up my neck. "As a Councilor, it is my duty to know my people. Your mother, however, became a very dear friend of mine when I was part of her Omada."

My jaw dropped, and all thoughts of the bedroom I was in vanished. "Wait… you're telling me…" I said, trying to connect the dots. "You, Libella, and my birth father were all part of my mother's Omada?"

He held up a finger. "You cannot forget about McGregor," he said, turning to the shelf along the wall nearest him. There were more books, but these appeared delicate and leather-bound, thinner than the ones downstairs. Oliver sifted through a stack of papers and finally pulled one out, closing the distance between us to hand me what he found. "We do not have the contraptions you use to capture such things here in Niccodra, but I was told this is called a photograph." One hand flew to my mouth while the other drew the picture closer.

The photo captured six people smiling and leaning on each other like a big group of friends. In the center were two girls tightly wrapped in each other's arms, with their heads leaning together, beaming brightly. I immediately recognized Ma, meaning the other girl must have been Analisa, my mother. She looked so much like Arabella and me that it was hard not to notice. Next to her was Libella, looking exactly as she does now, with the man I recognized as my birth father, Rafael, beside her. He was extremely handsome, his sharp features standing in stark contrast to the others in the photo. Next to Ma, Oliver stood with a huge grin, his gangly arms draped around her and the man beside him—

"My dad was part of Analisa's Omada? I thought he was part of mine," I whispered, studying the picture more closely, where everyone appeared friendly with one another. In a way, they seemed like a close-knit family. It reminded me of a picture I had back home of me, the twins, Arabella, Kaleb, and Mitch. I pushed the thought away, knowing that half of that group was now gone.

"He was part of your mother's first, but when he asked to stay back with Jordin, he relinquished all responsibilities of being in Analisa's Omada. However, the minute you and Arabella showed up on his doorstep, he was ready to step into those shoes once more."

I stared at the picture of my dad and Ma with the people from Niccodra. Ma was the only human, yet she seemed welcomed into their world—almost a part of it. It made me wonder if she'd ever dreamt of seeing Niccodra one day. She must have heard stories from her friends. Sure, she was here now, but she was locked away in the castle, completely unaware of what it was like outside those walls. Maybe I could sneak her out...

"Would you like to see the top level?" Oliver asked, breaking into my thoughts.

I shook the thoughts of Ma from my head, reminding myself to ask about seeing her when I returned to the castle. "Sure." My answer was more absentminded than genuinely curious, but he led me up the stairs anyway. "Are my parents still alive?" I inquired, trailing behind him up the last few steps.

"Yes." His response came so quickly and definitively that there was no room for questions.

"Where are they?"

Oliver didn't answer, standing in front of me on the upper level of the house and chewing on his lip.

When it became clear he wasn't going to respond, I rephrased the question. "Why didn't they ever come back for me?" I hadn't intended for the question to come out so quietly and emotionally, but tears stung the back of my eyes when I asked.

His gaze softened as he stepped toward me, reaching for my hands. I let him take them, noticing his gaze several inches above mine. "The hunter on your mother's trail is far more vicious than Koladon and Adarachi," he said, his thumbs swiping across the back of my hands as he spoke. "She has only managed to evade him once—just long enough to hide you—before he found her again. For whatever reason, he is determined to capture your mother for his own advancement, not giving a second thought to you and Arabella. She has been on the run since she left you with Jordin and McGregor, with your father helping her cover her tracks and lead them away from herself and you. There are times when years go by without him finding her, but when he does," he paused, taking a measured breath, "Well, to put it simply, he does not make it easy for her to escape."

"What do you mean?" I asked, hanging on his every word.

"He has an array of elegant—" he stopped suddenly, turning to face the open air over the ocean. There was nothing there but the beautiful view from the roof, but it was abruptly blocked by a portal that Nikylo was rushing through.

"We need to go. Now," he commanded, grasping my hand.

His harsh tone and urgency made me want to fight him, but something within me said to just go with him. I placed my hand in his, letting him lead the way. "Why? What happened?" I asked as he pulled me down the stairs to the main level. He didn't answer until we were stopped in front of a door opposite the main door, and he touched the elegant symbols similar to those on the door in his chambers.

He glanced over his shoulder at me as the light flashed behind the door. His shoulders were tense, and his face was masked with anger, yet his eyes betrayed his worry. "They moved up Mitch's trial."

The blood drained from my face as my whole body went numb at his words. "To when?" I whispered.

"Twenty minutes ago."

TWENTY-FIVE
Truth Comes Out

"I thought Mitch's trial was after Kaleb's ceremony," I whispered frantically to Nikylo, who had pulled me through the portal door and stopped us before another set of doors.

"Talekor," he corrected, then reached to adjust my hair, which I knew was out of place. I had no time to prepare for a trial, let alone make myself presentable. "And it was supposed to be. I'm not sure why they moved it up, but there's no stopping it now. We must go in, and you need to follow my instructions exactly. I didn't have the time I thought I would to get you ready for this." He lowered his voice, placing both hands on my shoulders, capturing my full attention. "This trial won't be easy. Some things will upset you, but you can't let anyone's actions affect you." He took a deep breath before continuing. "When we walk through those doors, I need you—" he stopped himself, pursing his lips. My concern was justified when he spoke again. "I need you to act as if you've completely forgotten about your brother. As if he never existed."

"What? Why?" I nearly shouted, but he raised a finger.

"We don't have time for me to explain. I need you to trust me, okay?" That was a big ask, but then I thought about the conversation Oliver and I just had and nodded. "There will be a moment when you'll know to act as if you suddenly remember him. But until that happens, you cannot act like you know what this trial is for, okay?"

So many questions ran through my head, but I nodded again. He dropped his hands from my shoulders and turned to the doors. He placed one hand on my lower back and opened the door with the other, his posture relaxing into that of the Prince I'd seen walking around.

Someone had been speaking when the doors opened, but they stopped as soon as we entered. Silence greeted us as several heads turned to see who was bursting in mid-trial. I swallowed the lump in my throat at the sudden onslaught of attention and wrung my fingers for distraction.

Nikylo guided me inside, his hand resting on my lower back as he led me down the aisle. People looked on as we moved in silence. I tried to avoid glancing around to see who was present, but I caught sight out of the corner of my eye that the benches were filled to capacity. Every person I had known or met in the past few days was in that room. Not a single seat was unoccupied. The trial seemed to be an event that no one wanted to miss.

Near the entrance where we first walked in, Tietra, Cleo, and Romeo stood against the back wall. Libella, Theo, Tom, and—somehow—Oliver were seated near Marta and Kaley. Mari and Kendall sat toward the front, while Leighton and Talekor were on the opposite side.

A short, hip-high wall with a gate separated the crowd from where the trial took place. Koladon sat on the far left side, shackles around his ankles and wrists, looking drained and pissed when our eyes met. Mitch was on the opposite side, restrained but appearing tired and uncertain about what was happening.

At the center of it all were the King and Queen, the latter sitting on one of the high-backed crystal thrones on a dais. The former was standing, watching Nikylo and me enter, but his body faced the space between the thrones and Mitch, where Ma sat with silent tears streaming down her face at the sight of me.

I held back the urge to cry. I knew they would bring Ma onto the stand for the trial, grilling her for more answers than she had been able to give in the dungeons, but I hadn't had time to prepare for this. They'd thrown me into it after all I had already been through this morning. Of course, they couldn't have known about this morning's events by this hour, but keeping my emotions in check was still proving to be difficult.

I fixed my face into one of confusion and nervousness, figuring those two emotions could describe my feeling if I were walking into a room with no idea of what was going on.

The King watched as Nikylo and I took our seats. As expected, I ended up on the same bench as Talekor and Leighton. I slid in beside her and gave her a weak smile. She was about to return it, but Talekor, unsurprisingly, made her switch spots with him, not even giving me the opportunity to sit beside her. When he caught my eye, I sensed a challenge there. I saw red—not in the same way I did when my Ignala powers surfaced—in fact, I couldn't feel my powers at all in the room.

I tore my gaze from Talekor's to face the front but reached out to Nikylo. *Is there a reason I can't feel my powers in here?* The silence echoing in my head answered the question on its own. I figured it made sense that powers weren't allowed to be used in the room; after all, some of their abilities could manipulate minds into saying something completely untrue. I ground my teeth at not being able to ask any questions privately, turning my attention back to the front where the King had turned to Ma again.

"Could you please repeat that last answer?" he asked her, his tone gentle.

Ma nodded, swallowing hard and wiping her tears. "Mitch has never shown any signs of power. Greg—" she pursed her lips, struggling against more tears. "Greg told me he would never develop them." I tried not to balk at her words. Why was she revealing these things as if she knew he wasn't human? Libella had told me she insisted he was human, that he was from Earth…

"What else did your late husband tell you?" the King asked, standing remarkably still as he questioned her.

Ma seemed to struggle with everything she had to hold back her words but ultimately lost the battle when she finally whispered, "He could never set foot in Niccodra, or he would be killed for his mixed bloodline." It took everything in me not to react to that. *Killed?* What was the point of the trial if he was already supposed to be dead? It's like they wanted to drag it out, to make it worse for us—for Mitch.

The King merely nodded, turning to the Queen. "Do you have any questions for Mrs. Foster?" The Queen shook her head timidly, wringing her hands in her lap. He turned back to Ma and lowered his chin. "You may return to your seat."

Ma stood up slowly, not out of nervousness but because of weakness. I could see it in the way her arms trembled and her legs shook. She grasped at anything within reach to take a few steps before the King himself offered his arm to help her back to the gate. Once she passed through, Libella relieved the King and helped her to her seat beside Theo.

"Kendall, is it?" the King said, catching my attention once more. Ken was staring at him with little emotion on her face but nodded. "Will you please take the stand?"

She stood up quickly, passed through the swing door, and took the chair that Ma had vacated. Once seated and facing the crowd, she found me, clenched her jaw, and nodded. I wasn't sure what the gesture meant, but I knew she would do everything in her power to prove that Mitch was not the monster these creatures feared he was.

"Place your hand on the arm of the chair and repeat after me," the King said, watching Kendall follow his instruction. Then he said, "*Aftínekla thaftó órkden dhapsevdó.*"

A slight wince crossed her face as she repeated the words, but when she finished, she lifted her hand from the arm of the chair and brought it to her lap to cradle. I strained to see what was in her hand, but Nikylo placed a hand on my knee, giving me a slight shake of his head—a warning. I was being too curious, too aware. I huffed quietly and settled back on the bench, pretending to twiddle my thumbs. Why did I have to pretend not to know why we were there? Forgetting Mitch wasn't impossible; I had obviously been so distracted the first few days that I actually had forgotten about him briefly, but what good did pretending do for anyone? Unless… I glanced at Nikylo sideways again. Could it be true?

Before any further thoughts could invade my mind, the King turned to the crowd. "Who modified her memories?"

I stared at the King in disbelief. Did he really erase Mitch from everyone's memories? My shock intensified as Nikylo stood beside me. His father signaled him to come forward, and he stepped through the gate but didn't approach Kendall. The King merely nodded at Nikylo, who glanced at Ken for a moment before retreating through the gate and taking his seat next to me again. His knee brushed mine in a silent plea for me to stay calm despite the realization I had. When our eyes met, I silently questioned him with my own, hoping he understood. He gave me a slight shake of his head, and I exhaled. He hadn't actually erased her memory of him. But why? And why had the King ordered it in the first place?

Before I could wonder any longer, he began his questions with Kendall. "How long have you known Mitchell?"

Ken turned slightly to take in the weakened Mitch beside her, offering him a small smile before facing the King again. "I met him when I was six years old," she recited as if she had practiced the words. When I glanced at Mari, I noticed her concentrating intently on Ken. Something was happening that I clearly wasn't informed about. Nikylo had said so himself. But what was it?

"Were you around him often? Did you play with him as a child?"

"I spent a lot of time at Rayleigh's house, yes. We would have Nerf gun battles and sword fights with toy swords in the grove. Mitch joined us most of the time, balancing the teams from five to six." Again, her response felt rehearsed and polished.

The King nodded. "Did he ever display signs of clumsiness or strength that seemed unusual or out of place for a child?"

Ken shook her head, the effort seeming difficult. "He was always good at camouflaging himself and had incredible aim," she blurted out. What was causing her to act this way? Did it relate to what he made her repeat? I hated having no information going into this trial.

"It is best not to fight against the vow, tavi." The words sounded like a scolding, but he maintained the same gentle tone he'd used every other time I'd seen him. However, those words confirmed my theory: the vow she repeated had something to do with telling the truth. I glanced down at my hand, at the cut I'd made for a vow that felt like it was made ages ago, but in reality, it was less than an hour. My eyes drifted across the aisle to where Oliver sat. His gaze was already on me, and he nodded just slightly. I wasn't sure how he knew what I was thinking, but his nod only confirmed my theory.

I turned back to find Kendall swallowing hard, briefly closing her eyes, then nodding for the King to continue. He lifted his chin. "Was there ever a time you questioned whether he might not be human?"

"No." Kendall answered quickly and easily. I knew it was the truth because none of us had even realized there were non-humans in our lives, so we had no reason to question it, let alone Mitch.

"Have you ever felt unsafe around him?"

"No. He was my best friend's little brother. There was no reason to be afraid of him." This was another one of her practiced responses. Mari must have prepared her for the trial with potential questions they might ask.

"He was never aggressive when playing pretend or too intense?" the King asked, still using that gentle tone.

"I mean, it was just pretend fighting," Ken began, a smile lighting up her face. "Of course, we got rough with each other, but never dangerously so." That wasn't a rehearsed answer, and when my gaze flew to Mari, I noticed her eyes had widened in fear.

"So none of you were ever hurt during these pretend fights?" His voice had shifted slightly to one of genuine curiosity.

Kendall must not have glanced at the crowd but instead held the King's gaze. If she had looked, she would have seen Mari with a fearful warning in her eyes, trying to communicate something to her. But Ken said, "Well, there were some injuries. We were kids. Accidents happen." Her eyes met mine. There was something that didn't seem quite right as she smiled at me. "Rayleigh was the clumsiest of all of us. She got hurt almost every single time."

"Who hurt her?"

"Oh, she mostly hurt herself—tripping over tree branches and slipping off a log." Her eyes scanned the crowd until they met mine, and she tilted her head. "But there was that one time…" Her smile faded as whatever memory she was about to spill invaded her mind. She opened her mouth to speak, but another voice interrupted her.

"Gus, dear," the Queen said, her gaze drifting around the room, pausing on Mari's face, Mitch's, and then on mine, before finally resting on the King's. "I don't believe this boy would have harmed his sister in the way you're imagining. It was just child's play. You know as well as I do that these things—"

"Enough," he said, raising his hand. "Let her finish."

The Queen bowed her head, but not before catching my eye. I noticed the sincerity in her actions that indicated she had done all she could, which made me appreciate her even more.

Kendall's voice brought me back to her story. "We were at the meadow with Rayleigh's family a few years ago."

The blood drained from my face. I knew exactly where this story was headed, and my whole body shook as oxygen slipped away from me. My hands trembled, my vision fading. My fingers sought refuge under my thighs, searching for the texture of the bench I sat on. Then, a hand covered mine—rough with callouses and radiating a warmth I recognized. I turned to find Nikylo staring straight ahead, waiting for Kendall to continue, but his hand held mine firmly, preventing me from hiding it under my leg. I felt the urge to resist, to pull my hand away from his, but then the words he shared with me after my explosive outburst rushed back. I didn't give myself time to analyze it or think twice, knowing I needed comfort more than the disgust and panic that threatened to take over.

I slowly turned my hand over and laid it palm to palm with Nikylo's, our calluses aligning perfectly. He tensed at the movement but then relaxed his hand and, with an agonizing pace, threaded his fingers through mine. Oxygen flooded my brain as I inhaled deeply, overwhelmed by the emotions that surged through me at the contact. This was neither the time nor the place to acknowledge anything happening, but I couldn't deny it either. He curled his hand around mine, and I exhaled the breath I'd been holding. Tension had my hand frozen in an extended position, but I forced myself to relax and let his comforting gesture calm me as I curled my fingers around his.

"We were swimming in the lake," Kendall continued, pulling my attention away from our clasped hands. The King must have encouraged her to keep talking while I was distracted. "Rayleigh hadn't gone in yet, saying the water was too cold. She was taking her time, standing near the edge with only her feet in." She paused, searching for me in the crowd again, her expression sad. "Mitch thought it would be funny to tackle her into the water, something he'd done a thousand times before, but this time," she swallowed, taking a deep breath, "when he surprised her from behind, she screamed in joy and laughter just before going under. When Mitch resurfaced, laughing, Ray didn't come up with him." Her voice grew softer as she continued, aware that this story hadn't been retold since the incident. "None of us panicked at first, thinking Ray was just showing off and swimming to another part of the lake before coming back up, but then she floated to the surface facedown."

I squeezed Nikylo's hand so tightly that I was sure my knuckles were white, yet he didn't pull away. He held my hand steady, warmth radiating from his palm into mine. His thumb made gentle strokes on mine. I let the movement ground me.

"Greg rushed into the water and pulled Rayleigh out. She was unconscious, bleeding from her head, and not breathing. He started performing CPR to expel the water from her lungs, yelling at us to call 9-1-1 and find something to cover the wound on her head." Kendall had tears streaming down her face at the memory, and I did too. Because that was the last time we had gone to the meadow before Arabella died. It was our annual end-of-summer trip. The twins had tagged along because Tom was out of town and they had been staying with us. It was supposed to be a fun trip, but it turned into a disaster very quickly. "Greg successfully got her to breathe again, but she was still unconscious. He scooped her up, told us to gather our things, and meet him back—

"I've heard enough," the King said. "Thank you, Kendall." He turned to the Queen. "Do you have any questions for her?" Again, she shook her head, her eyes dropping to her lap. It occurred to me then that even if she had questions, the King likely wouldn't permit her to ask them— not after how he reacted to her interruption. "Very well, you may return to your seat."

Kendall shot out of the interrogation chair, and as soon as she passed through the gate, she froze, her eyes locking onto mine. A look of horror crossed her face as she must have realized what she had just done. Whether it was against her will or not, I still felt a pang of betrayal from her as she stepped closer to me. "Rayleigh—"

"Please take a seat, Kendall." Again, the words felt like a reprimand, but the tone was gentle. This male was clearly skilled at deceiving people with his voice. It made me question everything he had told me since our first meeting.

Ken hung her head and walked back to her seat with her tail between her legs. I tried to remind myself that she was under a vow, but it didn't help that she had basically just said Mitch almost killed me. That day in the hospital, Mitch never left my side, aware that his playful spirit might have gotten a bit out of hand. But there was no malice or intention in hurting me that day. Anyone there would have told you so. However, with Ken unable to finish the story to tell the King that, he might never know that Mitch would never harm a fly, let alone me.

A squeeze of my hand brought me back to reality, and I realized I still had a death grip on Nikylo's. I relaxed my fingers to release him, but he didn't seem inclined to let go. I glanced up to find him watching me, a hint of concern on his face—one I didn't think I'd seen from him before. His fingers remained curled around my hand, and another wave of emotions washed over me. He had warned me that the trial wouldn't be easy. That there would be things said that I might not like. But I never imagined they would come from the mouths of people I loved so dearly.

"It won't get easier," he said, his voice low enough that no one else could hear. "Don't let them see," he whispered, his thumb caressing mine once more.

A tear escaped my eye, but I quickly wiped it away, nodding as I held his steady green-eyed gaze.

The King called Leighton to the stand next. She hurried through the gate, sitting on the chair with hardly any emotion. He had her place her hand on the arm and told her to repeat after him.

I jumped up from my seat without thinking and yelled, "You'll have to write it down."

Nikylo kept hold of my hand, gently tugging on it, silently urging me to sit back down.

The King turned to face me. "What did you say?"

"The words. She won't be able to repeat them out loud." I caught Leigh's eyes, wide with realization. "She has—something that makes it difficult for her to repeat words aloud that she doesn't know."

His Highness looked from me to Leighton and back again. He must have determined I was telling the truth because he waved a hand toward the Queen. "If you will," he said, gesturing to her as if she were capable of doing something. She nodded, and a piece of paper and a writing utensil landed in her lap. She quickly snatched them up, wrote down the incantation, and handed it to Leighton.

Her eyes remained locked on mine as she mouthed, "Thank you."

I gave her a slight nod. This time, when Nikylo gently pulled on my hand, I listened and sat beside him. Our knees brushed again, but neither of us pulled away this time. I wasn't going to deny the comfort he offered in a trial where I still wasn't sure what would happen, and it didn't seem like he was about to take back his offer, either.

Leighton read the words off the parchment with her hand on the arm of the chair. When she was finished, the King turned to the crowd to ask who modified her memory. But it was the Queen who cleared her throat, raising her hand timidly. When he turned back to face her, there was a thick silence before he ordered her to return the memories. She nodded, turned to Leigh, and did as she was told.

Leighton's questioning echoed Kendall's, yielding similar answers but producing no surprises against Mitch. When I caught a glimpse of him sitting before the crowd, I felt like bursting into tears. He sat slumped forward in a way that I could only describe as defeat. The lack of sun and proper nutrition was even more apparent under the light streaming through the windows. The King claimed he had brought no harm to him, but didn't a deficiency in food and exercise count as harming him? How was he supposed to battle the monster trying to take over his mind without a proper meal? Without some fresh air? As much as I wanted to believe the King was doing everything possible to prevent Mitchell from becoming a monster, it seemed like he was doing nothing at all.

"Thank you, Leighton," the King's voice broke into my thoughts. "You may return to your seat."

She returned to our bench, trying to sit on the end where she had been before, but Talekor stood, gesturing for her to step past him. I had been ignoring the fact that he was only a few inches away from me until that very moment. Leigh glanced between Talekor and me twice, probably wondering why he had made her switch in the first place, before moving to take his vacated spot. She gave me a shy smile as she sat down inches from me, and I returned it with tears in my eyes, remembering the last time I had seen her—what Talekor had said to me.

He locked eyes with me as he sat beside her—a wicked grin spreading across his face. He knew I couldn't do anything in this situation, and if I tried to reach out to her now, he would just pull her away from me again. Clenching my teeth, I held his gaze, only breaking it when the King called the next witness to the stand.

"Rayleigh." Hearing my own name had never filled me with such terror. "Will you please approach the stand?"

TWENTY-SIX
Even If It Hurts

I stared at the King, who was watching me from his place on the dais, wondering what questions he might have for me. I mean, sure, Nikylo had warned me. Libella mentioned it was possible. But nothing they said could have prepared me for the overwhelming urge to run away and hide.

With a final squeeze, Nikylo's hand slipped from mine, taking his warmth and comfort along with it. Yet, the sensation of his hand in mine lingered, like a phantom hand still holding onto me. I interpreted his release as a sign to stand up. Nikylo stepped into the aisle so I could pass by. My pulse raced, but I kept my eyes fixed on my destination, reminding myself not to acknowledge Mitch until it was time.

The Queen watched my every move, her wide eyes attempting to convey something to me, but I couldn't decipher what it was. However, as soon as I passed through the gate, a voice echoed in my mind.

Do not speak of your visit to Mitchell's room, she said, repeating it over and over. Shaking myself from the shock of another voice in my head, I finally gave a nod so subtle that only she might understand it. The Queen dropped my gaze, adjusting herself as I took my seat next to her. It hadn't occurred to me that anyone else could communicate with me like Nikylo; I had forgotten that Lunnoxia's powers worked similarly to our bond, but only when in close proximity. He must have inherited that power from her.

But why did the Queen care so much about this? What role did she play in all of this? How did she even know I visited Mitch's rooms last night? My questions would have to wait until later, as the King faced me from his fixed position on the floor.

"Please place your hand on the armrest and repeat after me."

I did as he said, sensing a slight pressure in the center of my hand, then repeated, "*Aftínekla thaftó órkden dhapsevdó.*"

As I repeated the words, a slight burn scorched my hand. It wasn't as intense as when Drako chose me—or had that been a joint effort between him and Nikylo? Pushing the thought aside, I pulled my hand into my lap and examined the burn—two opposing spirals whose tails met in a figure eight that divided them. Mentally, I reminded myself to jot down my questions about the mark and the incantation later.

His Majesty turned to the crowd, but Nikylo was already standing. In fact, I don't think he had sat down since I left his side. With his eyes locked on mine, he walked through the gate.

His voice invaded my mind immediately. *If you have to answer a question where the truth will incriminate Mitch, tell a half-truth.* He spoke so quickly that I thought he might want to say more, but instead, he took a moment to hold my gaze. His eyes conveyed so much; emotions flowing through them that I'd never seen from him before. As I stared into his deep green eyes, something deep within me stirred. *Don't let them see,* he whispered, then turned on the ball of his foot and returned to his seat without a backward glance.

His last words struck a chord in me, bringing up feelings I didn't want to acknowledge right now, or possibly ever, but tears stung my eyes anyway. Figuring I'd use them for the act I was supposed to perform, I turned to Mitch, allowing a sob to escape. His eyes were already on me, filled with worry and love, just as they had been when I left him last night.

"Mitch," I whispered, reaching my hand out to him but quickly retracting it when I realized where we were. I pursed my lips, unsure of what to do or say. The tears should have been enough to convince them that I had just remembered he existed, but honestly, I probably should have jumped out of my chair to hug him or something.

The King cleared his throat, pulling my attention back to him. "Rayleigh, when did you realize you were not human?"

Well, he wasn't wasting any time with formalities… What a strange question to start with, though, given that the trial was meant to be about

Mitch. But I answered anyway, "When I was told I wasn't human."

"And who told you that you weren't human?"

"Theo." I spotted him in the crowd, and he offered me a warm smile, though I could see the apprehension in his eyes.

"And when Theo told you that you weren't human, did you question your family's heritage as well?"

"Yes," I replied swiftly, realizing that when Theo first told me, I still believed they were my biological family.

The King stood so utterly still that it was unsettling. "Was there anything you believed could justify them being non-human?"

"No, because I didn't know the difference between human and fae."

"And since then, have you thought of anything that might qualify them as something other than human?"

Before the answer I wanted to give could slip through my lips, it got stuck in my throat. I couldn't say the word "no" as I intended. As I thought about why that was, I realized it was because I *had* thought about it since then. But it wasn't anything that would put any pressure on Mitch since they already knew he wasn't human. So I replied, "Yes."

"What might that be?" the King inquired.

"Well, Mitch was hit by a car going pretty fast. He should have died, but he survived."

"Does anything else come to mind?"

I shrugged, "Not to deal with Mitch, no." I figured it didn't matter what I thought about my dad, and honestly, I didn't really want to think about him right now anyway.

The thought was short-lived as the King said, "What about your father?"

I took a deep, unsteady breath, willing the tears to stay at bay. "Just that he was incredibly strong, and his singing seemed magical." The words rushed out, barely registering in my mind before they left my mouth.

"And your mother?"

My head snapped to him. "No. Nothing about her seemed inhuman." My brows furrowed at his question, wondering how they could even think she wasn't human, especially since she was deteriorating so quickly in Niccodra.

The King nodded, satisfied with my answer enough to go on. "Have you ever been hurt by your brother?"

I gulped, then remembered what Nikylo had said about half-truths. "Yes, in the story you heard Kendall tell. But it was an accident."

"Were you afraid of your brother after that incident?"

"No."

"Have you ever felt afraid of him?"

"No." I had expected the word to stick in my throat as last night's events flashed through my mind, but I was simply caught off guard and scared *for* him, not *of* him.

The King's eyebrows shot up at my response. It made me wonder why he thought I should be afraid of Mitch. He recovered from his surprise quickly, asking, "So you feel safe alone in a room with Mitch?"

"Yes."

The King smiled gently. "And the last time you saw him, did you feel unsafe?"

My blood ran cold. He knew. He had to know. There was no way he *should* know, but with that question and the smile that accompanied it…

There was no escaping the truth. No half-truths to tell. The mark on my hand burned as I tried to think of a way around the answer, the pain beginning to creep up my arm. I tried to avoid his gaze, my eyes drifting across the front of the room. Koladon was there, a maniacal grin spread across his face. The last time I was meant to see Mitch was in that cave. Where I didn't feel safe. An idea formed, but it needed to be carefully worded.

"No, I didn't feel safe."

"And why did you not feel safe?" the King's voice was again that deceiving, gentle tone.

"Because I was being attacked."

"Who was attacking you?"

"A monster." Even though I knew the words meant the monster within Mitch, I forced myself to glare across the room at Koladon when I said the word, accusation heavy in my tone. The vow I'd taken seemed satisfied with my answers, and the burning sensation disappeared.

Just as I planned, the King followed my gaze and sighed. "Ah, yes. The events in the cave." For the first time, the King paced in front of me. He hadn't moved during anyone else's questioning, remaining eerily still while they were on the stand. So why start now? "Did you know that a demifae's powers do not develop unless they are in Niccodra?" he asked.

My heart sank. "No," I whispered. The thoughts racing through my mind all led back to the same person, and I spotted his honey-brown eyes shining brightly from the front row. He wasn't smiling or gloating at all. In fact, he seemed apologetic, and that somehow made it worse.

"However, if they are close to a portal when it opens, they can also develop."

I furrowed my brows, seeing the King still pacing in front of me. "What do you mean?"

"The portal to this world from Gaia is in a meadow, one I've heard you're familiar with, no?" The King didn't actually look at me as I was compelled to nod because of the vow. "If he had been anywhere near the portal when it opened at any point in his life, the magic from Niccodra would have seeped into his system, starting the process of developing his powers." The King stopped suddenly to face me again. "Unfortunately, you've given me new questions that you won't be able to answer. So if you will—"

"What is the point of this trial?" I asked abruptly, surprising even myself.

The King appeared taken aback, and several gasps echoed through the crowd, followed by whispers. Had no one ever asked the King questions from the stand? I almost shrank back into my seat, but something within me urged me to stand my ground. When he finally regained his composure, the King cleared his throat. "To determine if your brother poses a danger to himself and our community."

"But if it's against the law for humans and Niccodrans to procreate, why aren't you following the repercussions of that law?" The question didn't sound like my own voice; it was more profound and demanding than I'd ever thought I could be. Yet, it was a question that had bothered me ever since I was told they knew he wasn't human.

The King studied me, his rigid stance gone as he stood before me, replaced by one of fluidity and freedom. "That law was made decades ago. We haven't seen a full-grown demifae in Niccodra since that law was enacted. When Mitch was brought to Niccodra, I was told there were signs that he wasn't human, and I've since seen them myself. What I haven't seen is the part of him that's a so-called monster." He hadn't raised his voice, but I felt like cowering away from him. His gentle tone was still deceptive, but what he said was perplexing. If what he was saying were true, then… "I'm trying to prevent an execution if it's unnecessary."

This time, I did sink into my chair. After everything, he was trying to save Mitchell?

"I understand this isn't easy for you, but I meant what I said on your first day here. You and yours were not meant to be harmed when you were brought here." He stepped closer to me and lowered his voice, locking his gaze with mine. "I'm only following protocol as advised. I would have returned them both to Gaia immediately if I had been the only one aware."

I let his words sink in. This King wasn't as bad as some had made him out to be. Sure, he wasn't someone I would trust with everything I knew, but he was proving to be better than the person I had imagined. It made me question how he and the person who trained Kaleb to be so evil and manipulative could be one and the same. That thought alone kept me wary of him.

He straightened, offering me his hand. "You may return to your seat now."

My nerves kicked into high gear as I returned to my seat and sat heavily beside Nikylo. Being next to him was a comfort in itself, and I wasn't sure what the next part of this would involve, but it didn't feel right to reach for his hand again, so I just clasped them in my lap as the King turned toward the back of the room.

"Please bring in our next witness," he said to someone near the doors.

How many others would he question? I knew he was just following protocol, but why go to such lengths for a trial if he was merely trying to prevent Mitch's execution? Besides, who else could possibly know anything about Mitch and his demifae abilities?

The answer came to me just as the doors behind us swung open. A hush fell over the room at the arrival of whoever entered, and I craned my neck to see who they had brought in. My heart sank as the person I dreaded stepped into view.

Dr. Smiles, or Stefano, confidently strolled up the aisle. No restraints, no guards, just him. When he made eye contact with me, he offered a small smile. "Lovely to see you again, Rayleigh," he whispered as he passed me on his way to the dais.

A chill ran through me. Another person I had trusted my entire life was now here to possibly ruin it. But why say the words he always used to greet me with when I saw him at the hospital? What was he up to?

Stefano went through the same ritual as everyone else, reminding me of the burn on my hand from when I was testifying. When I looked down, it was completely gone.

"It only stays as long as you're in the chair," Nikylo whispered next to me, drawing my attention. He still wasn't looking at me, but he was relaxed into the bench beside me, arms crossed over his chest and surveying the room around us. Since he couldn't use his powers here, he wouldn't know what I was thinking, which meant he must have been watching me study it before looking away.

I pushed that thought aside, placing my hands back in my lap as I tried to focus on what Stefano was saying. "—injuries were healed internally when he left my care."

"Did you notice any differences in his anatomy or blood work?" the King asked.

"Nothing I hadn't seen before," he replied coolly.

The King appeared to appreciate his answer, moving on without requesting further details. I found it odd that he didn't ask him to elaborate because, as a doctor, he had encountered normal human anatomy and bloodwork, yet within Niccodra, I'm sure he had also seen Fae anatomy and bloodwork. If they even had that kind of medical care here… He could have been alluding to either Fae or humans with his answer, which would indicate avoidance… I squinted at the deceitful doctor.

"Do you believe he shouldn't have survived the accident?" the King questioned, his sure and steady stance unwavering.

Stefano sighed, tilting his head back and forth before responding. "It's hard to say. The injuries from his accident all pointed to being fatal, even with Theophilus finding him shortly after it happened." I nearly choked at what I assumed to be Theo's full name. No one noticed because Stefano continued, "I would say it was a miracle he even survived long enough for Theophilus to perform a quick healing."

The King started to pace. "Do you think that may be due to his powers being activated?"

Stefano hesitated but then said, "It's a possibility."

The King paused in front of Mitch, studying him briefly before starting to pace again. "You reported that his injuries were not as fatal as when Theophilus discovered him."

"No. Theophilus provided me with a complete report of his findings before leaving him in my care. He told me he performed minor patches on severe internal bleeding and organ damage, just enough to get him to the hospital."

"Were his injuries as Theophilus described when *you* began treatment?"

"No."

A collective gasp echoed through the crowd, making me jump. As I turned to discover what happened, Nikylo shook his head slightly for me to see, then nodded toward the King and Stefano.

The latter appeared somewhat uncomfortable as he shifted in his chair, almost as if he hadn't intended to answer that question so quickly. The former seemed to contemplate his brief response.

"Were you the one who helped Rayleigh when her brother tackled her into the water?" the King asked.

"Yes."

"Did you observe anything unusual about her injuries?"

Stefano took a deep breath, scanning the crowd until he found me. "Her head had been slammed into a rock, likely due to the tackle, but the amount of water filling her lungs shouldn't have been as excessive as it was. I'm not entirely sure how she swallowed so much, unless…" Stefano stretched his head to the side, appearing uncomfortable. "Unless she was held under for too long."

The whispers began immediately, but my gaze darted to Mitch. He wouldn't have held me underwater. I knew that. But when I noticed the tears streaming down his face, I knew he thought it was possible. He might not have done it intentionally, but even the slightest chance of his powers being triggered made Stefano's answers feel ten times worse. It didn't seem like Mitch had any chance of surviving this trial. I didn't try to stop the tears from blurring my vision. How was I going to survive after losing him?

Drako's words floated through my mind. They chose me for my strength, but that was the last thing I felt. What I truly felt was powerless.

"Thank you, Stefano. You are free to go." The King watched as Stefano stepped down from the dais and left the courtroom, the whispers subsiding after his departure. His Majesty's gaze shifted to the person beside me. "Nikylo, I will need your assistance with the next two."

I felt as if I had been plunged into cold water when Nikylo stood up and walked through the gate. He didn't glance back at me until he was standing behind the chair. He pursed his lips, and I knew that signified things were about to get worse. And, of course, he wasn't by my side to —

Someone slid into the spot he had vacated, and I turned to see Oliver settling in beside me with a slight smile on his face. I returned the smile and faced Nikylo again. He was still watching me, so I mouthed, "Thank you," to him and received a curt nod in response. I knew that as soon as he left my side, he must have signaled Oliver, knowing I would need someone to hold on to during whatever was about to happen.

Taking a deep breath, I relaxed as much as possible while the King crossed the floor toward the man who was chained up and sneering. "Brother," the King said, gesturing for him to stand.

Koldaon sneered at him. "Typically, family doesn't imprison each other, *brother*," he spat.

"Nor do they torture each other." I couldn't help but give the King some credit for how calm he remained. If I were in his position, I would have been throwing punches by now. Even though Kaleb turned out to be evil all along, I hated how Koladon had controlled me, tortured my family, and made me believe I had killed Kaleb. I still wanted to give him a piece of my mind.

Koladon was led to the chair where Nikylo stood, chains and all. Once seated, the King glanced at Nikylo, who nodded and grabbed Koladon's shoulders while the King produced a key to unlock the shackles on his wrists. The process took only a few seconds, but I understood why Nikylo was up there and not someone else. With the power to control both mind and body, he could prevent Koladon from doing anything against his will.

Surprisingly, Koladon didn't resist Nikylo's hold at all. He calmly allowed them to help him get settled and placed his hand on the arm of the chair when instructed. He recited the words and then waited patiently for the King to start his questioning.

"Did you know my son's identity when you captured him?" That was when I realized the King might be killing two birds with one stone during this trial. Koladon had been accused of torturing three innocents and taken to the dungeons because of it.

"No," Koladon drawled, making himself more comfortable in the chair as he sank into it. Nikylo's hands rested on his shoulders, likely maintaining contact because it was easier to control him that way.

"Did you know that Mitchell wasn't human when you first encountered him?"

"No, Your Majesty. I knew nothing of either lineage."

"If you had, would you have brought them to me?"

Koladon sneered, "Your son? Sure. The boy? No." When the King asked why, he replied, "Because I know the law, brother. I would have followed through with it, as I was instructed when hunting down the other half-bloods. Besides," his eyes found me in the crowd, "I was the one who tried to kill him in the first place."

My hand flew to my mouth as an arm wrapped around my shoulders, drawing me close for comfort. I knew Koladon had been behind the attacks, but hearing him admit it so bluntly was jarring.

"Why did you attempt to kill him if you were unaware he was a demifae?" the King inquired, diverting Koladon's attention from mine.

"I was just following orders," he said. No one responded, so he continued, "I assumed that's what you would want me to do: isolate Rayliana."

There was that name again, reminding me how much I hated it. While I wanted to know where it came from, I more so wanted to burn it from his vocabulary and my mind.

"What would isolating her do for me?" He was pacing again.

Koladon sighed, seemingly unable to tell any more half-truths. "Nothing for you, I suppose."

His Majesty halted, turning sharply to his brother. "Explain." His gentle tone had vanished. This was the voice of a King.

A sly grin crept slowly across the Kool-Aid Man's face. "No, I don't think I will."

The room fell so quiet that I could hear a pin drop. When I was sitting in that chair, it was impossible not to answer the questions being posed to me. So how did Koladon so easily deny answering one? Or perhaps that was the point. The King hadn't technically asked a question; he simply instructed him to explain. Were there rules to the way the vow worked?

Nikylo watched me, a fierce determination etched on his face as sweat dripped down his temple. *Wait a minute…* If he was sweating, that meant he was working much harder than he appeared to be. I moved to stand, intending to point out this obvious difference in Nikylo's demeanor, but he shook his head just as I felt a tug on my shoulder where Oliver had draped his arm around me.

"Nikylo has this handled," he whispered close to my ear. "But if you cross that threshold, Niko will lose his focus, and Koladon will have access to you."

I slowly turned to face him at his words. Did he realize how much more he conveyed than just the words he spoke? I glanced back at Nikylo, whose focus was now on the back of Koladon's head. The veins in his neck were visible, and sweat trickled further down his face. I shook my head, practically begging, "Something's wrong. He's working too hard. You have to help him, Oliver."

"And if something goes wrong, it is my duty to remove you from the danger of the situation. You cannot be the source of Nikylo's distraction, nor can we let you fall back into the hands of the enemy." Oliver's eyes bore into mine, urging me to grasp whatever it was he wasn't saying, but I had no idea what he meant. It seemed like they were preparing for something terrible to happen at this trial. Was Koladon truly that powerful? Could he overpower the three royals and create chaos? There were so many other formidable beings in the courtroom. How could Koladon possibly defeat them all?

The King hadn't spoken since his brother refused to answer him. He was staring at him, clenching his jaw. I wondered if their feud had begun long before Koladon tortured Kaleb or my family. Finally, he wiped his hand across his face, clasped both hands behind his back, and stood before his brother again.

"When did you realize Mitchell was not human?"

Wait, he was going back to questioning about Mitch? Just like that?

"The first time I branded him with a hot iron rod."

I was going to be sick. My gaze darted to Mitch, who glared at Koladon from where he sat, still shackled at his ankles and wrists. How long had he been in the cave with Koladon? It couldn't have been since the day he left the hospital because he came to my house searching for him. That meant Koladon didn't know where he was when Theo and Chief—er, Bastiel, took him and Ma away. Did they go to the hospital after my house was destroyed? Is that when they roped in Dr. Smiles— er, Stefano? If his behavior during his testimony told me anything, it was that he was either a really good actor or...

Or he had been controlled by Koladon back on Earth.

My gaze snapped back to where the Kool-Aid Man sat, already watching me. I opened my mouth to shout some sort of warning, hoping to let them know something was wrong, but I was too late.

The doors at the back of the courtroom burst open, and everyone turned at the sudden noise. However, I kept my eyes on Koladon, jumping out of my seat when people standing obstructed my view of him.

"You're Majesties!" someone shouted. The Queen reached for the King, who grabbed her hand. The person who must have shouted for them also grabbed her hand. The room constricted, transporting them from the courtroom.

A scream echoed at the horror of what was happening in the back of the room, but I strained to see what the monster at the front was up to. Chaos erupted throughout the room as more shouts of terror echoed. Whatever they were witnessing in the back was causing mass panic, and the room constricting multiple times teleported members of the crowd from the space. How were their powers working now?

I pushed my way through the crowd, keeping my eyes on Nikylo and Koladon. He was so focused on controlling Koladon that he didn't notice the person approaching him from behind.

"Kyler!" I shouted, forgetting to use his real name, but it didn't matter. He didn't hear me.

The person behind him whispered something in his ear, making him relax his grip on Koladon and turn to face them. He didn't say anything or make any move to resist this person. I couldn't see their mouth moving, but I knew they were speaking, and Nikylo stepped closer, drawn forward by some unseen force. A hood covered the other person's face, so I didn't recognize their features, but I knew that gangly stature anywhere.

"Mitch," I whispered, his name a question on my lips. Nikylo faced him now, having long forgotten about Koladon, who disappeared as soon as Nikylo's hands left his shoulders. The screams around me grew louder, and I did my best to push through the crowd to get to the front. "Mitch!" I shouted over everyone else, but my voice was drowned out by the echoing shouts of others.

Mitch lunged forward, closing the distance between them, and Nikylo doubled over. My hand shot to my mouth as Mitch pull his hand back—

No. That wasn't a hand.

In the spot where his hand should have been were razor-sharp claws, resembling a bird's, covered in blood.

A strangled cry escaped me, and Mitch's gaze flew to mine. They were clearer than they'd ever been, the deep green sparkling even from this distance. I blinked away the tears, and he was gone. Disappeared. As if he had just vanished on site. But he couldn't do that; he didn't have—

Magic.

A fresh wave of panic surged through me as I made a final push toward the gate to reach Nikylo, who had to be bleeding out on the courtroom floor. But then, arms wrapped around my waist, yanking me backward. "No! Stop!" I cried, struggling against the grip I knew was Oliver's. "Nikylo's hurt!" I fought with everything I had to get Oliver to let go of me, but he wouldn't budge. He dragged me through the crowd that was rushing out the doors, kicking and screaming.

Once through the door, Oliver pushed and shoved people aside, making his way toward a hallway against the crowd. When we reached it, I realized it wasn't a hallway at all but a bridge overlooking the giant waterfall. He stopped, pulling me to one of the railings and turning me to face him. "Rayleigh, I need you to calm down," he instructed, his calmness unthinkable at a time like this. My breathing was ragged from screaming, and I tried to steady it, but my mind was elsewhere. Oliver pressed on, "We have to get you to safety. We will come back when everything has calmed down, but right now, we need to get you out of here. You are our first priority." I looked over Oliver's shoulder, searching for a familiar face in the crowd. Nikylo should be rushing out after us, his stubborn possessiveness unable to let someone else get me to safety.

But he wasn't there. He wasn't going to be there.

Two familiar faces emerged from the crowd, hurrying toward us. "Oliver, what are you still doing here? You need to get her out of here," Mari urged, with Kendall following closely behind her. "*Now.*"

"I know! I am trying, Amarietta," he said, whirling to meet her gaze. "She is worried about Nikylo's injuries."

Mari pursed her lips, her eyes darting to me before she nodded slightly. "Theo went to get him, but you can't worry about him, Rayleigh. You need to get out of here." When she noticed my lip quiver, she stepped between Oliver and me, placing her hands on my shoulders. "I know you're worried about him, but Niko would kill us if we didn't get you to safety; you know that. I'm sure he'll be fine," she said, though her words lacked conviction. "But you *have* to go with Oliver."

Tears had begun streaming down my face at some point, and I knew I wouldn't be able to stop them anytime soon. I nodded, and Mari stepped back to Kendall, taking her hand and pulling her to the railing. She wrapped her arms around Ken from behind, and before I realized what was happening, they both went hurtling over the ledge.

"What the hell—Mari!" I shouted, leaning over the railing to watch as they fell. Then I caught sight of iridescent wings flashing in the light of the setting sun amidst the water spray from the waterfall far below. My shock at their jump off the bridge faded, but I still couldn't fathom throwing myself off a bridge like that.

Oliver gently grabbed my face, pulling my gaze to his. "Rayleigh, focus." I blinked away the tears and fear and met his grey eyes. "Do you trust me?"

I shook my head. How could he ask me that right now? My trust in anyone had been shattered over the past month. He knew that.

"I promise I will let no harm come to you," he said, leaning in closer to keep my attention because my gaze was starting to drift behind him again, searching for that tall, familiar figure with deep green eyes. "Can you trust me just for right now? For the next five minutes?"

My thoughts were fixated on my brother's not-hand and how it had come away from Nikylo's stomach, bloodied. How I had left Nikylo crumpled on the ground, disappearing from sight and injured. How Mari and Kendall had simply free-fallen from a bridge above a waterfall.

"Rayleigh," Oliver said urgently, pulling me back to reality. "Please, we must go."

I shook the thoughts from my head and nodded vigorously at Oliver. "Yes, alright," I said, knowing that his vow with me made his words valid.

He reached out and wrapped his arms around my waist. "Hold on tight."

"What do you mean?" I asked, scrambling to do as he said.

He didn't respond. Instead, he bore my weight and hurled us both off the bridge, just like Mari did with Kendall, sending us plummeting toward the base of the waterfall as I screamed.

TWENTY-SEVEN
Your Touch

There I was again, freefalling down the side of a waterfall—no parachute, no wings, just gravity dragging me down into the darkness below.

The mist felt cool on my face and in my open mouth—because I was still screaming from our sudden jump.

At least in the dream, I knew it wasn't real. But this was *very* real. Panic coursed through me. I couldn't prevent us from smashing into the ground below by simply waking up. Oliver was no dragon, so throwing us off the bridge without any way to fly gave me every reason to scream bloody murder as we hurtled into the unknown.

A rush of air met us from below, slowing our descent and… changing our direction?

I must have been hallucinating, having passed out from the fear of the fall because there was no *way* he was using his power to fly us through the air. That was impossible…wasn't it?

But there we were, soaring away from the mist and through the sky without wings or a parachute. I was certain that the scenery beneath us was filled with meadows, forests, rivers, and lakes, all stretching to the edges of the island in every direction. Yet, I couldn't see it because I clung to Oliver, my face buried in his neck, my back to the ground below.

"What is happening?" I screamed, unsure if Oliver could hear me over the winds rushing past our ears. Then the wind vanished, leaving only the cool breeze on my face.

"This would be immensely easier," Oliver said through gritted teeth, "if you were not so squirmish."

I froze. "I wouldn't be so squirmish if you hadn't just thrown me off a bridge!" I shouted, still forcing myself to stay as still as possible.

"Going stiff is not helping either, love."

"What do you want me to do? Go as limp as a noodle?" I retorted as hysteria swept in.

"Hold on to me, and let me guide us," he said plainly, as if I should have known.

"I *am* holding onto you! What do you call this death grip I have around your neck?"

Oliver chuckled. "I've got you, love. There is no need for said death grip."

I felt his arms around my waist, his fingers wiggling along my rib cage. My arms were wrapped tightly around his neck, pulling myself completely flush against him at our torsos, but my legs dangled. With nowhere to put them, they hung loosely below us, likely making whatever he was doing harder than it needed to be.

"If you would wrap your legs around me, it would make this much smoother." There was no teasing in his tone, no sarcastic remark or smirk. Just a suggestion with no meaning behind it. It felt strange to hear something like that said without any snide smirk or comment accompanying it.

But I nodded, ignoring the unwanted flush that rushed to my cheeks as I locked my ankles behind his back. I also let my arms loosen enough to pull my face away from his neck. This kind of flying was incredibly different from flying on the back of a dragon, and I wasn't sure if I liked it as much. I had no control or stability. I had to place my life in his hands, completely trusting him to get me to safety.

"Where are you taking me?" I asked, feeling my face too close to his. There was nowhere to go but closer to him, so I stayed where I was to talk.

"We are headed to the crystal cove on this island," he stated, not turning his face to look at me. "Until we hear from the royals that everything is safe, we will lay low there."

"What happened besides... well, besides what I saw?" I asked, the bird claw covered in blood flashing in my mind. I tried to blink away the image, but even with my eyes closed, it remained.

"One of the Queen's handmaidens burst into the courtroom covered in blood," he said, pursing his lips. "Unfortunately, the injury was to her throat, so she could tell no one what happened. Bursting into the room was her only way of warning."

"Someone slit her throat?" I balked. "And she was well enough to burst into the courtroom and warn everyone else about the attack?" My mind raced. Of all the things Oliver could have told me, that didn't even make the top five.

"Her injuries—" he cut himself off, taking a measured breath before completing his thought. "Her injuries are the kind that someone in our world gives as a warning."

"What do you mean a *warning*?" My voice had risen an octave. "Slitting someone's throat is a death sentence!"

Oliver weighed his head back and forth. "Not for our kind..." he trailed off, still avoiding eye contact. "The only infallible way to kill Drakalasson is by severing their spinal cord at the neck or causing irreversible damage to their heart."

I blinked, swallowing hard. I opened and closed my mouth several times, and finally said, "What?"

He furrowed his brow but started to repeat himself.

"No. Stop," I demanded, squeezing my eyes shut. "I didn't mean for you to repeat yourself. I heard you. I just—" I took a deep breath. "That is just very specifically detailed."

He lowered his head a bit. "Sorry. I know you prefer straightforward answers, so I—"

I snapped my eyes open. "How do you know that?"

"Someone told me."

I narrowed my eyes. "Who?"

"It does not matter. You deserve answers to your questions, and I will gladly provide them whenever possible."

I stared at him, but he still avoided my gaze. There was something he wasn't saying. I knew he had likely learned those answers from someone in my Omada, but why wouldn't he tell me who? My guess was Theo since he was the only one who really answered my questions so openly.

Yet, something about the way Oliver was evading my gaze and the question made me wonder if that wasn't the case at all.

Oliver cleared his throat. "Would you mind not staring at me?"

I averted my gaze, but not before I noticed the color creeping up his neck. That was when I realized just how close we were to each other and how that might be affecting him. Instead of being shy about it, as I usually would be, I said, "Have you never been this close to a girl before, Oliver?" I smirked as the red of his ear deepened.

"Of course I have," he shot back. "What do you take me for? A three-hundred-year-old prude?"

I leaned in to whisper, "Then why are your ears so red?"

"Stop—stop that!" he stuttered, twisting his head back and forth to evade my lips. "I am betrothed!"

I chuckled. "What a shame."

I don't know what made me say those things—the delirium, the fatigue from using my powers, or the fact that I knew he was betrothed and wanted to see if I could make him squirm. He came off so prim and proper that I was starting to wonder if he could even be embarrassed. *Well, that answers that*, I thought to myself.

The weight of our predicament bore down on me. Oliver must have felt it, too, because he said, "We are landing soon. Hopefully, we will have some answers when we arrive."

I pursed my lips. "Will Kyler be okay?" I whispered, realizing too late that I had used that damn name again.

Oliver didn't answer. Did he even know? Did anyone else see what happened? He was trying to keep Koladon under control, but his power was stretched too thin. It felt like he was taking on more than he could handle. How had he weakened so easily? Wasn't he fully recharged this morning after sleeping on his crystals? Why did he let Koladon go when Mitch approached him from behind? Why didn't he fight him?

There were too many questions, and no one could answer them because no one else knew. Mitch was gone, the monster was taking over, and he wouldn't know who I was anymore. He wouldn't recognize me, Ma, or anyone else that he loved and cared for—all because he had been brought to this realm where his magic could develop.

Oliver sighed. "Are you ready?"

"Ready for what, exactly?"

"To land. It's a bit more difficult than the flying aspect."

Right. We were still flying. My view hadn't changed from the twilight sky, so I twisted my head to see what was around us. We were close to the ground, circling above what appeared to be a forest against the mountains. There was a gap in the trees where I could see light below, but no sign of anyone else, neither Drakalasson nor Fae. "What do I need to do?"

"I will be cushioning our landing with the air that is supporting us, but it will remove the shield I have around us. I need you to keep hold of me until my feet touch the ground. Do not release your legs or start to panic. Understood?"

I wasn't sure why he thought I would do any of those things, but I nodded.

The air that kept us aloft diminished, and I felt the weight of gravity pulling us down. I tried not to wiggle or squirm as I trusted Oliver to land us safely. Once we were past the treetops, a gust of wind greeted us, and he pulled his legs under us, landing both feet gently on the ground. I knew if I tried to stand, my legs would be unsteady and untrustworthy, so I waited a moment, mentally checking my muscles to prepare them for standing.

Oliver chuckled softly, his breath brushing the back of my neck. I hadn't noticed that I had buried my face in the crook of his neck again. "You alright, love?"

"No. No, I'm not alright," I said honestly, knowing that everything that happened back in the castle was about to come crashing down in a whirlwind of emotions. The distraction of making him squirm was welcome, but it was no longer effective.

"Oh, thank goodness you made it." The voice came from somewhere behind me, and I released a choked sob at Mari's presence. Her gentle, familiar hands grasped either side of my waist, lifting slightly to help me down. "I've got you, Rayleigh. You can let go."

Slowly, I unhooked my ankles from Oliver's waist, leaning into Mari as she helped me toward a break in the trees leading to a cave. What was it with me and caves? At least I wasn't being kidnapped, but what would I find inside?

My answer came almost immediately.

The cavern had a single hole in the ceiling through which light poured, alongside a rainbow waterfall. The pool below glowed with a luminescent light, with smaller streams trickling from other points along the walls. The dark walls were adorned with glowing flowers in shades of purple, gold, and teal. It was beautiful—like nothing I had ever seen before—in person, that is. Because I knew this cavern. I'd seen it in a painting back at the Dengalow. It had called to me then, and it called to me now, pulling on my magic where it rested within me.

After absorbing the beauty of the cave, my gaze shifted to the figures scattered throughout the space, my heart sinking when I noticed how few people were present. Theo, Libella, Tom, and Kendall—that was it. No Leighton or Nikylo. No Ma or Mitch. My lip quivered as Kendall sprang up from her spot on a rock to greet me at the entrance. I wrapped my arms around her and allowed myself to fall apart. She didn't say anything, just let me cry.

Never in my life did I think it would come to this. Learning that I was from a different realm was one thing, but I imagined it would be a fun adventure of discovering my powers and exploring a world I could never have envisioned. While those things were happening, my life was being torn apart at the seams. Nothing was as I believed it to be. No one was safe, and everyone I loved was either held captive by a monster, dead, or dying, except for the one who held me steady as I cried on her shoulder.

Mitch was the one person in my life who was supposed to be a normal kid. He was meant to grow up, become a star athlete in swimming, marry a sweet girl like Lily, and be happy. But now, there was a monster manipulating his mind, transforming him into someone who wouldn't recognize himself in the mirror, let alone those he loved. When he attacked me the other night, I thought it was just a fluke—a result of being trapped alone with only his mind for company, the monster growing stronger. But after what happened in the courtroom, I knew that wasn't true.

Then, there was Nikylo. Mitch had attacked him—taken control of him in that courtroom, if I remembered correctly. How had he, someone barely able to use their magic, managed to overpower the strongest Lunnoxia in the Kidemos? A *prince* of the Drakalasson.

But I'd seen it. Nikylo had relaxed his grip on Koladon and willingly turned to face Mitch. Then the claw with impossibly long talons appeared where Mitch's hand should have been, covered in blood after he'd thrust it into Nikylo's abdomen. Oliver had said Drakalassons were not so easily killed. Perhaps Nikylo was okay. But why was I so worried about his safety? Why wasn't I more concerned about my brother, who had vanished from the courtroom as if he possessed the power to manipulate time and space—

I lifted my head from Ken's shoulder, wiped away my tears, and faced the others in the cavern. "Does anyone know what happened?"

Theo stepped forward, but Oliver raised a hand, causing him to step back again. It was odd to see Theo take such orders from Oliver, considering he had assumed the leadership role back on Earth. But Oliver held more authority here. Was it because he was a Councilor? Or was there another reason everyone looked to him for guidance? "Tell us what *you* saw, Rayleigh."

My gaze shifted between those listening. Kendall still hugging me around my waist, but off to the side. I relished her comfort as I relayed what I'd seen happen in the courtroom.

"After Nikylo collapsed," Theo said when I finished, "did you see him lying on the ground?"

My brow furrowed. That's when I realized Theo was the one who was supposed to retrieve him. "No. There were too many people in the way for me to see."

"Weren't you sitting in the second row?" he asked, studying me.

"Yes. I—"

"So there shouldn't have been anything obstructing your view of the floor, dearie," Theo said, his tone not accusatory but curious. "Think, Rayleigh. What did you see?"

My mind replayed the memory. Mitch retracted the bloody claw. Nikylo doubled over. I screamed. In a single blink, he was gone. But where was Nikylo? "Mitch disappeared, and I tried to reach Nikylo… but I couldn't see him. Just a puddle of blood on the ground," I confessed, searching the scene in my mind for any traces of Nikylo or Mitch.

Theo pursed his lips and turned to Libella. "Can you check his chambers?" When she nodded, he turned to Oliver. "The Verdanvale?"

Oliver nodded. He faced Tom. "The Kytos?" With a final nod from Tom, Theo said, "I'm going to check the portal—"

"What's going on?" I shouted, finally realizing Theo's frantic tone.

No one spoke, glancing around at each other for someone to respond. Finally, Oliver stepped up, placing his hands on my shoulders. "It seems Nikylo may have taken your brother."

"*What?* No!" I protested, pushing Oliver's comforting hands off my shoulders. "Mitch whispered something to Nikylo that made him let go of Koladon—who, by the way, also escaped!" My heart raced and my senses became overwhelmed. "Why would Mitch attack him if Nikylo was trying to help him escape? What was the point of the girl rushing into the room, or Koladon escaping, or Mitch stabbing him—"

"Rayleigh, take it easy," Oliver coaxed.

But it was too late. My hyperventilation had already begun, and my body collapsed onto the rocky ground. I reached for the gritty floor, scraping my hands against it, but they were numb to the pain. I grasped at my shirt, hoping the softer fabric would pull me back, but it *wasn't working*. My coping methods were failing me. My body felt both numb and heavy at the same time. I gasped for air, trying to get it to my brain, but I couldn't release it. The voices around me were garbled and unintelligible.

Why would Nikylo, the one person who seemingly hated me, try to help my brother escape? And how could he let the monster who tortured my entire family go free? Why did I care so much that he would do this to me? If Mitch had escaped, why were the people around me acting as if Nikylo's actions were unacceptable?

Surprised that I hadn't lost all sense of self, I tried to focus on the sounds around me. There was a commotion—someone was shouting, and I was bumped into something—but I couldn't determine what was happening. The panic attack had pulled me deep, too far from the real world—down into the black abyss I hadn't been in for years. The darkness enveloped me, and no one could reach me down there as the scenes of that horrible day replayed in my mind.

Until I felt it.

A gentle caress down my temple. *Breathe, Sunshine.*

The hyperventilation began anew. *I… I c-c-can't,* I managed, my stutter evident even in my mind.

The caress came again, and I centered my attention on that sensation, aware of the request but unable to locate the oak door amidst the whirlwind of anxiety.

Feel this? Nikylo asked, stroking my temple again.

Yes.

Focus on that, he instructed, continuing the sensation while I poured all my focus into it.

I pushed away the scenes replaying in my mind—the courtroom, the firestorm, the panic—shoving it all out instead of burying it deeper. I didn't want the anxieties in my head anymore.

Good. What else do you feel?

I shifted my focus to other parts of myself. *The ground,* I recited, wiggling my fingers back to their senses enough to feel the rough texture of where I'd fallen. *Warmth,* I added, feeling my legs pressed against something soft and warm but unable to identify it.

Alright. Take a deep breath for me now and try to open your eyes.

I took one of the slowest breaths I could, dragging it out until I couldn't inhale any more air. When I released it, I opened my eyes.

My first instinct was to jerk backward, but I held steady, absorbing what I could. The stroke down my temple hadn't been in my head at all. Nikylo was holding my face to his, leaning his forehead against mine. His bright green eyes were only inches away from me. He had positioned himself facing me, his legs bent over either side of mine, as we sat on the ground just inches apart.

"How?" I squeaked, hoping he understood what I meant.

He sighed, his eyes closing briefly before they met mine again. "I don't know," he said honestly. "But I knew that if he escaped, he would be hunted down and killed for what he did."

"What do you mean?" Tears filled my eyes, uncertain of where he was headed with this.

He hadn't stopped stroking my face, nor had he pulled away, so I felt his body shake as he inhaled before saying, "He attacked a royal. It doesn't matter now whether his monster can be controlled or not." He paused, his eyes closing for another brief moment before they shone green again. "My father has placed the hunter's mark on him."

"The what?" I screeched, tears streaming down my face as I recoiled from Nikylo. Even though I had never encountered that term before, it seemed clear enough.

His hands slipped from my face as I pulled away, leaving them hovering in the air between us. He dropped them and propped his elbows on his knees as he leaned back slightly, a flash of something in his eyes. Hurt? That couldn't be right. "The hunter's mark," he repeated. "After the final event tomorrow, the King will order him to be found and brought back to him."

He didn't need to say it. I could tell from his hesitation. The King wouldn't care if he was brought back dead or alive. I swallowed the lump in my throat, blinking back more tears. "Where is he?"

"Safe."

"*Where?*" I demanded through clenched teeth.

His voice lowered. "I can't tell you."

"The last time someone didn't tell me about my little brother's whereabouts, he was kidnapped, tortured, and taken to a realm where he turned into a monster," I seethed, my anger surging. "Now tell me, w*here is Mitch?*"

Nikylo pursed his lips, glancing over my head at whatever was behind me—or whoever—before taking a deep breath and locking his gaze on mine again. "He's at the Verdanvale. In the basement."

The basement? Oliver never mentioned a basement during the tour. "Take me to him."

"I can't do that."

My skin prickled as I struggled to control my emotions. "It's not a request."

"I know," he bit back. "If I take you to him, they'll discover where he is."

"What? How?"

Another sigh. "They can track your power. If you don't return to the castle tonight for the ceremony, they will assume you were involved in this."

"How could they even think that? I was sitting in the courtroom just like everyone else! I couldn't have done anything!" Tears streamed down my face, growing hot.

Nikylo lifted his hand to—what? Wipe them away? But I flinched. *Flinched.* I don't know why. He hadn't done anything to make me react that way, but I noticed the clear hurt on his face as he pulled back, giving me space. This distance allowed me a better view of him, and I noticed the sweat beading on his brow—his paler complexion. I had only seen him like this once before. I glanced down at his abdomen, where Mitch's clawed hand had impaled him.

Sure enough, a stain of blood pooled there. It didn't appear to be flowing freely, but rather oozing. Instinct drove me to close the distance between us again, all questions momentarily leaving my mind. "You need healing." It wasn't a question, and I wasn't about to wait for someone to give me orders. I scanned the cavern until my eyes found Mari's. She was sitting on a rock with Ken but moved immediately toward me at my unspoken command. Turning back to Nikylo, I reached for his shirt, but he grabbed my wrist to stop me.

"You don't have to do this." His words were gentle, strained, yet firm. My eyes met his as he spoke, and I held his gaze for a moment. The green was slightly duller than usual but still sparkled like emeralds.

"I know," I responded, just as gently but firm. "I..." Hesitating, I chewed on my lower lip, briefly drawing his attention. Because if I finished the thought I was having, the impulsive response, everything might change. I shook my head slightly, then lifted my chin. "I want to."

His throat bobbed once, then twice. He licked his lips and blinked rapidly. Then his body trembled with a deep, shuddering breath, and he nodded as he released my wrist.

Mari stopped nearby, clearly waiting for whatever had just happened between Nikylo and me, but knelt down next to me at his nod. "Remember, this won't be pleasant," she said.

Oh, I remembered, alright. But the way they described this made it sound like I should have been in pain, especially if I was taking away his... right? I added it to my never-ending list of questions, internally cursing myself for never bringing my notebook anywhere.

This time, when I reached for Nikylo's bloody shirt, he didn't stop me. The fabric clung to his skin because of the dry, sticky blood, but I peeled it away, earning a sharp inhale from Nikylo.

"Easy there, Sunshine," he hissed.

I huffed a laugh. "You were a much easier patient when you were unconscious," I muttered, glancing up at him.

A smile danced on his lips, and that annoying dimple appeared. "Always here to save my ass, huh?"

"At least you still have a pulse this time." The comment was intended as a joke, but something deep inside me stirred. It reminded me of the feeling I had when he nearly died. I'm not sure why I reacted so strongly, but I knew I never wanted to experience that again. Perhaps it was the bond we shared, but the thought of losing this protective asshole who I was unfortunately attracted to was not something I wanted to entertain.

Unfortunately, his voice echoed in my mind.

I jolted, surprised by his voice. I clenched my jaw. *Can't you just leave me to my thoughts?*

A chuckle resonated in my mind. *Not when you think such things about me.* His voice had lowered, sending an unwelcome shiver down my spine.

This is why I said, 'Unfortunately.' I bit back, ripping the rest of his sticky shirt from his injury and earning a wince from him.

Don't lie to yourself. You enjoy our ability to converse privately even when others are around. He was mocking me, likely to distract from the pain he was obviously experiencing.

As I assessed his injury, I knew removing his shirt was the best way to access it properly. My other hand grabbed the clean side of his shirt and lifted it up over his head.

This is not how I imagined you taking my shirt off for the first time.

Heat rushed to my cheeks as something stirred deep within me. He imagined this? What did he mean by 'the first time?' As if there would be more... But then I realized: he *was* distracting himself. This was how he distracted me when I was anxious; now he was doing it for himself. His ragged breathing came from the injury, not from the intimacy of the moment. I could play along with it. *Oh?* I teased, hoping it helped keep his mind off the pain. *And how often do you fantasize about such nonsense?*

Every. Damn. Day. His confession was sultry and had me dragging my gaze up to his. Sweat still glistened on his forehead, but his eyes pulsed like a breeze whipping through a grassy plain.

Are there any other nonsensical scenarios that trouble your mind that I should know about? I placed a hand on his bare shoulder and pushed him backward, urging him to lie back so the wound could heal properly.

Oh, plenty. When his inner voice quivered, I knew his pain was overwhelming. What could Mitch have done to cause this much damage? *One of them includes me like this, while you crawl on top of me.*

The blush rushed to my ears this time. I hoped those around us realized we were conversing and didn't think I was blushing because I took off his shirt and made him lie down. Either way, I was sure to hear about it later. *I remember you mentioning something about that once before,* I chided, returning to the task at hand and placing my hands over his wound. It had been a while since I had encountered blood so closely, but it still didn't bother me as one might expect.

His gasp was either from pain or—

"Mitera, your hands are *freezing!*" he said through gritted teeth.

I couldn't help but giggle. "It's good that you can warm them up then." His skin was hot to the touch, his body struggling to heal itself without success.

Mari rested her hand on my shoulder. "You ready?"

I nodded, watching Nikylo for his affirmation as well.

The power struck me just as it had the first time, but I was prepared for it and the glowing fingers that came with it.

What I wasn't prepared for was the voice in my head returning, but this time, it was full of heady desire, skittering along my mind. *Tell me, Sunshine. Did it feel like this when I healed you?*

I focused on stitching his wound together, but a rush of bliss washed over me. I knew I had to keep my hands on his injury and my mind on healing him, yet I found myself leaning closer, meeting his gaze as another surge of bliss coursed through me. *Yes,* I admitted. *And it's incredibly confusing.*

A dark chuckle reached my ears. He was laughing through his pain. *I concur.* His hand lifted to tuck a strand of hair behind my ear. *Another unfortunate circumstance?*

The skin beneath my hands was closing its final gap as I pushed onto my knees, looking down at him. *It's only unfortunate because you're an ass most of the time.*

I could be charming if you'd like.

I hadn't meant to, but I scrunched up my face in disgust. Nikylo being charming was not something I wanted to experience, and I wasn't quite sure what that meant. *No, because then I'd have a hard time finding reasons to hate you.*

Ah, he mused. *And we can't have that, can we?*

I lifted my hands from his injury as Mari removed her hands from my shoulder. I turned to her and said, "Thank you."

"Anytime, Rayleigh." She stood, her eyes darting between Nikylo and me before walking back to Ken.

Nikylo sat up and immediately invaded my space, forcing me to sit back on my heels. It didn't make much difference, as he continued moving until he was standing right in front of me. I looked up at him as he extended a hand to help me stand. I took it, and he pulled me up, not stepping back when I was mere inches from him.

"Thank you, Rayleigh," he whispered, his gaze fixed on mine.

Shock coursed through my body, tingling along my skin as I stared at him. He used my name. I could count on one hand the number of times he had done that. I swallowed hard, "Why do you use my name so rarely?"

"Do you not like when I use it?" he asked sincerely.

"No, it's just…" The way he said it made it sound like a prayer. I knew he would sense my thoughts, so I tried to mask them by saying, "You only call me that when I'm in trouble or—"

"Sorry to interrupt, love," Oliver said, causing me to jump a foot away from Nikylo. I had forgotten everyone else was there. "The royals have deemed the area secure and expect us back in the next few moments. We will have to discuss all other matters after Talekor's ceremony."

When I faced him, I noticed his jaw muscles working as he glared at Nikylo, who merely glared back. After shifting my focus between them a few times, I finally asked, "They're still holding the ceremony today?"

Neither of them looked away from each other, but Nikylo replied, "Yes. The dragons won't reschedule on such short notice. Gathering their unbound in one place is not easy."

"I thought they were connected from birth," I said, recalling my conversation with Libella.

"They are," Nikylo said, finally facing me. "But if the final bonding fails, someone else can bond with the shifter."

I furrowed my eyebrows. "Why would it fail?"

"All bonds are a choice."

The mystery of that statement made me search for Kendall across the room; her side was empty without her twin. "Not all bonds," I whispered.

"Come," Oliver said, placing his hand on my lower back. "We mustn't waste any more time." He then led me out of the cave, with Nikylo falling into step behind us.

I was left wondering two things: what was the glaring standoff about, and why did Nikylo allow Oliver to lead me away from him, let alone touch me?

TWENTY-EIGHT
Nevermind

Nikylo

I was drying my hair with a towel when a soft knock sounded at the door. Knowing it could only be one person, I wrapped the towel around my waist and swung open the bathroom door.

Rayleigh's gaze fell to my exposed abdomen and shot back to my face much quicker than I had hoped. She cleared her throat, clearly still trying to keep her eyes from wandering too low. I smirked. "Libella told me to bathe before the ceremony."

"I'm just finishing up." I gestured for her to enter the bathroom and stepped back to return to the vanity. I grabbed the hair paste from its compartment on the counter and ran it through my wet locks.

"What should I expect from this ceremony?" Her voice was softer than usual, and when I turned to see her looking at me, I understood why.

"Still admiring my back dimples, Sunshine?" I asked, turning back to the mirror to adjust my curls.

She scoffed, and a rush of water filled the room, followed by the closet door opening and closing before she replied, "You're incredibly conceited."

A soft chuckle escaped me as I turned to face her, leaning against the sink. "I can't tell you what to expect. Each ceremony is different for various reasons. My brother's," she stiffened at the word. I understood why, but I wished I could help ease her mind about it. Not here…

Hopefully soon. We had no free time to fill her in on any details. The lack of privacy in this castle was astonishing. One might say the walls could talk. "Talekor's will be more crowded since he's a prince. His dragon will likely be strong and highly temperamental if Tal's demeanor is any indication."

She rolled her eyes, yet I noticed the trepidation in her expression. "Is there anything else I should know?"

Her voice didn't betray her fears, but what I heard internally had me saying, "I won't let him near you, Rayleigh." Her name rolled off my tongue like honey, and I noticed that reaction again. The same one I'd seen in the cavern when I used it.

Surprisingly, she hadn't pressed on that question on our way back to the castle.

Oliver had led her to a clearing where he offered her the choice of flying with him or with me. I was surprised when she chose me, but considering the lack of control she had while flying with Oliver, it shouldn't have been so unexpected. I knew she preferred to see the world around her. We weren't often outside, but when we were, her eyes would wander to take in the scenery, savoring the beauty.

Holding onto Oliver as he used the winds to fly them around didn't give her that freedom.

Even when she was indoors, her eyes would wander to the portraits, the crystal ceilings, or out the window to take in the view. I remembered her curiosity on the deck of the Dengalow, the way she wandered to the edge to take in the beauty of the waterfall below.

Being a Fae naturally connected her to the elements she embodied, yet she was drawn to them all. The way she moved her hand against the wind while driving was mesmerizing. Her fascination with her meadow and flowers was palpable. Although she couldn't control water, she still felt a deep connection to it. The only element I hadn't seen her near was fire. I knew she was terrified of the destruction it could do if her firestorm was any indication, but I hoped that one day she would realize it wasn't so frightening.

Once airborne, she asked if my parents would have any questions about Mitch. I had informed her they wouldn't need to see her, only sense her within their walls to know she wasn't involved in Mitchell's disappearance. I had taken a risk disappearing with him like that, but I hadn't been gone long enough for them to worry, and they had stopped tracking my power ages ago, as they were doing with Rayleigh's.

She relaxed only a little, then asked if Verdanvale was safe. I almost laughed, knowing the enchantments around that place were stronger than most. I told her it only allowed entry to those Ollie and I permitted, and that list was very short. The rest of the trip was silent, but I sensed tension from her. For once, I occupied my mind with anything except her thoughts, knowing she needed time to process everything that happened in that courtroom and afterward.

Looking at her now, I took a hesitant step toward where she stood near the tub. She was watching me, her hands wringing in front of her. "You asked me why I use your name so rarely." Another step. I could have sworn she leaned forward as she nodded. I was only a step away from her when I stopped. Her shoulders relaxed as she held my gaze. "I fear that if I say it too often, I will become accustomed to it on my lips."

She chewed on her bottom lip, instantly capturing my attention. "You make it sound like that's a bad thing."

I dragged my gaze from her mouth and took another step, closing the distance between us. "Names are sacred in this realm," I whispered, my eyes dancing between hers. "Using someone's name creates a deeper connection in the already established relationship between two people, making it more intimate."

Her breath hitched, but she nodded, considering my words before tilting her face back to look up at me. "That doesn't quite answer my question."

"What question?"

"You said you feared becoming accustomed to my name on your lips."

At the last word, her eyes flitted to my mouth and— *Mitera, save me…* if I didn't have the control I did… "I don't hear a question in there, Sunshine."

She squinted at me. "Why, asshole?"

There she was. I leaned down, my lips brushing against the shell of her ear as I whispered, "For the same reason I asked you to stop calling me Kyler." I never thought our situation would lead to this—sharing secrets I vowed to keep, confessing things like this. I felt her shudder.

"Our relationship cannot be so publicly intimate. It is forbidden."

She pressed her hand against my chest and I allowed it. When she met my gaze, she said, "Why not just use Rayliana like everyone else?"

"Because you hate that name." She simply stared at me, unwilling to admit I was right. "Besides, I know how saying your name affects you. How it makes you want me even more."

"I don't want you, Nikylo."

She said my name with such bite, as if she knew the effect it would have on me. I grinned, showing one of those dimples she loved so much. "You can lie to yourself and everyone else, Sunshine," I tapped my temple. "But you can't lie to me."

"There's only one person I can't lie to." She glared at me, but her words made me furrow my eyebrows.

"What do you mean?"

Her expression shifted to something unfamiliar. "I made an *órkomatos* with Oliver."

A growl echoed in my head, but I ignored it, closing the distance she had created between us. "You did what?"

"I told him I felt like I couldn't trust anyone, not even him. So he offered me the oath, and I took it." That bite never left her tone. I should have known Ollie would do something like this. "He's the only one who's been completely honest with me, while you've only kept secrets. Helping Mitch escape, while good, was just another secret you kept—from everyone." I stepped back, feeling the blow as if it were physical. "When will you realize that the only way I will ever trust you is if you start trusting me?"

I tightened my jaw. "There are countless reasons—"

"Name one."

"What?"

"Name one reason."

"You can't shield your mind!" I shouted, confused about how our conversation had reached this point. Just seconds ago, I could have kissed her, and now she was pushing me away.

"Then teach me!"

"It's not that simple," I began, stepping toward her again, but she pulled back.

"When you're ready to teach me how to block my thoughts and keep *you* out of my mind, we can revisit this conversation. Until then, there's no reason for me to trust you." She gestured toward the door. "Get out."

I blinked several times. "You're dismissing me from my own chambers?"

"I'm telling you to leave me alone while I bathe. Where you go is up to you."

Too stunned to speak and too drained to argue, I turned and left her standing in my bathing chambers, reeling from how quickly everything had changed.

۱ ﻣ ۲ ﺭ

I smoothed out the crumpled paper on my desk, reading the note again before grabbing my pen from the top drawer. I jotted down several different responses before my door creaked open. I quickly shoved the paper to the back of the drawer before standing up to find—

A hand fisted in the collar of my tunic and shoved me face-first into my desk.

"What the hell?" I shouted, puzzled by how anyone could sneak up on me. I attempted to twist in their grip to find—

"Do not act so surprised, Niko." Oliver's white hair contrasted sharply with his now red features. He was right in my face, his breath warm against my cheek. I had never seen him this angry before.

"Ollie, stop." I tried to grasp his fist to loosen his grip, but a sharp wind wrapped around my wrist, pulling it behind me, along with my other hand.

"Are you out of your damn mind?" he shouted at me.

"What are you talking about?" I shouted back, having no idea how to deal with his anger. Sure, we'd had our disagreements before, but he had never been physical with me. I could fight well enough without my power, so I let it lie idle while trying to break free from his grip.

He scoffed as if the answer should be painfully obvious. "I thought the moment after the firestorm was just a fluke, but you froze time, did you not?"

I froze. No one had ever been able to tell when I stopped time. No one—except Ollie. We could never figure out why, but he always knew when I tampered with time while he was around. I thought I'd gotten away with it because he hadn't mentioned anything. I was obviously wrong. Nodding, I said, "Why—"

"And just now in the cavern? Did you stop time then, too?"

"No," I replied hastily. "I was too weak."

"Do not lie to me!" He tightened his grip on my tunic.

"I'm not lying, Oliver!" I finally broke his magic's hold on my wrists and spun around, shoving him back and freeing myself from his grip. "What's gotten into you?"

He was breathing heavily, pacing as he raked his fingers through his hair. That was when I realized it wasn't anger that was riling him up—it was fear.

I relaxed my shoulders and approached him, attempting to rest my hand on his, but he shrugged me off, continuing to pace. I sighed, "What is it, Ollie?"

He wouldn't meet my gaze. His mind was swirling with the words he struggled to say so eloquently, and I couldn't make sense of them. So I waited, knowing that patience was what he needed right now, and that pushing him for an answer wouldn't help matters.

Finally, he stopped pacing and turned to me. "You were flirting with her, Nikylo."

It wasn't a question. "No, Ollie. I—"

"Spare me any denials," he interrupted. "I saw it clearly enough. Whether it was carelessness or intent, I cannot say, but I would expect my closest friend to know better."

"What are you referring to? Maybe I can help clarify things."

"When she was healing you," he said. "Her face was flushed in the silence between you. We all know you were conversing. She would not be blushing if she were simply doing the work to heal you."

I sighed, having forgotten how observant he was. I had also been delirious enough to forget there was an audience in the cavern. Although, I wasn't sure I would have acted differently if I *had* realized they were there. "It was harmless, Ollie."

"Are you honestly denying it? It is obvious she is attracted to you—"

But I interrupted him. "Yes. it's hard not to be, isn't it?" I joked, finally slapping my hand on his shoulder. "But believe me, she can't get past the great parts of my personality that Valisdrako contributed." My sarcasm was thick.

Again, those make you more intriguing. Drako's voice echoed in my mind. He had been unusually silent today, but naturally, he would pick this moment to speak up. *And you are lying to yourself if you think it's harmless. You know how she thinks.*

Yes, but Oliver doesn't need to know that.

"Tell your fire-breathing menace to mind his own affairs," Oliver snapped.

I felt Drako rising beneath my skin. *Let me out,* he commanded when I resisted the shift.

Absolutely not. You're not roasting my best friend.

He insulted me.

He did not, you big baby. Just relax.

His growl rattled my brain. *If you do not let me out, I will force you to shift.*

If you don't calm down, I'll put gonos on myself so you can't get out.

He let out another growl, but I sensed him retreat into my mind as he muttered, *I will pay him back one day.*

I shifted my focus back to Ollie, who still looked upset. I figured a bit of honesty wouldn't hurt in this situation. "I needed to distract myself from the pain." I absentmindedly rubbed the latest scar on my abdomen, recalling the pain that shot through my body from Mitch's clawed hand as it pierced my stomach. "The poison didn't hit my vitals, but it blocked access to my full power. I couldn't shift, and I barely managed the trip to the Verdanvale. The pain was excruciating, and I used my remaining energy to skith back to the cavern. I couldn't even heal myself enough to stop the bleeding; I was too drained. The only thing I had left when I reached Rayleigh was our myados." I took a deep breath. "Her voice... it distracted me." I locked eyes with Oliver. "I didn't expect her to understand that I needed the distraction and flirt back. She had never done that so blatantly before. But I swear it was harmless."

"And after her firestorm? Why did you freeze time?"

I hoped he'd forgotten that after my confession. I sighed. "She needed to hear words from me that I hadn't shared yet." Ollie looked at me expectantly. "She was denying her ability to get through this, denying her strength. I had to remind her that she was chosen *because* of her strength."

Oliver relaxed his shoulders and let out a long breath as he stared at me, whispering, "I cannot stand to lose another, Niko."

Something twisted in my gut, knowing he was right. "I'm not him, Ollie. I wouldn't do that."

"Sami said the same thing."

"Yes, well, he crossed that line knowing the consequences," I stated, trying to keep the emotions down that his name brought up. "I won't make the same mistake."

Oliver stared at me for what felt like an eternity before he finally nodded.

I crossed my arms, aware that what I was about to say would change the course of the conversation drastically. *Do not hold back,* Drako commanded. But I knew it wouldn't do any good to beat around the bush anyway.

"An *órkomatos,* Ollie? Seriously?"

His head snapped to mine. "She told you."

"More like she rubbed it in my face," I said, recalling the smug look she gave me. "But yes."

He sighed but straightened to his full height. "She needed someone she could trust, and you were not providing that for her."

"But an *oath?* Wasn't there another way to earn her trust?"

"I am certain over time she would have been able to, but Niko, she almost lost it today. Twice." I furrowed my brow but waited for him to explain. "After you left, she practically collapsed as she processed all the betrayal and loss she has experienced as of late." He waited for my reaction, but I couldn't give him anything more than a clenched jaw, knowing I'd partially caused that. So he continued. "Offering her my honesty through the oath was something tangible for her to feel—to know I cannot lie to her. I would never lie to her, as it is, but she would not know that either way and does not currently have the capacity to trust me. I hope that one day, before she learns of our betrothal, she will want to nullify it. But until then, I have to meet her where she is and provide her what little comfort I can."

I let out a long sigh. "I guess you're right." I sank back into my chair. "Have you ever nullified an *órkomatos* before?"

Ollie sat on the edge of my bed, full of crystals. "No, and I am not entirely certain I know how. The answers are not in my collection of tomes."

I narrowed my eyes. "Let me guess: you want me to fetch the answer for you?"

He shrugged. "You do have immediate access to the Kyllindro."

"Yes, but not that section of it," I countered.

"Evie would open the *Shadow Archives* if you simply smiled at her."

I scoffed, "She would not."

"Niko, she all but handed you a scroll that was never meant to leave the Shadow Archives just because you asked how she was faring."

The memory of the Nosí I first encountered decades ago resurfaced. She was a petite female, her age evident in her weathered skin. I had gone in search of information about the realm's power source, wondering how its disappearance was impacting climate change. She guided me to the scrolls that contained the information I needed and left me to conduct my research. When I returned several years later for hidden information regarding lineages of power, she was the one who welcomed me again. I asked her name, which surprised her. She told me no one had ever asked her name before.

Every time I returned since, I brought Evie something from the castle, whether it be baked goods or flowers. She didn't get to see the surface much since the Kyllindro was deep underground, and bringing her things she couldn't access was easy enough. In return, she always managed to retrieve the exact information I was looking for, even if it was classified.

"Fine," I finally replied. "I have to make a trip there anyway." I paused, considering the tomes and scrolls I already had to examine. "Rayleigh will need to come with me, though."

"Where are you taking Rayleigh?" A sharp voice echoed from my doorway. That made two people who had snuck up on me in the last ten minutes. I was losing my touch.

"Hello, Naila," Oliver said, rising to greet her with a kiss on the cheek.

"Oliver," she replied, returning the gesture. "It's nice to have you back in the castle."

"I assume Theo relieved you?" I asked from my desk.

"Isn't that what you sent him to do?"

"Anything new from the prisoner?"

"Still wants to see Rayleigh."

"Still not going to happen."

"Why does he want to see her?" Oliver interjected.

"He won't say," Naila said, crossing the room to my closet. "But he's quite persistent."

"I'll deal with him after the ceremony," I said, standing and following Naila.

"What do you mean by 'deal with him'?" Ollie followed us into my closet. The space was spacious enough, but it was certainly a tight fit for three people.

"Same way I dealt with Deakon." I suppressed a shiver as I recalled the Drakalasson who got too handsy with someone at the Luminae Ball. It had been a long time since I'd had any fun with my Lunnoxia powers, but Adarachi... His punishment would be more personal.

"Wait, did you say after the ceremony?" Ollie asked.

I shot him a grin over my shoulder. "Care to join me?"

Oliver's look of apprehension turned gradually into curiosity. "Who would stay with Rayleigh?"

"I've arranged for her and the twins to have some time tonight."

Naila gasped, "Talekor actually agreed to it?"

"Talekor will be with me."

"To interrogate Adarachi?" Oliver's confused expression made me laugh. He still hadn't grasped what I meant. So, I waited, watching as he puzzled it out. His eyes widened as he exclaimed, "You plan to risk something like that on a night like this?"

"That's what I said," Naila murmured.

"Do you want to keep her safe?" I countered.

"The answer is obvious, Niko. But would it not be easier to bring her with you?"

My nostrils flared as I growled, "She will never go near him again."

"Wait, I thought you *were* taking Rayleigh somewhere," Naila said, rummaging through my drawer of journals.

"Yes, to the Kyllindro, not the Kytos." I smacked her rummaging hand and pushed the drawer shut, then opened the one with the journal she was looking for and handed it to her.

"Thank you," she said in her sing-song voice. She made her way out of the closet and sat at my desk, grabbing my pen to start her report.

I snatched the purple-ink pen and exchanged it for a black one.

"It's a pen, babe," she mocked.

"Yes. *My* pen. Get your own."

She narrowed her eyes at me but took the black pen and started her report.

"How are we going to stop your parents from tracking her to the Kyllindro?" Oliver asked as he leaned against the closet doorframe.

"I was hoping you and the other Councilors might entertain them."

"Oh?" His surprised tone sounded mocking. "And what do you suggest we entertain them with?"

Raising an eyebrow, I said, "You could start with your betrothal."

"Betrothal?" Naila's head snapped up, spotting Oliver across the room. "Who are you betrothed to? Maybe she and I can plan together." Her voice dripped with sarcasm. She turned back to the notebook and muttered, "I've already been planning four years too long."

Oliver's death glare made me change the subject. "Or you could just ask my mother about the ball tomorrow. I'm sure she'd love to give you every detail. You are her favorite, after all."

His glare softened slightly. "That will still leave your father."

"He won't leave my mother's side after today. It was one of her handmaidens who was attacked, after all." I winked.

"Fine," Oliver conceded. "I will set up a lunch tomorrow with your parents and the other Councilors. You will not have more than a couple of hours, though."

"I realize. Shouldn't take too long, anyway. I'm planning to test her skithing in training tomorrow morning." After she passed out or threw up the last three times Adarachi or I had done it, I realized that training her to withstand it would be necessary sooner rather than later.

Especially since she is ours, Drako chimed in. *On top of that, you need to teach her to shield her mind.*

Stop reminding me.

Then stop holding off simply because you enjoy her thoughts.

That isn't— but I caught myself, realizing that if I initiated that discussion, I would end up losing. *I haven't had the time.*

No, you have not made time.

"Am I interrupting an important conversation?" Nalia fluttered her eyelashes at me, thumping the report journal against my chest. "I'm going to bed. Don't expect me at the ceremony."

She turned away as I cleared my mind of the conversation with Drako. "You are to report—"

"I know." She waved her hand above her head and walked through the door. "Don't bother me until then."

Oliver chuckled from where he stood. "She will certainly be a handful for you."

I didn't bother answering, as we both knew I had no intention of sticking around to follow through with that.

"Why did you mention my personal business in front of her?" Oliver's voice was soft and contemplative. He was usually good at understanding my tactics, but that one stemmed more from spite than anything, something he'd rarely witnessed from me. The thought of his betrothal to Rayleigh put me on edge. It was hard enough watching him leave the cavern earlier with his hand on her back. Drako muttering and grumbling the whole time didn't help either. I understood the reasons; I just didn't like it. Not that it mattered anyway. She could never be anything more to me than my rider.

"I have no explanation." The words weren't entirely false. Jealousy wasn't really an explanation. Watching her with Kaleb was one thing. I knew she was betrothed to Oliver at that time, but I couldn't tell her. I also understood he wouldn't be allowed to come to Niccodra with us. Or at least, I thought I did.

Watching her with Ollie… that was worse. Because they deserved each other.

"Valisdrako is fond of her, and I fear I'm starting to feel the same way," I confessed.

Oliver smiled at me as he crossed the room to where I was leaning against my desk. He placed a hand on my shoulder. "My betrothal to Rayleigh will not alter your friendship with her. I am not taking her away from you." He put his hands in his pockets and shrugged. "Besides, if everything goes according to plan—" He stopped short, noticing my expression. "Why are you looking at me like that?"

Because my eyes widened at the sight of the female standing in the doorway of my room. Her hair was still dripping wet from her bath, a towel secured around her—and those were tears welling in her eyes.

Shit.

I stood up abruptly, turning Oliver to face her, and watched his already pale complexion drain of what little color remained.

Rayleigh swallowed, worked her jaw, and met my gaze. "I need clothes." Her voice carried a false strength, but I could hear the thoughts of betrayal swirling in her mind. Again.

"Rayleigh," Oliver started toward her.

She raised a hand, stopping him in his tracks. "Clothes."

I hurried to my closet, grabbing a robe for her to wear while Libella got her ready for the ceremony. I shut the door behind her and found Ollie still frozen by my desk.

"What do I do?" His soft voice barely reached my ears.

I shrugged. "You offered her the *órkomatos*. It seems like the truth is your only option."

He closed his eyes. I knew he was beating himself up for being so careless with his words. He was usually so meticulous about what he said. Neither of us had expected her to walk into my room; it was completely warded against unwanted visitors. But she wasn't an unwanted visitor. And truthfully, I'd forgotten she was in there. It had been a long time since my rooms were shared with a Fae.

"Why are you being so hard on yourself, Ollie?"

"Because," he sighed, allowing the tension to ease from his shoulders. "She was aware I am betrothed, just not to her."

I furrowed my brows. "How does she only know half the truth if you took the oath?"

"The oath allowed me to tell her that I am betrothed to someone I do not yet know because I do not *know* her." His whispers were slightly panicked as he continued, "I do not know what food she likes or whether she prefers coffee or tea. Whether she enjoys the rain or the sun, the night or the morning, the flowers blooming in spring or the changing leaves in fall." He raked his fingers through his hair and clenched his fists in frustration. "Her favorite things are a mystery to me, and I do not know if I will ever learn them now."

Before I could reassure him, the closet door swung open. Even in a robe, freshly washed with damp hair, she looked beautiful.

Tears still welled in her deep blue eyes as she bit out, "I expect nothing less than secrets from you." It felt like being stabbed by Mitchell all over again, but I held her stare. It was better if she pushed me away. Her gaze found Ollie, still stuck across the room. "But you…" She swallowed the emotion lodged in her throat. "I thought I could trust you."

"You can—" he tried, but she cut him off.

"You said you wouldn't be able to lie to me, that the oath would make sure I knew if you did."

"It will—"

"Then why didn't it flare up when you claimed you didn't know who your betrothed was?" she shot back.

"Because my intention behind that word was not that I did not know your name. It was that I did not know what makes you, *you*." Oliver's voice cracked.

Her lip quivered, taking in his confession as he stood there with pleading eyes, hoping she would believe him. "And everything else you said?"

"It was the truth—every word."

They stared at each other, and I wondered what else could have been said when I'd left them alone on that island. But I knew what I was doing. Oliver needed time with her, and Rayleigh needed someone caring and kind. And I realized long ago that that was not something she would accept from me.

"I need time," she finally said. A single tear rolled down her cheek, but she quickly wiped it away and turned to me. "Tell Libella I need help with my hair." Before I could respond, she turned and made her way to the vanity outside the bathroom. She plopped down just as Oliver sank into the chair at my desk, both of them with their heads in their hands.

Next time, we should have popcorn, Drako said.

TWENTY-NINE
One Day

Rayleigh

"Are you ready?" Libella asked.

"Yes." No. At this point, I didn't really have a choice. Libella had kicked the boys out over an hour ago, telling them to get ready somewhere else. She didn't say it outright, but I knew it was because I needed the time and space to think things through.

With everything that had already happened today, I wasn't sure I was ready for yet another dangerous encounter, especially if it involved temperamental dragons and Talekor. I was still trying to come to terms with the fact that Mitch was holed up somewhere—again—fighting a mental battle with a monster that was trying to take over his mind and body. I hadn't seen Ma since she'd been transferred to her own rooms, and I had no idea if anyone even told her what was happening. Leigh was still trapped with Talekor, I hadn't had any time with Ken, and I was still being kept in the dark about everything going on.

And to top it all off, I was betrothed to Oliver.

I sighed as she reached out to adjust my dress, ensuring it lay correctly off my shoulder. The dress was beautiful, but it was far from comfortable. I had asked if I could wear anything else, but Libella made it clear that this was the only dress I could wear to the ceremony, mumbling something about protection. Of course, I knew it was likely embedded with Nikylo's xousía, but couldn't they have found a more comfortable one?

She allowed me a few more seconds before opening the door. I wasn't sure who I expected to find on the other side, but I dropped my head back, closed my eyes, and forced myself to take a deep breath before lowering my chin again to see Nikylo *and* Oliver waiting for me.

Great.

Oliver took in my dress, smiling softly at me. "You look—"

"Nope," I said plainly. "I don't want any false compliments or pretty words to try and make up for what you did."

"I cannot give you false compliments, love." He offered his elbow to me. "But I will honor your wishes."

I took his arm, if only because the heels Libella put me in were just as uncomfortable as the dress. She didn't say the shoes were necessary, but the length of the dress required some height added to mine. I could almost look Oliver straight in the eye, but Nikylo still had several inches on me.

"He can escort you there, but you have to enter the ceremony with me." Nikylo's voice was devoid of emotion, and when I turned to acknowledge his words, I noticed that his face reflected the same emptiness. How intriguing, considering the moments we shared today. From the firestorm to healing him to our conversation in the bathroom, so much had been said, but it also left a lot unspoken.

I expected nothing less, but I still asked, "Why can't I enter with Oliver?" As hurt as I was by him not telling me, it didn't change the fact that we were, apparently, betrothed. I had so many questions.

"The entirety of Niccodra does not know of our arrangement yet," Oliver replied.

"You make it seem like I have a choice in this," I mumbled, following his lead up the seemingly endless hallway.

"You do."

Perplexed by the lack of warmth from the mark on my chest, I glanced sideways at him. "Someone else offered me to you—"

"No," Oliver interrupted. "I offered myself." Again, there was no burning sensation.

"This isn't the time to discuss this," Nikylo whispered between our heads. "Unless you want everyone to know about your betrothal before *you* can announce it."

I rolled my eyes. "It's never the right time for *any* discussion." When I glanced over my shoulder, Nikylo was several steps behind us. They both wore similar tunics: Nikylo's was a darker blue, matching the color of my dress, while Oliver's was a much lighter blue. "Will I ever get answers to my questions?" Every time I wrote new questions, I checked my notebook for that familiar purple handwriting, but it was never there. I hated how disappointed that made me.

"Eventually," Nikylo replied, avoiding my gaze.

I turned to face forward again, realizing the paintings had changed into ones I hadn't seen before. "I miss Theo's presentations," I mumbled.

Nikylo scoffed. "You got so overwhelmed by those that you needed a break."

"You would, too, if you just discovered that magic and dragons exist in a world you thought was normal!"

Oliver placed his hand on mine, where it rested in the crook of his elbow. "Easy, love. You are attracting unwanted attention." His eyes darted to one of the paintings.

The hallway was empty, aside from being lined with strictly dragon portraits, all of which had eyes that seemed a bit too real. If what Oliver was implying were true… I took a deep breath. "At least I was getting my questions answered at the Dengalow."

"You will receive some answers sooner than you think, love. You must practice patience until then."

I shot him a glare. Patience—the one thing I was running out of. My notebook was filled with unanswered questions, with more piling on each day. Nikylo wasn't wrong; I did get easily overwhelmed by information, but that didn't mean I didn't want *any*. That reminded me. Over my shoulder, I said, "You still owe me a trip to the library."

"I owe you nothing, Sunshine."

"Oh, stop being so cryptic, Niko," Oliver said, leaning closer and whispering, "He is taking you to the Kyllindro tomorrow."

"What?" Unable to contain my excitement, I turned to Nikylo. "The *Kyllindro?*" I stared at him in awe, realizing that it wasn't just any library; it was *the* library. The one filled with all the scrolls and the collection of tomes and books that the knowledge hoarders had gathered. What did he call them? The Nosí? "What made you change your mind?"

He clenched his jaw, shooting Oliver a sharp glare. "Nothing. But I need to go and can't leave you behind."

I almost asked why but decided against it, knowing the answer had something to do with his possessiveness. I had been wondering about the Kyllindro ever since Theo mentioned it. I never thought the day would come when I would actually get to visit.

Oliver stopped walking and pulled his elbow from my grip. "Niko will take you from here. I will see you soon."

When I nodded, he disappeared. Not like, around the corner. No, completely out of sight. In the blink of an eye. A wind whipped around my feet, causing me to wobble in my heels as I stared at the floor, where the breeze tugged the skirts of my dress toward the end of the hall.

With my jaw still on the floor, I turned to Nikylo. "Did he just *disappear?*"

Nikylo sighed, shaking his head as if he were annoyed. "Yes. The wind can take him anywhere." He stepped next to me, placing a hand on my lower back and guiding me forward. His hand was burning against my bare skin, and I pushed down the thoughts that arose from seeing his bare back earlier. "It's how he beat us to the trial."

"How does that even work?" Nowhere in my lessons with Theo did he ever mention that kind of power.

"The caves have not just produced power for the Drakalasson. Some of them created flowers that held special power for the Fae—including Oliver's ability to travel among the winds," Nikylo said. When he didn't elaborate, I opened my mouth to ask about the flowers in the cavern we were in earlier, but he interrupted, saying, "Are you ready?"

I pursed my lips. That was the second time I had been asked that question within a matter of minutes.

We were stopped outside a pair of massive oak doors. They remained closed, but I figured it was for the same reason the courtroom doors had been closed earlier.

I chewed on my lip, my stomach suddenly filled with fireflies—an unruly combination of fireworks and butterflies. The constant reminder that this ceremony was dangerous was enough to keep me on edge. Add in the fact that it was for Talekor… I shuddered, recalling the sensation of his finger as he dragged it down my face.

A low growl resonated in my ears. When I locked eyes with Nikylo, his gaze shifted between green and blue. "He touched you?"

"Stay out of my head," I snapped, turning away from him.

But he seized my wrist, whipping me back to stand before him. "When did this happen?"

It was difficult to ignore the command to respond: "Before the dinner."

"What did he say to you?"

"Nothing. He was just taunting me."

"*What* did he say?" The sharpness in his words alone made me want to retreat. His anger was palpable.

"He said, 'As long as I have one of you, I have all of you.'" A shudder ran through me, but I added, "And some other choice words that I don't remember." Which wasn't entirely true. But the other words? They played back in my mind endlessly. How could I forget his claim over all of us just because he had Leighton under his control?

Nikylo clenched his jaw as he looked me over. Then, with a gentle grip, he pinched my chin between his thumb and forefinger, turning my head slightly to examine my cheek. How he knew exactly where he'd touched me, I'll never know. After a few seconds, he turned my face back to his, mere inches away. "What did I say about telling me if someone touches you?"

My anger clashed with his, and I swatted his hand away. "This isn't the time for the possessive asshole to make an appearance!"

Before I could push him away, he pulled me into an alcove I'd overlooked, away from the doors, and pushed me against the wall. "Do you honestly think there's no reason for the things I require of you?" His shout was quiet but had the same effect.

"Do you honestly expect me to be truthful with you when you don't extend the same courtesy?" I retorted.

"Dammit, Rayleigh!" His hand smacked the wall above my head, causing me to jump. "I'm trying to keep you safe!"

"What does Kaleb making me feel like a fool for loving him have to do with you?" My voice cracked. I hadn't meant to argue with him so fiercely about this. Being honest with him was probably the only way he would reciprocate, but this one hurt too much to admit. The moment my voice cracked, tears filled my eyes against my will. His tense posture relaxed slightly, but I could still sense his anger. "He came to your chambers to remind me that he controlled everything. To remind me that our relationship was manipulated from the beginning. Every second of it." I swallowed but held his gaze. "He came to show me just how much of a monster he really is, knowing that all he had to do was threaten Leigh, and I would do anything he wanted. He told me he would break her in ways I never thought possible." The last words barely made it past the emotion clogging my throat.

Nikylo let out a long breath.

"This isn't just about you," he confessed. Wait, was he actually about to tell me something? I held back tears as I waited for him to continue. "I've provoked him enough with my possessiveness to make him come after you." My confusion must have been evident on my face. "I didn't know he was my brother before we returned to Niccodra, but he did. He could see how I was with you on Gaia. I tried to tolerate him for you, I really did…" he trailed off, gripping my chin between his fingers once again, more gentle this time, and examining my cheek. "What did it feel like?" His voice was soft, his breath brushing against my cheek.

I swallowed thickly, ignoring my body's insistence to lean into him. "Like he dragged a hot knife down my face."

His growl echoed again as he turned me back to face him. "We don't know his powers yet, but something as simple as that could mark you. Will you *please* tell me if he touches you again?"

I nodded but asked, "Mark me? What does that—"

"Nikylo." A loud voice called from behind him.

He straightened up quickly, releasing my chin. Play along. I felt something in my hair as he stepped back to reveal who had interrupted us. "Sorry, Father. I got a little distracted seeing her in this dress." His arm slid around my waist and pulled me closer. A fire ignited inside me, but I couldn't tell if it was from anger or the way he was holding me. It wasn't aggressively possessive like I had imagined it might be. It was… gentler. Still possessive, but gentle.

The King stood just outside the alcove, Queen Kahlea beside him, her arm looped through his. "Yes, she does look quite ravishing tonight, doesn't she?"

Kyler's nose was suddenly pressed against my cheek, sending a chill down my spine as he said, "She tastes just as good as she looks."

I stiffened. *What did you just say?*

If there was anything else I could have done, believe me, I would have. Nikylo's voice was filled with regret. *But please, for the love of Mitera*—he paused, his warm breath cascading down my neck—*You need to imagine me kissing you in this alcove just moments ago.*

What?! I tried to jerk back, but felt his power holding me in place. *I've never—I could never imagine—*

I'm not saying you have, but you need to do so now. They are searching for proof of what we were just doing, and they cannot know about our conversation. I need to show them this.

Let them see a false memory? Why not just sift through my mind right now?

I am shielding you, as I always do, but they need to see it from your perspective; otherwise, they will think it is fabricated.

Because it is! This was ridiculous. Why would they care about what we were talking about anyway? *Can't you just make them see it with your mind powers?*

Sunshine, please.

I huffed. *Fine. What am I supposed to…picture?*

An image filled my mind, and I blushed at the thought. *Why not just ambush me when they walked up? Wouldn't that have been more realistic*

Because when I kiss you, Sunshine, his voice turned husky, *it will be because you want me to.*

He did not just say that… *I am betrothed,* I replied, failing to find any other excuse.

His eyes flashed an emotion too quick to catch. *They don't know that.* I could feel the desire radiating from him. I knew it was just to sell the moment, but damn, did it feel real. When he noticed the fight leaving me, he said, *Make it believable.*

I met his emerald green eyes and held them as I mentally returned to when he had shoved me into the alcove. Instead of him pushing me against the wall and slamming his hand above my head, I imagined his lips crashing into mine. A presence lingered at the edge of my mind, but I focused on the image of us kissing, imagining the hunger in his insistence and the kiss filled with heady desire. He wouldn't have taken his time, but instead would have taken what he wanted, and I would have given it freely, matching his frenzied pace. My hands would tangle in his curls while his traveled to the small of my back where the dress was open. His bare hands would have pulled me closer—

"Eh-em." That was Queen Kahlea. I released the fake memory and turned to where she stood, a blush on her cheeks, hoping one would show on mine to sell it. "I think we should let them be, dear." She tugged at the King, who was standing there studying me. "They still have a few moments before they're needed."

I took a deep breath as the King shifted his gaze to Nikylo. "I trust you remember the consequences if that leads to more?"

"Better than anyone, Father." Nikylo's voice remained low, but he cleared his throat. "We'll meet you outside."

When his parents left, I slumped against the wall. Nikylo slowly turned to face me, raising an eyebrow and wearing that familiar smirk. "Never imagined it before?"

"Oh, shut up." I smacked his shoulder, pushing the fake memory far from the front of my mind. "You told me to make it believable." It occurred to me then what had just happened and what it implied, and I felt all the color drain from my cheeks. "Wait…" The moment in the hallway at dinner flashed back to me—when Cleo found us in a compromising position—she hadn't seemed surprised, only embarrassed. "Are you telling me it's not just normal, but expected for Fae to—"

"Yes," Nikylo interrupted. "That's why I haven't claimed another Doulos since before my ceremony."

Shock rippled through my body as I stared at him, both truths hitting me hard. "You had a Doulos?" His rooms weren't prepared for me. They had always been like that: ready for a Doulos he would never claim.

He seemed to be somewhere far away, yet he nodded. "In my early years, I made the mistake of becoming too close to her. Nothing more than friends; the curse would never allow it, but a friendship nonetheless." The mention of the curse had me perking up, adding to my list of questions. Would they ever end at this point? He cleared his throat, refocusing on me. "I never… used her for that. But when I failed to protect her and she defied my father," he dropped his gaze, letting out a long sigh. "He doesn't take disobedience lightly."

He didn't need to say it, but I knew she was dead. "Here I was trying to decide if he was good or bad," I murmured, kicking myself for thinking a man who snapped necks effortlessly could be anything but evil. I was starting to think that if I *blinked* wrong, he might snap *my* neck.

"He is everything he made Talekor to be," he practically growled.

I stared at him, open-mouthed. Everything he had just confessed raced through my mind. Had I truly misread him all this time? "Wait, so you don't agree with what he expects from Fae?" I asked cautiously, aware that his answer would change everything.

He gave a small smirk, tugging on a loose curl before tucking it behind my ear. "Anyone with a heart would disagree with my father. Don't you remember what I told you about the Doulos bond?"

That night flashed in my mind. We were both sitting on my bedroom floor in the Dengalow. It had been so different and exciting to sit and learn things from him. He had shut down when I used the wrong word while talking about our bond—"claimed" instead of "chosen"—and told me there was a huge difference. "Yes," I said quietly.

"It still holds true, no matter how hard I've fought against it in the past." He was quiet for a moment before fully stepping out of the alcove and offering me his hand. "Come. We're the last ones to arrive."

With my mind racing and heart pounding, I took his hand. How were we supposed to shift from what just happened to this ceremony? Would everyone be there? What was I supposed to expect?

Expect the worst, Nikylo said.

I don't even know what the worst could be.

If he rejects the bond, he has the option to select another dragon. With him being a prince, things could get ugly.

Just the thought made me shiver. A fight among dragons sounded intense and chaotic. I hadn't been a part of the battle in the meadow, but I heard it all. It didn't sound pretty. When Mari was thrown out of the sky, I got lucky. She barely missed me, even though she couldn't have known where I was. Who knew what a whole gathering of dragons could do to one another? Would they fight to be bound to Talekor if he chose another?

Will I be able to see both Talekor and his dragon in this alternate dimension? The question sounded so strange when I said it aloud. A month ago, I thought the idea of a different realm was crazy. Look at me now, discussing dimensions as if I'd known about them my whole life.

Yes. Their minds will be entirely separate, as will mine and Drako's.

The theory I had swirling in my mind about Talekor trickled into my thoughts. I hadn't mentioned it to anyone because, well, I didn't want to upset them. But something had been nagging at me ever since he came to see me in Nikylo's rooms. The memory of him touching me burned all other thoughts away.

I pulled Nikylo to a stop. "What if his dragon tries to come after me?" If he was anything like Nikylo described, he was ruthless and temperamental. Dragons were possessive and fought for what belonged to them. What if he—

My breathing became uncontrollable, and my vision blurred due to the lack of oxygen. But the panic dissipated almost instantly. My hand fell against a soft fabric with detailed threading throughout. A heartbeat thrummed wildly beneath it. I focused to find it lying on Nikylo's chest, his hand flat against mine to keep it in place. His other hand was cupping my face, callouses rough on my cheek.

"He will not touch you, Rayleigh. I promised, remember?" The hand that was holding mine on his chest moved to gently cup the other side of my face, drawing my full attention to him. "You have everything you need to protect yourself in there. Drako and I will back you up, but you*'re* strong enough on your own. Remember what I told you earlier?"

I shook my head. "Don't let them see." The words came out in a whisper, but he nodded.

"You're the only one who can let people see your weaknesses, so *don't show them.*"

"You make it seem so easy."

"Because I know you can do it. I've seen how you stand up to your enemies. Your strength knows no limits, and your clever tongue can get you out of any situation." He smirked when his comment drew a genuine laugh from me. His confidence in those words seeped into me, boosting my own. I inhaled it, letting the words calm my nerves. "Good. Now, one more time. Are you ready?"

I nodded, wrapping my arm around his as we made our way into the ceremony.

If I weren't careful, I would start getting used to this side of Nikylo. Ever since he explained why he wanted me to stop calling him Kyler, everything started to fall into place. The conversation we just had about his father, his actions since we arrived in Niccodra, the possessiveness— they were all understandable. This didn't help my struggle to suppress everything I'd been feeling since he started showing that side of him again. The Kyler I had become friends with. The one I cared about.

But now that I understood what happened to his Doulos—why he reacted so viscerally and why his father posed that question before he left… I couldn't allow that to happen again, even if it wasn't the same kind of bond. The King didn't know that.

THIRTY
Burn It All Down

Nikylo pushed open the doors, and we stepped outside. It wasn't the glen where the twins and I trained, but rather somewhere in the heart of the castle—a kind of courtyard.

A large crowd gathered across the open lawn. Some people I recognized, like Romeo, Tietra, and Cleo, along with the Councilors, but no one else seemed familiar. On the opposite side, Talekor sat in the grass near the King and Queen. At the sound of the doors closing, every head turned our way. Nikylo was right: we were the last to arrive.

He ushered me along, and we made our way to an open lawn across from his parents and Talekor.

"Why is everyone sitting on the ground?" I asked out of the side of my mouth.

"This field aligns with where the ceremony will occur in the other dimension. It is also the island's strongest source of magic, aside from the caves."

"That doesn't explain why they're sitting on the grass." I tried to refrain from snapping, but his answer was not even remotely close to what I had asked.

A chuckle grazed my ear. "Our minds will abandon our bodies here to go to the other dimension. Lying in the grass ensures you won't fall over and hurt yourself."

I bugged my eyes at him and gritted out, "There's no way I can sit on the ground in this dress." It fit snugly around my torso, tight enough that I could have blamed it for losing my breath earlier.

Nikylo chuckled. "I'll help." His whisper tickled my ear once more, and suddenly, my feet were knocked out from under me. It happened so fast that I fell backward like a freshly cut tree. The scream I intended to release got caught in my throat as an arm wrapped around my waist before I hit the ground. Green eyes met mine as he lowered me to safety. "There. Easy."

"Asshole!" I thought better of punching, mentally decking him down the bond.

Ouch. His tone was sarcastic. *I caught you.*

You're the one who knocked me over!

Still caught you, though. He winked.

"Ugh." I tilted my head back onto the grass, absorbing the pinks and purples of the sky. *This* was what I needed to recall when he started acting like Kyler again. Remembering the asshole side would always bring me back from whatever thoughts I was having.

"Now that everyone is in attendance," the King's voice boomed, thick with annoyance. "The Drakalasson will ascend to the plane of the dragons."

Just the Drakalasson? What was I supposed to do? Lie here while this whole ceremony unfolded? I remembered Libella mentioning something about Nikylo allowing me to witness the ceremony, but would he really do that? Or would he leave me wondering what was happening on that other plane of existence?

I didn't think talking out loud would be a good idea, so I whispered down the bond. *Are you going to let me see what's going on?*

I wouldn't bring you here if that were not the case, he said, raising his eyebrows as if it were obvious. *Besides, I am not planning on just showing you; I am bringing you with me.*

Wait, what? How does that work? The only thing I could imagine was how he had invaded my mind in the past: back at school and in the dining hall for a memory— *Wait, how did you know they were searching for a memory in the alcove? I thought they had to be touching me.*

Asking for permission in the dining hall was a courtesy so they wouldn't scare you. They don't need to touch you to see your memories. That's why I constantly shield you.

Both of them have that power? I didn't miss that last sentence, but I also didn't want to dwell on it too much. Because that meant that his constant presence in my mind was to protect me.

I sensed him nodding mentally. *That's why mine is so strong.* He paused for a moment before answering my other question. *It will be similar to when I saw through your eyes, yes. But you will enter my mind while we journey to their dimension.*

Well, that's not what I expected. *How do I…do that?*

He chuckled. *I'll open my mind to you. You simply have to walk through the door.*

I turned my head away from the sky and found him lying beside me, his sparkling green eyes fixed on mine. *It's that easy?*

When you trust someone, yes.

I stared at him. *But you don't trust me enough to tell me anything.*

It's not you I don't trust, Sunshine.

I turned my gaze back to the sky, unable to think of a response. *Alright. Let's do this.*

His hand wrapped around mine. I knew it was likely connected to the whole traveling to another dimension thing, but I couldn't help but think back to when he held my hand in the courtroom. The way it steadied me so quickly, keeping me present. Wanting to feel grounded while we were among a group of dragons, I flipped my hand and intertwined my fingers with his. He didn't hesitate to curl his fingers around mine.

A warmth spread through me as the sky vanished from sight. I couldn't feel his hand anymore, yet his presence lingered.

I was alone, walking down a quiet corridor. The restrictive dress was gone, replaced by the riding leathers I had come to love more than I cared to admit. The walls towered out of sight, their color a familiar midnight blue. As I walked forward, I stopped at a single door. It stood stark white against the walls, a pearlescent hue swirling within its design. I reached out to place a hand on it. A humming sound reverberated through my body as the door creaked open.

Two sets of eyes stared back at me from the darkness beyond: one green pair and one bright blue. They both watched as I took a hesitant step into Nikylo's mind, and the world around me transformed.

At first, there was only a wide-open field that reminded me of the one from Theo's presentation about the dragons' power. I thought I might have walked through the wrong door, but then the others appeared. Dragons and their human forms were spread throughout the area. The dragons varied in size and color, scattered around the edges of the gathering. If they had a bond, they were seated before them in what looked like thrones. The empty thrones told me the dragons positioned behind them weren't bound.

Or their bond isn't present, Nikylo said as my gaze landed on a familiar golden dragon.

Where is Theo? I asked, seeing the empty throne.

On duty.

Unsure of what that meant but knowing now wasn't the right time, I followed the line of dragons around the circle until a familiar blue dragon came into view. He was settled directly behind Nikylo. I fought the urge to go to him, wanting to nestle against his warmth as I had— gosh, was that only last night? *Hi, Drako,* I said instead, waggling my fingers at him.

Hello, Little Ember. He winked, those bright blue eyes shining with pride, but something else lurked there, too. *I must warn you: the others here may sense your power and approach you. Do not let them get too close. They will try to tap into your power.*

That would have been nice to know… I mumbled, finding Nikylo watching me from the pearl stone throne he sat on before Drako.

I won't let them near you, he promised. That was the third time he'd said so. *Just stay close to me.* He patted the arm of the throne he was sitting on.

I squinted at him. *This is your mind. How can I wander away from you? Come to think of it… How can I see you? Aren't I supposed to be seeing through your eyes?*

He grinned and moved to stand directly in front of me. *You're in the mind of someone who can control what you see. You may be in here,* he said, tapping his temple, *but I'm also in here.* He then moved to tap mine.

That is some weird magic.

I know. He shrugged.

My gaze snapped back to the crowd as I felt a pair of eyes on me. I slowly scanned the field, searching for the gaze that felt like it was burning a hole in my head. When I reached the dais where Talekor stood, he was listening intently to whatever the King was saying. But the pair of copper eyes behind him were fixed on me. A magnificent creature, burnt orange in color, was watching me just like Drako had that first night on the lawn at the Dengalow.

A voice I didn't recognize echoed in my mind. *You were meant to be mine.*

How was another dragon speaking in my mind? Nikylo must've known this was happening, right? When he stepped up beside me, his eyes on the orange dragon as well, I shivered. *I am no one's,* I said with the confidence he had helped me realize.

The copper eyes flicked to where I knew Drako was positioned behind me. *He seems to think otherwise.*

We chose each other. That doesn't make me his.

The orange dragon released smoke from his nostrils. *Well, that changes everything, doesn't it?*

Shit. My eyes flew to Nikylo. "Did he not know?"

"I thought he did," Nikylo seethed. "Perhaps he was just speculating."

"Well, he certainly knows now!"

"Clearly." His jaw ticked. "It shouldn't change anything."

"Shouldn't or won't?"

He didn't respond. I clenched my teeth, biting my tongue so I couldn't use it anymore.

Biting your tongue won't help with how the dragons communicate, Sunshine.

Damn it. *Maybe you should have just left me behind.*

Another voice entered my mind, this one feminine. *So you are the one the rumors are about?*

I scanned the lineup of dragons for one whose attention was on me. Clear across the field, I spotted a massive lavender dragon with deep purple eyes locked onto me. The throne in front of her was vacant.

It depends on what the rumors are, I said, trying to keep my cool as more dragons turned their heads in my direction.

An Evanian has returned to our midst.

My head was filled with whispers as my eyes darted around to the different dragons. How could I hear all of them at once? I bit down on my nerves and found the purple eyes again. *I am what you claim.*

Her nostrils flared. Was she…*smelling* me from across the field? *All that power…* she hummed. *I sense air, earth, and…is that…fire?*

That is my fire you sense, Sylvarra. I felt Drako's presence behind me, so close that I knew his foreleg would be there if I leaned back. *Let me make this very clear*, his voice boomed, and all the dragons and human forms alike turned to him. *Rayleigh is not up for negotiation. Her bond is with me and will remain with me. If any of you try to change that—* he lifted his head toward the sky, and raging blue fire surged from his mouth. Some of the dragons had the sense to back up several steps. Hell, even I wanted to hide. That fire was *hot*. Drako cut off the flames and found Sylvarra again. *That fire will not be aimed at the sky.*

Sylvarra held his stare.

One dragon, with his bright red scales standing out among the crowd, countered Drako's fire with his own. The red flames licked so close to my head that I instinctively lifted my hands to push it away with my air. It worked, but I flinched back from the heat, bumping into Nikylo. He steadied me with his hands on my shoulders, though his focus remained on the dragon.

"That's Koladon's dragon," he murmured.

Naturally, the Kool-Aid man's dragon was red.

His torrent of flames ceased, and he snapped his jaws to the side. It came so close to the pale yellow dragon beside him that I thought he had chomped down on its neck. But the yellow dragon was ready to retaliate. It had spikes longer than my arms protruding from its tail, and it arched over and bit into the hind leg of Koladon's dragon, making him roar so loud that the ground shook.

"And that is the son of Koladon's dragon," Nikylo murmured. "He's turning out to be more ruthless than his father." His comment was echoed by another roar from Koladon's dragon as its son raked his claws down his red-scaled foreleg.

"This doesn't seem like a safe place for me," I murmured, my hands starting to tremble. I clenched them into fists to hide my fear, but I felt that any dragon in this field already knew.

"Enough!" King Gustav's voice resonated through the crowd. The two dragons stopped almost instantly, lowering their heads slightly in respect to him.

Silence fell over the crowd as the two dragons resumed their positions, and I paused to scan the thrones for familiar faces, wondering who I might have missed in the field. Libella was seated near the dais and nodded quickly when our eyes met. Her jade dragon was comfortably settled behind her, beside a nearly identical dragon of the same color positioned directly behind the Queen.

I didn't recognize anyone else. Where was everyone?

"It is time." The King stepped onto the dais, facing Talekor, and extended a fancy-looking goblet toward him.

A single finger hooked around my pinky, prompting me to turn, and I found Nikylo watching me. *The other dragons need to see Drako is serious,* he coaxed. *Sit with me.*

I nodded, trying to calm my fraying nerves, which were fueled by what had just happened and the anticipation of what was about to unfold. I let him guide me back to the throne, where he prompted me to stand beside it, and I wondered how long I'd have to remain there. My legs were already on the verge of buckling beneath me. But then his hands grazed my hips, and my gaze shot to his.

"May I?" he asked.

I swallowed. Every nerve in my body honed in on where his hands were still barely touching me. "May you what?"

"Help you onto the arm of my throne?"

My eyes flickered between his. He wanted me to sit on his throne with him? *Wouldn't that give them the wrong idea?* He simply smirked. I pursed my lips but nodded my permission.

His hands gripped my hips firmly and lifted me onto the arm of the pearl throne in front of Drako. Once I was perched, he asked, "Comfortable?"

"If I said 'no,' would you believe me?" Because that would definitely be a lie. My trembling legs were already thanking me.

"No." He sat in his spot and—damn him for knowing that leaning into me would only make me feel more at ease. His shoulder pressed gently against my waist, and I allowed it to ground me, just as his hand had before we traveled here.

"So we're just…lying on the ground outside the castle—unguarded?"

"Not unguarded, but yes. The Councilors and other Fae within the castle are keeping an eye on us." He glanced up at me, a grin on his face. "Don't worry. I'm still holding your hand."

Heat rushed to my cheeks as I turned away. Why was he still flirting with me when it was clear that nothing could happen between us? Sure, the flirting was fun, mostly limited to times when one of us needed a distraction. But with my betrothal and the curse, nothing would come of it. Not to mention, it wasn't something I wanted.

"Before us stand two souls," the King began, pulling my full attention to him and my thoughts away from Nikylo. He faced the crowd, his ivory dragon directly behind him, with Talekor and his soon-to-be dragon on either side. "Entwined since birth, yet free to choose their path. This bond is not one of servitude, but of trust, strength, and unity. This elixir will seal your destinies as one—" he held up the goblet, "—or set you free to walk separate roads." It sounded a bit old-fashioned, but perhaps that was part of the ritual.

He turned to my ex-best friend. "Do you, Talekor, willingly accept the bond, vowing to honor, protect, and grow alongside your dragon for as long as your paths align?"

However, Talekor's attention wasn't on his father. His gaze was fixed on me, where I sat beside Nikylo on his throne.

"No."

That single word made my stomach drop. Nikylo had warned that this could happen, but it was the *worst*-case scenario. He told me to prepare for the worst, but I never thought it would actually come to pass.

Talekor faced the King once more. "This bond doesn't suit me. It's made me feel things I don't wish to feel: compassion, care, mercy. I refuse to be chained to such frailty." His gaze shifted to the orange dragon, whose eyes were a familiar caramel hue that I recognized. That I'd seen before. I gasped. "You are too soft," Talekor sneered at the dragon, "too kind. I need a strength that matches my own, one that won't hold me back. I will not bond with a dragon so *weak*." He spat at the dragon's feet.

A few gasps resonated through the crowd at the display of disrespect.

"Talekor, by rejecting your dragon, you sever that bond permanently." The King didn't seem upset by this at all. In fact, he almost sounded proud. "There is no going back once he steps away from this dais. Do you accept this risk?"

"I do," Talekor replied, lifting his chin. "If I'm going to be bonded, it will be to a dragon who makes me unstoppable—not one that causes me to doubt myself."

The orange dragon did not react. There was no retaliation, no protest, or fight to stay. Before I could question how a dragon could drink from a goblet, he dipped his head and opened his jaw. The King poured the liquid into his mouth, and he swallowed with a visible shudder before bowing his head and stepping back from his position on the dais—as if he had anticipated this moment.

He searched for a new spot among the dragons and found it near the jade one behind Libella. When he settled into place, those honey-brown eyes met mine. *I'm sorry I failed you.*

His voice surprised me, sounding different than it did before. *Me?* I balked, trying to understand why this dragon was apologizing to me. *What do you mean?*

My influence of kindness and compassion wasn't enough to overcome the monster within him.

Oh. That was all I could say as my theory was turned upside down.

Libella told me it was rare for dragons to appear when the bond was not complete, but not impossible. This one, though I had no idea, had been there the whole time Kaleb and I were friends. Those honey-brown eyes were present more often than not.

I let this revelation wash over me as I stared at the dragon. *What did you mean earlier when you said I was meant to be yours?*

I hoped that, together, we could bring him back.

Back? I furrowed my brow. *Was he not always like that?*

The first several years you knew him, he fought against becoming a monster like his father. However, once he was taught to block me out, he transformed into the person you see before you now.

I glanced at Talekor, who was engaged in a heated but whispered conversation with his father. Completely detached from his dragon, I could see the darkness in his eyes, how much closer to black his brown irises had become.

Here I'd thought the dragon was influencing him to be evil. Little did I know, it was the exact opposite.

Keep your vigilance, Rayleigh, the orange dragon drew my attention back to him. *He can't harm you anymore if you don't allow it.*

Tears filled my eyes for the dragon as I nodded. *Can I call you something other than... well, dragon?*

His eyes crinkled. Was that a smile? *You can call me Lukas.*

I smiled back. *I hope you bond with someone worthy of your kindness, Lukas.*

The dragon bowed, and I brushed a tear away before it could roll down my cheek.

"Talekor has rejected his birthright bond and has chosen to invoke the right of challenge," the King announced. When another round of gasps echoed through the crowd, I turned to Nikylo. His body was tense on his throne, jaw tightened and eyes locked on the dais.

What's the matter? I asked, feeling a fresh wave of fear wash over me.

"He may challenge a source shifter only once," the King continued before he could respond. "If he fails, he will choose an unbound instead."

Cries of outrage erupted. Nikylo turned his head to Drako. *That's not usually the case, is it?*

Drako lowered his chin. *If he were anyone other than a Prince, he would be denied another dragon if he lost.*

Nikylo turned back to the dais, working his jaw while still avoiding eye contact with me.

"Who do you choose to challenge?" I snapped my gaze back to the King and Talekor.

A wicked grin spread across Talekor's face, his gaze fixed on his brother. "Prince Nikylo."

At this point, I don't think the crowd stopped murmuring between surprises because they only grew louder, drowning out my gasp of horror. He said the worst was that he could deny the bond, not that he could challenge someone for their dragon.

"Your dragon possesses the power and strength I require," Talekor continued. "He can command an entire horde of dragons due to the fear he instills. That is the dragon I deserve." He stood tall, all traces of the boy I once knew gone. "I challenge you, Nikylo, son of Gustav."

"By law and custom," Gustav said, "the challenge must be answered. Nikylo, do you accept, or will you yield?"

A hush fell over the crowd as Nikylo slowly rose to his feet, his warmth leaving my side as I watched in utter shock. He rolled his shoulders back, stretched his neck to each side, then crossed his arms over his chest.

"I accept your challenge, brother."

THIRTY-ONE
Don't Say I Didn't Warn You

Nikylo

My father's face didn't reveal a hint of surprise, meaning he knew Talekor would challenge me. Hell, he probably suggested it.

There was a time when I looked up to my father, respected him even. But in my three centuries of living I'd learned that you can't trust anyone blindly, not even those closest to you.

Unfortunately, or perhaps fortunately, that was something Rayleigh learned early in life, courtesy of the bastard on the stage.

I turned back to her, sensing her shock and horror at Talekor's challenge and my acceptance of it. Even if I didn't have my mental shields up around her, I would have known she felt that. It was written all over her face as she glanced between my brother and me.

I stepped into her space, bracing my hands on her shoulders, making sure I was the only one she could see. If I had one ounce less of self-control, I would have kissed her right then and there, if only to pull her from wherever fear had taken her. That damn curse was the only thing stopping me. Well… and Oliver. The curse was something I had never thought to research, accepting that it was just the way things were. But given the way I felt about her… that's why I needed to go to the Kyllindro. That, and to help her find a way to save her brother. I had to find out where the hell this curse came from. Sami had been on to something all those years ago.

But I couldn't worry about tomorrow's agenda today. Rayleigh's breathing had grown erratic, and she was still trying to look around me to see where Talekor was preparing for the challenge.

You did not prepare her well, Drako growled. *I warned you this was highly probable.*

Not helping, I snapped.

"Hey, look at me," I coaxed, dragging my hands up to her face, but she still avoided my gaze. I moved until my nose was inches from hers, fully aware of how it would affect her. I was right—her breath caught, and those stunning blue eyes finally locked onto mine. "This doesn't change anything," I lied. Because the moment she let slip that our bond was a Kavaltis, *everything* changed. "I will win, and he will be stuck with another dragon. I won't let him take you."

"Take *me?*" she squeaked. "What do you mean, *me?*"

Shit.

Well done, Drako scolded. *Now tell her, or I will.*

She can't know everything!

But she deserves to know this.

I glared at Drako, who was still sitting comfortably behind the pearl throne, before shifting my focus back to the woman before me. I sighed, knowing this was one of those things she had to hear, but I hated that it came to this. "If I were to lose, and the bond between Drako and Talekor were formed," I paused to swallow. Knowing this wasn't going to happen was enough, but the thought of it was horrifying. "The bond would transfer with Drako since he is who you are bonded to."

"No," she breathed, squeezing her eyes shut. She shook her head vigorously, telling herself mentally that it was all just a nightmare. That none of it was real. That all she had to do was wake up. But when she opened her eyes again, reality sank in. Tears pooled in her eyes at the thought of being bound to Talekor, the one thing we'd been trying to prevent since she arrived.

I moved my hands from her shoulders to her face, preventing her from turning away. "It won't happen, Rayleigh. Talekor can't beat me in a fair fight." I spoke with a confidence that had been instilled in me. If my father had trained him, it would be like our sparring match back on Gaia. I scoffed, realizing then how close he had come to beating me. If someone else trained him… "The challenge prohibits the use of power, instead focusing on Kontas Nami—"

"Are you serious?" she shrieked, pulling away from my grip. "Nikylo, *I* can beat you at that!"

I huffed a laugh, "That's because we were on Gaia, Sunshine. Remember?"

"You claim your power is stronger here," she said, shoving her finger toward Tal behind me. "That means his is, too!"

"Fine," I conceded, crossing my arms. "Then you were well-trained. Talekor didn't have such training."

"Yes, he did! He had trophies at home!"

"That didn't reflect on the mat," I stated, which wasn't entirely true because it had during our fight with the staff. But those weren't allowed in the first round.

"He was playing you!" she shouted, as if it was obvious. "He trained in martial arts."

"It's not the same, Sunshine."

She shook her head. "You don't know that." Her voice had lost its strength. I could see her giving up, accepting the loss that had yet to occur. I reached for her, but she pulled away from me. "What else does the challenge entail?" she snapped. I could feel her battling her emotions, trying to figure out how to keep me from losing. She worked her jaw, eyes darting between mine, then behind me—no doubt watching Tal. Concentrating on the fight was the only thing preventing her from breaking down.

I exhaled. "In the second round, weapons are introduced. The first to draw blood wins. If the same fighter wins both matches, they win the challenge." I could see her calculating the possibilities, aware that the fight was undoubtedly mine.

She dragged her hands through her hair and started to pace. "And if there's a tie?"

"Then a third round is fought, and the dragon in question decides whether it's with or without weapons."

She quickly turned to Drako. "Weapons. If it comes to you, choose weapons."

I am beginning to think you do not trust me, Little Ember. Drako was generous enough to let me hear his response to her. He didn't always do that, but at times he would cut me off when he deemed it was private between them.

She ignored him and turned back to me, her jaw clenched, but those stubborn tears remained in her eyes. "If you lose, I'll kill you."

"There she is." I flashed her a wild smirk and stepped toward her once more. This time, she stood her ground. "Tell you what, if I lose, I'll owe you a favor—anything you want, no questions asked."

Her mask of anger faltered slightly, and I took another step, forcing her to look up at me. "And if you win?" she asked, that crack in her mask revealing just how scared she was of me losing.

"If I win, well… I'll get the same." I winked, flashing a dimpled smile to ease her tension just a bit more. When she simply grinned, I added, "Come on, Sunshine. Have a little confidence in me."

She dropped her chin to her chest as she stepped back. "My confidence in you is outweighed by my fear of Talekor somehow pulling another one over on us."

Recognizing that this was her inner battle, I didn't reach for her again. I stepped back instead, pulling my tunic over my head. The movement made her head snap to where I stood, now shirtless. The fancy pants I had worn to the ceremony transformed with a thought, and I found myself in the loose linens for sparring. She held my gaze, the emotions there stirring something within me, and I almost closed the distance between us again.

"Challengers, prepare yourselves," my father declared. I had one minute to get into the challenge ring.

I wouldn't let her know, but my nerves kicked into high gear. There wasn't much that scared me, but losing her like this? I gave her one last cheeky grin, if only to hide my fear. "What? No good luck kiss?"

Finally, a laugh. And a genuine smile? Damn, she was beautiful. "If you win, maybe that could be your favor." Shock crossed her face as she realized what she said.

I'm sure it reflected my own, but I quickly hid that, too, and said, "Deal," before she could change her mind. She struggled to contain a smile as red crept up her neck. If fighting for her wasn't enough motivation, that definitely kicked it up a notch.

Without a second thought, I turned and made my way into the

challenge ring that appeared while my back was turned. It was customary to give participants time to prepare after accepting a challenge, but I had spent my five minutes reassuring Rayleigh that I wasn't going to lose her. I didn't regret it, but it meant I had lost the time I needed to really study Talekor. My powers would be cut off as soon as I entered the ring.

Any final words? I asked Drako.

Don't do anything stupid.

I mentally rolled my eyes. *Any* useful *words?*

Do not expect him to play fair. He does not understand integrity or nobility. You will fight with honor, but do not expect the same from him. I felt him sigh. *Lukasarion informed me that Talekor vowed to do whatever it takes for Rayleigh to be his.*

Noted. I clenched my jaw. A power grab was one thing, but deep down, I knew Talekor had other reasons for wanting her.

As I stepped into the circle, I felt my connection to Drako sever, along with the bond between Rayleigh and me. I turned to watch her retreat to the throne. When she passed it by and approached Drako, I nodded at him. He would keep her safe; I knew that. She wasn't tied to me, after all. My connection to her was merely a byproduct of their bond. So why did I feel so empty now that I couldn't feel it?

Knowing that the only way to get it back was through this fight, I faced my brother across the ring. I had a few inches on him, but in a fight like this, that wouldn't matter. He had discarded his shirt, and the muscles I'd glimpsed in our last spar were even more evident now. Rayleigh was right; he had been trained in something, but I didn't think it was simply martial arts. If he had undergone any of the training I had, this would be an interesting fight.

"First round is Kontas Nami only. No power, no weapons." My father stood at the edge of the ring, his voice booming so that everyone could hear. "The match ends with a tap out. Fighters, are you ready?" Both Tal and I nodded. "Begin."

The air felt heavy, thick with tension as the crowd's murmurs fell silent. Talekor was coiled like a spring, ready to pounce, his muscles tense beneath his scarred skin. I had no doubt that each of those scars came from our father.

I kept my stance loose, my feet shifting just enough to maintain balance. The dirt squished underfoot, grounding me. I learned to fight here, while he trained on a mat. Perhaps that would make the difference. We bowed slightly, locking gazes from just a few feet apart. My focus sharpened on Talekor's every move.

We both understood what was at stake.

Just as I suspected, he lunged first, dropping low and aiming for my legs. Instinctively, I threw my weight forward, forcing him to the ground before he could topple me. With a quick twist, I gained control, wrapping my arm around his neck from behind.

But Tal wasn't having it. He shoved hard against my chest, twisting his body with a burst of strength that broke my grip and forced me back. Before I could blink, he rolled onto his feet, resetting his stance and facing me again.

I hadn't expected this to be easy by any means, but I'd be lying if I said I wasn't disappointed.

I barely had time to take another breath before he rushed at me again, grabbing for my arm and trying to throw me off balance. I twisted free, planting my feet firmly in the dirt, and shoved him back. But the moment I created space, he surged forward, slamming his shoulder into my gut and knocking me to the ground.

Shit.

I hit the ground hard, my shoulders taking the brunt of the fall. Talekor was already attempting to pin me, pressing his weight onto my chest and trapping my arm. I gritted my teeth, refusing to let him win like this.

Planting my feet, I thrust my hips and pushed upward with all my strength, loosening his grip just enough to scramble free. My lungs burned, but I ignored the pain and rolled away. I jumped to my feet, brushing the grass and dirt off my chest, squaring up again.

Talekor followed suit, eyes narrowed and chest heaving. He flashed me a devilish smirk and said, "That all you got?"

I simply smiled back, allowing my stance to shift. "Not even close."

I didn't allow him time to process my words. I moved quickly, sweeping his legs with a sharp kick and sending him to the ground. Talekor hit hard, but before I could regain control, he wrapped his legs around my waist and pulled me down with him, twisting so that he was on top.

The dirt dug into my back as I struggled to escape, prying at his grip. His arms and legs felt like iron, holding me too close to gain any leverage. Sweat dripped down my temples as I pushed hard against his hold, finally breaking free and rolling away.

But I didn't reset; instead, I feinted to one side before rushing him, wrapping my arms around his waist and trying to slam him down. *Dammit!* I swore, because he saw it coming. He shifted, throwing me off balance, and twisted sharply, slamming me onto my back instead. The impact knocked the air from my lungs.

He didn't give me a moment to recover. He was on top of me, pinning my shoulders with his weight. I struggled, planting my feet and trying to throw him off, but he held firm. His forearm pressed against my throat, his body bearing down on me.

No! This wasn't how it was supposed to go. I twisted and pushed, straining against his grip. Rayleigh was counting on me. I knew if I won this round, there would be one more. I would win.

But Talekor shifted his weight, trapping one of my arms as he leaned down to whisper, "You know, the plan *was* to claim her, to bond with a dragon who would actually do it," he seethed, his mouth too close to my ear. "But stealing both her *and* your dragon?" A dark chuckle reached my ears. "It's just too good to pass up."

"You can't have her," I spat, fighting to breathe as he pressed his elbow against the side of my neck.

He flashed a maniacal grin. "Oh, but she's already mine—you just don't know it yet."

With one final push, the pressure in my head intensified, cutting off my air supply.

Coach says you shouldn't wait to tap out. Rayleigh's words echoed in my mind as I fought with everything I had to break his hold. My vision blurred as I clawed at his arm, twisted my torso, and bucked my hips. But it was no use. My strength was waning.

I was going to lose.

As her words echoed again, I summoned my last bit of strength to strike the ground twice with my open palm.

Talekor released me immediately, standing and stepping back as I rolled onto my side, gasping for air. My chest heaved with fresh oxygen as Tal crouched before me. "How embarrassing for you," he taunted. "Should have yielded when you had the chance." I was still gasping for air, but I wanted to strangle him. I wanted to see the life drain from his soulless eyes. I fought the urge, aware of the consequences of fighting between matches. "I do hope your skill with a weapon will give me more of a challenge."

I simply glared at him, knowing that my weapon skills far exceeded his. Without saying another word, he stood up, leaving me lying in the dirt to catch my breath.

When I finally pushed myself up, Rayleigh was crouched outside the ring several feet away, watching me. All I could see was the defeat etched on her face. With a heavy sigh, I stood and met her outside the barrier.

She gazed up at me with an expression I had never seen from her before. "Why didn't you listen to me?" she asked quietly.

Still catching my breath, I furrowed my brow. "What do you mean? Didn't Drako tell you? The bond was—"

"No!" she exclaimed, desperation lacing her voice. "I wasn't using the bond! I was yelling at you! Screaming for you to think outside the box, to find a way out. There's always a way out." Those damn tears returned, welling in her eyes but never falling.

I dropped my chin, meeting her gaze. "The challenge prevents all meddling." Her lip wobbled as I said, "I couldn't hear you." The fact that she was trying to coach me through it, trying to help me win… I didn't deserve her for more reasons than one, but this only added to those reasons.

She sniffed, pressing the heels of her hands into her eyes. When she pulled them away, the tears had vanished, replaced by determination. "You're good with weapons, though, right? This will be easy for you?"

"Still the lack of confidence."

"Can you blame me?" There was no teasing tone in her question. I hated this. I hated that she had so much doubt in me.

"No," I said honestly. "But if you could just trust that I know what I'm doing and that everything will be alright, it would help."

She eyed me, searching for an answer I couldn't provide. Then she relaxed her shoulders. "You're right. It's not like you just gave him the win. I saw you fighting it. You were," she paused, her lips twitching slightly, "alright."

"Was that almost a compliment?" I teased, grateful that she stepped back from the panic, if only for a moment.

"I'm not answering that."

"It was. I could feel it." I nudged her, finally catching her lips twitching upward. "I have him on the weapons, Sunshine. That favor isn't going to win itself." When she rolled her eyes, I smiled.

"I have a feeling I'm going to regret that…"

"The favor or the kiss?"

"Yes."

"Trust me, Sunshine," I leaned in to whisper, "the only thing you'll regret about kissing me is that you didn't do it sooner."

I expected it when she shoved me, but I let her, stepping back with a chuckle. She glared at me, though I could tell she was fighting a smile as she crossed her arms.

Just as she was about to say something, my father's voice rang out once more, "Challengers, choose your weapons."

Fear filled her eyes as she uncrossed her arms, then recrossed them, lifting her chin and setting her jaw. "Don't do anything stupid."

Those words coming from her? I gave her a two-fingered salute. "Wouldn't dream of it." I turned on my heel before I broke that promise.

The dais held a sparse collection of weapons, but I knew they were all sharpened and ready for the match. There were duplicates of each weapon: two swords, four daggers, two short swords, and two scimitars. Talekor watched as I picked up one of the swords, and he grabbed its twin. Typical.

The crowd buzzed around us, undoubtedly wondering how I was beaten by someone who wasn't raised here. However, I wasn't named one of the top three Kidemos because of my hand-to-hand. That was only one factor in the equation. Weapons, intelligence, discipline, and adaptability were the others, not to mention power. I excelled in three of those categories, with weapons being one of them.

Talekor followed me into the circle, silencing the world around us. He strolled in as if he'd already won, a smug grin plastered on his face. It made my blood boil.

"I hope you're prepared to lose her," he said, raising his sword.

"The only thing I'm losing today is that first match," I growled, mirroring his stance.

"Challengers ready?" With a nod at each other, Father said, "Begin."

Talekor lunged immediately, his blade coming down hard and fast. I blocked it effortlessly, pushing him back with a quick twist of my wrist. "Predictable," I muttered, dancing around him.

His face darkened as he came at me again, slashing wildly with a sword that wasn't suited for him. He fought as if he had something to prove—angry and reckless. I deflected each strike, my movements sharp, deliberate, and strictly defensive.

"Your footwork is sloppy and slow," I remarked casually, blocking him again.

He roared, swinging wide, and opened the door for me too easily. Stepping to the side, I brought my sword down across his forearm. Not a deep cut, but it didn't need to be. Blood welled instantly, and the fight was called.

Talekor stared at the minuscule cut, as if he couldn't believe it. His jaw tightened with each passing second.

"Better luck next time," I said, lowering my blade. "That is, if you ever learn to control that temper of yours." I walked away as the final announcement of my win was made. While hanging up my sword, I sensed her nearby.

I turned to see her sauntering toward me, still fighting the smile on her face. "Do you keep track like Theo does?"

Squinting, I asked, "Why? Did my time impress you?"

She shrugged, still unable to compliment my skills. "I still think I could take you."

My eyebrows shot up. "I'd love to see you try." I picked up a set of daggers, knowing we weren't allowed to use the same weapon in the second fight. I flipped one of them, grinning as she watched. "Does that mean your confidence in me winning has increased?"

Another shrug, but she was pursing her lips. "Is it too late to rescind my offer?"

"Far too late."

"In the event of a tie," the King's voice interrupted us. "The dragon in question will determine which form of combat will be used in the final round." Father turned to Drako, who was still settled behind the pearl throne. "Left claw signifies weapons, right means no weapons."

"Why not just ask him in his mind?" Rayleigh whispered.

"The answer could be switched since not everyone can hear his reply. This way, everyone can see his choice." Her eyes narrowed, pondering my answer. "I've never seen anyone do that, but usually, rules like that are only made because it has happened before."

Drako raised his left claw high enough for everyone to see before settling back down. His gaze landed on Rayleigh, who nodded and turned back to me with a grin. "He and I have a bet, too, you know."

"Oh?" I glanced back at him, but he remained silent, the mischief in his eyes dancing. "And what would that be?"

"He thinks you'll win in less than a minute."

I raised a brow, "And you?"

"I said two…"

Shaking my head, I eyed her. "And the stakes?"

She smiled, "If I win, he has to take me on a flight to another island."

With a sharp glare at Drako, I tried to conceal my annoyance at that promise. Turning back to her, I asked, "And if you lose?"

She sucked on a tooth, momentarily looking away from me. "If he wins—"

"Challengers, prepare yourselves."

I stepped closer to her, holding her gaze as her fear resurfaced at the announcement. "Tell me after I win what you'll have to do. Because I'm much better with a dagger than a sword." With a wink, I turned back to the ring and saw Talekor entering as well, his twin daggers in hand.

It felt different this time. He didn't have that confident smirk on his face. He twirled his dagger in his hand, his eyes blazing with hatred as he glared at me from across the ring.

I met his stare, not bothering with pleasantries. "I see that temper is still out of control."

A sneer confirmed that I was right, but he added, "My weakness won't cost me this fight."

Before I could respond, the start of the fight was announced. With a short bow of my head and Tal mirroring it, our father called for the fight to begin.

We clashed instantly.

Tal moved faster this time, his blades a blur as he came at me. I dodged and countered, slashing toward his ribs, but he twisted out of reach. Our daggers clashed again, and the sound of metal striking metal rang through the air.

I shuddered, noticing how focused he was this time—how calculating his moves had become. He wasn't fighting out of anger this time. He was fighting to win. Drako might actually lose his bet with Rayleigh.

I managed to slice his shoulder, but it wasn't deep enough to draw blood. He didn't wait to see, instead pressing forward and striking faster, harder.

"You're desperate," I taunted, slightly breathless but blocking him with every move.

His grin was sharp, borderline cruel. "You think?"

His gaze flicked from me to somewhere behind me and back. It was quick, but I knew it was intentional. Knew he was trying to get me to look, but I wasn't about to fall for it. Rayleigh was back there, probably watching on the edge of her seat. The first minute had to have passed by now, so she'd won her bet—if I could win in the next minute.

I went to strike, but he jumped back, which wasn't at all what I expected. When I lunged again, his arm snapped back, sending one of his daggers flying toward my head.

I dodged, tracking the path of the dagger just enough to know he'd missed his target, and then—

Tal was grinning.

My blood ran cold. *I wasn't his target.*

Internally, I told myself she would be fine, but instinct had my head snapping back to the dagger. My muscles tensed as I tried to reach for it, to snatch it out of the air.

But it slipped through my fingers and soared toward Rayleigh at the edge of the ring. She was frozen in a silent-to-me scream, her hands raised, as the dagger flew end over end toward her and—

And struck the invisible barrier, falling harmlessly to the ground.

That's when I felt the searing hot pain of a dagger in my side.

No. How could I have been so stupid? I knew there was a shield around the ring, that no sound could enter, but nothing could escape either. Another rule created because it had happened before. So why did I react so impulsively? Why did I fall for his deception? I met Rayleigh's gaze for a single moment, and that was all it took to see that hope had vanished from those deep blue eyes. Drako was right; Tal didn't have integrity, honor, or nobility. And I hadn't prepared Rayleigh properly.

I swung back to Tal, clutching the wound as blood seeped through my fingers. It wasn't deep, but it still stung all the same.

Sound erupted around us as the barrier fell, but all I could hear was the pounding of my heart in my ears; all I could feel was the fire coursing through my veins.

"You *coward!*" I hissed, moving toward him.

"I told you," Talekor smirked, meeting me head-to-head. "My weakness wouldn't cost me the fight. But yours just did.

THIRTY-TWO
Nothing Is As It Seems

He lost.

The challenge. His dragon. *Me.*

He lost it all when Talekor threw that dagger. Drako yelled something in my mind, but it was drowned out by the scream I let loose. And then the dagger clunked against an invisible wall.

Nikylo had exploded at him, but Talekor grinned, leaning in to whisper something unintelligible. Whatever it was, I couldn't hear it over the sudden murmur of the crowd. When Talekor walked away, Nikylo slowly turned to me, a distraught look on his face, and all I felt was emptiness inside. It was as if everything I had fought for had just slipped through my fingers.

Because it had.

When he won the second round so quickly, my tension eased more than it should have. My confidence spiked as I watched him move effortlessly with a blade. I let myself hope that he would actually win the third round, that he could defeat Talekor in less than two minutes. If I was being honest, I agreed with Drako, believing he could do it in one. His skill with weapons truly was incredible. But that didn't outweigh Talekor's knack for exploiting weaknesses. And now I knew I was one of Nikylo's.

He made his way over to me, defeat evident on his face. "Rayleigh," his voice strained, likely from the pain and fighting. All I could do was stand there in shock, every fear I'd shoved down earlier seeping up into my every thought. Talekor was going to bond with Drako. Then he was going to claim me. I would be his to control, and none of Niccodra would be safe. My friends would be in danger. And Nikylo—

I met his gaze. "You're going to lose Drako," I said, my voice emotionless. But he wasn't *just* losing Drako; he was losing Drako, me, *and* his powers. Would he bond with another? Or would he be powerless for the foreseeable future? How did it work when someone lost their bond with a dragon?

"I'll be fine. Just listen to me." He was still holding the wound on his bare torso, but his other hand lifted my chin. "*You* will be fine. He can't win if you don't let him."

"He's already won!" My emotions erupted as the tears I'd been trying to hold back the whole time streamed down my face. "Don't you see? He got exactly what he wanted: *me*."

"Rayleigh, please—"

"After a close match," the King's voice rang out yet again. "Talekor was the first to draw blood, thus winning the final round and the overall challenge."

The crowd's reaction told me they were unsure how to react. Some clapped but lacked enthusiasm. Others exchanged worried glances with those around them. Even I wouldn't know how to react. That is, if I wasn't at stake in this, too.

But my terror was surfacing, and I knew Nikylo could sense it. The bond had been restored when the barrier fell, and I felt all his regret down the bond. He reached for me, and I let him, knowing I was about to crumple to the ground if someone didn't catch me.

Just as his hand gripped my elbow, the King spoke again. "Nikylo, please join us at the dais."

His jaw flexed as his hand dropped from my elbow, and he turned, not to the dais but to Libella, who had crossed the field and was now standing behind him. "Make it quick."

She nodded, reaching for the wound on his side, and it knit itself shut at her touch. He barely even flinched.

With one last glance at me, he said, "Stay with Libella." He didn't turn back as a shirt materialized from thin air, which he pulled over his head while walking to the dais. I turned to look for Drako, but he wasn't where I had left him. Confused, I scanned the crowd and found him settled behind the dais near the King's dragon.

Tears streamed down my face again. I had to stand there alone as I lost the only thing that had been keeping me sane lately. The only thing that grounded me. I felt an emptiness inside that was unexplainable. An arm wrapped around my shoulders, but I barely felt the comfort she was trying to offer because it wasn't who I needed.

It wasn't who I wanted.

Sure, being bound to Nikylo hadn't been my first choice, but that changed over the time I'd known him. The times when the part of him I recognized as the real Nikylo had shone through. He only acted like an asshole to keep me at arm's length, but I knew there was a part of him that genuinely cared—and not just about my power. I'd known for a long time; I just hadn't allowed myself to admit it.

And I was about to lose him—the one person I was slowly learning to trust, even after everything he'd kept from me. Talekor would probably never let me near him again. He definitely wouldn't leave me alone with him for any length of time. Was that our last conversation? What would it feel like to sever the bond? Even just blocking the bond during the challenge had left me feeling empty. I couldn't imagine what it would be like to sever it completely.

When Nikylo stepped into place, the King turned to Talekor. "With your victory against Nikylo, he will be required to relinquish his bond with the dragon behind me. That will leave him to forge a new bond and you to take his." He lifted the goblet with the elixir. "However," I held my breath, wondering what other bombshell would be dropped today. "As always, the bond is a choice." I blinked when he paused. What was it with the dramatic pauses? Of course, it was a choice! But it didn't seem like one right now. "For both parties."

My jaw hit the ground.

A spark of hope ignited within me, consuming all the fear I'd let take control as a sob escaped my lips. All the terror dissipated as my gaze met that of the blue dragon behind the dais. His eyes flared with a familiar emotion—one I had neglected to recognize as tied not only to his possessiveness with me but with everything he believed was his.

The King turned to Drako. "Do you, Valisdrako, willingly relinquish your bond with Nikylo, severing your power from him and leaving yourself free to bond with another?"

The crowd fell utterly silent, holding their breath as the dragon rose to his haunches and stared directly at me.

No.

The whispers began immediately, but the one word that had previously made my stomach drop was now easing every worry and fear I had felt when Talekor said it. My body wanted to collapse in on itself as the tension faded, but Libella helped me remain standing, watching as the dragon I had grown so fond of rejected the severance of our bond that would have meant my doom.

But Drako wasn't finished. He turned his head to Talekor, who glared at the dragon with such fury that I could almost see smoke filtering out his ears. *The bond I chose with Nikylo was based on his honor, nobility, strength, and integrity. None of which you possess. Even if that were not the case, the moment you threatened my bond,* his eyes fell on me again, *you lost all hope for my agreement to this.* He turned back to Talekor for the final blow. *You are blind to power and rage, and you will do well to temper that before attempting to bond with another.*

Talekor appeared ready to explode. Rage seeped into his eyes as he tore his gaze from Drako and began scanning the lineup of dragons that he was left to choose from.

I trembled from head to toe as the adrenaline from the day left my body. The King dipped his head in acceptance of Drako's rejection, ignoring Talekor's outrage. "Thank you for your wisdom, Valisdrako." That was the second time a non-dragon had spoken his name… "You and Nikylo may return to your thrones to restore the balance."

Drako stood on all fours, taking the few steps necessary to position himself comfortably behind the pearl throne once again. Nikylo followed, and I couldn't contain the joy that bubbled up inside me. However, glancing over his shoulder at the King made me tense every muscle to stop myself from meeting him halfway. The King had been unnaturally attentive to me since my moment of weakness during the Kontas Nami round. His earlier comment to Nikylo in the alcove was the only thing that kept me waiting for him beside Libella. Otherwise, I would have run to jump into his arms.

When he appeared beside me, his eyes sparkled in the brightest green

I'd ever seen, swirling with the same joy I felt. "You couldn't have told me?" I asked, trying to suppress a smile.

"That Drako would deny the bond?" When I nodded, he shook his head. "He never tells me his plans. I only had an inkling." When I furrowed my brow slightly, wondering why he hadn't confided in me, he clarified. "I didn't want to get your hopes up. Drako…" His gaze darted to where I knew the dragon was behind us. "He can be unpredictable sometimes. And dramatic. *Very* dramatic."

It would be wise to consider your next words carefully.

"However," Nikylo continued, glaring at him, "his unpredictability is what has shaped who I am today. He has taught me to adapt in situations I never could have imagined. " His gaze returned to mine. "Choosing you was one of those moments. So no, I didn't know he would reject Talekor. But I should have realized he would have some choice words for him and that he would take such a public moment to deliver them."

A dark chuckle echoed in my mind as I turned to Drako. *He had to learn the hard way that a bond with a dragon cannot be formed by the source-shifter alone.* He lowered his chin as he met my tear-filled eyes. *Did you really believe I would subject you to a bond with that monster?*

I let out a strangled laugh and shook my head. *No. I just… I didn't know.*

Even if you were not in danger, I would have rejected his bond.

Really? Nikylo's shock reflected my own.

The muscle above Drako's eye twitched, and I suppressed a chuckle at the humanlike gesture. *Your surprise wounds me, Niko.* But then he leaned his head forward, coming nose-to-nose with Nikylo. *I did not choose you by mistake or out of pity. You would do well to remember that.* Nikylo nodded a bit sheepishly, leading Drako to pull his head back behind the throne before his gaze dropped to the dais. *Talekor has made his decision.* The growl in Drako's voice made me turn my head to see why.

When I found the dragon positioned behind the dais, goosebumps peppered my skin. "You said he was worse than the Kool-Aid Man's dragon." My voice was barely a whisper, but I felt Nikylo nodding.

It appeared that Talekor had already made his vow, drinking from the goblet that the King offered him.

He turned to the yellow dragon, whose ruthlessness was evident from this distance. Scars covered a lot of his wings and exposed underbelly. Some of his scales were missing. A scar bisected his brow, likely the cause of the cloudy portion of his eye beneath it. I never wanted to be near that dragon. *Ever.* "And do you, Morvax, willingly accept the bond, vowing to guide, protect, and share your strength with Talekor, as long as your paths align?"

Why can he use the dragon's full name? I asked, remembering he'd used Drako's earlier, too.

Special circumstances, Nikylo replied. *These ceremonies require full names. It isn't considered disrespectful during them.* I suppose that made sense.

Morvax nodded in agreement, his fiery orange eyes fixed on Talekor, who smirked with an aura of pure evil.

"Then drink, and let the elixir solidify the bond that no force, aside from death, can sever without ceremony." Morvax lowered his head and opened his jaws. The King poured the liquid into his mouth, withdrew the goblet, and allowed the dragon to retreat. "By your will and shared strength, the bond is eternally forged. Your fates are now intertwined, your powers have merged into one, and henceforth, you shall be honored as Drakalasson."

My eyes fluttered open to reveal the twilight sky above us and the uncomfortable dress pinching my ribs. I tried to sit up, but a sharp pain in my abdomen forced me to stop. I turned to find Nikylo helping himself up after releasing my hand.

"A little help?" My sass was evident.

He grinned, crossing his arms as if nothing that happened in the other dimension was real.

"Please," I added. He rolled his eyes but extended his hand, pulling me to my feet the same way I'd fallen—like a tree. It wasn't graceful, and it wasn't pretty, but he steadied me on my feet with an arm around my waist.

I looked up to find his face just inches from mine. "This dress might be uncomfortable," he said before stepping back to give me a slow once-over. "But you look extravagant wearing my scales."

My eyebrows shot up. "You mean Drako's scales?" Of course, I hadn't known they were *real* dragon scales. I thought they were just a symbol of possession as we walked into the ceremony. But now, the uncomfortable aspect made sense. Dragon scales were unyielding and impenetrable.

"What's mine is his." He shrugged, tracing his finger along the scales encircling my torso. I couldn't feel his finger through the scales, but something ignited within me when he touched me so gently. I wondered if it was because it was right along where the madí was…

"Why am I wearing a dress made of dragon scales?" I nearly shouted the question at him, struggling to suppress my emotions.

Those emerald green orbs locked onto mine, mischief dancing within them. "I wasn't sure what Talekor would be willing to try—if he had any Fae under his command on patrol during the ceremony. I have no doubt he would have attempted to take you from me forcefully." He shifted his gaze back to the bodice. "These are not only embedded with my xousía, but when I'm touching you while they're on, you cannot be separated from me."

There was that possessiveness again. But I'd be lying if I said it didn't make me feel things other than anger this time. I wanted to hate it

"You appear to have made it out in one piece," Oliver's voice carried across the field.

I turned away from Nikylo, breaking the tension his touch had caused. "Barely," I said, finding him striding straight for us.

He showed no signs of concern aside from the slightly furrowed brow. "What happened up there?"

Nikylo stepped up beside me. "Talekor challenged me. I lost. Drako rejected him. He chose the son of my uncle's dragon."

Oliver blinked several times. "I apologize; I must have misheard. Did you just admit defeat?" The teasing tone made me suppress a giggle.

"If you're implying that I don't do so often—"

"Oh, I am not implying anything, Niko. This is me calling you out on years of your bullshit."

Nikylo let out a mocking gasp, his hand flying to his chest. "Did you just curse?"

"I curse plenty, asshole." But the word didn't sound right coming from him, and neither Nikylo nor I could hold back our laughter when he mumbled to himself, "That was not how I imagined that word would sound." He glared at both of us, holding back a smile before finally saying, "How did this conversation turn into mocking me? Tell me what happened."

Nikylo sighed, relaying his loss and what it nearly cost him. As he did that, I observed Oliver as he took in the information, my smile fading as I recalled our last conversation.

We were betrothed.

His blue eyes were fixed on Nikylo as he spoke. There was no denying how handsome he was, with his soft yet defined features and white-blonde hair unkempt but also like he placed it perfectly. I barely knew anything about him, though. I knew he was flirtatious and possessed great leadership skills—if being a Councilor said anything. He was mostly honest, even though technically he had to be with me. He was caring and understanding, never pushing me to do anything I didn't want to. But would it always be like that? Or would he start to pressure me about the betrothal as time passed?

The rest of our earlier conversation came to mind. He told me he realized that his betrothed could also be the one who matched his soul. He had been talking about me the whole time, and that alone was a significant statement. On one hand, we barely knew each other, but on the other, everything came so easily between us. Our conversation flowed naturally, and being around him brought me a comfort I didn't know I needed. He was incredibly patient and kind, and as similar as that was to Kaleb, it was what I craved in someone close to me.

But that didn't change the fact that just beneath the surface, I was still angry. He'd made this vow with me and then found a loophole to share half-truths. It didn't sit well with me, but honestly, what else could he have done? Telling me the truth then would have only added to my already insane day.

"Rayleigh?"

I pulled myself from my thoughts, finding both Oliver and Nikylo looking at me expectantly. "Sorry, what did you say?"

Oliver smiled, likely trying to draw one from me as well but it wouldn't work. "Libella is going to escort you to your chambers to prepare for the evening."

I turned to see Libella behind me before refocusing my attention on Nikylo and Oliver. "Where are you going?"

"It's customary to celebrate with friends after the ceremony." Nikylo clenched his jaw. "My mother asked me to accompany Talekor." He met Oliver's gaze, then mine again. "Oliver is joining us."

"Your mom is making you hang out with your brother…because he doesn't have any friends?" I scoffed. That definitely seemed like something a mom would do, but it was still strange.

"Essentially, yes. Others will likely join us there."

"Who is staying with me?"

"Actually, you won't be staying at the castle tonight." When my eyebrows shot up, he grinned. "You'll be staying at the Verdanvale this evening. Kendall and Mari will join you. I'm trying to arrange for your mother to be brought as well." I couldn't contain my excitement. Not only was he sharing information, but he was also letting me see my friends. *I thought you might want to spend time with Mitch in a place where the magic doesn't affect him.*

"What?" I blurted out, realizing too late that he had said that last part in my mind. *How?*

I switched out the gonos he was wearing for a different pair. These are stronger and appear to be working well.

But are they draining him like the last pair?

Nikylo shook his head. *That wasn't because of the gonos. He wasn't being properly nourished, much like you and your friends in the dungeon.*

I eyed him, curious if he would answer my next question. *Why did your father act like he didn't put us in the dungeons?*

Because he didn't, he said plainly. His eyes darkened before he said, *The person Talekor is in league with put you in those cells.*

Perplexed by that, I asked, *Who is he in league with?*

That's what we're trying to figure out.

THIRTY-THREE
Everything or Nothing

Libella and I made it to Nikylo's chambers without anyone stopping us. He had mentioned before leaving the field that Talekor could appear anywhere. His powers were still unknown, but once the elixir settled into place, the madí between him and his dragon would manifest on his chest or back. They would announce his powers at the ball tomorrow.

That didn't mean Talekor would wait to use them. He could have been tracking me from the moment I left the dragon dimension, or he could have accessed my mind, sifting through my thoughts and memories. Nikylo assured me that Talekor's powers wouldn't be strong right out of the gate. It would require training and growth for them to develop into what Nikylo's powers were today.

Once back in my—er, Nikylo's chambers, I slammed the door and glared at Libella. She merely stared back with concern etched on her brow. "What is it, dear?"

"Will you *please* get me out of this dress?"

She gave a knowing smile but immediately started undoing the dress, and I finally felt like I could take a full breath. Between that dress and the day I'd had, I didn't know how much more I could handle. The days here weren't measured by the sun, but my body was still measuring by the hours back on Earth. I would bet my life that I'd already been up far longer than I would have been on a normal day back home.

I stepped out of the beautifully crafted dress, and Libella hung it up while I washed off the light makeup she'd put on me.

I met her in the closet where Nikylo apparently kept all the clothes he made me wear. I wasn't aware that we were sharing a closet since I never needed to retrieve anything for myself. Libella had a small satchel placed in the middle of the floor for me and pointed out where I could find my things: undergarments, socks, nightgowns, training linens, and flying leathers. The dresses I had worn to the events hung at the far end. No new dress, though. I turned to see her heading out of the closet.

"Libella?" She paused, glancing over her shoulder. "Will I be wearing one of those dresses for the ball as well?"

She smiled. "No, dear. Your dress hasn't quite arrived yet."

I groaned, "It's not another uncomfortable one, is it?"

"No." Her eyes danced like she was keeping a secret she couldn't wait for me to discover.

"Okay." She turned again, but I called her name one more time. When she looked this time, a smile lit up her features. "I don't know what to pack for tomorrow…" I admitted.

"A set of training linens and riding leathers should be enough. Oh, and don't forget a nightgown for the evening. But you'll need to return here to get ready for the ball." I nodded, heading back to the closet filled with mine and Nikylo's things. Something in the corner caught my eye. "Anything else, dear?" Libella cooed from the doorway.

"Um, no. Thank you." I stepped toward the corner but hesitated, not wanting her to stop me if it was what I thought it was.

"I'll be in the foyer when you're ready."

I waited for her to leave before dropping to the floor and pulling the box away from the wall. Sure enough, behind it was a small door. However, there was no handle on it. What had Drako said to do? Touch it? I figured it wouldn't hurt to try. I pressed my palm against the door, and a small snick echoed in the closet. When I removed my hand, the door came with it, opening to reveal a box full of mostly journals, along with some other items.

As I pulled out several of the journals and sifted through them, I realized I should have asked Drako which ones contained the information I needed. None of them were labeled except for a number on the edge. They were in order but skipped several numbers at a time, with the highest being three hundred and fifteen. Wondering if it could be related, I decided to take a chance.

Nikylo, how old are you? Oliver had mentioned it, but with everything that happened today, I'd already forgotten.

What? He sounded distracted.

How old are you? I repeated.

After a long pause, he said, *Three hundred sixteen years.*

Damn. I hadn't meant to say that to him, but that was *a lot* of years. *You're old.*

A sharp chuckle reached my ears. He must have been nearby because he said, *You just made me scare the hell out of Libella.*

If he was with Libella… shit. I needed to figure this out quickly. Trying not to think about the journals, I asked, *Why are you back here? I thought you were going out.* I shuffled through the journals, hoping my intuition was correct, and found some I hoped were dated over a hundred years ago. Mari had said it had been more than a century since Niccodra had looked like that painting. To be safe, I grabbed four—165, 182, 197, and 209—and stuffed them into the satchel.

I need to clean up before I go. Is everything okay? he asked, likely hearing my grunt as I shoved the box of journals back into the compartment and quietly closed the door, pushing the other box back to conceal it.

I jumped up, wanting to ensure no one found me on the floor, and said, *Yeah, just gathering my things.*

Okay… There was a tone of suspicion, but he must not have cared enough. *Theo will be here in five minutes.*

Hastily, I grabbed some clothes and shoved them into the satchel, emerging from the closet as nonchalantly as I could a few minutes later. I walked into the foyer—where I awkwardly shouted, "Oh my—" cutting myself off, I whipped back around to the bedroom. "I'm sorry!" I shouted again, pressing myself against the wall just inside the door. My face was surely bright red.

Because I had accidentally walked in on Theo and Libella kissing. And that… well, it felt like I had walked in on my parents.

Libella's voice drifted into the room as I buried my face in my hands. "Rayleigh, dear, you can come out now." She sounded as if she were giggling, making me want to hide in the closet again. "I promise there won't be any more kissing from us."

"Well… Ellie, darling. I haven't seen you in weeks…" Theo's

whispered voice carried.

"Theo, no. Stop!" An exaggerated kissing sound filled my ears, and Libella burst into giggles. "Dammit, Theo! Stop it!"

My curiosity got the best of me, and I peeked around the corner to see Libella beaming, pushing Theo away from her with his exaggerated, puckered lips. Libella stood about six inches taller than Theo, giving her the upper hand in keeping him at bay. The scene was so ridiculous that I couldn't hold back my laughter.

Theo finally glanced at me sideways without giving up on his advances, but Libella released him, causing him to stumble into her due to my distraction. She wrapped her arm around him, pulling his back to her in a hold I had practiced many times during training.

Theo laughed. "Okay, okay, Ellie, darling," he tapped her hand twice, " you win this one."

She let him go with a shake of her head, but she was smiling. "Leave it to you to embarrass the children."

When she released him, I stepped a few paces into the foyer, smiling. Witnessing the love they shared was incredibly comforting. Having a mate must be amazing. Their distance didn't create any tension between them; it simply made them miss each other. Although… Theo had been back for the same amount of time I had, so why was this their first reunion?

Theo turned to me, smiling brightly, and said, "Oh, sorry, dearie! I didn't see you there." The sparkle in his eyes made me roll mine. "Are you about ready to go?"

I lifted my satchel in response but realized one thing was wrong with this situation. "How are we getting there? I thought I could only fly with Nikylo." The annoyance I meant to add to that statement fell flat.

"Oh, well, yes," Theo started, and boy, did I miss his quirkiness. "Niko will be granting us entry once everyone is here."

"Granting us entry? And who else is coming?"

"Niko's little hideaway is enchanted, so only he and his co-conspirator can access it. No one else can enter without them." Theo stepped closer and whispered, "Kendall and Mari will be here soon with your mother."

I already knew that, so I whispered back, "Why did you need to whisper that?"

Theo's eyes scanned the walls around us, but his head remained still. It was rather comical. "These walls can talk."

"That's just an expression, dearest." Libella had followed Theo across the room, grasping his elbow to pull him out of my space.

But Theo shook his head dramatically. "Oh, no, Ellie, darling. I don't think so." His gaze fell on a portrait near the main archway. "That one in particular looks like a true gossiper."

Libella gave him a deadpan expression. "That's Nikylo's portrait, Theo."

He nodded with his whole body. "That is what I'm saying! Gossiper!"

I laughed, shaking my head at Theo. "You're in a goofy mood today."

"Oh, this is just about every day, dear," Libella said. "Did you not spend time with him at the Dengalow?"

I nodded, recalling his notion of locking his mouth with an invisible key. "I suppose you're right. I guess I've just been missing the silliness lately. I've been…" I trailed off, contemplating all the events of the past few days.

"Yes, yes. You've been through quite an ordeal, haven't you?" Theo said, stepping forward again, his arms outstretched. He didn't say anything more or close the distance; he just kept his arms open wide for me.

Tears welled in my eyes as I nodded and stepped into his embrace. The hug was everything I needed.

"There, there. I've got you. Cry as much as you need, dearie."

We stood there for a while before the bathroom door open and multiple voices came from inside. I gently pulled away from him and met his gaze. "Thank you, Theo. I… I didn't realize how much I needed that."

"My pleasure, dearie. I'm here for you to lean on anytime you need." I chuckled lightly, but he added, "Truly. I am here whenever you need me. Just let Niko or Ellie know." He extended his hand to Libella, and I nearly burst into tears again. It truly was heartwarming to witness such a loving relationship.

"I will," I said truthfully, knowing there would certainly be another opportunity soon.

"Are we ready?" Nikylo asked from across the room. He stood near the door I had gone through to see Mitchell for the first time. Next to him were Mari, Kendall, and—

"Ma!" I rushed across the room but slowed down just before crashing into her. She still looked frail, and I didn't want to hurt her more. However, she was standing on her own, allowing her to wrap both arms around me when I hugged her. "I missed you!"

"I missed you, too." Her voice was barely audible, and I pulled back to see a small tube beneath her nose, connected to a tank on rollers behind her. It was strange to see such an ordinary thing in a realm where things like that didn't exist. "How are you holding up, sweetheart?"

"I should be asking you that!" I said, hugging her again before pulling back to respond. "It's been a crazy few days... I have so much to tell you."

"Yes, yes. Lots to discuss." Theo made his way to the door Nikylo was now facing. "But not here. Plans are in place, and we must make haste."

Ma chuckled as I linked her arm with mine and extended my other hand to Kendall, who stood beside Ma with a small smile.

"Everyone will need to be holding on to each other for this to work," Nikylo said, stepping back from the door he was fiddling with.

A blue glow filtered through the cracks, and as it grew brighter, Theo and Libella, already holding hands, reached for Nikylo and Mari, who grabbed Kendall's other hand. Once we were all linked, Nikylo opened the door, revealing a familiar face standing in the living room. Nikylo pulled us through, and as I passed through the doorway, I felt a tingling sensation slide over my entire being. That must have been the enchantments Theo mentioned. I wonder why I hadn't felt them when I came here with Oliver.

Once everyone was through the door, we all let go of each other except for me and Ma. Swallowing my anger for a moment, I helped Ma over to where Oliver stood in the middle of the room. She released a small gasp because, if I was calculating correctly, they hadn't seen each other in almost twenty years. Maybe even more. He gave me a warm smile before turning to Ma and saying, "It has been quite some time, Jo."

"Ollie?" Tears filled her eyes as she gazed at him. "I haven't seen you in..." she trailed off, staring at his face as if she'd seen a ghost. "You look exactly the same."

He tilted his head, widening his smile. "And you... well, time has been more generous to me, it seems."

My jaw dropped, but Ma laughed, causing her tears to fall as she said, "Well, not all of us can cheat time, Ollie. Some of us have earned our wrinkles." She smiled broadly at him, proudly displaying some of those wrinkles.

He relented and closed the distance between them to wrap her in a warm hug. "It is marvelous to see you, Jo." The gesture felt so… casual. Familiar. As if the time between seeing each other was non-existent. "This hug is meant to make up for the times I could not be there over these past few years, my friend." Ma shook as quiet sobs escaped her.

I decided to let Ma have her moment with her friend and turned to find Ken. It was strange enough that I was betrothed to someone I didn't know, but even stranger that he knew my mom. And not like recently—he had known her since before I was born. I knew they didn't age the same way here, but it was still odd to think that a man older than my mom was betrothed to me.

If it helps, Nikylo chimed in, *you can think of him as a quarter century old.*

It doesn't, because he's not, I snapped, spotting Ken on the couch with Mari and settling between them. Ken laid her head on my shoulder right away, but my gaze found Nikylo's in the kitchen. The green was so striking I had to suppress a shiver. *Besides, it's weird talking to you about it.*

Oh? The corner of his lip quirked up. *Why's that, Sunshine?*

Instead of giving him an answer, I turned to Mari. "Is this that safe place you told me about? Where we can talk about things?" The journals were one source of information. The Kyllindro tomorrow was another. But hearing it straight from the source? That was my favorite kind of information.

"Yes," she chuckled. "If I have the answer, I'll share it with you."

I scanned the living area but didn't find what I was looking for, so I asked, "Where did Theo and Libella go? I have questions for them, too."

"They'll be back soon," Nikylo said. "I sent them on a perimeter check."

That alone gave me a slight reason to worry. What were they looking for? Weren't there enchantments or something to keep danger away or warn us about threats?

Before I could voice my questions, he pushed away from the counter.

"Ollie and I have to go." He met my gaze, his lips twitching. "The kitchen is stocked. Feel free to make whatever you want." I tried and failed to hide my smile. The thought of being able to cook again—to bake. Perhaps I had underestimated Nikylo for letting me come here... "After we leave, access to magic within the house will be cut off."

"What?" I sputtered. "That doesn't sound safe."

With a raised brow, he said, "Let me finish, Sunshine." I sank back onto the couch, gritting my teeth. "When we leave and the magic is gone, feel free to bring Mitch upstairs."

I shot out of my seat before he could finish, but I had no idea where to go or why I'd moved. He said it wouldn't be until after they left. But seeing him? Spending time with Mitch and Ma—Kendall? It was all too exciting to just sit around waiting. I had to stand—to pace—to do something. Out of the corner of my eye, Ma sank down onto the couch. Sighing, I joined her, resting my head on her shoulder. Did she know about Mitch? About his monster? I figured I'd find out soon enough.

Nikylo fought a smile. "Theo, Libella, and Mari will take turns on guard duty outside, but keep Mitch inside. We don't want any accidents tonight." He rounded the counter and pulled a box from the kitchen floor onto it. "This should keep you occupied while you're here." It was large enough that he had to hold it with both hands, but it didn't seem heavy. He signaled to Oliver, who met him at the door and opened it for both of them. "If everything goes to plan, I'll stop by again tonight."

"And if it doesn't?" I asked, wondering what the plan was but knowing he wouldn't take the time to answer. Not when he already seemed to be in a rush.

"Then I'll be here when you wake up."

I pursed my lips but nodded. "You'll tell me then?" I knew it was a long shot—that he probably wouldn't, considering he never shared his plans with me anyway. But if things really had changed between us the way I thought they had...

He stared at me for what felt like an eternity, though it was probably less than five seconds. This was one of those moments when I wished I could read his mind. Hear what he was thinking like he could with my every thought. Then he dipped his head and headed out the door, with Oliver on his heels.

THIRTY-FOUR
All My Friends

As soon as it shut behind them, a ripple coursed through the house, and I stood as a door appeared in the middle of the wall near the bookshelf. I knew it probably had to have something to do with the magic disappearing, but it was still shocking. No wonder I hadn't noticed it during my tour with Oliver. But I knew exactly where it led.

I approached the door and opened it slowly. Ken followed, peering over my shoulder down the staircase. It glowed from what seemed like a fire at the bottom, and I took a deep breath. "Mitch?"

A scuffling sounded before his curly brown hair popped into view at the bottom of the stairs, and tears filled my eyes when he said, "Ray?"

With a quick glance at his normal hands, I bounded down the stairs with a grace I didn't possess a year ago. I jumped into his waiting arms, wrapping mine around his neck. "You know who I am!" It was wild to think that just last night, he hadn't recognized me at all—not until it was almost too late. I pulled back, cradling his face in my hands just to look at him. "You're okay! You're still you." I shifted my hands to his to check up close. "And you don't have claws."

Tears flowed down his face as he nodded vigorously with a laugh at the absurd statement. He appeared freshly cleaned and well cared for. It made me curious who had been with him during the ceremony. I didn't care enough to find out, so I grabbed his hand and pulled him up the stairs. "Come on. Everyone is waiting."

Ma almost burst into tears when she saw him. She couldn't move very quickly, but Mitch could. Damn, they must've given him one of those special baths because even his body seemed to have some of its strength back.

I let Ma and Mitch have their moment since I'd already seen him, and I joined Mari back on the couch. "Do you know what Nikylo meant about his plan for tonight?"

She shook her head. "I only know that they plan to go out with Talekor."

"Yeah, same." It still left me wondering…

"So…" she started, eying me sideways. "Those questions you had for me. Did you get any answers?"

That conversation felt like it happened ages ago. "Uh, not all of them." I thought about what I had intended to ask her, mostly about Nikylo. "How did you not know Nikylo was the prince? I mean, your mom is the Queen's handmaiden. You had to have known who he was, right?"

"My mother wasn't always a handmaiden." She shrugged, and I stared at her, waiting for her to continue. "My father worked at the castle, but she stayed with me in the nearby village. When I was old enough to train, I was sent to training camps where Nikylo served as a captain of sorts. I had never met the prince or visited the castle because I didn't have a reason to. So, the only Niko I knew was the captain who trained me harder than anyone else. He said he saw something in me." She shrugged, pulling her knees to her chest. "He was right. I outrank him in the Kidemos."

"You *what?*" I knew she was strong, but I hadn't anticipated her saying that. "You don't outrank Theo, though, right?"

She barked a laugh, "Definitely not. Theo outranks me by a long shot."

"Huh." Considering everything I had learned, I took a different approach. "So if you're one of the best in the Kidemos, that means your dragon must be pretty strong too, right?"

She looked at me sideways. "Yes… our training included that."

"I thought you were just a healer or—what is it called? Dynkoi?"

She nodded and said, "That's my dominant power."

I waited for her to continue, but she didn't this time. I narrowed my eyes and asked, "What is your other power?"

Ken plopped down beside me. "Good luck getting her to spill. I've spent the last two days with her, and she won't tell me a damn thing." She shot Mari a wicked grin, who just smiled back. "Even channeling Leigh's super observant skills hasn't helped me figure it out."

Still watching Mari, I asked, "Why is it a secret?"

"Technically, it's not." Her smile had turned devious. "But that's part of why I'm ranked so high. My secrets are mine until I allow you to know them."

My jaw slackened. But I shook myself free from that thought because my question had a purpose. "I really think the plan to get Leigh back will work." We hadn't really made a plan per se, but we had discussed it.

Mari hesitated before saying, "I don't know, Ray. His new dragon might be more powerful than mine."

"But his dragon bond is so new," I argued. "There's no way he can outrank you yet." The challenge between Nikylo and Talekor was different because there was no magic—it relied solely on physical strength and skill. With magic, Nikylo would have won. Mari would be stronger than him. I was sure of it.

So, we started strategizing. I shared my idea for distracting Talekor, and they proposed their plan to lure Leigh to a safe place. It seemed plausible, and the only person I'd have to deceive was Nikylo. Now, I just needed to figure out how to keep him out of my head.

I got up to wander around the kitchen and see what food was available when I remembered the box Nikylo had set out on the counter. Ken jumped up to join me, and we both peered inside. Once we saw what was in there, our eyes met, and we grinned at each other.

"Hey, Mitch!" I shouted, reaching into the box and lifting up two Nerf guns. "You missed the last one. Want to see if you've still—"

A knock sounded on the door.

I dropped both guns back in the box, and everyone else jumped to their feet at the noise. Weren't Nikylo and Oliver the only ones who could access the place?

A muffled voice I recognized came through the door. "If Mitch is near this door, get him to the kitchen." *Nikylo.* He had told us he might be back. And with the magic not working, it made sense that he wouldn't be able to tell me he was coming down the bond. But why had he returned so soon? Did that mean everything went according to plan? "I don't want to risk him being too close to magic."

"I've got him," Mari said, trailing after Mitch, who was already on his way to the kitchen. It seemed he didn't want to take any chances either.

"Okay," I said once he was positioned as far from the door as possible. "He's in the kitchen."

The door clicked and swung open, revealing Nikylo occupying most of the doorway.

Everyone simply stared at him, waiting for him to say something. But he didn't need to say a damn thing. He just had to step to the side for both Ken and me to scream in surprise.

Leighton practically ran over the threshold as soon as Nikylo moved, and Ken and I met her halfway.

She was here. Away from Talekor. Hugging us. Laughing as joy bubbled up through our tears.

I never thought I'd see her again without Talekor close by. I can't imagine what Kendall had been thinking all this time. If it were Arabella and someone had her just out of reach, I would have been devastated— lost without her. Losing Arabella was one thing, but being separated and unable to see her? Knowing she was alive but in the hands of a monster? That sounded much worse.

I tried to pull away from them to let Ken have this one, but she held me tight. So did Leigh. It wasn't just a twin hug; it was a sister hug. Fresh tears spilled down my face. After all we'd been through together over the past several weeks—finding out we were Fae, learning our magic, being separated—first by bars and then by walls—and navigating a new realm surrounded by those we weren't sure we could trust... It was nice to be given this time together.

Nikylo still stood in the doorway, hands in his pockets and leaning against the frame. Tears continued to stream down my face as I mouthed, "Thank you," knowing our bond wouldn't work right now anyway. There were many other things I would have said if it were, so perhaps it was a good thing.

He offered a slight bow of his head, then turned and left once more.

How had he known? How had he pulled it off? Wasn't he supposed to be with Talekor right now? Had he somehow persuaded him to let

Leigh come? In the end, I didn't care. She was here. And that was all that mattered.

A couple of hours later, we were cuddled up on the twin couches with the cookies I'd made: oatmeal chocolate chip. The ingredients were slightly different, but they were similar enough in consistency that the cookies turned out just as gooey and delicious as I intended. The dinner I prepared included the milot meat I'd had a few times, some potato-like foods, and a fruit that was a mix between a pear and an apple. It took some experimentation with the new spices, but it seemed my culinary skills transcended any realm. There was more than enough for everyone, so Mari, Theo, and Libella all took turns eating. Mari had just returned to join us in the living room.

We'd given Leigh space, letting her know she didn't have to tell us anything yet. We told her to just enjoy her time with us because we weren't sure if or when it would happen again. But she finally said she was ready to talk about it. She was cuddled up against Mari on the couch opposite Ken and me. Ma and Mitch took up the chairs.

"The time I spent with Talekor over the last few days has been… strange." She seemed distant as she spoke. "There were moments when I really didn't think he knew what he was doing. Other times, he was… nasty toward me. Like when he got back from his ceremony today. He…" She paused, watching her thumbs as they fidgeted in her lap. "He was really angry. He mentioned that something unexpected had happened. So he…he said he had to…he—"

I gasped. "He had to reclaim you." It wasn't a question. It was something that hadn't even crossed my mind until then. She nodded, a tear slipping down her face. I quickly recapped the story of what had happened during the ceremony since I was the only one there. "So when he severed his bond with Lukas… that must have severed the Doulos bond."

Leigh nodded. "I did feel something strange while he was gone. My leg felt tingly for a moment, and then suddenly, I felt completely alone.

Before that moment, it was like someone was always with me." She fell silent again, taking a measured breath. When she spoke again, her voice was soft. "I didn't think much of it until he came back."

Mari wrapped her arms tighter around Leigh, pressing her lips to her head. I knew asking Mari about changing our plan would be pointless. The house had no magic, and no one wanted to risk going outside. Not only would it affect Mitch, but having Leigh here could also mess things up. So we just stayed inside like we were told, and I promised myself the plan for tomorrow would work.

Plus, if it didn't go as planned…

"Has he mentioned anything else to you?" Ken wondered, no doubt trying not to be too pushy.

She bit her cheek, lost in thought. "The only time he really opens up is when he's angry. After the dinner, he went on about Dad trying to get too close to me. The Queen warned him not to get too worked up about it because the Councilors might become suspicious."

"Suspicious of what?" Ken asked, stifling a yawn next to me.

"From what I understand, they aren't convinced the Fae are treated well at the castle," I said sarcastically.

"Well, Talekor hasn't really done anything except ask me to follow him around." Leigh shrugged. Her face suddenly brightened. "He did say something about needing to change plans again."

"Change plans? Did he tell you his original plans?" I asked, leaning forward on the couch.

"I mean, I assume his original plan was to bond with Nikylo's dragon, right?"

That made sense. "Well, did he happen to mention anything about the new plans?"

She looked as if she were scanning her memories before she said, "He said he would have to meet up with… someone. Owen, perhaps?"

Mari went deathly pale. Her relaxed state shifted suddenly rigid and she slowly pushed Leigh up, turning her to face her. "Are you sure that's what you heard?" Leigh gave a nervous nod, prompting Mari to swear violently. I had never heard such a thing come from her mouth.

"Mari… who is Owen?" I asked, almost dreading the answer.

She shook her head, not focusing on anything. "Not Owen. Orvyn."

She finally turned to me. "He was exiled a long time ago for trying to overthrow the King. If he's been in contact with Talekor…" She stood abruptly, making Leigh lose her balance and nearly fall back onto the couch. "I have to tell Theo and my mother."

I caught her wrist as she passed me. "Wait, Mari. There's something else, isn't there?"

She scanned my eyes, probably realizing that I wasn't going to let this drop. Finally, she said, "He's the King's other brother."

I released her hand as if she'd burned me. Three brothers? One already powerful, and two striving to gain that power. Mari rushed outside, leaving the rest of us staring after her.

"So." Naturally, Ken broke the tense silence. "Did he mention anything else? Take you anywhere interesting?"

Leigh nearly laughed at her twin's knack for picking up right where they left off. Shaking her head, she said, "I've been almost everywhere with him, except for training with you two yesterday and the Ceremony today."

"Why didn't he bring you to the ceremony?" I asked, sinking back into the couch and trying to shake off the nerves from Mari's strange departure. I didn't think Talekor would have left her behind if it was that important.

She shrugged. "He left me locked in his chambers. Told me not to try to leave, or something bad would happen."

"I wonder if the magic works both ways," I mumbled, glancing at the door where Mari had vanished. She would know. When Leigh and Ken both looked confused, I explained what Libella had told me. It made perfect sense for it to work both ways. If it could prevent you from entering a room, why wouldn't it be able to prevent you from leaving one? Especially with the Fae being essentially slaves here.

"That would also explain why I felt trapped in my rooms." Mitch's voice startled me. He had been pretty quiet this entire time, probably not accustomed to being around others. "I always thought I was losing my mind because I couldn't find a door, even though I knew someone opened one whenever they came to visit. It only added to my hysteria some days. The little food I received would just materialize out of nowhere, the water pitcher would refill itself, and I had a bathroom, but that was all. I never knew what time it was since the sun never moved, but it felt like an eternity would pass before I saw anyone. And even then, it was never more than a few minutes." He took a shaky breath, and Ma reached across the space between them to take his hand. "The crazy part is, there are moments when I was sure I was awake but would blackout. I'd wake up hours later, curled into a ball, aching all over and wondering what had happened."

He'd hardly seen *anyone*? Unless the times they visited him were during his blackouts… that made me more nervous just thinking about it. "Do you remember anyone who came to see you?"

"The only one I remember clearly was Kyler." The name had something within me stirring to life. Nikylo had been to see Mitch? When? Why? What happened when he saw him? I mean, it made sense since he knew where Mitch was all along, but still. Why didn't he warn me about his "attack first, talk later" bit? Unless… unless he never attacked Nikylo. "You've got your thinking face on, Ray. What's going on up there?" He pointed to my head.

"I just find it strange that you attacked me as soon as you saw me. But did you ever attack Nikylo—er, Kyler?" Apparently, he wasn't required to use his proper name. When he shook his head, I pursed my lips. "It just seems odd to me. You didn't attack him in your rooms, but you did in the courtroom. Why?"

Mitch's eyes grew wide. "He didn't tell you?"

Of course he didn't tell me. "Tell me what?"

"He was talking me through the entire trial."

"What?" four voices echoed. Ma, Ken, and I leaned forward. Mari returned from outside, her face grim as she sat back down next to Leigh and pulled her close once more. She gave me a slight shake of her head when our eyes met. Theo and Libella didn't know anything either, then.

"Well, not when he was outside the gate," Mitch continued. "But every time he entered, he tried to help me silence the monster's voice in my head."

I blinked slowly. "So, wait, then why did you attack him?"

"The monster snapped." He shuddered. "I felt it pacing behind whatever shield Kyler had helped me put in place. While Kyler was keeping Koladon under control, he was telling me to prepare for something. I didn't understand what he meant until the door suddenly flew open." Did Nikylo know something was going to happen? Or did he realize it too late? "He'd already stretched his powers so thin that, with the new threat, his shield keeping the monster at bay slipped just enough for it to break through. That's when I lost consciousness."

We all listened with rapt attention. The trial was so chaotic toward the end that I didn't know what happened to everyone else. Obviously, they all made it out, but what happened to that poor handmaiden? Did they ever find out who attacked her? Hopefully, I'd get answers to those and all my other questions soon. But now was not the time.

Taking a deep breath, I gave an audible, exaggerated sigh.

"I don't know about you guys, but I just want to take a break from the madness for a while." I pushed off the couch, brushing away the cookie crumbs that had collected on my hands, and made my way to the box in the kitchen. "I say we see if Mitch is still any good at Nerf wars, finish off these cookies, and then get a good night's rest." I pulled out two guns and offered them to Mitch and Ken, who had stood up at my suggestion, smiles on their faces.

"It's only been a month, Ray," Mitch teased as he loaded the foam bullets into his weapon. "I'll still hit you square in the forehead."

"You haven't gone up against Mari before," Ken said, quickly locating her starting position in the kitchen. "She shot Kaleb straight down the throat last time."

The memory carried a pang of grief, but I let it pass through, knowing the memories I shared with him were no longer mine to cling to. "Yeah, she's the best shot in the house. Don't let her sweet demeanor fool you." I grinned at Mari, who winked back.

"You're catching on, Ray," she said. "But I still have some tricks up my sleeve, remember?"

When everyone had their guns, there was one left in the box. I glanced at Ma, still sitting in the chair. "Do you want to join?"

Ma smiled, but it was a weak smile. "I think I'm going to head to bed, sweetheart. This day has taken a lot out of me." My expression fell, but she shook her head. "No, I don't want you to worry about me or cancel this game or war or whatever it is. I want you to enjoy your time with your friends while you can. I'll be here when you're done, okay?"

"I'll have my mom come help you upstairs," Mari said.

Ma nodded, then looked back at me, reaching for my hand. I laid mine in hers and dropped down beside her chair. There was a shuffling of feet behind me, and I looked back to find Mitch standing there. Grabbing his hand, I tugged him down with me, making it easier for Ma to see us both.

She moved both hands to cup his face and mine. "I'm so glad you two get to spend some time together after everything that's happened."

"Me too," Mitch said. "I'm sorry you're not feeling well, Mama. I was looking forward to kicking your butt in Nerf wars." His smile was watery.

Ma let out a gentle laugh, but then she really looked at him, her smile fading. "I'm sorry you were never told about your father." Her voice cracked, bringing tears to my eyes. "We wanted to tell you both," she said, eyes darting between us. "But with the uncertainties that knowledge could've brought you, we waited. Too long, it seems." Her eyes crinkled, causing the tears that had been welling to fall.

"This feels like goodbye again," I sniffled. Mitch rested his head on my shoulder, holding my arm with one hand and Ma's hand with the other.

"Well, I should be heading back home soon, sweetheart. The trial, though chaotic, has concluded. They no longer need me." She wiped away one of my tears, then brushed Mitch's away and held his gaze. "Kyler is going to look for answers for you tomorrow. He's hoping taking you back home will prevent your magic from fully developing." When had she spoken to Nikylo about that?

A door clicked shut, and Libella was there to help Ma up the stairs. "Mari will return once I get your mother settled."

Both Mitch and I stood up. I hugged her first. "I love you, Ma. I'll see you in the morning."

"I love you too, sweetheart," she said. Summoning all the strength she could, she pulled away and lifted her chin. "Do you remember what you promised me?" I nodded, but she reminded me anyway. "Keep training hard, learn as much as you can, and don't you ever give up." Her voice wavered as she added, "And know that I am so proud of you, sweetheart." I nodded as she cupped my face in her hands, wiping away some of my tears. "Your father would have been proud of you, too."

I choked back a sob but nodded again. Mitch's sniffle prompted me to step out of her embrace so he could say goodnight, too. I wiped my tears as two sets of arms wrapped around me. Ken and Leigh sniffled, too, as they hugged me. Saying goodbye to Ma was certainly not something I expected to experience again so soon.

As Libella helped Ma up the stairs, I realized just how much the month spent here had taken a toll on her. As much as I would miss her, she needed to return home soon.

૧ મ ૨ ૮

The girls were fast asleep, and all four of us were able to fit in the bed upstairs. It was a tight squeeze, but honestly, none of us minded. Leigh and Mari were snuggled up close together, and Ken had her arm draped over my waist from behind. Just like old times… well… almost.

When all of their breathing was steady, I carefully removed Ken's hand and slid out from under the covers. On light feet, I made my way to the satchel I'd placed strategically near the stairwell to the roof. At the top, I prayed the door wouldn't squeak, sighing in relief when it moved on silent hinges. I stepped through the threshold, feeling the magic ripple over me as I stepped out of its hold and shut the door quietly behind me. I approached the far wall of the rooftop porch where Nikylo had appeared earlier and sat against it, pulling the bag into my lap to retrieve the four journals. Hopefully, Nikylo didn't go looking for them tonight.

I opened the one numbered 167. The pages weren't blank, but they were in a language I'd never seen before. How was I supposed to read this? But Drako hadn't told me to read it, had he? What did he say I should do? Ask them specific questions, and they would show me? *Well, here goes nothing.*

"What happened when Niccodra went into Palekliedo?" I whispered, feeling a little silly for asking a book a question. But I waited. And waited. And… nothing happened. Maybe I had the wrong journal? I closed that one and picked up the next in the series. Opening it, I asked the same question.

This time, the journal floated out of my hand and turned several pages by itself to one marked with the number 191. As it floated, the words on the page appeared to morph and change as I—

THIRTY-FIVE
Anxiety

Nikylo

125 years ago

"Sami, come *on!* We're already running late." I shifted the pack on my shoulder. It wasn't unusual for us to be sent out on errands to other islands. Still, it felt somewhat trivial to request a visit from the Drakalasson royals when the Councilors should have been able to manage it—which was likely why Father was sending us.

"Relax, Champ." Sami strolled out of the bathroom with damp hair and a towel wrapped around his waist. A mirror image of me, but with Ma's lighter-toned skin and brown hair, his dark green eyes were the only trait he got from Dad. He moved more slowly than a parlej through the mud, and they usually stopped to roll around in it... "Marta didn't specify a time," he said, disappearing into the closet. "She'll probably have us sit down and eat first anyway."

"Ugh." I threw myself onto the armchair, leaning back with my eyes closed, and forced myself to take a deep breath. You would think the older one would know to be on time when they were summoned. He wasn't wrong, though. Every time we visited Marta for anything, she had a full meal prepared for her entire family and two extra seats for us.

My frustrations weren't really with Sami, though—Father had pulled me from my training sessions today. I'd been working with my elite Aidí, and I had to come up with an excuse for them to run exercises this afternoon without me. Amarietta had given me shit on the mat earlier, and I wanted to put her in her place with weapons training, but alas, here I was, following orders again. I let out a long sigh.

"Everything okay, Nikylo?" A gentle voice reached my ears. Valisdrako perking up clued me in on who it was.

I opened one eye to glance at Megdaline, offering her a half-hearted smile before shutting it again. "Just heading out to Fotypas to meet Marta. As usual, we're late."

"We're not late," Sami said. I opened my eyes to see him emerging from the closet without a shirt, and Meg quickly turned away as a flush of red spread across her cheeks. Sami wiggled his fingers at her. "Hi, Megi."

"Your Grace," she squeaked, bowing. Sami rolled his eyes at her formalities as he disappeared into his room.

"You can stay here and mingle with Tietra or Claude," I told Meg, aware that she enjoyed having free time with the other Fae in the castle. "I shouldn't need you while I'm gone."

She nodded, clasping her hands as she waited. Even after almost two centuries, she remained so quiet around me. When I took her places, she would find an excuse to siphon off some of her power as we flew over the water, creating waves and aquatic animals to join us on our journey. She would giggle when Valisdrako broke them apart with his tail in annoyance. I knew she enjoyed having some fun, but her persistent quietness made me wonder what she did in the free time I gave her. Did she talk to Tietra the way I spoke to Oliver? Or was she this quiet around everyone? "Do you anticipate when you'll be back?" she asked, still avoiding looking up.

"Before nightfall." It was midafternoon, but I'd calculated the time for Marta's dinner in there. "Feel free to have dinner in my chambers with your friends." I offered her a smile, to which she bowed in thanks. I turned to Sami, who had slung his pack over his shoulder and finally appeared ready to leave. "Where *is* Tietra?"

"Probably off gallivanting with Oliver or something." He shrugged on his pack of supplies and clapped his hands. "Come on, Niko! We're late," he teased, gesturing at me, still seated.

I rolled my eyes and stood up, leaning in to press a kiss on Meg's cheek. "Don't do anything stupid."

"I probably wouldn't even if you asked me to," she laughed.

Sami swept in, wrapping his arm around her waist and surprising Meg with a kiss on her other cheek. "Save me a zymi," he said, releasing her as quickly as he had grabbed her.

Her hands flew to her face as she steadied herself on her feet. "Your mother would not approve, Your Grace."

"I told you: call me Sami," he chided, tapping the tip of her nose.

"Perhaps someday, *Your grace*."

I grabbed his elbow before he laid it on too thick. "We'll see you later, Meg."

She waved goodbye as I opened a rift in the world to take us to Fotypas.

We stepped through to find Marta pacing on her front porch. The awning consisted of branches from the twisted trees among which she had built her home. Rearranging the forest required the skilled hands of an Udarian who knew what they were doing, which was an understatement for Marta. She had discovered this place in the forest a few centuries ago and decided it was where she would raise her family.

"Sami!" a small voice called from behind Marta, his little braids bouncing as he bounded down the stairs, barely making it to the bottom in one piece.

Sami bent down to catch Romeo as he tripped on nothing and flew into his arms. "Hey, Romi! Any luck with Ryga?"

The five-year-old rolled his entire head. "No! The daisy didn't work!"

"Aw, shucks," Sami said, his voice slightly higher to match Romeo's. "Maybe she likes roses."

"You think so?" he asked, his face brightening. When Sami shrugged, he practically deflated. "Roses are *really* hard."

"You can't give up now!" Sami lightly punched his shoulder. "Watch. One day, you'll be one of the greatest Udarians ever to walk the planet!" he exaggerated, then raised a finger. "But *only* if you keep practicing."

Marta had observed the whole exchange between Sami and Romeo with a tight yet affectionate smile. I watched with a twinge of jealousy at how effortlessly my brother stepped into those shoes.

You need only observe your brother to know how to interact with younglings, Valisdrako said.

Can you just keep your thoughts to yourself today? I asked, already worried that Marta had been pacing when we arrived.

Romeo sighed. "Okay..." He glanced up at me, then back at Sami. "Are you going to eat dinner with us?"

Sami stood up, catching Marta's eye. "Perhaps." The question was only apparent to Marta and me.

"Why don't you run along and practice those roses, child," Marta cooed. "I need to take Sami and Niko here to the glen for a little while."

"Ugh, okay..." he groaned, then bear-crawled back up the stairs and into the house, slamming the door behind him.

I glanced at Sami, whose brow was furrowed. She hadn't even invited us inside...

"Thank you for taking the time to come today, boys." Marta started toward the glen. "I'm afraid this one won't be so easy to ignore."

Sami and I exchanged glances. "Have there been any other signs of unusual activity?"

"No. This glen is the only one that shows any signs."

"Signs of what?" I asked, trying to recall what she'd said in the letter.

"You'll see."

There was a break in the trees ahead, and when she stepped aside so we could see, she warned, "Don't step past that vine. It indicates where the effects begin."

The world seemed to pause as Sami and I took in the sight before us. The glen, filled with vibrant flowers and many fruit-bearing plants, appeared as if gravity had given up. While the roots typically grew underground like any other plants, they had sprouted above ground, seeking refuge among the branches overhead, with the plants now turned upside down. Some plants were simply floating in midair but remained stationary—as if they were planted there.

I turned to Marta. "Have you tested your powers against it?"

She tilted her head. "Now, child, if that had worked, why would I have called you here?" The look she gave me suggested she knew I was smarter than that. But she answered me anyway, "My magic doesn't affect them the way it normally would."

This is not any power of ours. Valisdrako's voice was ominous, but I wanted to try anyway. Turning back to the glen, I focused on the berry plant a few paces away. I pushed and pulled with all my might, but it didn't move an inch.

Sami nudged me. "Did you try, too?"

I just nodded, staring at the strange phenomenon before us.

A power bigger than all of us has caused this. You will do well to check our sources. I knew he meant the Xouta.

I'll mention it to Father when we return.

It wasn't the first time something strange had been reported. Earlier in the week, we visited Taj and Lysan on Gitapodi. A primary water source had practically dried up within a day, leaving the nearby villages without it. We sent some of the Udarians and Omonians to check if the waterfall had somehow been blocked, but the flow had changed directions down the mountain and carved an entirely new path on the other side. Fortunately, there were no villages there. It was a sheer drop from the top of the mountain followed by a steep incline leading to the drop-off. It was one of the few islands where the mountain was situated on the edge rather than in the middle. With the skills of the wielders we had gathered, we were able to reroute the river again.

The problem before us didn't seem like something we could resolve.

I turned to Marta, whose face revealed none of the uncertainty I knew she was feeling. "We'll report this to my father and try to come back in a week to see if there are any changes, okay?"

Her eyes darted from me to Sami and back. "You don't think this is some Drakalasson trying to manipulate a power play again?"

I shook my head, but Sami replied. "Neither Niko nor I could do anything, either. If it were related to Drakalasson, we'd be able to maneuver it. This is…" he trailed off, glancing back over his shoulder at the floating roots and plants. "This feels like something else." When he met my gaze, I shook my head.

"No. It's not him," I said. Sami's shield had slipped just enough in his worry that I knew what he was thinking—or rather, who. "He took his darkness elsewhere."

You are naive to believe Orvyn would accept his banishment without seeking revenge, Valisdrako said.

I ignored him, watching as Sami pursed his lips and glanced at Marta again. "Was that your thought, too?"

"Yes." She swallowed thickly, her hands wringing together. I had never seen her this worried about anything before. She was always the one calming others, soothing their worries and fears before they could surface. "The regicide occurred centuries ago, but the destruction it caused? The chaos throughout the realm?" She seemed distant as she continued. "Orvyn doesn't seem like the type to give up just because he was banished." The similarity of her words to Valisdrako's sent a shiver down my spine. There was no way she knew what he had said.

Which meant I needed to explore the possibilities that Orvyn could be behind these strange events.

10 years later

> *The sun has remained in the sky for nearly three days, and although it is finally setting, the relentless heat has already taken its toll. Our crops have begun to wither—most are already dead or dying.*
>
> *The once-glorious waterfall that cascaded from our mountain has dwindled to a mere trickle, leaving the lakes it once fed dry and cracking. Desperate creatures from the forests and lakes now seek refuge in our diminishing water sources, forcing them closer to our homes. Their habitats are gone. I fear ours will be next.*
>
> *We have sheltered as many as we can, but the heat is becoming unbearable, and every new soul we take in only adds to the strain. We cannot endure like this. There must be another way—another place to go.*
>
> *Please, send aid before it is too late.*

I placed the letter on top of the pile I'd started. It was the seventh one this week from those on Fotypas. The pile for Gitapodi was smaller, with their complaints even stranger.

Perhaps you should tell your Father about the glowing water sources, Valisdrako suggested. *Maybe that will draw his attention enough to make him visit the islands.* His sarcasm alone communicated his frustrations with my father.

Nothing will make him leave this island, I mumbled, raking my fingers through my hair and pulling. *He's avoided going to see the damage this long. I don't think anything will make him go. It makes him* uncomfortable.

A knock sounded at my door, and I released my grip on my hair, pushing myself away from the desk. "Come in," I called, heading to the foyer to pour myself a drink. I hadn't been much of a drinker before all this started, but with the direction things were going… I needed it.

"Hi, Niko," Tietra's soft voice came from the door. "Sami sent me to retrieve you. The Councilors have all arrived. They want to start in twenty minutes."

"Thank you, Tietra." She reached to close the door, but I called her name again. When her head peeked back in, I asked, "Have you seen Meg today?"

Tietra pursed her lips, avoiding my gaze. "She's been in Sami's chambers. With me." She shifted on her feet as I kept my gaze on her, waiting for the other shoe to drop. "Would you like me to fetch her for you?"

I ground my teeth. "No, I'll meet you in his room soon." I downed the entire contents of my glass and poured another measure. "Be sure to tell your sister that if I'm noticing, then it's likely Father is, too." She nodded, twitching her lips as if she wanted to say something. "Spit it out, Ti," I urged.

"It's just… he knows, right?" Her voice was timid, but I could sense the worry she felt for her sister.

"Sami? Or my father?"

We both know who she was referring to, Niko. I resisted the urge to roll my eyes. He was particularly sassy today.

"Sami."

I sighed, taking a sip of my drink before answering. "He knows. He doesn't seem to care. Says he found something." When Ti raised an eyebrow, I shook my head. "Nothing to get rid of it, but something about the origins. He thinks the answer is in the Shadow Archives."

"Is that why he's going there tomorrow?"

I whirled around to her. "He is not going there tomorrow! We're supposed to transport—" Tietra's eyes widened at my raised voice. I forced myself to take another deep breath, finishing the rest of my drink and setting the cup down on the table. I approached her where she stood in the doorway. "Sorry," I said, leaning down to kiss her cheek. "I didn't mean to scare you, Ti. Go on back to his rooms. I'll... deal with him later."

"Should I tell him you're coming?" she asked, dipping her head at my proximity. I understood why she never tilted her head back far enough to maintain eye contact this close. Her height would have made it look almost comical. But it was more submissive of her than usual.

"Tell him I'll meet him in the council chambers."

She nodded and turned on her heel toward his room. I waited until she was out of sight, then opened my mind to search for a thread of power similar to Tietra's but much stronger. He was in his usual guest suite.

My chambers. Now, I said into his mind as I turned back towards the portal door on the opposite side. Nothing happened while I walked over to it, but just before I reached it, a white light glowed from behind the door, and it opened to reveal my best friend.

He strode right in, extending his arms to pull me into a hug. I returned the embrace, allowing him to pat me on the back a few times before stepping out of it. "How are you holding up, Niko? Sounds like your father has you all over the place."

I sighed, nodding—or was I shaking my head?—before answering, "I've visited every island except two. None of them are faring well."

"And no source of the issue has been revealed?"

This time, I knew I was shaking my head. "After this meeting, I'm supposed to head to Krevastistos. It seems to be on the cusp, but Father wants me to check the cave."

Ollie's eyebrows knitted together. "Why the cave? Is he sensing something wrong?"

I raked my fingers through my hair and started pacing. "Everything seems wrong! The islands to the west are getting too much sun, while those to the east are experiencing a lack thereof. Yet, the crystals from Gitapodi and Fotypas both had a strange glow when harvested. After some testing, we discovered they were draining power instead of providing it."

We held a council the night before to discuss the possibilities of the newly harvested crystals. Some believed they would grant different powers, while others thought they possessed double the power. When asked if anyone was willing to test them, the only one brave enough to volunteer was Theo. His well of power ran deeper than anyone outside the royal line, and even then, it was deeper than most of ours. His reserves were about half full when he touched the crystals, but the moment he did, his power was cut off, and he immediately began to weaken. He held onto it for what seemed like a minute, but the more he tried to draw power from it, the faster it drained him. He eventually dropped it, stumbling into the arms of his mate, barely able to stand. She used her power to restore his health, but his powers had been completely drained. He was sent for a full day of recharging to refill his reserves again.

"Does it do the same to Fae?" Oliver's soft voice pulled me back. He had never been scared of much, but there was a hint of fear in his tone.

"None of those present last night were brave enough to test it."

"I could—"

"No." The voice came from my chamber door, causing both Ollie and me to turn toward the commanding tone. Sami shut the door behind him and crossed the floor in a few long strides. He hooked his arm around Ollie's neck faster than a viper. "If I hear you volunteered to drain your powers, I'll knock you unconscious and drag you out of that room. Got it?"

Sami's hold on Oliver was loose, and his tone was light, but we both knew he was serious. "Better me than some elder—"

"No! Better someone with deeper reserves of power than my brother's best friend," Sami interrupted, tightening his grip. "We don't know what will happen if it drains all your power."

"Fine!" Ollie exclaimed, his voice straining under the pressure as he tapped Sami's arm twice. "I'll refrain from volunteering," he managed to say.

"Good." Before he released him, he ruffled his hair with his fist. "That's for not coming to see me first."

He let him go, and Ollie could barely maintain his glare for half a second before pulling Sami into a hug. "Always so protective, Sami."

"Neither of you will be making stupid decisions on my watch," Sami said, giving Ollie's back a reassuring pat and glancing at me.

"We're not the ones I'm worried about making stupid decisions," I fired the accusation at Sami, who met my gaze with a hard one of his own. Knowing this wasn't the right moment to discuss it, I lifted my chin and asked, "Why are you here? I told Tietra I'd meet you in the council chambers."

"There's only one person you turn to in secret when things get tough, Niko." He raised an eyebrow, looking at Ollie. "I missed him too, you know."

He made it sound much weirder than it was, but he wasn't wrong. Oliver was the one I turned to for everything, especially when things got tough. He hadn't been around lately because of all the issues arising, and the fact that he was here today spoke volumes about how dire the situation was. His mother only brought him to council meetings when his safety was at risk.

"We have to go, though," Sami said. "Head back to your chambers. I'm sure your mother will fill you in on the meeting once we're finished."

Oliver gave a playful salute as he turned to me. "I am terribly sorry you have to endure a council like that. I cannot, however, say that I am sorry to miss it."

I clapped a hand on his shoulder with a soft laugh. "If you'd like to join me on my trip to Krevastistos afterward, meet me here." I glanced around the empty chambers. "Or just relax here while I'm gone. My space is your space, after all."

Oliver flashed a mischievous grin. "So, does that mean your dragon would allow me rummage through his impressive collection of tomes?"

If he touches one thing that is mine, he will be ashes in the wind he loves to travel on, Valisdrako rumbled.

I cracked a grin. "He says go right ahead."

I didn't even give Ollie time to prepare. When my door swung open, he jumped up from the armchair, and I grabbed his elbow, creating a rip in the world to step through. Of course, we couldn't get to the island by skithing, so we stepped into midair. Oliver immediately gathered the air to hold himself up while I shifted, allowing Valisdrako to spread his wings. It had been a while since I'd let him out, but he'd been begging me to fly for weeks. Since all of our trips were urgent, I'd been skithing everywhere. But this one *required* flying.

This does not count toward letting me out, Valisdrako grumbled as Oliver settled onto his back.

Yes, it does, I replied. *You were the one who neglected to specify what you meant by flying.*

You forget I can force you to shift.

And you forget the crisis we are in right now, I snapped back. *My priorities do not align with your need to fly for fun.*

The meeting had me on edge, and I knew Valisdrako was aware of that, but it was frustrating nonetheless. Nothing reported was good. Every island faced some dire situation. They were either drying up from too much sun, or the lack of sunlight was causing the plants to die, and the ground was chilling. Bodies of water were freezing over, and there was barely any warmth apart from what the few fire-wielders could provide. The only water sources remaining fully intact were on Nykeraki, where our castle was located, and Pipistrella, home to the Councilors and their families. Both islands had several villages of Fae and Drakalasson, but none of them had the space and resources to accommodate the displaced families from the other islands.

The hour-long flight was silent, even though I felt Oliver poking me as a clear sign to open a line of communication. However, a dragon on edge was not one I wanted to upset further by letting Ollie into my head.

When we arrived, the Fae villagers were crowded and waiting for us. Valisdrako landed, sending a whirlwind of dry earth swirling up. Before Oliver could dismount, one of the villagers rushed forward.

"Haven't you taken enough from us?" she shouted. "Or did you come here to finish the job yourself, you monster—"

The dragon didn't let her finish, blocking me out while spewing a torrent of flames from its jaws.

You bastard! I shouted, pounding on the walls he had confined me to in my own mind. *She's just trying to protect her family!*

She should have known better than to speak so carelessly.

That doesn't give you the right to burn her alive. I retorted as he released me. *This plague has everyone terrified of those in power, and your lack of control isn't helping.* The screams of the remaining Fae echoed, and they scrambled away from the ashes Valisdrako had left in place of the Fae who'd insulted him.

Disrespect demands retribution.

Retribution? I shot back. *We're here to* help, *not to rule through fear.*

His voice was deadly when he responded. *Her insult was not directed at me, Nikylo.*

Understanding that his fuming rage was not for himself only made my guilt worse. *Then you should have let me handle it,* I said, tugging on the thread between us. When it didn't budge, I added, *Shift. You can't fit through the cave entrance.*

I can make it bigger, he offered malevolently. His thunderous footsteps made the earth tremble in a way that would put the Udarians to shame.

Shift! I demanded, tugging harder on the thread. He relented, and my feet hit the ground seconds later.

The smell of burnt flesh lingered in the air, heavy and accusatory, much like the glares of the villagers as I walked past them. I knew this incident would be reported back to my father, and the death would be on my hands. Valisdrako and I were viewed as one and the same by these people. We were not separate, and I understood that defending my dragon's actions would fall on deaf ears. So, I ignored the staring Fae and made my way to the tunnels of the cavern.

Oliver caught up with me but didn't say a word. He held strong opinions about how dragons should behave, yet he recognized that I was doing everything I could to control mine. He wasn't as ruthless as he used to be, but that didn't mean his temper was entirely gone.

We stepped into the cavern, and I halted abruptly, making Oliver bump into me.

"What is it? Is someone here?" he asked, peeking around me. He went completely still when his gaze landed on the reason I had stopped. He muttered, "Mitera, save us."

Because in place of Niccodra's power source—the giant orb of humming energy, now missing—there was a letter written in the familiar scrawl of my banished uncle:

> *Power is never lost.*
> *Only claimed.*

THIRTY-SIX
A Little Bit Bad

Nikylo
Present Day

"There is no age restriction here as there is on Gaia," Oliver said, following Talekor into The Whispering Winds after dinner. Tal had wondered why no one was checking identification when they walked in. "The libations here in Niccodra do not have the same effects as those on Gaia. Children are still not allowed to partake, but that changes after their training years." Thankfully, Oliver was much better at maintaining a conversation with Tal. He excelled at separating emotions from the task at hand, which made him an excellent fit for his position as Councilor.

It felt strange to be out with Tal, though. My brother. It still bothered me that I hadn't noticed it before. We looked similar enough that someone else should have seen it too. The genes I inherited from our father were more physical, while Tal got most of his from our mother. The opposite was true for our personalities. Tal definitely inherited the evil gene from Father, while I took after Mother's gentler side. Father's ruthlessness was not to be trifled with, but Talekor was definitely starting to rival it.

Our outing had originally been my punishment from Mother, who claimed I was too callous at Tal's dinner. But Oliver and I devised a plan to get Tal drunk enough that he would barely remember making it back to his rooms. So, we found the best tavern in the village just south of the castle.

There was a healthy mix of Drakalasson and Fae throughout the village, but most of them were bound. The ones who weren't owned the taverns, restaurants, and markets we visited. Ollie was well-loved at the tavern we chose, and he headed straight to the Fae behind the counter while Tal and I found a booth in the back corner. Some Fae entertained the crowd with dances, while other patrons partnered up and danced on their own. These places were definitely not my usual scene, and most people here didn't recognize me—mainly because when I typically came here, I altered my appearance. I never left the castle walls without masking myself. I became the captain everyone knew me as, which didn't set me apart from them as much as my proper title would have.

Oliver returned to the table with three mugs, setting a random one in front of Tal before placing mine down and taking a seat next to me. Tal squinted at his drink and then glanced between Ollie and me.

"Cheers to you and your dragon, Tal," I said, raising my glass in cheers.

"May your bond be strong and unbreakable," Ollie said, raising his mug beside mine.

"Wait." Tal glanced once more between his mug, mine, and Ollie's before saying, "Switch drinks with me." He lifted his mug toward me.

"Why would I do that?" I asked, taking a gulp of my drink. Oliver did the same.

He narrowed his eyes, but Ollie stepped in. "Here, Talekor. Take mine." He slid his mug across the table and pulled Tal's back to his side, raising it in cheers once more. I glanced at my friend, but he just lifted his brows as if shrugging with his eyes.

Tal took his new mug without hesitation and lifted it to clink against ours, taking a big swig before setting it down. "Is this like the drinks from dinner last night?" he asked, watching the deep indigo liquid shift between blue and purple.

"Spondí? No, that one sharpens the sixth sense." I lifted my mug, took another sip, and let out a satisfied sigh. "This is Starlight Mead. A Drakalasson specialty—aged beneath the open sky, infused with a touch of magic to make the world feel lighter."

Tal shrugged and took another big gulp. "You're right. This really does make everything feel lighter." His words were already starting to slur. Damn, that one was strong. Tal leaned forward and gave me what

I'm sure he thought was a coy grin, but it looked like his left cheek had been injected with paralysis venom from the glowing tree frogs. "Ya know," he drawled, "I'm not giving up on my girl."

I raised a brow, lifting my mug to my lips as they twitched. "Oh?" I took a drink. Surprisingly, this was the first time he mentioned Rayleigh all night.

"N-nope. She'll come around. You'll see." He lifted the mug to his mouth and downed the rest, slamming it on the table. "Another!"

Oliver and I exchanged glances and grinned. This would be much easier than expected. The scrape of a chair caught my attention, and I turned to see Tal weaving through the crowd of dancers with the grace of a young Fae just learning to walk. I jumped up to catch his elbow. "Tal, come sit back down," I coaxed.

He ripped his elbow from my hand, mumbling, "See, I told you she'd come back to me." He pointed to a couple dancing on the other side of the open space, heading straight for them.

"Rayleigh isn't here, Tal," I said, reaching for his elbow again. He stumbled before I could catch him and ended up sprawled on the floor, laughing. "Dammit, Tal," I growled, yanking him up by the back of his tunic.

"Is he okay?" a female asked, and I turned to find the Fae Tal had pointed at, standing right in front of us. I stumbled back a step, nearly dropping my brother. The female before us looked eerily like Rayleigh, but at the same time, not at all. Her pointed ears and sharp features distinguished her from the female I knew. "Your Grace?" her voice echoed.

I shook my head while nodding. The title rang in my mind. I had forgotten that I was the Prince here. "He's fine, just had a bit too much mead."

The male she had been dancing with stood behind her, his hands resting gently yet protectively on her shoulders. His dark hair and features resembled my own, except for his deep blue eyes, which were focused on me in a way that made me straighten my spine. He carried the scent of ashes and smoke, while she smelled of freshly dug dirt. Fae, then. But a fire fae this close to the castle and unbound? I narrowed my eyes.

"Well, if that's the case, we'll let you be." The woman smiled, and all traces of Rayleigh disappeared. There was no crinkle in her nose or dips in her cheeks that hinted at dimples. Her brown eyes lacked the same sparkle as Rayleigh's ocean-blue ones. She gave a slight bow of her head, the male behind her doing the same before he moved his hand to the small of her back and led her back to the dance floor.

I tore my gaze away from them and dragged Tal back to the table where Oliver lounged with his arms stretched along the back of the bench. "What was that all about?"

"He thought he saw Rayleigh." Ollie tilted his head, appearing intrigued by the story, so I relayed a quick version of the interaction.

Oliver turned to Talekor with a smirk. "If you wanted to sweep her off her feet, Tal, maybe you should start by staying on yours," he teased.

If my brother hadn't been lost to the lismóni, I probably would have worried for my friend's life. Tal barely managed to mumble an incoherent response. "He was Ignalian, Ollie," I said, hoping for some kind of reaction other than what I got.

His eyebrows raised slightly as he peered past us for a moment before shrugging and locking eyes with me again. "With the other Councilors and myself in town, perhaps they feel safer to mingle."

Before I could process that, my brother's weight suddenly dropped, and I had to use both hands to heave him into the booth. I set him down unceremoniously and glanced at Oliver, sighing. "We need to get him back. He'll be impossible to move in about ten minutes."

Oliver nodded, finishing the rest of his mead. The small amount of lismóni he had consumed reflected in his glossy eyes and the smirk plastered on his face. It was the perfect sensation of weightlessness. He stood up. "Before we embark on the next chapter of this grand misadventure, I need to visit the washroom." He smirked again, then vanished into the crowd. I took his seat and watched as my brother tried and failed to keep himself upright on his side of the bench.

Putting the lismóni in my drink would have worked, but Oliver knew I would never trade drinks with someone who thought theirs was poisoned. So Ollie, the genius he was, put it in his mug, knowing Tal wouldn't think twice after Oliver took a sip. One sip wasn't enough for the effects to drag him into the distorted reality of blurred memories and hazy dreams. But the amount Tal consumed in less than five minutes? He'd be out until tomorrow.

Oliver reemerged from the washroom across the tavern, and I finished my drink before standing up to throw Tal over my shoulder. When I turned back to head out the door, Oliver was not where I expected him to be. He should have been back at the table by now, but he was nowhere in sight. I narrowed my eyes, scanning the entire crowd for the familiar white hair.

Are you daft? Drako's voice nearly made me jump out of my skin. He had been quiet since the ceremony, having used a significant amount of his strength to bring everyone to the dragon dimension. He hadn't done it alone, of course, but it still required a lot of power.

Go back to sleep, I scolded, then reached for Oliver's power. I traced it back to him, but he had his damn shield up. What the hell?

If he were in danger, he wouldn't have shut me out. I pursed my lips and made my way out the front door, knowing he'd eventually be out there. Tal's weight was becoming noticeable, so I didn't want to linger around for him to show up. Once outside, I realized why I hadn't seen him inside the tavern. He was standing at the end of the path, talking to two cloaked figures. I trudged up the path, gravel crunching under my feet as I breathed in the cool air.

"Follow this road until you reach a crossroads; take a left, and you'll find the Skyborne Inn on the right," Oliver's voice carried the last ten yards. "Tell Glynn I sent you." He flashed them his infamously warm smile, and the cloaked figures made their way down the road. Oliver turned to me as I closed the gap between us. "Ready?"

I shot him a glare. "You typically don't keep things from me."

"Correct." Oliver blinked.

I shifted Tal on my shoulder and pointed an accusing finger at him. "Why start now?"

"I do not know what you are referring to."

"Bullshit. Those were the two Fae I encountered inside. I could smell them."

"Correct."

"Ollie, come on. I'm not stupid." When he just stared at me, I huffed. "Fine. If you won't tell me how you know them, I'll find out myself," I said, shouldering past him. The couple wasn't too far ahead, so I shouted, "Hey! You there!"

They didn't turn, but I felt Oliver's hand on my elbow to stop me. "Let it go, Niko. We do not have time for this.

I whirled on him. "How do you know them, Ollie?

"They needed a place to stay! I sent them to my cousin's inn."

"You don't just send anyone there! Who are they?"

"You want to know why I sent them there? Because he is *Ignalian*. The most sought-after Fae by any Drakalasson. If any of them had caught his scent like you did, he would have been claimed faster than you can throw a dagger." He was red in the face, struggling to keep his voice steady, but it was seeping with rage. "My cousin has enchanted rooms for those seeking to maintain a low profile, and I thought he might appreciate the sentiment." He jabbed a finger at my chest. "Do not assume I am always keeping things from you. That is *your* specialty. Not mine."

He didn't wait for me to respond before shouldering past me toward where we would skith back to the palace.

I took a deep breath as I turned to follow him. Drako's voice sounded sleepy as he grumbled, *Your friends have never given you reason to doubt them. Do not start now.*

<hr />

I dropped Talekor onto his bed. He moaned something about a bucket, so I opened a pocket to the bathing chambers and grabbed the small trash can. I shoved it into Tal's hand just in time for him to heave the contents of our dinner into it. He didn't entirely make it. The room immediately smelled of bile.

Sending a message to his attendant, I skithed from his room to mine, finding Ollie staring out the window at the sun hanging in the sky. I sighed. "I didn't mean to upset you, Ollie. I just… I wish you didn't feel like you had to go behind my back to do these things."

His shoulders tensed , but they relaxed as he turned to face me. "The Fae are my responsibility, Niko. I cannot burden you with the pursuit to protect them when you should be focusing on safeguarding those closest to you." The words I wanted to say were on the tip of my tongue, but he raised a hand. "As much as I would like to have this conversation with you, there are more pressing matters to address right now. We can discuss this after we complete our mission for the night."

He is right, Niko. We have limited time. The castle is buzzing even now. Somehow, Drako always knew what was happening throughout the castle. *If you wish to make your moves, now would be the time to do so.*

I sighed, nodding at Oliver. "Later." I turned, creating a tear in the world with my hand, but before extracting it, I made two full circles counterclockwise around the tear. I took Oliver's hand, catching his nervous glance. "Ready?"

"No," he said sincerely, gripping my hand regardless. He knew I had done this once before, but I had gone alone.

"Focus on me and don't let go," I instructed, not giving him a chance to back out as I pulled us both through the rip.

We appeared in my chambers as if the rip had never existed, but I knew that just ten minutes ago in this timeline I'd led the crew through the portal door to the Verdanvale. Knowing it all had to be perfectly timed, I turned to Oliver. "We need to make a stop before heading to the Kytos."

Oliver raised a hand to his mouth, not to show his shock, but because his face had turned a sickly shade of green.

"Shit." Naturally, traveling back in time had its consequences, but I had forgotten how different types of travel affect the Fae. I grabbed his elbow and guided him into the bathroom. Fortunately, *he* made it in time and didn't miss the target. Figuring he needed a few minutes to recover, I patted him on the back and said, "I'll be back in a few."

From the foyer, I skithed to the alcove hidden near Talekor's chambers. If I wasn't mistaken… Yep. Tal, Ollie, and my past self emerged from Tal's chambers. Oliver was rambling about the restaurant we were headed to, Tal half-heartedly listening, while I trailed behind them. I waited until all three of us were almost down the hall, and my past self glanced back over my shoulder to where I hid among the shadows and wink. I remembered winking at the alcove, but I hadn't seen myself. I just knew my plan to be there. I grinned.

You are going to get caught if you linger much longer, Drako warned.

Shaking off my own brilliant plan, I crossed the hall and knocked three times, followed by two, then four, before stepping back to wait.

The door creaked open, and Leighton peered out.

"Did you receive my note?" I asked, crossing my arms over my chest.

She opened the door fully revealing a pack slung over her shoulder. "Where are you taking me?" Her voice was softer and more upbeat than her twin's.

"It's a surprise." I offered her a small smile. She looked back over her shoulder, and I didn't need to read her mind to understand what she was thinking. "You'll return before he notices you're gone."

She faced me again, and her shoulders relaxed as she nodded and stepped into the hall, closing the door behind her.

"Just like that?" I asked, curious how she could trust someone so blindly after the little she'd seen of me in this castle. I hadn't been very nice, after all.

Leighton shrugged and offered me a coy smile. "If Rayleigh trusts you, then so do I."

"I'm not so sure she does," I admitted.

She looked down at her feet before meeting my gaze again. "She may not admit it, even to herself, but I can see it."

I accepted it for what it was and offered her my arm. She linked hers through it, and I led her back to my rooms, avoiding the main halls and taking the paths reserved for royals. Leighton was quiet during the walk, but it was a comfortable silence as she admired the paintings we passed. When we reached my chambers, I guided her straight to the portal door.

"Stand behind me," I instructed her. Once she was in position, I touched the symbols on the door I had carved for the Verdanvale, then knocked. The chatter on the other side cut off and said, "If Mitch is near this door, get him to the kitchen. I don't want to risk him being too close to magic."

As soon as Rayleigh confirmed, I opened the door, carefully keeping Leighton out of sight. Everyone stared at me expectantly. I stepped aside and ushered her over the threshold toward Rayleigh and Kendall's excited squeals. Morale had been awful lately, and I knew I needed to find a way to help. The girls and Mari mentioned Leighton at least twice a day since they'd been separated, and I figured a night away from the castle would benefit everyone.

I gave Rayleigh a nod at her thanks and retreated into my chambers, closing the door only to discover Oliver standing directly behind it.

"You must be out of your damn mind, Niko." Oh, he was furious.

"Her absence won't be noticed," I said, pivoting back to the center of my room once more.

"Not be noticed? Nikylo," Oliver grabbed my shoulder, but I shrugged out of his grip, creating the rip in the world we needed to reach Kytos. "You are taking bigger risks tonight than necessary." There was that hint of fear in his voice that he rarely displayed.

I turned to him, sighing. "Giving Leighton a break from Talekor's abuse is the least I can do, not just for her but for Rayleigh." At her name, he recoiled in shock. "But this is yet another thing we don't have time for. We can discuss this later."

Oliver ground his jaw but nodded, taking my extended hand as we stepped into the rocky alcove. Naila leaned against the entrance, waving at me with all her fingers.

"You're late," she said, stepping forward to greet Oliver. "I'm surprised you actually joined him." She pressed her cheek against his, then returned to her position at the entrance.

He still looked a bit pale but gave her a faint smile. "It would be unwise to leave him alone with Adarachi."

She raised an eyebrow at me. "He's not wrong," I said with a shrug. If I had come alone, I likely would have killed him with the first thing he said against Rayleigh. "If you don't see us in an hour, come get us."

"And if I hear screaming?" she mused.

"Pretend you didn't," I said, shouldering past her into the tunnel. I had discovered these tunnels long ago when I needed a place to escape from my father but wasn't allowed to leave the island. It wasn't a location many sought to explore because they were located on the rocky underside. I had done my fair share of exploring while learning to skith, though.

I rounded the corner of the tunnels to find Adarachi behind the crystal bars I installed years ago. He wasn't the first one I needed to contain and interrogate. The gonos only did so much, but these bars slowly drained the power from whoever was imprisoned behind them. If he touched them, it would've only sped up the process. It looked as if he learned that the hard way.

The wounds Theo inflicted on him remained unhealed, with blood still oozing from the gash in his stomach. The collar around his neck was one I'd stolen from the team that assaulted us when Rayleigh was captured on Gaia. It separated him from his dragon. Theo and Naila were instructed to keep him fed and nourished so that I could be the one to drain his life force, but they couldn't make him eat or drink what they provided. His latest meal lay untouched just inside the bars.

"There he is," Adarachi rasped. He coughed several times. "I was wondering how long it would take you to pay me a visit." He crawled from his cot in the corner into the light of the torch, and I noticed the effects of the bars more clearly. His skin tone was nearly gray. I'd forgotten how quickly they drain power and health. He peeked around me to see Oliver and let out a disappointed tsk. "That's not who I asked you to bring."

"I will not bring her down here. Ever. So either tell me what you were going to say to her, or we're leaving."

Adarachi cackled, making himself cough again. "You conducted all the research on your own. You should already know."

I crossed my arms over my chest, leaning against the tunnel wall. "Please, enlighten me."

After he repositioned himself against the wall, he studied me for a moment before he spoke. "I want real food." I gestured to the plate he hadn't touched. "Bread and cheese don't sustain us, and you know it. At least bring me some protein."

I rolled my eyes but sent a request to the kitchens for a plate of milot and root vegetables, even adding a request for a few zymis. Several minutes later, he was devouring his meal while Oliver and I sat against the wall, enjoying our own treats.

"You have your food," I spat. "Now, speak."

Adarachi glared at me but spoke around his mouthful of food. "The pull is stronger with her, isn't it?"

"The Kavaltis bond is stronger than the Doulos," I said as if it were obvious—because it was. "I was drawn to Meg once the bond formed, but my dragon was drawn to Rayleigh before he chose her."

"In your *thorough* notes," he winked, "you mentioned feeling her presence even when she wasn't speaking to you."

"Yes, and upon further research in the libraries *here*, I have discovered that there is more to the Kavaltis bond than most tomes reveal, including why I can sense her at all times." If he was trying to convince me it wasn't that type of bond, he was in for a rude awakening. I had spent hours in the libraries after my return, searching for everything I could find about the bond. I only had a few unanswered questions, and Adarachi was not the person who could answer them.

He tilted his head with a grin spreading across his face. "How did Kaleb—or whatever his name is—take the news?"

I narrowed my eyes. How could he have known Tal found out? He never managed to get the information to him before we brought him down here. I shot a glance at Oliver, but he just shrugged. That grin was still plastered on his face when I asked, "Who told you?"

He chuckled, "You did. Just now." When I merely raised an eyebrow, he continued, "I knew something would come up, that someone would let it slip. It was only a matter of time. Your reaction just now confirmed I was right."

"But how could you know he'd find out?"

"I told you before, the only thing he wants is to claim her as his own. Learning about the bond probably led him to, what, challenge you?" The confidence in his tone sent ice trickling through my veins.

Someone was telling him things. No one knew what happened on that field unless they were present… But who was it?

I stood and walked straight up to the bars, careful not to touch them. "Where is it?"

"Where is what?" His expression of feigned innocence made me see red.

I lifted my hands to raise the bars, but Oliver was standing beside me. "Niko, do not let him provoke you. He wants you to open the cage. You have just given him enough sustenance to restore his strength. Lifting those bars could mean him disappearing."

I was breathing heavily, but I heard him—I knew he was right. Somewhere in that cage, though, was a letter. Someone was sending him correspondence. "Who is your informant?" I demanded.

He ignored me and turned his attention to Oliver. "Now you… I'm surprised you haven't told him."

I whirled to face my best friend. "What is he talking about?"

"I have no idea, Niko."

"*Don't* lie to me."

"I would not lie about this!" he shot back. "He is speaking in riddles. I have no idea what he is referring to."

"Oh, but I think you do, *Councilor*," Adarachi mused.

Oliver didn't take the bait or tear his gaze away from mine. He held it, conveying everything he could with that stare. He had his own secrets, but if he knew what Adarachi was talking about he would have confessed. This was Rayleigh we were talking about—someone we both cared for in ways that neither of us could confess to each other fully.

Drako's words echoed in my mind. I couldn't start doubting him now. Taking a deep breath, I clenched my jaw and faced the prisoner again. One minute, he was taking a bite of his food; the next, he was choking on it as my power held him by the throat against the wall I threw him into. With his air supply cut off, he thrashed against my grip, clawing at the invisible force holding him in place. "When I release you, the next words out of your mouth had better be a non-cryptic explanation. Understood?"

I felt more than saw his agreement and released him. After a coughing fit, he looked up. But it wasn't my gaze he met; it was Oliver's. "You know the secrets they hoard." He heaved another breath, coughing several times.

"*Who?*" I demanded, barely restraining myself from storming into the cell and wrapping my bare hands around his throat this time.

A slow, wicked grin revealed all of his teeth before he said, "Her parents."

THIRTY-SEVEN
that way

Rayleigh

"Again."

I pushed myself up from the ground with a groan.

Nikylo picked us up from the Verdanvale after what felt like only a couple of hours of sleep. He said Leigh needed to be back in Talekor's chambers before he woke, and Ken and I needed to get some training in before leaving for the Kyllindro.

I woke up with a severe headache and pressure in my ears, but I was only given some glykos before he took us all back to the castle without offering anything else. What changed between our time together yesterday and this morning that made him return to his asshole self? No idea. But he definitely wasn't easing up on training, this time wanting me to focus on *purposefully* using my wielding.

So far, I had only managed to get knocked on my ass by Naila several times as she vanished from in front of me, only to reappear behind me and knock my feet out from under me. I'd been trying to fight back using air, but I was always one step behind her movements.

Nikylo had grown tired of my constant losing, saying, "Switch it up, Sunshine. Whatever you're trying to do clearly isn't working." I wanted to deck him. Since then, the vines and earth I attempted to harness barely did what I wanted them to as I yanked on my powers to give me *something* to fight with.

The rage I felt when I sparred against Naila last time was what made me accidentally wield, but Mari was standing nearby with instructions to keep that rage subdued. So now I was just annoyed.

"Tell me again why I can't use my rage to wield?" I asked, preparing to get my ass handed to me again.

"Bringing strong emotions into a fight will either distract you or cause you to lose control." Nikylo's tone was clipped. "You can use your emotions, but don't rely on them."

Oh, he was in a *mood*. Turning back to Naila, who wore her usual grin, I raised my hands. The thread of green connecting me to my Udara powers was faint but shimmering. Instead of yanking on it like I had done the last few times, I focused on coaxing it to my fingertips. I could feel it awakening. The glow of the thread brightened as I gently nudged it toward my hands. Naila lunged just as I felt the power reach my fingertips.

I exhaled sharply, planting my bare feet in the grass, and whispered to my powers, "Please work."

Naila flickered and then disappeared altogether. I hated that she kept using that ability. It made it nearly impossible to fight her when I couldn't even see her.

"Don't trust your eyes," Nikylo advised. "Utilize the other senses available to you."

Grasping the thread of white that was almost always readily available, I coaxed the wind to detect any disturbances in the air. Turning in a slow circle, I reached for the vines buried in the dirt, channeling my powers into them just as the air shifted behind me. The vines shot up as I spun around, curling toward where I sensed her presence, but the sharp ring of steel pierced the stillness as she appeared and sliced through the vines coiling around her with the short sword I'd noticed on her hip moments before. I changed tactics, throwing my hands toward her feet, and the ground trembled as it opened to swallow her, but she propelled herself skyward in an impossible leap, landing in a roll directly to my left.

I followed her with my arms, poised to strike again, but she swung her blade, and I felt the sting across my forearm just as something slammed into the back of my legs. *Dammit!* My back hit the ground—again—as her blade pressed lightly against my neck. Naila chuckled beside my ear. "Better. But still not good enough."

She pushed away from me, leaving me to help myself up. I pressed my hand into the dirt as I attempted to catch my breath.

"At least you were able to wield two elements that time," Nikylo said, standing at the edge of the sparring area with his arms crossed over his chest. I thought I caught a glimpse of pride, but it disappeared immediately.

"I still don't understand why she gets weapons." Standing up, I brushed the dirt from my linens and looked at the mess I'd made of the ground after summoning the vines and the hole to swallow Naila. We weren't on the castle grounds, still uncertain if I could control my powers well enough to leave the foundation intact, but the glen we'd come to wasn't the one I'd destroyed the other day either. A canopy of trees shaded this one, secluding us in a forest clearing.

"While you control physical elements, she requires something to counteract them. She doesn't possess physical manipulation like I do."

I mirrored his sassy-ass stance. "Then why don't *you* come spar with me?" His crankiness and my suppressed rage were pushing my limits. I needed to pin *someone*, and I knew I could pin him.

He dropped his arms and stalked across the field. "Sparring is over." Turning to Naila, he said, "Take Kendall, Mari, and Cleo back. I have business to attend to with my bonded." His gaze returned to me, a wicked gleam in his eyes.

Unsure of what he meant by that, my skin still tingled from the look. Ken, Mari, Cleo, and Naila walked across the field and disappeared into the forest beyond. It had been nice having a chance to use my powers without having to worry about them exploding out of me. I also got to watch Kendall fight Cleo. She had shown Ken how to craft the water weapons and use them during a lesson I missed. Apparently, she had more time to train than I did. I was busy with ceremonies and getting kidnapped, which left me with less time to train and hone my skills. Granted, we'd only been free from the dungeons for a few days, but Kendall was getting *really* good.

Slowly, I turned back to Nikylo, wondering what the hell we had to "attend to" that required everyone else to leave. He had found a tree trunk to lean against and was watching me from several yards away.

"You ready to tell me why you're so cranky?" I asked.

"Long night."

I squinted at him. "Which consisted of?"

"Too much mead."

I took a step toward him, prompting him to straighten up. "You expect me to believe that all it takes for you to go back to being an asshole is a hangover?" I was just steps away from him when I halted my advances. "After everything that happened yesterday?"

He shrugged and shouldered past me as if I hadn't said anything. "We need to work on two things today: shielding your mind and getting accustomed to skithing."

"Skithing?"

"Traveling through space." Of course, it had a weird name. They couldn't just call it teleporting... "Teleporting is a made-up word by humans," he said, undoubtedly reading my every thought. "First lesson." He crossed his arms. *Close your mind.*

It isn't open, I snapped.

Yes, it is. Anyone can currently walk right into your mind. A gentle tug in my mind had the thought of me decking him from earlier pop up. *You need to block me out.*

Grinding my teeth, I summoned the door in my mind that I'd opened many times for him. It was firmly closed. *See! Closed.*

Not that door, Sunshine. That is reserved exclusively for Drako and me. A smirk tugged at his lips. *I'm talking about the fact that you don't have any walls or anything to conceal your mind. You haven't since the day I met you. This means you're an open book to anyone with Lunnoxia powers.*

Great. I suddenly felt grateful that he had been kind enough to shield me from everyone in the castle. Who knows what thoughts might have run through my mind? I also finally understood why he never shared anything with me...

Thinking about when I entered *his* mind earlier, I recalled the hallway I had walked down, leading to the pearl door at the end. It was the sole entrance to his mind, surrounded by walls that stretched out of sight.

You can think of it however you like. A hallway worked for me, but that might not be the case for you.

Glaring at him for once again sifting through my thoughts, I closed my eyes and imagined what might be encompassing my mind. I contemplated my powers and how they could wrap protectively around me, shielding me from prying minds.

A rocky wall loomed before me, deep purple swirling with blue.

A wall. Good, Nikylo reassured. *Keep going.*

I stepped closer to the wall, extending my hand to feel the heat radiating from it. The blue wasn't just part of the stone; it was flames filling the cracks of the purple stone, sealing off any hidden paths into my mind. I turned in a circle, watching as the walls I summoned rose toward the endless height of my mind, forming a circular dome around me. I wasn't sure what type of stone these walls were made of, but it didn't matter. They surrounded my mind, encompassing every part of it —

Almost. There's still a way in. Find it.

I scoured the exterior of the swirling purple dome, the blue fire filling the empty pockets it required to breathe, but there were pinholes. Summoning the only thing I had left, I asked, *Does it have to be solid?*

Solid is subjective; it exists in your mind. If you deem it solid, it will be—

But I didn't catch the rest of his explanation. The wall of wind I created surrounded the dome, making it impossible for anything to get past it to even search for the pinholes.

"You won't be able to maintain that," Nikylo said, interrupting my concentration and halting the winds. *Try something more permanent.*

He made it sound much easier. Maybe I was overcomplicating things… Something Oliver said echoed in my mind, reminding me just how intense my fire could get. Refocusing on the heat within the walls, I used the wind to summon sand outside the dome, layering it over the stone wall and pushing more heat into the blue flames. I felt the sand begin to liquefy as it met the fire. Once the entire dome was coated in liquid sand, I reduced the heat and pushed cool air along the outside to solidify it.

I admired the dome I'd created, captivated by its beauty and wishing I could share it with someone—

That is truly remarkable.

I jumped in the space of my mind. Standing *inside* the dome with me was Nikylo. His eyes were scanning over what I'd created. *How the hell did you get in here?*

You opened the door. Not taking his eyes off the dome, he gestured to the oak door he claimed was just for him. Sure enough, it stood wide open. There was another door opposite his, not nearly as intricate. It was a simple red one that resembled the front door of my childhood home. It was shut tight.

Well…shoo, I said, waving him out the door, unsure how I felt about him just walking into my mind like that. *Tell me if it worked.* Then again, according to him, he was always there, creating his own version of a shield around my mind.

I opened my eyes as soon as I was sure the oak door was sealed shut behind him. Nikylo stood in the middle of the clearing, a stupid grin on his face. "Well done. Now, keep it up." He stalked toward me. Something in his eyes made me stumble back a step. Then another. He wasn't stopping; he was—

He was testing my ability to maintain the shields. Duh. I took one more step back, and the bark of the tree behind me pressed into my back. "Stop," I said, my voice shaky as he closed the distance between us. "Scaring me won't make me drop—"

He stopped inches from me, his gaze locking onto mine, the green swirling in his eyes in a way I'd only seen a select few times. "Who said I was trying to scare you, Sunshine?" The piercing stare flicked to my lips as he lifted his hand between us and lowered himself to the ground.

My shoes. He'd grabbed my shoes that I'd kicked off to help with my Udara powers. His hand gently wrapped around my calf, lifting my foot—

"I can put on my own shoes," I said, trying and failing to sound annoyed.

He glanced up at me as he slid on the first shoe, a wild smirk playing on his lips. Only after I double-checked my shield did I allow myself to think about how damn attractive he was. He released my leg only to grab the other one, his hand sliding a few inches down my calf in a gentle caress before lifting it to put on the shoe he held.

Slowly, he stood, not backing away from me. Once he rose to his full height, there was hardly any space to breathe, let alone move. Before I could try, he lifted an arm above my head and placed it on the tree I was still pressed against, leaning in closer. I could feel his breath skimming across my lips, and all I could do was swallow my nerves.

Why was he making me so nervous? I *knew* what he was doing—I could feel him skimming the edge of my mind, searching for a way in. It wasn't going to happen. Yet the tension felt so real. So intense and magnetic, the energy between us crackled within the incremental space he'd left between us.

"Do you know how ravishing you're going to look tonight in the dress I've chosen for you?" His voice had dropped to a tone I'd never heard from him. His eyes wandered to my shoulders, where I felt a whisper of a touch, the warmth seeping through my linens. "It falls off your shoulders, just so," he traced the top of my bicep, sending shivers down my spine, "and the sleeves are sheer all the way down to here." He followed the path of my arm, his fingertips now skating along my bare skin to the underside of my wrist. Somehow, that was the most sensitive place he'd touched, making my back stiffen.

His hand traced the same path back up my arm, then withdrew completely. He lowered it to my torso, lingering over my hips as he breathed, "The bodice will hug your hips in a way I've dreamed of doing many times." His hand traveled back up until it gripped my chin, lifting it so I could meet his gaze. I felt his lips move as he said, "And the back?" His other hand dropped from the tree and landed on the lowest part of my back, right where the hem of my shirt met the waistband of my pants. My breath caught as he pulled me into him while keeping my face in place by my chin. "It will fall right here, exposing your back for me to touch like this," he said, his fingers tracing the now-exposed skin at the bottom of my shirt.

My heart rate had jumped on impact and soared even higher as his eyes flicked between mine, a whisper of space between our lips. Was he going to kiss me? He said he wouldn't until I wanted him to. Did I want him to? Would I stop him? My immediate answer was yes, but I knew I was lying to myself. My eyes drifted to his mouth in a moment of weakness, and a slow grin spread across his face. My gaze moved back up to his just as his eyes crinkled with that smile, and he said in my head, *You lose.*

Gritting my teeth, I slammed the dome into position, simultaneously shoving Nikylo with all my strength. "Asshole!"

He stumbled back from my shove, chuckling and running his fingers through his hair as he backed away from me into the clearing. "Have to keep them up at all times, Sunshine. Even in *moments of weakness*," he mocked.

"Moment of weakness, indeed," I mumbled. Because I certainly wouldn't be falling for that again. I couldn't believe I had actually let my guard down for something so clearly designed to make me do just that. "Can we move on?" I asked, unsure if I was more frustrated with myself or with him for knowing how he affects me and using it against me.

"Not until you can keep it up without thinking about it."

"What else could you possibly do—" I screeched as my body lifted off the ground, soaring toward the trees above. "Put me down!" I shouted while also checking on the dome. It remained steady.

My weight returned, and I plummeted toward the ground. I threw my hands out, pushing air down to break my fall, landing rather clumsily in a roll.

A slow clap echoed behind me. "You're starting to rely on your powers. Good."

I pushed myself off the ground, stomping across the clearing toward him. "You were going to let me *fall?*"

"I could have caught you, but… well, you did it yourself." He shrugged, stepping out of my way just as I swung at him.

Twisting, I spotted him clear across the field. I gritted my teeth. "Fine. Test it. I won't let you in again—"

The ground beneath me vanished, and I was falling once more. This time, I was high above the trees when I fell, and, making sure my dome was still in place, I reached for the thread of green. I didn't need to coax it this time. It followed my lead, connecting and weaving a net with the branches in the canopy. But I crashed straight through before it had a chance to strengthen.

I screamed, reaching back for air but knowing I'd be too late this time. Air rushed up beneath me, anyways, twisting me so my back sped toward the ground, but it slowed my descent more than I thought I was capable of.

That was until an arm was wrapped under my shoulders and another under my knees, telling me I hadn't been my own savior this time. I opened my eyes, which I'd apparently closed during my fall, and found a pair of ice-blue ones staring back at me. *Ah… that explains it.*

"Is Niko giving you a hard time, love?" Oliver mused.

As I caught my breath, I shook my head. "Trying to make sure my glass dome stays up."

"Your glass dome?" he asked, raising an eyebrow toward his messy white locks.

"Testing her shields," Nikylo explained. "You're interrupting a training session."

"I realize," Oliver replied, giving in to my squirming as he set me down.

Because as much as I was grateful for the catch... "I'm still mad at you," I said, stepping back from him and crossing my arms.

He let out a sigh. "That makes two of us."

I squinted at him. "You're mad at yourself?"

He dipped his chin. "For the way you found out. It should have come directly from me."

"Yes. It should have," I agreed.

"Will you let me make it up to you?" he asked. My eyebrows shot up in response. "I would like to make you dinner after the ball tonight and answer any questions you might have."

I pulled my lips into my mouth. He *was* really good at giving me straight answers. And a home-cooked meal sounded lovely, as did spending some time with Oliver. I held his gaze for a moment longer, then looked back at Nikylo, feeling like I needed his permission on this one since I knew we wouldn't be at the castle. His jaw was clenched, but after a quick glance at Oliver and back, he gave me a curt nod. I turned back to Oliver, failing to hide my smile and holding up a finger. "Only if I can help cook."

His smile lit up his entire face, and I'd be lying if I said it wasn't contagious—and dare I say, beautiful. "It would be my honor," he said, giving a slight bow of his head.

With a bright smile, I said a bit louder than necessary, "It's a date."

I didn't hear it, but I felt a low grumble outside the dome that I'd successfully kept up the entire time. He'd been hovering during our conversation, waiting for my shield to weaken even the slightest bit, but it didn't. I also knew his growl hadn't come from being locked out. I was grinning like an idiot for more than one reason as Oliver leaned in to kiss my cheek. His lips were soft where they left their mark, and my stomach did an unexpected flip at their touch. He lingered a little longer than necessary, but I may have pressed my cheek into the kiss before he pulled away and whispered, "I hope you will save a dance for me tonight as well."

My stupid self giggled. "Of course," I said, trying to stop myself from grinning even wider. What was happening to me?

Blood rushed to my cheeks by the time Oliver stepped back and looked past me at Nikylo, his smile fading as he said, "Lunch is in an hour. I will keep them entertained for as long as I can. You have a maximum of two starting now."

I turned to see Nikylo give Oliver a firm nod, his jaw still clenched as he avoided my gaze. "Send word if anything goes wrong."

Oliver nodded, smirking at me before disappearing with a gust of wind through the field.

One of my questions later would definitely be how in the hell *that* worked.

Nikylo cleared his throat behind me, and I spun around to see him *still* clenching his jaw. "A date? Really?"

"Hey, you said yes." I raised my hands in surrender. "Besides, we're betrothed. We have to start somewhere."

He scoffed, "Well, even with his distraction, you kept your shield up."

"What, no 'good job' or 'well done'?"

A smile danced on his lips. "Do you need to hear those words from me?"

"No." Yes. I had no idea what I wanted from him, but it definitely wasn't to hear praises come from his mouth or to be alone with him any longer. "Can we just practice skiing or whatever you called it?"

"Skithing," he corrected with a grin. "And yes, because we only have an hour before we need to use it properly without you fainting."

"And how exactly do you expect me to get used to it without making me pass out several times?"

"We'll start with short distances, gradually increasing to longer ones." He tilted his head. "Once I can get you from here to the Verdanvale, we can skith to the Kyllindro from there."

"And if I pass out?"

"I suggest you don't. We're on a tight schedule."

I rolled my eyes. "Fine. How do we do this?"

He stepped closer, leaving about a foot between us as he turned slightly, slowly slicing the air beside us. A shimmering line appeared and widened as he pulled his hand away from the hole he had created. He extended his other hand toward me. "Shall we?"

I looked from his hand to his face—he really meant business because there wasn't even a hint of a smile. I thought that agreeing to dinner with Oliver would make the feelings he'd stirred in me earlier disappear, but my damn heart was racing at the thought of spending an entire afternoon alone with Nikylo.

Realizing I had no real choice if I actually wanted to help Mitch, I took his hand, and he pulled me through the tear he'd created in the world.

THIRTY-EIGHT
Feel the Light

It didn't take nearly as long for me to get used to skithing as Nikylo predicted, which he said could be due to Aaidan forcing me to skith a long distance.

The first time, we simply reappeared on the other side of the field, and although the electric charge coursing through my body felt strange, I didn't feel like I was about to faint. The second time, we passed through the rip in the world to a glen just outside the forest we were in. That one made me a little dizzy, but it quickly passed along with the prickling sensation against my skin.

He skithed us straight into his chambers on the fifth try, claiming he needed to grab something before heading to the Kyllindro. My headache had resurfaced during training, so I requested some glykos, suddenly questioning whether too much of the liquid was harmful. Nikylo didn't seem to think so; he handed me a bottle after retrieving a pack from his room, allowing me to drink the entire contents before summoning yet another rip in the world to the Verdanvale.

The pressure was greater than it had been on any previous trips, but Nikylo had warned me that longer distances might affect me differently. While I recentered, Nikylo quickly prepared some food, saying we wouldn't have much time to eat before the ball. Since the Nosí at the Kyllindro forbade eating near the tomes, we had to eat before we left. We had a quick meal of sandwiches and fruit, with the pinkish bread adding a sweetness to the sandwich that I never thought I would enjoy, but it was delightful.

As I finished putting the dishes away, Nikylo dried his hands and said, "There's a tome upstairs I need to get; then we can leave from the terrace." He didn't wait for me to respond and headed upstairs.

By the time I reached the second floor, I found him staring at the cover of a book and grinding his teeth. "What's that?" I asked, stepping closer to see if I could read the title.

His gaze flicked to me and then back to the book, finally landing on me again, squinting. He shook his head. "Nothing. Just something I need to show Oliver." He waved a small piece of paper I hadn't noticed before, which he tucked into his pack along with the book.

Odd, I thought. When Nikylo didn't react to my inner dialogue, I knew that meant my shields were staying in place. I brushed off the strange feeling his behavior gave me and asked, "Ready?"

He gave me a curt nod and gestured for me to head up the stairs to the roof. I hadn't mentioned his journals, wondering if he would be angry about my taking them. Would he believe me if I blamed Drako? Probably. The strange occurrences in Niccodra made me eager to see what the other islands looked like now, but I knew I had already witnessed the destruction of one of them... The island with the cave Aaidan took me to was where Orvyn had left that note.

I chewed the inside of my cheek, uncertain if asking would reveal my secret. I decided it didn't matter, especially after how Mari reacted last night. "Did you have a chance to talk to anyone else in my Omada this morning?" I casually tossed the question over my shoulder as I opened the roof door, which greeted me with sunshine.

"No. Why?" The door swung shut behind him, but he didn't move to skith right away either. He must have sensed that whatever I had to say was important.

"It's just... we believe Talekor might be working with Orvyn."

The color drained from Nikylo's face. "How do you know this?"

"Leighton said he let the name slip after his plan to bond with Drako didn't work. Said he had to meet up with him or something to change the plan."

His jaw flexed. "We're certain that's what she heard?"

"Well, no. She heard Owen, but with Leigh—"

"Right. Repeating things isn't her strong suit," he sighed. "We'll have to deal with that later." With that, he sliced the sky and pulled me into the darkness beyond.

The distance to the Kyllindro had me retching as soon as we hit the sand. A bottle of regular water was thrust into my line of sight. I snatched it, spitting out the bile from my mouth and taking a swig to wash away the taste. After spitting that out as well, I drank the remaining water and glared at Nikylo.

"You could have warned me about the nausea?"

He shrugged. "I haven't skithed a Fae that far. I wasn't sure what to expect."

"But you had this ready?" I chucked the now-empty bottle at him.

"Just a precaution. Glad I brought one, though, right?"

Rather than answering him, I took in our surroundings. Sand stretched in every direction for about ten feet, followed by water that extended as far as the eye could see. Gradually, my gaze lifted to the sky, and my jaw dropped at the sight.

Because we weren't just on another island—we were *beneath* them.

We stood on a sandbar among the water that the islands floated above. The closest island looked enormous, its rocky underside resembling an upside-down mountain. At the bottom, still high above the water-filled planet, water flowed up into its center, ignoring everything I knew about gravity. Apparently, the laws of science didn't apply to magic.

"How in the world…?" I whispered, mostly to myself

"Come on. We don't have much time," Nikylo said. I turned to find him standing in the middle of the sandbar…with nothing else around him.

"Come where, exactly? It doesn't seem like there's anywhere to go but the water," I gestured at the miles of water surrounding us.

He shook his head. "Trust me. You don't want to go in that water."

Eyeing him, I asked, "Why?"

"There are creatures in that water that will pull you under for fun.

They don't care if you can swim or not." He adjusted the pack on his shoulder, then tapped a random spot in the sand with his foot. "You have to be permitted." He nodded to a pole that jutted out of the sand next to him.

"And if I'm not?" I asked, panic threading through my voice. He hadn't mentioned anything about permissions to enter.

"Trust me. If anything, they'll let you in simply because of your lineage."

"But what if they don't let me in because of my fire? Or because I still can't control my powers?"

"All magic is blocked within the Kyllindro." He weighed his head back and forth. "Except for the power it possesses on its own. They don't want to risk the scrolls."

"*The scrolls?*" I balked. "As in the ones that magically update tomes? They're *here?*" When he nodded, a shiver of excitement ran through my body. I couldn't believe I was going to the Kyllindro, let alone visiting the place where the sacred scrolls were kept. A note of fear crept into my voice when I remembered how precious they were. "I won't be able to get close to them, right?" As much as I would have loved to see them, I had this irrational fear that I might somehow destroy them.

He chuckled. "You won't be able to destroy them if that's what you're worried about." I mentally checked my shields and found them intact. I cursed my facial expressions for betraying my thoughts. "Only those Mitera deems worthy can access them, remember?"

Nodding, I stepped up beside him, noticing that the pole had a round plate on top, large enough for a hand. He placed his hand on it and lifted it away to reveal a mark—similar to the one he'd left on my torso —which faded with a flash of green. Willing my hand not to shake, I placed it on the plate and felt a tingling sensation before lifting it away to discover a mark like the one on Nikylo's hand, indicating my power. I waited with bated breath until it, too, faded with a flash of green.

The ground beneath us shifted. I bent my knees slightly to maintain my balance and suddenly realized we were being lowered into the ground. "What the hell? The Kyllindro is *underground?*"

Nikylo's answering grin was so big that his dimples threatened to appear. "You never ask the *right* questions, Sunshine."

As much as I hated to admit it, he was right. While I'd asked what it was, I didn't inquire about anything else: where it was, what kind of magic it had, or how it was accessed. But how would I even know to ask those questions? Speaking of questions… I smacked my forehead. "I forgot my notebook."

"Did you?" he asked, lifting his pack filled with tomes with a knowing look.

I stifled my smile. "You hate that notebook."

"I never said that."

"It was implied well enough."

"You just ask a lot of questions."

"You haven't even answered any of them this time!"

"My journals didn't answer any of your questions?"

My jaw dropped. "How did you…?"

"You're not as sneaky as you think you are." He winked.

Damn. I pressed my lips together, concentrating on anything but him as we continued our descent.

The walls were adorned with a spiral of glowing yellow crystals, illuminating the space just enough for us to see each other. The hole in the ground above us, leading back to the surface, sealed with another circular platform as soon as the walls closed in around us. One section of the circular wall opened up, and our descent stopped when there was enough room for Nikylo to step out without hitting his head. I followed him into the cavern, taking in the crystals scattered throughout the space. They looked nothing like the Xouta the dragons used to recharge, having a more orb-like shape to them.

Nikylo approached what appeared to be an empty desk. He tapped something on it, and a sharp ring echoed through the cavern. Footsteps shuffled in the hallway beyond the desk just before a head popped into view around the corner.

"Ah, Nikylo. Evie has been wondering when you would stop by again." The small male climbed onto something behind the desk, providing a better vantage point for him to focus on me. "You, on the other hand, are new here." He studied me briefly, then perked his ear toward the hallway as if he was listening to something. His face was lined with age, and long gray hair cascaded to his shoulders. When his hazel eyes fell back on me, a slow smile spread across his face. "It has been quite a while since we've seen a Castellan."

"A what?" I blurted.

He ignored me and turned back to Nikylo. "What is it you require today, sire?"

"We come seeking knowledge on a few things," he said, reaching into his pack and pulling out a list to give to the man.

He scanned the paper and glanced up at Nikylo through his brows. "You seek information about the sirens?" Sirens? Weren't those like mermaids?

With a firm nod, Nikylo said, "That and the nullification are the most important."

The man arched an eyebrow. "The answer for the latter is standing right beside you."

Nikylo's gaze shot to mine. I shrugged, prompting him to turn back to the man. "Can you just—we need tomes with answers, Claude. Not cryptic information."

The name rang a bell, but I didn't have time to figure it out. Claude smiled. "Of course, sire. Please," he stepped down from whatever he was standing on to make himself taller and entered the hallway, "follow me."

Nikylo adjusted the pack on his shoulder again, then hovered his hand over my lower back to usher me down the hallway.

"What's a Castellan?" I whispered to Nikylo.

"No idea."

Claude led us to a small space with a table and two chairs, instructing us to wait while he fetched the books we requested. Nikylo set his pack on the table, pulling out the ones he had collected from within, along with a journal and my notebook, which he set in front of me as I sat down. Claude returned with the other tomes, and Nikylo immediately started making two stacks, sliding one of them to my side of the table when he finished.

"The references I wrote for you." He gestured toward my notebook, then opened his journal and the first tome on his stack, immediately finding something and writing it down.

"When did you have time to answer these?" I asked, flipping through the notebook to find several of my questions had simple answers or references. For the ones that didn't, I assumed we'd be searching for the answers together.

"Last night," he said, not looking up from his work.

"You certainly did a lot after dropping us off," I mumbled.

"I didn't have anyone distracting me." I could *hear* the smile in his tone.

"You can't blame me for you getting distracted."

"Yes, I can. It's entirely your fault when I can't focus." He looked up from his writing. "Right now, for example."

I leaned forward and lowered my voice. "You and I both know it's not my talking you were referring to." I snatched the book from the top of my pile and spotted the title on the side: *Niccodran Creatures and Monsters.*

"That might not be the only distracting thing about you, but it is certainly part of it." He returned to writing before I glanced up at him.

I chose to ignore that comment and open to the page he referenced for my questions about Mitch. Apparently, Dad was Annysian—according to Nikylos' answer in my book—that meant the air magic within my brother was manifesting as a siren. As I flipped through the pages, I discovered that sirens weren't mermaids but bird-like creatures that lured their enemies or prey to death by word or song. That explained the claws I'd seen in the courtroom…

"So sirens have the same ability as Oliver? Disappearing among the winds?" The description lacked detail, but it sounded similar. I looked up to see him scribbling something from his book, but I couldn't make out the title.

"It's not exactly the same," he said, scanning his book once more and jotting something else down. "Oliver walks with the winds. Sirens camouflage into their surroundings."

I swallowed hard and asked, "And they're definitely all…bad?" I didn't want to use the word evil, but the way the book described how they left their prey had my insides churning.

Nikylo finally looked up at my hesitation, his face softening a touch. "I've never encountered one, so I can't say for certain." He reached over and closed the book, pulling it to his side of the table. "But he's not going to make it to that stage." He tapped the book he was studying. "We're going to stop the transformation, okay?" I nodded, unsure if he was speaking with false confidence or if he'd actually found something. He pulled another book from my stack and slid it over to me. "Do me a favor and see if you can find a way to nullify your *órkomatos*."

"What? Why?" That oath was meant to reassure me that he wouldn't lie to me, and I didn't feel ready to let that go—even if he had found a way around it once before.

"For future use," Nikylo suggested. When I simply stared at him, he continued, "Far in the future, if you want. But Oliver just wants to make sure he has the information if it's needed."

I had thought about that, too—wanting to trust him enough to forgo the oath someday. So, I pulled the tome titled *Bonds, Oaths, and Curses* closer to my side of the table. This was one of the volumes Claude had brought, so I had no reference point to flip to. There was also no table of contents to consult, so I started flipping through the pages, hoping to find the right one. After browsing for a few pages, I realized they were organized in alphabetical order. I then set the book upright on its spine, found the middle, and opened it.

It landed on an oath called *echemon*—something about a vow of silence you can't break without risking a curse called thrypsis, which is referenced later in the book. After flipping through several more pages, I discovered *synásfeia*—a bond between souls for life. It made me think of how Mari described the mate connection between Theo and Libella. I flipped back a couple pages, finally locating *órkomatos*.

The description matched exactly what Oliver had told me, elaborating on where the souls connect and how the magic senses a lie to alert the other. It was designed to build trust between a pair but never meant to be permanent, which is why the second page included a section on nullifying it.

When I scanned the paragraph, it mentioned two methods. The first involved connecting blood between the pair and reciting a phrase that would simply release them from each other. The only hiccup in that plan was that it had to occur in the presence of both moons rising. I hadn't even seen a moon since I'd arrived, which likely meant they were probably stuck in the same way the planet was.

Skipping to the second option, I read it quickly, pausing midway through to go back and reread it. "That doesn't seem right..." I mumbled, reading it a third time just to be sure.

"Did you find something?" Nikylo asked, still focused on his tome. When I didn't reply, he finally looked up and saw me frozen, staring at the book. "What's wrong?"

Slowly, I tracked my eyes to his and turned the book around, sliding it towards him. He scanned the page. "The rising moons will be an issue because—" He must have reached the second option. Because his head snapped up, locking his gaze with mine for a split second before returning to the book and reading aloud, "As with any other oath or unilateral bond, Evanians have the ability to nullify the órkomatos on anyone but themselves."

"How?" My voice came out as barely a whisper.

"There's a reference guide," he said, flipping to the back of the tome and scanning a page, turning to the next when it didn't contain what he was looking for. "Here. 'Due to the inherent instability and fusion of magical essences within their bloodline, Evanians can dismantle the following oaths and unilateral bonds, rendering them void through a process of arcane interference and lineage-based disruption: alétheon, akrisios, antimneme, diathemis, doulos, echemon, phragmós, órkomatos, and thesi.'" He looked up at me, wonder in his eyes like the night he discovered I was Evanian. "No wonder your lineage is so powerful. Most of these are oaths, but it mentions two bonds that can also be nullified."

The shock of the news washed over me, but then I finally processed the other things he listed. "Did you say doulos?" He nodded. A trickle of hope seeped into my heart. "I could save her." Tears blurred my vision, but I blinked them away.

"Claude!" Nikylo shouted, prompting hurried footsteps from down the hall.

"Yes, sire," Claude said as he appeared, slightly breathless.

"Can you fetch Evie for me?" he asked, jotting down something on a note and folding it twice before giving it to Claude.

He hesitated reaching for the paper, stumbling over his words as he said, "But sire, Evie—well, she's on duty in the archives."

"You can hold her position while she gets that for me." When Claude hesitated, Nikylo practically shouted, "Now, Claude."

He scurried away, mumbling something about pompous royalty.

I twisted my fingers, catching Nikylo's attention. He placed his hand on mine, redirecting my focus to him. "This is a good thing, Sunshine."

"But what if I can't do it?" The words barely made it past the lump in my throat. "It's not like I have a teacher to guide me through this. I'm the only Evanian left."

"You don't have to do this."

"I can't leave her tied to Talekor like that! If there's something I can do—"

"Then have more confidence in yourself. Limiting your intelligence to what you already know is doing yourself a disservice." His intense gaze made me drop mine.

He was right, though. Everything I'd learned over the past month of my life felt impossible. Yet here I was, in a magical library after a training session with magic that had terrified me just a week ago. This magic worried me not because it put the life of my friend in danger, not if I succeeded, but if I *failed*. Deep down, I hoped Mari would succeed, so I wouldn't have to.

"Niko!" a shrill voice called out, its source tripping over her own two feet as she entered the room. She was smaller than Claude, which was saying something, but she seemed to be aging just like he was. "I was just asking Claude when he thought you might be stopping by!" She looked like she was about to burst with excitement. "Did you bring me anything today?"

Nikylo gave her a warm smile, one I had never seen him use before. "You'll have to wait to open it until you get home," he said, rummaging through his bag for a small package and handing it to her. "Chocolate-filled zymi from Tietra."

"Oooo, chocolate! You never bring chocolate!" She held the package to her nose and took a deep sniff, sighing with contentment as she released her breath. Eyeing Nikylo, she said, "You're missing out."

"Don't know what I'm missing when I've never tried it," he teased. "Did you find the scroll?"

My jaw dropped. "You had her bring a scroll *here?* I thought only those considered worthy by Mitera could access them."

Evie jumped at my words, seemingly unaware of my presence. She gasped as soon as her gaze landed on me. "A Castellan!"

"Okay, what is that?"

"Not a what, a who, silly!" She waved her hand at me dismissively. "Your family line."

I scrunched my brows. "Wait, are you saying my last name is Castellan?" When she nodded, my confusion deepened. "How can you tell that just by looking at me?"

She laughed. "Well, for one, it's my job to know everything there is to know. And two, you look like every other Castellan female I've ever met." She blinked as if my questioning her at all was ridiculous.

"The scroll, Evie," Nikylo gently scolded.

"Oh, sorry, sire. Yes, here." She pulled a small scroll from her tunic and placed it in his outstretched hand. "I regret to inform you that there isn't much more on the scroll than precisely what you requested."

"That's alright, Evie. Our trip today is brief anyway. Maybe you can collect other scrolls for a time when Rayleigh and I can return?"

Evie's eyes sparkled with excitement. "It's been decades since you last visited! Are you telling me I'll get to see you twice within a single decade?"

"It does seem plausible. Head back to the archives and start your search. I'll want everything you can find on the Evanians, okay?" Evie nodded, tucking her chocolate zymis into her tunic as she hurried out the way she had come in. Nikylo unrolled the scroll and caught my eye. "Can you hold this open?"

I shook my head. "You should have asked her to do it."

"You're not going to damage it." When I hesitated, he sighed. "Fine, can you come over here and copy it down in your notebook?"

Deciding I'd rather do that than touch an ancient magical scroll, I grabbed my notebook and walked to stand beside him. The scroll contained information on the incantations to nullify oaths, the ones with the Evanian and without. I jotted both down just in case we somehow found both moons rising.

When I was finished, Nikylo stood, rolled it back up, and called for Claude. After instructing him to return it directly to Evie, he turned to me. "Unfortunately, we have to head back now." I groaned, having not found anything to help Mitch, just details explaining his transformation and what it would do to him. "Fortunately," he continued, "the nullification isn't the only thing we're leaving with." He closed the gap between us and held out his journal, open to the page he had been taking notes on.

After scanning it, my head snapped up. "This means—"

He nodded. "Mitch will accompany your mother on her trip back to Gaia."

THIRTY-NINE
Empty

Nikylo

A knock woke me from where I slept in the armchair. I blinked away the grogginess, placing the book I had fallen asleep reading on the table before heading to the door.

As soon as it swung open, Sami rushed past me, frantic and wild-eyed.

"Sami, it's the middle of the night. What are you doing here?" I closed the door and turned to see him leaving tracks in the carpet as he paced.

He worried his bottom lip. "We need to leave."

I furrowed my brow at him. "What do you mean, leave? And who is we?"

"You, me, Ti, and Meg. We have to leave Niccodra."

"Is this about the plague?"

"What?" He stopped pacing and stared at me. "No, this is about the curse."

"Mitera, save me," I mumbled, pinching the bridge of my nose. I didn't have time for this. "Let me guess—you finally figured it out? The secret that no one else could uncover in the last *millennia?*"

"This isn't a joke, Niko!" he shouted. "I told you once before, and I'll say it again—this curse hasn't always been a part of us. *Someone* created it —decided we couldn't be with them."

"You're grasping at straws here, Sami. The curse has always existed."

My exasperation was coming in strong. This wasn't the first time we'd had this argument, and I'm sure it wouldn't be the last. He was shaking his head, so I pressed on. "What? You think that if you dig deep enough, you'll uncover some hidden secret—some loophole? *There isn't one.* So stop searching!"

"How do you know that?" he shouted, throwing his hands up. "Have you ever even questioned it? Ever tried to fight it?" He stepped nose to nose with me as he spat, "Or have you just accepted the chains that Father has placed around your neck? Accepted your role as the good little *Prince?*"

I shoved him hard. "You think I haven't questioned it? Think I don't hate it as much as you do?" I jabbed my finger into his chest. "You think I don't watch how you are with Meg and wonder why the hell you two can't be together?" They were playing with fire, sneaking around with stolen moments and spending more time than usual together, but I never grew tired of watching them. The way Sami looked at Meg, or how he understood even her slightest movements and facial expressions. Their defiance of the curse, while futile, was also admirable. I even envied how Meg, my Doulos, stood by Sami despite the danger it put them in. I sighed. "But Sami, wishing the curse wasn't real won't make it go away. It's in our blood. You can't outrun it, and you sure as hell can't break it.

He stepped back. "And you're just fine with that? With letting some ancient, twisted magic control our lives?" His resigned tone was worse than yelling, but I could see it in his eyes—not giving up on the curse, but on me.

"Of course I'm not okay with it, Sami! But I know better than to throw myself against something immovable and pretend that I'll be the one to break it."

"Fine. Stay here and rot. Live under a curse you refuse to fight. But don't expect me to do the same." He pushed past me, reaching my door faster than I expected.

"Sami, please don't do this!" I shouted, reaching for his elbow.

He ripped it from my grasp and spun around to face me. "I'd rather burn trying to break free than live in a prison I never questioned." He turned and wrenched the door open to find Tietra there, hand raised to knock. The anger in his voice shifted to concern. "Tietra, what are you doing here? I told you to stay with Meg."

The tears welling in her eyes had Valisdrako completely invading my mind. He'd been fast asleep, but the sense of danger skyrocketed at Meg's absence, pulling him from his slumber. *Megdaline is not well*, his sleepy voice said.

Even if he hadn't said that, I would have known. Tietra never cried.

"Where is she?" I growled.

Her lip quivered as she whispered, "Your father summoned her."

"Shit." Sami and I said simultaneously. "Did he give reason?" Sami asked, appearing ready to rush out the door.

He does not need reason. He is King. Validrako growled, now fully awake.

Tietra shook her head and extended her hand. "He's summoned all of us."

The small piece of paper she held was a bit crumpled, but I could make out the official summons. If we didn't respond within the next minute, the castle would haul us there by force.

I turned to Sami, placing my hands on either side of his face because I knew he was about to spiral if he didn't have an anchor. "Stay with me, Sami. What do you feel?" I felt his fingers sink into my tunic and watched as he opened his eyes to focus on various things around the room before falling back to me. "We don't know what this is—"

"Yes. We do." Sami inhaled sharply, releasing the breath slowly. "He knows. Somehow, he found out we were leaving. He *knows*."

"Sami, I need you to stay with me." Our father had clearly been watching Sami. I knew he would notice how often Sami and Meg were together—mainly because she wasn't his bonded. I just didn't think he would act on it. "Listen, we have about thirty seconds before we must be in the throne room. You know what happens if we're not." His eyes were still unfocused, and I could feel him on the brink of an attack. "Think of Meg. She needs you right now."

He clenched his jaw and nodded. I reached for Tietra's hand. She placed the one with the summons in mine, and I skithed us to where the paper led.

When we stepped into the throne room, it was eerily quiet. The heavy silence was suffocating—like the calm before a storm.

Father stood with his back to us, hands clasped behind him, gazing at the floor-to-ceiling windows and taking in the newly permanent scenery of the sunset on the horizon. He turned when he sensed our presence, slowly making his way to his throne. He snapped his fingers before sitting, and the doors opened to reveal two guards, Meg hanging loosely between them.

"Megi!" Sami shouted, dooming himself with that single cry. They dragged her to the steps of the dais and dropped her at my father's feet. If anyone should have expressed worry for her safety, it was me. She was my bonded—my Doulos. But I couldn't find the words to speak. Couldn't push past the fear that lodged itself in my throat the moment we entered the room. Meg lifted her chin defiantly despite the bruises marring her skin and her hands bound behind her back.

Guards seemed to materialize from thin air, restraining Sami while those who had brought Meg in positioned themselves behind Tietra and me.

Steady, Ti, I said, sensing her trembling next to me. *I'm right here.* I sent a gentle caress down her mind and felt her tension ease just a little.

Sami had his shield clamped tight against everyone, not wanting Father to see what he likely already knew. But that also meant I couldn't reach him. There was no way to calm him. He struggled against the guards, rage twisting his features as he stared down our Father.

Father had his fingers steepled against his temple, while his other hand rested on the armrest, fingers drumming. His gaze was fixed on Sami with a cold amusement that made my stomach churn.

"Tell me you weren't actually thinking of running away, Samdrien." His voice was deceptively calm, but the steel in his words made it clear —he was furious. Sami only held his gaze, matching his fury. Father straightened at Sami's silence, resting his elbows on his knees and letting his hands hang between them. "You would disgrace our bloodline by gambling with a curse?"

"Let her go." Sami's voice was rough, strained—barely containing his rage. "This is between you and me."

Father chuckled. "Oh, no, son. This is between all of us." His gaze briefly flicked to me before settling on Tietra. "You should have been more careful about whom you confided in."

I whipped my head toward Ti and saw a tear slip down her cheek. She wouldn't have betrayed Meg to anyone. She didn't talk to anyone except

Claude and Meg. Who could she have confided in that told Father?

He turned to Meg. "Tell me, girl. Did you really think this would end in your favor? That you could defy fate and find happiness with my son in another realm?"

Meg didn't respond. Didn't even flinch. She held his gaze, unwavering. *If only I had her confidence.*

"Pathetic." He stood up, stepping down from the dais one slow, deliberate step at a time, his dark gaze fixed on Sami. His boot steps echoed across the marble. "You were born into power, Samdrien. Born to rule. And you were willing to throw it all away for a female? A *Fae* female?" He clicked his tongue at Sami's answering scowl. "You, my *son*, should know that such...fusion is forbidden."

Sami roared, lunging against the guards' hold, but they wrenched him back. "I don't care about your *throne*," he spat. "I don't care about power. I only care about *her.*"

Father sighed, shaking his head. "And that is why you are unworthy of either." He lifted his hand, a dagger flashing in his grasp.

I tensed, a knot of dread tightening in my chest. *Speak, Nikylo,* Valisdrako commanded, *or forever wish you had.* But the only words I could muster were, "Father, please—"

"You allowed this to happen!" he roared, aiming the dagger at me. "You will *watch.*" My stomach dropped as he turned to where Meg knelt before his throne.

My ears were ringing, drowning out all other sounds in the room. My body went completely numb, unable to move in any direction.

Everything happened in slow motion.

Father stepped up behind Meg, grabbing a fistful of her hair. He yanked her head back, exposing her neck. She gazed at the ceiling, silent tears streaming down her face. Her lips formed what I recognized as "I love you," as her eyes found Sami's. Those were her final words as Father drew the dagger across her throat and then plunged it into her heart, sealing her fate. Her blood spilled onto the dais, and her lifeless body followed as Father released his grip on her hair.

The world sped up as the dragon within me roared, and Sami's screams filled my ears. Tears welled in my eyes at his raw sorrow. He struggled against the guards until Father waved a hand, releasing him.

He hurried to where Meg had fallen, scooping her into his arms. He cradled her head, brushing back her hair. "No, no, no… Megi, I'm so sorry. Please, Megi. Megi." He begged through his tears for her to come back to him, wishing for all of this to be a nightmare.

Father exhaled, slow and deliberate, wiping the blood from the dagger on a handkerchief he pulled from his tunic. He stepped around Sami, his gaze devoid of remorse, his voice almost…disappointed. "Look at you. Reduced to nothing over a Fae." He knelt beside Sami, head tilted and eyes glinting with pure cruelty. "I told you, boy. Love makes you weak." He reached out, almost mockingly, brushing a hand through Sami's hair as he had when we were young. "And now you will die weak."

"NO!" I yelled, lunging for the dais as the King thrust the dagger into Sami's chest and twisted. It was only then that I realized I was held back by the guards beside me. I expected Meg's death the moment we walked into the throne room, but Sami's? It never occurred to me that he would kill his own son.

My knees buckled, slamming hard onto the marble floor as the guards released me, and I crawled toward him. *"Sami!"* His gaze locked on mine, his lips moving, but I couldn't make out his final words as blood poured from his mouth and the life drained from his eyes.

Father yanked the dagger from the gaping hole in Sami's chest, swiping it once more across his kerchief as Sami's lifeless body bowed over Meg's.

"What have you done?" The words barely escaped my lips as I wrapped myself around Sami and Meg, as if I could shield them from any further harm—as if their lives hadn't already slipped away. Tears streamed down my cheeks as the weight of the loss settled deep into my bones.

Nikylo, you need to stand up, Valisdrako said, his voice far from its usual sharp tone. *This weakness is what just killed your brother. You must not show it.*

He's gone. They're both gone. I can't—

You can. And you will. Now stand. Valisdrako had never used his power on me. Not since we bonded nearly two centuries ago. But there was no mistaking it. I felt his magic wrap around me, forcing my muscles to obey his command. I wanted to fight it, to hold onto them until I woke up from this nightmare. But I knew it would be pointless. I seized control of my body, turning to face my father—no. The King. "You're a monster."

The King gave a dark chuckle, pushing the dagger's tip into his finger as his silver eyes met mine. "Oh, I'm not finished. This lesson will not be one you forget, son." I hadn't realized he had moved, but he now stood beside Tietra. Placing a hand on her shoulder, he turned her toward him. "Open, little traitor."

Tietra was trembling from head to toe, avoiding the King's gaze. *Tietra…* I reached for her, knowing that whatever he was about to do would not be pleasant. *Do you want me to make it go away?*

Niko, please. Her inner voice choked on the sobs that wracked her body.

I'll take care of you, I whispered.

"Open, before I lose patience."

Do it, Ti. I've got you.

As soon as she did, he lifted the dagger to her mouth. I couldn't bear to watch. I closed my eyes and reached into Tietra's mind, finding a place for us where pain didn't exist. Where she wouldn't feel the blade on her tongue. Where she wouldn't remember that her friends were dead on the dais steps. Where the monster who cut out her tongue couldn't touch her.

"Niko!"

I frowned at the sound of Tietra's voice. No, that wasn't right. She couldn't speak.

Niko! The female voice echoed again. Then, I felt a firm yet gentle shake from the hands on my shoulders. *Niko, wake up!*

My eyes snapped open to find Tietra hovering over me in the armchair. I must have fallen asleep when we returned from the Kyllindro. I sat up, placed the book I had been reading on the table, and shook my head, disoriented by the similarities between the nightmare and reality. Sweat dripped down my temple, and my training linens clung to my body.

Tietra stared at me, then said down the bond I'd created for us, *You were projecting.*

I shut my eyes and sighed. *I'm sorry, Ti.*

They're happening again, aren't they?

I could only nod. My hands flexed as I rubbed my knees, trying to steady myself and push the memories back where they belonged.

For the first decade after it happened, I relived those moments every night. As time passed, they became less frequent—less suffocating. But lately, they had been returning with full force, as if I were that younger version of myself, powerless as the people I loved were slaughtered.

Rayleigh is with Mari.

I blinked, only now realizing that my gaze had been scanning the room. *Why are you here?*

Libella sent for me. She said you might need me.

Of course. Libella probably sensed it.

Do you want to talk about it? Tietra asked, twidling her fingers.

I exhaled sharply. *What's there to talk about, Ti? You and I were both there.*

I know. Her throat bobbed as a single tear slipped down her cheek. *I miss them too, you know.*

The weight in my chest grew heavier. I stood, opening my arms for her. "Come here." She didn't hesitate, burying her face in my chest as I wrapped my arms around her. Her breath was shaky, but she didn't sob —she never did—and I felt the way she held it all in. How her fingers curled into my shirt as if it were the only thing keeping her steady.

After a long moment, she pulled back slightly to sign, *"You were loud."*

I sighed. "I know."

Her lips pressed into a thin line. *"I hate that you're going through this again."*

"I'll be fine," I murmured, though we both knew it was a lie. There was a reason behind the nightmare resurfacing: it reminded me of what would happen if I didn't follow orders. Drako had likely saved my life that day, pulling me from my sorrow to make me stand up to my father, even if it was just to call him a monster. He showed my father that I wasn't weak—wasn't disposable, both things he'd called Sami since that day. The thought sickened me.

But I knew that if I showed the same weaknesses with Rayleigh, he wouldn't hesitate to repeat history, especially now that he had another son ready to take his throne. One who inherited his desire for power and control.

Ti gave me a look but didn't argue. Instead, she signed, *"You should talk to someone about it."*

I let out a breath through my nose. "And who might that be?"

She signed without hesitation, *"Rayleigh."*

I huffed a quiet laugh. "Rayleigh has enough to deal with without taking on my nightmares."

Tietra searched my face. *"So do you."* I let out a slow breath, but before I could argue, she nudged me. *"Go bathe. You smell."*

I barked a laugh, flicking her nose. "Always so honest."

She gave me a mischievous smirk. *"Someone has to be."*

Without another word, she turned and left my room. If it hadn't been for her and Drako, I don't think I would have made it through the years that followed Sami's death.

Sighing, I dragged my hand down my face, hoping to erase any traces of the nightmare. Then it hit me... *Why didn't you wake me?*

Drako didn't answer immediately, but when he finally spoke, it sent chills down my spine. *You did not relive the nightmare alone, Niko.*

That rarely happened. Sharing a mind was one thing, but both of us asleep and experiencing the same nightmare? *It seems we both needed the reminder.*

Adjusting the sleeves of my tunic, I waited outside Mari's door. We were cutting it close on time, and I knew Father would notice if we weren't there for the announcement. I'd told Naila to meet me near the ballroom doors since she practically shoved me out of her room when I went to get a report. Apparently, she'd hardly gotten any sleep after her shift. She was crankier than Drako when I woke him from his slumber.

The door to Mari's room opened just enough to reveal Kendall standing there, a broad grin on her face. She wore a stunning black dress adorned with blue sequined accents. Mari truly had a talent for designing dresses. Kendall glanced back over her shoulder. "It's Nikylo," she said. Turning back to me, she lowered her voice, "Wait until you see."

"I've already seen the dress, Kendall." I'd imagined it on her several times since Mari showed me the design. Telling Rayleigh about it earlier was a moment I wouldn't soon forget. The way her breath caught when I touched her wrist and the warmth of her skin as I ran my fingers across her lower back. Being so close to her was intoxicating, and while I *was* testing her shields, I was also testing my self-control. "We need to leave, though. Can you please open the door?"

She raised her eyebrows as if I had missed something, then turned back to whoever was inside and asked, "Is she ready?"

"Ready." Rayleigh's soft voice came from inside. She sounded nervous for some reason, and suddenly, *I* felt the same.

Kendall stepped behind the door and pulled it open further to reveal the room. The foyer resembled mine, but it was much smaller, featuring just a bed for Kendall and a couch positioned against the window. Mari stood beside the bathroom door with a knowing grin. I took a moment to admire the dress worn by my highest-ranking soldier, as I was not accustomed to seeing her in anything other than training gear. It flowed to the floor, the color different at every angle, depending on how the light hit it. The low-cut front and sleeveless design shimmered against her olive skin. Her literal magic touch was evident in her work. Her dark hair cascaded in waves but was pinned back on one side with a shimmering pin resembling her dragon's wing. "You clean up well, Aidi."

"As do you, Lochi," she said, giving a slight bow of her head.

I stepped into her room, scanning for Rayleigh but not seeing her. "Where—?" But I was silenced by the swish of a dress coming from the bathing chamber and turned to see her emerging.

Time stopped.

There was no telling if I'd done it or if it was just in my head. But the moment my eyes landed on her, all sense of anything else in the room vanished.

There was only *her*.

I drank in the sight of her, my eyes roaming over her from head to toe, committing this moment to memory. I had been mistaken. She wasn't just ravishing. She was exquisite. A beauty crafted by Mitera herself and forgotten by time. No words could express what I saw in this female before me.

The blue satin skirt beneath the sheer black layer matched Drako so closely that even he rumbled his approval. The bodice hugged her just like I had told her it would; the black lace design had no fabric behind it, revealing the spot on her torso where her madí rested. The enchantment concealing the mark on Gaia was absent here, so even though I felt compelled to, I didn't have to run my fingers across the mark to make it visible. It was permanent now. The low-cut lace design dipped low on her chest and traveled out around her arms, just off her shoulder, with the lace extending down her arms in a loose sleeve. I knew the back fell low without seeing it, but I would be spinning her later to take in the entire dress.

Mari cleared her throat. "As you can see, her headache earlier was not *just* a headache."

I closed the distance between Rayleigh and me, continuing to ignore everything else in the room. A giggle escaped from Kendall as I walked past her. Rayleigh's breath caught when I took my final step, maintaining a small space between us but close enough to observe her new features. I lifted my hand but paused to ask, "May I?" When she nodded, I used a single finger to tilt her chin and slightly turn her face. Her cheekbones and jawline were fuller and more pronounced. Her curled hair, likely styled by Libella, was half pinned, cascading loosely around her face and arranged to accentuate her now pointed ears. I lifted my hand, running my finger along the new shape and her breath caught at my touch. When I lowered my hand, tilting her face back to me, her ocean blue eyes shone brighter than the last time I'd seen her.

"Say something," she whispered, her nerves were getting the best of her.

Slowly, I removed my finger from her chin and extended my hand to her. "We should go," I said, lowering my voice so only she could hear, "Before I forget why we can't stay."

Her cheeks flushed pink as she fought a smile. "And if I said I would rather stay?"

I took a deep breath, aware that I was about to ruin the moment. "Then I would have to remind you of the dance you promised your betrothed."

FORTY
Lose Control

Rayleigh

"Announcing Councilors Kaledra, Marta, Oliver, and Thomas."

Oliver descend the stairs, escorting Kaley while Tom accompanied Marta. As Oliver met my gaze on his way down, he offered a smile that was meant just for me, even though everyone could see it. I felt heat rush to my cheeks as I smiled back. He looked incredibly handsome in his chosen attire. His perfectly tailored tunic was a pale blue with billowy sleeves that tapered at the wrist, cuffed in silver. The detail of the charcoal gray vest stood out against his pale complexion, adding to the air of nobility he carried so effortlessly. The slim-fitting gray trousers accentuated his toned legs and ended at sleek knee-high boots.

He winked as they passed by, making their way to a raised dais next to the thrones, which remained empty.

Kendall had her arm linked with mine, giving a slight squeeze while her gaze was fixed on her twin across the room. Leigh stood by herself, watching the top of the stairs as if no one else in the room existed.

I placed my hand on Ken's and squeezed, momentarily pulling her attention. "It's going to work."

Tears welled in her eyes, but she nodded. "I know. It's just odd that she hasn't even acknowledged me."

"Knowing Talekor, he probably forbade it." I followed her gaze back to Leigh, whose eyes were still fixed on the entrance at the top of the stairs. Taking a quick look around, I asked, "Where's Mari?" Kendall had been escorted to the ball by Romeo, which she found utterly annoying because he wouldn't stop flirting with her. I thought it quite hilarious, having seen Romeo as a child in Nikylo's journals and knowing he'd been trying to woo females since he was young.

"She said she had duties to attend to for the first part of the ball." Hmm. Why hadn't she mentioned it while she was helping me into my dress? The stunning gown took long enough to get into; she had plenty of time…

"Announcing His Royal Highness, Prince Nikylo, and his betrothed —" my head snapped so quickly to the top of the stairs that my neck cracked, "—the esteemed Lady Nailaria, daughter of Kastiel." He was betrothed to Naila? Oh, everything made sense now. The first time I met her, and the subsequent times after, validated the subtle jabs and hostility. In Naila's mind, Nikylo was *hers*. And I was Nikylo's *property*.

"I was *not* expecting that," Ken whispered as Nikylo and Naila appeared at the top of the stairs. Her dress clung to her from her chest to her hips and then flared out into an A-line skirt. It looked like a dress far too modest for her—until she took a step. There was a slit that ran all the way up both legs, ending *above* her hip and leaving hardly anything to the imagination. Beautiful, but not something I would ever feel comfortable wearing.

"Me neither." I should have, though. I should have guessed there was some other reason he tolerated her presence the way he did. Although she never came around his chambers, despite her threats—only to escort me places Nikylo requested. Which made me wonder if there was something else he wasn't telling me about her. As they descended the stairs, his eyes locked on mine. The green held a hint of mischief, and I let down my shields enough to say, *That's something you could have told me.*

What's wrong, Sunshine? Jealous that someone else gets to be my bride?

I just feel bad she won't know the truth.

He raised an eyebrow as he walked past me. *Oh? And what's that?*

She may hold the title of your betrothed, but she doesn't hold your attention.

I could say the same about Oliver and you.

No, you can't. I paused long enough to let him ponder the words, then added with a smirk, *Oliver, while still someone new, has held my attention since we met.*

Not all of it, Nikylo murmured as he settled into the throne on the far right, with Naila standing beside him, his gaze never leaving mine. *I can guarantee he won't have any of your attention while I'm holding you during our dance later.*

I tilted my head, allowing my smirk to deepen. *You didn't ask me to save you a dance,* I teased. Then, before he could reply, I added, *And unfortunately for you, I'm all booked.*

The announcer called out the arrival of the King and Queen, diverting my attention from Nikylo. I put my shields back in place, blocking him—and hopefully everyone else—out. It might have been my imagination, but I felt something else settle over the glass dome— another layer of protection. I stole a glance back at Nikylo, who continued to watch me. He pursed his lips and gave a tight nod.

I knew he trusted my shields, but since they were still new to me, I appreciated that he continued protecting my mind from prying eyes.

The Queen sat two chairs away from Nikylo, with the King occupying the empty seat between them. He didn't release her hand, instead resting it on the armrest between the thrones. For the briefest moment, his gaze met mine. There was a softness there, reminiscent of the first day I encountered him, but it was difficult to think of him as anything other than the cruel King who killed anyone beneath him for the slightest disobedience.

"Presenting His Royal Highness," the announcer called out, capturing the full attention of the ballroom. "Prince Talekor." The doors opened to reveal the prince himself, his dark brown eyes lacking any honey coloring as he surveyed the crowd. Unlike the others who entered, he remained at the top of the stairs. A Fae stepped up beside him, his pointed ears identifying him—as they also identified me.

My hand traveled up to one of my exposed ears, feeling the point it now came to. After my bath earlier, I had to do a double take when I saw my reflection. The pointed ears were one thing, but it felt as if my entire facial structure had changed. It was like the bath had taken years off my life, making me feel suddenly fully grown and developed. My body had changed too—not drastically, but enough that Mari had to adjust my dress slightly when I put it on. It was strange; it felt like I was in a whole new body, while the one I'd had before seemed all wrong. Now, everything just felt so right. I was terrified of what other aspects might have changed with my full Fae features now evident.

Talekor placed his hand on a plate that the Fae held out—similar to the one Nikylo and I had used to enter the Kyllindro. The Fae ran the disc down the stairs and presented it to the King, who stood right in front of his throne. A furrow in his brow lingered for only a moment as he took in what the plate revealed.

"In my hand, I hold proof of Talekor's power," the King declared, his voice resonating through the ballroom. Many people were present, much like at the dinner—a mix of Fae and Drakalasson alike, all dressed in splendid outfits, with every eye on the King. "Power has been passed down through generations, sometimes bestowing two powers and, rarely, three. In tonight's instance, it seems my third son takes after my second, harnessing the strength of three bloodlines." Cheers erupted in the hall, reflecting the excitement of the King's announcement. Three sons… That's *right*. Sami. The journals had shown him to me, but why had I never met him? Where was he now? With a proud smile, the King raised his hand for silence. The room quieted immediately as he lifted the disc. "His first power, unsurprisingly, as both his mother and I possess it, comes from the Lunnox line." The cheers were slightly quieter, but the excitement remained. "His other two powers come from my queen's lineage," he said, smiling at Queen Kahlea. Her face lit up at his announcement, and she leaned forward in her seat in anticipation. "Fyxenal and Ravault."

When the final two powers were revealed, I felt a gentle but urgent caress on my temple and turned to Nikylo. Our eyes met, and his voice filled my mind as soon as I opened the door that only he could access. *Do not, under any circumstances, let him touch you.*

You already told me that!

Yes, but he has Fyxenal powers, just like Aaidan. When I gave him a puzzled look from across the room, he said, *He's a tracker, Sunshine. If he touches you, he could mark you.*

Dread coursed through my body. *But he touched my face—*

I know. I'm letting Theo know now. He can shield you.

I thought you were shielding me.

Only your mind. I can't— his voice *cracked*. If his words hadn't been enough, the fear in his eyes would have pushed me over the edge. *I can't fully shield you. Not like Theo can.*

I scanned the room for that familiar tan beanie, then realized he probably wouldn't wear one to a ball. The crowd parted on my left, and his eyes instantly met mine. He winked, pausing with a few people still between us. I felt it then—power gliding along my skin as what I assumed was a shield locked into place around me. It formed to my body, but I could still feel Kendall's touch on my arm as she held me. I still felt the fabric of the dress hugging my body. It didn't dull my senses, but I could tell it would prevent magic from touching me.

Do not leave his sight tonight, Nikylo said, snagging my attention once more.

Nodding, I turned back to see the King displaying the disc of powers. *What were his other two powers?* I asked, trying to recall all the powers.

Ravault grants the ability to skith and manipulate time. Lunnox is mind manipulation.

Great. Talekor possessed three of the powers that had given me the most trouble since I found out about magic…

The King shared the tale of Talekor's dragon and how he had chosen another. Apparently, this was a rare occurrence, as the crowd gasped in shock and awe while the King recounted the story.

Ken squeezed my arm, reminding me of her presence. "Why *did* he challenge Nikylo? Surely there were other, stronger dragons?"

"He's only ever wanted one thing: me." The truth of that was becoming harder to ignore. "And he'll do everything he can to get what he wants."

He won't win, Nikylo reminded me. I'd apparently left the door open for him, but I didn't mind his presence.

I wanted to challenge that statement but decided that believing in it might help make it true. *He won't win,* I agreed.

Talekor descended the steps, heading toward what I assumed was the dance floor instead of the dais. As he passed Leighton, he extended a hand to her, and she effortlessly matched his stride as she joined him on the dance floor. Watching her behave like an obedient dog made me nauseous.

The rest of the royalty and councilors joined him, the latter pairing off with one another. As they spun around the dance floor, I wondered if my two left feet would cause a problem now that my full Fae powers had emerged. Clumsiness was part of being a youngling, but based on everything I had learned about Fae, I was fully grown, with all my powers accessible and my pointed ears developing. Did that mean I could finally bid farewell to my clumsiness?

"Oliver looks pretty handsome tonight, doesn't he?" Kendall said, nudging me.

I tried to hide my smirk. "He does."

"Oh, come on, Ray. You're betrothed. You don't have to hide your attraction to him."

"I'm not," I said, elbowing her. "I just… there's more to consider."

"You mean there's another *man* to consider."

I turned my head slowly, eyes wide, lips parted in an exaggerated look of betrayal. "Excuse you?"

Ken pursed her lips. "You can't tell me there's nothing between you and Nikylo. Not with what I saw earlier."

I couldn't decide if I wanted to run away from the embarrassment or fight for my dignity—not that I had much left.

Before I could decide, Oliver and Tom strode across the floor toward Ken and me. Oliver stopped a step away from me, bowing and extending his hand. I took a deep breath and gently placed my hand in his. Kendall shot me a wild grin before doing the same with Tom, and they swept us onto the dance floor.

Oliver paraded me around in a circle before pulling me close. He guided my hand to his shoulder, grasping the other before placing his free hand on my waist. I had never learned ballroom dance and suddenly felt very aware of that fact. Oliver leaned in slightly, saying, "Let your magic find mine, and it will show you what to do."

"My magic knows how to dance, but I don't?" Oliver simply smiled. The idea seemed absurd, but I allowed myself to grasp the thread of white, and his magic immediately tangled with it. A small gasp escaped my lips as a sense of certainty settled into my body, and Oliver spun me across the dance floor.

"Mari has truly outdone herself," Oliver whispered as he held me in his arms, guiding me around the floor as if we were floating on air—which we very well could have been. "She understood her canvas perfectly."

I did my best to hide how those words affected me, but I realized I had no reason to and smiled. "Is that the line you use on all the pretty girls?"

"Oh, yes. I have said that to every female who captures my attention." He smirked, his icy blue eyes glimmering.

The spot in my chest stayed quiet, so I asked, "And how many have captured your attention?"

"Tonight? Or in my lifetime?" He seized my moment of hesitation to spin me around before drawing me back to him. I swear we were closer this time, and a ripple of excitement rushed through me.

Catching my breath, I pondered his question. As much as I wanted to hear him say it was only me, I replied, "Your lifetime."

This time, he *did* pull me closer, his hand gliding slowly from my waist to rest on my bare lower back. He closed the remaining distance between us, his whisper brushing my ear as he said, "Only one."

The órkomatos had to be faulty. There was no way that could be true. Yet, when I pulled back to meet Oliver's gaze, there was nothing but honesty shining in his eyes. "You've seriously never dated anyone? In your three hundred years?"

He shrugged. "Never anything serious. There was a time when I embraced the livelihood of the Fae around me and gave in to the whims life had to offer. But when I stepped back and considered the person I truly wanted by my side, I became more careful about whom I shared those intimate parts of myself with. Shifting my priorities helped me realize that I would rather be alone than with the wrong person."

"And then you were betrothed to someone you didn't know."

He didn't answer right away, holding my gaze as we glided around the floor in time with the music. He took a deep breath and exhaled slowly, the feel of it brushing against my exposed collarbone. "Then I offered myself in betrothal to you, yes."

"Why?" My voice had lost all its strength from the way he looked at me—held me. As if I were truly the only person who had ever captured his attention. I cleared my throat. "Why is this betrothal so important?"

Oliver furrowed his brows. "To be completely honest with you, the details regarding the importance and the agreement are a bit unclear."

Surprised by his response, I waited as he struggled to find the answer to my question, "What do you mean?"

He met my gaze again. "Nikylo and I briefly discussed this last night. It seems the discussion regarding my agreement with your parents is somewhat muddied."

Eyeing him, I asked, "What does that even mean? Muddied how?"

He sighed. "Niko and I believe—"

"May I cut in?" came a voice I did not want to hear, let alone dance with its owner.

But who could refuse the King?

"Absolutely, Your Majesty," I replied, nodding in gratitude toward Oliver. He would fill me in on the rest of that story later. For now, I needed to concentrate on keeping my shields in place and not disrespecting the King. One wrong move, and I'd be done for.

Oliver bowed to the King and then to me as he released me and stepped aside. I instantly missed the warmth he'd brought with his presence and the sense of comfort he had given me. When his magic disentangled from mine, it felt like I'd been hollowed out. I turned back to the King and placed my hand in his outstretched one.

Are you there? I asked, already knowing the answer but wanting to make sure Nikylo knew who had asked me to dance.

Nikylo replied instantly, as if he had never left. *For you? Always.*

The King's grip was firm but not painful as he lifted my hand to guide me onto the dance floor. It was too firm to be casual, too steady to be anything but controlled. My pulse throbbed in my ears, but I forced myself to keep my expression neutral.

"You have my sons in quite the quarrel for your attention, Rayleigh." His voice was smooth, almost amused, as he guided our movements around the floor. "It appears I can now add a certain Annysian to that list as well."

I swallowed hard, keeping my tone even. "I wasn't aware those vying for my attention were under the watchful eye of royalty, Your Highness."

His lips twitched, but his eyes held something sharper. "It's a dangerous thing to draw the eye of a king." His fingers flexed over mine. "More so when it isn't truly his own."

A chill ran down my spine at his cryptic words. "I don't—" I hesitated. "I don't know what that means," I whispered.

He exhaled deeply, his gaze flicking past me as he surveyed the room. "For centuries, I've played the role assigned to me, whether I wanted to or not." When I simply stared at him, his voice dropped to just above a whisper. "Not all curses are what they seem."

I stiffened, my stomach in knots. None of what he said made sense. It felt like trying to solve a puzzle with several missing pieces. Maybe someone else would understand him. *Are you hearing this?*

Yes, but I have no idea what he's talking about.

Mirroring the King's tone, I asked, "Why are you telling me this?" *And being so cryptic about it?* I didn't add.

He worked his jaw, a flicker of frustration crossing his face. It seemed he wanted to say more—needed to say more. But then, just as quickly as it had appeared, his expression softened. The sharp glint in his eyes dimmed, and his grip relaxed. "You should enjoy the ball, Rayleigh," he said, his voice lighter now—easier.

The music swelled, and he released me as the dance concluded. I stepped back quickly, my heart racing, but the King had already turned away, disappearing into the crowd.

I stood there, sifting through everything he had just said, an uneasy feeling crawling along my skin.

A hand landed on my shoulder, making me jump. "Everything alright, dearie?" Theo extended his hand to me at the start of the next song.

"I don't know." My legs were shaking, and I wasn't sure I could handle another dance with these thoughts rolling through my head.

Dance with him. Nikylo said. *You're drawing attention.*

I placed my trembling hand in Theo's and let him lead, my nervousness fading with his confidence on the dance floor. After allowing the silence between us to linger for half a song, I caught Theo's gaze. "How long have you known the King?"

"I have held the highest rank in his Kidemos since the very beginning of his reign." The casual tone was laced with apprehension. "As one might expect, a friendship developed over time, and with it came the title of Dikitís."

"Dikitís?"

"Oh, I suppose 'captain' is the closest equivalent. In short, I oversaw the Kidemos—led them, managed them, ensured they didn't turn into an absolute disaster. That sort of thing." He smiled

Realizing what that meant, I stared at Theo in awe. "You were the *Captain of the Guard?*" He nodded and gave me a wicked smirk. It shouldn't have surprised me; he outranked everyone. But being the Dikitís would have meant he had to protect the King at all costs. And Theo was part of *my* Omada. I narrowed my eyes. "What happened?"

His brown eyes darkened in a way I never thought Theo's could. "Over time, Gustav made choices—decisions that, despite my best efforts, I simply could not support. Wholeheartedly disagreed with them, actually. And so, I found myself at a crossroads. I could not, in good conscience, continue to stand by his side. I remained within the Kidemos, yes, but I stepped down from my position and, in doing so, severed our friendship."

"Just like that?"

"Just like that." He shifted his gaze from mine to glance over my shoulder briefly. "Nikylo approaches. Our conversation was muffled, but I cannot do the same for yours. It will seem too suspicious."

I nodded, and he spun me out of his grip right into Nikylo's arms. My hands came up to stop myself, landing flat against his firm chest, while his hands found my hips, warmth seeping through the lace fabric. His heart raced beneath my fingers, mine matching the quick tempo. I shifted my gaze from my hands to his face and felt my lips part as I took him in. My vision *must* have been enhanced with my other features because, damn him, he was even more gorgeous than I remembered.

His green eyes scanned my face as they had earlier, absorbing all the changes. I shamelessly did the same, committing every angle and line to memory, noting where his dimples appeared when he smiled and how his eyes crinkled *only* when he smiled at me.

"Where is your betrothed?" I asked. The teasing tone I meant to add lost its strength when I noticed the way he looked at me.

"Following orders," he said, his eyes scanning mine. *Relieving Mari from guard duty. Naila would much rather be wearing leathers.*

I couldn't decide if I was surprised by that or not. Nikylo was still staring at me, neither of us moving. "We should dance," I breathed, leaning into the warmth radiating from him, "or people will wonder why we're just standing in the middle of the dance floor."

I just need a moment. The world seemed to halt as he reached up and brushed a strand of hair from my face, the trail of his fingers stealing the oxygen from my lungs. His eyes were fixed on mine, the green pulsing with that emotion I couldn't quite place. I had only caught it briefly in the past, but it didn't happen often enough for me to know what it was.

People are staring. Or at least it felt that way, but I couldn't tear my gaze away from his to confirm.

No, they're just frozen, he said casually, his hand sliding down to my bare shoulder, brushing the hair away that covered it. The cool air was quickly replaced by the warmth of his skin as he traced the lace sleeve all the way to my fingertips. When he reached them, he gently gripped my fingers between his own and slowly lifted my hand to his dipped chin. My breath caught as his lips brushed against my knuckles, the softness and warmth igniting fireflies within me. *Someone will notice if I don't release them soon, though. So I cannot take the time I wish I could to admire you tonight.*

Wait, did he just say he froze the entire ballroom of attendees? His words barely registered as I became lost in the sensation of his wandering touch, mesmerized by the trail of warmth it left behind. He finally placed my hand on his shoulder and reached for the other, intertwining his fingers with mine, sending another wave of that blissful feeling through my body. His other hand found its place beneath my shoulder blade as he pulled me closer.

The world exploded with sound around us, the music continuing with a slow-paced song while the crowd adjusted their dancing to match the rhythm. How had I not noticed that the entire crowd had gone silent? Nikylo was becoming an increasingly bad influence on me. He distracted me from the world to the point that I didn't even realize it had stopped. We were toeing a dangerous line.

Nikylo's gaze wandered over my face again, as if trying to memorize every detail, his fingers tightening slightly around mine as we moved. "Stopping time was probably not the best idea, but seeing you in this dress has robbed my mind of all sensible thoughts," he murmured, holding my gaze.

Heat crept up my neck, but I smirked, allowing it to reach my eyes. "That sounds like a *you* problem."

His lips quirked, eyes glinting. "Oh, it is. A very persistent, very *distracting* problem." He spun me around, catching me off guard but making it seem effortless. When he pulled me back to him again, there was no space between us. His breath hit my lips as his hand settled on the part of my back that was completely exposed to him—just like he said it would be. His fingers traced the outline of the lace that formed the bodice of the dress, and he let out a shaky breath. "The worst part is, I can't find it in me to look for a cure."

Not sure how to respond, I lowered my gaze to his chest, taking in the intricate details of the jacket he wore while trying to fight the urge to tell him what I wanted. He spun us around as I memorized the swirling patterns of black woven through the blue satin of his tunic. He definitely looked like a prince in this outfit, just as he had the other night at Talekor's dinner. The King's words echoed in my mind, and I let out a small laugh.

"What?" Nikylo asked.

"Your father told me he saw how the three of you fought for my attention." I glanced up at Nikylo through my lashes and said, "I find it amusing that I've not only caught the attention of one prince, but two— and a Councilor." With a mischievous smirk, I scanned the room to see if I could spot the latter. Sure enough, Oliver sat in his chair among the Councilors, seemingly conversing with Kaley, but the way his hands were clasped in front of him suggested otherwise. His white knuckles indicated he knew exactly what was happening on the dance floor.

I swallowed the rising guilt. It was getting harder to dismiss flirting with Nikylo as just a distraction.

Nikylo's lips grazed my ear as he said, "If I were a better man, I would step aside and let Oliver have the chance at love he deserves." My gaze shot to his at the confession, the words settling deep within me as his piercing green eyes bore into mine from inches away. That gaze softened, and for a long heartbeat, he held my stare. When he spoke again, his voice was low and uncharacteristically raw. "And yet…I can't seem to walk away."

"Oh, but you will be," a familiar voice interrupted. Nikylo stiffened under my hands. I turned my head sharply to where Talekor stood, a wild grin aimed at Nikylo. "Walking away, that is." His brown eyes—so dark they looked black—locked onto mine. "It's my turn for a dance."

FORTY-ONE
Evil Is My Middle Name

Taking a deep breath, I nodded to Talekor but said to Nikylo, *I know you told me not to let him touch me, but I need to do this.* I stepped back from his hold on me and gave a small curtsy. "Thank you for the dance, Nikylo."

You cannot be serious. Even with those words, he took a brief bow. "The pleasure was all mine."

"I'm sure it was," Talekor scoffed.

Please trust me. I glanced behind Nikylo and saw Theo positioned near the edge of the dance floor with Libella, moving to the music. He didn't look at me but nodded, telling me everything was in place. His shields still thrummed around me, so I found Nikylo's gaze again and said, *Theo has me. Find Mari. She might need your help.*

I didn't give Nikylo a second glance. Instead, I extended my hand to Talekor, who took it eagerly and pulled me close. I had forgotten what it felt like to have his arms around me. Why did I ever enjoy this? It felt icky and gross as his greedy hands held me the way he wanted: too close for comfort.

Block me out until he releases you. The second his presence left my mind, I slammed the oak door, locking it securely.

"Tell me, girlie," Talekor sneered. "What will it take for you to release yourself from Nikylo's bond?"

"I would rather try stabbing you again," I said with a false sweetness. "Maybe this time it'll stick." I smiled innocently.

"Oh, you'll never get that opportunity again. I'm more powerful than you now."

"Are you?" I asked, prompting my own spin to scan the edge of the ballroom. I spotted exactly what I was looking for: two heads disappearing through a side door, one with long reddish-blonde hair and the other with dark brown hair pinned back with an iridescent wing.

"Definitely," he said, pulling me back to him possessively. I wanted to squirm out of his arms, but I had to give Mari time. That's all she needed. And this was my role in the plan.

"I defeated Nikylo no problem on the mat, and he's a top-ranked warrior." I leaned in, lowering my voice. "Who's to say I can't do the same to you?"

He grinned. "Always so sure of yourself." This time, he spun me, but instead of letting me go, he held both of my hands and spun me until my back was against his front, pinning my arms across my body. "Tell me, which of your friends should I threaten to make you do as I say?"

The way his breath grazed my ear made me arch away from him. "You won't hurt anyone."

"Your confidence in that statement is misguided." He released one of my hands to splay his on my abdomen and drew me closer to him, eliminating the space I'd tried to create between us. "I've already hurt people to get what I want. Your friends won't be any different."

Every inch of my body screamed to get as far away from him as possible. "They were your friends too," I spat, resisting the urge to throw my head back into his face.

"No," he whispered, his voice darkening. "That weakling of a dragon was the friend you knew." Talekor spun me back to face him so quickly that I lost my sense of direction. His hand gripped my hip possessively, leaving no space between us. "He insisted on taking the reins some days, so I let him, too tired to think about playing nice. Unfortunately, he became attached to you. To the friendships he made."

"What?" I recoiled at his harsh words, already aware of this from Lukas during the ceremony, but playing along was what mattered. He didn't know I'd spoken to Lukas. "You mean to tell me that the friend I thought I had in you... that was *your dragon*? All this time?"

"Not the whole time. I had to pretend for most of it—to get information from you, to plant seeds of doubt. But the damn dragon never shut up about the Nerf battles and the courtyard walks." The annoyance in his voice was unmistakable. "Hell, he was the one who helped you through your panic attacks. All I wanted to do was shake you like a ragdoll until you snapped out of it."

I shivered at the thought of Kaleb doing something like that. Or should I call him Lukas now? Who knows if I would ever see the dragon again? I needed to thank him properly for everything he'd done for me.

"But I suppose it worked out in my favor," Talekor continued, monologuing as I hoped he would if given the chance. "His insistence on helping you made you dependent on me." His jaw tightened. "That is, until Nikylo showed up," he growled.

"I didn't even like him," I scoffed. Why did it seem like Talekor was jealous of Nikylo? He only wanted me for my power.

"No, but I knew that, given time, he would win you over—just like he's doing now." I tried not to let my concern show, but if Talekor and the King could both see it… We had to be more careful. "I knew if I didn't make a move, your focus would shift, especially with the magic you had yet to learn."

I narrowed my eyes. "What do you mean, 'make a move?'"

"A series of moves, really. First, it was the Prom, which I'm still sad we missed." He stuck out his bottom lip in a mock pout. "It would've been fun to make a spectacle of that instead of being kidnapped from that damn house." He rolled his eyes, still leading us around the floor. "Then it was picking you up from the hospital, leading Adarachi to you without him knowing who I was… you know, the usual undercover work." He shrugged. "The real kicker, though—and daresay my most necessary move—was the first day Nikylo brought me to the Dengalow."

I'd forgotten just how deep this betrayal went. Every moment of our relationship was fake—all of it. None of what he felt was real, even if it was for me. "Ah, the day you two were at each other's throats," I said, trying to make him think I wanted to hear his version. In truth, all I really wanted was to walk away from this conversation and never listen to another word he said. "Yes, what *did* happen between you two in the car? You acted like a lovesick puppy the next day." I batted my eyelashes at him and might have regretted it when he squeezed my hip hard enough to leave a bruise, but I didn't even flinch. *Don't let them see.*

"That's because I had to play the part," he said through clenched teeth. Then he seemed to remember where we were and offered me a tight smile. "I let Lukas handle all the 'I'm worried about my best friend' shit at the house, but in the car? I had to show my brother just how much Kaleb meant to you." Hearing him refer to himself in the third person was unsettling. "Surprisingly, he didn't start by mocking me, instead telling me the first kiss is always the most awkward." Nikylo had given Kaleb advice? "But then I started rambling about how I didn't want to ruin our friendship and whether I'd made a mistake by kissing you, and he immediately got annoyed. I couldn't let him think it was one-sided, though. So I told him you were the one who made the first move."

My lips parted in shock, but I quickly masked it with a small cough. "I mean, technically, I did." I shrugged, remembering the moment on that piano bench with disgust rather than the happiness it once brought me.

Talekor ground his jaw. "Stop interrupting my story." His eyes flashed a hue I almost missed, but I knew the yellow wasn't just my imagination. "Anyway. That had Nikylo scoffing. He didn't believe for a second that you made the first move. But then I launched into a rant about our friendship, how much you counted on me, how I was there when your dad died, and for your sister, and then when your brother was hit by a car." He grinned, his eyes taking on a manic look. "I saw him process every word I said, jaw tightening with each one. Because he knew you'd never leave me behind. Knew you would fight to keep me around. But then his jaw relaxed, and his face softened as he turned and gave me this wicked grin," Talekor's voice turned dark, "and said, 'Sounds to me like you're just trying to convince yourself how much you mean to her.'"

I couldn't stop the laugh that burst out of me. I reeled it back in as much as I could but smiled brightly as I said, "No wonder you were distraught."

"This is no laughing—" His growl cut off, stopping us mid-dance, and his head snapped toward the door Leigh and Mari had gone through. Then, slowly, his gaze found mine again. "What did you do?" Lethal—that was the only word to describe the tone of his voice.

My smile was gone, replaced with a blank expression. "I don't know what you're talking about."

"Bullshit." His head whipped toward the door again, and suddenly I found myself being dragged through the crowd. Dread filled my stomach as the crowd parted for us without question. Had I given Mari enough time? Did it work? How did Talekor know about it? As we approached the door, I prayed they hadn't been reckless enough to stay right outside the ballroom. I glanced back to see Theo following us through the crowd at a safe distance. I felt his shields still fully intact around me, but if Talekor pulled me too far out of his sight, I'd lose that protection. I clung to Theo's magic, hoping it would help somehow.

Talekor kicked the door open, and I let out the breath I had been holding when only an empty hallway was revealed. The doors to the ballroom closed behind us, and Talekor resumed his search. Thinking he was distracted enough, I cracked open Nikylo's door and asked down the bond, *What happened?*

Silence. *Shit.* Trying not to let it worry me, I slammed the door shut again, afraid that Talekor might somehow find a way through it.

He was still dragging me down the hall at a pace I could barely keep up with without running. He stopped at a crossroads, glancing both ways before turning back to me. He released me, both hands flying to his head as he pulled his hair and screamed in rage, his eyes locked on mine. "What is she *doing?*" he roared.

"I don't know!" I shouted back.

The next thing I knew, my face slammed against the wall. The rough surface of the stones pressed into my cheek, and I felt a warm liquid trickling down my face. Talekor had one arm pinned behind my back and the other above my head. His body pressed against mine, making it impossible for me to move. "If you don't tell me what's going on right now," his mouth was right next to my ear, his hot breath raking over my face like coals, "someone is going to get hurt." He pushed me further into the wall, pain shooting up my arm as he twisted it further behind my back. "And it won't be you, girlie."

"I—I don't know," I forced out, trying to catch my breath as my lungs struggled to expand fully. But then I laughed, realizing that whatever Mari was doing *was working.* "Oh, I hope you lose her—"

The words barely escaped my lips before I was spun around. He slammed me against the wall again; this time, my head cracked against the stone, and I let out a grunt—the only sign of pain I'd show him. His hand was around my neck, squeezing tight enough to show his control but not cutting off my air supply. His eyes searched mine, and I could see flecks of black in the brown of his eyes this close. Then they widened as he breathed, "She's trying to take her from me." I didn't need to answer for him to know. His head slowly tilted to the side as his thumb moved from my neck to the hollow spot beneath my jaw, pressing until my chin lifted to look straight up at him.

I could have kneed him in the groin or disabled him somehow, but Mari needed more time. My dome was still in place, so he couldn't get into my head. I still felt the thrum of a shield surrounding me, so I wasn't in danger there either. I could keep him here, if only for a little longer.

A smile spread across Talekor's face. One filled with malice and greed as he leaned in closer, his hot breath making me squirm. "She won't win." The confidence in that statement drained the blood from my face. "I told you, having one of you means I have all of you." His finger traced down my face as it had in Nikylo's chambers, but this time, I felt nothing. Anger flashed in his eyes. "A Fyxenal is shielding you. Who?" When I met his furious gaze with one of my own, he tightened his grip on my neck, not completely cutting off my air supply—not yet. "That's alright. It can't really stop me, anyway. Wanna know why?" I felt the power of Theo's shield shudder as Talekor leaned in to whisper in my ear. "Because I have the power to break it."

The shield around me shattered, and I let out a piercing scream, flinging open the door in my mind to Nikylo and screaming his name.

Talekor let out a sinister laugh. "No one can hear you scream."

Shit. How had he learned so fast? I'd barely figured out my powers after a few days. He *just* got his.

"Now, where was I?" He lifted his finger to my cheek again but hesitated. His eyes darted from mine to his finger, his brow furrowing. His hand shook as he stared at it. "What the—?"

"I would think twice before laying a single finger on what is not yours." The cool voice seemed to come from nowhere and everywhere all at once.

Talekor still had a grip on my throat, squeezing tighter and causing my vision to fade, preventing me from searching for the source. But his head whipped back and forth, searching for something I knew he wouldn't find.

Because I felt it then—the breeze wrapping around my ankles.

"You would do well to release her, young prince," the invisible voice continued. "Or you might find it suddenly difficult to breathe."

Talekor growled, his fingers digging into the hollow of my jaw, finally cutting off my air supply. "Show your—

The hand was ripped from my throat, and a scream that wasn't mine filled the hall. I dropped to the ground, landing on my hands and knees, gasping for precious air. A thud echoed nearby, cutting off the scream. I glanced up to find Talekor pinned to the wall—ten feet off the ground. He was grasping for purchase on the air that held him in place. His face was turning purple, a mix of rage and the inability to draw in oxygen. His gaze was fixed on the person beside me.

A hand appeared, and I lifted mine to fit into Oliver's, allowing him to help me stand. "Are you alright, love?"

I nodded, my eyes fixed on the spot where Talekor was struggling against Oliver's winds. "You were almost late," I remarked as if the whole thing had been planned.

"You seemed to have it under control." I turned to find his icy blue eyes fixed on me, with a slight crinkle in them. "I did not want to overstep."

Suppressing the emotions those words stirred in me, I asked as casually as I could, "How long before he passes out?"

"If he keeps struggling? Probably thirty seconds." Oliver winked and then turned to Talekor, his voice taking on a darker tone. "We are going to return to the ball—where some have already noticed your absence— to enjoy a refreshment or two. If you were wise, you would follow suit. The other Councilors have voiced their concerns about your rather… inelegant handling of Rayleigh on the dance floor." He stepped closer, gazing into Talekor's bulging eyes. "If any of them had found you in this predicament, you would be stripped of any Fae you currently possess and denied the right to claim any others. I know that will not stop you from claiming them. However," Talekor slid down the wall, his feet not quite touching the ground when he stopped. Oliver stepped up to him, standing nose to nose. His voice was eerily calm—far more unsettling than shouting. "If I catch you attempting to lay claim to my betrothed again, you will learn just how quickly I can suffocate your very existence."

Talekor collapsed to the ground, gasping for breath as I had moments before. "When my father—"

"Do not threaten me with a man I have dealt with far longer than you can fathom." Oliver extended his arm, and I wrapped my hand around his elbow. "I will not cower before a tyrant." With that, he turned away from Talekor and led us back toward the ballroom. Once we were far enough away, his tense posture relaxed, and he glanced at me. "We need to get you cleaned up before we return."

I nodded, letting him guide me through a door that appeared a few feet before the ballroom. We stepped into the dining hall, and as soon as the doors shut behind us, I released the breath and tears I had been holding back.

When Oliver noticed, he stopped me, his features softening as he lifted a hand to wipe them away. "I know you said yes out there, but I will ask again. Are you alright?"

I shook my head, and he immediately wrapped his arms around me without further question. The comfort and warmth seeped into me as I let the tears fall and made myself breathe. I wasn't shaking from sobs but from the need to release the emotions I'd suppressed as Talekor proved to be the monster I knew he was. I couldn't let him see the fear he had instilled in me, so I'd shoved it deep down until now.

Oliver held me close, my arms pinned between us. I realized I hadn't wrapped my arms around him. It was a strange feeling to be held and not reciprocate. It was as if he didn't expect anything from me but offered his comfort while I processed my emotions on my own. I wiggled my arms free from their trap and twined them around his waist, feeling him give a slight chuckle as I did so. My head nestled under his chin, but I felt him lift it, and then his cheek was pressed to my head.

We stayed there for a moment before I pulled away, gasping when I took in his tunic. "I got blood on your shirt!"

"Just takes a little potion to get it out, love." He shrugged. "But we should take care of your wounds," he said, gesturing to my cheek. "I believe your head is bleeding as well."

I reached up and touched the back of my head, wincing at the sensitive spot. Sure enough, blood covered my fingers. "I guess being slammed against a wall is bound to cause some damage."

"Depends on the intent," Oliver murmured, then smirked when he saw my jaw drop. "I am not a three-hundred-year-old prude, remember?"

I grinned, letting him lead me to the table. Instead of setting me in a chair, he lifted me onto the tabletop and leaned against my knees. He pulled his kerchief from inside his vest and dabbed at my cheek, cleaning up the blood. His closeness suddenly gave me a funny feeling in my stomach. Wanting to ignore it, I said, "Where is everyone else?"

He answered without hesitation. "Nikylo is with Mari and Leighton. Theo and Libella are dealing with the Councilors. Romeo is guarding Kendall." Strange that Tom wasn't with Kendall... His words were so matter-of-fact. So why did they make me feel so--

"Wait. Mari—*Leighton?*" I couldn't find the words to ask the question, but I didn't have to.

"She did not fully succeed."

My heart dropped to my stomach. "What?" My voice was barely a whisper. "Then why did Talekor…"

"He sensed her effort to undermine their bond. Although that did not succeed, his dragon still alerted him to the attempt."

"But he was in pain." I winced as he dabbed a particularly sensitive spot on my cheek.

"I suppose someone attempting to overpower his magic was unpleasant." Oliver pulled the kerchief away, most of its surface stained with blood. He placed it on the table and waved his hand. I felt a breeze sweep past my hair, and then he held what appeared to be several cloth bandages.

"Where did those come from?" I asked, turning to find a place behind me where they might have been stashed.

But a gentle grip on my chin turned my head back. Oliver's blue eyes pierced mine with a slight crinkle to them. "Stay still, love. Our absence has already been noted, and there is still another wound I need to clean."

I gave a shy nod at his gentle tone. His thumb and forefinger lingered for a moment before slipping away from my chin, continuing to dab at my cheek. He started humming, and I don't know why, but it made me feel so much more relaxed. Again, trying to ignore the rising emotions, I returned to our conversation. "You said Mari didn't *fully* succeed."

"Yes." The clipped answer was not what I wanted, but the corner of Oliver's mouth ticked up as he continued to hum. So I waited for him to continue, watching his face as he studied my bloodied cheek. "While she failed to overpower his Doulos bond, they successfully formed a Kavaltis bond."

Shock rippled through my body. "*What?*" Nikylo had mentioned the possibility of a Fae having two bonds with different dragons, but I hadn't thought it would actually happen. "How? And why didn't Mari's dragon choose her sooner?"

"Not every dragon is as impulsive as Nikylo's," Oliver smirked. "In fact, most are deliberate in every choice they make." He leaned forward just as his thumb traced the cut on my cheek, blowing cool air over the wound. It sent a shiver down my spine—

That wasn't just a shiver. My eyes locked with Oliver's. "Was that *magic?*"

His smile lit up his entire face. "Our ability to heal does not compare to those of the Dynkoi, but a simple tune carries the power to soothe and stop excessive bleeding." He placed the newly soiled cloth on the table, then braced his hands on either side of my hips. "Remind you of anyone you know?"

The momentary distraction of his closeness made my breath hitch, but I swallowed and thought about what he said—*a simple tune.* My eyes lit up. "My dad," I breathed. "He was Annysian." Oliver nodded, his face so close that I felt the movement. His eyes roved my face, a look of something I couldn't quite place, and my stomach tightened with each second that passed without him moving. Finally, I broke the silence. "Why are you looking at me like that?"

He shook his head and leaned back. "No reason." He held out a hand to help me from the table, but I just stared at him as he avoided my gaze.

Because those two simple words caused a burning sensation right above my heart. "Oliver."

"It is of no consequence," he said, his cheeks suddenly stained pink.

"Apparently, it is," I said, laying a hand where the mark of our órkomatos burned again.

"Now is not the time."

"And when is the time?" I asked, helping myself off the table and stepping toward him.

His eyes shot to mine, likely sensing what I realized. They softened as he took in my smile. "Perhaps this evening. After our dinner?"

I smiled, my heartbeat racing as I nodded. "I'll hold you to that."

He swallowed thickly but smiled. "I do not believe that will be necessary."

I shrugged. But before I could respond, the doors banged open.

The King, Queen, and Talekor barged in, Libella and Theo hot on their heels. Not who I was expecting, but I stepped back into the table again, waiting for the accusations to ring out as Talekor's hateful gaze fell on Oliver.

Oliver stepped to my side, his shoulder brushing mine.

"The King heard you were injured, Rayleigh," Theo explained, crossing the room with Libella straight to me. "He insisted on seeing to it himself."

My gaze shot to the royals, who stood several feet away, their eyes fixed on me. "I'm fine. Just—" How was I supposed to pretend that Talekor wasn't the one who attacked me? "Just a little shaken up."

"Did you see who attacked you?" The King demanded, eyes falling on Oliver.

Seeing exactly how the prince hoped this would go, I straightened my spine and placed my hand just over my heart. "It was no one I recognized," I said, gesturing to the male beside me. "Councilor Oliver stepped in to save me, sending Talekor to fetch you while he tended to my injuries."

Talekor's jaw clenched at my words, then Oliver added. "The Drakalasson skithed away as soon as I stepped in. Unfortunately, I did not get a good look at his face." The spot above my heart seered, and I was thankful I remembered to cover it, unsure if they could see it. "The other Councilors and I are becoming slightly concerned with how some of the Fae here are treated, Your Highness."

"I assure you," the King said, bowing his head ever so slightly, "We are working to rectify the issue at hand. As you know, Rayleigh's safety is highest on our list of priorities." A gleam of genuine sincerity shone in his eyes.

"There are more Fae in this castle than just Rayleigh," Oliver stated coolly.

A gentle caress down my mind had me opening the door for Nikylo. *Where are you?*

Dining hall. I said, holding the King's gaze. *You?*

"That brings me to my next point," he said, glancing at Talekor before meeting Oliver's eyes again. "My son seems to think Rayleigh was not the only targeted Fae. His bond appears to be missing as well."

Ballroom. Nikylo confirmed. *I'm coming to you.*

No. Stay there.

What?

Trust me. My gaze flicked to Talekor. *Is Leighton with you?*

Yes.

"Last I saw, she was heading to the bathroom," I lied smoothly. "Have you checked there?"

"That's what I suggested," the Queen mumble. My eyes flicked to hers, and I had to suppress a smile.

"She wouldn't have taken this long," Talekor said, returning my attention to him. He tried to hide his sneer behind a false sense of worry, but I saw right through it.

"Dresses like these aren't easy to maneuver in the bathroom." I smiled innocently. "I can go check the bathroom if you'd like?"

"That will not be necessary," the King said. "Your injuries are healed, Rayleigh?" He was studying my cheek, where I'm sure a bruise was forming.

"There is one on the crown of her head I still need to attend to," Oliver piped in. "She will return momentarily to the ballroom."

The King held his gaze for a moment before nodding stiffly. "Libella can stay here to help." Something caught his attention on the table behind us. "Do see that you remove those bloody bandages from my table." His eyes snapped back to Oliver, whose eyebrows had shot up. "I have standards. This is one of them."

He then extended his arm to the Queen, who accepted it and was escorted out of the room. Talekor levelled me with a gaze that I'm sure was meant to scare me, but I just raised my hand and waggled my fingers at him, whispering, "Better run along. Mommy and Daddy are waiting."

He clenched his jaw but turned on his heel and followed them out the door. As soon as it shut, I took a deep breath, relaxing into the table behind me. Libella helped heal the back of my head, and I couldn't help but wonder if that had all been a little too easy. Talekor could have told them the truth. Could have informed them that someone was trying to take Leighton from him. But then he would have revealed that he was the one who hurt me in his search for answers.

Which led me to question: Why were the King and Queen so concerned about *my* safety?

FORTY-TWO
My Heart's Grave

I sat waiting in Nikylo's chambers, trying to compose myself before he returned. I knew the moment would come, that the distractions of the night would only last so long before I would have to say goodbye.

The minute the door creaked open, my efforts to compose myself failed. Tears streamed down my face as Ma walked in, using Nikylo as her support. Libella trailed them, carrying the things she'd collected while here over the past few days. A small bag of clothes and one full of her vitamins that had been provided.

I crossed the room, wrapping my arms around her, but not too tight. I couldn't find my voice, so I just conveyed everything I felt with the hug.

"We don't have much time before she arrives," Nikylo said, having stepped aside the moment I had Ma in my arms. "Once the memories have been modified, Libella is going to make her sleep on our way to Gaia."

I found Libella with my eyes from where my head lay on Ma's shoulder, not wanting to let go. "You'll get her there safely?"

Libella nodded. "She'll be safe with me. I'll ensure she's tucked in and safe before we leave."

I nodded, looking back to Nikylo. "And Mitch."

On the way back to the castle from the Kyllindro, he'd explained that my brother's magic wouldn't develop fully if he wasn't around a power source. While he'd shown signs of it, complete transformation didn't happen until the magic fully flooded their system—similar to my powers developing my Fae features. Mitch was still a couple of years away from when a Fae male usually hit their fully developed years, so the hope was that getting him back to Gaia would stop the progression.

At least, that's what every tome Nikylo read had said.

"Naila will be taking him."

"*Naila?*" I balked, lifting my head from Ma's shoulder and shifting to support her weight.

His mouth quirked up on one side, but he nodded. "As cunning and bitchy as she is, she swore her loyalty to me long ago."

"Like, an oath loyalty? Or betrothal loyalty?"

"Technically both, but separately." When I eyed him suspiciously, he sighed. "She can't spill my secrets without the consequences of thrypsis."

"Thyrpsis... Isn't that a curse?"

"Exactly," he smirked, a sense of pride rolling off him. "I see you've been reading."

I shrugged, but he was right. I'd taken time when we returned to read more about the oaths, bonds, and curses, wanting to understand them. The curses stuck out, especially that one. It resulted in a fracturing of the body, mind, and magic, which sounded absolutely terrifying. I didn't want to admit that I'd read through the curses searching for the one everyone kept eluding to: between the Fae and Drakalasson. It hadn't been in that book, though, which made sense. That book only talked about the curses that were the effect of breaking oaths. *That* curse was active and affected the entire realm. None of the other books Nikylo let me bring back had anything about it. I just wanted some sort of explanation of what the curse *was*. What happened if a Fae and Drakalasson got together? And why didn't it happen when the Fae were forced to do anything the Drakalasson wanted in the castle? Or maybe it did, and it just wasn't as obvious?

"We both know Naila wouldn't risk her power," I sighed. While I still questioned her attitude toward me, I knew she was probably an asset for Nikylo. "So you're taking Naila and Libella?" He nodded. "That leaves Kendall and me with Theo, Mari, and Oliver?"

"Mari will be on guard duty until we get back," Nikylo said.

"Yeah. That's what I said." When he shook his head, I tilted mine.

Who could he be—? Then it clicked. "*Aaidan?*" I asked, jaw dropping. "He's still alive?"

"For now."

"But you said—"

A knock sounded at the door. *Shit.* I'd spent the whole time I had left with Ma doing anything except saying goodbye. I turned back to her, finding a smile on her face. Nikylo went to answer the door as I gave Ma one more hug. "I love you, Ma."

"I love you, too, sweetheart." Her voice was weak, and I knew she was saving her strength for the trip back to Gaia. Not that she really needed to have strength for the journey, but I didn't let her lack of words affect me. Her encouragement at the Verdanvale—that was her goodbye.

When I released her, I turned to see Nikylo ushering in the Queen, Naila trailing her. His mother gave me a warm smile, which I tried to return without tears. Mari told me that the King didn't like to mess with the memories himself, but he still had to trust the person he delegated the task to. So, that left his wife. Nikylo had assured me his mother wouldn't erase her memories altogether, but she had to do enough that if the King followed up with her, she could show him she did her job. I wasn't sure how much I trusted her, but Nikylo seemed to. And right now, that had to be enough for me.

She didn't waste any time, crossing the room to take Ma's hands as I supported her around the waist. "Are you ready, Jordin?" Ma gave a gentle nod. "You might initially feel a strange sensation, but it should disappear after a few seconds. When I'm done, Libella will prepare you for transport. You won't wake until you are safely back on Gaia, alright?" Ma gave another nod, strangely confident as she stood there holding hands with the Queen. Perhaps she didn't know who she was... "Libella, could you please get into position?"

"Yes, Majesty." Libella stepped beside me, and I knew my help was no longer needed. Releasing Ma, I stepped back so Libella could take my place, the tears slipping down my face.

"This will only take a moment," the Queen told me, closing her eyes to concentrate on erasing me from Ma's memory—if only temporarily. I wrapped my arms around myself, wishing I had my friends to comfort me. Then, an arm wrapped around my shoulders. When I felt him request access to my mind, the door opened without hesitation.

She'll be safer this way, Nikylo said.

I nodded, leaning my head on his shoulder. *Knowing she'll be safe and eventually remember who I am doesn't make never seeing her again any easier.*

I know, Sunshine. His thumb made gentle caresses on my shoulder. *But if the portal stays, those hunting Mitch will still be able to get to him. We have to destroy it.*

That was another thing he'd mentioned on the trip home from the Kyllindro. It was the only way to ensure Mitch's mind stayed his. No portal meant no accidental magic seeping into the world. I sighed. *I just wish I had more time.*

"All done," the Queen said quietly, releasing Ma's hands so Libella could scoop her unconscious body into her arms. Turning to Nikylo, she said, "Make haste. Your father will expect a report within the hour." And with that, the Queen was gone.

"Within the hour?" I said as the door shut behind her. "That doesn't seem like much time."

"It's not," Nikylo said, already crossing to the portal door. "We're already cutting it close."

I hurried after him, Libella and Naila following silently. While we waited for the door to open, I eyed Naila sideways. She was already watching me with a wicked grin. "Just because Nikylo trusts you doesn't mean I do."

"Oh, I know, kató," she said, waving me off. "I don't trust anyone either. Keeps life more interesting this way."

That was not how I wanted to live my life. But I supposed I was holding my trust close to my heart these days. "Just don't hurt my brother."

"No promises."

"Naila," Nikylo growled.

"Ugh, fine. I promise I won't hurt your brother," she leaned in, "too much."

"Naila!"

She scoffed, turning to where Nikylo stood by the open door. "You're no fun." She walked toward the door, saying over her shoulder, "No harm will come to your brother under my care."

Despite how nonchalantly she said it, I believed her.

Libella followed Naila through, and I made to follow suit, but Nikylo grabbed my hand, making my eyes snap to his. He didn't say anything, just studied me. Something in his gaze made me ask quietly, "What?"

He was quiet a moment longer before finally saying, "Try not to let all of this distract you from your time with Oliver."

Surprise rushed through me, warming my cheeks at the sudden wave of guilt. I swallowed hard. "I thought you weren't stepping aside."

"I'm not," he said, searching my eyes. "But you wanted this date, right?" When I nodded shyly, he smiled, "Then I will not stand in *your* way."

१ ओ २ र

"Trust me, this one enhances the sweetness," Oliver said, holding the spice I was trying to use hostage behind his back while offering one that smelled like basil.

After a teary goodbye with Mitch, Libella used her power to knock him out, and they left with Naila carrying him and Nikylo skithing them from the front lawn of the Verdanvale. Oliver suggested that our date could wait for another time, but I knew the distraction would be better than moping about after they left. Kendall and Theo had been kind enough to sit outside by the fire, giving Oliver and me full access to the kitchen—alone. He'd already had everything prepped for us to cook, so I let him take the lead. It had been fun working alongside someone with a familiar love of the kitchen and the creativity it allowed with food— until he suggested adding sweetness to *meat*.

"But I don't want it to be *sweeter*," I whined, trying to reach behind his back. He evaded me—again. "Cooking is supposed to be savory. Leave the sweet for my baking!"

"Ah, but that's just it, love. *Your* specialty is baking. *Mine* is cooking." Oliver's eyes sparkled as I crinkled my nose at him.

"Ugh, fine," I said, stepping back and holding out my hand. "Then let me put it away."

"That will not be necessary." The small jar of the savory spice floated over my head toward the cabinet, ruining my plan of sneaking it into the meat sizzling over the stove.

Thinking quickly, I tried another route, placing my hand on his chest and dropping my voice. "You know, I don't normally like it when someone tries to take over my kitchen." Oliver lifted his brows at my claim on his kitchen, retreating into the counter behind him as I closed the space between us. I walked my fingers up his chest and heard his breath catch. "But with you," my fingers jumped from his chest, landing a single finger on his lips, "well, I can't make any exceptions."

The meat on the stove sizzled as the savory spice fell onto half of it. Oliver's gaze snapped to the pan and then back to me. He slowly shook his head in disbelief—or was it awe? My distraction gave me the opening I needed. I used the powers I'd been practicing all night to snatch the spice from Oliver's magical grasp with a vine from the plant on the windowsill near the stove.

I reached for the basil-scented spice still in his hand and sprinkled it on the other half of the skillet. "There," I said, adding one more shake of each. "Now you have your sweet-enhancing spice, and I have my savory one." I held out both jars to him with a grin, knowing I won, but really, so did he.

Oliver chuckled, grabbing the spices from me. "Niko was right about you." He tapped my nose with a finger and moved around me to put the spices away.

I whipped around to follow him because there was no way I was letting him just get away with saying that. "What's that supposed to mean?"

He smirked over his shoulder as he placed the spices on their shelf. "Your ability to distract from the task at hand is…what was the word he used?" He closed the cupboard and faced me, crossing his arms. "Uncanny?"

I smiled, brushing invisible lint from my shoulder. "It doesn't work on every male—just the incredibly attractive ones."

"Oh?" he said, arms dropping as he took a single step toward me. "And how many has it worked on?" Another step.

"Well, there's Nikylo," I held up one finger, "and Aaidan." Another finger, another step. "Talekor." I couldn't stop my smile as Oliver took the last step between us and placed his hands on the counter on either side of me. "Does Koladon count? He's kind of old." I tapped my finger on my chin. "But then again, so are you…"

I could feel his breath on my lips as he grinned. "Is that your way of including me in this list of those you find *incredibly attractive*? By referring to me as old?"

"I could put you on a different list." I shrugged, leaning back on my elbows.

"What list might that be?"

I grinned. "The insufferable ones." Oliver let out a soft chuckle, dropping his head closer to mine. I leaned in to whisper, "Or the ones who get so distracted by a pretty girl they forget about the food on the stove."

His head snapped up, and he simultaneously threw a hand out behind him. The action removed the skillet from the fire and turned off the stove. His eyes hadn't left mine, though. He sniffed the air. "It will only be slightly crispier than I intended."

I raised a brow, smirking. He was still caging me against the counter, waiting for…what? I didn't know. But there was a sparkle in his eyes as they wandered my face. "You're doing it again."

"Doing what?"

"Looking at me like that." His closeness and intense gaze made my heart race, wondering if he would follow through with his promise from earlier.

"Like what, love?"

"I don't know… like…"

"Just say it."

"Like you want to kiss me," I said, struggling to catch my breath due to his closeness.

"Because I do," he confessed in a whisper.

Unable to stop myself, my gaze fell to his lips, mere inches from mine, before flicking back to his intense blue eyes. "What's stopping you?"

His eyes locked on mine. "Only you."

How was I stopping him? I hadn't pushed him away or stopped his physical advances. If anything, I encouraged them. Was he waiting for me to ask for it? To give him permission? Did I *want* to? The way I instinctively leaned into him told me one thing. Did normal people kiss on the first date? But this wasn't a typical first date because we were betrothed. Ugh, why was I so bad at this?

A knock sounded. Oliver sighed, "And apparently, whoever is at the door."

He made to push off the counter, but making a bold decision, I grabbed the front of his tunic. "Wait." My move had pulled him within millimeters of my face, and my heart was beating wildly, but I swallowed my fear and said, "I'm not stopping you. And whoever is at the door can wait."

Oliver's look of surprise quickly shifted to something darker—more intense. His hand cupped my face, fingers threading around me ear as he closed the distance between our lips–

The knock sounded again. Reluctantly, I laid a hand on Oliver's chest and pushed, not bothering to hide the disappointment on my face. On my way to the door, I shouted, "Kendall, if that's you, I'm going to kick your ass." I grabbed the doorknob and glanced at Oliver, barely containing my smile at the look on his face that told me he had wanted that as much as I did. "You were interrupting—" But the words caught in my throat when I opened the door. Every warm feeling I was experiencing left my body as I took in who stood there.

"Interrupting what, girlie?" Talekor asked, holding a bloodied up Mari hostage with a crystal dagger to her throat.

I stumbled back into the room. Oliver was by my side in an instant, hand on my back to keep me steady.

Mari's eyes found mine as blood leaked out of her mouth. "I'm sorry," she choked out.

I shook my head, not knowing how the hell this happened. There was only one way to find out. Glaring at Talekor, I spat, "What do you want?"

He chuckled, reaching behind him. "Come on, pet," he purred. "We all have to be touching to go through."

My heart plummeted when he pulled Leighton into view behind him. "She's not a *pet!* She's a *person!*"

He ignored me, though, pushing Mari over the threshold while pulling Leighton in behind him. The door shut behind them as soon as they were through. He dropped Leigh's hand and, in one quick movement, sliced the dagger across Mari's throat.

"NO!" I shouted, lunging for her, but Oliver caught me around my waist, pulling me back just as Talekor made a grab for me. He'd completely abandoned his hold on Mari, dropping her in a heap on the floor as her blood spilled onto the carpet. Tears streamed down my face as I lunged for Talekor, screaming, "You *monster!*"

Oliver backed me further into the room, whispering, "Love, you must calm down." We stopped in the middle of the living room, surrounded by furniture. "He has powers now, remember. He could skith you out of here the minute he touches you."

Duh, powers! I reached for the thread of white within me, not as confident in my earth-wielding without direct access to the roots. The power I managed to gather and throw at Talekor bounced off a shield ten feet from him. *Damnit!*

"It's going to take more than a feeble blast of air to get past my shields, girlie," Talekor taunted, stepping around Mari's lifeless form.

Shit. I wasn't strong enough. But I also wasn't the only one with the ability to fight. "Why aren't you using *your* powers?" I hissed at Oliver, trying to rip my eyes away from where Mari lay.

He grunted. "Currently fighting his control over my mind. I cannot release you."

My blood ran cold. Talekor was controlling *Oliver?* "How did he—?"

"My shields were down. I didn't— I wasn't—" he grunted again, breathing labored.

"Why did you have your shields down?" I asked, unable to stop myself from asking.

"Because it was just you," he whispered, his voice strained. I couldn't read minds, so it made sense. But— "Focus on him. Niko taught me to fight this."

I heaved several breaths, focusing on Oliver's grip and his breath hitting my ear to keep me grounded. Talekor wiped the blood from the dagger on his sleeve and then handed it to Leighton before he moved to stalk the perimeter of furniture around us.

Leighton had barely reacted, but I swear there were tears shining in her eyes as she stole a glance at Mari's lifeless form on the ground. They'd just made that damn bond between them and now it was gone.

Mari was *gone*. I knew Leigh was under some kind of mind control, but all I wanted to do was scream at her to do something—*anything* besides just standing there.

"So," Talekor said, amusement shining in his eyes as he glanced at Oliver, hands clasped behind his back as he paced. "Now that we've established that I am, indeed, a monster." He glanced around the room as if expecting someone else to be there. "Let's address your question since you asked so nicely…" He stopped pacing, pulling a hand from behind his back to point at me. "*You* are the only thing I want."

"Why? Why is having me so important to you?" I screamed, still fighting the tears streaming down my face.

"Uh uh…" he tsked, shaking a finger at me. "That's for me to know and you—"

The door burst open. "Rayleigh!" Ken rushed in, her back to us as she watched something out the front door. "I don't mean to barge in on your date! But Theo sent me inside because some dragons showed up and—"

"Kendall, no!" I shouted at the same time Talekor said, "Ah, Kendall. Perfect timing."

Ken whipped around at the sound of his voice, the color draining from her face. "Kal—er, Talekor? What the hell—?"

"Go get Theo!" I yelled, trying to escape Oliver's grasp again, but he held tight.

"They're almost here. Just hold on." His breathing was almost normal, but I could tell he was still fighting to shove Talekor from his mind. How had Talekor gotten so strong so quickly?

A smirk slowly worked its way across Talekor's face. He was unfazed by Kendall's surprise or my outburst. "Leighton," he barked, eyes flicking to where she stood. "Do it. Now."

FORTY-THREE
Unstoppable

Nikylo

"Keep them on until sundown tomorrow," I told Mitch, holding out the key for his gonos. "Magic will linger for several hours after the portal is destroyed, and I don't want you risking anything."

The sun was peeking up above the trees in the early morning hours. Seeing the sunrise and fall during my time on Gaia was something I hadn't realized I missed about Niccodra. Hopefully, that would change soon. Something about having Rayleigh back was messing with the power. There hadn't been storm clouds in the sky for nearly fifty years, but I'd glimpsed some the day of Talekor's dinner. Nothing came of them, but I knew it wasn't random. Things were changing.

"I don't think I want to take them off. Ever," Mitch confessed. "This is the first time I've felt like myself since...well, since my accident."

I chuckled. "You can leave them on as long as you like. Or, take them off and if you feel like you need to put them back on," I shrugged. "Use your best judgment."

He nodded, then chewed on his cheek as if he wanted to say something else.

"Spit it out, champ." The nickname left my mouth before I could stop myself, bringing a pang of grief with it. I shook the feeling, focusing on Rayleigh's little brother.

"You promise Ray will be okay?" he asked.

My stern gaze softened at his worry. "She has the best team of warriors protecting her."

"That didn't answer my question," he glared at me.

Did he know that was an impossible promise to make? That the danger in Niccodra was unpredictable. With signs of Orvyn resurfacing again, I could only imagine the things coming our way. But I sighed, reaching out to grip his shoulder. "I promise you I will do everything in my power to protect your sister. She means a lot to so many people."

He clenched his teeth, but I couldn't tell if it was out of anger or to suppress a smile as he said, "That includes you, right?"

I held his gaze, searching for the answer he wanted to hear, but then decided on the truth. "Yes."

Mitch huffed a sigh. "I was pretty sure she hated you, you know."

I laughed. "Oh, she did. Pretty sure she still does sometimes."

"She doesn't," he stated plainly. When I gave him a questioning look, he clarified, "She doesn't trust people she hates."

"Well, she definitely doesn't trust me," I said. Then, mumbled more to myself than him, "I haven't given her a reason to."

Mitch shook his head. "The last time she said goodbye to us, we were kidnapped. You think she would trust just anyone to get us here safely?"

The only surprise I showed was my eyebrows flicking up. Her reaction when I told her Mitch was safe after the trial but wouldn't tell her where was proof enough that she didn't trust me. He was right, though. Something changed her mind. Was it the ceremony? Our trip to the Kyllindro? I'd have to ask her when I returned.

Although, who knew what I would return to? She was supposed to be having her date with Oliver. I'd said I wouldn't stand in her way, but leaving her there? Knowing what was likely going to happen? Easily one of the most challenging things I'd done. Everything about leaving her with him felt wrong. Not because Oliver wasn't a good male—hell, he was the best one I knew. But whatever I felt between Rayleigh and me was magnetic—like nothing could have kept us from finding each other. Across realms and dimensions, we would have found a way to each other. I felt it in my soul.

But the damn curse meant I couldn't cross that line with her. Any act of intimacy with feelings involved would set us straight on a path to death—not to mention the destruction it would cause elsewhere.

A door clicking shut snapped me back to reality. "She's settled," Libella said, eyes falling to Mitch. "When she wakes, make her drink the water beside the bed. The lack of magic in the world shouldn't change the effects of the glykos."

Mitch nodded, then asked, "How long until she wakes?"

"Shouldn't be too long," Libella smiled. "But her body is weak. It will take time for her to regain her strength." She turned to me, holding out a bag. "I thought you might want this. Or rather, she might."

I took the bag, peering inside, and grinned to myself. "I'm sure she'll be happy to have it." I closed the bag, throwing Rayleigh's old backpack over my shoulder. "We should go. Our hour is almost up." Libella nodded, skirting around Mitch and me. Clapping a hand on his shoulder, I said, "The Dengalow is yours. I'm taking the books I need, but feel free to scour them if you want information on the world your dad came from."

His brow furrowed. "Are you sure destroying the portal will stop magic from working?"

"Positive. Why?"

"Well, Rayleigh's magic still developed here. And you can still shift into dragons—which is really cool, by the way. I never thought I'd see a real-life dragon." He grinned, likely remembering waking up on the flight from the meadow to here. He thought he was dreaming, and, not wanting to freak him out, I let him believe that until we landed on the lawn. But the freaking out never came. He stared in awe at Drako's form, taking in every possible angle before I shifted. "But does magic only exist here because of the portal?"

I shrugged. "Earth may have its own magic, but cutting off the source of *our* magic should keep yours at bay." He eyed me warily, so I gestured to his wrists again. "You have those just in case. They'll work as long as our magic does. So either way, you're protected."

"Niko," Libella's voice echoed down the hall.

"I have to go. Take care of your mother."

"I will," he said, and I turned to go. "And Kyler?" The name sent a jolt of something through me, but I turned, finding him focusing on a piece of folded paper he was messing with in his hands. When he lifted his gaze to meet mine, his eyes shone with sorrow. "Take care of my sister."

Nodding, I gripped his shoulder, meeting his gaze with a sincerity I didn't use often. "You can count on me, champ."

Naila had been guarding the portal to make sure no one followed us here. With the Hunter's Mark, it was unclear if Mitch could be found with the gonos and a shield around him, but we hadn't wanted to risk it. That was the main reason I had Naila join me on the journey. As soon as Libella and I flew over the treeline into the meadow, she turned to open it. I'd sent her back after dropping Mitch off to prep for the destruction.

A deep rumble came from within me. *Something is wrong,* Drako said, instantly chilling me to the bone.

What do you mean? Did someone come through the portal? I asked, unable to look around as I'd given him control.

No, he said, diving straight for the swirling vortex in the center of the giant, twisted tree. *With Rayleigh.*

How can you— That's when I felt it—a tug of urgency and terror in my chest. Why hadn't I felt it sooner? Was it because I'd given him control? But then again, how could she be in danger? The Verdanvale was the safest place for her in Niccodra. Theo and Oliver were there. No one could get in or even see the little house tucked into the cliffside.

We shot past Naila as she shifted. I knew she would follow us through even if we didn't stop. *Drako, the portal! We need to destroy it!*

Naila has already seen to that. He didn't slow down as we passed through the opening in the tree, and the pressure was almost too much at the speed we were traveling.

An explosion filled the air behind me, and I realized he was right. Naila couldn't resist the opportunity to blow something up. She'd always had a fascination with destroying things or watching them burn. Her father, the Dikitís, had made sure to curb her love of destroying stuff for fun decades ago, but when she was given a task to do so, she never disappointed.

The heat of the blast chased us through the portal, lighting up the path as we broke through the other side. Naila's unusual speed had her right on our tails as we flew out into the glen where the portal connected the realms. The fire shot out of the portal just as her tail cleared it, and she let out a cry of triumph.

Drako would have echoed it if he weren't hellbent on getting to Rayleigh as quickly as possible.

Rayleigh's in trouble, I said to both Naila and Libella. *Chain up.*

Neither of them questioned my command, banking to fall in line behind Drako. He slowed enough for Libella's dragon to clamp onto his tail, Naila's doing the same to hers.

Drako didn't waste time, skithing us to just off the bank of the Verdanvale within seconds. I could tell he was furious from his lack of words. As soon as the house in the cliffs came into view, my entire being went into fight mode.

Three dragons were stuck in combat outside the shields of the Verdanvale, and I swore. I recognized all three of them. Theo's gold dragon shot skyward from the fray, Koladon's red dragon rushing after him. The gold dragon did a spiraling reverse bank and slammed straight into the red dragon's flank. A mighty roar echoed from the collision as we closed in, Naila and Libella falling into formation.

The other red dragon was what caught my attention, though. He shouldn't have been there, but if Adarachi was, that meant something had happened with Mari. I shoved the thought aside as I reached for the bond.

Rayleigh? I shouted, but her shields were solid against me. I tried my usual caress down the side of them to let me in, but she either didn't feel it or didn't think letting me in was a good idea. *Shit.* Plan B, then. I searched for my friend's thread of power, finding it right next to Rayleigh. His shields were half up, but someone else was there, too. Invading his mind. Forcing him to keep hold of her. *Oliver!* I shoved my way into his mind, pushing past the half shield and using all my power to force the invading presence out. Whoever it was, their claws were sunk deep into Oliver's mind. How had he even gotten past his shields? *I'm almost there, Ollie,* I reassured him. With immense effort, the hold whoever it was had on my friend released, and I added an extra shield to his mind as I felt him build his back up around me.

Talekor is here, he said, making me swear violently. *He has Leighton holding Kendall hostage.* Oliver sounded exhausted. How long had he been fighting for control over his own mind?

How did he even get there? I shouted.

I knew the answer right as he said it, *Mari.*

That sense of dread regarding her resurfaced, and I hesitated to ask, *Where is she?*

Bleeding out. Rage filled my soul. *He slit her throat.*

Libella! I shouted, banking to head for the house. She was headed for the battle between Theo, Koladon, and Adarachi, likely sensing Theo's need for backup. But Naila could handle them. *Mari needs you inside.*

I felt her slight panic as she changed course, following me through the shields around the Verdanvale—

Something crashed into me from below, knocking Drako off course. He and I both roared as talons clamped into his hind legs and ripped us away from the shields that would have protected us. Libella hesitated just outside the shields, but I yelled, *Go! Help Mari and the others!*

She followed the instruction, diving through the shields to safety. Although, with Talekor on the other side, I wasn't sure how safe that would be for much longer. Turning my focus to Adarachi, I snapped at his neck. Sharing control with Drako was my favorite way to fight. His ruthlessness and intelligence complemented my strategic and calculated moves. It made us one hell of a fighter.

Our minds melded and became one.

I folded in my wings, my entire weight causing Adarachi's grip on me to slip. I didn't reopen them immediately, continuing my dive straight down about a hundred feet before snapping them out and soaring away from the shields. If I had crossed over those shields with him clinging to me, they would have granted him access. I had to get him as far away as possible before going through.

I flew straight for Theo and Naila, battling Koladon, his red dragon maneuvering out of their grasps with the precision I thought only my soldiers had. How did he even know where to go? Was he the one who freed Adarachi?

Focus on the now, Niko, Drako commanded.

Adarachi's dragon was slightly smaller than mine, making him faster but not wiser. He snapped at my tail, but I swung it out of range with seconds to spare, slamming it down on his head. He dropped several feet upon impact, shaking his square head free of the concussion I likely gave him.

Theo! I shouted, flying straight for him as Naila engaged Koladon in a chase. *Tailstrike!*

He didn't turn toward me, blasting fire at Koladon as he passed, but I knew he heard me as I closed in. Adarachi had caught up to me, his jaws snapping closer this time at the base of my tail, but I dove right before colliding with Theo. Flipping midair, Theo brought his tail down on Adarachi's back, and I unleashed a torrent of blue fire straight into his jaw as he roared in agony. The combination sent him spiraling down as I flipped back over, spreading my wings and shooting out of the way.

Naila's dragon roared in pain. My gaze shot to where Koladon's talons pierced her purple wing. The sound of him shredding the membrane echoed her agony before he tossed her aside. He let her fall, turning when he noticed me flying straight for him. Sending my blue fire out to meet his torrent of red, I closed the distance quickly. Cutting off my flames, I dove to where Naila struggled to right herself with a half-shredded wing. Theo crashed through the flames, his talons stretching toward Koladon's dragon's eyes and raking over them. The screech that followed told me Theo hit his target dead on.

Letting him take point in that fight, I positioned myself beneath Naila and shouted down our bond. *Shift!*

She didn't hesitate, screaming as she fell the distance to my back. But I knew it wasn't terror causing that scream. Shifting when your dragon was injured, depending on the injury, was basically torture for both parties. She landed on the spot between my spines where I needed Rayleigh to be to know she was safe.

I banked a hard left, avoiding the spray of blood that Theo caused above us as he dug his talons into Koladon's eyes and jaw. I had no doubt that injury would transfer to his human form—that is, if Theo left him alive.

Circling them, I double-checked that Adarachi was nowhere in sight, then made for the Verdanvale. *Oliver, get Rayleigh to the roof—*

Niko dive! Naila shouted, pulling herself flat against Drako's spine as I dove. The scorching heat of the flames I dodged seared my back. Naila had her shields up and the fire couldn't penetrate my scales, but damn they were hot.

Who was that? I yelled, knowing it couldn't be Koladon or Adarachi, as one was still locked in Theo's talons. The other was likely still disoriented by the flames I'd shot down his throat, trying to fight his way back up.

I don't know! Naila shouted back. *I've never seen that dragon before.*

It shouldn't have surprised me that they'd recruited others, but one we hadn't seen before? That was almost impossible. I swooped low, not planning on letting the newcomer stop me from getting to Rayleigh. When I nearly collided with the underside of the island, I pulled up. The angle was sharp enough to have Naila's legs clinging to the underside of my wings as we climbed. I felt the enchantments of the Verdanvale swallow us as we broke past the surface, and I spun to right myself before flying toward the cliffs. Rayleigh still wasn't on the roof. Neither was Oliver. What was taking them so long?

Ollie! But my voice bounced back against his shields. *Dammit Ollie!* I circled the cliffs, staying well within the enchantments. *Drako, let me shift,* I pleaded, knowing it was likely out of the question in his state. He was only quiet when sleeping or when fury engulfed his entire being.

Absolutely not, he growled. *It leaves you too vulnerable.*

But you can't get into the house!

She will come out.

I shouldn't have let you take control. I mumbled as we faced the fight still happening beyond the shields. The newcomer was a silver dragon, currently fighting against my enchantments, while Theo was still engaged in battle with a blinded Koladon. *Have you seen that dragon before?*

The only response I got was a menacing growl.

"Nikylo!" A voice shouted from the ground. I banked, finding the source of the voice. Libella. She was waving her hands, but when she had my attention, she pointed to the door. "I can't get in."

Before I could even think about what that meant, a blood-curdling scream came from inside.

FORTY-FOUR
Friends

Rayleigh

Leigh's body stiffened at the command.

No.

Her fingers twitched at her side. Her jaw was clenched as if fighting to scream.

The tears in Leigh's eyes as they locked on her twin were the only thing that told me she was still in there. She wasn't just some mindless soldier that he was controlling. She was still there. Fighting.

A fresh wave of dread flooded my body. Talekor wasn't going to just make her do it—he was going to make her *watch* as she did.

Leighton stepped forward—toward Kendall—her movements slow. Unnatural. Like a puppet on strings.

"Kendall," my voice was barely more than a whisper. "Run."

But Kendall didn't move. She stared at her sister, eyes locked on hers.

Talekor smirked, deepening the creases in his cheeks where the smile I loved so much used to land. "Oh, she won't be running anywhere." He shifted his gaze back to Leigh, who was fighting another step forward, her body shaking.

"Leigh," Kendall's broken voice whispered. "It's me. It's Ken."

"Talekor, *please*," I begged, unable to stay silent. "Let her go. She has nothing to do with this!"

"Oh, but she has everything to do with this," he sneered. "The only reason they're here is so that you'll cooperate. And if you don't," he snapped a finger. Leigh flinched at the harsh sound, but her hand moved of its own accord, trembling as it reached for Kendall's arm.

"*Stop!*" I screamed, my hand shooting out a stream of power to try and stop Leighton, but Talekor moved faster, throwing a shield up in front of them.

"Do as you're told!" he growled, his manipulation forcing Leigh's hand to move with purpose instead of hesitation, clamping down on Kendall's wrist, knuckles white.

"Leigh," Kendall's whisper didn't hold any fear as she kept her eyes locked on her sister. "This isn't you. I know it isn't you. Fight it. Fight *him*." She still didn't run. Still didn't try to pull away from her.

Leigh shook her head, tears spilling down her cheeks. "I can't. It—it goes against the bond." She squirmed as the words left her lips, as if saying that went against it.

"Do not speak to her," Talekor demanded. But it wasn't aimed at Kendall. That command was for Leigh, whose mouth snapped shut instantly. A whimper escaped through her lips.

Leigh's hand was shaking, her lip quivering, but she lifted the dagger, the tip of it resting against Kendall's sternum.

"Good." Talekor straightened his spine. "Now. Let me tell you how this is going to go." Talekor went on as if nothing else were happening. As if he wasn't forcing my friend to point a dagger at her twin's heart.

"*Fight*, Leigh," I pleaded. "*Please.*"

Oliver's mouth was next to my ear. "It will not work, love. The Doulos bond is almost impossible to disobey."

I clenched my jaw, refusing to believe him. "Keyword: almost."

"You will break the bond with Nikylo," Talekor continued, "Or Leighton will drive that dagger through her sister's heart." He was still skirting the perimeter of the furniture around Oliver and me, his voice sending chills through my entire body. "If that doesn't convince you, she will drive it through her own. Then you'll have *three* dead friends. Shall I go on?"

"No," I snapped.

"No, I shouldn't go on or no to breaking the bond?"

"Leigh," I said, ignoring Talekor. "You need to fight him with *everything* you have. *Please.* I can't—" my voice cracked. "I can't watch you die."

"Pity," Talekor spat, tilting his head as his eyes gleamed with cruel amusement. "Do it." Leigh fought his control, shaking her head as her hand trembled.

"Kendall," I whispered, dread settling in as the panic in Leigh's eyes heightened. "Move." Because as much as I believed Leighton could fight it, he was too strong.

"I can't," she sobbed. And that's when I realized—Kendall hadn't just been standing there because she was unafraid. She'd been standing there against her will. She masked her fear because she didn't want her twin's last memory of her to be that she was *scared* of her.

"Now." Talekor's command rang through the room.

Leigh gasped as her own hand betrayed her.

I lunged, but Oliver's hold on me hadn't loosened. "Let me go!" I cried.

But it was too late. The crystal dagger flashed.

"Kendall!" The scream ripped from my throat

The dagger sank into her chest. And I froze as the sound of it echoed in my very soul.

Kendall staggered, eyes wide, lips parting—but no sound came out. Her knees buckled. Leigh caught her before she hit the floor, but her body shook from the sobs, trembling from the horror of what had just taken place. Every inch of her face showed how completely and utterly broken she was.

Just like Talekor promised.

"Kendall," Leigh sobbed, her knees hitting the floor with their combined weight. "No, no, no—please." She hastily moved the strawberry blonde hair from her face, the blood on her hands staining it red.

Kendall's breath hitched, shallow and uneven. Her eyes fluttered, finding Leighton's face, her gaze unfocused but soft. There was no anger there. No fear. Just love. "It's okay, Lele," she murmured.

But it wasn't okay. *None* of this was okay.

Leigh sobbed through the tears. "I didn't mean to—I couldn't stop —"

Her breath caught as Ken reached to cup Leigh's cheek, her trembling thumb wiping away her tears. "Remember the mat?"

Leigh froze. "What?"

Ken's lips curved into a weak smile, blood seeping out the corner. "That day I let you win… it wasn't because I was weak." Tears streamed down Leigh's face. "It was because you needed to know how strong you were." Ken coughed, blood staining her lips and Leigh's shirt. "You still are, Lele."

"I'm so sorry," Leigh choked out, dropping her forehead to Ken's.

Ken was quieter still, "I don't blame you." With a shuddering breath, the smile left her face as she exhaled. Her chest didn't rise again.

My vision tunneled.

Memories of our lives swam through my head: Nerf wars, swimming in the lake, sleepovers, giggling about boys, trips to the mall, learning sign language just to communicate in class, learning our magic, and her strong and steady friendship. I could see it all so clearly, as if remembering might somehow bring her back. But it wouldn't. There were no more memories to make. No more laughing until my sides hurt. No more late-night talks or whispered promises that we'd always have each other. Just an aching, empty space where she used to be.

The vilest chuckle met my ears. "Well. That was disappointing."

I snapped, and a blood-curdling scream left my mouth. I wrenched Oliver's arms from around me and launched myself at Talekor, fire crackling in my veins.

"You are going to *die* for making her do that."

He had the gall to rub his hands together like this was what he'd been waiting for. "Finally. Some excitement." His black eyes shone as dark as his soul with a smile so cruel—

The door burst open.

Both Talekor and I spun toward the intruder.

Nikylo.

He flew through the door, eyes finding mine before falling to Mari's lifeless body and Leigh still hugging Ken's close to her as she sobbed.

Talekor hissed, snapping his hand out to Leigh. She lurched forward, her body yanked from where she was clutching Kendall. It was like invisible chains dragged her to her feet and Talekor's side. It all took less than a few seconds for it to happen, and by the time Nikylo realized what was happening, it was too late.

"No!" I shouted, the distraction of Nikylo's appearance finally banking. I surged forward, not for Talekor but for Leighton.

The rip he'd made in the world glowed as he darted through, pulling her behind him. My hand grazed her fingers right as it closed, but someone pulled me back before I could close my hand around hers. The jump point closed. I screamed obscenities at the person who stopped me, trying to rip their hands from around my waist. "You'll lose a hand if it closes on you!" they shouted.

"I need to get her back!" I cried, my body suddenly craving oxygen that I couldn't catch. "I need to—I need—" I collapsed into the arms holding me as the full weight of what happened hit me. Sobs wracked my body as he pulled me upright, the comfort I needed right there. I twisted in his embrace, my hands finding purchase in the soft-textured tunic that smelled of smoke and strawberries. His arms wrapped around me, pulling me closer as sobs tore through me. I let myself catch my breath. I allowed myself this one moment to feel the emotions that would fuel my vengeance.

With all the strength I could muster, I lifted my head to Ken's body lying on the ground. Oliver was kneeling beside her, checking her neck for a pulse. His eyes met mine as he slowly shook his head.

Dropping to my knees, I crawled across the space between us. I lifted her head from where it lolled to the side, laid it in my lap, and found her eyes—too still, too dull.

A sob escaped me. "You promised we'd figure this out together." My voice trembled as I brushed her damp strawberry blonde hair from her forehead. "You swore I wouldn't be alone."

Tears blurred my vision, but I blinked them away, forcing myself to find the dagger still embedded in her chest. Slowly, I pulled it out, letting it fall aimlessly to the ground, where it clattered loudly in the silence.

My hands were shaking as I cradled her against my chest. "How did you survive weeks of torture and learning our magic to end up—" My voice broke, cracking something open within me. All I could do was pull Kendall closer as if I could undo what Talekor had done. I pressed my forehead against hers and whispered my confession, "I couldn't save you." The words settled into my bones as I lifted my head and said with fierce determination, "But I can still save her."

I pressed my lips to Kendall's forehead, sealing my promise. Slowly, I moved her from my lap and onto the floor. Feeling their gazes, I let it ground me as I finally lifted my head.

I met Nikylo's gaze first. His expression was unreadable, but his eyes burned with something deep—something unspoken. He saw my pain— perhaps even felt it in a way he couldn't explain. I noticed it in the tension of his jaw and the way he clenched his fist. He wanted to reach for me again, but held back.

My eyes flicked to Oliver. He didn't bother hiding the sorrow in his gaze. It was raw, open, making my throat tighten all over again. His usual eloquence was gone, replaced with a silent understanding. He seemed to be waiting—to see if I'd break, ready to jump in and catch me if I did.

The air was thick with things unsaid. But I didn't have time to find the words. Not yet.

Because Leighton was still out there. And I wasn't going to lose her, too.

I swallowed the emotions and lifted my chin. "We have to save her."

They both nodded. Nikylo cleared his throat. I met his gaze, something like guilt shining there as he said, "There's something you should know before we go."

"Now is not the time—" I started but was interrupted by someone else.

"Rayleigh?" came a soft rasp, and I twisted toward the voice.

Mari, with fresh blood soaking the front of her shirt, was sitting up, leaning against Libella for support. Her eyes were open. Aware. Locked on me.

The place where her throat had been sliced open was sealed.

I gaped at her. She was alive. Breathing. "*How?*" I asked softly, pushing away the need to scream.

"I told you once before, love," Oliver said, stepping up beside me. "There are only two ways to kill our kind. Severing the spinal cord or—" his gaze fell from mine, "—extensive damage to the heart."

I clenched my teeth, closing my eyes to absorb the information being given to me. A word that shouldn't have surfaced but did floated to the tip of my tongue: unfair. I shoved it down, along with every other feeling trying to push its way out. Finding the box where I kept all my emotions, I forced them in and slammed it shut. There would be time to process them all later, but right now, I needed to focus. The longer we lingered here, the farther away Talekor got with Leigh.

And I made a promise.

I opened my eyes to find Mari watching me with the hopelessness I'd felt moments ago. "I'm glad you're okay," I said, trying and failing to smile. "But I'm still trying to process Kendall's—" I cut myself off, unable to finish that sentence. Trying again, I said, "What Talekor made Leigh do."

Mari gasped. I tried not to let it affect me.

"She didn't deserve to die, and Leighton doesn't deserve to live with the guilt either." Mari nodded through her tears, forcing herself to sit up further, Libella helping her to do so. I went on, "Talekor wanted to break her. Wanted to show me he could. He will let this eat her alive, will probably tell her it was all her fault." I swallowed the emotions trying to prevent me from going on. "I need to nullify the bond. To get her as far away from him as possible." I lifted my chin. "But I can't—" I choked on the words but forced myself to take a breath and tried again. "I can't do this alone."

"I'm in," Nikylo said.

"Me too." Oliver nodded.

"How can I help?" Libella.

"Where do you need me?" Mari asked quietly.

The hope I felt fill my chest was overwhelming. I answered Mari first. "I need you to be prepared to get her out of here as soon as the bond is gone." When she agreed, I turned to the other three. "Are Theo and Naila still in commission?"

"Theo and his dragon, yes," Nikylo answered. "Naila, yes. Her dragon, no."

I nodded, opening my mouth to explain my plan, but then I met Nikylo's eyes. What I saw there made me pause. It was what Drako's eyes reflected every time they popped through. But it was Nikylo's green eyes staring back at me now, with the same determination. No hesitation. No doubt. He would follow me into this fight, just like he did when I went to save Kaleb. He hadn't cared for him—for good reason

—but he still tried to help me save him. He would do the same this time. Without question. Without fear.

Because it was me.

Releasing some control, I said, "Last time I made the plan, we all ended up captured." His piercing gaze didn't waver.

"Perhaps I can add some insight?" Oliver said, catching my attention.

I dipped my chin, clenching my teeth as I faced him and asked, "What did you have in mind?"

FORTY-FIVE
Sweeter Than Revenge

"A truce?" Naila balked, staring at my outstretched hand.

"Only until we've won," I promised.

While we were inside, Theo successfully blinded the Kool-Aid Man's dragon, sending him away, roaring in pain. Aaidan had apparently disappeared—again. Which left Theo to fight the silver dragon *and* stop Talekor from getting away. Luckily, Naila had been cunning enough to wield her powers from land, throwing a shield up to keep Talekor trapped. With the strength of his powers that he'd already displayed, I wasn't sure how Naila's power compared, but I had to give her props for holding her ground against him. By the time we reached her, she was nearly drained, and there were no crystals here for her to recharge them. But she had enough for this.

Nikylo had taken to the skies immediately, telling me Drako had a personal score to settle with Talekor and would keep him busy until I was ready for my part. Libella followed, determined to help Theo against the silver dragon. No one recognized it, making everyone a little wary of what was happening, but it didn't stop us from fighting.

Naila tentatively took my hand, shaking it. "What do you need from me?"

I explained the maneuver for which I needed her skills, and she smiled wickedly. "Oh, that sounds dangerous."

"It is," I agreed. "But for it to work, I need you. Nikylo said you could do it."

"Oh, I can. Can you?"

"We're about to find out," I said, straightening my spine and turning to Oliver. "Promise you'll catch me?"

"I have caught you once before, love. Do you truly believe I would not be able to do it again?"

I smiled weakly. "So long as you keep catching me."

"I will." His eyes sparkled with something I couldn't process right then.

Thankfully, I wouldn't have to.

A roar sounded from the battle in the skies. That was my cue. Turning from Oliver's soft gaze, I asked Naila, "Ready?"

She tilted her head both ways, cracking it while stretching her arms out in front of her. "Let's do this, cató."

I suppressed a smile, turning to the edge of the roof. Drako's form was flying our way, Talekor's yellow dragon hot on his tail. The distance made it nearly impossible to tell, but I knew Leighton was likely clutching tightly to him while he flapped his wings wildly to catch Drako.

You are more daring than I assumed, Little Ember. Drako's voice reverberated through me.

Not bothering to suppress my smile, I asked, *Did you get your revenge?*

Not even close, he growled. *But I have to save some of him for you.*

A torrent of flames spewed from Talekor's dragon—what was his name? Morvax? The fire silhouetted Drako in a way that made him look absolutely majestic as he banked a sharp turn and then a steep dive down. The maneuver caught Talekor off guard, but he dove after him, both of them disappearing from view below the edge of the island.

"Should we hold hands?" I yelled at Naila, unsure of the best way to do this.

"Ew, no," she said, the disgust evident in her voice. "Just stay close."

Now! Drako shouted.

I took off, running as fast as I could toward the edge, feeling Naila beside me. With a coordinated leap, we launched ourselves into the air and over the edge. For a moment, I felt weightless, the wind whipping past me with only the water-filled planet thousands of feet below. Then Drako's massive form appeared, his wings beating fiercely as he flew straight toward me from below. Time seemed to stretch as we fell, the wind biting into my skin. With me plummeting and him ascending, we would collide much faster than I had imagined. But as the space between us closed, there was a flap of yellow wings directly behind Drako as he snapped at his tail. I reached for Naila, hauling her into position and yelling, "*Now!*"

I felt her power crawl along my skin and watched her transform into me. Drako was close enough that I could see the way his scales shone, and then his head shot past me. Naila reached out and hooked her arm around the spine to hold her onto Drako's back, and his momentum yanked her in the opposite direction. I used my foot to push myself away from him as he passed, avoiding the rest of his spines and his tail. Morvax came into view and I locked in on my target.

Her blue eyes were rimmed with red, and her strawberry-blonde hair whipped in the wind as she clung to the spine in front of her. Morvax continued to charge after Drako, his head barely missing me as I angled myself. Right before impact, I opened my arms and crashed into Leighton, ripping her from the dragon's back and feeling the winds pushing us away from his tail as it whipped in his pursuit to catch Drako.

Leighton tried to scream, but I held her face in my shoulder and shouted, "It's me. I've got you."

She screamed again, starting to thrash in my arms. *Shit.* I hadn't planned on her not cooperating in this. I thought she would want to be saved, but I'd forgotten about the bond and how it might affect her.

The winds pulled us up and up until we were level with the surface of the island again, pulling us to safety where Mari waited on the ledge, arms outstretched. As soon as my feet hit the ground, I released Leighton into Mari's waiting arms and ran the remaining feet to my supplies.

Throwing myself down on my knees, I grabbed the dagger and sliced my hand open. The book of *Oaths, Bonds, and Curses* lay open on the ground, and my eyes roamed the page for the words I needed to say. While Mari was helping me prepare for the ball earlier, we'd made a backup plan for freeing Leigh if Mari's attempt to save her failed. I'd studied the book to ensure I knew what to do and tried memorizing the words, but I hadn't had enough time. I read the incantation several times while Mari carried a struggling Leighton to where I waited.

"Use your powers, Mari!" I shouted, needing Leigh to be still for this to work.

"I said I would never—"

"Now is not the time for sentiments!" I retorted. "You can apologize when she's free!"

The battle raged above us, dragons roaring and fire-spewing left and right.

Mari set her jaw, realizing I was right, and Leigh instantly stopped struggling. I surged forward right as a dragon roared. I whipped my head to find Morvax's yellow gaze settled on me several yards away. Then Drako slammed into him, and the struggle for power between them began.

"Now, Ray!" Mari yelled.

Snapping back to my task, I gripped Leigh's arm where she'd told me Talekor's new mark had been made. A scream flew past her lips, her body seizing as I guided my magic into her arm. I locked my gaze with Mari's. "Don't let go."

"Never."

I dropped my eyes to the page on the ground, finding the incantation, and read, "Láthito desmós, oú pote prókeitai na yparchí." Another scream ripped from Leighton's throat, sounding strangled as I felt my magic start to disentangle the bond. The madí reflecting Talekor's powers began to glow.

When I felt it working, I released a breath, relaxing my shoulders. No one was certain this was going to work. With no Evanians to consult and no other books talking about the nullification, it was a considerable risk. One everyone was willing to take. The pronunciation was the thing I was the most unsure of, so I had asked Oliver to help me with it before our date. When I asked if he knew what it meant, he said it roughly translated to "Let the bond be undone, for it was never meant to be." There wasn't time to understand its meaning, only to hope it would work.

I repeated the phrase twice, feeling the last of the bond unravelling as the glowing subsided. I pulled my hand away from her arm and saw no evidence of Talekor's brand.

Leigh's screams faded into the night, replaced with a thunderous roar that shattered the silence. A sound of rage and loss so powerful it seemed to shake the very ground beneath me.

Slowly, my gaze turned toward the noise, and a maniacal grin spread across my face. Morvax was glaring at me with murder in his eyes, as if he hadn't already committed the act. He was outside the enchantments of the Verdanvale, pushing for a way in. To get to me. But they held firm, keeping him out.

I turned, finding Leighton cradled tightly in Mari's arms as she stood. "Get her out of here. Don't tell me where." Mari gave me a curt nod, turning toward the house. "And Mari?" She turned, finding my gaze. "Keep her safe."

"Mari." A great gust of wind hit me from both sides, but I glanced toward the voice, finding Oliver as he touched down a few feet away, covering the distance between us in a few strides. He pulled Mari to the side and whispered something in her ear.

Her head snapped to him. "You're sure?"

Oliver nodded. Mari searched his eyes for a moment and then turned and disappeared into the house.

"What was that about?" I asked.

"I suggested a place to hide," he said, turning to me. He glanced past my head to where I knew Morvax waited, then met my eyes. I could see the acceptance there, but he still said, "He is still a threat, but do not let him get into your head, love. You do not have to do this."

"I know." I looked over his shoulder to where Mari had just disappeared with Leighton. "But I need to. For Leigh. For Ken."

He held my gaze for a moment, then nodded. "Then I will fight by your side if that is what you want."

I chewed on my lip. My only request during the planning was that if Oliver didn't have to fly into battle, he wouldn't. Which was why he stayed on land. Not only was he a Councilor and not supposed to be here, but he had unfortunately made it to the list of people I cared about. Dropping my gaze to the ground, I whispered, "I can't lose anyone else."

He closed the space between us, cupping my face and making me meet his piercing stare. "Then I will be here when you get back." I nodded, eyes burning as he pressed his lips to my forehead.

Sensing what was coming, I moved my arms away from my body,

allowing Drako's tail to slip around my waist. He had been the cause of the other gust of wind and patiently waited for my moment with Oliver to play out. But he was done being patient. I swore I could also feel a touch of jealousy as I was lifted away from Oliver, making his hands slip away from my face. But I knew it wasn't the dragon who was jealous of the encounter.

Drako's tail placed me gently between his shoulder blades, and his blue eyes found mine as I tore my gaze away from Oliver. As soon as I was in position, I fixed my eyes on Talekor's dragon and said, *Drako?*

Yes, Little Ember?

Let's finish him.

With pleasure, Little Ember. Drako's massive wings spread wide, and we shot into the sky, aiming straight for the yellow-eyed demon.

Taking a deep breath to steady myself, I reached for the power within me. The tendrils of magic came easily, sensing the battle they were about to take part in. *I wish I had more training.*

You have training enough for this. He is but one dragon.

I knew he was right, but his words didn't calm my nerves like I thought they would. I pulled on the white thread, the one I was most confident—

Put your confidence not in your ability to control the elements but in your ability to wield them, Drako said, baring his claws as we closed in on our target. *The elements do not bow to strength—they bow to understanding.*

We had seconds before we would meet Morvax in the air. I closed my eyes, taking a moment to focus on my power, feeling each of the three threads as they rose to greet me.

The white one swirled around my fingers, making its way up and around my torso, my lungs expanding as the power fueled me. The weightless, boundless feeling existed everywhere and nowhere all at once. I surrendered control and was met with the feeling of being unchained and untethered from gravity—like I could slip between the breeze and become a part of it.

The green one wound around my arms, mingling with the white around my torso. It released a deep, steady thrum as it pulsed beneath my skin, grounding me. Strength rippled through my limbs, a slow and unshakable force—like the earth shaking and waiting to rise at my command. My heartbeat synced with the pulse of power, solid and unwavering, as I surrendered control to the steady presence that whispered of unyielding power.

When greeting the final thread of my power, I hesitated for only a moment. But it came to me, licking up my arms like red veins, the comforting warmth seeping into my skin. As it sank into my chest, it roared with a steady hum of untamed power, wild and hungry but mine to wield. It coaxed me to release control, and the moment I did, the power rushed through my blood, igniting every nerve. My pulse thrummed with the crackling energy of a firestorm just waiting to break free.

I opened my eyes, feeling every element ready and waiting for my command. Time seemed to have slowed while I found my power, but it was moving fast again as Drako crashed into Morvax, talons first. The impact surprised me, but my grip didn't falter as Drako threw Morvax to the side, tearing scales away when his claws broke free.

I summoned the fire within and unleashed the blast, aiming for where the scales had been ripped away. It hit true to its mark, but Morvax didn't even react, escaping the flames as if they were nothing.

Drako banked, adjusting midair. *Raw power is not enough. Focus it.*

While I appreciated his wisdom in battle, I was slightly disappointed I wasn't fighting alongside Nikylo.

I'm here, Sunshine, Nikylo said, making my heart jump out of my chest. *I just don't want to distract you.*

I smiled, mentally reaching a hand out to him. *Distract me later. Help me now.*

Nikylo took my hand, the feeling fueling my power even more. *Push air behind Drako's wings,* he suggested. *Accelerate his attack. Don't give Talekor time to react.*

Drako was headed straight toward Morvax again, whose yellow eyes flashed black, gleaming with fury.

You make it sound easy, I teased, channeling the winds in time with Drako's wing beats, increasing our speed effortlessly.

You make it look *easy.*

I grinned. We were a blur in the sky, Drako diving for Talekor. But before Drako could crash into him, the yellow dragon disappeared.

Nikylo swore as Drako spread his wings to slow our flight. Drako's voice rumbled with an unsettling timber, *He is drawing strength beyond what should be possible.*

Thinking back to the struggle in the house, I said, *How many minds can someone with his power control at a time?*

Two max, Nikylo said. *But splitting the power would mean he wouldn't have complete control of either.*

He wasn't just controlling Leighton but both Kendall's and Oliver's movements, too. Neither of them could move.

Something is amiss, Drako commented, his voice ominous.

Yeah, no shit, Drako, Nikylo scoffed.

Drako growled but didn't respond. He had halted midair, beating his wings to keep us aloft, but was searching the skies for Morvax. A roar came from beneath us, and I sent a panicked blast of air into Drako's side, knocking him out of Morvax's path in the nick of time. He plowed through the space where we had just been, a torrent of flames shooting after us as Drako pulled a sharp turn to face him.

Firestorm! Nikylo shouted.

Pushing the winds into a circular motion around the flames, I added my own to it, creating a vortex of wind and flames, the combination expanding it exponentially. A sweat broke out on my temple, but I pushed the cyclone of fire straight toward the yellow dragon. But the storm halted, meeting a force midair.

"What the—?" I started, trying to push it forward again, but then the firestorm changed direction and rushed toward us. I screamed, feeling the pull of skithing just before the fire singed my skin. We appeared behind Morvax, enough space between us that I could comfortably ask, *How is he using* my *power?*

He is not using it, Drako said. *He is somehow interfering with it, bending it to his will.*

But my shields are up! I yelled, double-checking anyway. *How can he control the elements? Unless…*

Finally figured it out, girlie? His voice crawled along my skin.

My gaze shot to the yellow dragon hovering in place, his black, soulless eyes on me. He wasn't in my mind; my shields were locked in place. But I could still hear him—feel him raking the claws down the outside of my shields. His power was beyond what I knew Drakalasson could do. Beyond what anyone should be able to control. It was like he had stolen power—

Orvyn. Nikylo's voice echoed in my head, apparently on the same train of thought. He'd just gotten there first.

He's using the planet's stolen magic, I breathed. *That's why we can't overpower him.*

Very good, his voice scraped along the outside of my shield. I felt Nikylo's shield reinforce mine, but it did nothing to kick Talekor out. *But knowing won't change the outcome. You can't defeat me.* His confidence had me sneering. *Surrender,* he commanded.

Never, Drako rumbled. *While he may possess strength, we can leverage our intellect to gain the upper hand.*

You can certainly try, Talekor said, and I could hear the smirk in his tone.

With him in our heads, there was no way we could devise a plan without him knowing what it was. But then I smirked. *Nikylo, did you know you can scream in your head as loud and as long as you want without taking a breath?*

What a brilliant idea.

Drako rumbled with laughter from beneath me, and all three of us did just that. Drako's roar was piercing alongside Nikylo's yelling and my blood-curdling internal scream. Using the shield of our screams, I fed them both the idea with images, and we didn't waste any time. Drako shot forward, my air pushing him from behind to make us a blur in the sky.

Morvax charged, beating his wings to meet us in combat. Drako's torrent of blue flames flew from his mouth as Nikylo formed the rip in the world right before we collided. Suddenly, we were coming at Morvax from a different angle, straight into his underbelly— his most vulnerable spot, according to Drako. I summoned my fire, ready to—

A sharp cry was my only warning before something slammed into us, knocking us from our winning blow and sending us tumbling away from Morvax. Drako roared in pain, the sound slamming into me as if I'd taken the blow myself. I clung to the spine in front of me, my legs gripping as tight as I could when a blur of silver shot past us. *No.* That was the dragon Theo and Libella were fighting, but I couldn't look for them to see if they were okay. I could hardly tell which way was up, let alone where my friends fought. *Please let them be okay.*

Before I could even make my next move, another roar pierced the sky just as a silver tail appeared out of nowhere and slammed into me. The impact sent me sailing from Drako's back. I opened my mouth in a silent scream as my vision blurred and spun as I fell.

Rayleigh! Nikylo's voice echoed in my head. I was yanked to a halt by what I knew were Nikylo's powers. He was lifting me back toward him, Drako circling back to me with blood flowing from his hind leg. When had he gotten hurt? Dark spots clouded my vision, causing me to see double of the blue dragon. A glint of something caught my attention as it flew through the air, straight toward Drako.

Kyler… Even my inner voice was hard to find. *Gonos.*

But it was too late. The collar slapped against Drako's neck, snapping into place with a sharp click. The bond was cut off.

Drako released a furious roar as his body shifted against his will. I blinked, my eyes opening to find his wings retracting and scales melting away to flesh.

"Hold on, Ray!" Nikylo's green eyes locked on mine as I blinked again, slower this time.

I opened them to find my view of Nikylo blocked by claws closing around me.

Then, there was nothing.

FORTY-SIX
The Rumble

A gentle breeze skated across my skin, cool and refreshing. I breathed it in, trying to remember where I was.

My body was pressed against something warm, the feeling familiar, but I couldn't quite place it. The warmth seeped into my bones as I checked my other senses. My eyelids felt like sandpaper as I dragged them open, the room's brightness forcing me to blink several times before anything came into focus.

The ceiling resembled branches woven together to create the roof, but light seeped in through the little spaces they left. This wasn't the castle, but it didn't seem like a dungeon either.

What happened? Where am I?

The question was mostly to myself, so when someone responded, I jolted.

You're where you were always meant to be. That voice. I'd heard that voice before.

I tried to sit up, to find the source of it, but my whole body protested when I flexed the muscles to do so. Groaning, I relaxed and tried turning my head instead.

A pair of huge copper eyes settled on me, swirling from where he watched me several feet away.

"Lukas?" My voice rasped as I realized the warmth I lay against was his dragon scales. He was curled up inside the room, and we were nestled on a cushion not unlike the one in Nikylo's bed chambers back at the castle. "How are you here?"

That's something I think our hosts should explain. He dipped his chin, the honey brown swimming as he held my gaze. *Shall I call for them?*

I swallowed, wondering who could possibly have brought us here—wherever here was. "Um…yes?"

You hesitated. Why?

"Because the last thing I remember was being thrown off Drako's back before he was forced to shift. Then Nikylo and I were falling and—" My gaze shot to Lukas. "Nikylo?"

The dragon shook his head.

"No…" Tears pricked my eyes as I thought of all that had happened before I lost consciousness. Mari and Leighton. Oliver. *Kendall.* I swallowed the emotions and asked, "What happened to him?"

Morvax grabbed him before our hosts could. The reluctance in his voice told me enough: he'd been taken hostage.

I fought the urge to jump out of the bed and demand to be taken back. My body was too weak to even sit up, let alone charge into another battle. There was nothing I could do on my own, especially with no information about where we were. And how Lukas was here. Who had he bonded with? "What about everyone else? Oliver? Theo and Libella? Naila?"

Some are here. Others have resumed their positions undercover. Smoke filtered through his nose. *Our hosts were generous enough to offer their home as refuge.*

"But who are they?"

It's better to let them introduce themselves.

I narrowed my eyes. "Can you tell me anything?"

There's a lot I would like to tell you. But I don't think I should until you know who they are.

I sighed, realizing he wouldn't tell me anything until I met them. "Fine. Call them or whatever."

Lukas dipped his head, then lifted it to the branches above and released a series of whistles. After a few seconds of silence, his call was answered with a series of similar whistles. His eyes fell to mine again. *They're on their way.*

Wanting to make myself presentable, I asked, "Can you at least help me sit up?"

Lukas huffed a laugh, his warm breath skating over my skin. *Of course.*

His tail appeared and hovered above me on the bed. *Grab hold.*

I did as he said, and he lifted me from my position on the bed to sit up. When I released his tail, it snaked around my torso and moved me back against the wall of his warmth once more to relax against him again. "Thank you," I said, settling in and letting my mind wander back to the battle. "Nikylo was hurt," I whispered.

He's okay.

I met his gaze. "How can you know that?"

You'd be in far more pain if he were dead.

"What?"

Those honey-brown eyes churned with emotions. *The bond would have torn you apart from the inside out if you lost him like that.*

"Oh." I didn't know much about our bond, and Nikylo had still been researching it. I had no idea it ran that deep.

Our hosts approach. His gaze turned away from me, and I followed it.

The room was scarce of anything else, but I drank in the beautiful colors of the space. The walls were similar to the ceiling, branches woven together, but they were covered in a beautiful green moss, eliminating the need for decor.

Across the room was a wide opening onto a balcony, big enough for the dragon swooping in to land. My jaw dropped at the sight of the magnificent creature, its scales a purple so dark it was almost black. But that wasn't what caught my attention.

Sliding from the dragon's back was a beautiful female. Her eyes met mine, their rich brown boring into me as she crossed the room. I knew this female, although in the picture I'd seen of her, she didn't have the pointed ears. But it was like looking in a mirror, her brown eyes the only difference.

"Hello, Rayleigh," Analisa said, her eyes shining with tears as they drank in the sight of me. "I have long been waiting a lifetime for our reunion."

I stared at her, having a hard time believing that my real mother was standing right in front of me. Then, before I could find the words to respond to her, the dragon behind her shifted. His scales melted away, and the male stepped into the room, wearing a brilliant purple silk robe. His dark hair and features mimicked Nikylo's, but he looked nothing like him. His deep blue eyes trained on me as he wrapped a possessive arm around Analisa.

She glanced up at him with a smile. "And this is Rafael," she said, turning back to me. "Your father."

To Be Continued…

Acknowledgements

Full Playlist (in a different order…)

Wow. Two books. And I wouldn't be here without any of my support. Since writing and publishing Forgotten Flare, I have met so many new people, mostly through socials, but some in person! All of them are irreplaceable and have been the biggest support system throughout this entire journey.

The OG Lollipop gals: Erin, Jenna, Kaley and Lauren. I know I dedicated this to them, but they deserve more recognition. They are my biggest support system and always talk me through the tough parts of the writing process. They read the stuff that didn't make it and helped rework some things that needed it. This book wouldn't be what it is without them.

To my editor, Alexis, who had to put up with my repetition of the words sand, hand, and tome… Just be glad you didn't have to put up with those! She was also so encouraging throughout the entire process and made everything easy to understand and rework. I haven't ever worked with someone so understanding and professional while also being relatable and honest throughout the process.

My parents and siblings are the reason I am where I am today and have always encouraged me on all the journeys I've been on, but this one the most. If they haven't read it, they've told everyone they know to read it. I don't think I would be able to do what I do without their support.

To my cast of characters for the audiobooks (coming to you soon!), I thank you for always being in my corner and being willing to be a part of this journey that I've got going. Your support means the world to me, as does your lending your voice to my characters.

Dom, David, you're the best brothers from another mother a gal could ask for. Your constant jokes, conversations and hilarity inspired some of the conversations in this book, even though it may not seem like it. Having friends like you has really helped my understanding of different lifestyles in the best way.

For those of you that I met on socials and encouraged me through every writing sprint, I appreciate you. For those in my life that checked in when I was holed up writing, I appreciate you. And for those who keep bugging me to send you the book, I appreciate your patience.

There are many others I could list, but just know if I know you and you're reading this. I appreciate *you*.